# THE GIANT BOOK
## OF
# CRIME
## STORIES

**Edited by George Hardinge**

MAGPIE BOOKS
LONDON

Magpie Books
11 Shepherd House
5 Shepherd Street
London W1Y 7LD

This edition first published by Magpie Books in 1991.

Previously published by Robinson Publishing as The Mammoth
Book of Modern Crime Stories, 1987.

First published by Macmillan London Ltd as
The Best of Winter's Crime, Vols. 1 & 2

Collection © Macmillan London Ltd 1986

Cover illustration by Brent

A copy of the British Library Cataloguing in Publication
Data is available from the British Library.

ISBN 1 85487 116 1

Printed and bound in Great Britain by The Guernsey Press
Co. Ltd., Guernsey, Channel Islands.

# CONTENTS

# PUBLISHER'S NOTE

*The Mammoth Book of Modern Crime Stories* was originally published in hardback as *The Best of Winter's Crimes*, Volumes 1 and 2. *Winter's Crimes* have been published annually by Macmillan London Ltd. since 1969, containing the best of the year's crime stories. This collection was made by the distinguished editor, George Hardinge, who founded the series and edited all but six of the volumes. In his introduction to the two volume edition, he describes the genesis of the series: 'I owe many debts, one of them (once again) to my friend Julian Symons. At the very start he acted as an unpaid and more or less unthanked adviser: the concept of the *Winter's Crimes* series was worked out with his help in the bar at the Charing Cross Hotel many years ago.'

He goes on to describe the difficult process of choosing the stories: 'To make my choices I have re-read all of the one hundred and ninety-three stories that appeared in the annual volumes referred to above. Coming again to these stories I found myself in an absolute Aladdin's Cave of marvellous things. If I had really been the editor who sponsored and conjured so many wonderful gems of invention and craftsmanship into being, had I not something to be proud of?

The real answer, I think, is luck: luck in having such support from an immense range of authors including many who have been and mostly still are personal friends. And already some of these friends who have had more than one story in the series have been pointing out to me, in the kindest possible way, that I have chosen the wrong one. They may well be right; these are subjective questions.

Obviously all these stories have been published before, some more than once and in different media. But they have not been published together, and I am going to have the temerity to suggest that this is an absolutely stunning compendium of crime short stories: the author's names are a roll-call of distinction and success in crime-writing in the second half of the twentieth century, and in their inventions for the *Winter's Crimes* series they have often reached the height of their powers.

I hope many readers new and old will come to share the huge pleasure I have derived from re-reading these stories.'

# ERIC
# AMBLER

---

# The Blood Bargain

Ex-President Fuentes enjoys a peculiar distinction. More people would like to kill him now that he is in retirement than wanted to kill him when he was in power.

He is a puzzled and indignant man.

What he fails to understand is that, while men like General Perez may in time forgive you for robbing them, they will never forgive you for making them look foolish.

The *coup d'état* which overthrew Fuentes' Social Action Party government was well organised and relatively bloodless.

The leaders of the *coup* were mostly Army officers, but they had understandings with fellow-dissidents in the Air Force and Navy as well as the discreet blessing of the Church. A price for the collaboration of the Chief of Police had been agreed upon well in advance, and the lists of certain left-wing deputies, militant trade union officials, pro-government newspaper editors, Castro-trained subversives and other undesirables whose prompt arrest would be advisable, had been compiled with his help. Similar arrangements had been made in the larger provincial towns. Although the conspirators were by no means all of the same political complexion, they had for once found themselves able to sink their differences in the pursuit of a common goal. Whatever might come afterwards, they were all agreed upon one thing; if the country were to be saved from corruption, Communist subversion, anarchy, bankruptcy, civil war and, ultimately, foreign military intervention, President Fuentes had to go.

One evening in September he went.

The tactics employed by the 'Liberation Front' conspirators followed the pattern which has become more or less traditional when a *coup* is backed by organised military forces and opposed, if it is opposed at all, only by civilian mobs and confused, lightly armed garrison units.

As darkness fell, the tanks of two armoured brigades together with trucks containing a parachute regiment, signals units and a company of combat engineers rolled into the capital. Within little more than an hour, they had secured their major objectives. Meanwhile, the Air Force had taken over the international airport, grounded all planes and established a headquarters in the customs and immigration building. An infantry division now began to move into the city and take up positions which would enable it to deal with the civil disturbances which were expected to develop as news of the *coup*, and of the mass arrests which were accompanying it, reached the densely populated slum areas with their high concentration of Fuentes supporters.

A little after eight-thirty a squadron of tanks and a special task force of paratroopers reached the Presidential Palace. The palace guard resisted for a quarter of an hour and suffered casualties of eight wounded. The order to surrender was given personally to the guard commander by President Fuentes 'in order to avoid further bloodshed'.

When this was reported to General Perez, the leader of the *coup*, he drove to the Palace. He was accompanied by five senior members of the Liberation Front council, including the Chief of Police, and no less than three representatives of the foreign press. The latter had been flushed out of the Jockey Club bar by an aide earlier in the evening and hastily briefed on the aims and ideals of the Liberation Front. General Perez wished to lose no time in establishing himself abroad as a magnanimous, reasonable and responsible man, and his regime as worthy of prompt diplomatic recognition.

The newsmen's accounts of the interview between President Fuentes and General Perez, and of the now-notorious 'blood bargain' which emerged from it, were all in substantial agreement. At the time the bargain seemed to them just another of those civilised, oddly chivalrous agreements to live and let live which, by testifying to the continued presence of compassion and good sense even at moments of turmoil and destruction, have so often lightened the long, dark history of Latin American revolution. The reporters, all experienced men, can scarcely be blamed for misunderstanding it. They knew, as everyone else knew, that President Fuentes was a devious and deeply dishonest man. The only mistake they made was in assuming that the other parties to the bargain had made due allowance for that deviousness and dishonesty and knew exactly what they were doing. What the reporters had not realised was that these normally wary and hard-headed officers had become so intoxicated by the speed and extent of their initial success that by the time they reached the Presidential Palace they were no longer capable of thinking clearly.

President Fuentes received General Perez and the other Liberation Front leaders in the ornate Cabinet Room of the Palace to which he had been taken by the paratroopers who had arrested him. With him were the other male occupants of the Presidential air raid shelter at the time of his arrest. These included the Palace guard commander, the President's valet, the Palace major-domo, two footmen and the man who looked after the Palace plumbing system, in addition to the Minister of Public Welfare, the Minister of Agrarian Education, the Minister of Justice and the elderly Controller of the Presidential Secretariat. The Minister of Public Welfare had brought a bottle of brandy with him from the shelter and smiled glassily throughout the subsequent confrontation. Agrarian Education and Justice maintained expressions of bewilderment and indignation, but confined their oral protests to circumspect murmurs. The thin-lipped young captain in charge of the paratroopers handled his machine pistol as if he would have been glad of an excuse to use it.

Only the President seemed at ease. There was even a touch of impatience in the shrug with which he rose to face General Perez and his party as they strode in from the anteroom; it was as if he had been interrupted by some importunate visitor during a game of bridge.

His calm was only partly assumed. He knew all about General Perez' sensitivity to foreign opinion, and he had immediately recognised the newsmen in the rear of the procession. They would not have been brought there if any immediate violence to his person had been contemplated.

The impatience he displayed was certainly genuine; it was impatience with himself. He had known for weeks that a *coup* was in preparation, and had taken the precaution a month earlier of sending his wife and children and his mistress out of the country. They were all now in Washington, and he had planned, using as a pretext his announced wish to address personally a meeting of the Organisation of American States, to join them there the following week. His private spies had reported that the *coup* would undoubtedly be timed to take advantage of his absence abroad. Since the *coup* by means of which he himself had come to power five years earlier had been timed in that way, he had been disposed to believe the report.

Now, he knew better. Whether or not his spies had deliberately deceived him did not matter at the moment. A mistake had been made which was, he knew, likely to cost him more than temporary inconvenience. Unless he could retrieve it immediately, by getting out of the country within the next few hours, that mistake would certainly cost him his liberty, and most probably his life too.

He had risked death before, was familiar with the physical and mental sensations that accompanied the experience, and with a small effort was able to ignore them. As General Perez came up to him, the President displayed no emotion of any kind. He merely nodded politely and waited for the General to speak.

For a moment the General seemed tongue-tied. He was sweating too. As this was the first time he had overthrown a government he was undoubtedly suffering from stage fright. He took refuge finally in military punctilio. With a click of the heels he came to attention and fixed his eyes on the President's left ear.

'We are here . . .' he began harshly, then cleared his throat and corrected himself. 'I and my fellow members of the Council of the Liberation Front are here to inform you that a state of national emergency now exists.'

The President nodded politely. 'I am glad to have that information, General. Since telephone communication has been cut off I have naturally been curious as to what was happening. These gentlemen' – he motioned to the paratroopers – 'seemed unwilling to enlighten me.'

The General ignored this and went on as if he were reading a proclamation. In fact, he was quoting from the press release which had already been handed to the newsmen. 'Directed by the Council and under its orders,' he said, 'the armed forces have assumed control of all functions of civil government in the state, and, as provided in the Constitution, formally demand your resignation.'

The President looked astounded. 'You have the effrontery to claim constitutional justification for this mutiny?'

For the first time since he had entered the room the General relaxed slightly. 'We have a precedent, sir. Nobody should know that better than you. You yourself set it when you legalised your own seizure of power from your predecessor. Need I remind you of the wording of the amendment? "If for any reason, including the inability to fulfil the duties of his office by reason of ill-health, mental or physical, or absence, an elected president is unable to exercise the authority vested in him under the constitution, a committee representative of the nation and those responsible to it for the maintenance of law and order may request his resignation and be entitled. . . ." '

For several seconds the President had been waving his hands for silence. Now he broke in angrily. 'Yes, yes, I know all about that. But my predecessor was absent. I am not. Neither am I ill, physically or mentally. There are no legal grounds on which you are entitled to ask for my resignation.'

'No legal grounds, sir?' General Perez could smile now. He pointed to the paratroopers. 'Are you able to exercise the authority of a president? *Are* you? If you think so, try.'

The President pretended to think over the challenge. The interview was so far going more or less as he had expected; but the next moves would be the critical ones for him. He walked over to a window and back in order to give himself time to collect himself.

Everyone there was watching him. The tension in the room was mounting. He could feel it. It was odd, he thought. Here he was, a prisoner, wholly at their mercy; and yet they were waiting for him to come to a decision, to make a choice where no choice existed. It was absurd. All they wanted from him was relief from a small and quite irrational sense of guilt. They had the Church's blessing; now the poor fools yearned for the blessing of the law too. Very well. They should have it. But it would be expensive.

He turned and faced General Perez again.

'A resignation exacted from me under duress would have no force in law,' he said.

The General glanced at the Chief of Police. 'You are a lawyer, Raymundo. Who represents the law here?'

'The Council of the Liberation Front, General.'

Perez looked at the President again. 'You see, sir, there are no technical difficulties. We even have the necessary document already prepared.'

His aide held up a black leather portfolio.

The President hesitated, looking from one face to another as if hoping against hope that he might find a friendly one. Finally he shrugged. 'I will read the document,' he said coldly and walked towards the cabinet table. As he did so he seemed to become aware again of his fellow prisoners in the room. He stopped suddenly.

'Must my humiliation be witnessed by my colleagues and my servants as well as the foreign press?' he demanded bitterly.

General Perez motioned to the paratrooper captain. 'Take those men into another room. Leave guards outside the doors of this one.'

The President waited until the group from the air raid shelter had been herded out, then sat down at the table. The General's aide opened the portfolio, took out a legal document laced with green ribbon and placed it in front of the President.

He made a show of studying the document very carefully. In fact, he was indifferent to its contents. His intention was simply to let the tension mount a little further and to allow the other men there to feel that they were on the point of getting what they wanted.

For three minutes there was dead silence in the room. It was broken only by

6

the sound of distant machine-gun fire. It seemed to be coming from the south side of the city. The President heard a slight stir from the group of men behind him and one of them cleared his throat nervously. There was another burst of firing. The President took no notice of it. He read the document through a third time then put it down and sat back in his chair.

The aide offered him a pen with which to sign. The President ignored it and turned his head so that he could see General Perez.

'You spoke of a resignation, General,' he said. 'You did not mention that it was to be a confession also.'

'Hardly a confession, sir,' the General replied drily. 'We would not expect you voluntarily to incriminate yourself. The admission is only of incompetence. That is not yet a criminal offence in a head of state.'

The President smiled faintly. 'And if I were to sign this paper, what kind of personal treatment might I expect to receive afterwards? A prison cell perhaps, with a carefully staged treason trial to follow? Or merely a bullet in the head and an unmarked grave?'

The General reddened. 'We are here to correct abuses of power, sir, not to imitate them. When you have signed you will be conducted to your former home in Alazan province. You will be expected to remain there for the present and the Governor of the province will be instructed to see that you do so. Apart from that restriction you will be free to do as you please. Your family will naturally be permitted to join you.'

'You mention the house in Alazan province. What about my other personal property?'

'You will be permitted to retain everything you owned when you took office.'

'I see.' The President stood up and moved away from the table. 'I will think about it. I will let you have my decision tomorrow,' he added casually.

The silence that followed this announcement did not last long, but one of the newsmen reported later that it was one of the loudest he had ever heard. Another remembered that during it he suddenly became conscious of the presence and smell of a large bowl of tropical flowers on a side table by the anteroom door.

The President had walked towards the windows again. General Perez took two steps towards him, then stopped.

'You must decide at once! You must sign now!' he snapped.

The President turned on him. 'Why? Why now?'

It was the Chief of Police who answered him. 'Son of a whore, because we tell you to!' he shouted.

Suddenly they were all shouting at him. One officer was so enraged that he drew his pistol. The General had difficulty in restoring order.

The President took no notice of them. He kept his eyes on General Perez, but it was really the newsmen he was addressing now. As the din subsided he raised his voice.

'I asked a question, General. Why now? Why the haste? It is a reasonable question. If, as you say, you already control the country, what have you to fear from me? Or is it, perhaps, that your control is not in fact as complete and effective as you would have us believe?'

The General had to quell another angry outburst from his colleagues before he could answer, but he preserved his own temper admirably. His reply was calm and deliberate.

'I will tell you exactly what we control so that you may judge for yourself,' he said. 'To begin with all provincial army garrisons, air force establishments and police posts have declared for the Liberation Front, as have five out of eight of the provincial governors. The three objectors – I am sure you will have guessed who they are – have been rendered harmless and replaced by military governors. None of this can come as a great surprise to you I imagine. You never had much support outside the capital and the mining areas.'

The President nodded. 'Stupidity can sometimes be charted geographically,' he remarked.

'Now as to the capital. We control the airfields, both military and civil, the naval base, all communications including telephone and radio and television broadcast facilities, the power stations, all fuel oil storage facilities, all main traffic arteries, all government offices and city police posts together with the offices and printing presses of *El Correo* and *La Gaceta*.' He glanced at his watch. 'In connection with the broadcast facilities, I may mention that while the television station is temporarily off the air, the radio station will shortly begin broadcasting an announcement of the establishment of the new Liberation Front regime, which I recorded two days ago. As I told you before, everything is now under our control.'

The President smiled and glanced significantly at the newsmen. 'Are the *sumideri* under control, General?'

*Sumideri*, meaning sinks or drains, was the popular slang term used to describe the slum areas on the south side of the capital.

The General hesitated only an instant. 'The southern area is effectively contained,' he replied stiffly. 'The first infantry division reinforced by the third tank brigade has that responsibility.'

'I see.' The President looked again at the newsmen. 'So the civil war may be expected to begin at any moment.'

With a quick motion of his hands the General silenced the chorus of objections from his colleagues. 'We are fully prepared to deal firmly with any mob violence which may occur,' he said. 'Of that you may be sure.'

'Yes,' said the President bitterly, 'perhaps civil war is not the phrase to use for the planned massacre of unarmed civilians.' He swung around suddenly to face the newsmen and his voice hardened. 'You have been witnesses to this farce, gentlemen. I ask you to remember it well and let the civilised world know of it. These men come to ask for my resignation as head of state. That is all they want! Why? Because outside in the streets of the city their tanks and guns are waiting to begin the slaughter of the thousands of men and women who will protest their loyalty to me. And the way to bring them out for the slaughter is to fling my resignation like so much filth in their faces!'

General Perez could stand it no longer. 'That is a lie!' he shouted.

The President turned on him savagely. 'Do you think they will *not* come out? Why else are they "contained" as you call it? Why else? Because they are my people and because they will listen only to me.'

8

A glow of triumph suffused General Perez' angry face. 'Then their blood will be on *your* hands!' he roared. He stabbed a forefinger at the newsmen. 'You heard what he said, gentlemen. *They do what he tells them!* It is his responsibility, then, not ours, if they oppose us. *He* will be the murderer of women and children! Let him deny it.'

This time the President made no reply. He just stood there looking about him in bewilderment, like a boxer who has staggered to his feet after a count of ten and can't quite realise that the fight is over. At last he walked slowly back to the cabinet table, sat down heavily and buried his head in his hands.

Nobody else moved. When the President raised his head and looked at them again his eyes were haggard. He spoke very quietly.

'You are right,' he said, 'they are my people and they will do as I tell them. It is my responsibility. I accept it. There must be no senseless bloodshed. I think it is my duty to tell them not to protest.'

For a moment they all stared at him incredulously. The Chief of Police started to say something, then stopped as he caught General Perez' eye. If the man were serious this was too good an opportunity to miss.

General Perez went over and addressed the President. 'I cannot believe that even you would speak lightly on such a matter, but I must ask if you seriously mean what you say.'

The President nodded absently. 'I will need about an hour to draft my statement. There is a direct line to the radio station here in the Palace and the necessary equipment. The station can record me on tape.' He managed a rueful smile. 'In the circumstances, I imagine that you would prefer a recording to a live broadcast.'

'Yes.' But the General was still reluctant to believe in his triumph. 'How can you be sure that they will obey you?' he asked.

The President thought before he answered. 'There will be some, of course, who will be too distressed, too angry perhaps, to do as I ask,' he said. 'But if the officers commanding troops are ordered to use restraint, casualties can be kept to a minimum.' He glanced at the Chief of Police. 'There should be moderation, too, in respect of arrests. But the majority will listen to me, I think.' He paused. 'The important thing is that they must believe that I am speaking as a free man, and not out of fear because there is a pistol at my head.'

'I myself can give them that assurance,' said the General. The fact that he could make such an ingenuous suggestion is an indication of his mental confusion at that point.

The President raised his eyebrows. 'With all respect, General, I don't think we could expect them at this time to believe you of all people. I also think that the news that I am to be kept under what amounts to house arrest in Alazan province will not help to convince them either.'

'Then what do you propose? You can scarcely remain here in the capital.'

'Naturally not.' The President sat back in his chair. He had assumed a statesmanlike air now. 'It is quite clear,' he said, 'that we must achieve an orderly and responsible transfer of power. I shall, of course, resign in order to make way for the Liberation Front. However, in your place, I must say that I would regard my continued presence anywhere in this country as undesirable.

These people to whom I am to appeal tonight will only respond with restraint because of their loyalty to me. That loyalty will continue as long as they are able to give expression to it. You would do better really to get rid of me. As soon as I have spoken to my people you should get me out of the country as quickly as you can.'

'Exile?' It was the Chief of Police who spoke up now. 'But if we exile you that looks no better than house arrest in Alazan. Worse, possibly.'

'Exactly.' The President nodded approvingly. 'The solution I suggest is that I am permitted to announce to my people that I will continue to serve them, the nation and the Liberation Front, but in a different capacity and abroad. Our embassy in Nicaragua is without an ambassador at present. That would be a suitable appointment. I suggest that after I have recorded my broadcast I leave the country immediately in order to take up my post.'

The council discussion that ensued lacked the vehemence of the earlier exchanges. The strain of the past twenty-four hours was beginning to tell on General Perez and his colleagues; they were getting tired; and the sounds of firing from the south side were becoming more insistent. Time was running out. It was one of the newsmen who drew their attention to the fact.

'General,' he said to Perez, 'has it occurred to you that if the President doesn't talk to these people of his pretty soon they're all going to be out on the streets anyway?'

The President recognised the urgency, too, but refused to be hurried. As he pointed out, there were matters of protocol to be dealt with before he could make his appeal to the people. For one thing, his resignation would have to be redrafted. Since, he argued, he was now to be appointed his country's Ambassador to Nicaragua, references in the present draft to his incompetence would obviously have to be deleted. And there were other clauses which might be interpreted as reflections on his personal integrity.

In the end, the President wrote his own act of resignation. It was a simple document but composed with great care. His radio speech, on the other hand, he scribbled out on a cabinet desk pad while technicians, hastily summoned by jeep from the central radio building, were setting up a recording circuit in the anteroom.

Meanwhile, telephone communication had been restored to the Palace, and the Controller of the Presidential Secretariat had been released from arrest and put to work in his office.

His first task had been to contact the Nicaraguan Ambassador, give him a discreetly censored account of the current situation and request him to ascertain immediately, in accordance with Article 8 of the Pan-American Convention, if his government would be prepared to accept ex-President Fuentes as *persona grata* in the capacity of ambassador to their country. The Nicaraguan Ambassador had undertaken to telephone personally to the Minister of Foreign Relations in Managua and report back. His unofficial opinion was that there would be no opposition to the proposed appointment.

With the help of the air force council member present the Controller next spoke to the officer in charge at the International Airport. He learned that of the two civil airliners grounded earlier that evening, one had been southbound to

Caracas, the other, a Colombian Avianca jet, had been northbound to Mexico City. Fortunately, a Vice-Consul from the Colombian Consulate-General was already at the airport, having been summoned there by the Avianca captain to protest the grounding. The Controller spoke with the Vice-Consul who said that Avianca would be willing to carry ex-President Fuentes as a passenger to Mexico City if the Mexican Government would permit him to land. A call to the Mexican Embassy explaining that ex-President Fuentes would be in transit through Mexican territory on his way to his post as an accredited diplomatic representative to the republic of Nicaragua secured the necessary permission.

The President already had a diplomatic passport which needed only minor amendments to fit it for its new role. All that was needed now to facilitate his departure was confirmation from the Nicaraguan Ambassador that he would be accorded diplomatic status in Managua. Within an hour, the Nicaraguan Government, acting promptly in the belief that they were helping both parties to the arrangement, had replied favourably.

The escape route was open.

President Fuentes made two tape-recordings of the appeal to his supporters, one for the radio, the second for use by a loudspeaker van in the streets of the *sumideri*. Then he signed his resignation and was driven to the airport. General Perez provided an escort of armoured cars.

The plane, with ex-President Fuentes on board, took off a little after midnight. Five hours later it landed in Mexico City.

News of the Liberation Front *coup* and of the President's voluntary resignation and ambassadorial appointment had been carried by all the international wire services, and there were reporters waiting for him. There was also, despite the early hour, a protocol official from the Department of External Relations to meet him. Fuentes made a brief statement to the reporters, confirming the fact of his resignation. On the subject of his appointment as Ambassador to Nicaragua he was vague. He then drove to a hotel in the city. On the way there he asked the protocol official if it would be convenient for him to call upon the Minister of External Affairs later that day.

The official was mildly surprised. As Ambassador Fuentes was merely passing through Mexico, a brief note of thanks to the Minister would normally be the only courtesy expected of him. On the other hand, the circumstances of Fuentes' sudden translation from President to Ambassador were unusual and it was possible that the Minister might be glad of the opportunity of hearing what Fuentes himself had to say on the subject. He promised that he would consult the Minister's personal assistant at the earliest possible moment.

The Minister received Ambassador Fuentes at five o'clock that afternoon.

The two men had met before, at conferences of the Organisation of American States and on the occasion of a state visit to Mexico paid by Fuentes soon after he became President. It was a tribute to the Minister's natural courtesy as well as his self-discipline that Fuentes believed that the Minister liked him. In fact the Minister viewed him with dislike and disapproval and had not been in the least surprised or distressed by the news of the Liberation Front *coup*. However, he had been amused by Fuentes' ability to emerge from the situation not only alive and free but also invested with diplomatic immunity; and it modified his distaste for the man. He was, one had to admit, an engaging scoundrel.

After the preliminary politenesses had been disposed of the Minister inquired courteously whether he could be of any service to the Ambassador during his stay in Mexico.

Fuentes inclined his head: 'That is most kind of you, Mr Minister,' he said graciously. 'Yes, there is one thing.'

'You only have to ask.'

'Thank you.' Ambassador Fuentes straightened up a little in his chair. 'I wish,' he said, 'to make formal application to be considered here as a refugee, and formally to request political asylum in the United States of Mexico.'

The Minister stared for a moment, then smiled.

'Surely you must be joking, Mr Ambassador.'

'Not in the least.'

The Minister was puzzled, and because he was puzzled he put into words the first obvious objection that came into his head.

'But in the United States of Mexico, even though you are not accredited to the Federal Government, you already, by virtue of the Pan-American Convention, enjoy diplomatic status and privileges here,' he said.

It was a statement which he was later to regret.

Ambassador Fuentes never took up his post in Nicaragua.

One of the first official acts of General Perez' Council of the Liberation Front was to set up a committee, headed by the Professor of Political Economy at Bolívar University, to report on the financial state of the Republic.

It took the committee only a few days to discover that during the past three years ex-President Fuentes had authorised printings of five hundred peseta banknotes to a total value of one hundred million dollars and that twenty of those hundred millions could not be accounted for.

The Governor of the National Bank was immediately arrested. He was an old man who had spent most of his life in the National Archives gathering material for a scholarly study of colonial Spanish land grants. He had been appointed to the bank by Fuentes. He knew nothing about banking. He had merely carried out the orders of the Minister of Finance.

Fuentes had been his own Minister of Finance.

Interviewed on the subject by the press in Mexico City, ex-President Fuentes stated that the committee's revelations had shocked, horrified and amazed him. He also said that he had no idea where the missing twenty millions might be. Regrettably, he was unable quite to refrain from smiling as he said it.

Ex-President Fuentes' retirement has not been peaceful.

During the five years he held office as President there was only one serious attempt on his life. Since he resigned the Presidency, ceased to concern himself with politics and went to live abroad, no less than three such attempts have been made. There will doubtless be others. Meanwhile, he has had to fight off two lots of extradition proceedings and a number of civil actions directed against his European bank accounts.

He is wealthy, of course, and can afford to pay for the protection, both physical and legal, that he needs; but he is by no means resigned to the situation.

As he is fond of pointing out, other men in his position have accumulated larger fortunes. Moreover, his regime was never unacceptably oppressive. He was no Trujillo, no Batista, no Porfirio Diaz. Why then should he be hounded and harassed as if he were?

Ex-President Fuentes remains a puzzled and indignant man.

# JOHN
# BINGHAM

# Mr Bulmer's Golden Carp

Mr Bulmer stood patiently in the Underground train waiting for it to arrive at Green Park Station. He hung on to the overhead strap, swaying slightly with the movements of the train, looking at the faces of his fellow-travellers. Most of them looked pinched and pale, hating the start of a new week made more miserable by the winter dark, the touch of fog, the freezing cold in the streets.

He never felt unhappy on Monday mornings, or indeed any other morning. He was always raring to go, whatever the weather, because he had his hobby to keep him warm.

So now, while other passengers drugged themselves with the morning newspapers, or sniffed and dabbed their noses, or stared at nothing with glazed eyes, Bulmer hummed to himself a silly little tune resurrected from the past:

> '*I saw two cods cuddling,*
> *Down in the deep blue sea—*
> *I saw two cods cuddling,*
> *But I don't think they saw me—*'

He paused, fumbling for the next lines, then, right or wrong, went on humming:

> '*Back I went to the shore again,*
> *And shouted out with glee—*
> *I saw two cods cuddle-luddle-luddling—*
> *Down in the deep blue sea.*'

He looked again at his fellow-passengers, seeking a face which might indicate a feeling as cheerful as his own. He thought he might find one if somebody had won a good-sized Premium Bond, or believed he had done well with the football pools.

But they all still looked sunk in Monday morning gloom.

He thought impatiently of Bonds and Pools, those fishing lines baited to hook a fish sufficiently large to release people from work for ever. Bonds meant locking up cash, assuming you had it; and Pools involved baiting the hook with money, and you normally only threw the hook in once a week.

His own line was always in the water. Day after day. And the hook was large, strongly barbed and unbaited. That was the beauty of it. No bait was needed.

In their frenzied enthusiasm the fish could hardly swim fast enough towards it or impale themselves with greater eagerness. In certain cases he jerked the hook away, because he was choosy, and some fish might actually bite the hand that had provided the hook, and others were too small. He had never bothered with small fish.

It wasn't worth the risk.

Usually there was a struggle, of course, but it added fun to the profitable sport, demanding skill, experience, expertise, and his line was tough and smooth. He prided himself on the smoothness of his line of talk, too. Mr Bulmer loved a play on words.

As he swayed with the train he thought again that his line was smooth. Smooth and nearly unbreakable, though one or two fish had got away in his early, inexperienced days.

He began to recollect, affectionately, the details of how his first small fish had wanted to hook itself, and how he had shooed it away; although of paltry value itself, it had revealed to him the worth of a hobby which could be a constant source of pleasure and profit, and keep him warm for the rest of his life.

It was not to be risked for a tiddler.

The train drew into Green Park Station, and he had to interrupt his memories.

He walked quickly, because it was sleeting, towards the small dry-cleaning business near Curzon Street of which he was the manager. He had been in charge of bigger suburban branches, but when he heard that the firm was finding difficulties in replacing a good manager for the little struggling Mayfair branch he had most sportingly offered to take it over, though following the wage structure, based on turn-over, it meant a drop in salary.

Mildly, with his best Honest Old Bulmer look, he had pointed out that as an unmarried man his needs were modest, he was over fifty, the firm had treated him generously in the past twenty years, and no doubt they would do so when he came to retire – and if he could help them out he was prepared to.

He was convinced that he would be helping himself, too, and without fiddling the books or deceiving the accountants or auditors in any way.

So he had sat back, looking at the managing director benevolently, brown eyes magnified by thick lenses, hearing words of appreciation, as he stroked his bald head and then temporarily rested his small white hands on his small round paunch.

It was all delightfully friendly.

Afterwards, he had gone along to a narrow street in Soho which catered for his own peculiar pleasures and desires, because he knew that all work and no play would make Bulmer a dull boy.

It was an occasion for celebration.

The Mayfair branch, though modest in size, should be no ordinary fish pond. It should hold carp – big, old and heavy.

Golden carp.

Now, as he came to the Four Star Dry Cleaners, he looked up at the notice in the window calling attention to the four virtues of the firm: cleaning on the premises, pressing while you waited, mending and repairs, and speedy free delivery.

He had recently redesigned it himself, and giggled, as he often did, at a play on words in the first of the four starred lines:

*Dry Cleaning *Done On the SPOT*!

On the SPOT was good! Witty! Hinting at alert, lively minds.

He smiled into the driving sleet and let himself in by the side entrance. It was thirty minutes before opening time. The rest of the staff would not arrive for twenty minutes.

He always got in early partly because although in winter the building would be cold he had his hobby to keep him warm, and partly to see that the books and everything else were punctiliously in order. That was most necessary for his hobby.

He glanced briefly at the giant drum where the forty-pound bundles of clothes revolved in Perchloroethylene, known briefly as Perk to the staff, then at the big ironing board, where the spotter went over the clothes for obstinate stains.

The steam gun, capable of blowing wet or dry steam on to stains, lay on the board and by its side the little bottles of chemicals; simple meths for such things as ink, and amyl acetate, and sulphuric acid, and peroxide for certain whites, and ammonia, and hydrochloric acid. Ammonia and hydrochloric acid were useful for blood stains.

As he hung up his thick grey coat and scarf and hat he was thinking dark inconsequential thoughts about wine, and how it used to be easy to remove wine stains. Now it wasn't. They seemed to dye the material, and he wouldn't be surprised to learn that colouring was added to the cheaper red wines to make them look richer.

Then, eagerly, he stepped with his little bouncy gait to the front of the shop where the customers' clothes, cleaned and ready for collection or delivery, hung in rows on rails.

This was his fishpond.

It was not large, and he had been there three months without catching anything, but as in some small remote mountain lake, where the fish were rare but magnificent, so in this Mayfair branch with a limited but rich clientele he knew his line was in the right water.

It was only a question of patience.

He ran his eye along the row of clothes, noting the colour of the tags pinned to them. Each tag was a piece of short wide tape, bearing three rows of figures written in indelible ink.

The first row bore the same numerals as in the receipt book, and the customer had the top copy. The second row showed the number of items involved in each cleaning – a man's two-piece suit would bear the figure '2', a jacket by itself the figure '1'. The third row gave the date the clothes were handed in.

Red tags meant normal cleaning service. A red and a yellow tag meant normal cleaning but refer to desk for instructions about repairs. A blue tag meant Express, wanted in twenty-four hours.

A white tag meant things left in pocket, collect from cupboard under counter.

Mr Bulmer, the hard-working little manager who always came in before the others, stood staring at the clothes, rubbing his hands, looking for a white tag.

He was checking stuff which had come in on Saturday, when he had taken a morning off, and was due to go out that Monday. The rest he had already checked or could do so at his leisure.

So he stood, feeling the old familiar thrill, eyes shining and large behind the pebble lenses. Perhaps this grey morning he would get stuck into one of the Big

Fellows, a fish worth thousands. Perhaps ten thousand. Perhaps more.

There were five blue Express tags. Two on women's clothes, others on a dinner jacket and trousers, a sports jacket and trousers, and a black jacket and striped trousers. He saw no white tags, and turned away, disappointed, to switch on the central heating.

Then, passing the black jacket and striped trousers, he saw a white tag pinned to an arm of the jacket. It had been partly obscured by one of the women's dresses.

Delicately, with a white podgy little hand, he lifted a sleeve of the jacket, to which were pinned the white and blue tags, noting the number, 112451.

There was a jar on the reception counter in which there was an assortment of old pencils and ball-point pens in need of refills. The key of the cupboard under the counter, containing stuff found in customers' clothes, was kept in the jar in an attempt to foil burglars and pilferers.

He shook the key out and unlocked the cupboard and gazed at a row of buff envelopes on the shelf. Scribbled on the outside were numbers corresponding to tag numbers.

He went through them, looking for 112451.

It was surprising the things people left in their pockets, especially men. Slim gold cigarette cases, lighters and bank-notes were not uncommon in the Mayfair branch. He was not interested in such things, nor in more intimate things, bought at a chemist's shop and which, if found by a wife, might or might not cause the most appalling domestic scene. Mr Bulmer was always insistent that the staff should use their heads about what, how and to whom property should be handed back. If in doubt they could refer to him.

Family harmony was vital in this day and age, he would point out, and if, now and then, the Four Star Dry Cleaners could play a humble part in avoiding the break-up of a marriage, then it was their duty to do so – and without hope of reward, except the feeling of social duty conscientiously performed.

The envelope marked 112451 was flat and light. This was a good omen. Bulky or heavy envelopes were invariably disappointing.

He stood looking at it for a few moments, holding it in his hand unopened. He always did this with a likely envelope, enjoying the anticipation of seeing what was inside, knowing that the nature of his hobby meant that he must almost always be disappointed. Almost always. But not always.

He had often noticed that before a man started to eat what he hoped would be a good dish a very slight smile would flicker round his lips as he picked up his knife and fork.

Mr Bulmer smiled slightly and opened the buff envelope.

Inside was a plain white envelope. He approved the expensive quality of the paper. It was addressed, 'Sir Henry Bendetter'. In the top left-hand corner were the words, 'By hand', and 'Personal only'. On the back, as a reinforcement, was written 'Private'.

The writing was large, bold and probably feminine. The envelope had been raggedly, probably hurriedly, torn open.

When he had read the note inside Mr Bulmer felt the stillness which always came over him in moments of sudden pleasurable surprise. It was as though all sounds had ceased for him except the noise of his slowly accelerating heartbeats.

He read the note a second time:

My darling,

Clever you! He has taken your advice, and flies to Geneva for a consultation on Thursday morning, returning Sunday. HRH not due back till Monday. I have booked our room at Oakleigh, as agreed. Pick me up at the usual place, Thursday noon. Darling, it's been so long!

Your own Nutkin
XXX

There was a song in Mr Bulmer's heart all day.

Staff complained about the wintry weather, were sour to customers and at times downright rude to each other, but Mr Bulmer hummed intermittently to himself. This was noted by the staff behind the steamed-up windows of the Four Star Dry Cleaners, and it annoyed them. Old Bulmer had no right to be happy on such a day. But Mr Bulmer felt he had every right to be happy, and the tune he hummed more than any other was: '*I saw two cods cuddling, down by the deep blue sea, I saw two cods cuddling and I don't think they saw me.*'

It was appropriate, since Oakleigh was by the sea, on the Sussex coast.

He kept repeating the last line – '*and I don't think they saw me*'. They certainly wouldn't see him, not till it was too late.

But as the morning drew on he changed one of the words.

The reference book which he kept in his desk drawer had yielded information which expanded the song in his heart.

Sir Henry Bendetter was a Fellow of the Royal College of Surgeons, had had a distinguished career and doubtless hoped to continue it, since he was only forty-nine.

At the age of thirty-eight he had married Elizabeth Maker, widow of the late Sir James Maker, and there was one s., James, and one d., Mary. They had an address in Kensington, and there was another, obviously a consulting-room, in Harley Street.

Mr. Bulmer glanced again at the letter from Nutkin, with its reference to HRH and again his heart beat fast.

Nutkin was clearly a scatty woman. His mind briefly went back to his childhood and Beatrix Potter's little book about Squirrel Nutkin. Most squirrels were scatty, they often forgot where they had buried their nuts.

This particular Nutkin had even written on her own writing paper.

He consulted the street directory, then, with increased excitement, he again consulted a reference book.

It seemed too good to be true.

Nutkin's address was that of Lord and Lady Catterley. There was a valuable reference to an honorary Court appointment.

This was unique. Two big fish, not one, perhaps to be played separately, with luck, each struggling desperately.

Therefore he had changed the word in the song from Cod to Carp, and hummed gently, '*I saw two carp cuddling, down in the deep blue sea*'.

Golden carp – at last.

At the end of the day, he made his way once more to the little basement club in the dingy Soho street where he indulged his peculiar sadistic pleasures. It cost him a good deal of money, but he had earned and saved good money from his other hobby, and now the golden carp would bring him more, and once again he told himself as he went there that all work and no play would make Bulmer a dull boy.

At around nine o'clock, he made his way back to Notting Hill Gate and let himself into a tall Victorian house, with pillars each side of the door, and plodded up to the second floor where he had his living-room and bedroom, and the closet in the wall furnished with a gas-ring, which was called a kitchenette. On the half landing, on the way up, was the bathroom and lavatory which he shared with the people below.

He did not smoke, or drink spirits or beer, but on rare occasions he indulged in a glass of sweet cider. In view of the excitements of the day, and the more recent excitement of the early evening in Soho, he opened a bottle of cider and carefully poured it out, and settled down in an easy chair in front of the electric fire.

Normally, he only switched on one bar. In really cold weather, two bars. Tonight, in view of the weather and the day's events, he switched on all three. Money should be no object.

Before sitting down he took his accounts book out of a locked drawer in a shoddy table, and glanced at it, noting that he had savings of approximately £17,000.

Now that he had got stuck into the golden carp, the sum might be increased to £37,000. Maybe even £47,000. Maybe £50,000 – as a round figure.

And there'd be fun.

Surely there'd be fun.

He turned on his little radio and tuned in to some Beethoven music, and stretched his short legs happily towards the fire, and took from a paper bag the two big cream buns he had bought at lunchtime. He might be plump, and short, too, he thought, and corrected himself, because he prided himself on accuracy. He *was* short. But so were Napoleon and Mussolini and Winston Churchill, and other powerful people, including some well-known murderers.

He began to think about murder, savouring the sickly sweetness of the buns, soothed by the Beethoven music, telling himself that killing was the ultimate exercise of power, for what did it profit a man if he gained the whole world and lost his life? Therefore to take away a life was the final triumph of man over man. Or woman. He repeated aloud the phrase, 'Killing is the ultimate exercise of power,' because he liked the sound of it.

Some of the cream had oozed out of the bun he was eating on to his fingers. He licked it off and contemplated his small white hands. They had never been stained with blood from a killing. But you didn't need hands to kill.

Not even a finger to press a trigger.

The subtlest refinement of murder was to make the victim do the work for you himself. Therein lay art, his own unique art.

First, the extraction of money, for money was sweet, sweeter than the love of women, he felt sure, since nature in her wisdom had ordained that he should not be able actually to make love to women. Then the observation of despair. Then the implementation of his power – leading to the self-killing.

It was when he played a fish so that both these aims were fulfilled that he felt the greatest achievement from his hobby. It was rare, but it made the effort and waiting so infinitely worthwhile.

His first attempt to bring off what he termed a 'double' had been bungled. He saw that now. He had been over-confident. It looked a sure-fire success, in the days when illegal operations could mean ruin.

The young doctor had been married with two children. He had extracted £1,500 in instalments from the doctor and was inclined to believe the man when he had said that no more was available.

So he had demanded £5,000 within one month, and during that month had left London, first to attend a launderers' and dry-cleaners' conference, and then to go on holiday. On holiday, he had sent the doctor a picture postcard each week.

But when he came back the fish had disappeared.

It had been very annoying, because the doctor must have had within his own surgery ample means to kill himself. But he had emigrated. Swum off to deeper and richer and safer waters in America.

It seemed at the time almost a breach of trust.

Still, he had learned his lesson. You had to keep the pressure up, the line tight, you couldn't relax.

His first success had been a brief, brisk affair involving a bank manager, the payment of £4,000, a demand for a further £10,000 and a 'shooting accident'. Satisfying, as a first 'double event', because at the final interview the man had seemed truly distressed, indeed tearful – but for money and exquisite pleasure it did not compare with the Susan Barclay operation two years ago.

That had been a beauty.

Materially, it had brought £6,000 in four payments of £1,500 each, the result of her shares and jewel sales, because her husband was a very rich and jealous American.

Furthermore, she had loved her husband, despite one temporary lapse.

Mr Bulmer finished his second cream bun, and took some sips of cider, going over in his mind once again the final interview with Mrs Barclay, watching the tears, listening to the pleas that £10,000 more was impossible.

It had indeed been the ultimate exercise of power.

The coroner's verdict had been that Mrs Barclay had taken her own life by an overdose of sleeping tablets while the balance of her mind had been disturbed. It was a merciful verdict, since nobody could say why the balance of her mind had been disturbed, except Mr Bulmer, of course, and he wasn't telling.

At 9.45 p.m. Mr Bulmer telephoned the Plough Arms at Oakleigh-on-Sea and booked a room for himself for the nights of Thursday and Friday. The Plough was a one-star hotel in his motorist guide-book. There were only two hotels. The other was a four-star hotel called the Bay Hotel.

22

He knew for a certainty who would be staying there, and in a double room, too, while he was at the modest Plough. He had no intention whatever of staying in the same hotel as Sir Henry Bendetter and the woman with the revoltingly twee nickname of Nutkin.

He went happily to bed at ten-thirty punctually. For a while he thought up certain formalities, such as ringing the dry-cleaner's on Thursday morning to say that he had a stomach upset and might not be in until Monday. Nobody would object. They'd better not, since he was the manager.

Then he thought out his plan of action. Finally, he fell asleep thinking of the goings on in the Soho basement club that evening. Murder by what you might call remote control couldn't be organised often. You had to have a substitute to fill in the gaps, that is, if you wanted to keep happy and well-balanced mentally. He'd read psychological books, he knew about these things.

Making love for a man was a way of exercising power. If you'd never made love, never could, you found power in other ways.

Killing was the ultimate exercise of power, but if the opportunity was not to hand you must find a substitute, maybe a second-rate substitute, like inflicting pain.

Better than nothing, he told himself, and fell happily asleep.

Once, in the night, he woke and thought again of Susan Barclay. That had indeed been a good exercise. Perfect in its way. For a few minutes he lay speculating about how long the present one could last. Probably quite a long time. And the end?

He had a sudden thought which made him catch his breath. Might there, in the distant end, even be a double suicide, a double killing by remote control, his control?

He shook his head in the dark and composed himself for sleep again.

That was too much to hope for.

Mr Bulmer drove down to Oakleigh on the Thursday morning, starting early, and booked in at the Plough Hotel around noon. February was a dead month for hotels. They were glad to see him.

He felt sure that not only would the Bay Hotel be glad to welcome Sir Henry Bendetter, and the woman who was pleased to call herself Nutkin, but that he would have no difficulty in spotting them, even though they would certainly have booked in under an assumed name.

He knew these hotels. He could recognise the aged 'permanent' residents, who were kicked out in the summer to make room for holiday-makers, and graciously permitted to return in winter when business was slack; the casual one-night businessmen; and the others. In February visiting couples would be rare indeed, and he guessed Sir Henry Bendetter and his woman would stick out like sore thumbs.

He spent the afternoon driving around the district, seeking a place where the first, long, vital interview could take place. There would, of course, be a skirmish first, some argy-bargy, indignation, denials, protests, a reference to the police, but that did not rank as the first *real* interview.

The first *real* interview was all-important.

It was here that the tone was set. And the scale of payment. It was here, too, that danger was at its height. Here the barbed hook could be jerked deeper, but here, too, the line might be snapped by ham-fisted action.

There were other more obvious hazards, such as microphones and tape-recorders, which was why Mr Bulmer always conducted the first vital interview at a place of his own choosing. And that place was preferably in the open air, away from the contamination of sophisticated eavesdropping.

He drove around for about an hour and a half before he found what he wanted. The search was made more difficult because the wintry weather which had ushered in the week was still gripping the countryside, and he did not relish conducting the main negotiations in a snowstorm. At one time he thought of a cosy chat in his own car. But that meant removing the number plate, which was a bore, and not without danger.

Suddenly, about four miles from the coast, in the hills overlooking the little harbour, he found what he sought. A couple of hundred yards from a side road, a cart track ended in a cul-de-sac consisting of some broken-down walls which had been a farmyard, and a small abandoned farmhouse, the roof partly open to the sky, the front door drooping on its hinges.

Here he would talk. It would be cold. It would be cheerless.

That was all to the good.

He drove slowly back, noting certain landmarks so that Sir Henry Bendetter would have no difficulty in following his directions with the aid of the sketch map he would give him.

Mr Bulmer's mental image of a well-known surgeon was a conventional one: a tall, distinguished-looking man, aged about fifty, with clean-cut features, hair greying elegantly above the ears and fine, sensitive hands with long fingers. The hands of a musician, really.

Bendetter turned out to be quite different. He was a short, thick-set man, with coarse black hair and strong, square hands. Mr Bulmer might not even have identified him, he might have mistaken him for a top-class salesman or an advertising executive. But he had a stroke of luck.

Mr Bulmer did not rely on good luck. He hoped for an absence of bad luck, and that was all, but if good luck came his way it was an unexpected bonus, and that evening he had a small bonus.

From 6.30 p.m. onwards he had sat in the lounge of the Bay Hotel, watching a trickle of people eventually pass him to the dining-room, because he liked to have a sight of a victim beforehand. It was a winter collection. A few old ladies, some walking slowly with sticks. A portly red-faced man who looked like a caricature of an old-time Indian Army colonel. A middle-aged married couple with a strong Yorkshire accent, comparing the place with one they had stayed in at Scarborough.

At 7.30 p.m., after two tomato juices, he began to grow uneasy.

A notice prominently displayed in the vestibule stated peremptorily, in British hotel fashion, that dinner would be served from 6.45 to 7.45 p.m.

He wondered if things had gone wrong, plans been changed, and at 7.35 p.m. he wandered out to the reception desk. The receptionist, a girl of about nineteen, crudely made up, stared at him hostilely and said, 'Yes?'

The hotel registration book was open on the counter before him.

'I expected some friends of mine to stay here tonight,' he said mildly. 'A Mr and Mrs Ives de Boisculaire.'

'Who?'

'Boisculaire – a French couple. Perhaps they've been held up by bad weather.'

The foreign name, the query and his tentative explanation occupied enough time to enable him casually to glance at the column for new arrivals.

He heard the girl, bored, say, 'Nobody of that name. Only one couple arrived today. Not that name.'

It certainly wasn't that name. Nor was the name Henry Bendetter. The entry showed a Mr and Mrs H. Bendit, of London, W1, British, occupying Room 12. It was good enough for Mr Bulmer.

'Thank you,' he said gently, and at that moment heard a voice at his side say:

'Mrs Bendit is not feeling very well – would it be possible to have some clear soup and plain boiled fish and creamed potatoes sent up to her in Room 12, please?'

The receptionist did not exactly snarl, she just said it was not usual to serve meals in rooms with a skeleton winter staff. She would have to ask the chef.

'Thank you, and you may present my compliments to the management, if need be, and inform them that if it is not possible for the chef to perform this small service I shall certainly write to the Hoteliers Association or whatever the appropriate body is.'

Mr Bulmer felt his nerve ends tingle with excitement. This was going to be a fish worth landing, this one was a fighter. He would need all his expertise with this one. He might even have to use Nutkin to soften him up. He felt confident that Nutkin would cave in easily, what with her husband's Court connections. He made a quick dive for a play on words and told himself Nutkin would be a soft nut to crack, and giggled softly as he followed his man towards the lift.

At the lift door he made his first cast.

'Sir Henry Bendetter,' he said quietly, in a voice which stated a fact and did not pose a question. The fish made no attempt to escape.

'Yes?'

'I believe you and – er – your wife are staying here under a different name.'

Mr Bulmer smiled in a friendly way.

'I would be grateful if you would keep your knowledge to yourself. Unfortunately I am fairly well known, through the Press. We frequently travel incognito.'

'Like Royalty,' Mr Bulmer murmured, and was pleased at his sly reference to Court circles.

'What can I do for you, Mr—?'

'Palmer, Mr Harold Palmer is my name. We have not met. It is a private matter.'

Sir Henry Bendetter hesitated.

'Perhaps after dinner, Mr Palmer. My wife is—'

It was time to give the first quick jerk on the line.

'Not after dinner – now.'

'Is it so urgent?'

Mr Bulmer nodded and adjusted his pebble-lensed spectacles.

'We need a quick talk at once, Sir Henry. A couple of minutes. That's all.'

'May I ask what it is about?'

'Nutkin,' Mr Bulmer said as bleakly as he could say such a ridiculous name. He saw his victim stiffen, his face go blank. It was a square face, naturally pale, but he thought it turned a shade paler. Certainly the grey eyes flickered, and the words, when he spoke, were hardly audible.

'What or who is Nutkin?'

'A woman. As we both know.'

'What about Nutkin?'

'This about Nutkin,' said Mr Bulmer, and handed over a photostat copy of the note. 'My principal has the original, of course.' He balanced himself on the balls of his feet, ready to jump back. There was always the chance that a man might lose his head, and try to hit him.

'Your what?'

'My principal – the gentleman for whom I act, see?' He found it more delicate to pretend that he was acting for somebody else.

Sir Henry Bendetter sighed, turned and led the way to a table and chairs in a corner of an adjacent room. They were alone. Everybody else was at dinner.

'I suppose you want money?'

Mr Bulmer raised his hands deprecatingly.

'Not me, my principal. My principal, he doesn't like immoral liaisons, see? He believes those who offend in this way should be heavily fined. Get it? It is his way of helping to clean up the permissive society, see?'

'How much? A thousand pounds?'

Mr Bulmer shook his head.

'My principal is a hard man, see? We must talk further – tomorrow. At about four-thirty. By then you will have had time to think things over, get it? This sketch map will show where we meet. And you won't try any bloody tricks, will you? No tape-recorders, microphones, any of that sort of lark, none of that?'

He was putting the pressure on now, and when he did so Mr Bulmer's voice always grew suddenly hard, the slight cockney accent more pronounced, the phraseology more rough.

He watched Bendetter shrug, then nod reluctantly.

'And no capers with the police, right? They try and keep names out of the papers, but it all leaks out, don't it? Often, it does. My principal would see that it did in your case, not half he wouldn't, and to the right people, too. Get it?'

He tossed the sketch map on the table and got up. As he walked away he said:

'See you tomorrow. Give my love to Nutkin – or should I say Lady Catterley?'

That night in bed he ran over his mental film sequences of the fun he'd had with Susan Barclay. She'd been a good-looking woman, a big, tall blonde, with an oval face and large blue eyes, and arched eyebrows, and a very short upper lip, and a big dimple on the left of her mouth which quivered in and out when she cried and pleaded with him. She'd done a lot of that. She'd been real good value, in more ways than one.

Sir Henry would probably be dull, at least at first, but Nutkin might be fun.

Mr Bulmer arrived punctually at the farmhouse. It was bitterly cold and snowing and darkness would fall earlier than usual.

Sir Henry Bendetter's car was already there. He noted with approval that it was a Bentley. It was empty, and he guessed that Bendetter had already gone up to the ruined building. That was good, punctuality on these jobs showed nervousness.

But he approached the building carefully, looking for signs of anybody else's presence. Inside, he paused in the dark hall where the wallpaper was hanging in shreds, and listened. There was no sound.

Then he heard a slight noise, a footstep, from a room on the left, and walked quickly in, and stopped abruptly in the doorway, because the figure at the window with its back to him was not that of Bendetter.

It wasn't a man.

When the tall woman turned to face him he felt his heart churning over, then slowing down, then turning somersaults, then thundering in his ears as he looked at the blonde hair, the short upper lip, the big dimple to the left of the mouth, the large blue eyes now as cold as the ice outside.

'I've only seen you once before, you bastard,' she said softly. 'I caught a glimpse of you, once, when you were leaving my sister Susan's house. It's taken me two years to track you down through your firm's laundry tags, you little hyena.'

He didn't know that the revolver she was holding was empty, a bluff, a deterrent in case he thought of attacking her. He only saw the weapon, he saw nothing else but the weapon – that, and the ice in her blue eyes.

'You killed my sister, my twin sister,' he heard her say, above the roar in his ears. 'When you killed her you as good as killed me. That's how it goes with twins.'

He managed to gasp out three words:

'We can talk.'

'What about?'

Now it seemed as though there were large marbles running across his chest, and a pain was creeping up his left arm from the elbow. He stared at her, horrified, and whispered:

'Bendetter and the woman Nutkin—'

She laughed impatiently.

'I am the woman Nutkin, and Sir Henry is my husband, you silly little swine, and we used the Catterley writing paper for the trap we set you. We could prosecute you for blackmail, but on the whole I think I will kill you.'

He stared in panic at the revolver she was caressing.

The pain from his left elbow was spreading across his chest, now, reaching down his right arm towards his right elbow.

He lost consciousness, his hobby no longer keeping him warm.

Sir Henry Bendetter came from another room when she called him, and looked down at Mr Bulmer, and then examined him, and got up from his knees and said:

'He was about the right age and plumpness for it, and he had an emotional disturbance. He oughtn't to move at all, but he will certainly try to, later.'

'What are you going to do?'

'I am going to do what Susan may or may not wish me to do.'

'Meaning?'

'I'm going to do nothing.'

'Nothing?'

'It should be cold in here tonight, if he survives till then. Cold is one of the worst things for these cases, my dear,' said Sir Henry Bendetter woodenly, and led his wife back to the car. Her face was relaxed and peaceful.

On the Monday, they collected the spaniel, HRH, from the vet.

By then Mr Bulmer was no longer interested in his warming hobby, or anything else, since there was no warmth in him at all, which was just as well, because if there had been any warmth left in him then there would have been something seriously wrong with the municipal morgue, which is not what rate-payers expect in these days of high taxation.

# CHRISTIANNA BRAND

## Bless This House

They were beautiful; and even in that first moment, the old woman was to think later, she should have known; should have recognised them for what they were. Standing there so still and quiet in face of her own strident aggression, the boy in the skin-tight blue jeans, with his mac held over his head against the fine drizzle of the evening rain – held over his head like a mantle; the girl with her long hair falling straight as a veil down to the pear-shaped bulge of her pregnancy. But though suspicion died in her, she would not be done out of her grievance. 'What you doing here? You got no right here, parking outside my window.'

They did not reply that after all the street did not belong to her. The girl said only, apologetically: 'We got nowhere else to sleep.'

'Nowhere to sleep?' She glanced at the ringless hand holding together the edges of the skimpy coat. 'Can't you go home?'

'Our homes aren't in London,' said the boy.

'You slept somewhere last night.'

'We had to leave. The landlady – Mrs Mace – she went away and her nephew was coming home and wanted the place. We've been hunting and hunting for days. No one else will take us in.'

'Because of the baby,' said the girl. 'In case it comes, you see.'

Suspicion gleamed again. 'Well, don't look at me. I got nothing, only my one bed-sit, here in the basement – the other rooms are used for storage, all locked up and bolted. And upstairs – well, that's full.'

'Oh, of course,' said the girl. 'We didn't mean that at all. We were sleeping in the car.'

'In the car?' She stood at the top of the area steps peering at them in the light of the street lamp, shawled, also against the rain. She said to the boy: 'You can't let her sleep in that thing. Not like she is.'

'Well, I know,' he said. 'But what else? That's why we came to this quiet part.'

'We'll move along of course,' said the girl, 'if you mind our being here.'

'It's a public street,' she said illogically. But it was pitiful, poor young thing; and there was about them this – something: so beautiful, so still and quiet, expressionless, almost colourless, like figures in some dim old church, candle-lit at – yes, at Christmas time. Like figures in a Christmas crèche. She said uncertainly: 'If a few bob would help—'

But they disclaimed at once. 'No, no, we've got money; well, enough, anyway. And he can get work in the morning, it's nothing like that. It's only. . .Well,' said the girl, spreading slow, explanatory hands, 'it's like we told you. The baby's coming and no one will take us in. They just say, sorry – no room.'

Was it then that she had known? – when she heard herself saying, almost without her own volition: 'Out in the back garden – there's a sort of shed. . .'

It was the strain, perhaps, the uncertainty, the long day's search for accommodation, the fading hope; but the baby came that night. No time for doctor or midwife; but Mrs Vaughan was experienced in such matters, delivered the child safely, dealt with the young mother – unexpectedly resilient despite her fragile look, calm, uncomplaining, apparently impervious to the pain – settled her comfortably at last on the old mattress in the shed, covered over with clean bedclothes. 'When you're fit to be moved – we'll see.' And to the boy she said sharply 'What you got there?'

He had employed the waiting time in knocking together a sort of cradle out of a wooden box; padded it round and fitted it with a couple of down-filled cushions from their car. Taken nothing of hers; all the things were their own. 'Look, Marilyn – for the baby.'

'Oh, Jo,' she said, 'you always were a bit of a carpenter! You always were good with your hands!'

Joseph. And Marilyn. And Joseph a bit of a carpenter, clever with his hands. And a boy child born in an outhouse because there was no room elsewhere for his coming . . . She got down slowly on to her thick, arthritic knees beside the mattress and, with something like awe in her heart, gathered the baby from his mother's arms. 'I'll lay him in the box. It'll do for him lovely.' And under her breath: 'He won't be the first,' she said.

The boy left money with her next day for necessities and went out and duly returned that evening with news of a job on a building site; and carrying in one scarred hand a small, drooping bunch of flowers which he carefully divided between them, half for Marilyn, half for Mrs Vaughan – 'till I can get you something better' – and one violet left over to place in the baby's tiny mottled fist. 'And till I can get *you* something better,' he said.

They gave him no name . . . Other young couples, she thought, would have spent the idle hours trying to think up 'something different' or christened him after a pop-star, some loose-mouthed, long-haired little good-for-nothing shrieking out nonsense, thin legs kept jerking by drugs in an obscene capering. But no – it was 'the baby', 'the little one'. Perhaps, she thought, they dared not name him; dared not acknowledge, even to themselves . . .

For the huge question in her mind was: how much do they know?

For that matter – how much did she herself know? And what? – what in fact did she know? The Holy Child had been born already, had been born long ago. Vague thoughts of a Second Coming wandered through her brain, but was that not to be a major, a clearly recognisable event, something terrible, presaging the end of all things? The End. And the other had been the Beginning. Perhaps, she thought, there could be a Beginning-Again? Perhaps with everything having gone wrong with the world, there was going to be a second chance . . .?

It was a long time since she had been to church. In the old days, yes; brought up the two girls to be good Catholics, washed and spruced-up for Mass every Sunday, convents, Catechism, the lot. And much good it had done her – married a couple of heathen GIs in the war and gone off to America for good – for good or ill, she did not know and could no longer care; for years she had heard not a word from either of them. But now . . . She put on her crumpled old hat and, arthritically stumping, went off to St Stephen's.

It was like being a schoolgirl again, all one's childhood closing in about one; to be kneeling there in the stuffy, curtained darkness, to see the outlined profile crowned by the black hump of the biretta with its pom-pom a-top, leaping against the little iron-work grille that was all that separated them. 'In the name of the Father and of the Son and of the Holy Ghost . . . Yes, my child?'

He talked to her quietly and kindly, while waiting penitents shifted restlessly outside, and thought, among their Firm Purposes of Amendment, that the old girl must be having a right old load of sins to cough up. About chance, he spoke, and about coincidence, about having the Holy Child in one's heart and not trying to – well, rationalise things . . . She thanked him, made of old habit the sign of the cross and left. 'Them others – *they* didn't recognise Him either,' she said to herself.

And she came to her room and saw the quiet face bent over the sleeping baby lying in its wooden cradle; and surely – surely – there was a light about its head?

On pay day, Jo brought in flowers again. But the vase got knocked over almost at once and the flowers and water spilt – there was no room for even the smallest extras in the close little room, now that Marilyn was up and sitting in the armchair with the wooden box beside her and the increasing paraphernalia of babyhood taking up so much of the scanty space. The car was being used as a sort of storage dump for anything not in daily use. 'During the week-end,' said Jo, 'I'll find us a place.'

'A place?' she said, as though the idea came freshly to her. But she had dreaded it. 'Marilyn can't be moved yet.'

'By the end of the week?' he said.

'You've been so good,' said Marilyn. 'We can't go on taking up your room. We'll have to get somewhere.'

But it wasn't so easy. He spent all his evenings, after that, tramping round, searching; but as soon as he mentioned the baby, hearts and doors closed against him. She protested: 'But I don't want you to go. I got none of my own now, I like having you here,' and she knelt, as so often she did, by the improvised wooden-box cradle and said, worshipping: 'And I couldn't lose – Him.' And she went out and bought a second-hand bed and fixed that up in the shed, brought Marilyn in to her own bed, was happy to sleep on a mattress on the floor, the box-cradle close to her so that if the child stirred in the night, it was she who could hush it and croon to it and soothe it to sleep again. Is He all-knowing, she would wonder to herself in the dark, does He understand, even though He's so small, does the God-head in Him understand that it's I who hold Him? Will I one day sit at the right hand of the Father because on this earth I nursed His only begotten Son . . .? (Well, His – second begotten Son . . .? It was all so difficult. And she dared not ask.)

She had no close friends these days, but at last, one night, a little in her cups, she whispered it to Nellie down at the Dog.

'You'll never guess who I got at my place.'

Nellie knocked back her fifth brown ale and volunteered a bawdy suggestion. 'A boy and a girl,' said Mrs Vaughan, ignoring it. 'And a Baby.' And she thought of him lying there in his wooden bed. 'His little head,' she said. 'Behind His little head, you can see, like – a light. Shining in the darkness – a kind of a ring of light.'

'You'll see a ring of light round *me*,' said Nellie, robustly, 'if you put back another of them barley wines.' And to the landlord she confided, when Mrs Vaughan, a little bit tottery, had gone off home, 'I believe she's going off her rocker, honestly I do.'

'She looked all right to me,' said the landlord, who did not care for his regulars going off their rockers.

'They're after her stocking,' said Nellie to the pub at large. 'You'll see. Them and their Baby Jesus! They're after what she's got.'

And she set a little trap. 'Hey, Billy, you work on the same site as this Jo of hers. Give him a knock some day about the old girl's money. Got it in a stocking, saving it up for her funeral. Worried, she is, about being put in the common grave. Well, who isn't? But she, she's proper scared of it.'

So Billy strolled up to Jo on the site, next break-time. 'I hear you're holed up with old Mother Vaughan, down near the Dog. After her stocking then, are you?' And he pretended knowledge of its place of concealment. 'Fill it up with something; she'll never twig till after you've gone. Split me a third to two-thirds if I tell you where it's hid?'

And he looked up for the first time into Jo's face and saw the look that Jo gave him: a look almost – terrible. 'He come straight home,' Mrs Vaughan told Nellie in the pub that night, 'and – "they're saying you got money, Mrs V," he says. "If you have, you should stash it away somewhere," he says, "and let everyone know you've done it. Living here on your tod, it isn't safe for you, people thinking you're worth robbing."' And he had explained to her how to pay it into the post office so that no one but herself could ever touch it. Only a few quid it was, scrimped and saved for her funeral. 'I couldn't a-bear to go into the common grave, not with all them strangers . . .'

'Never mind the common grave, it'll be the common bin for *you*, if you don't watch out,' said Nellie. 'You and your Mary and Joseph – they come in a car, didn't they, not on a donkey?'

'You haven't got eyes to see. You don't live with them.'

'They've lived other places before you. Did them other landladies have eyes to see?'

What was the name – Mrs Mace? Had Mrs Mace had eyes to see, had she recognised, even before the baby came—? 'Course not,' said Nellie, crossly. 'She chucked 'em out, didn't she?'

'No, she never. She was moving out herself to the country, her son or someone needed the flat.' But if one could have seen Mrs Mace, consulted with her . . . 'Don't you ever visit your last landlady?' she asked them casually. 'Does she live too far?'

'No, not far; but with the baby and all . . . All the same, Marilyn,' said Jo, 'we ought to go some day soon, just to see she's all right. Take you along,' he suggested to Mrs Vaughan. 'You'd enjoy the drive and it's a lovely place, all flowers and trees and a little stream.'

'Oh, I wouldn't half like that. I dare say,' said Mrs Vaughan, craftily, 'she thought a lot of you, that Mrs Mace?'

'She was very kind to us,' said Marilyn. 'Very kind.'

'And the baby? She wasn't, like – shocked?'

'Shocked? She was thrilled,' said Jo. And he used an odd expression: 'Quietly thrilled.'

So she *had* known. Mrs Mace had known. The desire grew strong within Mrs Vaughan's anxious breast to see Mrs Mace, to discuss, to question, to talk it all over. With familiarity, with the lessening of the first impact of her own incredulous wonder, it became more difficult to understand that others should not share her faith. 'I tell you, I see the light shining behind His head!'

She confided it to strangers on buses, to casual acquaintances on their way to the little local shops. They pretended interest and hastily detached themselves. 'Poor thing – another of them loonies,' they said with the mirthless sniggers of those who find themselves outside normal experience, beyond their depths. She was becoming notorious, a figure of fun.

The news reached the ears of the landlord, a local man. He came round to the house and afterwards spoke to the boy. 'I've told her – you can't all go on living in that one little room, it's not decent.'

'There's the shed,' said Jo. 'I sleep out in the shed.'

'You won't like that for long,' said the man with a leer.

Billy had seen that look, on the building site. But the boy only said quietly: 'You couldn't let us have another room? She says they're only used for storage.'

'They're let – storage or not, no business of mine. For that matter,' said the man, growing cunning, 'it's no business of mine how you live or what you do. Only . . . Well, three and a kid for the price of one—'

'I'll pay extra if that's it,' said Jo. 'I could manage that. It's only that I can't find anywhere else, not at the price I could afford.'

'Just between the two of us, then. Though how you put up with it,' he said, as the boy sorted through his pocket book, 'I don't know. The old girl's round the bend. What's this about your kid got a light around its head? – and your girl's a—' But the look came once more. A strange look almost – frightening. 'Well, like that other lot, Jesus and all. She's mad.'

'She has some ideas,' said the boy. 'That doesn't make her mad.'

But not everyone agreed with him. The greengrocer's wife tackled Marilyn one day when she went out for the shopping, Mrs Vaughan left worshipping the baby at home. 'They're all saying she's going off her rocker. You shouldn't be there, what with the baby and all. It could be dangerous.'

So still and beautiful, the quiet face framed in its veil of long, straight hair. 'Mrs Vaughan – dangerous? She's kind. She'd do us no harm, she loves us.'

'She told us last time that the baby lies with its arms stretched out like a – well, like a cross. She said it knows how it's going to die. Well, I *mean!* It's blasphemous.'

'He does lie with his arms stretched out.'

'Any baby does, sometimes. And she says he shines. She says there's always a light around his head.'

'I put the lamp on the floor once to keep the brightness out of his eyes. It did sort of gleam through a crack in the wood. We explained it to her.'

35

'Well, she never listened then. And I say it's not right. Everyone's talking. They say . . .' It took a little courage to persist, in face of that quiet calm. 'They're saying you ought to fetch a doctor to her.'

Mrs Vaughan rebelled, predictably, against any suggestion of seeing a doctor. 'What for? I'm not ill. Never better.' But it alarmed her. 'You don't think there's something wrong with me?'

'We just thought you looked a bit pale, that's all.'

'I'm not pale, I'm fine, never been better in my life. Even them arthritics nearly gone, hardly any pain these days at all.' And she knew why. Alone with Him, she had taken the little hand and with it touched her swollen knees, had moved it, soft and firm, across her own gnarled fingers. 'Look at 'em,' she had insisted to Nellie next evening in the pub. 'Half the size. All them swollen joints gone down.'

'They look the same to me,' said Nellie and suddenly saw Mrs Hoskins through in the Private and had to hurry off and join her. 'Barmy!' she said to Mrs Hoskins. 'I don't feel safe with her. How do I know she won't suddenly do her nut and start bashing me? It should be put a stop to.'

Only one thing seemed to threaten Mrs Vaughan with any suggestion of doing her nut and that was mention of her precious little family going away. If Jo searched for rooms now, he kept very quiet about it. To outside representations that she ought to let them go, that young people should be together in a place of their own, she replied that it wasn't 'like that' between them; that Marilyn was 'different'. All the same, they were young and shouldn't always be cooped up with an old woman, and she fought to be allowed to move out to the shed and let them have her room; there was the bed out there now and in this weather it was warm and dry – she'd like it. In other days, she would have gone off to the pub in the evenings and left them free, but the Dog wasn't what it had been, people didn't seem so friendly, they looked at her funny and sometimes, she suspected, made mock behind her back of her claim to be housing God. Not that that worried her too much. In them old days, no one had believed in Him then, either. And I'll prove it to them, she thought, and she would watch the children playing in the street and when she saw a tumble, bring in the poor victim with its bruises and scratches and cajole it into letting the baby touch the sore places with its little hand. 'Now you feel better, love, don't you?' she would anxiously say. 'Now it's stopped bleeding, hasn't it? – when the Baby touched you, it was all better in a minute? Now you tell me – wasn't it?' 'Yes,' the children would declare, wriggling in her grasp, intent only upon getting away. 'It's dangerous,' said their mothers, gathering outside the shops in anxious gossip. 'You don't know what she might do, luring them inside like that.' And a deputation at last sought out Jo. 'You ought to clear out, you two, and leave her alone. You're driving her up the wall with these ideas.'

'That's just what we can't do now,' said Jo. 'She gets upset if we even mention it.'

'It could be the last straw,' admitted Mrs Hoskins, who knew all about it from Nellie at the Dog. 'Properly finish her off.'

'And then she'd be there without us to look after her.'

'You can't spend your whole lives in that one room.'

36

'If we could get a place and take her with us . . . But we can't find anywhere, not that we could possibly afford; let alone where she could come too.'

'What? – you two kids, saddle yourselves for ever with a mad old woman? You couldn't do that.'

'She saddled herself with us,' said Jo. 'Where'd we be now, but for her?'

All the same, clearly something must be done. With every day of her life with them, Mrs Vaughan's obsession increased. She could not bear the baby out of her sight, would walk with Marilyn when she carried it out for a breath of fresh air and almost threateningly warn off the curious who tried for a glimpse of the now quite famous child. If they came to worship, well and good. If not . . . 'If you don't make some arrangement about her,' said the greengrocer's wife at last to Jo, 'I will. She's terrorising the whole neighbourhood.'

'She wouldn't hurt a fly. She believes our baby's – something special. What harm does that do anyone else?'

'You never know,' said the greengrocer, supporting the missis, though in fact he was fond of Mrs Vaughan – as indeed everyone had been in easier days. 'They do turn queer, sometimes. Why not just take her to the doctor and ask him, or take her to the hospital?'

'She won't go to any hospital, she won't go to any doctor.'

'They can be forced,' said the wife. 'Straitjackets and that. They come and fetch them in a padded van.' But anyway, she repeated, if something were not done and soon, she herself would ring up the police and let *them* deal with it. 'She's keeping custom from the shop. It can't go on.'

He promised hastily and later convened a little meeting of the malcontents. 'Well, I've done what you said. I went to the hospital and they sent me to some special doctor and I told him all about it. They're going to send her to a place where she won't be too suspicious and they'll have her under observation there, that's what they call it, and then there'll be psychiatrists and that, and she can have treatment. He says it's probably only a temporary thing, she can be cured all right.'

'Well, there you are! You and Marilyn can be finding somewhere else in the meantime and when she gets back and you're not there, she'll just settle down again.'

'We'll go anyway even if we don't find anywhere. We couldn't let it start all over again.'

'These things aren't as quick as all that. You'll have time to look around.'

'It's not very nice,' he said, 'us there in her room and her in the bin.'

'If you ever get her there. How'll you persuade her to go?'

'I've thought of that,' he said. 'Our last landlady—'

'Oh, yes, that Mrs Mace she's always talking about! Mrs Mace would understand, she keeps saying, Mrs Mace knew all about it . . . You tell her she's going to see Mrs Mace.'

'That's what I thought. Mrs Mace is out in the country now and so's this place, fifteen, twenty miles. I can drive her there in the car. She'll go if she thinks Mrs Mace is there. I think it'll work.'

And it worked. Mrs Vaughan was prepared to leave even the precious Baby for a while, if she could go and talk to Mrs Mace. So many puzzling things that

Mrs Mace might be able to help her with. That about the Second Coming, for example, and then no Kings had arrived, not even a shepherd carrying a woolly lamb; and what about Herod killing off all them boy babies? Of course these were modern days, what would they have done with a live lamb, anyway? – and people didn't go around killing babies any more. But you'd think there'd be something to take the place of these events, something – well, sybollick or whatever the word was, and it might be important to recognise it. Mrs Mace would understand, would at least be sympathetic and talk it all over; she had known them since before the baby even started, had been brushed by the very wings of Gabriel, bringing the message: Hail Mary, full of grace, the Lord is with thee . . . She could hardly wait to gather up her few shabby clothes and pack them into the cardboard box that must do for a suitcase. 'You'll look after things, Marilyn, love, just the couple of days? I'd like to have some good long talks with Mrs Mace. You do think she'll let me stay?'

'It's a big place; like, sort of, a hotel,' said Jo. 'But lovely, all them trees and flowers. And lots of nice people,' he added, cautiously.

'I thought it was a cottage? It's only Mrs Mace I want to see. I can be with her?'

'Oh, yes, of course. We've written and told her,' fibbed Jo, 'how good you've been to us.'

'Me – good?' she said. 'When you think what you've done for *me*. Me being chosen. But still, there – the last time it was only a pub-keeper, wasn't it?' The thought struck her that perhaps in fact it had been meant that they should park outside the Dog that night, only a few doors down – that only through an error had they come to her. 'Well, never mind, even if I wasn't worthy to be chosen, fact remains it was me that got you – and reckernised you. First minute I saw you. I'll never forget it.' So beautiful, so quiet and undemanding, standing out there in the drizzle of the evening rain, Mary and Joseph and the promise of the Holy Child. And as they had been then, so they had remained: quiet, considerate, gentle; reserved, unemotional as she was emotional and out-giving; almost colourless, almost impersonal – a little apart from other human beings, from ordinary people like herself; and yet living with herself, close together in that little place with her for their only friend – the Mother and the Guardian of the Son of God; and the Word made flesh. She knelt and kissed the tiny hand. 'I'll come back to you, my little Lord. I'll always love You and serve You, You know that. It's only just that I want to know everything about You, I want to get things right, I want to ask Mrs Mace.' And all unaware of eyes watching from behind window curtains, balefully or pityingly or only with relief, she climbed into the battered little old car with Jo and drove away.

Marilyn was nursing the baby when he got home. 'You've got the place all cleared up,' he said, astonished at the change in it. 'You must have been slaving.'

'It kept my mind off things,' she said. But still she did not ask what must be uppermost there. 'Without Mrs Vaughan here, I must say there's more room. Not as much as we had at Mrs Mace's—'

'We couldn't stay at Mrs Mace's once the nephew was coming home.'

'No, I know. I was only saying.' And now she did ask at last: 'Did it go all right?'

'Yes, not a murmur. A bit surprised when we got there, of course, but I kept urging her on, saying she'd be with Mrs Mace.'

'You found the place again, no trouble?'

'Yes, I found it. A lovely spot, perfect, in the middle of all those woods.'

'And Mrs Mace?'

'Still there, quite OK. A bit lonely, I daresay. She'll be glad of company.'

'They should get on fine.' She smiled her own cool, quiet, impersonal little smile, shifting the baby on her shoulder so that its fluffy head pressed, warm and sweet, against her cheek. 'Well, she got her wish. You couldn't call that a common grave.'

'No, just her and Mrs Mace; and right in the middle of them lovely woods like I told her, and all them flowers and the stream and all.' He came across and ran a bent forefinger up the little channel at the back of the baby's tender neck. 'A shame to have to bash her. She was a kind old thing. But there you are, it's so hard to find anywhere – we had to have the place.'

'Yes,' she said. 'Especially now we got the kid.'

# SIMON BRETT

---

# Don't Know Much About Art

I have been described as not very bright. Partly, I reckon it's my size. People who look like me have appeared as dumb villains in too many movies and television series. And if you've had a background as a professional wrestler, you find the general public doesn't have too many expectations of you as an intellect.

Also, I have to face it, there have been one or two unfortunate incidents in my past. Jobs that didn't turn out exactly like they was planned. Like when I was in the getaway car outside the bank and I drove off with the wrong passengers. Or when I got muddled after that bullion robbery and delivered it all back to the security firm. Or when I wrote my home address on that ransom demand. OK, silly mistakes, sort of thing anyone could do in the heat of the moment, but I'm afraid it's the kind of thing that sticks in people's minds and I have got a bit of a reputation in the business as a dumbo.

Result of it all is, most of the jobs I get tend to be – to put it mildly – intellectually undemanding. In fact, the approach of most of the geezers who hire me seems to be, 'We couldn't find a blunt instrument, so you'll have to do.'

Now, of course, my own view of my mental capacity doesn't exactly coincide with that, but a chap has to live, and a recession isn't the time you can afford to be choosy. I mean, you read all this about rising crime figures, but you mustn't get the impression from that that villains are doing well. No, we feel the pinch like anyone else. For a start, there's a lot more blokes trying to muscle in. Side-effect of unemployment, of course, and most of them are really amateurs, but they do queer the pitch for us professionals. They undercut our rates and bring into the business a kind of dishonesty that I'm sure wasn't there when I started. The cake isn't that much bigger than it ever was, and there's a hell of a lot more blokes trying to get slices.

Result is, I take anything I'm offered . . . driving, bouncing, frightening, looming (often booked for looming I am, on account of my size). No, I'll do anything. Short of contract killing. Goes against my principles, that and mugging old ladies. As I say, it's no time to be choosy. When this country's got more than three million unemployed, you just got to put off your long-term ambitions, forget temporarily about career structure, and be grateful you got a job of any sort.

So when I was offered the Harbinger Hall job, never crossed my mind to turn it down. Apart from anything else, it sounded easy and the pay was bloody good. Five grand for a bit of petty larceny . . . well, that can't be bad, can it? Sure there was always the risk of getting nicked, but didn't look like there'd be any rough stuff. Mind you, never be quite sure in stately homes. Tend to be lots of spears and shotguns and that stuck on the walls, so there's always the danger that someone might have a fit of temperament and cop hold of one of those.

Still, five grand for a weekend's work in a slow autumn was good money.

The initial contact come through Wally Clinton, which I must say surprised me. It was Wally I was driving to Heathrow after that jeweller's job the time I ran out of petrol, so I didn't think I was exactly his Flavour of the Month. Still, shows how you can misjudge people. Here he was letting bygones be bygones and even putting a nice bit of work my way. Take back all that I said about him at the Black Dog last New Year's Eve.

Anyway, so Wally gets in touch, asks if I'm in the market and when I says yes, tells me to go and meet this bloke, 'Mr Loxton', in this sauna club off St Martin's Lane.

Strange sauna club it was. Not a girl in sight. I think it actually must've been for geezers who wanted to have saunas. All neat and tidy, no little massage cubicles with plastic curtains, no funny smell, no nasty bits of screwed-up tissue on the floor. Most peculiar.

Bloke on the door was expecting me. Give me a big white towel and showed me into a changing-room that was all very swish with pine and clean tiles. He told me to take my clothes off, put on the towel and go into the sauna. Mr Loxton would join me shortly.

Don't mind telling you, I felt a bit of a grapefruit sitting on this wooden shelf with nothing on but this towel. When I first went in I sat on the top shelf, but blimey it was hot. Soon realised it got cooler the lower you went, so I went to the bottom one. Still uncomfortably hot, mind. Geezer my size really sweats when he sweats.

I tried to work out why Mr Loxton had chosen this place for the meet. I mean, a sauna's good if you're worried the opposition might've got shooters. Isn't anywhere you can put one when you've got your clothes off. Nowhere comfortable, anyway. But this wasn't that kind of encounter.

On the other hand, it wasn't bad if you didn't want to be identified. The lights in the sauna was low and it was a bit steamy. Also, people don't look the same when they're starkers. Oh, I know they do lots of corpse identification from secret birthmarks and moles on the body and that, but the average bloke without clothes on doesn't look like himself. For a start, next time you see him, chances are he'll be dressed, and you'd be surprised how many clues you get to what a person's like from what they wear. I reckoned Mr Loxton was meeting there to maintain the old incog.

I felt even more sure of that when he come in. He had a big towel round him under his armpits like me, but he also got a small one draped over his head like a boxer. He didn't turn his face towards me, but immediately went over to a wooden bucket in the corner, picked out a ladleful of water and poured it over this pile of stones. Well, that really got the steam going, and when he did turn towards me, he wasn't no more than a blur.

'You are Billy Gorse.'

I admitted it. Wasn't spoken like a question, anyway, more a statement.

'Thank you for coming. Wally Clinton recommended you for a job that needs doing.'

He might have hid his face with all the towels and the steam, but he had a voice that was really distinctive. Private school, you know, and a bit prissy. I'm good with voices. Knew I'd recognise his if I ever heard it again.

I stayed stumm, waiting for the details, and he went on. 'What I want you to do, Gorse, is to steal a painting.'

'Blimey,' I said, 'I don't know much about art.'

'You don't need to.'

'But surely . . . paintings . . . I mean specialist work, isn't it? Not like walking in and nicking someone's video. If a painting's any good, it's got security systems all round it. And then finding a fence who'll handle them sort of goods—'

'All that side is taken care of. All I said I wanted you to do was to steal a painting.'

'You mean I'd be, like, part of a gang?'

'There's no need for you to know anything about anyone else involved. All you have to do is to follow instructions without question.'

'I can do that.'

'Good. Wally said you could. You do the job on the last weekend of October.'

'Where?'

'Have you heard of Harbinger Hall?'

I shook my head.

'Then I suppose you haven't heard of the Harbinger Madonna either.'

'Who's she?'

'"She" is the painting you are going to steal.'

'Oh. Well, like I said, I don't know much about art.'

'No.' His voice sounded sort of pleased with that. Smug.

He asked me where he could send my instructions. I nearly gave him my home address, but something told me to hold my horses, so I give him the name of Red Rita's gaff. She often holds mail for me, on account of services rendered what I needn't go into here.

Then Mr Loxton reached into his towel and pulled out a polythene bag. Thought of everything, he did. Didn't want the notes to get damp.

'Five hundred in there. Two thousand when you get your instructions. Second half on completion of the job.' He rose through the steam. 'Stay here another ten minutes. If you appear in the changing room before I've left the building, the contract's cancelled.' He reached for the door handle.

'Oh, Mr Loxton . . .'

His reaction was that half-second slow, which confirmed that he wasn't using his real name. No great surprise. Very few of the geezers I deal with do. Not for me, that. Always stick to 'Billy Gorse'. Only time I tried anything different, I forgot who I was half-way through the job.

'What did you want, Mr Gorse?'

I'd got what I wanted, but I said, 'Oh, just to say thank you for the job, Mr Loxton.'

He done a sort of snort and walked out the sauna.

Long ten minutes it was in that heat. When I come out I was sweating like a Greek cheese.

*     *     *

Instructions come the following week as per. I went down Red Rita's for reasons that aren't any of your business, and after a bit she give me this thick brown envelope. Just my name on it. No stamps, nothing like that. Just come through her letterbox. She didn't see who dropped it.

I didn't open it till I got back to my place next morning. First I counted the money. Fifties, forty of them all present and correct. Then there was this postcard of some bird in blue with this nipper on her knee. That was presumably the picture I was going to nick. I didn't take much notice of it, but unfolded the typewritten sheet of instructions.

No mention of my name and they wasn't signed either. Plain paper, no other clues to where it might've come from. It was all typed in capital letters, which I must say got my goat a bit. Reckon Wally Clinton'd been casting aspersions on my literacy, the cheeky devil. Anyway, what I had to do was spelled out very clear.

FIRST – FILL IN THE ENCLOSED BOOKING FORM, BOOKING YOURSELF INTO THE 'STATELY HOME WEEKEND' AT HARBINGER HALL FOR THE 29TH AND 30TH OCTOBER. SEND THE FULL PAYMENT BY MONEY ORDER. (ALL YOUR EXPENSES WILL BE REPAID.)

SECOND – THIS FRIDAY, 21ST OCTOBER, TRAVEL DOWN TO HARBINGER HALL AND TAKE THE CONDUCTED TOUR OF THE BUILDING (THESE RUN EVERY HOUR ON THE HOUR BETWEEN 10 A.M. AND 4 P.M.). WHEN YOU REACH THE GREAT HALL, LOOK CAREFULLY AT THE PAINTING OF THE MADONNA, NOTING THE VISIBLE SECURITY ARRANGEMENTS AROUND IT.

WHEN THE TOUR REACHES THE END OF THE LONG GALLERY UPSTAIRS, LINGER BEHIND THE GROUP. AS THE REST OF THEM GO INTO THE BLUE BEDROOM, OPEN THE DOOR LABELLED 'PRIVATE' AT THE END OF THE GALLERY. YOU WILL FIND YOURSELF AT THE TOP OF A SMALL STAIRCASE. GO DOWN THIS QUICKLY AND YOU WILL FIND YOURSELF IN A SMALL LOBBY. ON THE WALL OPPOSITE THE FOOT OF THE STAIRS YOU WILL SEE THE BOXES CONTROLLING THE BUILDING'S ALARM SYSTEM. THESE ARE OPERATED BY A KEY, BUT YOU WILL SEE THE WIRES WHICH COME OUT OF THE TOP OF THE BOXES. WHEN YOU ACTUALLY COME TO STEAL THE MADONNA, YOU WILL CUT THROUGH THESE WIRES. HAVING SEEN THEIR POSITION, RETURN AS QUICKLY AS POSSIBLE UP THE STAIRS AND REJOIN YOUR GROUP. COMPLETE THE REST OF THE TOUR AND RETURN HOME WITHOUT FURTHER INVESTIGATION.

FURTHER INSTRUCTIONS WILL FOLLOW NEXT WEEK. MEMORISE THE DETAILS IN THESE SHEETS AND THEN BURN THEM.

I done like I was told and before the Friday I got a confirmation of my booking on this 'Stately Home Weekend'. I read the brochure on that and I must say it didn't really sound my scene. Tours of the grounds, lectures on the history of the place, full mediaeval banquet on the Saturday night, farewell tea with Lord Harbinger on the Sunday. I mean, my idea of a fun weekend is going down Southend with a few mates and putting back a few beers. Still, I'd put up with a lot for five grand.

So, the Friday I do as I'm told. Get the train out to Limmerton, and from there they've got this courtesy bus takes you out to Harbinger Hall.

Not a bad little gaff old Lord Harbinger's got, I'll say that for him. Don't know any more about architecture than I do about art, but I can tell it's old. Don't build places like that nowadays, not with blooming great pillars in front of the door and all them windows and twiddly bits on the roof.

Nice position and all. It's high, like on top of this hill, looking out over all the rest of the countryside. That's how you first see it in the bus from the station. As you get nearer, you lose sight for a bit, because it's a really steep hill with trees. So you sort of zigzag up this drive, which is really a bit hairy and makes you glad the old bus's got decent brakes. And then suddenly you come out the top and you're right in front of the house and it's blooming big. And there's car parks off to the right and left, but the bus drops you pretty well by the front door.

I looked around as I got out. You know, some of these stately homes've got sort of zoos and funfairs and that, you know, a bit of entertainment. And, since I had to spend a whole weekend there, I thought it'd be nice to know there'd be something interesting to do. But no such luck. Place hadn't been developed like that. Maybe the grounds wasn't big enough.

In fact, not only hadn't the place been developed, it looked a bit tatty. I mean that sort of gaff isn't my style. Blimey, if I owned it, I'd knock it down and put up a nice executive Regency-style townhouse with double garage and Italian suite bathroom. But even I could tell this one needed a few grand spending on it.

And if my busload was anything to go by, the few grand wasn't going to come very quickly from tourists. OK, end of the season and that, but there wasn't many of us. Had to wait around till a few more come from the car parks before they'd start our guided tour, and then it was only about a dozen of us. Well, at a couple of sovs a head, takes you a long time to make money that way.

The guide what took us round had done the trip a few thousand times and obviously hadn't enjoyed it much even the first time. The spiel come out like a recording, jokes and all. Didn't look a happy man.

And what he said was dead boring. I never got on with history at school, couldn't see the percentage in it, so all his cobblers about what Duke built which bit and when didn't do a lot for me. And to think that I'd got a whole weekend of lectures on it coming up. I began to think I was going to earn my five grand.

Anyway, eventually we get to the Great Hall, and I see this picture all the fuss is about. Didn't go on it much in the postcard; the real thing's just the same, only bigger. Not big, though, compared to some of the numbers they got on the walls. I don't know, two foot by eighteen inches maybe. Don't know why they wanted to nick this one. Some of them was ten times the size, must've been worth a lot more. Still, not my decision. And a good thing, come to think of it, that they didn't want me to walk out with one of the twenty-foot numbers under my arm.

So the picture's just this Mum and her sprog. Frame was nice, mind. All gold and wiggly, like my brother-in-law's got round the cocktail bar in his lounge. And at the bottom of the frame there's this little brass plate nailed on. It says:

MADONNA AND CHILD
Giacomo Palladino
Florentine
(1473–1539)

Never heard of the git myself.

Anyway, I'd memorised my instructions like a good boy, so I have a good butchers at the pic. Can't see a lot in the way of security. I mean, there's a sort of purple rope strung between uprights to keep the punters six feet away from the wall, but that isn't going to stop anyone. Of course, there might be some photo-electric beam or some rocker device what sounds the alarm if you actually touch the thing. I step over the rope to take a closer look.

'Art-lover, are we, sir?' asks this sarcastic voice behind me.

I turn round and see this bloke in uniform. Not the guide, he's up the other end blathering about some king or other. No, this geezer's just some sort of security guard I noticed hanging around when we arrived.

'No,' I says, with what people have described as my winning smile. 'Don't know a blind thing about art.'

'Then why are you studying the Madonna so closely?'

I'm about to say that I'm just interested in what security arrangements she got, and then I twig that this might not be so clever, so I do this big shrug and step back over the rope and join up with the other punters. I glance back as we're leaving the hall and this guard's giving me a really beady look.

Upstairs I follow the instructions without sweat. Dawdle doing the old untied shoe-lace routine while the rest troop in to hear the history of the Blue Bedroom, quick look round to see I'm on my own in the gallery, then through the old 'Private' door and down the stairs.

It's just like they said it would be. These big metal-covered boxes opposite me with coloured lights and chrome keyholes on them. And at the top the wires. Not that thick. Quick snip with the old metal-cutters. No prob.

I think for a minute. I know some of these systems got a sort of fail-safe so's they sound off if anyone tampers with the wiring. For a moment I wonder if someone's trying to set me up. Certainly are one or two geezers what I have sort of inadvertently offended in the course of my varied career, but this'd be a bloody elaborate way of getting their own back. Anyway, there's the two and a half grand I already got. Nobody's going to spend that kind of bread just to fix me. I hurry back upstairs again.

I've just closed the door when I see the security guard coming in the other end of the Long Gallery. Don't know whether he saw me or not, but he still looks beady. 'Looking for something, sir?' he calls out, sarcastic again.

'Little boys' room,' I say, and nip along to the Blue Bedroom.

*     *     *

47

Next package arrives the Wednesday, three days before I'm due on my Stately Home Weekend. I'm actually round at Red Rita's when we hear it plop through the letter-box, but needless to say by the time I open the front door to see who brought it, there's nobody in sight.

Since the whole thing's getting a bit close and Red Rita's tied up with someone else, I open the package there. There's money in it, which I wasn't expecting this time. It's in fives and ones and a bit of change and covers my expenses so far. What I paid to book the weekend, return fare London to Limmerton, even the two quid for my guided tour. Someone's done their research. Makes me feel good. Nice to know you're dealing with geezers who know what's what. There's a lot of berks in this business.

As well as the money there's a car key. Just one, on a little ring attached to a plain yellow plastic tag. And of course there's the instructions. Block capitals again, which miffs me a bit. Again, they're so clear an idiot could understand them. I wonder if someone's trying to tell me something.

ON THE MORNING OF SATURDAY, 29TH OCTOBER AT 9 A.M., GO TO THE UNDERGROUND CAR PARK IN CAVENDISH SQUARE. THERE, IN BAY NUMBER 86, YOU WILL FIND A RED PEUGEOT WHICH YOU CAN OPEN AND START WITH THE ENCLOSED KEY. ON THE BACK SEAT WILL BE A LARGE SUITCASE, TO WHICH YOU WILL TRANSFER YOUR CLOTHES, ETC., FOR THE WEEKEND. *DO NOT REMOVE ANYTHING FROM THE SUITCASE.*

IN THE GLOVE COMPARTMENT OF THE CAR YOU WILL FIND MONEY TO PAY THE PARKING CHARGE. DRIVE DIRECTLY TO HARBINGER HALL. GIVEN NORMAL TRAFFIC CONDITIONS, YOU SHOULD ARRIVE THERE AT ABOUT HALF-PAST TWELVE, JUST IN TIME FOR THE BUFFET LUNCH WHICH OPENS THE STATELY HOME WEEKEND.

DURING THE WEEKEND TAKE PART IN ALL THE ACTIVITIES OFFERED AND GENERALLY BEHAVE AS NATURALLY AS POSSIBLE. ABOVE ALL, DO NOT DRAW ATTENTION TO YOURSELF.

THE MOMENT FOR THE THEFT OF THE MADONNA WILL COME LATE ON THE SUNDAY AFTERNOON WHEN THE TOUR GUESTS ARE ABOUT TO LEAVE. AT THE END OF THESE OCCASIONS THE TRADITION HAS DEVELOPED OF LORD HARBINGER, HIS FAMILY AND STAFF LINING UP IN THE FRONT HALL TO SAY GOODBYE TO THEIR GUESTS. THE PREMISES WILL BE CLEARED OF DAY VISITORS BY FOUR O'CLOCK ON THIS, THE LAST DAY OF THE SEASON. THERE WILL BE NO STAFF GUARDING THE MADONNA.

*FOLLOW THESE INSTRUCTIONS EXACTLY.* AFTER TEA WITH LORD HARBINGER, THE STATELY HOME WEEKEND GUESTS ARE GIVEN HALF AN HOUR TO PACK AND ASKED TO APPEAR IN THE FRONT HALL AT SIX TO SAY THEIR GOOD-

BYES AND GET THE COACH TO THE STATION OR GO TO
THEIR OWN CARS. DO ANY PACKING YOU HAVE TO AND GO
DOWN TO THE FRONT HALL AT TEN TO SIX, *LEAVING YOUR
SUITCASE IN YOUR BEDROOM.* WHEN MOST OF THE OTHER
GUESTS ARE DOWNSTAIRS, MAKE A SHOW OF REMEMBER-
ING YOUR SUITCASE AND HURRY BACK TO YOUR BED-
ROOM TO GET IT. *THE NEXT BIT HAS TO BE DONE QUICKLY.*
GO FROM THE PRIVATE APARTMENTS TO THE LONG GAL-
LERY AND DOWN THE STAIRCASE TO THE ALARM BOXES.
CUT THROUGH THE WIRES AT THE TOP OF THE BOXES.
THERE IS A DOOR TO THE RIGHT OF THESE WHICH LEADS
DIRECTLY INTO THE GREAT HALL. GO THROUGH, GO
STRAIGHT TO THE MADONNA AND REPLACE THE ORIGINAL
PAINTING WITH THE COPY IN YOUR SUITCASE. IT WILL JUST
BE A MATTER OF UNHOOKING THE PICTURE AT THE BACK.
WITH THE ALARMS NEUTRALISED, THERE ARE NO OTHER
RESTRAINING DEVICES.

PUT THE ORIGINAL PAINTING IN YOUR SUITCASE AND
RETURN UPSTAIRS THE WAY YOU CAME. GO BACK TO
YOUR ROOM AND THEN GO DOWN THE MAIN STAIRCASE
TO THE FRONT HALL. THE WHOLE OPERATION SHOULD
TAKE YOU LESS THAN FIVE MINUTES AND WILL NOT BE
NOTICED IN THE CONFUSION OF THE GUESTS' GOODBYES.
JOIN IN WITH THESE AND BEHAVE PERFECTLY NATURALLY.
ALLOW ONE OF THE STAFF TO TAKE YOUR SUITCASE OUT
TO YOUR CAR, AND ASK HIM TO PUT IT ON THE BACK SEAT.

DRIVE STRAIGHT BACK TO LONDON. RETURN THE CAR
TO THE CAVENDISH SQUARE GARAGE, PARKING IT IN BAY 86
OR AS NEAR TO THAT AS YOU CAN GET. REMOVE YOUR
OWN BELONGINGS FROM THE SUITCASE, BUT LEAVE THE
CASE ITSELF AND THE PAINTING, ALONG WITH THE CAR
KEY AND PARKING TICKET, INSIDE. THEN LOCK THE CAR BY
PRESSING DOWN THE LOCKING BUTTON INSIDE AND CLOS-
ING THE DOOR WITH THE HANDLE HELD OUT.

WHEN YOU RETURN TO THE ADDRESS USED BEFORE,
YOU WILL FIND THE SECOND TWO AND A HALF THOUSAND
POUNDS WAITING FOR YOU.

AS BEFORE, MEMORISE THESE INSTRUCTIONS *AND BURN
THEM.*

Now I got my principles, but crime is my business and it's a sort of natural
reaction for me to have a look at any plan what comes up and see if there's
anything in it for me. You know, anything extra, over and above the basic fee.

And, having read my instructions, I couldn't help noticing that, assuming all
went well with the actual nicking, from the moment I left Harbinger Hall on the
Sunday night I was going to be in temporary possession of an extremely
valuable painting.

Simon Brett

Now I been in my line of work long enough to know that nasty things can happen to villains carrying off the goods. You hear cases of them being hijacked by other gangs, mugged, somehow getting lost on the way to their hand-over, all that. And though I didn't fancy any of those happening to me, I wasn't so down on the idea of them *appearing* to happen to me. I mean, if I'm found on the roadside with the side of my motor bashed in, a bump on my head and the suitcase gone, the bosses won't be able to *prove* I knew the bloke who done it.

Don't get me wrong. I wasn't planning anything particular, just sort of going through the possibilities in my mind. Like I said, I don't know anything about art, but I do know that you need extremely specialised help if you're trying to unload a well-known stolen painting.

One of the advantages of Red Rita's line of work is that she does get to meet a big variety of people and when I mentioned, casual like, that I wanted a bit of background on the art scene, it turned out she did just happen to know this geezer who was a dealer in the less public transactions of international art-collectors. And he was another of the many who owed her a favour and yes, she'd be quite happy to fix up a meet. For me, darling, anything.

I suppose I shouldn't have been surprised, if I'd thought about it. I mean, bent bookies are still bookies, bent solicitors do their stuff in solicitors' offices, but I really hadn't expected a bent art dealer to work out of a posh little gallery off Bond Street. Still, that was the address Red Rita give me, and when I got there it seemed that Mr Depaldo was expecting me. The sniffy tart at the desk said she would just check he was free and left me looking at a series of pics of what seemed to be a nasty accident in the kitchens of a Chinese restaurant. I don't know how people buy that stuff. I mean, if you can't tell what it's meant to be, how do you know you're not being taken for a ride? Don't get me, wrong, I'm not against all art. My brother-in-law's got this collection of sunsets painted on black velvet and with those, well, you can *see* they're good. But a lot of this modern stuff . . . forget it.

So I'm shown up to Mr Depaldo's poncy little office, and he's a real smoothie. Striped shirt, bow tie, you know the number. If I didn't know about his connection with Red Rita, I'd have put him down as a wooftah.

But her hold is clearly strong. Plain from the start he don't want to see me, but Rita's threatened to blow the lid on something if he won't. So he just about managed to be polite.

I ask him if it's possible to sell a stolen picture and he says, through a lot of unnecessary grammar, that it is.

Then I mention the Harbinger Madonna, and he sort of perks up like a conman spotting a mark. And I ask him how much he reckons it's worth.

'Well, it's hard to tell. Prices at auction are so unpredictable. I mean, there aren't many Palladinos around, certainly no others of that quality. The last one to come on the market was a Saint Sebastian back in 'sixty-eight. Went to eight hundred.'

Didn't seem that much to me. I mean, paying me five grand and only getting eight hundred for the goods, well, that's no way to run a whelk-stall.

50

Old Depaldo must've twigged what I was thinking, because he says, rather vinegary, 'Eight hundred *thousand*, of course. But that was fifteen years ago. And an inferior work. If the Madonna came to auction now, she must go to at least two.'

'Two?' I queried, not wanting to be caught out again.

'Million.'

'That's at auction?'

'Yes. Of course, a . . . private deal wouldn't realise nearly as much.'

'Like what?'

You know, all fences give you the same pause before they come up with a figure. Doesn't matter if you're talking about a colour telly, a lorryload of booze or a *Last Supper*, they all hesitate before they cheat you. 'Maybe one. Say seven hundred and fifty to be safe.'

Even if he'd been telling the truth, it sounded like a lot of money. Made my five grand for actually taking the risk and doing the job look a bit pathetic.

'And if it did . . . become available, you could handle it?'

He nodded, looking sort of eager. Obviously he knew there was a lot more in it for him than he let on. 'There are only two people in London who could make the arrangements, and I'm one of them.'

'But I'm the first one who's talked to you about it?'

'Yes.'

So perhaps my bosses had got a deal set up with the other geezer. 'What's your commission rate, by the way?'

'Sixty per cent,' he says, cool as an ice-cream down the neck. 'You see, in these matters the risk must be judged in relation to how much one has to lose.'

Meaning he'd got his poncy gallery and his sniffy tart downstairs and his international reputation; and I was just a cheap heavy. I let it pass. Reckoned I could work out some fine tuning on the figures later if it became necessary.

'Any idea,' he asks, really keen now, 'when this exceptional property might come on the market?'

'No,' I tell him. 'Only asking for information, aren't I?'

He looks a bit miffed.

'But if it ever was to come up,' I go on, 'you'd be interested in handling it?'

'Oh yes,' he says.

I haven't made any plans yet, mind. But it is nice to have things sorted out in case you need them.

Saturday morning I do like a good boy should. Get to Cavendish Square car park on the nose of nine, find the car in Bay 86. Red Peugeot, like they said. Ordinary saloon, not one of the hatchback jobs. The key opens the door and fits the ignition. I try it on the boot, which seems to be locked, but it doesn't fit. Needs a different key. Never mind.

On the back seat there's this suitcase as per. One of those that sort of opens up like a big wallet with a zip three-quarters of the way round. Then inside there's straps to hold your clothes in. One side, strapped in, is this hard rectangular package wrapped in cloth. Got to be the copy of the painting, but I don't think it's the moment to have a dekko. I take my gear out of the polythene carrier I got it in and strap the lot in the other side. Just clothes, shaving tackle. And a pair of metal-cutters. Oh, and a thing called a priest. Little stick with a weighted tip. Fishermen use them to finish off fish. Mine's clobbered a few slimy customers in its time, and all. Wouldn't ever carry a shooter, but the priest's handy.

Car starts first turn of the key, so I reckon it had only been left there that morning. In the glove compartment there's the parking ticket. Clocked in 8:12. Pity I hadn't thought to arrive earlier. Be nice to know who I was dealing with, apart from the steamy 'Mr Loxton'.

There was the right money in the glove compartment for the parking. Seemed a bit steep for such a short stay, and I mentioned this to the bloke at the barrier.

'Rates just gone up, mate. Here's the new tariff.' And he give me a printed sheet with my receipt.

I shoved it in my pocket. I should worry. Wasn't my money I was spending.

I never really thought it wouldn't be, but the Stately Home Weekend was way off my scene. I mean, we was treated all right, you know, all the staff deferential and that, trying to give you the feeling of being privileged, but you got the feeling they didn't really mean it, like they was sniggering behind your back all the time.

OK, some things we was allowed to do that the ordinary day-trippers wasn't. We could leave our cars directly in front of the house, we could go through most of the doors marked 'Private', we was actually allowed to *sit* on the chairs. But all the time they was pretending to treat us like regular house party guests, the staff seemed to be just watching out for us to make fools of ourselves. I mean, like turning up in the wrong clothes or not picking the right knives and forks at meals, they really seemed to be on the lookout for that sort of thing. And I'm afraid for me it was particularly difficult. Social graces didn't figure large in the Borstal educational curriculum.

Mind you, the other punters seemed to lap it up. I saw they was getting the old sneers from the staff just as much as I was, but they didn't seem to notice. They really thought they was being treated just like house-guests, like they was there by personal invite of Lord Harbinger and not paying through the nose for the privilege of lounging around his gaff and seeing him for a rationed hour and a half of tea and farewells on the Sunday afternoon.

Also, let's face it, they wasn't really my sort of people. I daresay I got a lot of flaws in my character, but one thing nobody's ever called me is a snob. And that's what this lot was, every one of them.

A lot of them was Americans and in fact they was generally less offensive than the English ones. I mean, their grasp on culture was so sketchy that all they seemed to do was keep saying how old everything was. Apparently Harbinger Hall had been featured in some naff television series that they'd seen over there and they spent a lot of time walking round the place acting out their favourite bits and taking photos of each other in various settings. Funny lot, the Yanks, I always thought that.

Still, they was at least friendly. The English punters reckoned as soon as they saw me that I wasn't 'their sort of person'. Dead right they was too. I wouldn't want to be some nasty little factory owner who, just because he's made a bit of bread, reckons he can go around buying breeding. I may not have a lot in the way of social gloss, but at least it's all mine.

Anyway, the English ones certainly disapproved of me. I'd catch them talking behind their hands about me when I come in the room. 'Sticks out like a sore thumb,' I heard one cheeky little pickle-manufacturer say. 'You'd think they'd vet the applications of people who come on these weekends.'

Under other circumstances I'd have pushed the little git's false teeth out the other end, but I remembered that I wasn't meant to be drawing attention to myself so I laid off him.

You'll have got the impression by now that the company wasn't that great, and let me tell you the entertainment, so-called, was even worse. Dear oh dear. I already told you my views on history, and I really thought that old git of a guide had said everything there was to say and a bit more about Harbinger Hall when I done my day-trip. Don't you believe it. For the Stately Home Weekend they got in blooming Professors of History to take us through the lot, Duke by Duke. Then another berk come and took us through the family portraits and, as if that weren't enough, some bloody snooty old blue-rinse give us a lecture on eighteenth-century house-keeping. Tell you, I done some boring jobs in my time, but I'd rather spend a solid week watching for some fence to come out of his front door than ever sit through that lot again.

The Mediaeval Banquet wasn't no better. My idea of a good Saturday night is going out for a few beers and, if you're feeling a bit exotic, ending up at the Chinkie or the Indian; not sitting in front of seventeen knives and forks while gits march up and down holding up stuffed pigs and peacocks. As a general rule, I don't mind music, either – good sing-song round the Joanna or a nice tape of James Last, Abba, that sort of number; but please God may I never again be put in a position where I have to act natural while listening to a bunch of birds singing madrigals to a lute.

But I stuck at it, like a right little swot. Fixed my mind steadily on the five grand. Or maybe on a bit more than that.

Being the size I am, I got a pretty well-developed appetite, and all them lectures and that had sharpened it a bit, so, even though they wasn't serving anything I fancied, I had a good go at all this stuffed pig and peacock and fruit tarts and what-have-you. Even forced myself to drink some of the mead, which is not an experience I'd recommend to anyone with taste-buds.

Anyway, result of all this is, I wake up in bed round one in the morning with this dreadful heartburn. Well, it's more than heartburn, really. It's that round the chest, but it seems to be moving down the body and turning into something less tasteful. Not to put too fine a point on it, I have to get to the bog in a hurry.

Well, they're real mean with the wattage on the landings and, sense of direction never having been my special subject, I go through all kinds of corridors and staircases before I find what I'm looking for.

And, dear oh dear, when I get there, what a spectacle it is. Blooming great dark wood seat like something out of an old rowing boat, and the pan's got all these pink and blue roses all over it. Out the back there's this sort of plunger like it was going to detonate a bomb. You'd really think in a place like Harbinger Hall they'd get decent facilities. I mean, more like the sort of thing my brother-in-law's got – low-level avocado with matching sink and gold-plated dolphin flush-handle.

Still, I'm in no condition to bother about Lord Harbinger's lack of design sense. It's lock the door, down with the pyjama trousers and settle in for a long session.

Embarrassing though it is to confess, I'm afraid I must've dozed off. Mead must've got to me. Because next thing I know I'm hearing voices. I don't mean 'hearing voices' like loonies hear; I mean there's a couple of geezers nattering outside the bog door. So I holds my breath (amongst other things) and listens.

Well, first thing is, I recognise one of the voices. Told you I was good on them, didn't I? Yes, you guessed. Mr Loxton from the sauna, wasn't it?

'I saw our contact this afternoon,' he's saying. 'All set up for tomorrow evening. It'll be a quick handover.'

'That's not what I'm worried about. It's the bit before.'

'It'll be fine. I've talked to the staff and it sounds as if the other guests are certainly going to remember him.'

'But if he's as dumb as he appears, are you sure he's capable of actually doing what he's meant to?'

'It's not difficult. If he does blow it, we just call the police and have him arrested.'

'Not keen on that,' the other says sharply. His voice was older, real upper-crusty, sounded like a Cabinet Minister being interviewed, know what I mean? 'Police might want to investigate a bit too deeply. No, we've got to hope the whole affair goes through as planned.'

'I'm sure it will.' Mr Loxton sounds all soothing and . . . what's the word? You know, like a head waiter who thinks he's going to get a big tip.

'Yes. And you're sure he's not suspicious?'

'No chance. Picked with great care. He's as thick as two short planks.'

'Good. Good night.'

The older voice was moving away. I unlocked the door dead quiet and risked a quick flash through the crack. One who's just spoken's out of sight, but I see the other just as he's said 'Good night.' Mr Loxton's voice. Mean-looking bastard he is when you blow the steam away. But important thing is, he's wearing the striped trousers and that of one of the Harbinger Hall staff. As I suspected, I am part of an inside job.

That's not all I've learnt, though. Maybe it's the reference to 'two short planks', which I've heard more than once in my passage through life, but I feel sure Loxton and his chum was talking about me.

I've forgotten my gutrot by the time I get back into bed. Can't be distracted by things like that – need all my mind for thinking.

I can't work out what's happening yet, but I know it's something I don't like. I been set up a few times in my career, and there's a feeling you get when it happens. You don't know the details, but you know something's not kosher. Like when your bird's having it off with someone else.

I go through the whole thing to myself, listening out for the bits that don't ring true. I try to remember if there was any little bits struck me as odd at the time. And I come up with a few.

First, there's the fact that Wally Clinton put up my name. Now, like I explained, he had no reason to sugar-daddy on me. I nearly shopped him once and he had to give a very big birthday present to the boys in blue to get off the hook. Wasn't my fault, but Wally was never bothered by details like that.

My first thought is Wally is just out to get his own back, get me nicked when I cut through the alarm cables, but somehow that don't match the wallpaper. It's too complicated. He don't need to bring in Loxton and all this set-up. And two and a half grand's a month's takings to a smalltimer like Clinton. He's not going to throw it away on me.

'Picked with great care,' Loxton said. What's that mean? I begin to wonder. Think about my reputation in the business, where, as I happened to mention, I am reckoned a complete dumbo who'll do whatever he's told without question. That's it, of course. Loxton wanted someone guaranteed thick as a bunch of duvets; and Wally Clinton recommended me.

Hurtful though this conclusion is, I don't dwell on it. If that is the case, other things follow. Yes, I am being set up, but set up for something bigger than revenge for Wally. I try to think what else in the deal needs a deodorant.

I remember that right from the start I'd been impressed by the efficiency of the villains I was dealing with. Attention to detail. They'd given me instructions you couldn't go wrong with. They'd paid back my exact expenses. They'd even left the right money for the parking in Cavendish Square.

That thought stopped me. Cavendish Square Garage was where the car was meant to go back to. I was to drive there from Harbinger Hall. On my little lonesome. They'd set the whole thing up real tight until I left the Hall and then I could do what I liked. I know they thought I was thick, but surely even someone thick was going to realise that there was other things they could do with a couple of millions' worth of canvas than leave it in a garage. Considering the care they'd taken with everything else, they really hadn't thought that bit through. Why?

Something else suddenly barged into my mind. I went across to where my bomber jacket was hanging and felt in the pocket. The new price-list the bloke at the garage had given me.

There it was. Give me a nasty turn when I saw it.

*The Garage is closed all day Sunday.*

They hadn't bothered to think through the details of the hand-over once I'd stolen the painting, because they knew I wasn't going to get that far.

Then I remembered the other thing that didn't fit in. The locked boot of the Peugeot.

Picking locks isn't my Number One talent, but I got a decent set of skeletons and I get by. Could've done the Peugeot boot quicker with a jemmy, but I didn't want no one to see I been snooping. So I was patient and after about ten minutes had it open.

And what a treasure trove my little pencil torch lit up inside. Complete Do-It-Yourself burglar kit. Sets of chisels, jemmies, wire-snips, pliers, big crowbar, the lot. Stethoscope, too, presumably for the old listening-to-the-tumblers routine when opening safes. Not that many villains do that nowadays.

Don't use dynamite much either. Not in sticks. Plastic explosive's much easier to handle. Less likely to have accidents. Still, whoever had stocked out that car boot reckoned I might need dynamite for the odd safe-job.

They also reckoned I was going to need something else. The rectangular outline of the suitcase was familiar, and that of the cloth-wrapped object inside even more so. I felt the knobbly ridges of the frame as I undid it.

It was a painting, of course. Same size as the Madonna. Old, like the Madonna. But it wasn't the Madonna. Difficult to see what it was, actually. Or what it had been. The paint was all flaked and stained. Could have been anything. Can't imagine anyone would have given two quid for that one, let alone two million.

But the odd thing about it was that screwed to the frame at the bottom there was this brass plate, which said:

### MADONNA AND CHILD
Giacomo Palladino
Florentine
(1473–1539)

Someone was certainly setting me up, but I couldn't right then work out what for.

The Sunday was as boring as the Saturday. Some gamekeeper git give us a long lecture on grouse-shooting; there was a berk who went on about coats of arms; and the 'Traditional Sunday Lunch' was full of gristle. And whoever done the gravy ought to be copped under the Trades Descriptions Act. I mean, if the upper classes have been fed gravy like that since the Norman conquest, no wonder they're a load of wimps.

The afternoon was, in the words of the old brochure, 'less structured'. That meant, thank God, they couldn't think of anything else to bore us silly with. Guests were encouraged to wander round the grounds until the great moment of tea with Lord Harbinger.

I didn't bother to go out. I just lay on my bed and thought. I was piecing things together. Though nasty things have been said about it, there is nothing wrong with my intellect. It just works slowly. Give it time and it'll get there.

Trouble is, thinking takes it out of me, and I must've dozed off. When I come to, it was quarter to five and the old Royal Command tea had started at four-thirty. I got up in a hurry. Half of me was working out what was up, but the other half was still following instructions. I had to behave naturally, go through the weekend without drawing attention to myself.

As I hurried across the landing, I looked out through the big front window. I could see the red Peugeot parked right outside.

And I could see Mr Loxton closing the boot and moving away from it. Thought I'd be safely inside having my tea, didn't you, Mr Loxton?

The tea gave me the last important fact. As soon as I was introduced to Lord Harbinger, it all come together.

'Good afternoon,' he said with a reasonable stab at enthusiasm. 'Delighted to welcome you to Harbinger Hall.'

It was the voice, wasn't it? The bloke Loxton had been speaking to the night before. I realised just how inside an inside job it was.

And I realised other things that give me a nasty trickly feeling in my belly.

Half-past five the tea broke up. Lord Harbinger switched off like a lightbulb and, in spite of the Americans who would have liked to go on mingling with the aristocracy for ever, everyone was hustled out of the drawing-room to go and get packed. I went up to my bedroom like the rest.

Wasn't a lot to pack, was there? But for the first time I took a butcher's at the package in my suitcase. After what I seen in the car-boot the night before, could have been anything.

But no. It was a copy of the Madonna. Bloody good, too. I couldn't have told it apart from the real thing. But then I don't know much about art, do I?

Ten to six, following my instructions to the letter, down I go to the hall, leaving my suitcase in the bedroom. There's already a few of the punters milling around and piles of cases. Casual like, I take a glance at these and see, as I expected, that there's one there just like the one in the bedroom. Expensive for them on suitcases, this job. Mind you, if it all worked, they'd be able to afford it.

I hear Loxton's voice suddenly, whispering to Lord Harbinger. 'I'll get away as quickly as I can afterwards.'

'Fine,' says the noble peer.

Just before six, most of the punters have arrived and the Harbinger Hall staff are all starting to make a farewell line like something out of a television serial. The Americans think this is wonderful and start cooing.

'Oh, blimey,' I say loudly. 'Forget my own head next!' Then, for the benefit of the people who've turned round to look at me, I add, 'Only forgotten my blooming case, haven't I?'

They turn away with expressions of distaste, and I beetle upstairs. Do it by the book. To my bedroom, pick up the suitcase, to the Long Gallery, down the 'Private' staircase. Out with the old metal-cutters, reach for the cables at the top of the alarm boxes, snip, snip. I'm tense then, but there's no noise.

Into the Great Hall, put the suitcase on the table. Unzip it all the way round, take the copy of the Madonna out of its cloth wrappings, and do what I have to do.

Slam the case shut, back up the stairs, Long Gallery, bedroom, back down the main staircase towards the hall, stop on the stairs, panting a bit. Whole operation – three and a half minutes.

Now you've probably gathered that I have got this unfortunate reputation for bogging things up. Just when the job's nearly done, something always seems to go wrong. Bad luck I call it, but it's happened so often that some people have less charitable descriptions.

So, anyway, there I am standing on the stairs in front of all these people and I reach up to wipe my brow and – you'll never believe it – I haven't had time to zip up my suitcase again and I'm still holding the handle and it falls open. My aftershave and what-have-you clatters down the stairs with my pyjamas, and there, still strapped in the suitcase for all to see, is the Harbinger Madonna.

'My God!' says Lord Harbinger.

I say a rude word.

Various servants come forward and grab me. Others are sent off to the Great Hall to see the damage. Loxton's the first one back. He looks dead peeved.

'My Lord. The alarm wires have been cut. He's replaced the Madonna with a copy!'

'What!' Lord Harbinger blusters.

'Shall I call the police, my Lord?' asks another servant.

'Um . . .'

'All right.' I shrug. 'It's a fair cop. Story of my life. Every job I seem to screw up. And this one I really thought I'd worked out to the last detail.'

'Shall I call the police, my Lord?' the servant asks again.

'Um . . .'

'You better,' I say. 'I really have got caught with the goods this time. I'm afraid the police are going to want a really thorough investigation into this.'

'Ye-es.' His Lordship sounds uncertain. 'Under normal circumstances of course I'd call the police straight away. But this is rather . . . um . . . awkward.'

'Why?' I ask. 'I'm not pretending I haven't done it.'

'No, but, er . . . er . . .' Then finally he gets on the right track. 'But you are a guest in my house. It is not part of the code of the Harbingers to call the police to their guests, however they may have offended against the laws of hospitality.'

'Oh,' I say.

'Gee,' says one of the Americans. 'Isn't this just *wonderful*?'

Harbinger's getting into his stride by now. He does a big point to the door like out of some picture and he says, 'Leave my house!'

I go down the rest of the stairs. 'Better not take this, had I, I suppose?' I hold up the Madonna.

'No.'

I hand it over, sort of reluctant. 'You better keep the copy. I got no use for it now. And I suppose the police will want to look at that. Might be able to trace back who ordered it.'

'Yes,' says his Lordship abruptly. 'Or rather no. You take that back with you.'

'But—'

'No. If the police could trace you through the copy, I would be offending the rules of hospitality just as much as if I had you arrested. You take the copy with you.'

'But I don't want it.'

'YOU WILL TAKE IT, SIR!' he bellows.

'Oh, all right,' I say grudgingly.

'Oh, heck. This is just so *British*,' says one of the Americans. Made her weekend, it had.

They give me the picture from the Great Hall, I put it in my suitcase, and I'm escorted out by Loxton. The punters and staff draw apart like I'm trying to sell them insurance.

Outside, Loxton says, 'God, I knew you were thick and incompetent, but it never occurred to me that you'd be *that* thick and incompetent.'

I hang my head in shame.

'Now get in your car and go!'

'Oh, it's not my car,' I say. 'It's stolen. Way my luck's going, I'll probably get stopped by the cops on the way home. I'll go on the coach to the station.'

Loxton doesn't look happy.

Takes a bit of time to get all the punters on to the bus. Loxton stands there fidgeting while further farewells are said. I sit right at the back with my suitcase. Everyone else sits right up the front. I'm in disgrace.

The bus starts off down the steep zigzag drive towards Limmerton. I look back to see Loxton rush towards the Peugeot, parked right in front of Harbinger Hall. I look at my watch. Quarter to seven. All that delayed us quite a bit.

I see Loxton leap into the car. Without bothering to close the door, he starts it and slams her into reverse. He screeches backwards over the gravel.

But it's too late. The Hall's saved, but he isn't.

The back of the Peugeot erupts into a balloon of orange flame. From inside the bus the sound is muffled. A few of the punters turn curiously, but just at that moment we swing round one of the hair-pins and there's nothing to see.

I piece it together again in the train. They've left me in a compartment on my own. I'm still like some kind of leper. They all feel better having had their guesses at the sort of person I was confirmed.

Lord Harbinger had money problems. Cost a lot to keep the Hall going, and the trippers weren't coming enough. Stately Home Weekends might bring in a few bob, but they took such a lot of staff, there wasn't much percentage in it.

But he had got the Madonna. Couldn't just sell it, wouldn't look good, public admission of failure. Besides, either he or Loxton had worked out a scheme that'd make more than just selling it. They'd have it stolen, get the insurance *and* sell it. But they need a real mug to do the actual thieving.

Enter Yours Truly.

I had to raise suspicions when I came for my day-trip, then stick out like a sore thumb on the Stately Home Weekend. When I'd actually done the theft, switched the real Madonna for the copy, Loxton would have offered to take my bag to my car. He would have switched my suitcase for the empty one and put the Madonna in another car, in which he would later drive it up to London to do his deal with Mr Depaldo's rival.

I would have driven off in the Peugeot, maybe full of plans to doublecross my paymasters and do a little deal of my own. They weren't worried what I had in mind, because they knew that half an hour away from Harbinger Hall, the dynamite in the back of the car would explode. When the police came to check the wreckage, I would be identified as the geezer who'd been behaving oddly all weekend, the one who'd obviously cut the alarm cables and switched the paintings. My profession was obvious. There was my record if they ever put a name to me. And if not, there were all the tools of my trade in the boot of the car.

Together with the dynamite, whose careless stowing caused my unfortunate demise.

And some burnt-out splinters of wood and shreds of canvas, which had once been a painting. A very old painting, tests would reveal. And the engraved brass plate which was likely to survive the blast would identify it as Giacomo Palladino's masterpiece, *Madonna and Child*. Another great art work would be tragically lost to the nation.

Had to admire it. Was a good plan.

They only got one thing wrong. Like a few others before them, they made the mistake of thinking Billy Gorse was as thick as he looked.

I felt good and relaxed. Pity the train hadn't got a buffet. I could have really done with a few beers.

Go to Red Rita's later, I thought. Yeah, be nice. Be nice to go away with her, and all. Been looking a bit peaky lately. She could do with a change. South America, maybe?

I got my suitcase down from the rack and opened it.

Found it grew on me, that Madonna.

And I was very glad I hadn't changed the two pictures round in the Great Hall. I may not know much about art, but I'm beginning to realise what it's worth.

# GWENDOLINE BUTLER

## North Wind

As soon as I saw Harry Trask I guessed what he must be. He was one in the line of descent, an inheritor, a successor.

CIA, I thought: *he's* the man sent here to replace Jim Olsen. (Jim had been a friend of mine. Or, anyway, we'd seen a lot of each other.) Then I thought: if he is the man sent to succeed Jim, he's come here to watch someone. So the thing to do is to observe whom he cultivates, whom he sees most of.

It took me some time to realise that person was me.

A bubble of speculation, floating airily above me, had suddenly turned hard and white and hit me, like a golf ball driven in from outer space during some celestial competition.

In fact there was a golf ball at my feet where I walked by the sea. I picked it up and threw it back towards the green. The dog followed it.

When you live a great deal alone by yourself in an isolated but intellectual community, games get invented. I belong to such a group, living amidst schools, university and golf courses, and facing the bleak North Sea. The German Ocean, the Kaiser's Ocean, our grandfathers called it. We were far away from almost everywhere. The winds that lashed us came straight from the Urals.

The best game was about people, and I was the inventor. 'Bubbles' we called it. Half secret, half public was 'Bubbles'. We played it at drinks parties, on long quiet walks, in bed. You could play it together or alone. 'Bubbles' had no beginning and no end. So innocent, so inventive, so easy, a challenge to the imagination we thought it. In the time since, at moments when I have been alone, I have given much thought to the essential nature of the game we played and I would now call it destructive.

'A dangerous game it turned out to be,' I said aloud, stirring my coffee. The waiter, who did not understand very well, and small wonder, since I was but learning his tongue, thought I asked for sugar and brought me a bowl.

This particular 'Bubble' began at a party. A cold summer evening in a garden overlooking the sea, not a time to have drinks out of doors, but Clara and Jock ignored the thermometer's temperature when their roses were out.

Roses do bloom beautifully by the sea, but sometimes the salt spray burns and scorches them. This had happened now to Clara and Jock Oban-Smith's roses, so that the petals were brown and sere.

All the same, I picked one and sniffed. The sea air diminishes scents as well, but in this case the roses had triumphed. 'Lovely,' I said to Jock. 'Delicious. Better than ever. A good year.'

He was pleased; he knew it was a lie, roses, after all, aren't like vines and don't have a vintage, but he could accept a compliment to his own good husbandry. He and I were particularly good exponents of 'the game'.

There were about thirty people crowded into the small garden and I knew

63

every one of them. There were no more variations to be played in our small circle, we had done them all. I suppose it was what made our game so essential.

One notable omission among the guests that evening, I observed.

'Who's not here?' I said, testing.

'Jim Olsen, of course.'

Jim Olsen was a fat young American who had come to teach geography at the local boys' prep school. He was always beautifully dressed in grey, with a good deal of white about him. He seemed too rich and sophisticated (and also just slightly too seedy, there was a hint of secrets about him) to be teaching in a boys' school. We could never quite understand his presence, so he was a natural for our game.

'Why of course?'

'He has to obey his masters. He's been called back home.'

'Ah,' I nodded sagely. 'What a good notion.'

In this bubble of our imagining, Jim Olsen swam round and round like a goldfish in a bowl with Jock Oban-Smith after him. It was Jock's bubble really. I had just joined in, but I was taking it over. In it Jim Olsen was not really a school teacher but a representative of the CIA.

'Of course, if Jim *is* really CIA,' I had said originally when we were just starting this bubble, Jock and I, 'then he has to be here doing something.'

'Oh, that's simple,' said Jock Oban-Smith easily. 'There's a Russian spy at the airfield. Or a security leak of some sort. The Americans are alarmed, you know they use the airfield, although we aren't supposed to admit it. They've sent old Jim over to watch a suspect.'

'Yes, I accept that,' I nodded judiciously. 'We all know that more things than they ever admit to fly in the skies over that field. I am sure there are spies. And so counter-spies. Yes, I like that, Jock.'

Although we never talked much about the airfield I, for one, never forgot its presence. My husband had been a flyer there. Had been or was: of which tense I was never sure – was it what he did or what he aspired to? To me, he seemed to have so many ambitions.

Now Jock Oban-Smith said: 'Look, Elizabeth, I know how dreary it's been for you since your man went away. Rotten for you. Let me know if I can help.'

'Oh, Jock, it's not so bad,' I protested. 'He's not dead or divorced. He's coming back.' (I wasn't totally convinced of this, but never mind.) 'It's only a polar expedition.'

'But twelve months!' He looked at me with sympathy. 'Tough.'

Jock had never been six months away from his wife, and probably never would be, but Clara had confided in me that she wished for silence and a period of quiet and would have been grateful if the North Pole had called Jock.

'Oh, I *know*,' went on Jock, looking at me with sympathy. 'I've seen you taking your long walks across the sands, head down, pushing against the wind.'

To divert him I said, 'We never worked out who Jim was watching, did we? He hardly seemed to know anyone but us.'

'Oh, not so. He had a tremendous circle: all the boys at the school, all the staff. Oh yes, he had his circle. They'll miss him.'

'And he's really gone?'

'On Wednesday. Flew out. Naturally he'd kept it quiet. Been discreet. The school was told his mother had died. But that's a cover story. Anyway, he's gone. With hardly a word.'

As I took my customary long walk across the dunes that ran towards the airfield, I thought: if Jim Olsen was truly CIA and has now been withdrawn, then someone else will surely take his place, because the job is not done. I have only to watch and wait to identify his successor.

It was such an extension of our bubble that at first I decided to keep it to myself. The town seemed full of ghosts as I turned and walked towards it, leaving the sand dunes and the wild sea behind me. Some of them walked out of history, like Mary Stuart and John Knox, but others were my own private and personal hauntings. I think Jim Olsen had his own walk there.

By October a young American had arrived. He had short-cropped hair and an air of great neatness. He said he had been an army officer stationed in Athens, had become interested in antiquity and had come here to study the ancient Greeks. A likely story.

All right, I thought, if he is Jim Olsen's replacement come here to study a local spy, watch who he gets close to.

Rather shyly I told Jock Oban-Smith about my addition to the bubble and he agreed that it was a good one.

So I watched. The young soldier was called Harry Trask, which seemed a good name for him, whether it was his own or not. He was a nice boy and I liked him. Back home he had a pretty little wife called Livia; he showed me her photograph but, of course, anyone can have a photograph and call it what they like. A solitary soul, he seemed to make few friends outside the ancient world. I used to meet him walking on the beach, face screwed up against the onslaught of wind and sand and spray. He was musical, too, so I let him come and listen to Vivaldi and Handel on my record player. He didn't seem to like anything written later than seventeen sixty. If I had had Bronze Age music, I expect he'd have chosen that.

I was very slow. It was spring before I took in that the only person he seemed interested in was *me*.

Me. Why me? I thought.

Ironically enough, it was just about the time this sank in that I became convinced my bubble was no bubble but the truth. Hard to say exactly how I arrived at this conclusion, perhaps things he let drop, perhaps his very evasions and discretions.

Why me? Why was he watching me? What had I got that he wanted?

Well, I knew what I had got, even in his absence, and that was a husband attached to a highly strategic airfield. Far away from me at this moment, of course, but it might be presumed that I had noticed things about his life and work, – or had had secrets told me, as a wife. So if there was a leak, I was due for suspicion.

Or – a further puff for my bubble (now getting rather unpleasant and hard, like some grotesque physical cyst) – it might be thought that I was a spy.

Jock Oban-Smith was surprised that I no longer joined in our game. (Clara had never played.) How could I tell him that I seemed to be inside the bubble myself?

Jock liked immunity, you see. He liked to be the doctor identifying the disease, not the patient in fever with it. And he had all the right antigens to protect him from contemporary society, too, for he was rich and Clara was well born.

'You're getting dull, my dear girl,' he complained. 'I shall have to do something.'

'I don't know what, then,' I retorted.

'I'll ask Clara.'

Jock always asked Clara, although he didn't always do what Clara suggested. About me, for instance, I know she thought Jock shouldn't encourage me in our games. She thought he was in love with me, but he wasn't. Jock wasn't in love with anyone, not even Clara, only her family tree. He *did* love genealogy; it brought out the best in him. He would tell you about her descent quietly and gently, as a special privilege, when he felt you had earned the honour. Clara never mentioned it herself. She was above that sort of thing.

It was early summer when I learned, through the usual devious routes by which such news came to me, that my husband's return from the Arctic was delayed. I had suspected it already, of course. I began to wonder if he would ever come back. There comes a time in any long absence (does there not?) when you feel that the loved one will not come back at all. This fear had a great deal to do with what happened. I was anxious. And there were no letters from him, you see. From where he was no letters could come.

I let Harry see me as often as he wished from that time on, get as close to me as he seemed to want, because I was watching him watch me.

I thought that way I could find out what I was supposed to have done.

Inside the bubble values get distorted like a reflection in a crooked mirror, so that my behaviour seemed acceptable and even good sense.

As Harry got closer, and we met more often, I thought: if he's watching me then I'll give him something to watch. So I went to the airfield often. I had a lot of contacts there, it was an easy thing for me to do. I entertained some of the young pilots; they were lonely and came willingly to drink coffee and listen to music. It was harmless enough, they expected little of me except companionship, but the bubble distorted everything, and I suppose I looked like a woman amusing herself in her husband's absence.

Jock Oban-Smith it was who acquainted me of the next development. He stopped me in the street one day, the usual keen wind was blowing.

'You're crying,' he accused.

'No, I'm not. My eyes are watering in the wind, that's all.'

'Have you had bad news from that husband of yours?'

'I tell you there's nothing wrong with me.'

'You've had no news, though.'

'I expected none,' I said tersely. I tried to move, but Jock wouldn't let me.

'That young man's in love with you.' He meant Harry.

'I think not.'

'He's very very interested,' said Jock.

'Oh, fascinated,' I said.

'You wouldn't go doing anything silly? Couldn't blame you, I suppose.' His kind face looked concerned. 'I always said it was a pity, your husband being away so much.' He wagged a finger. 'And I'm thinking of that young man, too, as well as you. You've got a hard heart, he hasn't.'

'I have? Is that what you think? But I'll have a word with him,' I promised. 'I've been meaning to, really.'

The next day I met Harry on the sands. He had a small dog with him, a stray mongrel he had befriended. Everyone in the town knew the dog. It was known as 'the little lame dog'. They stopped when they saw me.

'It must be lonely for your wife,' I said. 'With you away.'

Harry and the dog turned to look at me, moving their heads simultaneously as if the same string pulled them both.

'It was her choice,' he said defensively. He hadn't talked about his wife much lately and I had begun to wonder if she really existed. Now it looked as if she did. 'Her own choice,' he said again. 'It's her life back home, her pottery and the shop where she sells it. No, she couldn't leave it.'

'Hasn't she ever moved about with you? I mean, as the army has moved you from country to country?'

'Only sometimes.' He was always tight-mouthed about his army life. Then he countered: 'You must know all about loneliness, with your husband so long gone.'

'Only it wasn't my choice; I was left.'

He gave me a wary look, almost exactly like the stray dog's. 'What's your husband's name? You've never said.'

'Edward. Always Edward.'

'What a funny way of putting it: as if he could change names.'

Inside my bubble the sound of his words was magnified and distorted. Was I hearing true? Now it sounded as if he thought the spy he was watching was not me after all, but my husband, and that because he could not watch Edward he was watching *me*. It figured, as they say where he came from.

'I only meant that some people shorten it to Ted or Ed or Eddie; he's always Edward,' I said. 'Still, he's been a long time away.'

The dog pawed at my leg, he was a friendly fellow, and I bent down to pat his head.

Harry said: 'For me, it's been a lovely time, I've had a lovely time. Knowing you, our walks together, the music. A good time for me.' He spoke awkwardly, offering me the words like a shy present.

I was terrified. Is it, then, not a spy story after all, but a tender love story between two lonely people? Had I made a terrible mistake?

'You do like me, don't you?' he said, still hesitantly.

'Oh, yes. I do.' I patted the dog's head again so that I need not meet his eyes. But instead I saw the dog's lambent gaze, and it was almost the same thing.

'I think you like Americans. There was another, wasn't there? Jim Olsen.'

'I wondered if you'd mention him.'

'He seems much missed. Everyone says how nice he was. I wish I'd known him.'

'You might meet him one day, I suppose.'

'America's a big country,' he observed mildly. 'He was from Boston and I'm from New York and never the twain shall meet. Oddly enough, though, I have sort of heard of him. My—' and here he hesitated for a word, the right, the true, the telling word. He came up with it. 'My folk know his folk.'

'Ah,' I said. 'So there's a connection.'

'And he's never got back home yet. They're getting a bit worried.'

'As you say, America's a big country. I expect he's visiting somewhere. He loved the sands here,' I said. 'I often used to meet him walking here. Or he met me. I don't know which way round it was, which of us kept meeting the other. But he certainly loved it here. Perhaps he never got any further home than these sand dunes.'

'But that's a terrible thought,' he protested.

'What, not happy for him among all the little crabs and molluscs? But I was only joking.'

'I'll never get used to your British sense of humour.'

'What you really mean is that it was a joke in incredibly bad taste.'

'Well, it was rather.' He was stiff.

'I'm a bit on edge, one way and another, about absent friends.'

'Were you so close to Jim Olsen, then?'

'Not really,' I said after a pause.

'You have the reputation for letting people get so close to you and then no closer.'

'That's about it,' I said.

'You see, I'm being completely honest with you.'

I sat down on the sand, where it was dry, and the dog came and sat next to me. After a bit Harry sat down too.

The sky was a clear, pale blue, the sort of blue washed with silver that you only get in those northern days. Towards the west it was banded with pink and gold.

'It's coming towards the longest day,' he said, looking at the sky.

'Yes, so it is.' The season of the white nights, so the Russians called it. The further you got into the Arctic Circle, the longer the day.

'And the shortest night,' he went on. 'Hardly any night at all. Already the hours of darkness are shorter than I expected.'

'Yes.' I did not take my eyes off the sky. 'It's being so far north. Next week I am going to Norway, to take a trip on a small ship that goes round the fjords. It goes right through the Arctic Circle to Kirkenes. I shall leave the ship there and go right up to the Russian border. I'm going to study the birds and the flowers.' I did look at him then, and saw his eyes bright and hopeful. But who knew quite what the hope was for? 'Why don't you come too?'

'I could come,' he said slowly. 'I could get away.'

'I shall go right up to the Russian border. If you've never seen the tundra country you'll love it.' I spoke sweetly. I meant him to accept. I was punishing somebody and I wasn't quite sure who.

If any letters had come then from Edward, I believe I would have shown them to Harry, and said: 'Look, read them and see for yourself. Make up your own mind what he is and what I am. Is he just a nice, shy, inarticulate man who has gone away on a scientific trip, or is he something more devious? And if he is, then what am I? An innocent victim or his assistant?' But no letters came.

'How do you get there?' he asked.

'Well, if you really don't know, and I'm sure you do, you fly to Bergen and get on the boat there. Then leave it at Kirkenes. The boat gets booked up well ahead, but I'm sure you will find a berth.'

He didn't rise to the implication of my remark, but said: 'Are you sure *you* will?'

'Oh, I have had mine booked for months.'

'I can see you plan ahead,' he said.

'You have to,' I answered briefly. 'Well, what about it?'

There was nothing explicitly sexual about my invitation. He could make what he liked of it. He had offered me a show of affection, love even, and I had replied in kind. He would have to come to Norway, I thought. If he was a CIA agent, as postulated in my bubble, he would have to accept.

'I'll come.'

'What will you do about the dog?'

'You've got a cat, haven't you? What are you doing with her?'

'Clara Oban-Smith is looking after her. It's all arranged.'

'Will she take the dog too?'

'Clara always says yes to everything. It's what makes her such a good wife.'

'You can be a bitch sometimes, can't you?' he said coolly. Oddly enough, it was at that moment I believed that he might be in love with me.

I shrugged. 'Successful wife, then.'

'And you are not?'

'Manifestly, I am not. Successful wives are with their husbands, not left behind.'

'But that is due to an Arctic trip. Wives, women, can't go on such trips, can they?'

I paused. 'Well, I tell you: it was just a little bit more than that. The trip, I mean.'

'What?' The question was wrung from him.

'You don't sound surprised. I'm sure you've suspected. Jock Oban-Smith has.' I thought for a moment. Yes, I was nearly sure that Jock's imaginings stretched that far.

'You mean he *has* left you? Your husband has left you?'

'Not quite that. I mean the Arctic trip had its secret side. As well as doing all the official scientific things.'

'You mean spying?'

'But of course you've already guessed it.'

He didn't answer, but stared at me with a completely blank expression. I suppose that's how you look when your cover is blown. That's what they call it, isn't it?

'If that is what the party including your husband is really up to, I don't believe you'd know it,' he said coolly.

'You mean that my husband wouldn't dare to tell me?' I said as coolly back. 'That would depend, wouldn't it?'

'On what?'

'On what sort of a husband he is, and what sort of a wife I am,' I said, still cool. 'I suppose you don't tell your wife anything. Poor Livia. I pity that girl.'

He stared hard for a minute, then suddenly burst out laughing. Loudly. 'What a girl you are for a joke,' he said. 'You almost had me believing you. Like the suggestion you'd got Jim Olsen buried here beside you.'

We walked back into the town, not talking much, and the dog loped beside us.

Over the next few days I got on with my arrangements for the voyage, and I presume he did the same. Jock Oban-Smith said he deplored my departure, but he did nothing to stop my going.

'I suppose you've dropped all that story about Harry Trask now?' he said.

'Oh, completely.'

'You've fallen in love with him, that's why.'

'Oh, rubbish.'

'It's true.' He sighed. 'And it was such a good game. "Bubbles", I mean. Of course, I can never play it now.'

'Yes, you can, Jock,' I said kindly. 'You'll never stop. You're playing it now: me in love with Harry Trask. That's a prime example of a good bubble.'

'I admit it,' he said after a bit. 'And in my bubble you're doing it to pay your husband back for something.'

'For what?'

'That I don't know. Leaving you alone so long – something like that. I'll give it thought.'

'You're quite cold-hearted under that friendly exterior, Jock,' I said.

'Never you mind. Remember I'm looking after your cat while you're away. Doesn't that show a kind heart?'

'I'll see you about that, Jock,' I said.

Jock Oban-Smith put on his spectacles; they were a tiny, round, steel-framed affair, an affectation which increased his likeness to a fluffy-haired owl. He was long-sighted, Clara short-sighted; they were a perfect match.

'And shall I see you tomorrow before you go?'

'Oh, probably. Yes, I'm sure, Jock,' which meant, as I knew he guessed, no, he wouldn't.

'And where are you off to now?'

'Just for a last look at the sands.'

'I'll say goodbye now, then.'

'Goodbye, Jock. Goodbye.'

He kissed my cheek. 'I see you've got your shopping bag with you,' he called after me.

It was lonely on the beach, with only the hungry cries of the seagulls, and I wanted it that way so that I could say goodbye.

I was kneeling on the sand in the shelter of a low range of dunes topped with rough sea grass, still thinking I was alone, when I heard my name. I looked round, trying to hide what I was doing.

'Oh, Harry, you?' I leaned back on my heels.

Quickly he said: 'I wasn't following you.'

'No, of course not.'

'I just wanted to take a look at the places where we've walked. You can understand that, can't you?'

I nodded; I wished he would go away. I knew he wouldn't, though.

'What have you got in your hand?' he asked. He was staring at me. 'It's a little spade. A children's spade.'

'I found it on the sands,' I lied.

But his eyes had wandered beyond me. 'You're burying something.' He moved to see better. 'It's your cat. Your own cat.'

'He was very old,' I said. 'He might have died while I was away. I wanted his last hours to be with me. Besides, I didn't quite trust Clara Oban-Smith's care of him. She's decent, of course, but she has no imagination. People with no imagination can't be really kind.'

'My God, you are ruthless,' he said.

'I couldn't help it. It really is much kinder this way.'

'But if it had to be so, couldn't you bury the creature in your own backyard?'

'Oh no, here is best,' I said swiftly. 'More natural, more beautiful. But I must bury him deep, because of the seagulls. You can help, if you like.'

'No, the job's nearly done. You'd better finish it yourself.'

He watched me sprinkle the last sand on the furry face. 'You did love the creature.'

'Oh, yes.'

'And yet you killed it.'

'I had to.' I stood up. 'Honestly, what I did was best.'

Both of us started to walk away, the town lay ahead of us; behind us the sea and the dunes.

'Clara's all right for your dog, though,' I said. 'As a matter of fact she's looked after him before. He's anyone's dog, really.'

'Don't tell me Jim Olsen had him before me,' he said.

'There was a relationship,' I admitted, not willing to meet his eyes.

We walked on in silence for a few minutes. Then: 'Do you know what I'm wondering as I plod beside you?'

'No.' There was a strange note in his voice. I glanced at him quickly, there he was, shoulders hunched and head down.

'I'm wondering whose dog he will be next.'

'I think you will be his last owner,' I said seriously. 'But you needn't come with me. Stay here. Be his master.'

'No, I'm coming with you.'

We boarded the boat at Bergen and sailed slowly, and with many stops at the Norwegian towns up the coast and down a fjord or two. Bergen, Trondheim, Tromso, Harstad lay behind us.

I think he enjoyed it. We went sightseeing at each port, and then ran to catch the *Arctic Queen* before, on the minute with Norwegian punctuality, she sailed.

There was an American couple on board not on good terms, I thought, for they bickered constantly. I thought that perhaps it was the way they liked to live, but it seems not, since they began to look more and more miserable. The wife said to me: 'Do you ever have a cold war with your husband?'

'Yes, and a hot one too sometimes,' I said.

I think she imagined Harry and I were husband and wife, and I suppose we did seem like a pair, which in a way we were, although, if she had bothered to observe, she would have seen we had separate cabins.

At Kirkenes we left the *Arctic Queen* and moved into rooms in the small modern hotel where it seemed as though only businessmen came briefly, to look at the open-cast iron mine. Or perhaps there was the occasional educator visiting the school.

One other class of visitor there was, and I was not surprised to see them: neatly dressed men with quiet faces and well-drilled shoulders, an air of discipline and quiet authority belying their unobtrusiveness.

We were two days at Kirkenes and several such men were there during that time. I knew why they were there. A few miles away ran the Russian border, and on their side of the frontier were red telephones in guard huts that rang for emergencies only. And beyond the line of demarcation, and on this side too, were who knew what bits of sensitive military equipment? One does not leave frontiers like this guarded only by fresh-faced militiamen.

I wondered what languages the unobtrusive men spoke when they called at the military HQ outside the town. Any one of the NATO languages, I supposed.

Harry fitted into their background remarkably well, he looked just like one of them.

'I've enjoyed this trip so far,' he said on our first evening after dinner. 'And it has been perfectly educational.' I looked at him sharply. 'But I haven't seen any sign so far of your interest in the flora and fauna.'

'Tomorrow,' I said. 'We'll take a picnic and walk. It's marvellous country for walking.'

'You've got a map, have you? It's not the sort of country to wander in, I should say.'

'Oh, I have a map.'

The next day, early, we set off together. True to my word, I had a picnic lunch (thick smoked sausage and cheese sandwiches) in a bag hanging over my shoulder.

Until that moment I hadn't been quite sure that Harry would come. I thought that in the night he might have packed his bags and gone away. Or even had me arrested. I was sure he could have done either of those things and kept within his remit.

Instead, he walked beside me quietly. The further we had travelled inside the Arctic Circle, the better the weather had become. Behind us we had left a cold, windy Scotland, here it was warm and still. The landscape was golden, the grasses tall and the trees tiny and fragile. A small stream traced a winding path across the grassland.

'It's like the landscape of the moon, isn't it?' I said. 'Or what one used to imagine the moon might have been like before one knew it was covered with dust and dry boulders. This is timeless and quiet.'

'Lovely now, but it must be grim in winter,' said Harry.
'Snow and ice,' I said.
'I hope you know where we are.'
'The river follows the frontier,' I said, pointing. Distantly we could see the wooden watch-towers from which unseen Russian eyes might even now be watching us.
'The Norwegians presumably have something here also,' he said looking round.
'Bound to have. I expect we could find it if we wanted. But, of course, they wouldn't let us get too close.'
'To the frontier, you mean?'
'To anything,' I said lightly. 'And we won't even stare at the Russians in their turrets, in case it provokes them.'
'Could it?'
'I don't know. Depends how they're feeling, I suppose. But sometimes I believe the Russians and the Norwegians meet. Fishing in that river. It's a salmon river, you see.'
'So they catch salmon?'
'I suppose it's all there is to catch up here,' I said. 'You haven't got a camera on you, have you?'
He shook his head. 'No, no camera.'
'You must be hot in your jacket. Why don't you take it off?'
He mopped his brow. 'It *is* getting hot. Never thought of the Arctic Circle being so hot, somehow.' He didn't remove his jacket, however.
I looked up at the sun. 'Nearly noon. I suppose it's as hot now as it ever will be.'
By now I was deeply puzzled. We had come all this way together and so far he had offered me nothing but simple, unquestioning companionship. Perhaps my bubble was all wrong. Perhaps he was just what he seemed, a man who had abandoned the army for scholarship.
But no. Life could not be as innocuous as all that, and if it was, then he was not. There were lines about his mouth such as simple scholars never had.
We were quite close to the river bed now, and for a while we walked along a narrow track with birches and tall grasses on one hand and the silver river on the other. Then the river seemed to twist away out of sight.
A small hollow with a tree to lean against seemed to invite us to sit down. 'Let's have our lunch here, shall we?' I said.
I sat down. He remained on his feet, looking down at me. I held out my arms. He knelt. 'I waited for a long time for you to ask me to kiss you.'
'I think I've been asking all the time.'
'Ah, you don't know yourself.'
Even as I kissed him, I was experiencing a moment of shock. Not to know yourself, not to be sure what signals you are sending out is dangerous. So I had not given to him exactly the impression I thought I had?
As our hands explored each other, I thought: dammit, he's feeling me to see if I have a gun.
I drew away a little. 'No, I haven't got a camera, either,' I said.

'What do you mean?' He sounded puzzled.

'Never mind. Let's have our picnic now.' I unpacked my bag and spread the food out in front of us. I was hungry and ate quickly, keeping one eye on the countryside and another on Harry as I ate.

We leaned back against the tree in companionable silence. At least companionable on my part. I don't know what it was on his.

'Of course, I haven't got a camera,' I said. 'Neither have you. Neither of us would be silly enough to bring a camera right up to the Russian border.'

'If you say so.'

'Neither have I got a gun. You wondered about that, didn't you? I felt you wondering,' I said drily. 'We've been speculating about each other, haven't we? About what we are, and why we are both here. And if I haven't got a gun, *you* have. I felt it when you kissed me.'

'Yes, I have got a gun,' he said. 'Many Americans carry guns.'

'Oh, yes? On pleasure trips? Let me spin you a tale of what I imagined about you. I thought that you had come into my circle of friends to succeed Jim Olsen as a CIA agent. Jim having gone—' I hesitated, 'gone away. After a while, I decided that you were watching *me*. And it is certainly true that through, or because of, or even in spite of my husband, I could know secret matters. Jim had watched me. Jim had gone away. You had come in to take his place. That's what I thought. So I thought I'd lead you a dance.'

'You've certainly done that,' he said.

'Haven't I? And perhaps we're both innocent. Perhaps you're not what I think you are, nor am I a spy.'

'I suppose it's your sense of humour again,' he said. 'I reckon you ought to take it in hand. It spoils you, Elizabeth.'

'Never mind.' I settled myself comfortably against the tree. 'I know how we can work things out. I have a plan. And it depends on where we are.'

'I know where we are. Just this side of the Russian border.'

'No. I don't think you realised how the border winds. It does follow the river, roughly, but then the river loops too. We are now across the border. We are in Russia.'

'What?' He stood up quickly with alarm.

'Yes,' I said calmly, still sitting where I was. 'But dinna fash yourself, as they say where we have both come from, all may yet be well. We shall both be arrested, but if I am an innocent tourist and you are innocent also, then eventually we shall both go free. Probably not at the same time, and probably not together. But if I am guilty of what you suspect, you are guilty of what I suspect . . .' I shrugged.

'Then what?' he said.

'We shall still be arrested, but only one of us will go free.'

'Is this another specimen of your sense of humour?'

I ignored the jibe. 'I have a plan: let's make an arrangement to meet for coffee in McVitie's in Prince's Street in six months' time.' I smiled. 'If we are both there, well then, we are both innocent of everything.'

'I wish I knew what to make of you.'

'Well, it doesn't matter now.' I had my eyes on the skyline. 'I can see two men approaching, and they are Russian soldiers.'

Then I too stood up, waiting.

Six months later I finished my drink. The coffee hadn't been bad. Not good, but not bad either. Considering.

I called out to the waiter. 'Can I pay for my coffee?'

The waiter bowed and smiled. 'You enjoyed it? A good cup, eh?' which was clever of him since he was not speaking his own language.

'Delicious,' I lied, speaking in his.

'And your companion?'

'He enjoyed it too,' I said.

My husband, comfortably out of his Arctic trip and suitably apologetic for not having written ('I really couldn't, Liz, circumstances, you know. I dare not communicate with you'), came into the café then and heard the conversation. 'Your Russian's coming on,' he said. He sat down with us, making a third.

'I've worked at it.' I looked around me. 'I'm beginning to settle down. What about you, Jim?'

'Slowly, slowly,' said Jim Olsen. 'Give me time.'

'We did the only thing,' said my husband. 'Once we'd turned you, Jim, once you were one of *us*, people determined to upset the structure of society as we grew up in it, we all had to clear out. As much to protect you as anything, Jim.'

'I hope you're right,' said Jim.

'Oh, you're safe enough,' I said. 'Harry thinks I've killed you and buried you in the sands. I had to sacrifice my poor old cat to make sure. Still, I'd never have left him with Clara Oban-Smith anyway.'

My husband said uneasily: 'I suppose Harry was what you thought? We never really heard, you know.'

I shrugged. I didn't know. I was still wondering. For that matter, *he* may have been wondering about me. And that's what I mean about the bubble being dangerous. I may have ruined a perfectly innocent life.

# AGATHA CHRISTIE

# The Harlequin Tea Set

Mr Satterthwaite clucked twice in vexation. Whether right in his assumption or not, he was more and more convinced that cars nowadays broke down far more frequently than they used to. The only cars he trusted were old friends who had survived the test of time. They had their little idiosyncrasies, but you knew about those, provided for them, fulfilled their wants before the demand became too acute. But new cars! Full of new gadgets, different kinds of windows, an instrument panel newly and differently arranged, handsome in its glistening wood but, being unfamiliar, your groping hand hovered uneasily over fog lights, windscreen wipers, the choke, et cetera. All these things with knobs in a place you didn't expect them. And when your gleaming new purchase failed in performance, your local garage uttered the intensely irritating words: 'Teething troubles. Splendid car, sir, these roadsters Super Superbos. All the latest accessories. But bound to have their teething troubles, you know. Ha, ha.' Just as though a car was a baby.

But Mr Satterthwaite, being now of an advanced age, was strongly of the opinion that a new car ought to be fully adult. Tested, inspected, and its teething troubles already dealt with before it came into its purchaser's possession.

Mr Satterthwaite was on his way to pay a weekend visit to friends in the country. His new car had already, on the way from London, given certain symptoms of discomfort, and was now drawn up in a garage waiting for the diagnosis, and how long it would take before he could resume progress towards his destination. His chauffeur was in consultation with a mechanic. Mr Satterthwaite sat, striving for patience. He had assured his hosts, on the telephone the night before, that he would be arriving in good time for tea. He would reach Doverton Kingsbourne, he assured them, well before four o'clock.

He clucked again in irritation and tried to turn his thoughts to something pleasant. It was no good sitting here in a state of acute irritation, frequently consulting his wrist watch, clucking once more and giving, he had to realise, a very good imitation of a hen pleased with its prowess in laying an egg.

Yes. Something pleasant. Yes, now hadn't there been something – something he had noticed as they were driving along. Not very long ago. Something that he had seen through the window which had pleased and excited him. But before he had had time to think about it, the car's misbehaviour had become more pronounced and a rapid visit to the nearest service station had been inevitable.

What was it that he had seen? On the left – no, on the right. Yes, on the right as they drove slowly through the village street. Next door to a post office. Yes, he was quite sure of that. Next door to a post office because the sight of the post office had given him the idea of telephoning to the Addisons to break the news that he might be slightly late in his arrival. The post office. A village post office. And next to it – yes, definitely, next to it, next door or if not next door the door after. Something that had stirred old memories, and he had wanted – just what was it that he had wanted? Oh dear, it would come to him presently. It was mixed up with a colour. Several colours. Yes, a colour or colours. Or a word. Some definite word that had stirred memories, thoughts, pleasures gone by, excitement, recalling something that had been vivid and alive. Something which he himself had not only seen but observed. No, he had done more. He had taken part. Taken part in what, and why, and where? All sorts of places. The answer came quickly at the last thought. All sorts of places.

On an island? In Corsica? At Monte Carlo watching the croupier spinning his roulette wheel? A house in the country? All sorts of places. And he had been there, and someone else. Yes, someone else. It all tied up with that. He was getting there at last. If he could just . . . He was interrupted at that moment by the chauffeur coming to the window with the garage mechanic in tow behind him.

'Won't be long now, sir,' the chauffeur assured Mr Satterthwaite cheerfully. 'Matter of ten minutes or so. Not more.'

'Nothing seriously wrong,' said the mechanic, in a low, hoarse, country voice. 'Teething troubles, as you might say.'

Mr Satterthwaite did not cluck this time. He gnashed his own teeth. A phrase he had often read in books and which in old age he seemed to have got into the habit of doing himself, due, perhaps, to the slight looseness of his upper plate. Really, teething trouble! Toothache. Teeth gnashing. False teeth. One's whole life centred, he thought, about teeth.

'Doverton Kingsbourne's only a few miles away,' said the chauffeur, 'and they've a taxi here. You could go on in that, sir, and I'd bring the car along later as soon as it's fixed up.'

'No!' said Mr Satterthwaite.

He said the word explosively and both the chauffeur and the mechanic looked startled. Mr Satterthwaite's eyes were sparkling. His voice was clear and decisive. Memory had come to him.

'I propose,' he said, 'to walk along the road we have just come by. When the car is ready, you will pick me up there. The Harlequin Café, I think it is called.'

'It's not very much of a place, sir,' the mechanic advised.

'That is where I shall be,' said Mr Satterthwaite, speaking with a kind of regal autocracy.

He walked off briskly. The two men stared after him.

'Don't know what's got into him,' said the chauffeur. 'Never seen him like that before.'

The village of Kingsbourne Ducis did not live up to the old world grandeur of its name. It was a smallish village consisting of one street. A few houses. Shops that were dotted rather unevenly, sometimes betraying the fact that they were houses which had been turned into shops or that they were shops which now existed as houses without any industrial intentions.

It was not particularly old world or beautiful. It was just simple and rather unobtrusive. Perhaps that was why, thought Mr Satterthwaite, a dash of brilliant colour had caught his eye. Ah, here he was at the post office. The post office was a simply functioning post office with a pillar box outside, a display of some newspapers and some postcards, and surely, next to it, yes there was the sign up above. The Harlequin Café. A sudden qualm struck Mr Satterthwaite. Really, he was getting too old. He had fancies. Why should that one word stir his heart. *The Harlequin Café.*

The mechanic at the service station had been quite right. It did not look like a place in which one would really be tempted to have a meal. A snack perhaps. A morning coffee. Then why? But he suddenly realised why. Because the café, or perhaps one could better put it as the house that sheltered the café was in two portions. One side of it had small tables with chairs round them arranged ready for patrons who came here to eat. But the other side was a shop. A shop that sold china. It was not an antique shop. It had no little shelves of glass vases or mugs. It was a shop that sold modern goods, and the show window that gave on the street was at the present moment housing every shade of the rainbow. A tea set of largish cups and saucers, each one of a different colour. Blue, red, yellow, green, pink, purple. Really, Mr Satterthwaite thought, a wonderful show of colour. No wonder it had struck his eye as the car had passed slowly beside the pavement, looking ahead for any sign of a garage or a service station. It was labelled with a large card, as 'A Harlequin Tea Set'.

It was the word 'harlequin' of course which had remained fixed in Mr Satterthwaite's mind, although just far enough back in his mind so that it had been difficult to recall it. The gay colours. The harlequin colours. And he had thought, wondered, had the absurd but exciting idea that in some way here was a call to him. To him specially. Here, perhaps, eating a meal or purchasing cups and saucers might be his own old friend, Mr Harley Quin. How many years was it since he had last seen Mr Quin? A large number of years. Was it the day he had seen Mr Quin walking away from him down a country lane, Lover's Lane they had called it. He had always expected to see Mr Quin again, once a year at least. Possibly twice a year. But no. That had not happened.

And so today he had had the wonderful and surprising idea that here, in the village of Kingsbourne Ducis, he might once again find Mr Harley Quin.

'Absurd of me,' said Mr Satterthwaite, 'quite absurd of me. Really, the ideas one has as one gets old!'

He had missed Mr Quin. Missed something that had been one of the most exciting things in the late years of his life. Someone who might turn up anywhere and who, if he did turn up, was always an announcement that something was going to happen. Something that was going to happen to him. No, that was not quite right. Not *to* him, but through him. That was the exciting part. Just from the words that Mr Quin might utter. Words. Things he might show him, ideas would come to Mr Satterthwaite. He would see things, he would imagine things, he would find out things. He would deal with something that needed to be dealt with. And opposite him would sit Mr Quin, perhaps smiling approval. Something that Mr Quin said would start the flow of ideas, the active person would be he himself. He – Mr Satterthwaite. The man with so many old friends. A man among whose friends had been duchesses, an occasional bishop, people that counted. Especially, he had to admit, people who had counted in the social world. Because, after all, Mr Satterthwaite had always been a snob. He had liked duchesses, he had liked knowing old families, families who had represented the landed gentry of England for several generations. And he had had, too, an interest in young people not necessarily socially important. Young people who were in trouble, who were in love, who were unhappy, who needed help. Because of Mr Quin, Mr Satterthwaite was enabled to give help.

And now, like an idiot, he was looking into an unprepossessing village café and a shop for modern china and tea sets and casseroles no doubt.

'All the same,' said Mr Satterthwaite to himself, 'I must go in. Now I've been foolish enough to walk back here, I must go in just – well, just in case. They'll be longer, I expect, doing the car than they say. It will be more than ten minutes. Just in case there is anything interesting inside.'

He looked once more at the window full of china. He appreciated suddenly that it was good china. Well made. A good modern product. He looked back into the past, remembering. The Duchess of Leith, he remembered. What a wonderful old lady she had been. How kind she had been to her maid on the occasion of a very rough sea voyage to the island of Corsica. She had ministered to her with the kindliness of a ministering angel and only on the next day had she resumed her autocratic, bullying manner which the domestics of those days had seemed able to stand quite easily without any sign of rebellion.

Maria. Yes, that's what the Duchess's name had been. Dear old Maria Leith. Ah well. She had died some years ago. But she had had a harlequin breakfast set, he remembered. Yes. Big round cups in different colours. Black, yellow, red and a particularly pernicious shade of puce. Puce, he thought, must have been a favourite colour of hers. She had had a Rockingham tea set, he remembered, in which the predominating colour had been puce decorated with gold.

'Ah,' sighed Mr Satterthwaite, 'those were the days. Well, I suppose I'd better go in. Perhaps order a cup of coffee or something. It will be very full of milk, I expect, and possibly already sweetened. But still, one has to pass the time.'

He went in. The café side was practically empty. It was early, Mr Satterthwaite supposed, for people to want cups of tea. And anyway, very few people did want cups of tea nowadays. Except, that is, occasionally elderly people in their own homes. There was a young couple in the far window and two women gossiping at a table against the back wall.

'I said to her,' one of them was saying, 'I said you can't do that sort of thing. No, it's not the sort of thing that I'll put up with, and I said the same to Henry and he agreed with me.'

It shot through Mr Satterthwaite's mind that Henry must have rather a hard life and that no doubt he had found it always wise to agree, whatever the proposition put up to him might be. A most unattractive woman with a most unattractive friend. He turned his attention to the other side of the building, murmuring,

'May I just look round?'

There was quite a pleasant woman in charge and she said,

'Oh yes, sir. We've got a good stock at present.'

Mr Satterthwaite looked at the coloured cups, picked up one or two of them, examined the milk jug, picked up a china zebra and considered it, examined some ashtrays of a fairly pleasing pattern. He heard chairs being pushed back and, turning his head, noted that the two middle-aged women still discussing former grievances had paid their bill and were now leaving the shop. As they went out of the door, a tall man in a dark suit came in. He sat down at the table which they had just vacated. His back was to Mr Satterthwaite, who thought that he had an attractive back. Lean, strong, well muscled but rather dark and sinister-looking because there was very little light in the shop. Mr Satterthwaite looked back again at the ashtrays. 'I might buy an ashtray so as not to cause a disappointment to the shop owner,' he thought. As he did so, the sun came out suddenly.

He had not realised that the shop had looked dim because of the lack of sunshine. The sun must have been under a cloud for some time. It had clouded over, he remembered, at about the time they had got to the service station. But now there was this sudden burst of sunlight. It caught up the colours of the china through a coloured glass window of somewhat ecclesiastical pattern which must, Mr Satterthwaite thought, have been left over in the original Victorian house. The sun came through the window and lit up the dingy café. In some curious way it lit up the back of the man who had just sat down there. Instead of a dark black silhouette, there was now a festoon of colours. Red and blue and yellow. And suddenly Mr Satterthwaite realised that he was looking at exactly what he had hoped to find. His intuition had not played him false. He knew who it was who had just come in and sat down there. He knew so well that he had no need to wait until he could look at the face. He turned his back on the china, went back into the café, rounded the table and sat down opposite the man who had just come in.

'Mr Quin,' said Mr Satterthwaite. 'I knew somehow it was going to be you.' Mr Quin smiled.

'You always know so many things,' he said.

'It's a long time since I've seen you,' said Mr Satterthwaite.

'Does time matter?' said Mr Quin.

'Perhaps not. You may be right. Perhaps not.'

'May I offer you some refreshment?'

'Is there any refreshment to be had?' said Mr Satterthwaite doubtfully. 'I suppose you must have come in for that purpose.'

'One is never quite sure of one's purpose, is one?' said Mr Quin.

'I am so pleased to see you again,' said Mr Satterthwaite. 'I'd almost forgotten, you know. I mean forgotten the way you talk, the things you say. The things you make me think of, the things you make me do.'

'I – make you do? You are so wrong. You have always known yourself just what you wanted to do and why you want to do them and why you know so well that they have to be done.'

'I only feel that when you are here.'

'Oh no,' said Mr Quin lightly. 'I have nothing to do with it. I am just – as I've often told you – I am just passing by. That is all.'

'Today you are passing by through Kingsbourne Ducis.'

'And you are not passing by. You are going to a definite place. Am I right?'

'I'm going to see a very old friend. A friend I have not seen for a good many years. He's old now. Somewhat crippled. He has had one stroke. He has recovered from it quite well, but one never knows.'

'Does he live by himself?'

'Not now, I am glad to say. His family have come back from abroad, what is left of his family that is. They have been living with him now for some months. I am glad to be able to come and see them again all together. Those, that's to say, that I have seen before, and those that I have not seen.'

'You mean children?'

'Children and grandchildren.' Mr Satterthwaite sighed. Just for a moment he was sad that he had had no children and no grandchildren and no great-grand-children himself. He did not usually regret it at all.

'They have some special Turkish coffee here,' said Mr Quin. 'Really good of its kind. Everything else is, as you have guessed, rather unpalatable. But one can always have a cup of Turkish coffee, can one not? Let us have one because I suppose you will soon have to get on with your pilgrimage, or whatever it is.'

In the doorway came a small black dog. He came and sat down by the table and looked up at Mr Quin.

'Your dog?' said Mr Satterthwaite.

'Yes. Let me introduce you to Hermes.' He stroked the black dog's head. 'Coffee,' he said. 'Tell Ali.'

The black dog walked from the table through a door at the back of the shop. They heard him give a short, incisive bark. Presently he reappeared and with him came a young man with a very dark complexion, wearing an emerald green pullover.

'Coffee, Ali,' said Mr Quin. 'Two coffees.'

'Turkish coffee. That's right, isn't it, sir?' He smiled and disappeared.

The dog sat down again.

'Tell me,' said Mr Satterthwaite, 'tell me where you've been and what you have been doing and why I have not seen you for so long.'

'I have just told you that time really means nothing. It is clear in my mind and I think it is clear in yours the occasion when we last met.'

'A very tragic occasion,' said Mr Satterthwaite. 'I do not really like to think of it.'

'Because of death? But death is not always a tragedy. I have told you that before.'

'No,' said Mr Satterthwaite, 'perhaps that death – the one we are both thinking of – was not a tragedy. But all the same . . .'

'But all the same it is life that really matters. You are quite right, of course,' said Mr Quin. 'Quite right. It is life that matters. We do not want someone young, someone who is happy, or could be happy, to die. Neither of us want that, do we? That is the reason why we must always save a life when the command comes.'

'Have you got a command for me?'

'Me – command for you?' Harley Quin's long, sad face brightened into its peculiarly charming smile. 'I have no commands for *you*, Mr Satterthwaite. I have never had commands. You yourself know things, see things, know what to do, do them. It has nothing to do with me.'

'Oh yes, it has,' said Mr Satterthwaite. 'You're not going to change my mind on that point. But tell me. Where have you been during what it is too short to call time?'

'Well, I have been here and there. In different countries, different climates, different adventures. But mostly, as usual, just passing by. I think it is more for you to tell me not only what you have been doing but what you are going to do now. More about where you are going. Who you are going to meet. Your friends, what they are like.'

'Of course I will tell you. I should enjoy telling you because I have been wondering, thinking, you know, about these friends I am going to. When you have not seen a family for a long time, when you have not been closely connected with them for many years, it is always a nervous moment when you are going to resume old friendships and old ties.'

'You are so right,' said Mr Quin.

The Turkish coffee was brought in little cups of oriental pattern. Ali placed them with a smile and departed. Mr Satterthwaite sipped approvingly.

'As sweet as love, as black as night and as hot as hell. That is the old Arab phrase, isn't it?'

Harley smiled over his shoulder and nodded.

'Yes,' said Mr Satterthwaite, 'I must tell you where I am going though what I am doing hardly matters. I am going to renew old friendships, to make acquaintance with the younger generation. Tom Addison, as I have said, is a very old friend of mine. We did many things together in our young days. Then, as often happens, life parted us. He was in the Diplomatic Service, went abroad for several foreign posts in turn. Sometimes I went and stayed with him, sometimes I saw him when he was home in England. One of the early posts was in Spain. He married a Spanish girl, a very beautiful, dark girl called Pilar. He loved her very much.'

'They had children?'

'Two daughters. A fair-haired baby like her father, called Lily, and a second daughter, Maria, who took after her Spanish mother. I was Lily's godfather. Naturally, I did not see either of the children very often. Two or three times a year either I gave a party for Lily or went to see her at her school. She was a sweet and lovely person. Very devoted to her father and he was very devoted to her. But in between these meetings, these revivals of friendship, we went through some difficult times. You will know about it as well as I do. I and my contemporaries had difficulties in meeting through the war years. Lily married a pilot in the Air Force. A Fighter Pilot. Until the other day I had even forgotten his name. Simon Gilliatt. Squadron Leader Gilliatt.'

'He was killed in the war?'

'No, no. No. He came through safely. After the war he resigned from the Air Force and he and Lily went out to Kenya as so many did. They settled there and they lived very happily. They had a son, a little boy called Roland. Later when he was at school in England I saw him once or twice. The last time, I think, was when he was twelve years old. A nice boy. He had red hair like his father. I've not seen him since so I am looking forward to seeing him today. He is twenty-three – twenty-four now. Time goes on so.'

'Is he married?'

'No. Well, not yet.'

'Ah. Prospects of marriage?'

'Well, I wondered from something Tom Addison said in his letter. There is a girl cousin. The younger daughter Maria married the local doctor. I never knew her very well. It was rather sad. She died in childbirth. Her little girl was called Inez, a family name chosen by her Spanish grandmother. As it happens I have only seen Inez once since she grew up. A dark, Spanish type very much like her grandmother. But I am boring you with all this.'

'No. I want to hear it. It is very interesting to me.'

'I wonder why,' said Mr Satterthwaite.

He looked at Mr Quin with that slight air of suspicion which sometimes came to him.

'You want to know all about this family. Why?'

'So that I can picture it, perhaps, in my mind.'

'Well, this house I am going to, Doverton Kingsbourne it is called. It is quite a beautiful old house. Not so spectacular as to invite tourists or to be open to visitors on special days. Just a quiet country house to live in for an Englishman who has served his country and comes back to enjoy a mellow life when the age of retirement comes. Tom was always fond of country life. He enjoyed fishing. He was a good shot and we had very happy days together in the family home of his boyhood. I spent many of my own holidays as a boy at Doverton Kingsbourne. And all through my life I have had that image in my mind. No place like Doverton Kingsbourne. No other house to touch it. Every time I drove near it I would make a detour perhaps and just pass to see the view through a gap in the trees of the long lane that runs in front of the house, glimpses of the river where we used to fish, and of the house itself. And I would remember all the things that Tom and I did together. He has been a man of action. A man who has done things. And I – I have just been an old bachelor.'

'You have been more than that,' said Mr Quin. 'You have been a man who made friends, who had many friends and who has served his friends well.'

'Well, if I can think that. Perhaps you are being too kind.'

'Not at all. You are very good company besides. The stories you can tell, the things you've seen, the places you have visited. The curious things that have happened in your life. You could write a whole book on them,' said Mr Quin.

'I should make you the main character in it if I did.'

'No, you would not,' said Mr Quin. 'I am the one who passes by. That is all. But go on. Tell me more.'

'Well, this is just a family chronicle that I'm telling you. As I say, there were long periods, years of time when I did not see any of them. But they have been always my old friends. I saw Tom and Pilar until the time when Pilar died – she died rather young, unfortunately – Lily, my godchild, Inez, the quiet doctor's daughter who lives in the village with her father . . .'

'How old is the daughter?'

'Inez is nineteen or twenty, I think. I shall be glad to make friends with her.'

'So it is on the whole a happy chronicle?'

'Not entirely. Lily, my godchild – the one who went to Kenya with her husband – was killed there in an automobile accident. She was killed outright, leaving behind her a baby of barely a year old, little Roland. Simon, her husband, was quite broken-hearted. They were an unusually happy couple. However, the best thing happened to him that could happen, I suppose. He married again, a young widow who was the widow of a Squadron Leader, a friend of his and who also had been left with a baby the same age. Little Timothy and little Roland had only two or three months in age between them. Simon's marriage, I believe, has been quite happy though I've not seen them, of course, because they continued to live in Kenya. The boys were brought up like brothers. They went to the same school in England and spent their holidays usually in Kenya. I have not seen them, of course, for many years. Well, you know what has happened in Kenya. Some people have managed to stay on. Some people, friends of mine, have gone to Western Australia and have settled again happily there with their families. Some have come home to this country.

'Simon Gilliatt and his wife and their two children left Kenya. It was not the same to them and so they came home and accepted the invitation that has always been given them and renewed every year by old Tom Addison. They have come, his son-in-law, his son-in-law's second wife and the two children, now grown up boys or, rather, young men. They have come to live as a family there and they are happy. Tom's other grandchild, Inez Horton, as I told you, lives in the village with her father, the doctor, and she spends a good deal of her time, I gather, at Doverton Kingsbourne with Tom Addison who is very devoted to his grand-daughter. They sound all very happy together there. He has urged me several times to come there and see. Meet them all again. And so I accepted the invitation. Just for a weekend. It will be sad in some ways to see dear old Tom again, somewhat crippled, with perhaps not a very long expectation of life but still cheerful and gay, as far as I can make out. And to see also the old house again. Doverton Kingsbourne. Tied up with all my boyish memories. When one has not lived a very eventful life, when nothing has happened to one personally, and that is true of me, the things that remain with you are the friends, the houses and the things you did as a child and a boy and a young man. There is only one thing that worries me.'

'You should not be worried. What is it that worries you?'

'That I might be – disappointed. The house one remembers, one has dreams of, when one might come to see it again it would not be as you remembered it or dreamt it. A new wing would have been added, the garden would have been altered, all sorts of things can have happened to it. It is a very long time, really, since I have been there.'

'I think your memories will go with you,' said Mr Quin. 'I am glad you are going there.'

'I have an idea,' said Mr Satterthwaite. 'Come with me. Come with me on this visit. You need not fear that you'll not be welcome. Dear Tom Addison is the most hospitable fellow in the world. Any friend of mine would immediately be a friend of his. Come with me. You must. I insist.'

Making an impulsive gesture, Mr Satterthwaite nearly knocked his coffee cup off the table. He caught it just in time.

At that moment the shop door was pushed open, ringing its old-fashioned bell as it did so. A middle-aged woman came in. She was slightly out of breath and looked somewhat hot. She was good-looking still with a head of auburn hair only just touched here and there with grey. She had that clear ivory coloured skin that so often goes with reddish hair and blue eyes, and she had kept her figure well. The newcomer swept a quick glance round the café and turned immediately into the china shop.

'Oh!' she exclaimed, 'you've still got some of the Harlequin cups.'

'Yes, Mrs Gilliatt, we had a new stock arrived in yesterday.'

'Oh, I'm so pleased. I really have been very worried. I rushed down here. I took one of the boys' motor bikes. They'd gone off somewhere and I couldn't find either of them. But I really had to do something. There was an unfortunate accident this morning with some of the cups and we've got people arriving for tea and a party this afternoon. So if you can give me a blue and a green and perhaps I'd better have another red one as well in case. That's the worst of these different-coloured cups, isn't it?'

'Well, I know they do say as it's a disadvantage and you can't always replace the particular colour you want.'

Mr Satterthwaite's head had gone over his shoulder now and he was looking with some interest at what was going on. Mrs Gilliatt, the shop woman had said. But of course. He realised it now. This must be— He rose from his seat, half hesitating, and then took a step or two into the shop.

'Excuse me,' he said, 'but are you – are you Mrs Gilliatt from Doverton Kingsbourne?'

'Oh yes. I am Beryl Gilliatt. Do you – I mean . . .?'

She looked at him, wrinkling her brows a little. An attractive woman, Mr Satterthwaite thought. Rather a hard face, perhaps, but competent. So this was Simon Gilliatt's second wife. She hadn't got the beauty of Lily, but she seemed an attractive woman, pleasant and efficient. Suddenly a smile came to Mrs Gilliatt's face.

'I do believe . . . yes, of course. My father-in-law, Tom, has got a photograph of you and you must be the guest we are expecting this afternoon. You must be Mr Satterthwaite.'

'Exactly,' said Mr Satterthwaite. 'That is who I am. But I shall have to apologise very much for being so much later in arriving than I said. But unfortunately my car has had a breakdown. It's in the garage now being attended to.'

'Oh, how miserable for you. But what a shame. But it's not tea time yet. Don't worry. We've put it off anyway. As you probably heard, I ran down to replace a few cups which unfortunately got swept off a table this morning. Whenever one has anyone to lunch or tea or dinner, something like that always happens.'

'There you are, Mrs Gilliatt,' said the woman in the shop. 'I'll wrap them up in here. Shall I put them in a box for you?'

'No, if you'll just put some paper around them and put them in this shopping bag of mine, they'll be quite all right that way.'

'If you are returning to Doverton Kingsbourne,' said Mr Satterthwaite, 'I could give you a lift in my car. My chauffeur will be bringing it from the garage any moment now.'

'That's very kind of you. I wish really I could accept. But I've simply got to take the motor bike back. The boys will be miserable without it. They're going somewhere this evening.'

'Let me introduce you,' said Mr Satterthwaite. He turned towards Mr Quin, who had risen to his feet and was now standing quite near. 'This is an old friend of mine, Mr Harley Quin, whom I have just happened to run across here. I've been trying to persuade him to come along to Doverton Kingsbourne. Would it be possible, do you think, for Tom to put up yet another guest for tonight?'

'Oh, I'm sure it would be quite all right,' said Beryl Gilliatt. 'I'm sure he'd be delighted to see another friend of yours. Perhaps it's a friend of his as well.'

'No,' said Mr Quin, 'I've never met Mr Addison though I've often heard my friend, Mr Satterthwaite, speak of him.'

'Well then, do let Mr Satterthwaite bring you. We should be delighted.'

'I am very sorry,' said Mr Quin. 'Unfortunately, I have another engagement. Indeed' – he looked at his watch – 'I must start for it immediately. I am late already, which is what comes of meeting old friends.'

'Here you are, Mrs Gilliatt,' said the saleswoman. 'It'll be quite all right, I think, in your bag.'

Beryl Gilliatt put the parcel carefully into the bag she was carrying, then said to Mr Satterthwaite:

'Well, see you presently. Tea isn't until quarter past five, so don't worry. I'm so pleased to meet you at last, having heard so much about you always both from Simon and from my father-in-law.'

She said a hurried goodbye to Mr Quin and went out of the shop.

'Bit of a hurry she's in, isn't she,' said the shop woman, 'but she's always like that. Gets through a lot in a day, I'd say.'

The sound of the bicycle outside was heard as it revved up.

'Quite a character, isn't she?' said Mr Satterthwaite.

'It would seem so,' said Mr Quin.

'And I really can't persuade you?'

'I'm only passing by,' said Mr Quin.

'And when shall I see you again? I wonder now.'

'Oh, it will not be very long,' said Mr Quin. 'I think you will recognise me when you do see me.'

'Have you nothing more – nothing more to tell me? Nothing more to explain?'

'To explain what?'

'To explain why I have met you here.'

'You are a man of considerable knowledge,' said Mr Quin. 'One word might mean something to you. I think it would and it might come in useful.'

'What word?'

'Daltonism,' said Mr Quin. He smiled.

'I don't think—' Mr Satterthwaite frowned for a moment. 'Yes. Yes, I do know, only just for the moment I can't remember . . .'

'Goodbye for the present,' said Mr Quin. 'Here is your car.'

At that moment the car was indeed pulling up by the post office door. Mr

Satterthwaite went out to it. He was anxious not to waste more time and keep his hosts waiting longer than need be. But he was sad all the same at saying goodbye to his friend.

'There is nothing I can do for you?' he said, and his tone was almost wistful.

'Nothing you can do for *me*.'

'For someone else?'

'I think so. Very likely.'

'I hope I know what you mean.'

'I have the utmost faith in you,' said Mr Quin. 'You always know things. You are very quick to observe and to know the meaning of things. You have not changed, I assure you.'

His hand rested for a moment on Mr Satterthwaite's shoulder, then he walked out and proceeded briskly down the village street in the opposite direction to Doverton Kingsbourne. Mr Satterthwaite got into his car.

'I hope we shan't have any more trouble,' he said.

His chauffeur reassured him.

'It's no distance from here, sir. Three or four miles at most, and she's running beautifully now.'

He ran the car a little way along the street and turned where the road widened so as to return the way he had just come. He said again,

'Only three or four miles.'

Mr Satterthwaite said again, 'Daltonism.' It still didn't mean anything to him, but yet he felt it should. It was a word he'd heard used before.

'Doverton Kingsbourne,' said Mr Satterthwaite to himself. He said it very softly under his breath. The two words still meant to him what they had always meant. A place of joyous reunion, a place where he couldn't get to too quickly. A place where he was going to enjoy himself, even though so many of those whom he had known would not be there any longer. But Tom would be there. His old friend, Tom, and he thought again of the grass and the lake and the river and the things they had done together as boys.

Tea was set out upon the lawn. Steps led out from the French windows in the drawing room and down to where a big copper beech at one side and a Cedar of Lebanon on the other made the setting for the afternoon scene. There were two painted and carved white tables and various garden chairs. Upright ones with coloured cushions and lounging ones where you could lean back and stretch your feet out and sleep, if you wished to do so. Some of them had hoods over them to guard you from the sun.

It was a beautiful early evening and the green of the grass was a soft deep colour. The golden light came through the copper beech and the cedar showed the lines of its beauty against a soft pinkish-golden sky.

Tom Addison was waiting for his guest in a long basket chair, his feet up. Mr Satterthwaite noted with some amusement what he remembered from many other occasions of meeting his host, he had comfortable bedroom slippers suited to his slightly swollen gouty feet, and the shoes were odd ones. One red and one green. Good old Tom, thought Mr Satterthwaite, he hasn't changed. Just the same. And he thought, 'What an idiot I am. Of course I know what that word meant. Why didn't I think of it at once?'

'Thought you were never going to turn up, you old devil,' said Tom Addison.

He was still a handsome old man, a broad face with deep-set twinkling grey eyes, shoulders that were still square and gave him a look of power. Every line in his face seemed a line of good humour and of affectionate welcome. He never changes, thought Mr Satterthwaite.

'Can't get up to greet you,' said Tom Addison. 'Takes two strong men and a stick to get me on my feet. Now, do you know our little crowd, or don't you? You now Simon, of course.'

'Of course I do. It's a good few years since I've seen you, but you haven't changed much.'

Squadron Leader Simon Gilliatt was a lean, handsome man with a mop of red hair.

'Sorry you never came to see us when we were in Kenya,' he said. 'You'd have enjoyed yourself. Lots of things we could have shown you. Ah well, one can't see what the future may bring. I thought I'd lay my bones in that country.'

'We've got a very nice churchyard here,' said Tom Addison. 'Nobody's ruined our church yet by restoring it and we haven't very much new building round about so there's plenty of room in the churchyard still. We haven't had one of these terrible additions of a new intake of graves.'

'What a gloomy conversation you're having,' said Beryl Gilliatt, smiling. 'These are our boys,' she said, 'but you know them already, don't you, Mr Satterthwaite?'

'I don't think I'd have known them now,' said Mr Satterthwaite.

Indeed, the last time he had seen the two boys was on a day when he had taken them out from their prep school. Although there was no relationship between them – they had had different fathers and mothers – yet the boys could have been, and often were, taken for brothers. They were about the same height and they both had red hair. Roland, presumably, having inherited it from his father and Timothy from his auburn-haired mother. There seemed also to be a kind of comradeship between them. Yet really, Mr Satterthwaite thought, they were very different. The difference was clearer now when they were, he supposed, between twenty-two and twenty-five years old. He could see no resemblance in Roland to his grandfather. Nor apart from his red hair did he look like his father.

Mr Satterthwaite had wondered sometimes whether the boy would look like Lily, his dead mother. But there again he could see little resemblance. If anything, Timothy looked more as a son of Lily's might have looked. The fair skin and the high forehead and a delicacy of bone structure. At his elbow, a soft deep voice said,

'I'm Inez. I don't expect you remember me. It was quite a long time ago when I saw you.'

A beautiful girl, Mr Satterthwaite thought at once. A dark type. He cast his mind back a long way to the days when he had come to be best man at Tom Addison's wedding to Pilar. She showed her Spanish blood, he thought, the carriage of her head and the dark aristocratic beauty. Her father, Dr Horton, was standing just behind her. He looked much older than when Mr Satterthwaite had seen him last. A nice man and kindly. A good general practitioner, unambitious but reliable and devoted, Mr Satterthwaite thought, to his daughter. He was obviously immensely proud of her.

Mr Satterthwaite felt an enormous happiness creeping over him. All these people, he thought, although some of them strange to him, it seemed like friends he had already known. The dark beautiful girl, the two red-haired boys, Beryl Gilliatt, fussing over the tea tray, arranging cups and saucers, beckoning to a maid from the house to bring out cakes and plates of sandwiches. A splendid tea. There were chairs that pulled up to the tables so that you could sit comfortably eating all you wanted to eat. The boys settled themselves, inviting Mr Satterthwaite to sit between them.

He was pleased at that. He had already planned in his own mind that it was the boys he wanted to talk to first, to see how much they recalled to him Tom Addison in the old days, and he thought, Lily. How I wish Lily could be here now. Here he was, thought Mr Satterthwaite, here he was back in his boyhood. Here where he had come and been welcomed by Tom's father and mother, an aunt or so, too, there had been and a great-uncle and cousins. And now, well, there were not so many in this family, but it *was* a family. Tom in his bedroom slippers, one red, one green, old but still merry and happy. Happy in those who were spread round him. And here was Doverton just, or almost just, as it had been. Not quite so well kept up, perhaps, but the lawn was in good condition. And down there he could see the gleam of the river through the trees. More trees than there had been. And the house needing, perhaps, another coat of paint but not too badly. After all, Tom Addison was a rich man. Well provided for, owning a large quantity of land. A man with simple tastes who spent enough to keep his place up but was not a spendthrift in other ways. He seldom travelled or went abroad nowadays, but he entertained. Not big parties, just friends. Friends who came to stay, friends who usually had some connection going back into the past. A friendly house.

He turned a little in his chair, drawing it away from the table and turning it sideways so that he could see better the view down to the river. Down there was the mill, of course, and beyond the other side there were fields. And in one of the fields, it amused him to see a kind of scarecrow, a dark figure on which birds were settling on the straw. Just for a moment he thought it looked like Mr Harley Quin. Perhaps, thought Mr Satterthwaite, it *is* my friend Mr Quin. It was an absurd idea and yet if someone had piled up the scarecrow and tried to make it look like Mr Quin, it could have had the sort of slender elegance that was foreign to most scarecrows one saw.

'Are you looking at our scarecrow?' said Timothy. 'We've got a name for him, you know. We call him Mister Harley Barley.'

'Do you indeed?' said Mr Satterthwaite. 'Dear me, I find that very interesting.'

'Why do you find it interesting?' said Roly, with some curiosity.

'Well, because it rather resembles someone that I know, whose name happens to be Harley. His first name, that is.'

The boys began singing, 'Harley Barley stands on guard, Harley Barley takes things hard. Guards the ricks and guards the hay, Keeps the trespassers away.'

'Cucumber sandwich, Mr Satterthwaite?' said Beryl Gilliatt, 'or do you prefer a home-made pâté one?'

Mr Satterthwaite accepted the home-made pâté. She deposited by his side a puce cup, the same colour as he had admired in the shop. How gay it looked, all that tea set on the table. Yellow, red, blue, green and all the rest of it. He wondered if each one had their favourite colour. Timothy, he noticed, had a red cup, Roland had a yellow one. Beside Timothy's cup was an object Mr Satterthwaite could not at first identify. Then he saw it was a meerschaum pipe. It was years since Mr Satterthwaite had thought of or seen a meerschaum pipe. Roland, noticing what he was looking at, said,

'Tim brought that back from Germany when he went. He's killing himself with cancer smoking his pipe all the time.'

'Don't you smoke, Roland?'

'No. I'm not one for smoking. I don't smoke cigarettes and I don't smoke pot either.'

Inez came to the table and sat down on the other side of him. Both the young men pressed food upon her. They started a laughing conversation together.

Mr Satterthwaite felt very happy among these young people. Not that they took very much notice of him apart from their natural politeness. But he liked hearing them. He liked, too, making up his judgement about them. He thought, he was almost sure, that both the young men were in love with Inez. Well, it was not surprising. Propinquity brings these things about. They had come to live here with their grandfather. A beautiful girl, Roland's first cousin, was living almost next door. Mr Satterthwaite turned his head. He could just see the house through the trees where it poked up from the road just beyond the front gate. That was the same house that Dr Horton had lived in last time he came here, seven or eight years ago.

He looked at Inez. He wondered which of the two young men she preferred or whether her affections were already engaged elsewhere. There was no reason why she should fall in love with one of these two attractive young specimens of the male race.

Having eaten as much as he wanted, it was not very much, Mr Satterthwaite drew his chair back altering its angle a little so that he could look all round him.

Mrs Gilliatt was still busy. Very much the housewife, he thought, making perhaps rather more of a fuss than she need of domesticity. Continually offering people cakes, taking their cups away and replenishing them, handing things round. Somehow, he thought, it would be more pleasant and more informal if she let people help themselves. He wished she was not so busy a hostess.

He looked up to the place where Tom Addison lay stretched out in his chair. Tom Addison was also watching Beryl Gilliatt. Mr Satterthwaite thought to himself: He doesn't like her. No. Tom doesn't like her. Well, perhaps that's to be expected. After all, Beryl had taken the place of his own daughter, of Simon Gilliatt's first wife, Lily. My beautiful Lily, thought Mr Satterthwaite again, and wondered why for some reason he felt that although he could not see anyone like her, yet Lily in some strange way was here. She was here at this tea party.

'I suppose one begins to imagine these things as one gets old,' said Mr Satterthwaite. 'After all, why shouldn't Lily be here to see her son?'

He looked affectionately at Timothy and then suddenly realised that he was not looking at Lily's son. Roland was Lily's son. Timothy was Beryl's son.

'I believe Lily knows I'm here. I believe she'd like to speak to me,' said Mr Satterthwaite. 'Oh dear, oh dear, I mustn't start imagining foolish things.'

For some reason he looked again at the scarecrow. It didn't look like a scarecrow now. It looked like Mr Harley Quin. Some tricks of the light, of the sunset, were providing it with colour, and there was a black dog like Hermes chasing the birds.

'Colour,' said Mr Satterthwaite, and looked again at the table and the tea set and the people having tea. Why am I here? said Mr Satterthwaite to himself. Why am I here and what ought I to be doing? There's a reason . . .

Now he knew, he felt, there was something, some crisis, something affecting – affecting all these people or only some of them? Beryl Gilliatt, Mrs Gilliatt. She was nervous about something. On edge. Tom? Nothing wrong with Tom. He wasn't affected. A lucky man to own this beauty, to own Doverton and to have a grandson so that when he died all this would come to Roland. All this would be Roland's. Was Tom hoping that Roland would marry Inez? Or would he have a fear of first cousins marrying? Though throughout history, Mr Satterthwaite thought, brothers had married sisters with no ill result. 'Nothing must happen,' said Mr Satterthwaite, 'nothing must happen. I must prevent it.'

Really, his thoughts were the thoughts of a madman. A peaceful scene. A tea set. The varying colours of the harlequin cups. He looked at the white meerschaum pipe lying against the red of the cup. Beryl Gilliatt said something to Timothy. Timothy nodded, got up and went off towards the house. Beryl removed some empty plates from the table, adjusted a chair or two, murmured something to Roland, who went across and offered a frosted cake to Dr Horton.

Mr Satterthwaite watched her. He had to watch her. The sweep of her sleeve as she passed the table. He saw a red cup get pushed off the table. It broke on the iron feet of a chair. He heard her little exclamation as she picked up the bits. She went to the tea tray, came back and placed on the table a pale blue cup and saucer. She replaced the meerschaum pipe, putting it close against it. She brought the tea pot and poured tea, then she moved away.

The table was untenanted now. Inez also had got up and left it. Gone to speak to her grandfather. I don't understand, said Mr Satterthwaite to himself. Something's going to happen. What's going to happen?

A table with different coloured cups round, and – yes, Timothy, his red hair glowing in the sun. Red hair glowing with that same tint, that attractive sideways wave that Simon Gilliatt's hair had always had. Timothy, coming back, standing a moment, looking at the table with a slightly puzzled eye, then going to where the meerschaum pipe rested against the pale blue cup.

Inez came back then. She laughed suddenly and she said, 'Timothy, you're drinking your tea out of the wrong cup. The blue cup's mine. Yours is the red one.'

And Timothy said, 'Don't be silly, Inez. I know my own cup. It's got sugar in it and you won't like it. Nonsense. This is my cup. The meerschaum's up against it.'

93

It came to Mr Satterthwaite then. A shock. Was he mad? Was he imagining things? Was any of this real?

He got up. He walked quickly towards the table, and as Timothy raised the blue cup to his lips, he shouted.

'Don't drink that!' he called. 'Don't drink it, I say.'

Timothy turned a surprised face. Mr Satterthwaite turned his head. Dr Horton, rather startled, got up from his seat and was coming near.

'What's the matter, Satterthwaite?'

'That cup. There's something wrong about it,' said Mr Satterthwaite. 'Don't let the boy drink from it.'

Horton stared at it. 'My dear fellow—'

'I know what I'm saying. The red cup was his,' said Mr Satterthwaite, 'and the red cup's broken. It's been replaced with a blue one. He doesn't know the red from blue, does he?'

Dr Horton looked puzzled. 'D'you mean – d'you mean – like Tom?'

'Tom Addison. He's colour blind. You know that, don't you?'

'Oh yes, of course. We all know that. That's why he's got odd shoes on today. He never knew red from green.'

'This boy is the same.'

'But – but surely not. Anyway, there's never been any sign of it in – in Roland.'

'There might be, though, mightn't there?' said Mr Satterthwaite. 'I'm right in thinking – Daltonism. That's what they call it, don't they?'

'It was a name they used to call it by, yes.'

'It's not inherited by a female, but it passes through the female. Lily wasn't colour blind, but Lily's son might easily be colour blind.'

'But my dear Satterthwaite, Timothy isn't Lily's son. Roly is Lily's son. I know they're rather alike. Same age, same coloured hair and things, but – well, perhaps you don't remember.'

'No,' said Mr Satterthwaite, 'I shouldn't have remembered. But I know now. I can see the resemblance too. Roland's Beryl's son. They were both babies, weren't they, when Simon re-married. It is very easy for a woman looking after two babies, especially if both of them were going to have red hair. Timothy's Lily's son and Roland is Beryl's son. Beryl's and Christopher Eden's. There is no reason why he should be colour blind. I know it, I tell you. I know it!'

He saw Dr Horton's eyes go from one to the other. Timothy, not catching what they said but standing holding the blue cup and looking puzzled.

'I saw her buy it,' said Mr Satterthwaite. 'Listen to me, man. You must listen to me. You've known me for some years. You know that I don't make mistakes if I say a thing positively.'

'Quite true. I've never known you make a mistake.'

'Take that cup away from him,' said Mr Satterthwaite. 'Take it back to your surgery or take it to an analytic chemist and find out what's in it. I saw that woman buy that cup. She bought it in the village shop. She knew then that she was going to break a red cup, replace it by a blue and that Timothy would never know that the colours were different.'

'I think you're mad, Satterthwaite. But all the same I'm going to do what you say.' He advanced on the table, stretched out a hand to the blue cup.

'Do you mind letting me have a look at that?' said Dr Horton.
'Of course,' said Timothy. He looked slightly surprised.
'I think there's a flaw in the china, here, you know. Rather interesting.'
Beryl came across the lawn. She came quickly and sharply.
'What are you doing? What's the matter? What is happening?'
'Nothing's the matter,' said Dr Horton, cheerfully. 'I just want to show the boys a little experiment I'm going to make with a cup of tea.'
He was looking at her very closely and he saw the expression of fear, of terror. Mr Satterthwaite saw the entire change of countenance.
'Would you like to come with me, Satterthwaite? Just a little experiment, you know. A matter of testing porcelain and different qualities in it nowadays. A very interesting discovery was made lately.'
Chatting, he walked along the grass. Mr Satterthwaite followed him and the two young men, chatting to each other, followed him.
'What's the doc up to now, Roly?' said Timothy.
'I don't know,' said Roland. 'He seems to have got some very extraordinary ideas. Oh well, we shall hear about it later, I expect. Let's go and get our bikes.'
Beryl Gilliatt turned abruptly. She retraced her steps rapidly up the lawn towards the house. Tom Addison called to her.
'Anything the matter, Beryl?'
'Something I'd forgotten,' said Beryl Gilliatt. 'That's all.'
Tom Addison looked enquiringly towards Simon Gilliatt.
'Anything wrong with your wife?' he said.
'Beryl? Oh no, not that I now of. I expect it's some little thing or other that she's forgotten. Nothing I can do for you, Beryl?' he called.
'No. No, I'll be back later.' She turned her head half sideways, looking at the old man lying back in the chair. She spoke suddenly and vehemently. 'You silly old fool. You've got the wrong shoes on again today. They don't match. Do you know you've got one shoe that's red and one shoe that's green?'
'Ah, done it again, have I?' said Tom Addison. 'They look exactly the same colour to me, you know. It's odd, isn't it, but there it is.'
She went past him, her steps quickening.
Presently Mr Satterthwaite and Dr Horton reached the gate that led out into the roadway. They heard a motor bicycle speeding along.
'She's gone,' said Dr Horton. 'She's run for it. We ought to have stopped her, I suppose. Do you think she'll come back?'
'No,' said Mr Satterthwaite, 'I don't think she'll come back. Perhaps,' he said thoughtfully, 'it's best left that way.'
'You mean?'
'It's an old house,' said Mr Satterthwaite. 'An old family. A good family. A lot of good people in it. One doesn't want trouble, scandal, everything brought upon it. Best to let her go, I think.'
'Tom Addison never liked her,' said Dr Horton. 'Never. He was always polite and kind but he didn't like her.'
'And there's the boy to think of,' said Mr Satterthwaite.
'The boy. You mean?'
'The other boy. Roland. This way he needn't know about what his mother was trying to do.'

'Why did she do it? Why on earth did she do it?'

'You've no doubt now that she did,' said Mr Satterthwaite.

'No. I've no doubt now. I saw her face, Satterthwaite, when she looked at me. I knew then that what you'd said was truth. But why?'

'Greed, I suppose,' said Mr Satterthwaite. 'She hadn't any money of her own, I believe, her husband, Christopher Eden, was a nice chap by all accounts but he hadn't anything in the way of means. But Tom Addison's grandchild has got big money coming to him. A lot of money. Property all around here has appreciated enormously. I've no doubt that Tom Addison will leave the bulk of what he has to his grandson. She wanted it for her own son and through her own son, of course, for herself. She is a greedy woman.'

Mr Satterthwaite turned his head back suddenly.

'Something's on fire over there,' he said.

'Good lord, so it is. Oh, it's the scarecrow down in the field. Some young chap or other's set fire to it, I suppose. But there's nothing to worry about. There are no ricks or anything anywhere near. It'll just burn itself out.'

'Yes,' said Mr Satterthwaite. 'Well, you go on, Doctor. You don't need me to help you in your tests.'

'I've no doubt of what I shall find. I don't mean the exact substance, but I have come to your belief that this blue cup holds death.'

Mr Satterthwaite had turned back through the gate. He was going now down in the direction where the scarecrow was burning. Behind it was the sunset. A remarkable sunset that evening. Its colours illuminated the air round it, illuminated the burning scarecrow.

'So that's the way you've chosen to go,' said Mr Satterthwaite.

He looked slightly startled then, for in the neighbourhood of the flames he saw the tall, slight figure of a woman. A woman dressed in some pale mother-of-pearl colouring. She was walking in the direction of Mr Satterthwaite. He stopped dead, watching.

'Lily,' he said. 'Lily.'

He saw her quite plainly now. It was Lily walking towards him. Too far away for him to see her face but he knew very well who it was. Just for a moment or two he wondered whether anyone else would see her or whether the sight was only for him. He said, not very loud, only in a whisper,

'It's all right, Lily, your son is safe.'

She stopped then. She raised one hand to her lips. He didn't see her smile, but he knew she was smiling. She kissed her hand and waved it to him and then she turned. She walked back towards where the scarecrow was disintegrating into a mass of ashes.

'She's going away again,' said Mr Satterthwaite to himself. 'She's going away with him. They're walking away together. They belong to the same world, of course. They only come – those sort of people – they only come when it's a case of love or death or both.'

He wouldn't see Lily again, he supposed, but he wondered how soon he would meet Mr Quin again. He turned then and went back across the lawn towards the tea table and the harlequin tea set, and beyond that, to his old friend Tom Addison. Beryl wouldn't come back. He was sure of it.

Doverton Kingsbourne was safe again.

Across the lawn came the small black dog in flying leaps. It came to Mr Satterthwaite, panting a little and wagging its tail. Through its collar was twisted a scrap of paper. Mr Satterthwaite stooped and detached it – smoothing it out – on it in coloured letters was written a message:

CONGRATULATIONS! TO OUR NEXT MEETING

HQ

'Thank you, Hermes,' said Mr Satterthwaite, and watched the black dog flying across the meadow to rejoin the two figures that he himself knew were there but could no longer see.

# FRANCIS CLIFFORD

## Turn And Turn About

When he first set eyes on her she was billed as *L'Oiseau D'Or* and she was seventy feet above his head at a tented circus near Madrid. Now he called her Tony, short for Antonia, and she knew him simply as Clay – that, and no more. They never went far with names. She was as small-boned and beautiful and daring as a bird, and within seconds of seeing her he had felt for sure that she was the one for him.

'What are you doing with the rest of your life?' – old movies have such lines. Yet these were the words he'd used, and only five weeks ago. Since then the two of them had discovered the seclusion of this rented salt-white villa perched amid the spectacular coastal scenery of Sardinia. 'Love me, bird girl?' he would ask and, as often as not, she would wrinkle her nose and frown a bit and pretend to give it serious consideration.

She was, he guessed, in her very early twenties. Her hands were enormously expressive, compensating for occasional lapses in her slightly accented English. Her mother, he learned, was Spanish and her father came from Poland; both were circus people, still active with a juggling routine somewhere in the States. She had Modigliani eyes, brown, wonderfully alert, and her straight raven-dark hair was shoulder length. What her surname was she had never told him, and it didn't matter; Tony was label enough.

'Tony,' Clay said now, watching her, 'you're gorgeous.'

'Thank you.'

'More so every day.'

'You are a great flatter.'

'Flatter*er*,' he corrected.

'You're so clever, and I'm a dense.'

'Dunce.'

'All right, but a dunce in four languages.' The line of her lips was tighter than she realised. 'At least I am not a prisoner of my tongue, like you and all the other English.'

He grimaced amiably. '*Touché*.' Then he kissed her.

'Give me a cigarette, will you?'

Clay lit one and transferred it direct to her mouth. They were by the pool, stretched out on loungers. Olive skin and pink bikini – every time he ran his eyes over her he marvelled. He was thirty years old, stocky and muscular. His hair was short and crinkled, his eyes blue. Only an enemy could have suggested he was anything but handsome. He had told her he was a Londoner, which made straightforward sense, and explained that he was in the metal business – 'exclusively non-ferrous' – which didn't interest her enough to question whether it made sense or not.

'How about a drink?'

'Please,' she said. 'A Cloudy Sky.'

'Does that mean gin and ginger beer?'

He got up and began to pad around the pool's edge. 'Know something?' he said, turning his head. 'You're a gift, bird girl. A pure gift.'

He slipped as the last word left his mouth. For a few seconds he was all arms and legs, wildly trying to retain his balance. Finally, like a drunken dancer, he pirouetted on the wet tiles and crashed down.

'Clay! . . . Are you all right?'

For a moment he didn't move. Then he pushed himself into a sitting position. 'All right?'

He nodded. She began to laugh, head back. But when she looked at him again his face was contorted and he was gripping both ankles.

'Clay—'

'Wow.' His eyes widened with pain. '*Wow* . . .'

'What is it?' She squatted anxiously beside him. 'Broken?'

'Shouldn't think so.'

'I'll call a doctor.'

'Let's get up first.'

He struggled on to the nearest lounger and gingerly explored the damage.

'Well?'

'Really turned them over, didn't I?' He sucked in air between clenched teeth. 'Left one's not so bad. But the right – ayeeeee . . .'

Her hands fluttered. 'Is it bones?'

'Bones, no. Muscles, ligaments.'

'Muscles – ah.'

She rose at once and went into the house. When she came back she carried an ice bucket and a wad of table napkins. She wrapped crushed ice in a napkin and draped the compress gently round Clay's right ankle.

He said: 'You've done this before.'

'In a circus these things happen.'

'Hardly with my flair and style.'

'We are not all with your talent.'

'Bitch,' he said.

'Now you have to take it easy and look at the view.'

'I know all about the view. I've seen it before.'

'Only robbers and gipsies say you must never return. Which one of those are you?'

'Of all the bloody things to have happened . . . Tony, girl, you're looking at a prize idiot.'

'I know it.'

'All done by – ouch! – mirrors. Incredible, isn't it? Nothing up my sleeves.'

She slid away from him, pushing a cushion under the extended leg. 'You need to keep it high.'

'Is that so?'

'And tonight, if it isn't any better—'

'Tonight, if it isn't any better, the nurse will be in trouble.'

'Tonight,' she smiled secretly, 'if it isn't any better, your problem will be to catch the nurse.'

'I'll manage,' Clay said.

'It would not surprise me.'

He winced slightly. 'You, bird girl, are a great flatter.'

Later in the afternoon she drove the Fiat to the village. It was a corkscrew stretch of road, narrow and unpredictable, offering head-on glimpses of the sea one moment and mountain views the next. Figs and olives grew on the bordering slopes and goats scattered as the car passed, tyres sobbing through the turns.

'Take it easy,' Clay had muttered, half asleep as she left him. 'There's no safety-net out there.'

The village was piled around a small fishing harbour. A week ago, when Tony first appeared with her raffia basket and walked barefoot in trousers and bikini-top, the locals had no idea that anyone so desirably symmetrical could bring such drama and passion to the purchase of a few daily commodities. But word had since spread, and now she was greeted with respect as well as wonder.

Once or twice a week a coachload of crab-red tourists arrived and sampled the sucking pig at the restaurant on the quayside and ate the unleavened bread and went away; but today the village was spared. Tony finished her shopping and turned along the waterfront. Strangers nodded as she passed and she acknowledged each in turn. When she reached the restaurant she unslung the basket from her shoulder and seated herself at one of the tables on the paved area outside.

'*Un cappuccino.*'

She lit a cigarette and glanced at *La Stampa*. Only a handful of people were there – a blue-chinned priest intent on his office, a couple of middle-aged women, heads close together, a powerful-looking man with the *Herald Tribune* and a lip-line moustache who couldn't keep his eyes away from her. The coffee came and she added sugar. The world's news was as depressing as ever and she didn't dwell on it. She smoked the cigarette through, crumbled a biscuit for the pigeons, smiled to herself at the memory of Clay's involuntary fandango, paid the bill and left, retracing her steps to where she had parked the car.

Less than an hour after setting out she swung into the villa's short steep driveway. It had just gone five o'clock and the brassy glare had left the sky. She hauled her basket off the seat and made for the front door.

'Hold it!'

Startled, she turned. It was the man from the restaurant. As fast as light she wondered how on earth he could have got there so soon. And in the self-same instant she saw he had a pistol.

He was wearing a crumpled light-weight suit and carried an airline travel bag. With heightened awareness she noted his coarse brown thinning hair and the blue and white sweatshirt under his jacket.

He jerked the gun. 'Take me through.'

She wheeled around and did exactly as he said, opening the iron-studded door and leading him into the apparent darkness of the house. There was a yawning sensation in the pit of her stomach and, as they emerged on to the terrace beside the pool, the villa had never seemed so isolated. Clay was dozing, shaded by an umbrella, oblivious of his vulnerability.

'Who else is here?' the man said, right on her heels.

'Nobody.'

'No maid?'

'No.'

'Gardener? . . . Dog?'

'No.'

The questions were over-loud, and Clay stirred. He opened his eyes and gazed at them both with bleary affability.

'Hallo,' he said. 'You caught me napping.' Then he saw the gun and his expression changed. He sat up as if he'd been stung. 'What the hell—?'

'Stay where you are.'

'Who are you?' Clay squeezed his eyes against the light, bewildered now. Things like this happened to other people. 'What's going on, for Christ's sake?'

'He was outside,' Tony faltered. 'He was waiting for me.'

'Go and join him,' the man said. He used his head like a boxer. 'Get yourself over there and speak when you're spoken to.'

He was on the tall side, broad with it, all muscle. His accent was hard yet back in the throat. Whatever he was it probably wasn't American and certainly wasn't English.

To Tony he said: 'Why's flatfoot got the bandage?'

'He twist his ankle.'

'Oh yes?' The gun gave him complete authority. He came round the end of the pool. 'Fine time for it to happen.'

'Listen—' Clay began.

'You've got it inside out. My listening days are dead and gone.'

'What the bloody hell d'you want?'

'We're coming to that,' the man said. He sat on the edge of the second lounger, very sure of himself, looking them over. He put the travel bag down between his feet and took off his jacket, transferring the gun from hand to hand. His sinewy forearms were mahogany-brown; on one was tattooed MORGEN and on the other GESTERN. 'We're going to do each other a good turn, you and the girl and me.'

'We don't need any good turns.'

'The fact remains that when I say jump you're going to jump. When I say move you're going to move . . . Like now, for instance. By way of example.' He stood up and nodded at Tony. 'It's time you showed me around.'

She frowned.

'I want to see the house. And while we're inside,' he warned Clay, 'don't try anything foolish. Otherwise it'll be the worse for her, and I've no wish for that. My part of this deal's to cause you no harm.'

Tony led him into the villa. He was as quiet as a cat behind her. In the living room she checked between strides for her vision to adjust and felt the gun touch her spine.

'Where's the telephone?'

She took him to the main bedroom. She pushed the door open and stood aside, but he signalled her to go on through. 'What is the idea?' she began, white showing in her eyes, but the moment passed. He rounded the bed and ripped the telephone from the wall, a kind of savagery in the way it was done, as if to frighten from her mind any lingering suspicion that none of this was really happening.

He made a swift tour of the other rooms, not a word spoken, never more than a yard or two between them. In the kitchen he took a beer from the ice-box and drank it from the can; in the garage he showed passing interest in the rubber suits and aqualungs. Otherwise he didn't pause. Within minutes he was prodding her out on to the terrace again and Clay was staring at them both with sullen impotence.

'There's a sensible guy,' the man said. 'Congratulations.' The sun jazzed on the surface of the pool. 'Ever seen a marionette show?' He produced what amounted to a grin. 'The crudest pressures are the best – wouldn't you say that?'

'You're a bastard.'

There was no reaction. He went to where he had left the travel bag and tore the zip across. He reached inside and took out a walkie-talkie radio; it was black with white metal trim and had a shoulder strap fitment.

He said to Tony: 'What d'you make of it?'

'I don't make.'

'Specially designed for those who are out of sight but not out of mind.'

'I don't understand.'

'You will.' He took a second handset from the bag and pressed a red button; three feet of telescopic aerial extended with a series of soft clicks. 'Know how these things function?'

Tony shook her head.

'Come and learn.'

She met his gaze. 'And if I say no?'

'You don't look that stupid.'

'I am not stupid enough to have printings on my arms, either.' Her anger flared, out of control. 'Morgen and gestern – tomorrow and yesterday . . . What is it supposed to mean? Only peoples who have never grown up have words and pictures on their skin.'

The man let fly, the point of his shoe making contact with Clay's injured ankle. Clay yelped and twisted away, his mouth an O.

'See what trouble you can cause?' the man said reprovingly. 'Your friend could have done without that.' His tone changed. 'Get hold of that second handset and listen to me.'

Reluctantly she picked it up. He began to explain how to operate it: nothing could have been more simple and she had no questions. The gun was always in evidence, utterly persuasive. Once or twice she glanced at Clay, conveying alarm as well as defeat. The man told her to go to the far end of the terrace and make contact, *sotto voce*, from there. After several false starts and shouted instructions to push the SPEAK or LISTEN switch their exchanges became reasonably proficient. Tony finally came through with: 'Whatever you want we are not your kind of peoples. You made a mistake picking this house . . . Over.'

'I never said to push your luck . . . Over.'

'You are a bad dream.' She was as petulant as a child. 'Over.'

'I'm flesh-and-blood real, and you know it . . . Over and out.'

'For Christ's sake,' Clay tried again. 'Who the hell are you? Half an hour ago—'

'Half an hour ago, flatfoot, you were a non-contributing member of society. Once upon a girl's a good time, and so say all of us, but there's more to life than lotus-eating. Very soon now you're going to make yourself useful.'

Tony walked towards them. 'You are all hot air.' She was never able to hold her tongue. 'All talk, all the time talk.'

'Is that how it seems?'

'I think you are one big bluff.'

The man fired into the space between Clay and herself. The gun spat and jumped in his hand and a beachball exploded behind them – all in an echo-less split second, so fast they hardly flinched. A fraction afterwards they blinked, caught their breath, stiffened; and a moment later the shrivelled casing of the ball slapped into the pool.

'God almighty,' Clay whispered. In terms of the bullet's path about two feet separated him from Tony; no more. The back of his neck prickled, ice and fire.

'Don't put faith in the bluff idea,' the man said. 'You'll only regret it . . . Let's have that understood once and for all. There's just the three of us and we might as well be together in a locked room.'

A bougainvillaea-covered balustrade enclosed the near end of the pool. He crossed over to it, cryptic and shatteringly offhand, and looked out at the savage beauty of the scene beyond. Once upon a time the face of an entire mountainside had crumbled into the sea. Fantastic heaps of weathered rock now shaped the coastline, and the sea itself lay green and azure and gentian in a score of bays. The village was fudge-coloured in the near distance, and here and there were scattered a few medium-size villas, perched dramatically between sea and mountain, their stark newness redeemed by tamarisks and myrtle and splashes of flowers.

'Come and join me,' the man said. 'You, too, flatfoot. And bring the bag.'

With difficulty Clay hopped across, unable to equate the man's conversational style with his reckless use of the gun, imprisoned momentarily in disbelief about himself and Tony and their situation.

'You'll find binoculars in the bag,' he was told. 'And a tripod. Let's have them out.'

He had no choice. Despite their size the binoculars were surprisingly light.

'Try them.'

He sighted on the villa known as Castello di Roccia. In all respects it was a place apart, incomparable in size and setting, rising sheer from the very tip of a narrow finger of land which separated one bay from another. Its stucco was the palest of blues, its huge area of ribbed roof a reddish brown. Terraced gardens faced inland and a raised driveway led to wrought-iron gates set in high colour-washed walls. Clay fiddled the soft blur into focus and the detail leapt at him across a quarter of a mile, fantastically sharp and clear.

'Good, eh?'

Against his will Clay nodded.

'Steady it on the tripod and you'll find it's almost too good to be true.'

Sunlight lay across the sea like a bar of molten metal and the sea itself was a travel-brochure blue. The boat Clay used for water-skiing was moored in the horseshoe bay below.

'Listen,' the man said as lightly as if they were playing a game. 'Who's heard of the Rivers diamond?'

Clay and Tony exchanged glances, but neither answered.

'Don't you read the magazines?' He was close, standing back a little, but the gun made him safe. 'No? . . . Your education's incomplete. For your information the Rivers diamond is one of the big ones.'

'So what?' Clay frowned.

'The Rivers diamond,' the man said evenly, 'belongs to a certain Barbara Ashley. And the Barbara Ashley in question—'

'God,' Clay exclaimed, anticipating.

'—lives in the Castello di Roccia. And the Castello di Roccia, as you very well know, is straight in front of you.'

Something seemed to heave in Tony's brain. She looked first at the man, then at Clay, then back to the man transferring the same startled glance.

'Why are you tell us this?'

'Because,' the man said, 'I want the Rivers diamond for myself . . . And you're the one who's going to get it for me.'

Time seemed to miss a beat.

'*Me?*'

'Correct.'

'You're crazy.' Tony tossed her head, incredulity in her voice. 'I never hear such nonsense talk.'

'You're getting it, beautiful, and that's that.'

'How?' She fluttered her hands. 'How? . . . It isn't possible. Besides—'

'It's possible, all right.'

'Not by me.'

'You better than anyone.'

Clay said: 'You must be out of your mind. She isn't a thief.'

'There's always a first time. . . . Give her the glasses,' the man said curtly, 'and let her see where she's going.'

'You can't make her.'

'You know damn well I can, so shut up . . . Now,' he said with a nod at Tony, 'take a long look – and listen like you've never listened before.'

She lifted the binoculars to her eyes. He gave her almost half a minute to herself before speaking again.

'There's only one normal way in – along the driveway and through the gates. But that's hardly for you; Barbara Ashley doesn't exactly keep open house. And if you go over the wall you'll find the garden's alive with guards. What's more you'll still be outside the house. So you won't do anything like that.'

She glanced sideways at Clay, appalled, tongue-tied.

'Keep looking,' the man went on. 'Look left, all the way left as far as the cliff edge. See the wall there? – like an extension of the cliff itself?' He waited, restless as a guide. 'Right across from that cliff-edge part of the wall are two balconied windows on the second floor of the house . . . Got them? – between the casuarinas.'

He took her silence for assent.

'The windows are the Ashley woman's dressing room and bathroom – from left to right respectively. Nothing else need interest you.'

To Tony it seemed they were almost close enough to reach out and touch. Yet in reality they were an almost impossible goal. In a voice that didn't sound much like her own she heard herself say: 'This must be all a joke . . . Some kind of a joke.'

'Ten seconds inside that dressing room – that's all you'll need.'

'I could never get there.'

'A little help from me and flatfoot, and you'll surprise yourself.'

'Never,' she said. 'Never.'

'Tonight,' the man continued relentlessly, 'it's party time somewhere over Calagonone way – and the invitations include you-know-who. No ordinary party, believe me. The strongroom at the bank's already been visited with the occasion in mind. Which means that until the gates open and the white Mercedes drives her away the stuff I've set my sights on is in the villa for the taking.'

'Tonight?' – this was Clay.

'Tonight, yes.'

'Where did you hear all this?' Disbelief still sharpened his tone. 'How in the hell—?'

'I've got friends.'

'Not here you haven't.'

'Here,' the man said, 'I've got accomplices.'

Tony wheeled on him. 'Why me?' She gestured almost pleadingly. 'Why us?'

'Listen,' he said. 'When it's time we'll take the boat across to the base of the cliff. The two of us, yes . . . We climb the cliff together, descend together, return together. The only time you'll travel alone is from the top of the wall to the dressing room and back again – and even then you'll have flatfoot whispering in your ear.'

Clay scowled. 'I don't get you.'

'You'll guide her in by walkie-talkie. And the instructions you give will depend on what you see through the Zeiss. The requirement is an empty dressing room and with lighted windows and those binoculars you'll as good as have your own key-hole.'

'Suppose the curtains are drawn?'

'They never are. She leaves the windows open, too.'

'How d'you know?'

Again the man said: 'Friends.' He lifted his shoulders. 'Observation . . . What are friends for?' He seemed grimly amused. 'Barbara Ashley moves from dressing room to bathroom, then back to the dressing room again. Habit points to the dressing room being unoccupied for fifteen to twenty minutes. That's when you two come into your own. The rest will be roses.'

Tony had lowered the binoculars. She was pale and strained. 'Those guards you talk about . . .'

'We've cheated them already.'

'There is garden between the wall and that part of the house, the same as other places.'

'Take another look,' the man ordered. Then: 'What else d'you see?'

'Where?'

'From high wall to window.'

'Telephone wires?'

'Right first time . . . Just waiting for you to give a command performance.'

Her eyes as she turned were wide with amazement, but for seconds on end it was as if she had lost her voice. 'Do you mean . . .?' she faltered, got no further and tried again. 'Do you seriously mean . . .?'

The man filled the hanging silence. 'Why else d'you think I'm here, beautiful? They may not know it down in the village, but you're a very clever girl.'

'Those wires would never hold me.'

'Want to bet on it?'

'You bastard,' Clay said with useless venom.

The gun made it all inevitable. The man's changes of mood were unpredictable, but there were going to be no deviations from his plan; that was a certainty.

'I singled you out,' he told them, 'and I've chosen my time. Don't kid yourselves along with fancy ideas that I might decide to cut and run. This operation's going ahead just the way you've been told.'

Tony had no illusions left: the incredible was happening and she was part of it. They watched the day die behind the purple mountainside. Bats began to flit and darkness spread like a stain across the water. The lamps of the distant village trembled brightly under the early stars. The Castello di Roccia seemed suspended between sea and sky, its shadowy bulk pierced by a dozen lighted windows. Clay had the binoculars trained on the only two that mattered; lit up and enlarged they offered astonishing detail. 'Like I told you,' the man said. 'You'll be a regular Peeping Tom, so take care your attention doesn't wander.' He made them practise with the walkie-talkie, sending Tony out into the night, extending the range. 'Stay out of touch for more than thirty seconds and flatfoot's going to wish he never set eyes on you.'

She kept slavishly in touch, and she came back. 'Like a lamb,' the man said, arrogantly confident. He showed no sign of nerves, but Tony suffered – chainsmoking, unable to remain still. At eight fifteen he got her to rope Clay to a chair set behind the tripod-mounted binoculars, and at half past he followed Tony down the rocky slope to where the boat was. They were wearing the rubber suits from the garage and were soon invisible. His parting words to Clay were: 'Don't go silent on us, flatfoot. Don't ever let me get the idea you're trying to be smart.'

He had no trouble with the outboard; one swing and it fired. He nosed out into the bay, throttled back and running quiet, handling the boat with a sure touch. Once they reached the open water he cut the engine and fitted the oars and made Tony row.

Quite soon he said to Tony: 'Ask flatfoot if he can see us.'

She called Clay, her voice low and surly. She had the walkie-talkie slung like a bandolier.

'Yes and no,' Clay reported. 'Only because there's a reason to look.'

'Can you hear us?'

'No.'

The sea was dead calm. Tony rowed them steadily past their own blunt headland and started in a wide arc across the next bay, traces of phosphorescence in the water, the cliff they would scale already looming, the villa on its summit already blocking out the lowermost stars. At most it took about fifteen minutes to reach the base of the cliff, during which Clay must have reported all of a dozen times. 'Dressing-room and bathroom empty . . . No one there yet . . . Still empty, still no one there . . .' Only once was his whisper distorted, sucked away; otherwise he might have been with them.

The man steered the boat with uncanny precision, never hesitating, reading the darkness with impressive assurance. How he did it Tony neither knew nor cared; to the exclusion of everything else her thoughts were congealed around what awaited her at the top of the cliff.

'Both rooms still empty . . .'

Presently there was a soft grating sound. All at once the darkness was solid to the touch and they could smell the weed growths. The man grunted and ordered Tony to ship the oars. He worked the boat along with his hands. After about twenty yards they slid into a resonant gap beneath a flying buttress of rock where the water was as still as a pool. He made fast there, fore and aft, then clambered on to a ledge, hauling Tony after him. She could hardly see an inch and accepted his help, unconscious of the irony. Together they moved crabwise along the shelf until they were out from under the buttress and on the cliff face itself.

'Straight up.'

She hesitated.

'You first.' Even now he couldn't resist a jibe. 'What kind of fool d'you take me for?'

She began to climb. To her relief it was easier, less sheer, than she'd imagined. She had no fear of heights and there were holds everywhere, hand and foot. Almost the worst thing on the way were the reports from Clay which prodded her mind where it least wanted to go.

'No one in either room . . .'

She lost track of time. Once or twice something broke off and rattled down. She was breathing hard and so was the man. When she looked up the stars thudded in and out of focus with every beat of her heart. Eventually she reached the top and lay there panting. The villa's wall stood several yards from the edge like a massive cake decoration. She stared at it, thinking back, thinking forward, no prospect of refusal or defiance remaining in her. Somehow it had come to this.

'The crudest pressures are the best . . .' *Madre de Dios*. 'Do what he wants,' Clay had urged anxiously. 'He's trigger-happy. Try it, for Pete's sake . . .' All right. *All right.*

Presently she climbed on to the man's shoulders and hauled herself up on to the wall. It was incredibly quiet and she moved with immense caution. A narrow width of the shrub-filled garden lay between her and the house. The balconied windows she had last seen through the Zeiss were off to her right, ablaze with light and partly hidden by trees, and she edged along to bring herself nearer, on the look-out for the telephone wires.

Without warning someone cleared his throat and spat. She froze, scared out of her mind, the pulsing seconds stretched into great distortions of time. At last she spotted movement – a dark figure passing away from her, patrolling a path under the lee of the house. She waited, flattened on top of the wall, until the figure had gone from view, and an enormous effort was required to force herself on again.

It was only a short while before she saw the twin wires. They stretched from above the dressing-room balcony to a gibbet-type post planted just inside the wall; the gleam of glass insulators located them for her. She began to work her way closer, dry in the mouth, still unable to see into the windows because of the trees.

But suddenly a shadow blinked the light from inside. And, almost simultaneously, Clay was through on the walkie-talkie.

'She's in the room now.'

Clay watched Barbara Ashley enter the dressing room and start to disrobe. She was a well-built blonde in her late thirties with three husbands already dead and a millionaire fourth just divorced. In other circumstances it might have given him pleasure. Twice she flitted in and out of the bathroom. Once, half naked, she stood before an ornate mirror and held a heavy pendant to her neck.

'Still there.'

He was terse and to the point. He had had no glimpse of Tony and, since she called him from the boat, there had been no word from her either. It was beginning to seem as if he was talking to himself. Fretting, he pressed the SPEAK switch yet again.

'Still there.'

Barbara Ashley chose that precise moment to step out of her pants and saunter more positively into the adjoining bathroom. Clay waited, allowed her a chance to change her mind. If Tony made a false start across the wires it could be disastrous. He delayed for at least a couple of minutes before coming to a decision.

'All clear . . . You can go now.'

Once more he had this feeling that nobody listened. He screwed his eyes to the binoculars. A long time seemed to pass without anything happening and the beginnings of alarm stirred in his guts. Then, dramatically, he saw Tony silhouetted in space as she approached the window on the wires, small and compact, arms outstretched like a Balinese dancer. An exclamation escaped him. He watched as if mesmerised. She progressed with unnerving slow-motion and he sweated for her, the tension agonising. In a circus they would have been straining to applaud.

Eventually she came close enough to the balcony to be able to lower herself on to it. For a short while before she reappeared in front of the window she was lost to him against the dark of the house. The urge was to contact her, encourage her, but he fought it down. She darted like a shadow along the balcony, stopped, hesitated, then opened the window. A moment later she was inside and he held his breath as she hurried across the room, sharing the knife-edge seconds with her.

'Not only the Rivers,' the man had said. 'The rest as well.'

It astonished Clay how quickly she emerged. He supposed the jewellery was on the table from which Barbara Ashley had picked up the pendant; at any rate Tony didn't have to look far. She came out, busily stuffing something inside her rubber suit. It was child's play – except for the wires. Her return crossing started him sweating again. Half way over she suddenly stopped in her tracks, her silhouette absolutely motionless, and he guessed a guard was near. He pressed against the ropes, imagination on the rampage. When she finally moved again he began to tremble with relief, and by the time he reckoned she was off the wires and over the wall and on the way down the cliff relief had changed to exultation.

He continued his watch on the window. Barbara Ashley took her time in the bathroom and the boat was almost back at its mooring before she came out and theatrically discovered her loss. In fact Clay heard the boat throbbing softly into the small bay below at the self-same moment as the distant dumb-show panic in the Castello di Roccia got under way.

He waited impatiently for Tony and the man to arrive from the horseshoe beach. It was almost over; the future was about to begin again. After a while an area of darkness seemed to shift and he made out Tony on the path. But nobody else. Only Tony, walking up the path alone.

'Where is he?'

Even then he expected the man to answer. He peered past her, braced for the bullying voice.

'Where is he?'

'He won't be coming.'

She was through the gate on to the terrace. 'Not coming? How d'you mean?' There and then it seemed about the most unbelievable thing he'd ever heard. '*Why* isn't he coming?'

'Because I left him there,' she said.

His mouth was hanging open as she flopped into the chair beside him.

'What d'you mean – "left him there"?'

'He is at the bottom of the cliff.'

An awful thought struck him. 'Alive?'

'Of course alive.'

'God,' he said.

His brain seemed to have gone numb. He shot a glance across the water. Someone at the Castello di Roccia had switched on the floodlighting.

'He has what he deserve,' Tony was saying. 'Give me some cognac, please.'

'How can I?' She seemed to have forgotten that he was bound to the chair. 'Tony – what happened? For Pete's sake what happened?'

'I stole a lot of things, that's what happen.'

He shook his head frantically. 'To him.' He was repeating himself. 'What happened to him?'

'I gave him a push. . .Right at the finish, when we are both in the boat and the boat is not tied up, I gave him a push and drove off.'

'Oh my God,' Clay said.

'He was swearing something awful.'

Clay swallowed. 'Get me out of all this.' She started to loosen the ropes. 'What about the stuff you took?'

'He's got it.'

'Oh my God.'

'Not again.'

'Huh?'

'That's all you say – oh my God this, oh my God that.' She freed the last knot and flipped the rope aside. 'Get me the cognac, Clay.'

'But that man—'

'Excuse me, but I have been up a cliff and over some bad wires and into someone else's room and down a cliff—'

'And incriminated yourself . . . Me as well.' He was on his feet. 'Of all the damn stupid things to have done. Don't you see? We're in trouble unless he gets away – both of us.'

'I was made to steal. He force me. And you were tied up.'

'Try telling the police that.'

'It's the truth.'

'Not the kind of truth they'll believe.'

Clay went quickly to the binoculars and trained them on the base of the cliff, but he might as well have been staring into a dark tunnel. He straightened, agitated, urgency in every move he made.

'I'll have to go get him.'

'You'll *what?*'

'We're sunk if he's found.'

'Sunk . . . What is sunk?'

'To hell with that now,' he snapped. 'I'm going. Keep a look-out for me.'

He picked up the walkie-talkie he'd been using and started towards the gate. Tony made a final show of bewildered protest.

'You're crazy. The way he treated you and me.'

'That's not the point.'

'It is ridiculous to have all that again.'

'He won't come back here.'

'If he still has the gun you will have to take him where he wants.'

'All he'll want will be to get away. I'll dump him somewhere along the coast.'

'Why not let him swim?'

He wasn't listening any more. She got up and went to the balustrade and looked over, watching the night swallow him up as he hurried away. Her eyes narrowed in the star-green darkness.

'What happen to your ankle?' She'd intended waiting until later, but she couldn't resist it. 'All of a sudden you lost your limp.'

She went into the house and poured herself a cognac and got out of the rubber suit. She hadn't the slightest doubt about what she was going to do. Less than

112

five minutes later she was in the Fiat and on the road. Half-way to the village a couple of cars crammed with *carabinieri* screamed by in the other direction. Around the next bend she pulled on to the verge and switched the engine off.

'Clay?' she said softly into the walkie-talkie. 'Clay?'

He was soon there. 'Yes?'

'The police are on their way . . . Over.'

'Right.'

'. . . You found your friend yet?'

He parried it well. 'Friend?' She could hear the muffled engine beat.

'Partner, then.'

'What are you driving at?'

'You know. . .'

'. . . Sounds to me you're off your head.'

'Not any longer . . . flatfoot.' Her lips curled. 'Are you still listen?' She kept the thing on SPEAK. 'Tell your friend he made one big mistake. Those printings on his skin – morgen and gestern. I saw those once before. The face I'd forgot, but not the printings – or where I saw them. . . It was in Madrid. He was reading a poster of *L'Oiseau D'Or* and it was the same day you later came and said to me "Hallo". At first I did not think it was possible. I told myself that I was making a mistake. But on the way down the cliff he forgot his game for a moment and mentioned you as Clay – which he could not have known. And so all the questions I have been asking come up with the same answer. . . You have been using me, flatfoot man. You and your friend use me. You did a great big thing of make-believe together.'

She relented for a moment and let him speak. 'Tony?' he started. 'What's got into you, Tony?'

'Goodbye,' she said. 'In spite of everything I hope you escape the police. You know why? . . . You never intend it, but you have been so very good to me.' She laughed. 'Don't be angry with your clumsy friend. . . Over and out.'

She was far away when morning came; in another country. When she first opened her eyes in the hotel bedroom she couldn't for several long moments remember where she was; but everything soon jigsawed together. She felt under the pillow and pulled out what was there, staring with childlike wonder at the glittering brilliance of the Rivers diamond and the assortment of jewellery she had stuffed inside her rubber suit such an unreal time ago.

She was late down to breakfast, buying a newspaper from the stand on the way. An item with a Sardinia date-line in the second column leaped at her off the front page.

### VILLA THIEVES' HAUL
Early this evening thieves broke into the Castello di Roccia, the Sardinian home of Mrs Barbara Ashley, and stole a number of items of jewellery from her bedroom at a time when Mrs Ashley was taking a bath . . .

'Coffee?' a waiter interrupted.

. . . How the thieves entered the house is a mystery, since the grounds are extensively patrolled. However, despite the audacity of the theft, Mrs Ashley is not greatly concerned. . .

'Coffee?'

. . . 'It was all imitation,' she stated. 'No one in her right mind would leave the Rivers diamond just lying about. Or anything else of value for that matter. I have a special arrangement with the local bank whereby – irrespective of the hour – I am always able to call at the premises and visit the strongroom en route to wherever I happen to be going.'

'Coffee?' the waiter tried again.

Tears were rolling down Tony's cheeks; he hadn't noticed until now.

'I am sorry,' he apologised gravely. 'Is there anything I can do?'

She shook her head. To his surprise he realised she was laughing. In all his experience he had never seen such laughter. Baffled, he glanced at the newspaper.

'What is so funny?'

'Life,' he thought she said, but she was so convulsed by that time that it was impossible to be sure.

# EDMUND CRISPIN

We Know You're Busy
Writing, But We Thought
You Wouldn't Mind If We
Just Dropped In For
A Minute

(i)
'After all, it's only us,' they said.

I must introduce myself.

None of this is going to be read, even, let alone printed. Ever.

Nevertheless, there is habit – the habit of putting words together in the most effective order you can think of. There is self-respect, too. That, and habit, make me try to tell this as if it were in fact going to be read.

Which God forbid.

I am forty-seven, unmarried, living alone, a minor crime-fiction writer, earning, on average, rather less than a thousand pounds a year.

I live in Devon.

I live in a small cottage which is isolated, in the sense that there is no one nearer than a quarter of a mile.

I am not, however, at a loss for company.

For one thing, I have a telephone.

I am a hypochondriac, well into the coronary belt. Also, I go in fear of accidents, with broken bones. The telephone is thus a necessity. I can afford only one, so its siting is a matter of great discretion. In the end, it is in the hall, just at the foot of the steep stairs. It is on a shelf only two feet from the floor, so that if I have to crawl to it, it will still be within reach.

If I have my coronary *up*stairs, too bad.

The telephone is for me to use in an emergency. Other people, however, regard it differently.

Take, for example, my Bank Manager.

'Torhaven one-five-three,' I say.

'Hello? Bradley, is that Mr Bradley?'

'Bradley speaking.'

'This is Wimpole, Wimpole. Mr Bradley, I have to talk to you.'

'Speaking.'

'Now, it's like this, Mr Bradley. How soon can we expect some further

117

payments in, Mr Bradley? Payments out, yes, we have plenty of those, but payments in. . .'

'I'm doing everything I can, Mr Wimpole.'

'Everything, yes, everything, but payments in, what is going to be coming in during the next month, Mr Bradley?'

'Quite a lot, I hope.'

'Yes, you hope, Mr Bradley, you hope, you hope. But what am I going to say to my Regional Office, Mr Bradley, how am I going to represent the matter to them, to it? You have this accommodation with us, this matter of five hundred pounds. . .'

'Had it for years, Mr Wimpole.'

'Yes, Mr Bradley, and that is exactly the trouble. You must reduce it, Mr Bradley, reduce it, I say,' this lunatic bawls at me.

I can no more reduce my overdraft than I can fly.

I am adequately industrious. I aim to write two thousand words a day, which would support me in the event that I were ever able to complete them. But if you live alone you are not, contrary to popular supposition, in a state of unbroken placidity.

Quite the contrary.

I have tried night-work, a consuming yawn to every tap on the typewriter, I have tried early morning work.

And here H L Mencken comes in, suggesting that bad writing is due to bad digestion.

My own digestion is bad at any time, particularly bad during milkmen's hours, and I have never found that I could do much in the dawn. This is a weakness, and I admit it. But apparently it has to be. Work, for me, is thus office hours, nine till five.

I have told everyone about this, begging them, if it isn't a matter of emergency, to get in touch with me in the *evenings*. Office hours, I tell them, same as everyone else. You wouldn't telephone a solicitor about nothing in particular during his office hours, would you? Well, so why ring me?

I am typing a sentence which starts, *His crushed hand, paining him less now, nevertheless gave him a sense of.*

I know what is going to happen after 'of': *the appalling frailty of the human body*.

Or rather, I did know, and it wasn't that. It might have been that (feeble though it is) but for the fact that then the door-bell rang. (I hope that it might have been something better.)

The door-bell rang. It was a Mrs Prance morning, but she hadn't yet arrived, so I answered the door myself, clattering down from the upstairs room where I work. It was the meter-reader. The meter being outside the door, I was at a loss to know why I had to sanction its being scrutinised.

'A sense of the dreadful agonies,' I said to the meter-reader, 'of which the human body is capable.'

'Wonderful weather for the time of year.'
'I'll leave you, if you don't mind. I'm a bit busy.'
'Suit yourself,' he said, offended.

Then Mrs Prance came.

Mrs Prance comes three mornings a week. She is slow, and deaf, but she is all I can hope to get, short of winning the Pools.

She answers the door, but is afraid of the telephone, and consequently never answers that, though I've done my utmost to train her to it.

She is very anxious that I should know precisely what she is doing in my tatty little cottage, and approve of it.

'Mr Bradley?'
'Yes, Mrs Prance?'
'It's the HI-GLOW.'
'What about it, Mrs Prance?'
'Pardon?'
'I said, what about it?'
'We did ought to change.'
'Yes, well, let's change, by all means.'
'Pardon?'
'I said, "Yes".'
'Doesn't bring the wood up, not the way it ought to.'
'You're the best judge, Mrs Prance.'
'Pardon?'
'I'm sorry, Mrs Prance, but I'm working now. We'll talk about it some other time.'
'Toffee-nosed,' says Mrs Prance.

*Gave him a sense of – a sense of – a sense of burr-burr, burr-burr, burr-burr.*
Mrs Prance shouts that it's the telephone.
I stumble downstairs and pick the thing up.
'Darling.'
'Oh, hello, Chris.'
'How are you, darling?'
'A sense of the gross cruelty which filled all history.'
'What, darling? What was that you said?'
'Sorry. I was just trying to keep a glass of water balanced on my head.'
A tinkle of laughter.
'You're a poppet. Listen, I've had a wonderful idea. It's a party. Here in my flat. Today week. You will come, Edward, won't you?'
'Yes, of course, I will, Chris, but may I just remind you about something?'
'What's that, darling?'
'You said you wouldn't ring me up during working hours.'
A short silence then:
'Oh, but *just this once*. It's going to be such a lovely party, darling. You don't mind *just this once*.'
'Chris, are you having a coffee break?'
'Yes, darling, and Oh, God, don't I need it!'

'Well, I'm *not* having a coffee break.'
A rather longer silence; then:
'You don't love me any more.'
'It's just that I'm trying to get a story written. There's a deadline for it.'
'If you don't want to come to the party, all you've got to do is say so.'
'I do want to come to the party, but I also want to get on with earning my living. Seriously, Chris, as it's a week ahead, couldn't you have waited till this evening to ring me?'
A sob.
'I think you're beastly. I think you're utterly, utterly *horrible*.'
'Chris.'
'And I never want to *see* you again.'

*A sense of treachery*, I typed, sedulously. *The agony still flamed up his arm, but it was now—*
The door-bell rang.
*—it was now less than – more than—*
'It's the laundry, Mr Bradley,' Mrs Prance shouted up the stairs at me.
'Coming, Mrs Prance.'
I went out on to the small landing. Mrs Prance's great moon-face peered up at me from below.
'Coming Thursday next week,' she shouted at me, 'because of Good Friday.'
'Yes, Mrs Prance, but what has that got to do with *me*? I mean, you'll be here on Wednesday as usual, won't you, to change the sheets?'
'Pardon?'
'Thank you for telling me, Mrs Prance.'

One way and another, it was a remarkable Tuesday morning: seven telephone calls, none of them in the least important, eleven people at the door and Mrs Prance anxious that no scintilla of her efforts should lack my personal verbal approval. I had sat down in front of my typewriter at nine-thirty. By twelve noon, I had achieved the following:
*His crushed hand, paining him less now, nevertheless gave him a sense of treachery, the appalling frailty of the human body, but it was now less than it had been, more than indifferent to him since, after, because though the pain could be shrugged off the betrayal was a*
I make no pretence to be a quick writer, but that really was a very bad morning indeed.

(ii)
Afternoon started better. With some garlic sausage and bread inside me, I ran to another seven paragraphs, unimpeded.
*As he clawed his way out, hatred seized him*, I tapped out, enthusiastically embarking on the eighth. *No such emotion had ever before—*
The door-bell rang.
*—had ever before disturbed his quiet existence. It was as if—*
The door-bell rang again, lengthily, someone leaning on it.

*—as if a beast had taken charge, a beast inordinate, insatiable.*
The door-bell was now ringing for many seconds at a time, uninterruptedly.
*Was this a survival factor, or would it blur his mind? He scarcely knew. One thing was abundantly clear,* namely that he was going to have to answer the bloody door-bell.
He did so.
On the doorstep, their car standing in the lane beyond, were a couple in early middle age, who could be seen at a glance to be fresh out from the Duke.

The Duke of Devonshire is my local. When I first moved to this quiet part of Devon I had nothing against the Duke: it was a small village pub serving small village drinks, with an occasional commercialised pork pie or sausage-roll. But then it changed hands. A Postgate admirer took over. Hams, game patties, quail eggs and other such fanciful foods were introduced to a noise of trumpets; esurient lunatics began rolling up in every sort of car, gobble-mad for exotic Ploughman's Lunches and suavely served lobster creams, their throats parched for the vinegar of 1964 clarets or the ullage of the abominable home-brewed beer; and there was no longer any peace for anyone.
In particular, there was no longer any peace for me. 'Let's go and see old Ted,' people said to one another as they were shooed out of the bar at closing time. 'He lives near here.'

'Charles,' said this man on the doorstep, extending his hand.
The woman with him tittered. She had fluffy hair, and lips so pale that they stood out disconcertingly, like scars, against her blotched complexion. 'It's Ted, lovey,' she said.
'Ted, of course it's Ted. Known him for years. How are you, Charley boy?'
'*Ted*, angel.'
I recognised them both, slightly, from one or two parties. They were presumably a married couple, but not married for long, if offensive nonsenses like 'Angel' were to be believed.
'We're not interrupting anything,' she said.
Interested by this statement of fact, I found spouting up in my pharynx the reply, 'Yes, you sodding well are.' But this had to be choked back; bourgeois education forbids such replies, other than euphemistically.
'Come on in,' I said.
They came on in.

I took them into the downstairs living-room, which lack of money has left a ghost of its original intention. There are two armchairs, a chesterfield, a coffee-table, a corner cupboard for drinks; but all, despite Hi-Glow, dull and tattered on the plain carpet.
I got them settled on the chesterfield.
'Coffee?' I suggested.
But this seemed not to be what was wanted.
'You haven't got a drink, old boy?' the man said.
'*Stanislas*,' the girl said.

'Yes, of course. Whisky? Gin? Sherry?'

'Oh, Stanislas darling, you are *awful*,' said this female. 'Fancy asking.'

I had no recollection of the name of either of them, but surely Stanislas couldn't be right. 'Stanislas?' I asked.

'It's private,' she said, taking one of his hands in one of hers, and wringing it. 'You don't mind? It's sort of a joke. It's private between us.'

'I see. Well, what would you like to drink?'

He chose whisky, she gin and Italian.

'If you'll excuse me I'll have to go upstairs for a minute,' I said, after serving them.

*One thing was abundantly clear: Giorgio's map had been wrong, and as a consequence—*

'Ooh-hooh!'

I went out on to the landing.

'Yes?'

'We're lonely.'

'Down in just a minute.'

'You're doing that nasty writing.'

'No, just checking something.'

'We heared the typewriter. Do come down, Charles, Edward I mean, we've got something terribly, terribly important to tell you.'

'Coming straight away,' I said, my mind full of Giorgio's map.


I refilled their glasses.

'You're Diana,' I said to her.

'Daphne,' she squeaked.

'Yes, of course. Daphne. Drink all right?'

She took a great swallow of it, and so was unable to speak for fear of vomiting. Stanislas roused himself to fill the conversational gap.

'How's the old writing, then?'

'Going along well.'

'Mad Martians, eh? Don't read that sort of thing myself, I'm afraid, too busy with biography and history. Has Daphne told you?'

'No. Told me what?'

'About Us, old boy, about Us.'


This was the first indication I'd had that they *weren't* a married couple. Fond locutions survive courtship by God knows how many years, fossilising to automatic gabble, and so are no guide to actual relationships. But in 'Us', the capital letter, audible anyway, flag-wags something new.

'Ah-ha!' I said.

With an effort, Stanislas leaned forward. 'Daphne's husband is a beast,' he said, enunciating distinctly.

'Giorgio's map,' I said. 'Defective.'

'A mere brute. So she's going to throw in her lot with me.'

Satisfied, he fell back on to the cushions. 'Darling,' he said.

*As a consequence, we were two miles south-west of our expected position.* 'So what is the expected position?' I asked.

'We're eloping,' Daphne said.

'This very day. Darling.'

'Angel.'

'Yes, this very day,' said Stanislas, ostentatiously sucking up the last drops from the bottom of his glass. 'This very day as ever is. We've planned it,' he confided.

*The plan had gone wrong, had gone rotten. Giorgio had failed.*

'Had gone rotten,' I said, hoping I might just possibly remember the phrase when this pair of lunatics had taken themselves off.

'Rotten is the word for that bastard,' said Stanislas. Suddenly his eyes filled with alcoholic tears. 'What Daphne has suffered, no one will ever know,' he gulped. 'There's even been . . . beating.' Daphne lowered her lids demurely, in tacit confirmation. 'So we're off and away together,' said Stanislas, recovering slightly. 'A new life. Abroad. A new humane relationship.'

*But was his failure final? Wasn't there still a chance?*

'If you'll excuse me,' I said, 'I shall have to go upstairs again.'

But this attempt aborted. Daphne seized me so violently by the wrist, as I was on the move, that I had difficulty in not falling over sideways.

'You're with us, aren't you?' she breathed.

'Oh, yes, of course.'

'My husband would come after us, if he knew.'

'A good thing he doesn't know, then.'

'But he'll guess. He'll guess it's Stanislas.'

'I suppose so.'

'You don't mind us being here, Charles, do you? We have to wait till dark.'

'Well, actually, there is a bit of work I ought to be getting on with.'

'I'm sorry, Ted,' she said, smoothing her skirt. 'We've been inconsiderate. We must go.' She went on picking at her hem-line, but there was no tensing of the leg muscles, preliminary to rising, so I refilled her glass. 'No, don't go,' I said, the British middle class confronting its finest hour. 'Tell me more about it.'

'Stanislas.'

'H'm, h'm.'

'Wake *up*, sweetie-pie. Tell Charles all about it.'

Stanislas got himself approximately upright. 'All about what?'

'About Us, angel.'

*But the devil of it was, if Giorgio's map was wrong, our chances had receded to nil.*

'To nil,' I said. 'Nil.'

'Not nil at all, old boy,' Stanislas said. 'And as a matter of fact, if you don't mind my saying so, I rather resent that "nil". We may not be special, like writer blokes like you, but we aren't "nil", Daphne and me. We're human, and so forth. Cut us and we bleed, and that. I'm no great cop, I'll grant you that, but Daphne – Daphne—'

'A splendid girl,' I said.

'Yes, you say that now, but what would you have said five minutes ago? Eh?

Eh?' He looked at his empty glass.

'The same thing, of course.'

'You think you're rather marvellous, don't you? You think you've . . . got it made. Well, let me tell you one thing, Mr so-called Bradley: you may think you're very clever with all this writing of Westerns and so on, but I can tell you, there are more important things in life than Westerns. I don't suppose you'll understand about it, but there's Love. Daphne and I, we love one another. You can jeer, and you do jeer. All I can tell you is, you're wrong as can be. Daphne and I, we're going off together, and to hell with people who . . . jeer.'

'Have another drink.'

'Well, thanks, I don't mind if I do.'

They stayed for four whole hours.

Somewhere in the middle they made a pretence of drinking tea. Some time after that they expressed concern at the length of time they had stayed – without, however, giving any sign of leaving. I gathered, as Giorgio and his map faded inexorably from my mind, that their elopement plans were dependent on darkness: this, rather than the charm of my company, was what they were waiting for. Meanwhile, with my deadline irrevocably lost, I listened to their soul-searching – he unjustifiably divorced, she tied to a brutish lout who unfortunately wielded influence over a large range of local and national affairs, and would pursue her to the ends of the earth unless precautions were taken to foil him.

I heard a good deal about these precautions, registering them without, at the time, realising how useful they were going to be.

'Charles, Edward.'

'Yes?'

'We've been bastards.'

'Of course not.'

'We haven't been letting you get on with your work.'

'Too late now.'

'Not really too late,' lachrymosely. 'You go and write, and we'll just sit here, and do no harm to a soul.'

'I've rather forgotten what I was saying, and in any case I've missed the last post.'

'Oh, Charles, Charles, you shame us. We abase ourselves.'

'No need for that.'

'*Naturally* we abase ourselves. We've drunk your liquor, we've sat on your . . . your sofa, we've stopped you working. Sweetie-pie, isn't that true? Haven't we stopped him working?'

'If you say so, sweetie-pie.'

'I most certainly do say so. And it's a disgrace.'

'So we're disgraced, poppet. *Bad*,' she said histrionically. 'But are we so bad? I mean, he's self-employed, he's got all the time in the world, he can work just whenever he likes. Not like you and me. He's got it *made*.'

'Oh, God,' I mumbled.

'Well, that's true,' Stanislas said, with difficulty. 'And it's a nice quiet life.'

'Quiet, that's it.'

'Don't have to do anything if you don't want to. Ah, come the day.'

'He's looking cross.'

'What's that? Old Charles looking cross? Angel, you're mistaken. Don't you believe it. Not cross, Charles, are you?'

'We *have* stayed rather long, darling. Darling, are you awake? I say, we *have* stayed rather long.'

'H'm.'

'But it's special. Edward, it's special. You do see that, don't you? Special. Because of Stanislas and me.'

I said, 'All I know is that I—'

'Just this once,' she said. 'You'll forgive us just this once? After all, you *are* a free agent. And, after all, it's only us.'

I stared at them.

I looked at him, nine-tenths asleep. I looked at her, half asleep. I thought what a life they were going to have if they eloped together.

But 'It's only us' had triggered something off.

I remembered that on just that one day, not an extraordinary one, there had been Mrs Prance, the meter-reader, Chris (twice: she had telephoned a second time during working hours to apologise for telephoning the first time during working hours), the laundry-man, the grocer (no Chivers Peas this week), my tax accountant, a woman collecting for the Church, a Frenchman wanting to know if he was on the right road to the Duke.

I remembered that a frippet had come from the National Insurance, or whatever the hell it's called now, to ask what I was doing about Mrs Prance, and if not, why not. I remembered a long, inconclusive telephone call from someone's secretary at the BBC – the someone, despite his anxiety to be in touch with me, having vanished without notice into the BBC Club. I remembered that undergraduates at the University of Essex were wanting me to give them a talk, and were going to be so good as to pay second-class rail fare, though no fee.

I remembered that my whole morning's work had been a single, botched, incomplete paragraph, and that my afternoon's work, before this further interruption, had been little more than two hundred words.

I remembered that I had missed the post.

I remembered that I had missed the post before, for much the same reasons, and that publishers are unenthusiastic about writers who keep failing to meet deadlines.

I remembered that I was very short of money, and that sitting giving drink to almost total strangers for four hours on end wasn't the best way of improving the situation.

I remembered.

I saw red.

*A red mist swam before his eyes,* doing the butterfly stroke.

I picked up the poker from the fireplace, and went round behind them.

Did they – I sometimes ask myself – wonder what I could possibly be doing, edging round the back of the chesterfield with a great lump of iron in my hand?

They were probably too far gone to wonder.

In any case, they weren't left wondering for long.

(iii)

Eighteen months have passed.

At the end of the first week a Detective Constable came to see me. His name was Ellis. He was thin to the point of emaciation, and seemed, despite his youth, permanently depressed. He was in plain clothes.

He told me that their names were Daphne Fiddler and Clarence Oates.

'Now, sir, we've looked into this matter, and we understand that you didn't know this lady and gentleman at all well.'

'I'd just met them once or twice.'

'They came here, though, that Tuesday afternoon.'

'Yes, but they'd been booted out of the pub. People often come here because they've been booted out of the pub.'

Lounging on the chesterfield, ignoring its blotches, Ellis said, 'They were looking for a drink, eh?'

'Yes, they did seem to be doing that.'

'I'm not disturbing your work, sir, I hope.'

'Yes, you are, Officer, as a matter of fact. So did they.'

'If you wouldn't mind, sir, don't call me "Officer". I am one, technically. But as a mode of address it's pointless.'

'Sorry.'

'I'll have to disturb your work a little bit more still, sir, I'm afraid. Now, if I may ask, did this – this *pair* say anything to you about their plans?'

'Did they say anything to anyone else?'

'Yes, Mr Bradley, to about half the population of South Devon.'

'Well, I can tell you what they said to me. They said they were going to get a boat from Torquay to Jersey, and then a plane from Jersey to Guernsey, and then a Hovercraft from Guernsey to France. They were going to go over to France on day passes, but they were going to carry their passports with them, and cash sewn into the linings of their clothes. Then they were going on from France to some other country, where they could get jobs without a *permis de séjour*.'

'Some countries, there's loopholes big as camels' gates,' said Ellis biblically.

I said, 'They'll make a mess of it, you know.'

'Hash-slinging for her,' said Ellis despondently, 'and driving a taxi for him. What was the last you saw of them?'

'They drove off.'

'Yes, but when?'

'Oh, after dark. Perhaps seven. What happened to them after that?'

'The Falls.'

'Sorry?'

'The *Falls*. Their car was found abandoned there.'

'Oh.'

'No luggage in it.'

'Oh.'

'So presumably they got on the Torquay bus.'

'You can't find out?'

Ellis wriggled on the cushions. 'Driver's an idiot. Doesn't see or hear *anything*.'

'I was out at the Falls myself.'

'Pardon?'

'I say, I was out at the Falls myself. I followed them on foot – though of course I didn't *know* I was doing that.'

'Did you see their car there?' Ellis asked.

'I saw several cars, but they all look alike nowadays. And they all had their lights off. You don't go around peering into cars at the Falls which have their lights off.'

'And then, sir?'

'I just walked back. It's a fairly normal walk for me in the evenings, after I've eaten. I mean, it's a walk I quite often take.'

(And I had, in fact, walked back by the lanes as usual, resisting the temptation to skulk across fields. Good for me to have dumped the car unnoticed near the bus-stop, and good for me to have remembered about the luggage before I set out.)

'Good for me,' I said.

'Pardon?'

'Good for me to be able to do that walk, still.'

Ellis unfolded himself, getting up from the chesterfield. Good for me that he hadn't got a kit with him to test the blotches.

'It's just a routine enquiry, Mr Bradley,' he said faintly, his vitality seemingly at a low ebb. 'Mrs Fiddler's husband, Mr Oates's wife, they felt they should enquire. Missing Persons, you see. But just between ourselves,' he added, his voice livening momentarily, 'they neither of 'em care a button. It's obvious what's happened, and they neither of 'em care a button. Least said, Mr Bradley, soonest mended.'

He went.

I should feel guilty; but in fact, I feel purged.

*Catharsis.*

Am I purged of pity? I hope not. I feel pity for Daphne and Stanislas, at the same time as irritation at their unconscionable folly.

Purged of fear?

Well, in an odd sort of way, yes.

Things have got worse for me. The strain of reducing my overdraft by £250 has left me with Mrs Prance only two days a week and, rather more importantly, I now have to count the tins of baked beans and the loaves I shall use for toasting.

But I feel better.

The interruptions are no less than before. Wimpole, Chris, my tax accountant all help to fill my working hours, in the same old way.

But now I feel almost indulgent towards them. Towards everyone, even Mrs Prance.

For one thing, I garden a lot.

I get a fair number of flowers, but this is more luck than judgement. Vegetables are my chief thing.

And this autumn the cabbages have done particularly well. Harvest cabbages, they stand up straight and conical, their dark green outer leaves folded close, moisture-globed, protecting firm, crisp hearts.

For harvest cabbages you can't beat nicely rotted organic fertiliser.

Can I ever bring myself to cut my harvest cabbages and eat them?

At the *moment* I don't want to eat my harvest cabbages. But I dare say in the end I shall.

After all, it's only them.

# CELIA DALE

---

## Faery Tale

I, Edward Augustus Steynes, Associate of the Royal Academy of Arts, of Holland Park, London, wish to set down – yes, in hot blood while the events of the monstrous persecution of my ward are still fresh in my mind (not that they will ever fade but will remain branded on my memory) the truth as I know it of the misfortunes which culminated in scenes worthy of a Roman circus rather than an English Coroner's Court, and the effects of which are only now, some five weeks later, beginning to recede into the nightmare past but from which, I fear, the delicate sensibilities of a young girl may never entirely recover.

To understand fully the sequence of events which led to this monstrous persecution it is necessary to go back many years – to 1868 it must have been, when my cousin Rollo Ogilvy brought his motherless daughter Blanche back to England from India where he had held a commission in a cavalry regiment. Although the atrocious Mutiny was in the past, the anxieties and rigours of Army life, allied to a constitution always frail and further weakened by a second pregnancy, had been too much for Rollo's young wife Clara, to whom he was extravagantly attached, and she and the unborn babe had been laid to rest among, alas, so many of her compatriots in that alien land. Overwhelmed by grief, Rollo resigned his commission and returned to find refuge in the Oxfordshire home of his mother, Lady Ogilvy, my aunt, and widow for many years of a prosperous merchant knighted for his services to Industry and the Poor.

I was at that time establishing myself as a painter of classical subject pictures – my *Sweet Echo . . . within thy airy shell* attracted much critical commendation at the Royal Academy Exhibition that year – and I did not visit Long Basing until the Christmas after their arrival there. My aunt was a formidable woman who kept great state and, although one's creature comforts were excellently catered for, I had always found her rules and regulations irksome (one was not allowed to smoke even in the billiard room but must brave the elements on the terrace or, at best, the stables if in need of a cheroot). But Christmas was a Day of Obligation (as the Romans have it) and I always spent the two days of its festivities there, as much to honour my uncle's memory as my aunt's command.

My aunt had thought very little of Rollo's marriage. He was her only child and she had great ambitions for him, I presume. She had considered Clara to be weakly (and was correct), that to take her out to India would kill her (correct again), and that she was not of the stuff to breed good sturdy sons (once more, correct). But Rollo – a handsome fellow of great charm, whom many a duke's daughter might have looked on with favour – was head over heels in love, and duly bore his Clara off to those far reaches of our Sovereign's Might. Clara was only twenty-four when she passed away, and although I had met her only at her wedding I had always remembered her fragile gold-and-silver beauty, delicate as thistledown.

My first sight of Blanche that Christmas Eve made me catch my breath, for she was her mother in miniature. She was six years old at the time, brought to the drawing room by her nurse to watch the candles being lit upon the Christmas tree. She could have graced the tree herself, for she was a faery child of pink and white, her long fair tresses falling down her little back to cover the wide sash at her waist, her full frilled petticoats rustling atop little feet shod in bronze slippers and drawn-thread socks.

Her nurse, a large slab-faced woman of fierce mien, held her fast, but she pulled her hand away and sped towards her father, love and gladness shining in her face. My aunt admonished her and bade her curtsy first to herself and then to me. 'This is your cousin Edward,' she declared, 'who paints famous pictures.'

The child gazed upon me earnestly, and then, in the prettiest way possible, piped up, 'Will you paint a famous one of me?'

'Indeed I will, my dear,' I answered. And so indeed I did in the years to come.

The purity of childhood is unique. Beside it men and women are as dross, heavy, brutish, tainted with the knowledge of sin. But a child is all innocence, all Creation, the wonder of the world in her eyes, her little body fresh and resilient as a flower. Gaze into a child's face and see with a painter's eye the marble eyeball, lustrous and fringed with curving lashes, the tender flush of cheek, the rosebud freshness of lip and the pearly teeth within. Every portion of a child is a miracle of God's work, pure and untouched by the dark faces that bedevil men and women. And so their minds are too, each day a wonder of discovery, each hour one in which they can bestow their artless love on His creations. Fears they may have, of witches and ogres perhaps: but fears of the desires and appetites that lurk within the adult human soul they have no knowledge of. They are as God made them, unstained, fresh from His hand.

This I have always tried to capture in my works. Not for me the haggard and unwholesome visions of the Rossettis and their ilk! Rather I try to capture on canvas the pearly radiance of young flesh and spirit – caught well, I think, in my *Not Angles but Angels* (now in Stopford Art Gallery) or *Attendant on Queen Mab* (Wenham Town Hall). I have had my struggles, my dark nights of the soul – all men have wrestled with the Devil, art students not least of all. Depravity and destruction are all too easy to embrace. But the Soul must rise above it and shall be as a little child.

I returned to London and my studio after Christmas, but my thoughts often turned to that faery child and her piping query. And I wondered how she would fare, torn from the sultry land of her birth, motherless at so tender an age, under the cold authority of Lady Ogilvy and that intimidating nurse.

The answer was – badly. For her father, unable to reconcile himself to the loss of his young wife or to apply himself either to country life or to the building of some new career, had disappeared into America. 'He intends to take up what is called "ranching",' my aunt wrote in her spiked calligraphy, 'although since he is ignorant of even the basic principles of home farming I am dubious of his success.' More than this, Blanche herself fell grievously ill, and my aunt intimated (it was not in her nature to beg) that I should visit them at Long Basing, as the child sorely missed the attentions of a father.

I found her stretched upon a sofa, not in the nursery but in Lady Ogilvy's sitting room, the long windows open on to the rose garden. She was playing listlessly with her dolls and as she saw me advancing across the room her face lit up and she opened her little arms to me. 'Papa!' she cried: then, as the truth struck her, she fell back, her mouth trembling.

'It is Cousin Edward come all the way from London,' my aunt said.

The child brightened. 'To paint my famous picture?' she enquired.

'Very likely,' I said, sitting down on the couch beside her, 'if that is what you wish.'

'Oh yes!' she cried, and threw her arms about my neck. Her pale curls fell against my face and her little form trembled in my arms. She looked up, laughing. 'Oh, Cousin Edward, you have such silky whiskers!' she declared. And ever after, when we were alone, she would call me Silky. And I could call her Faery.

The facts of her illness emerged. She had been ill because, ignorant of the flora of our English countryside, she had wandered in the garden alone and espied what she took to be green pea pods lying on the path. Childlike, she had eaten some – but alas, they were not green peas but laburnum seeds and she was taken almost mortally ill.

Secondly, she was in my aunt's sitting room and not the nursery because Nurse Hodge had been dismissed. Her negligence in allowing Blanche to wander unsupervised and so meet with an almost fatal accident had led Lady Ogilvy to dismiss her without a character, and she had packed her bags and taken herself off not to London but to the village inn, with whose widowed host she had, it appeared, been on somewhat familiar terms. My aunt had decided to care for the child herself, teaching her her letters and simple arithmetic, a nurserymaid being sufficient to see to her physical needs.

'With my son gone, Blanche is the only Ogilvy,' my aunt said with her cold smile. 'It is my duty – and my pleasure – to bring her up with due regard to her inheritance.'

I stayed the month of August. During that time my faery regained her strength and spirits and ran about the house and gardens of Long Basing like some merry sprite. She was somewhat in awe of Lady Ogilvy and worked studiously at their lessons together, learning with the quickness of a singular intelligence. But between this faery child and myself there grew up an intimacy, a confidence which took me into the magic world of childhood. Hand in hand we explored the woods and fields of the estate, looked at the animals on the Home Farm, rode together, I on Rollo's neglected hunter, she on her fat pony. On rainy days we would play dominoes or Happy Families, or, while she read the *Tales from Shakespeare* or Maria Edgeworth's stories, I would take my pad and charcoal and sketch her as she sat, her cheek upon her hand, lost to the world.

She told me all her secrets and once, when we sat one twilight in the nursery, she curled like a kitten on my lap, her little arms round my neck, she whispered, 'I'm so glad that Nurse has gone.'

'Was she unkind to you, dearest?'

'She was horrid. She pulled my hair and hurt my arms putting on my clothes. It was worth nearly dying to make her go away.'

'But,' I said, mystified, 'you didn't know those horrid seeds were poisonous?'

'No, I did not. I shall remember another time. They hurt me awfully, but it was worth it to make Nurse go away and you to come.'

I returned to London. Time passed. It was some two years later that my aunt summoned me unexpectedly to Long Basing. Rollo was dead. A band of 'rustlers', as they are termed, had tried to drive away some of his cattle and in the fray Rollo had perished. My aunt, her face white marble in the cascading black of her mourning weeds, said stonily, 'Blanche is my heir. She will grow up different from her father. When I die, you shall be her guardian.'

Thereafter I was more often at Long Basing, and my faery was permitted to visit me in London several times a year, either with my aunt or, later on, with her maid Agnes.

These were joyous days indeed! Together we visited the Zoological Gardens, Madame Tussaud's, Maskelyne and Devants. At Christmas there was the pantomime, my faery entranced by the more tawdry fairies on the stage and by the drolleries of Dan Leno. I watched her grow from a chubby child into a slender ten-year-old, as white and gold as her mother had been but with a vitality that shone in the pulsing of the blood in her delicate veins and in the candid challenge of her eyes. She took an enchanting pleasure in pretty clothes, and it was my delight to buy her frills and flounces, little muffs, a bonnet or a small pelisse more frivolous than those allowed by my aunt, who kept her fairly strictly. She would throw her arms around my neck and shower kisses on me. 'Dearest Silky,' she would whisper, 'you are my best Papa.' And each time we parted, in the sunlit, stable-smelling caverns of Paddington Station, she would say passionately, 'I wish that we could be together always!'

It was the following spring that Lady Ogilvy had a stroke. It had been planned that she and Blanche, accompanied by their maids, should join me for two months in Dieppe, a small watering-place on the French coast much patronised by English artists (although mostly of a more radical school than myself). This plan had, of course, to be abandoned, and instead I repaired to Long Basing and spent the summer there.

It was a strange time. On the one hand there was the sickroom where my aunt, bed-bound and able to do nothing for herself, lay day after day, cared for by the servants and the regular visits of the doctor, a room of shadows and drawn curtains, low voices and the cloying odours of medicines, to which my faery made twice daily visits, to read or prattle to my aunt as best she could while the maid took a brief respite – a sunbeam glancing into that drear room, in duty bound.

On the other, there were the fields and gardens, where Blanche and I wandered, she with her dolls, I with my sketching things, and the handsome, empty rooms of the house of which she and I were now the sole monarchs. In the morning room, which faced north, I rigged up a studio, had the carpet rolled up and put away, the curtains taken down. And there, on many happy days, I made my pictures – sketches, drawings, studies – my model my enchanting faery, content to sit as still as any eleven-year-old can be, artlessly prattling or sometimes falling silent, her eyes remote, lost in who knows what thoughts. Some of my finest compositions grew from these sessions, worked up in my London studio at a later date – *Cupid and my Campaspe*, Blanche half draped, a wreath of roses in her hair leaning across a chequered board; and *Who shall be May Queen?* (now in Storrington Town Hall). These were idyllic days, in which beauty and innocence went hand in hand despite the dark shadow of the sickroom.

When the time came near – 'I shall not be able to bear it when you go back to London,' she whispered, her eyes luminous with tears. 'Why cannot I come and live with you?'

I smoothed her hair. 'Because you are all your grandmamma has. Because you owe her duty in her last days.'

'I cannot bear it,' she repeated, and turned away from me with that mutinous pout I loved so well.

She did not, poor child, have to bear it long, for a day or two before I was due to depart Lady Ogilvy was taken mortally ill during the night. Unable to help herself, her attendants sleeping, she succumbed to the ghastly symptoms of an acute disorder and died before morning.

I will draw a veil over the next few weeks or months – the grief, the condolences, the domestic and legal dispositions. Suffice it to say that, my aunt having indeed appointed me guardian of her grandchild and sole heir, I decided to maintain Long Basing, the only home Blanche had ever truly known, with the support of the excellent housekeeper and staff. I myself would divide my time between that household and my own in London, where the bulk of my clientele was to be found. The sketches and studies I made at Long Basing could be admirably worked up later in Holland Park. But the problem of my faery's education, hitherto undertaken by my aunt, remained. A series of governesses was the result.

I say a series for, alas, perfection was hard to find. Some were too strict, some not strict enough, some were true blue stockings, most were mere geese. My faery had the bright intelligence of unspoiled childhood, was quick to grasp a subject, had read widely in the books ranged on the library walls, was impatient of restraint. 'I don't need to learn French verbs like a parrot,' she would cry, curled on my lap in her old sweet way (although now, in her thirteenth year, she was no longer a kitten but, perhaps, a small, smooth, lissom cat). 'I will speak it well enough when we are in France together' – for I planned that holiday still. Or, 'Why do I need to know the water-table of Australia, I am never going to go there?'

Sometimes she came to me in tears. 'Miss X is cruel to me, she raps my knuckles,' or, with pretty disdain, 'Miss Y is so silly, she can only add up on her fingers.'

The governesses too were loud in their complaints, for few of them made allowances for the tragedies in my faery's short life; nor, when I was absent, could they readily accept the authority of the housekeeper and the sometime insolence of the servants, for a governess is neither fish nor fowl in the eyes of the lower orders.

Our most sunlit days were when she stayed with me in London, the faithful Agnes in attendance. Then, in her little ermine cape and muff, she would gaze wide-eyed at the wondrous displays in Regent Street or, in velvet and satin-sashed, clap her little hands at the antics of the clowns and harlequins. There were sunlit days too in Dieppe, the elegant, strolling crowds along the parade, the cakes and chocolate, the fellowship of brother artists gallantly curbing their sometimes raffish humour in deference to my young companion. Sunlit days indeed – in which the innocence of the child burgeoned into the radiance of the young girl, a child still but with the awareness of womanhood within her, half child, half woman, wholly mine.

More child than woman at first glance seemed Madeleine Fenton, daughter of an East Anglian rector and now cast upon the world at his death. But Miss Fenton's small and dainty person concealed a well-stocked mind and a character both pliable and firm. Barely a head taller than my faery (who had grown apace, as children will), she seemed more like an elder sister than a governess, and so it seemed that Blanche regarded her. A whimsical humour, a gentle but discerning tact, fitted Madeleine Fenton into our household as though she had been meant for it.

At last, it seemed, our troubles were done. Miss Fenton was only nineteen years of age, still close enough to childhood to feel and understand the innocent joys of simple country life, while her dainty stature, the fresh and laughing candour of her face, made her seem almost Blanche's twin. To watch them run together down the wide lawns of Basing, to see their two heads bent together in the lamplight as though two students, not mentor and pupil, was a joy inexpressible. It seemed that Blanche had given her her heart.

And so had I.

It is difficult for me to write of subsequent events, for the agony is with me still. But I must do so, for my sole purpose in penning these lines is to vindicate and protect my faery, no matter what my own pain.

I began to care for Miss Fenton in a way which no woman my own age could ever evoke in me. Mature women, women wise in the ways of the world and of polite society, their beauty no longer with the bloom of innocence upon it, had never made appeal to me. I have seen too much of the world's dark side, of the shame and torment of our adult appetites, ever to feel true tenderness for those of my own age. But in Madeleine Fenton the bloom still glowed; fresh from the Suffolk rectory, she knew nothing of the evils of humankind, but saw the world still with the fresh vision of childhood. Her father had trained her mind but he had left her heart unsullied. I began to look at her with different eyes; to wonder if it might not be that we three could enter a faery world together, that these two bright spirits might not in fact become my child and wife . . .

I cannot dwell on it. The bare facts can be read in the scurrilous gutter-press of the day.

Madeleine Fenton was taken ill during the night of July 27. Vomiting, pain unspeakable, fever, sweats. The doctor came, his potions eased her symptoms – but they returned. For three days she swung between life and death, and on the fourth day she died.

The doctor was mystified. He could not, he said, give out a Death Certificate. An inquest must be held.

It was held in the Parish Hall in Basing village. The Coroner was a jumped-up local solicitor with whom the Ogilvys had never been on good terms; my aunt had never received him as she had, for instance, the Rector or the doctor, and I believe he also nursed some resentment that he had never been put in charge of her affairs. These, which had been considerable, she had always deemed best to have handled by a London firm, a practice which I, as executor and Blanche's guardian, had continued. It was clear from the Coroner's opening remarks that he felt neither sympathy nor impartiality for the tragedy before him.

The acidulous – nay, malicious – tone of the proceedings soon captured the interest of the journalists sent by local newspapers. The Coroner's cross-questioning of Dr Pierce was not concluded by the end of the day, and when the inquest was resumed on the morrow the Grub Street jackals were there in abundance. TRAGIC EVENTS AT COUNTRY MANSION ran a headline in a London journal, MYSTERIOUS FATALITY AT FAMILY SEAT, DOCTOR QUIZZED ON HOUSE OF DOOM – for it had not taken the so-called Gentlemen of the Press long to discover and set out in paragraphs of lurid scurrility the sad facts in the family's past: the motherless child, the dramatic departure and subsequent death of the father, the sudden demise of Lady Ogilvy, and now that of Madeleine Fenton. In this sad catalogue the frail figure of the orphaned child stood out, a bright star in the midst of darkness, and on her the jackals fastened.

Only the doctor, myself and Mrs Poole, the housekeeper, had been required to attend the first day's proceedings. It was inconceivable to me that a child of tender years should be called on to do so, but when the doctor's evidence was at last concluded the Coroner ordered that Blanche should be called on the following day. I telegraphed Mr Forbes, our London lawyer, to be present, for at all costs I was determined to protect her by whatever means I could from the pain and confusion of what was fast becoming a Raree-show. The Coroner also ordered that the domestic staff be called, and spent much time in questioning Mrs Burgess, the cook, as to the food served on those fatal days; also the housemaid who had attended Madeleine in her sickness, the under-housemaid who had served and removed the trays sent up to her room, the kitchenmaid who had washed up the utensils. For no matter how Dr Pierce had hedged his statements, trying nobly to protect his friends and patrons from the innuendoes of the court, he had been forced in the end to admit that Madeleine had expired from the ingestion of some noxious substance. What terrible mischance could have achieved so dread an outcome?

Everyone who had been in Long Basing that fatal day, or days, was summoned to the witness-box. My own ordeal had been quickly over, for I had been in London for some days when Madeleine first fell ill and, summoned by telegraph by Mrs Poole, the housekeeper, had arrived, alas, too late to bid my dearest friend farewell. Loyalties and resentments were revealed as one by one the servants gave their testimony – petty jealousies, for as I have said, a governess is often in uneasy relationship with the domestic staff: an under-gardener who had been too familiar, the housemaid who had not cared for extra duties, and, strangest of all, the unsuspected presence of Blanche's one-time nurse, now wife to the village innkeeper, who had, unbeknown to us or to Lady Ogilvy, been a familiar visitor to the Servants' Hall, having formed a friendship with Mrs Burgess. So little does the master know his man!

And then, despite the protests of Mr Forbes, our lawyer, my faery was summoned to the box.

I can scarce describe it. For four long hours she stood there, pale and steadfast as an altar candle, clad in deepest black, her fair curls hidden beneath a bonnet whose black veil she had thrown back, her little hands in their black gloves clasped on the wooden rail before her. Once she faltered and seemed like to faint; but against the protests of our lawyer, she remained in the box, sipping a glass of water, her gaze fixed on the Coroner. Had she visited the sickroom? Of course. Had she administered any substance? Of course not. What were her feelings for Miss Fenton? She loved her – and here her voice broke and her eyes filled with tears. Was Miss Fenton in the habit of taking patent medicines? She did not know – perhaps such as were in common use. Such as? Perhaps cough mixture or for headaches, or to help (her pale cheeks flushed here) elimination. Cascara, senna pods? Yes. Did Miss Fenton ever administer such things to her? Sometimes. But she came to no harm from them? Never.

Like terriers the Coroner and Mr Forbes fought out their battle, the one determined to intimidate the frail child in the box, the gist of his questioning ever more loathesomely clear, Mr Forbes striving with all the energy at his command to open the field of speculation, to show how possible it would have been for Madeleine's death to lie at several doors, but, likeliest of all, at none. Disgruntled servants, even the long-nourished rancour of Nurse Hodge, dismissed, as she no doubt felt, unfairly and supplanted first by Lady Ogilvy (whose death, the Coroner dared to imply in his infamous summing-up, might also bear investigation) and then by a charming governess – all were possible. Most possible of all to any but his warped sensibilities, that Madeleine had accidentally dosed herself not with some common panacea such as senna pods but one which contained some unsuspected lethal substance.

The torture ended. Despite the Coroner's outrageous summing-up, the stalwart jurymen brought in an Open verdict. It was not what I had hoped, but at least it stilled most tongues and lifted from us the foul burden of the public gaze. For five days we had lived in the ferocious glare of the yellow Press, our words and actions reported in every detail, our visages sketched and reproduced across the page – for the spectacle of a young girl, beautiful and gently bred, made the centre of what, in all but name, came near a trial for murder was for the Press a Roman holiday.

Half-fainting, she clung to me as we fought our way to the carriage. In tears she lay in my arms as I bore her up to her room, the servants whose characters had been so variously revealed flustering about us. At last she slept. And I, alone with my grief, could weep.

We shall leave Long Basing. It is entailed and cannot be sold, but tenants will be found and we shall never live here again. We shall live in my house in Holland Park, my faery and I, and put the past behind us. I have a faithful staff, my work goes well; the dreadful events of the past months have not harmed my professional reputation, which is, I believe, secure. The world shall wound us no more, for I shall keep my faery safe. As she grows to womanhood she will still pose for me; although she must lose the soft radiance of childhood, she will remain as sweet and winningly wilful as I have always known her. No doubt one day some handsome fellow will come to claim her from me. I dread that day, but pray I may be spared for many years to shield her from the fortune-hunters that I fear abound – for on my death, together with her Ogilvy inheritance, my faery will indeed be well endowed with this world's riches. But, as the Bard says, 'Beauty provoketh thieves sooner than gold', and she is beautiful indeed, still with a childlike purity in her candid gaze.

I set all this down in the desperate hope of exorcising the dark memories of the past; to state the true facts as I understand them of that sad and singular sequence of events which resulted in so terrible an ordeal of suspicion and persecution; and to attest my deep and loving fidelity to my faery child, my Blanche.

Edward Augustus Steynes

*These papers were among the effects of Edward Augustus Steynes, ARA, seen but not used by the Crown Prosecuting Counsel in the trial of Blanche Clarissa Ogilvy, aged seventeen years, for his murder by laburnum poisoning, for which she was sentenced to death by Mr Justice Talbot at the Old Bailey. The sentence was subsequently commuted to life imprisonment. It is thought she emigrated to Australia after her release.*

# LIONEL DAVIDSON

---

# Indian Rope Trick

*The Spey is one of the greatest of the great Scottish east coast rivers. Its rate of flow is the fastest of any major river in the United Kingdom. Below Grantown it begins to swell into a big river flowing mostly through a dramatic and precipitous valley where it rushes and boils between a mixture of boulders and sandbanks.*

Bang on, thought Waring. That was exactly what it was doing. He could hear it. He was sitting and reading about it. He was doing this in a comfortable chair, in a comfortable lounge, some hundreds of yards from where the boiling and rushing was going on. Even at this distance the tumult of the mighty river was like an engine in the air. It excited him. He sensed great salmon beating up it, in darkness, in snow. *And doing it right now*. Right now Waring wanted to go out in the dark and see them.

However, he didn't. It was months since his operation but he still tired easily. He took a sip of whisky instead; an extra big sip.

'Darling,' his wife said warningly.

'Don't fuss.'

'Your heart will race.'

'Nag.' But he laid whisky and book aside. 'They do it to one,' he told Nigel.

'They want to hang on to one,' Nigel said.

Nigel looked sleepy; contentedly sleepy. Nigel had fished the Blackrock today and got three fine springers; now sacked and ready for smoking in Aberdeen. Waring had fished the smaller pool and had got nothing. His turn for the Blackrock tomorrow!

Again the sound of the river excited him and again he wanted to go out in the dark to it.

'What I wouldn't mind having a dab at in the morning,' he said to Estelle, 'is the Indian rope trick. If you feel up to it.'

'If *you're* up to it, and the river's up to it.'

'It's what I'd like,' he said.

'Brucie won't,' Nigel said.

'Bugger Brucie.'

'Brucie rules.' Brucie was the gillie.

'Not on our beat.'

Nigel's beat, actually. A beautiful little beat, two rods, syndicate water. By chance Nigel had managed to buy into it years before. The firm had held the syndicate covered against legal costs arising from accidents. When the scion of a tobacco family had managed to drown himself in the Blackrock Nigel had handled the matter and had been in a position to jump the queue and buy the scion's water; for the first two weeks of April. They had been coming up every year since.

142

'If the snow keeps up,' Estelle said, 'won't it do something to the water? Then there'll be no tricks of any kind.'

'Not this snow,' Waring said. 'It's settling.' But he didn't mind what it did. Snow-melt, peat-stain. He looked forward to using some big gaudy flies in it. A Thunder-and-Lightning, a flashy great Childers. Above all he looked forward to the Indian rope trick.

He felt very happy.

He felt happy just looking forward. Months ago there had been nothing to look forward to. Yet he hadn't minded. In this incredible year he had learned an incredible thing. Dying, he found that though he enjoyed what he had, he didn't mind seeing it all go. It was easy to die; everybody did it; a common affair. But now he had his life back he liked it. He appreciated it more. He appreciated his wife Estelle, and her great qualities. With this year's huge bills and the unlikelihood of his working much longer, his appreciation had rocketed. Estelle's main great quality was her thirty thousand a year.

He had never really lied about it. She knew he didn't love her in the way that she wished to be loved. But she loved *him*. That was the main thing. And he had denied her nothing, while able. He had early discovered another curious truth. Sexually unattractive women were very big on sex. Dame Nature seemed to make them so: some fine adjustment perhaps in the handicapping before the great race for renewal. Whatever the reason, Estelle was certainly a tigress at it. She enjoyed it awfully.

Pondering this, he looked round the big hotel room and wondered if anyone could guess at the jumbo appetites in his smallish plain wife. The room was full of bores all yawning away at their own potty wives, so he looked away again in case one of them should come and talk to him.

He looked at Nigel and caught him having the most enormous yawn himself. All of Nigel was yawning, from the tips of his outstretched fingers right down to his feet. One of these feet, Waring noticed, was close to Estelle's. He had an impression that moments before it had been touching; also that Nigel's tremendous stretching of himself had less to do with actual weariness than with a kind of limbering-up.

OK, Waring thought. Situation under control. Much less OK would have been a situation not under control, one that he didn't even know about. This one he knew all about.

He had an idea that Estelle had actually wanted to tell him: to explain that it didn't *matter*; that it was just something she had to do; that he was the one she loved and cherished. And he would have been glad if she had said this because he knew she always spoke truthfully.

However, she hadn't said it, and in the tricky situation he couldn't help her to say it. In any case, though she might think it true now, he knew it wouldn't go on being true.

He knew a tremendous amount lately. Since his brush with death he seemed to know practically everything. He felt special knowledge of the imperatives of life, of the programmes laid down for all the living.

Lying in hospital, his life slipping away, he had watched all the people coming and going; coming and going so seriously about their business. He had watched as if from the wrong end of a telescope, and he thought what a silly game! He had enjoyed the game while playing it but he saw that it had no meaning. With his life restored, the joy of the game had returned. What had brought back meaning to the game? He didn't know. Yet mysteriously it was back. Its imperative was back – the same imperative that brought the salmon back, every year, to this river.

The great fish came battling in from the sea, from thousands of miles away, to find just this estuary, just this river, and struggle up it (through rapids, through waterfalls), to spawn where they themselves had been spawned. They couldn't help it, couldn't stop it, had to do it.

As with Estelle: who also had to do what she was doing. Perhaps she thought it just a passing affair, and perhaps it would have been. Except that on this trip, he had seen most plainly, she was growing fond of Nigel. And Nigel was evidently meeting her needs in bed. There was not much doing with *him* in the bed line lately; nothing at all, of course, during his illness, and very little since. He knew each night, after his sleeping draught, that she slipped out to Nigel's room, and he didn't grudge her. But he saw what would come of it.

Estelle was not a woman to go chasing after men. But Nigel didn't need chasing. He was there, and an old friend; and one who had been showing signs lately of wanting to settle down himself. Yes, he could see it all coming. She had a *need* for sex, and a dislike of deception. She would want to regularise her life, and slowly a dissatisfaction with him would grow. She loved him now; he didn't doubt it. As Nigel had said, she certainly wanted to hang on to him. She didn't know herself the blind force, the life imperative, that would at first weaken and then destroy the tie between them. But Waring knew. He knew such a lot now.

He was honest with himself and knew that if he had to choose between Estelle and her thirty thousand he would go for the thirty thousand; even if it meant the sad demise of Estelle. But he did not have this choice. Estelle's money was life money. No Estelle, no money.

He thought the best formula would be for Nigel to go and get a wife for himself, preferably one who also had thirty thousand of her own. But he knew Nigel was indolent and probably wouldn't. So he had lately revised the formula to a more abbreviated and manageable one.

Nigel would simply have to go.

Estelle had been picking up her knitting, and they were now walking through the lounge, offering cheerful goodnights to those remaining.

Outside he could hear the muffled thudding of the river. It was going like an engine: rushing, boiling. His heart raced, but he didn't mind. Indian rope trick tomorrow!

It was still dark after breakfast, and still a few minutes early, but Brucie was already waiting. He was waiting in the vestibule; standing like a tree in it, smoking his pipe. He had the carrier's note for the Aberdeen salmon-smokers.

'Morning, Brucie,' Nigel said, taking the note with pleasure. 'How's the water?'

'High,' Brucie said.

'Fishable?'

'A touch colour.'

'Is it cold?' Estelle said, shivering.

'Healthy,' Brucie said, and took his pipe out.

Estelle tightened the leather belt round her fur coat and pulled her hat over her ears. She knew Brucie meant germs would not survive such healthy conditions.

Brucie had removed his pipe to stare curiously at the coil of rope Waring was carrying. For a moment Waring almost explained. Then he remembered and thought Bugger Brucie, and led the way himself out to the car.

Brucie had de-snowed the car, but with all their breaths and his pipe going it misted up at once. Nigel turned everything on, engine, headlamps, wipers, blower, and in a mild uproar and fuggy discomfort they circled the wide gravel and went slowly out into the village.

The indigo light was paling into a kind of gunmetal. Snow lay everywhere and a few flakes still drifted in the air. Behind them other headlamps swung out of the hotel and turned away.

Nigel kept slowly on, through the village, and out of it, and up, and up, to the hut.

They parked a couple of hundred yards from the hut, and walked up to it through the undergrowth. The chimney was already smoking in the hut. Brucie didn't live in the place but left various bits of gear more or less permanently outside. He left them quite untended, knowing no hand dare touch them. His own ham-like hands were known in the vicinity. For the same reason he never bothered locking the hut. He just went right at it now and pushed the door in without a word. He was offended at Waring for not explaining the rope.

An oil-lamp was burning in the hut and the kettle was singing on the side of the wood stove. By old routine Estelle made the tea while Brucie assembled the tackle and the two men got into their wading gear.

The chest waders, of a rubberised fabric, were stiff and unwieldy, iron cold to the touch. Waring took his shoes off and stepped into his and drew it up to his chest and slipped the braces over his shoulders. Then he sat down and pulled on his heavy woollen stockings and his nailed boots. He felt tired. He sat and drank his tea and watched Brucie continuing to assemble the tackle.

Brucie laid the two fly rods and the two spinning rods on the floor and went out and looked at the water. Then he came back and described it and asked what flies they wanted to use. He did this without expression (and without any mention of spinners, which he abjured); and when they had made their suggestions he told them what to use.

Waring barely listened to him. He had caught him looking at the rope again. He wondered if there was a rule against it. There were rules for practically everything. The bugger might well produce a rule or run off and phone somebody for one. He did not think there could be one; but he didn't know so he kept quiet. He thought he'd first get the rope in the water and then outface Brucie if problems arose. The position for Brucie to be in was of one obeying orders and not giving rulings or tendering opinions. It was important that Brucie should immediately do as he was told when Waring told him the important thing he had to do. He didn't think that Brucie's pride in its present state of offence would allow him to ask about the rope.

Brucie didn't ask about the rope, and he continued being offended. When they left the hut he picked up Nigel's tackle and went straight down with him to the small pool, leaving Waring to carry his own.

Waring didn't mind. With Estelle he collected the gear and they started the long walk down to the Blackrock.

Outside the hut everything was very beautiful. The snowbank was beautiful, and the trees, and the jagged broken valley of the river. The river was immensely beautiful. The air was now totally full of the sound of it, its force and vibration so shattering that Waring laughed out loud. He saw Estelle smiling herself, though her face was pinched with cold.

'You'll warm up!' he called in her ear.

'I'm warm. Let me carry the rope.'

'You're carrying enough.' He had the rope round his neck.

'You're not really going in with it today?'

'I'll see,' he said.

The water was so high he didn't know if he'd get in at all. It was reddish brown, and going fast. But when they reached the bank he saw it was possible. Five or six feet of beach were still exposed. The fingers of shingle were exposed. The fingers ran out to the stream, and he knew the ground on both sides, and it was not deep. Even where it deepened, it wasn't dangerous. It was a question of keeping his footing.

He shook out the rope and slipped the bight over his head.

'Henry, it's dangerous,' Estelle said.

'Don't fuss.'

'The water's much too fast.'

'You'll guide me out.' He tightened the rope under his shoulders. 'I'll wave to you. I'll blow my little whistle.' He dangled the whistle at her from its lanyard, having to shout now, unable to stop laughing. He saw she was laughing herself; lips puckered in alarm but laughing. It was the water. It was the astounding flood of water, endlessly rounding the Blackrock; spume-flecked, magnificent, spray smacking the air. A world of water, and in the water the salmon, wild things in from the sea.

'I'll try the fly,' he said.

Brucie had already put on a fly, a big sunk one.

'Don't, Henry.'

'Just a cast or two.'

'Henry, I'm asking you.

'And don't pull. You don't have to pull,' he said. 'It's only to guide me back.' But she couldn't hear him now. He was walking cumbrously out along the spit, rod in his left hand and gaff in the right. He used the gaff as a wading stick and came cautiously down off the spit, and took a step, and a few more, and right away knew it was dangerous. The river bed had changed. The water was quite suddenly over his knees, his waist. Even despite the evidence of his eyes he was shocked by the force of it.

He struggled to keep his balance, leaning hard on the gaff. The rod was almost torn from his hand, the long whippy length of it wrenching and thrumming in the water. He managed to lift it and edge farther out, feeling for level footing. He was confused and deafened by the uproar, by the dizzying race of foam. He didn't know how far he'd gone, and daren't turn to see. A backward glance would unbalance him, would have the water up over the top of his chest waders, filling them, sinking him. It had happened to the tobacco man.

He found rock, a solid boulder, and wedged his feet there, leaning against the current. The breath was almost battered out of him. He knew he had to turn and go. He had to do it immediately. His heart was thumping, head spinning with vertigo from the racing water. He closed his eyes against it, planning the moves. But just as he opened them again a salmon leaped. It leaped clean out of the spray, not ten yards from him. 'Oh, my God,' he said. It was big as a big dog, thirty or forty pounds at least. In the air the salmon looked at him. Its cold eye watched him all the way through its long arc until it re-entered the river.

Waring saw where it entered and knew why it had leapt. It had leapt the long ridge of rock that formed one wall of the pool. The salmon was now in the pool. Dozens of other salmon would be there with it, resting before the next onslaught up river.

'Jesus,' he said, and knew he would have to try. He would have just one try. His vertigo had gone suddenly, and he had got the feel of the current. He thought if he was careful he could stand unaided. He tried it and he could. He released the fly from its ring, stripping off line from the reel. He stripped four or five yards off, and raised the big rod double-handed, and got it swishing there and back till he had ten, then fifteen yards in the air, and he shot it. He shot it across and down and saw the heavy line snaking out through the spray and the few see-sawing snowflakes, and felt it belly at once as the current took it. He rolled the rod in the air, mending the line on the water, and it came round very fast. He couldn't see the end of the line but he saw the angle change sharply at his rod tip and knew he was over the pool, and that his fly was in it, bobbing down among the salmon. He willed one of them to come and get it and began drawing in line to keep the fly moving. He held a finger on the line to keep contact with the fly. If a salmon took, it would turn away, and as it turned the fly would check in its jaw; and his finger would feel it.

He stood deep in the current, feeling the adrenalin flowing in him. He was barely aware of the battering pressure now. He brought the line in slowly, brought all of it in, and no salmon took, and he thought *once more: just once*. The salmon were there – dozens, scores of them were there! But he knew it was madness, that at any moment vertigo could seize him again. Also there was the rope trick to be attempted, the *Indian* rope trick; and attempted now before Brucie appeared.

The moment he stopped fishing the vertigo hit him again. He stood stock still in the water, steadying himself with the gaff and closed his eyes and slowly turned, and didn't open them till he thought he was facing the beach. He wasn't quite facing it but he saw it there, thirty or forty feet away, and Estelle hopping on it, gesticulating at him. Her face was pink with cold and she was shouting. He couldn't hear her but he waved back, and almost at once tension came on the rope, and he realised she was pulling him in. He didn't want this. He didn't want it! He saw that every gesture counted, and motioned her to stop, but she couldn't understand. He pointed at the black rock, the huge hump that lay at the far side of the beach, and after a moment she nodded, and he began wading there.

All the river was coming at him now and he leaned into it, prodding with the gaff in front. He prodded carefully, finding the holes where boulders had been, where he could drown so easily now. He knew he was sweating heavily. He had to get beyond the black rock, but he made right for it and once there almost kissed it. He hung on to the gaff and hugged the rock tightly. There was just a narrow ledge under him now, and below it the pool, very deep, very dangerous.

He shuffled his way round the ledge, holding the rock with both arms, and found the beach at the other side, smaller than the one he had left; but still exposed.

He came down off the ledge exhausted but still with no time to rest. He laid his rod on the shingle and slipped the bight of rope over his head. He had marked a projection of rock yesterday, and he found it and attached the rope and tightened up. Then he let the slack of the rope go in the water and saw the current take it. He watched a moment and bent and felt it. The rope was thrumming in the water, but far away at the other end he could still feel Estelle, as he had felt the fly. Indian rope trick. A man went up a rope, and the rope stayed up. Was the man still at the end of the rope? Estelle knew he was at the end of this one. He looked at his watch and started counting.

And now he could rest. And he sat on the beach. At the far side of it was another outcrop of rock, quite small, and beyond that sloping shingle. From there it was just uphill and over the top to the position where Nigel would be fishing below; immediately below at the right time. It wasn't the right time yet.

By ten o'clock Nigel would be there, having worked down from the head of the pool. And once there, Nigel would have to remain there: for a good half hour. It was the only way the river could be fished at that point: too deep to wade. It had to be fished up, across and down, all from the same small point. There was no more than a yard of leeway at either side; and wherever Nigel stood in it, Waring could get him. He had already loosened the boulder. The thing must weigh a couple of hundredweight. It was firmly wedged but movable. Waring had already moved it, and he knew he could topple it without great effort. All understandable. Loosened by rain and snow. Not the gillie's fault. Not the angler's. Hazard of the sport.

It had taken him several minutes yesterday to get there and back from that point to this one. Now he gave it nine, to allow for contingencies.

The nine minutes ticked away, and he got moving. He fixed himself to the rope, picked up his rod and shuffled round the rock again. Estelle was watching most anxiously, and waved at once. He didn't wave back. Brucie hadn't appeared yet, but he might at any moment. He didn't want Brucie to see him coming from the rock.

He put distance between it. He struggled out to mid-stream. He stayed a full calculated minute watching the water before turning away. Then he waved. Then she pulled.

She pulled too hard. She'd have him over! He hung back on the rope, steadying himself. But the thing was a help. He was desperately tired now, heart thumping, and with double vision into the bargain. He knew he'd never make it if he had to watch the beach and the racing water in between. Guided by the rope he could concentrate on his feet, and in a few minutes was stumbling out.

Brucie was coming down the slope.

'Darling, that was *lunacy!*' Estelle cried.

Waring couldn't speak.

'I thought I'd literally have a *seizure!*'

She was babbling on but he barely heard her; still trying to catch his breath and remove the rope as Brucie arrived.

The giant stared at him open-mouthed. 'You planning to catch a whale?' he said.

Waring didn't answer. Estelle would babble in explanation soon enough. And there were things in store for Brucie yet.

Estelle almost immediately was babbling. 'I told him not to go in, that the water was too fast. The rope's supposed to guide him back. He can't get a fly out far enough since his illness. But he goes so far!'

'Why so?' Brucie said. 'The fly fishes from here.'

'The fly won't fish.'

'It fishes *parfectly*. Mr Clintock fishes the fly.'

'I want the spinner,' Waring said.

'The spinner?' The spinner was guaranteed to unhinge Brucie. 'Why the spinner? It's fly water. They want fly.'

'Take the spinning rod,' Waring said, 'and go to the next pool. I'll join you shortly.'

'They will take fly, Mr Waring,' Brucie said desperately. 'You must give them a chance, sir. You must have patience.'

The 'Mr Waring, sir' was an advance. And there was no nonsense about the rope: nothing about it frightening fish. There couldn't be a rule about it.

'Don't waste time, Brucie,' Waring said, pressing on. 'Take the spinning rod. Take all the tackle. Don't forget the gaff.'

He made Brucie come and get the gaff. Brucie bit hard on his pipe but he came and got it and stumped off, deranged.

'Henry, it was so dangerous,' Estelle said.

'You did well,' he told her.

'And you were so miserable to Brucie.'

'Brucie *will* do well.'

'I'll have to make it up to him somehow.'

'Easily done.' There was always a reliable way of making it up to Brucie. The flask was in her shoulder bag now. 'Only you don't have to pull so hard,' Waring said. 'The rope does all the work, and it only upsets you.'

'It's nothing to do with the rope.'

'It's everything to do with the rope,' Waring said.

It was a good ten-minute slog to the pool, and Brucie wasn't there when they arrived. The tackle was there, but Brucie himself had gone up to sulk in the hut. From the hut he could view all the beat.

And that was the next thing, Waring thought. Brucie had to be removed from his view of the beat. It was the reason for putting him through his paces today.

D-Day would be the day after tomorrow, when Nigel would once more be in position. That was also D for Departure day, for they'd be checking out after lunch. It would give him only the morning to do it. Not that he needed all morning. He needed nine minutes; and Brucie's instant obedience in the nine minutes.

He fished the spinner for an hour without success, then it began snowing hard. It was still early for elevenses but they went to the hut, and found Nigel there before them. He and Brucie were weighing a ten-pounder.

'Caught on the fly,' said Brucie heavily.

Estelle sweetened the brute with her flask, and soon had him telling of other great malts he had known so that the atmosphere became quite affable.

Waring distanced himself from all the affability.

No toadying, he told himself. Brucie had to be kept in his place. There was a job ahead for Brucie.

The snow kept on till lunch, and afterwards turned to driving sleet; which meant no more fishing for the day. They did the tweed factory instead. They usually did the tweed factory on every visit. This time Waring was distracted half out of his mind.

He stayed that way all through dinner. The wind driving the sleet had risen. He could hear it slamming away outside. He wondered what it would do to tomorrow's fishing; if there would *be* any fishing. On all the beats there were good stations and not so good ones; it accounted for the strict rotation of rods. If the river was not fishable, the rotation was simply held up. But he couldn't have it held up. He had to have the small pool tomorrow so that Nigel would get it the day after: D-Day.

Later on, in the lounge, the wind began fairly howling. It drowned the sound of the river, and he saw the keener anglers about the room anxiously tapping the barometer.

He kept his nerve, drank his whisky, read his book.

*'The kind of deep whirling water that often lies beyond these banks is the most likely place for a fisherman, encumbered with heavy equipment, to be sucked down and drowned. This is where he must keep his head. Unless help is close to hand and immediately available . . .'*

He read the passage again, and then once more, almost faint with longing. The vision it depicted of Nigel on D-Day was so perfect it was almost a prophecy. The deep whirling water was *just* beyond the bank. Nigel would not be keeping his head, not after a boulder had fallen on it. The only help close to hand would be Waring's, which would in no way be available.

Nigel had begun yawning again and Estelle was folding her knitting. Waring finished his whisky and rose.

Let tomorrow be fishable, he thought. Let it be!

He was slow in turning out in the morning so that Estelle went down before him. This gave him an opportunity to be sick in the bathroom. The snow was going horizontally outside. His legs were so weak he thought he'd faint.

He pulled himself together, however, went down, had his porridge, had a kipper, had two cups of coffee.

'I don't know about you,' Nigel said, peering out of the window. 'But it does not look top o' the morning, does it?'

'See what Brucie says.'

'Oh, Brucie,' Estelle said. Brucie had not yet found any conditions unfishable; which was Waring's remaining hope, and the only thing keeping his kipper down. He didn't know for certain but he seemed to recall a rule that stated that the whole rotation of a beat must proceed if any particular member chose to fish his part of it. He thought he was going to be that member. Brucie must have his say, though.

Brucie was waiting in the vestibule, pipe going.

'Well, Brucie,' Nigel said. 'How is it?'

'Fresh,' Brucie said. Beyond the glass panels of the vestibule something very like a tempest seemed to be in progress.

'Is it fishable?' Waring said.

Brucie took his pipe out and paused, causing Waring's heart almost to stop. 'It's no' *un*fishable,' Brucie said. 'It's nò *parfect*,' he amplified. 'There's a breeze.'

The breeze just at that moment very nearly took the door off.

'Will it be so bad down at the small pool?'

'*No-o*,' Brucie said cautiously. 'You have the high bank there. The small pool would be – fishable.'

'I'll fish it,' Waring said.

He said it quickly. Much too quickly. They all stared at him and Nigel burst out laughing. 'You old weasel,' he said. 'You stoat. You fox. You cunning old swine. You want the Blackrock tomorrow, don't you?'

'Well, I – I'm game to try today,' Waring said, toes curling in his shoes.

Nigel's laughter roared on, and even Brucie's broken teeth bared in a grin. 'Silly old sausage,' Nigel said, prodding him affectionately. 'Of course have it tomorrow. I've had the most marvellous bag. Be my guest, Henry.'

'I'm quite prepared to fish today,' Waring said stiffly.

'Oh, Henry,' Estelle said.

'Give it away, old boy! Take your chance on the Blackrock tomorrow if it's OK.'

'Tomorrow will be parfect,' Brucie said.

'Will it?' Waring said.

'Not a doubt. And there's elsewhere today.'

'Where?'

'The distillery,' Brucie said.

'Oh,' Estelle said.

'The Glentorran. If there's a whole *day*.' He'd been trying to sell them the Glentorran for years now; it was forty miles off, too far for an afternoon jaunt.

'Well, it's very big of you, Nigel,' Waring said.

'Nonsense. I've had splendid value this trip.'

So he had, Waring thought, taking one thing with another. 'OK, then. Fine.'

'Wonderful! Lead on MacBruce.'

Waring quietly glowed in the car; but retained his caution. There were details to be sewn up yet. His mind roamed over the familiar ones. Fingerprints on boulders. Could there be? But if so, why not? He'd been there many times. *Footprints in snow*. Yes. He'd have to work on that; work backwards, obliterating them. And on shingle, the upward path? But who would look? Foul play not suspected. A boulder had gone over, weakened by weather. Unless he dropped something in his excitement: a knife, fishing scissors, any of a dozen bits of paraphernalia he'd have with him. Even his fishing hat. But he'd be using the hat, to brush the snow. That one already worked out. Remove *flies* from hat. Flies so easily droppable. Memorise a check list. Above all, keep calm. He wouldn't even look after the boulder, to see what happened. There couldn't be any doubt, after all. And no one else would be looking. Brucie wouldn't. *That* was the vital element: still the one that needed working on. But before they reached the distillery he'd worked that one out, too.

The Glentorran was a small family pot-still whose raw product was in high demand for premium blends. Rarely, bottles of the mature single malt appeared in the haunts of butlers at the highest of Highland Flings. More rarely still, a sacred bottle of Partners' Reserve became available every millennium or so, for royalty and above. None of the Reserve was below forty years old, its padlocked oak casks under religious scrutiny by the Excise authorities. However there was a mysterious evaporation known as ullage . . . Brucie was still holding forth on this mystery as they entered the ramshackle gates.

Brucie had friends at the Glentorran and they were soon having tiny samples as they made the rounds. At Waring's behest Brucie discreetly enquired into ullage, and before they left a lorry driver was asking him as a special favour to deliver a small wee food parcel to an old auntie of his, now very infirm; and fifteen pounds of Waring's money had changed hands.

Waring took charge of the food parcel himself as they returned after lunch. There was barely half a pint in it, and it had not ulled from the oldest of the casks; but its antiquity still seemed to have Brucie in a trance.

'Should we no' just *try* a drop?' he asked.

'Tomorrow. At elevenses,' Waring said. 'As a final celebration. If I've caught anything to celebrate.'

He thought he would be needing a drop by then. He thought they all would; except one, of course.

And that sewed Brucie up. D-Day ahead.

D-Day dawned dim, but afterwards turned absolutely marvellous: the perfection prophesied by Brucie. The wind had dropped, the snow was hard, the sky was blue and a sun of exceptional cheeriness shone in it. Waring suspected all this. There was too much general goodness about. He saw he would need more and not less determination in such blithe conditions, and concentrated grimly on his check list.

Brucie met them with a face so unnaturally ravaged by smiles as to be almost unrecognisable. 'Mr and Mrs Waring, Mr Clintock! Did I deliver the right weather?'

'You did, Brucie, you did,' Nigel said genially.

'A fine bonny fish for you today, Mr Waring!'

'I hope so,' Waring said.

'For sure, for sure. Have we got everything? Your wee bit rope,' he said, nodding with great good humour at Waring's coil. 'Everything *else*?' His eyes were roaming.

Estelle patted her bag. 'All here, Brucie.'

'Ah, we'll have a grand morning!'

He got them in the car, and out of it, and bustled about the hut with such pleasing deference that it wasn't till he was striding ahead of them with the tackle to the Blackrock that Waring noticed Estelle was without her bag.

'He'll drive me round the bend this morning,' she said, vexed. 'It must be in the car. We can get it later.'

'He won't forget. His mind is wonderfully concentrated today.'

He kept his own mind that way.

'Brucie,' he said as they were on the river bank, 'a word in your ear. I want to catch something today.'

'You will, you will, Mr Waring. Make no doubt!'

'I'll try the fly, but I'd like to give the spinner a go, too.'

'Where's the harm in it?' said Brucie tolerantly.

'And I'll cover as much water as possible. So keep an eye on me, and when I give the word just run every bit of tackle I'm not using down to the next pool.'

'Good as done,' Brucie said. 'I'll be up yonder, watching the pair of you, you and Mr Clintock both.'

'I'll give you a wave. I'll blow the whistle. Just come right down and get the stuff and I'll follow you round.'

'Rely on me.'

'And if I'm lucky – a *special* celebration, remember.'

'Say no more, Mr Waring,' said Brucie, chuckling. 'If you're all set I'll just take a wee look at Mr Clintock, get him off right.'

'But watch out for me, mind.'

'I will, sir. Be of good heart.'

Waring's heart wasn't good. It was bumping unevenly. He couldn't believe he'd be doing it within the hour; in less than *half* an hour. It was gone half past nine now. Nigel would be in position in thirty minutes. It was happening too fast. And in conditions he hadn't expected. He'd imagined a harsh scene of wind and snow, himself doggedly going about the task, almost a part of the natural violence, a part he might later confuse, even forget. In this smiling day none of it seemed real.

He slipped the bight of rope over his head.

'Henry, do be careful. It's still very fast.'

'I'll be all right.'

'Don't go so far.'

He didn't answer her. He tightened the rope, took his fly rod and gaff and went out along the spit. He entered the water carefully, knowing about it now, using the gaff cannily. The force of it still almost knocked him sideways, but he braced himself and proceeded. Keep careful check of the time. He'd get in position and try a few casts. He'd have to do that.

153

He found the position, the boulder he'd found before, and steadied himself at it again. Everything seemed absurdly unreal; the uproar, the tumultuous water, his own physical danger in it, apart from the coming dangers. But he did not feel danger. Unreal, all of it. He thought perhaps he had to feel like this, that he'd subconsciously prepared himself for it. Some part of him was going on working. He was stripping off line. He was swishing the big rod there and back. He had his line out fishing. And it was part of the unreality that almost at once he was into a fish. He felt it, with his finger; felt it without any question. The unseen salmon took the fly, turned, checked. He let it go, didn't strike, felt the fly run free again. The powerful beast would take upwards of twenty minutes to play, to tire out, and then would have to be beached. He didn't have twenty minutes.

He looked at his watch and saw that he had fifteen: it was twenty to ten. Before ten to, he would turn and give Brucie the signal in his hut. At five to, he would check that Brucie was down on the beach and going off with the tackle: going off in the other direction. He could start moving then.

He cast half a dozen times more, all from the same position. He knew Brucie, if watching, wouldn't approve. You had to move steadily down the beat. He wasn't moving from where he was, not till necessary.

Before ten to, he halted and closed his eyes in the torrent and went over the check list. Then he opened them and checked the whistle. He did it balancing awkwardly, with the hand holding the gaff, and right away the whistle came off its lanyard. First damned thing. *After use, lose whistle.* He didn't want to lose it elsewhere. It unsettled him suddenly and a touch of vertigo came on. He closed his eyes again and put it out of mind; and with eyes still closed stripped off some line. He had to be seen to be in action. He opened his eyes and cast, and again as if in a dream was immediately into a fish.

He knew then it was going to be all right. There was an inevitable feeling about it. It was the feeling he'd had in hospital: something that seemed totally incredible was in fact happening.

He let the fish go, and checked with his watch, and got the whistle in his teeth, and turned and blew. He waved at the same time, and saw a tiny answering movement outside the hut, and with the strangest feeling knew that it was now on. It was on! He got the line out a couple of times more, not even watching it, and turned, and saw Brucie was picking up the tackle and walking away.

He was walking the wrong way.

He was walking towards Nigel.

Waring blinked, and shook his head to clear it, and looked again. Brucie was still walking the wrong way.

He blew the whistle. He blew as hard as he could, and waved, and saw Brucie turn and motion to him. But he still kept walking in the same direction and didn't look back any more.

Something had gone terribly wrong; Waring knew it. He blew and kept blowing, but Brucie didn't turn and he saw that he couldn't hear him.

Brucie heard quite well, and clucked to himself. The wee man could surely wait a few minutes. The missis had just this minute told him she'd left her bag with the Reserve in the car and would he take it in preparation to the hut. For sure he would! He'd have a quick wee glance to see how Clintock was doing below at the same time – tips due from both of them – and get the Reserve and pop it in the hut and from there run directly with the tackle down to the other pool. He had the tackle with him now. In a question of something like the Reserve did a few minutes here and there matter? The wee man was keeping on with his whistle, tooting away. It seemed more discreet just to keep on and no' look back. So Brucie didn't.

Waring spat the whistle out and started for the bank. There were still minutes in hand and he could still turn him around. He waved wildly at Estelle, and she responded at once. He felt the tension come on the rope.

It came too hard. She was pulling like mad. He signalled her not to pull so hard, but she kept on, and he clutched tightly on the rope, leaning back on it. He had to clutch so tightly, the rod slipped from his hand, and he let it go. He had the line still out, and it caught in some way about his ears, and then his neck. With the same sense of unreality he suddenly realised that he was into another fish. Or rather, the fish was into him. The fish had the fly. He did not have the rod.

At just about the moment that he realised this, Waring realised something else. Estelle had let go of the rope.

He was leaning heavily against its pull, and then there was no pull, and he was on his back, in the torrent.

He felt the icy water pouring into the top of his waders, and tried to stand, and couldn't. He was waterlogged. He was also in some way going backwards, at speed. He was no longer in control. Something else was in conrol. For fleeting moments he got his arms out and waved. He saw Estelle was waving back, and mouthing something. He couldn't hear her, but he saw she was smiling.

In a series of simultaneous impressions he registered a number of things. He registered a grating feeling under his back. He registered that Nigel was wrong and Estelle didn't want to hang on to him, for she had let him go. She had let all the rope go. He realised that the grating under his back was caused by the ridge of rock that formed the wall of the pool and that the salmon had just taken him into the pool. And he realised finally – with a kind of rage that he had not experienced when seeing it all go before – what it was that Estelle was mouthing as she continued to smile so. It was only one word, but she kept on mouthing it. And her hand kept waving goodbye too.

# COLIN DEXTER

## At The Lulu-Bar Motel

I shall never be able to forget what Louis said – chiefly, no doubt, because he said it so often, a cynical smile slowly softening that calculating old mouth of his: 'People are so gullible!' – that's what he kept on saying, our Louis. And I've used those self-same words a thousand times myself – used them again last night to this fat-walleted coach-load of mine as they debussed at the Lulu-Bar Motel before tucking their starched napkins over their legs and starting into one of Louis' five-star four-coursers, with all the wines and a final slim liqueur. Yes, people are so gullible . . . Not *quite* all of them (make no mistake!) – and please don't misunderstand me. This particular manifestation of our human frailty is of only marginal concern to me personally, since occasionally I cut a thinnish slice of that great cake for myself – as I did just before I unloaded those matching sets of leather cases and hulked them round the motel corridors.

But let's get the chronology correct. All that hulking around comes right after we've pulled into the motel where – as always – I turn to all the good people (the black briefcase tight under my right arm) and tell them we're here, folks; here for the first-night stop on a wunnerful tour, which every single one o' you is goin' to enjoy real great. From tomorrow – and I'm real sorry about this, folks – you won't have me personally lookin' after you any more, but that's how the operation operates. I'm just the first-leg man myself, and someone else'll have the real privilege of drivin' you out on the second leg post-breakfast. Tonight itself, though, I'll be hangin' around the cocktail bar (got that?), and if you've any problems about – well, about *anything*, you just come along and talk to me, and we'll sort things out real easy. One thing, folks. Just one small friendly word o' counsel to you all. There's one or two guys around these parts who are about as quick an' as slick an' as smooth as a well-soaped ferret. Now, the last thing I'd ever try to do is stop you enjoyin' your vaycaytions, and maybe one or two of you could fancy your chances with a deck o' cards against the deadliest dealer from here to Detroit. But . . . well, as I say, just a friendly word o' counsel, folks. Which is this: *some people are so gullible!* – and I wouldn't like it if any o' you – well, as I say, I just wouldn't like it.

That's the way I usually dress it up, and not a bad little dressing up, at that, as I think you'll agree. 'OK' (do I hear you say?) 'If some of them want to transfer their savings to someone else's account – so what? You can't live other folks' lives for them, now can you? You did your best, Danny boy. So forget it!' Which all makes good logical sense, as I know. But they still worry me a little – all those warm-hearted, clean-living folk, because – well, simply because they're so gullible. And if you don't relish reading about such pleasant folk who plop like juicy pears into the pockets of sharp-fingered charlatans – well, you're not going to like this story. You're not going to like it one little bit.

Most of them were in their sixties or early seventies (no children on the Luxi-

Coach Package Tours), and as they filed past the old driving cushion they slipped me a few bucks each and thanked me for a real nice way to start a vaycaytion. After that it took a couple of hours to hump all that baggage around the rooms, and it was half-past eight before I got down to some of Lucy's chicken curry. Lucy? She's a honey of a girl – the sort of big-breasted blonde that most of my fellow sinners would willingly seek to seduce and, to be honest with you— But let me return to the theme.

The cocktail bar is a flashily furnished, polychrome affair, with deep, full-patterned carpet, orange imitation-leather seats, and soft wall-lighting in a low, pink glow; and by about half-past nine the place was beginning to fill up nicely. Quite a few of them I recognized from the coach: but there were others. Oh yes, there were a few others . . .

He wasn't a big fellow – five-six, five-seven – and he wore a loud check suit just like they used to do in the movies. When I walked in he was standing by the bar, a deck of cards shuttling magically from hand to hand. 'Fancy a game, folks? Lukey's the name.' He was pleasant enough, I suppose, in an ugly sort of way; and with his white teeth glinting in a broad-mouthed smile, you could almost stop disliking him. Sometimes.

It was just before ten when he got his first bite – a stocky, middle-aged fellow who looked as if he could take pretty good care of himself, thank you. So. So I watched them idly as they sat opposite each other at one of the smooth-topped central tables, and it wasn't long before a few others began watching, too. It was a bit of interest – a bit of an incident. And it wasn't *their* money at stake.

Now Lukey loved one game above all others, and I'll have to bare its bones a bit if you're going to follow the story. (Be patient, please: we're running along quite nicely now.) First, it's a dollar stake in the kitty, all right? Then two cards are dealt to each of the players, the court cards counting ten, the ace eleven, and all the other cards living up to their marked face-value. Thus it follows, as day follows night and as luck follows Luke, that the gods are grinning at you if you pick up a ten and an ace – for that is vingt-et-un, my friends, whether you reckon by fahrenheit or centigrade, and twenty-one's the best they come. And so long as you remember not to break that twenty-one mile speed-limit, you can buy as many more cards as you like and— But I don't think you're going to have much trouble in following things.

It was the speed with which hand followed hand that surprised all the on-lookers, since our challenger ('Call me Bart') was clearly no stranger to the Lukesberry rules and five and six hands were through every minute. Slap! A dollar bill in the kitty. Slap! A dollar bill on top. Flick, flick; flick, flick; buy; stick; bust. Dollar, dollar; flick, flick; quicker ever quicker. Soon I'm standing behind Bartey and I can see his cards. He picks up a ten, and a four; and without mulling it over for a micro-second he says 'Stick'. Then Lukey turns over a seven, and an eight – and then he flicks over another card for himself – a jack. Over the top! And Bartey pockets yet another kitty; and it's back to that dollar-dollar, flick-flicking again. And when Bart wins again, Luke asks him nicely if he'd like to deal. But Bart declines the kind offer. 'No,' he says. 'I'm on a nice li'l winnin' streak here, pal, so just you keep on dealing them pretty li'l beauties same as before – that's all I ask.'

So Lukey goes on doing just that; and by all that's supersonic what a sharp our Lukey is! I reckon you'd need more than a slow-motion replay to appreciate that prestissimo prestidigitation of his. You could watch those fingers with the eagle eye of old Cortes – and yet whether he was flicking the cards from the top or the middle or the bottom, I swear no one could ever tell. In spite of all this, though, Bartey-boy is still advancing his winnings. Now he picks up a seven, and a four; and he decides to buy another card for ten dollars. So Lukey covers the ten dollars from his fat roll, deals Bartey a nine – and things are looking mighty good. Then Luke turns over his own pair (why he bothers, I can't really say, for he knows them all along): a six, and a nine, they are – and things look pretty bad. He turns over another card from the deck – an eight. And once more he's out of his dug-out and over the top.

'My luck'll change soon,' says Luke.

'Not with me, it won't,' says Bart, picking up the twenty-two dollars from the kitty.

'You quitting, you mean?'

'I'm quitting,' says Bart.

'You've played before, I reckon.'

'Yep.'

'You always quit when you're winning?'

'Yep.'

Luke says nothing for a few seconds. He just picks up the deck and looks at it sourly, as if something somewhere in the universe has gone mildly askew. Then he calls on the power of the poets and he quotes the only lines he's ever learned:

'Bartey,' he says,

' "If you can make one heap of all your winnings
    And risk it on one turn of pitch and toss . . ."

Remember that? What about it? You've taken seventy odd dollars off o' me, and I'm just suggestin' that if you put 'em in the middle – and if I cover 'em . . . What do you say? One hand, that's all.'

The audience was about thirty strong now, and as many were urging Bartey on as were urging him off. And they were all pretty committed, too – one way or the other. One of them in particular . . .

I'd seen him earlier at the bar, and a quaint little fellow he was, too. By the look of him he was in his mid- or late-seventies, no more than four-ten, four-eleven, in his built-up shoes. His face was deeply tanned and just as deeply lined, and he wore a blazer gaudily striped in red and royal blue. Underneath the blazer pocket, tastelessly yet lovingly picked out in purple cotton, was the legend: Virgil K Perkins Jnr. Which made you wonder whether Virgil K Perkins Snr was still somewhere in circulation – although a further glance at his senile son seemed to settle that particular question in the negative. Well, it's this old-timer who tries pretty hard to get Bartey to pocket his dollars and call it a night. And for a little while it seemed that Bartey was going to listen. But no. He's tempted – and he falls.

'Okey doke,' says Bartey. 'One more hand it is.'

It was Luke now who seemed to look mildly uneasy as he covered the seventy-odd dollars and squared up the deck. From other parts of the room the crowd was rolling up in force again: forty, fifty of them now, watching in silence as Luke dealt the cards. Bartey let his pair of cards lie on the table a few seconds and his hands seemed half full of the shakes as he picked them up. A ten; and a six. Sixteen. And for the first time that evening he hesitated, as he fell to figuring out the odds. Then he said 'Stick'; but it took him twice to say it because the first 'stick' got sort of stuck in his larynx. So it was Lukey's turn now. And he slowly turned over a six – and then a nine. Fifteen. And Luke frowned a long time at his fifteen and his right hand toyed with the next card on the top of the deck, quarter turning it, half turning it, almost turning it – and then putting it back.

'Fifteen,' he said.

'*Sixteen*,' says Bartey, and his voice was vibrant as he grabbed the pile of notes in the middle.

Then he was gone.

The on-lookers were beginning to drift away as Luke sat still in his seat, the cards still shuttling endlessly from one large palm to the other. It was the old boy who spoke to him first.

'You deserve a drink, sir!' he says. 'Virgil K. Perkins Junior's the name, and this is my li'l wife, Minny.'

'We're from Omaha,' says Minny dutifully.

And so Virgil gets Luke a rye whisky, and they start talking.

'You a card player yourself, Mr Perkins?'

'Me? No, sir,' says Virgil. 'Me and the li'l wife here' (Minny was four or five inches the taller) 'we're just startin' on a vaycaytion together, sir. We're from Omaha, just like she says.'

But the provenance of these proud citizens seemed of no great importance to Luke. 'A few quick hands, Mr Perkins?'

'No,' says Virgil, with a quiet smile.

'Look, Mr Perkins! I don't care – I just don't *care* – whether it's winnin' or losin', and that's the truth. Now if we just—'

'No!' says Virgil.

'You musta heard of beginner's luck?'

'*No!*' says Virgil.

'You're from Omaha, then?' says Luke, turning all pleasant-like to Minny . . .

I left them there, walked over to the bar, and bought an orange juice from Lucy, who sometimes comes through to serve about ten o'clock. She's wearing a lowly cut blouse, and a highly cute hair-style. But she says nothing to me; just winks – unsmilingly.

Sure enough, when I returned to the table, there was Virgil K Perkins 'just tryin' a few hands' as he put it; and I don't really need to drag you through all the details, do I? It's all going to end up exactly as you expect . . . but perhaps I'd better put it down, if only for the record; and I'll make it all as brief as I can.

From the start it followed the usual pattern: a dollar up; a dollar down. Nice and easy, take it gently; and soon the little fellow was beaming broadly, and picking up his cards with accelerating eagerness. But, of course, the balance was slowly swinging against him: twenty dollars down; thirty; forty . . .

'Lucky little run for me,' says Luke with a disarming smile, as if for two dimes he'd shovel all his winnings across the table and ease that ever-tightening look round Virgil's mouth. It was all getting just a little obvious, too, and surely someone soon would notice those nimble fingers that forever flicked those eights and nines when only fours and fives could save old Virgil's day. And someone did.

'Why don't you let the old fella deal once in a while?' asks one.

'Yeah, why not?' asks another.

'You wanna deal, pop?' concedes Luke.

But Virgil shakes his white head. 'I've had enough,' he says. 'I shouldn't really—'

'Come on,' says Minny gently.

'He can deal. Sure he can, if he wants to,' says Luke.

'He can't deal off the bottom, though!'

Luke was on his feet in a flash, looking round the room. 'Who said that?' he asked, and his voice was tight and mean. All conversation had stopped, and no one was prepared to own up. Least of all me – who'd said it.

'Well,' said Luke, as he resumed his seat, 'that does it, pop! If I'm bein' accused of cheatin' by some lily-livered coward who won't repeat such villainous vilification – then we'll have to settle the question as a matter of honour, I reckon. *You* deal, pop!'

The old man hesitated – but not for too long. 'Honour' was one of those big words with a capital letter, and wasn't a thing you could shove around too lightly. So he picked up the cards and he shuffled them, boxing and botching the whole business with an awkwardness almost unmatched in the annals of card-play. But somehow he managed to square the deck – and he dealt.

'I'll buy one,' says Luke, slipping a ten-dollar bill into the middle.

Virgil slowly covers the stake, and then pushes over a card.

'Stick,' says Luke.

Taking from his blazer pocket an inordinately large handkerchief, the old man mops his brow and turns his own cards over: a queen; and – an ace!

Luke merely shrugs his shoulders and pushes the kitty across: 'That's the way to do it, pop! Just you keep dealing yourself a few hands like that and—'

'No', cries Minny, who'd been bleating her forebodings intermittently from the very beginning.

But Virgil lays a gentle hand on her shoulder: 'Don't be cross with me, old girl. And don't *worry*! I'm just a goin' to deal myself one more li'l hand and . . .'

And another, and another, and another. And the gods were not smiling on the little man from Omaha: not the slightest sign of the meanest grin. Was it merely a matter of saving Face? Of preserving Honour? No, sir! It seemed just plain desperation as the old boy chased his losses round and round that smooth-topped table, with Minny sitting there beside him, her eyes tightly closed as if she was pinning the remnants of her hopes on the power of silent prayer. (I hitched the briefcase tighter under my right arm as I caught sight of Lucy behind the crowd, her eyes holding mine – again unsmilingly.)'

By half-past ten Virgil K Perkins Jnr had lost one thousand dollars, and he sat there crumpled up inside his chair. It wasn't as if he was short of friends, for the large audience had been behind him all along, just willing the old fellow to win. And it wasn't as if anyone could blame our nimble-fingered Lukey any more, for it was Virgil himself who had long since been dealing out his own disasters.

Not any longer, though. He pushed the deck slowly across the table and stood up. 'I'm sorry, old girl,' he says to Minny, and his voice is all choked up. 'It was your money as much as mine—'

But Luke was leaning across and he put his mighty palm on the old boy's skinny wrist. And he speaks quietly. 'Look, pop! You've just lost yourself a thousand bucks, right? So I want you to listen to me carefully because I'm gonna tell you how we can put all that to rights again. Now, we'll just have one more hand—'

'NO!' (The little old lady's voice was loud and shrill this time.) 'He *won't*! He won't lay down another dollar, d'you hear me? He's just – he's just a poor old fool, can't you see that? He's just a gullible, poor old—' But the rest of her words were strangled in her throat, and Virgil sat down again and put his arm round her shoulder as she began to weep silently.

'Don't you *want* to get all your money back?' Luke's voice is quiet again, but everyone can hear his words.

'Don't listen to him!' shouts one.

'Call it a day, sir!' shouts another.

Says Luke, turning to all of them: 'Old pop here, he's got one helluva sight more spunk in him than the rest o' you put together! And, what's more, not a single man jack o' you knows the proposition I'm proposin'. Well?' (Luke looks around real bold.) 'Well? *Do* you?'

It's all silence again now, as Luke looks across to Virgil and formulates his offer. 'Look, pop. I've been mighty lucky tonight, as I think you might agree. So, I'm going to give you the sort o' chance you'll never have again. And this is what we'll do. We'll have just one last hand and we'll take two points off my score. Got that? I pick up eighteen – we call it sixteen. And just the same whatever score it is. What do you say, pop?'

But old Virgil – he shakes his head. 'You're a good sport, Luke, but—'

'Let's make it *three* off, then,' says Luke earnestly. 'I pick up twenty – we call it seventeen. OK? Look, pop!' (He leans across and grips the wrist again.) 'Nobody's *ever* gonna make you any better offer than that. *Nobody*. You know something? It's virtually *certain* you're gonna get all that lovely money right back into that wallet o' yours, now, isn't it?'

It was tempting. Ye gods, it was tempting! And it was soon clear that the audience was thinking it was pretty tempting, too, with a good many of them revising their former estimate of things.

'What d'you say?' asks Luke.

'No,' said Virgil. 'It's not just me – it's Minny here. I've made enough of a fool of myself for one night, haven't I, old girl?'

Then Minny looked at him, straight on, like. A surprising change had come over her tear-stained face, and her blue eyes blazed with a sudden surge of almost joyous challenge. 'You take him on, Virgil!' she says, with a quiet, proud authority.

But Virgil still sat there dejected and indecisive. His hands ran across that shock of waving white hair, and for a minute or two he pondered to himself. Then he decided. He took most of the remaining notes from his wallet, and counted them with lingering affection before stacking them neatly in the centre of the table. 'Do you wanna count 'em, Luke?' he says. And it was as if the tide had suddenly turned; as if the old man sensed the smell of victory in his nostrils.

For a few seconds now it seemed to be Luke who was nervy and hesitant, the brashness momentarily draining from him. But the offer had been taken up, and the fifty or sixty onlookers were in no mood to let him forget it. He slowly counted out his own bills, and placed them on the top of Virgil's.

Two thousand dollars – on one hand.

Luke has already picked up the deck, and now he's shuffling the spots with his usual casual expertise.

'Why are *you* dealin'?'

Luke looks up and stares me hard in the eye. 'Was that *you* just spoke, mister?' I nod. 'Yep. It was me. And I wanna know why it is you think you got some goddam right to deal them cards – because you don't deal 'em straight, brother. You flick 'em off the top and you flick 'em off the bottom and for all I know you flick 'em—'

'I'll see you outside, mister, as soon as—'

'You'll do no such thing,' I replies quietly. 'I just ain't goin' to be outside no more tonight again – least of all for you, brother.'

He looked mighty dangerous then – but I just didn't care. The skin along his knuckles was growing white as he slowly got to his feet and moved his chair backwards. And then, just as slow, he sat himself down again – and he surprises everybody. He pushes the deck over the table and he says: 'He's right, pop. *You* deal!'

Somehow old pop's shaking hands managed to shuffle the cards into some sort of shape; and when a couple of cards fall to the floor, it's me who bends down and hands them back to him.

'Cut,' says pop.

So Luke cuts – about half-way down the deck (though knowing Lukey I should think it was *exactly* half-way down). Miraculously, it seems, old Virgil's hands had gotten themselves rid of any shakes, and he deals the cards out firm and fine: one for Luke, one for himself; another for Luke, and another for himself. For a few moments each man left them lying there on the top of the table. Then Luke picks up his own – first the one, and then the other.

'Stick!' he says, and his voice is a bit hoarse.

Every eye in the room was now on Virgil as he turned over his first card – a seven; then the second card – a ten. Seventeen! And all you've got to do, my friends, is to add on three – and that's a handsome little twenty, and the whole room was mumbling and murmuring in approval.

Every eye now switches to Luke, and in the sudden tense silence the cards are slowly turned: first a king, and then – ye gods! – an ace! And as Lukey smiles down at that beautiful twenty-oner the audience groaned like they always do when its favourite show-jumper knocks the top off the last fence.

And where, my friends, do we go from there? Well, I'll tell you. It was Lucy who started it all immediately Luke had left. She pushed her way through the onlookers and plunged her hand deep down between those glorious breasts of hers to clutch her evening's tips.

'Mr Perkins, isn't it? I know it isn't all that much; but – but if it'll help, please take it.' About seven or eight dollars, it was, no more – but, believe me, it bore its fruit two-hundred-fold. It was me who was next. I'd taken about thirty-five dollars on the coach and (once more hitching the old briefcase higher under my arm) I fished it all out of my back pocket and placed it a-top of Lucy's crumpled offerings.

'Mr Perkins,' I said sombrely. 'You should've been on *my* coach, old friend.' That's all I said.

As for Virgil, he said nothing. He just sat back all crumpled up like before, and with Minny sobbing silently beside him. I reckon he looked as if he couldn't trust himself to say a single word. But it didn't matter. All the audience was sad and sullenly sympathetic – and, as I said, they'd had their fill of Louis' vintage wines. And I've got to hand it to them. Twenty dollars; another twenty dollars; a fifty; a few tens; another twenty; another fifty – I watched them all as these clean-living, God fearing folk forked something from their careful savings. And I reckon there wasn't a single man-jack of them who didn't make his mark upon that ever-mounting pile. But still Virgil said nothing. When finally he stumbled his way to the exit, holding Minny in one hand and a very fat pile of other people's dollars in the other, he turned round as if he was going to say something to all his very good friends. But still the words wouldn't come, it seemed; and he turned once more and left the cocktail bar.

I woke late the next morning, and only then because Luke was leaning over me, gently shaking me by the shoulder.

'Louis says he wants to see you at half-past ten.'

I lifted my left arm and focused on the wrist-watch: already five to ten.

'You all right, Danny?' Luke was standing by the door now (he must have had a key for that!) and for some reason he didn't look mightily happy.

'Sure, sure!'

'Half-past, then,' repeated Luke, and closed the door behind him.

I still felt very tired, and I was conscious that the back of my head was aching – and that's unusual for me. Nothing to drink the night before – well, only the odd orange juice that Lucy had . . . orange juice . . .? I fell to wondering slightly, and turned to look at the other side of the bed, where the sheet was neatly turned down in a white hypotenuse. Lucy had gone – doubtless gone early; but then Lucy was always sensible and careful about such things. . . .

I saw my face frowning as I stood in front of the shaving-mirror; and I was still frowning when I took the suit off the hanger in the wardrobe and noticed that the briefcase was gone. But I'd have been frowning even more if the briefcase *hadn't* gone; and as I dressed, my head was clearing nicely. I picked up the two thick-sealed envelopes that had nestled all night under my pillow, put them, one each, into the pockets of my overcoat, and felt happy enough when I knocked on the door of Louis' private suite and walked straight in. It was ten thirty-two.

There were the usual six chairs round the oblong table, and four of them were taken already: there was Luke, and there was Bartey; then there was Minny; and at the head of the table, Louis himself – a Louis still, doubtless, no more than four-ten, four-eleven in his built-up shoes, but minus that garishly striped blazer now; minus, too, that shock of silvery hair which the previous evening had covered that large, bald dome of his.

'You're late,' he says, but not unpleasantly. 'Sit down, Danny.' So I sat down, feeling like a little boy in the first grade. (But I usually feel like that with Louis.)

'You seen Lucy?' asks Minny, as Bartey pours me a drop of Irish.

'Lucy? No – have you tried her room?'

But no one seemed much willing to answer that one, and we waited for a few minutes in silence before Louis spoke again.

'Danny,' he says, 'you'll remember that when we brought you into our latest li'l operation a few months back I figured we'd go for about a quarter of a million before we launched out on a new one?'

I nodded.

'Well, we're near enough there as makes no odds – a fact perhaps you may yourself be not completely unaware of? After all, Danny, it was one o' your jobs to take my li'l Lucy down to the bank on Mondays, now wasn't it? And I reckon you've got a pretty clear idea of how things are.'

I nodded again, and kept on looking him straight in the eyes.

'Well, it was never no secret from any of us – was it? – that I'd be transferrin' this li'l investment o' mine over to Luke and Bartholomew here as soon as they – well, as soon as they showed me they was worthy.'

I was nodding slowly all the time now; but he'd left something out. 'Lucy was goin' to be in it, too,' I said.

'You're very fond of my Lucy, aren't you?' says Minny quietly.

'Yep. I'm very fond of her, Minny.' And that was the truth.

'It's not bin difficult for any o' us to see that, old girl, now has it?' Louis turned to Minny and patted her affectionately on the arm. Then he focuses on me again. 'You needn't have no worries about my li'l daughter, Danny. No worries at all! Did it never occur to you to wonder just why I christened this latest li'l investment o' mine as the "Lulu-Bar Motel"?'

For a few seconds I must have looked a little puzzled, but my head was clearing nicely with the whisky, and I suddenly saw what he meant. Yes! What a deep old devil our Louis was! The *Lu*-cy, *Lu*-ke, *Bar*-tholomew Motel . . .

But Louis was still speaking: 'I only asked you down this mornin', Danny, because I was hopin' to wind it all up here and now – and to let you know how much I've bin aware o' your own li'l contribution. But – well, it's all tied up in a way with Lucy, isn't it? And I reckon' (he looked at Luke and Bart) 'I reckon we'd better call another li'l meeting tonight? About eight? All right?'

It seemed all right to all of us, and I got up to go.

'You off to town, Danny?' asks Louis, eyeing the overcoat.

'Yep.' That's all I said. Then I left them there and caught the bus to the station. I'd always noticed it before: whenever I'd felt a bit guilty about anything it was as if I sensed that other people somehow seemed to *know*. But that's behind us now. And, anyway, it had been Lucy's idea originally – not mine. She'd needed me, of course, for devising the cheque and forging Louis' signature – for though I'm about as hamfisted with a deck of cards as an arthritic octopus, I got my own particular specialism. Yes, sir! And Lucy trusted me, too, because I'd been carrying all that lovely money – 240,000 dollars of it! – all neatly stacked in five-hundred bills, all neatly enveloped and neatly sealed – why, I'd been carrying it all around with me in the old briefcase for two whole days! And Lucy – Lucy, my love! – we shall soon be meeting at the ticket-barrier on number one platform – and then be drifting off together quietly in the twilight . . .

At a quarter-to twelve I was there – standing in my overcoat and waiting happily. (Lucy had never been early in her life.) I lit another cigarette; then another. By twelve forty-five I was beginning to worry a little; by one forty-five I was beginning to worry a lot; and by two forty-five I was beginning to guess the truth. Yet still I waited – waited and waited and waited. And, in a sense, I suppose, I've been waiting for Lucy ever since . . .

It was when the big hand on the station-clock came round to four that I finally called it a day and walked over to look at the Departure Board. I found a train that was due for New York in forty-five minutes, and I thought that that had better be that. I walked into the buffet and sat down with a coffee. So? So, here was another of life's illusions lying shattered in the dust, and yet . . . Poor, poor, lovely Lucy! I nearly allowed myself a saddened little smile as I thought of her opening up those two big envelopes in the briefcase – and finding there those 480 pieces of crisp, new paper, each exactly the size of a 500-dollar bill. She must have thought I was pretty – well, pretty gullible, I suppose, when we'd both agreed that *she* should take away the briefcase . . .

A single to New York would cost about fifty or sixty dollars, I reckoned; and as I joined what seemed to be the shorter queue at the ticket-office I took the bulky envelope from the right-hand pocket of the overcoat, opened it – and stood there stunned and gorgonized. Inside were about 240 pieces of crisp, new paper, each exactly the size of a 500-dollar bill; and my hands were trembling as I stood away from the queue and opened the other envelope. Exactly the same. Well, no – not *exactly* the same. On the top piece of blank paper there were three lines of writing in Louis' unmistakably minuscule hand:

'*I did my best to tell you Danny boy but you never did really understand that filosofy of mine now did you? It's just what I kept on telling you all along. People . . .*'

By now, though, I reckon you'll know those last few words that Louis wrote.

I walked back across the buffet and ordered another coffee, counting up what I had in my pockets: just ten dollars and forty cents; and I fell to wondering where it was I went from here. Perhaps . . . perhaps there were one or two things in my favour. At least I could spell 'philosophy'; and then there was always the pretty big certainty (just as Louis said so often) that somewhere soon I'd find a few nice, kindly, gullible folk.

But as I glance around at the faces of my fellow men and women in the station buffet now, they all look very mean, and very hard.

# ELIZABETH
# FERRARS

# Instrument Of Justice

When Frances Liley read in the obituary column of *The Times* of the death of Oliver Darnell, beloved husband of Julia, suddenly at his home, she folded her arms on the table before her, put her head down on them and burst into violent tears. Anyone who had seen her then would have assumed that she was weeping at the loss of a dear friend. In fact, they were tears of relief, healing and wonderful. At last she was free. No threat hung over her any more. Or so she thought until she had had time to do a little thinking.

As soon as she had she sat back abruptly, dried her eyes roughly and sat staring before her, a dark, angularly handsome woman of forty, possessed by a new horror. For when a person died his solicitor or his executors or someone would have to go through his papers and somewhere they would find those terrible photographs. And God knew what would happen then. At least with Oliver, Frances had known where she was. Two thousand a year to him, which it had not been too difficult for her to find, and she had been relatively safe. But if someone else found the photographs and felt inclined to send them to Mark, her husband, he would immediately go ahead with the divorce that he wanted and would certainly get custody of their two children. That would be intolerable. She must think and think fast.

Luckily she had always had a quick brain. After only a few minutes she knew what to do, or at least what was worth trying. Telephoning Julia Darnell, she said, 'It's Frances, Julia. I've just seen the news about Oliver. I'm so terribly sorry. I can hardly believe it. It was his heart, was it? There was always something the matter with it, wasn't there? Listen, my dear, please be quite honest with me, but would you like me to come down? I mean, if you're alone now and I can help in any way. But don't say you'd like me to come if you'd sooner I didn't. Of course I'll come to the funeral, but I could come straight away and stay on for a few days, unless you've some other friend with you.'

Julia was tearfully grateful. She had no relations of her own and had never liked Oliver's, and though the neighbours, she said, had been very kind, she was virtually alone. And she and Frances were such very old friends, she could think of no one who could help so much to break the dreadful new loneliness of bereavement. Of course Julia had never known of her husband's brief adultery with Frances, or that he had supplemented his not very large income as a painter of very abstract pictures with a sideline in blackmail, and her affection for Frances was uncomplicated and sincere. Promising to arrive that afternoon, Frances telephoned Mark in his office to tell him what had happened and that she would probably be away for a few days. The children were no problem, because they were away at their boarding school. Packing a suitcase, she set off for the Darnells' cottage in Dorset.

By that time she had a plan of sorts in her mind. On the morning of the funeral she intended to wake up with what she would claim was a virus and say that she was feeling too ill to go out. Then, during the one time when she could be certain the cottage would be empty, she would make a swift search of it for the photographs. The probability was that they were somewhere in Oliver's studio, a very private place in which Julia had never been allowed to touch anything, even to do a little cautious dusting. If they were not there, of course, if, for instance, Oliver had kept them in the bank, then there was nothing for Frances to do but go home and wait for the worst to happen, but with luck, she thought, she would find them.

Unfortunately her plan was wrecked by the fact that on the morning of the funeral it was Julia who woke up with a virus. She had a temperature of a hundred and two, complained of a sore throat and could only speak in a husky whisper. Frances called the doctor who gave Julia some antibiotics and said that she must certainly stay in bed and not to go out into the chill of the February morning, even to attend her husband's funeral. Julia, with bright spots of fever on her plump, naturally pale cheeks, cried bitterly and said, 'But all those people coming back here to lunch, Frances – what *am* I to do about them? I can't possibly put them off now.'

For Julia had insisted that Oliver's relations, who were coming from a distance, and such neighbours as were kind enough to come to the funeral, must be given lunch in her house after it, and she and Frances had spent most of the day before assembling cold meats, salads, cheeses and a supply of rather inferior white wine for what Frances felt would be a gruesome little party, but the thought of which seemed to comfort Julia.

Again thinking fast, Frances said, 'Don't worry. I'll look after them for you. I'll go to the service, but I won't go on to the cemetery, I'll come straight back from the church and have everything ready for your friends when they arrive. Now just stay quiet and I'll look after everything.'

She gave Julia the pills that the doctor had left for her and also brought her a mug of hot milk into which she had emptied two capsules of sodium amytal which she had found in the bathroom cabinet. They would almost certainly ensure that Julia would be asleep by the time that Frances returned from the church, and though she would not have as long for her search as she had hoped, she might still be fortunate.

There were not many people in the church. A man sitting next to Frances, who started a low-voiced conversation with her before the coffin had been brought in or the vicar appeared, introduced himself as Major Sowerby and said that his wife was desperately sorry not to be able to attend, but she was in bed with a virus.

'There's a terrible lot of it around in the village,' he said. 'Is it true poor Mrs Darnell's laid up with it too?'

'I'm afraid so,' Frances said.

'Tragic for her. Most upsetting. She and Oliver were so devoted to one another. Of course I didn't understand his painting, but Isobel, my wife, who knows a lot more about that sort of thing than I do, says he deserved much more recognition than he ever had. Great dedication, she says, and such integrity.'

'Oh, complete,' Frances agreed with a sweet, sad smile, and thought that in its way it was true. Oliver had been dedicated to exploiting any woman who had been fool enough to be charmed by his astonishing good looks and to trust him. As soon as the service was over she hurried out of the church, leaving the other mourners to go on to the cemetery, and made her way along the lane that led to the Darnells' cottage.

As she entered it, she stood still, listening. All was quiet. So it looked as if the sodium amytal had done its work and Julia was asleep. But just to make sure, Frances went to the foot of the stairs and called softly, 'Julia!'

There was no reply. She waited a moment, then wrenched off her coat, dropped it on a chair and went swiftly along the passage to Oliver's studio. Presently she would have to attend to the setting out of the lunch for Julia's guests, but the search must come first. Opening the door of the studio, she went in and only then understood the reason for the quiet in the house. Julia, in her dressing-gown, was lying in the middle of the floor with her head a terrible mass of blood and with a heavy hammer on the floor beside her.

Frances was not an entirely hard-hearted person. Also, she was by nature law-abiding. Her first impulse, as she stared at the battered thing on the floor, was to call the police. But then a habit that she had of having second thoughts asserted itself. It was still of desperate importance to her to find the photographs and once the police were in the house she would have no further chance of searching for them. That made the situation exceedingly complex. For one thing, how were the police to know that it had not been Frances whom Julia, drugged and half-asleep, had heard downstairs in her husband's studio, and coming downstairs to investigate, been killed by her for it? If Frances called the police now, she thought, she might find herself in deep trouble.

But if she did not and searched for the photographs first, she would presently find herself with a cooling body on her hands and sooner or later would have to explain why she had failed to report it a few hours earlier. It did not help that she was almost certain that she knew who the murderer was. A virus can be a very convenient thing, and Mrs Sowerby, who had not attended the church, would not have found out that Julia was ill and would have assumed that the house was empty. Looking round the studio, where drawers had been pulled out and papers, letters, sketches, notebooks spilled on the floor, Frances wondered if the woman had found the photographs or letters that Oliver had presumably been holding over her before she committed murder, or if she was still in terror that someone else would find them. But even if she were, she was unlikely to come back for the present, knowing that a dozen guests would shortly be arriving. Taking the key out of the door, locking it on the outside and putting the key into the pocket of the suit that she was wearing, Frances went out to the kitchen to go on with preparing the lunch.

She took all the things that she and Julia had made the day before out of the refrigerator, spooned the various salads, the prawns with rice and peppers, the cucumbers in sour cream, the coleslaw and the rest, into cut glass bowls, arranged the slices of cold turkey, meat loaf and ham on dishes, and set them out on the table in the dining-room. She put silver and wine glasses on the table and drew the corks of several of the bottles of wine. The meal was only just ready when the first guests arrived.

They were the vicar, Arthur Craddock, and his wife. He was a slender, quiet-looking man whose voice, as he recited the psalms that Julia had chosen and described Oliver's improbable virtues, had seemed unexpectedly vibrant and authoritative. But any authority that he might achieve when he was performing his professional duties was sadly diminished, in a mere social setting, by his wife, a large, hearty woman who looked kindly, but accustomed to domination and who upset Frances at once by saying that she would just pop upstairs to have a few words with poor Julia, tell her how splendidly everything had gone off and how much she had been missed.

'But the infection,' Frances stammered. 'I believe it's all round the village and I know she wouldn't want you to be exposed to it here.'

'I'm never ill,' Mrs Craddock replied. 'Ask my husband. We were in India for a time, you know, and I've nursed patients through bubonic plague and never a whit the worse. I'm sure I could give Julia a little comfort.'

'Well, later, perhaps,' Frances said, recovering her presence of mind. 'I went up to see her myself a few minutes ago and found her asleep. The doctor gave her a sedative. He said rest was what she needed, and I'm sure he's right. I know she hasn't slept properly for days. But she's looking very peaceful now, so I don't think we should disturb her.'

'Ah, no, of course not,' Mrs Craddock agreed. 'Was that Dr Bolling? Excellent man. The best type of good, old-fashioned family doctor whom you can really trust.'

She let herself and her husband be shepherded into the dining-room and they had each just accepted a glass of wine when the doorbell rang again and Frances left them to admit the next guests.

They were a brother and a cousin of Oliver's, both of whom, he had once told Frances, he knew disliked him. The next to arrive was Major Sowerby and gradually the dining-room filled, the hushed tones in which everyone spoke on first arriving rising by degrees until the noise in the room resembled that of any ordinary cocktail party. The food on the table was eaten with appetite, the wine was drunk, and the atmosphere became one of what seemed to Frances a faintly gruesome hilarity, quelled only now and again by guilt when someone was tactless enough to remind the others that these were funeral baked meats that they were consuming.

Slightly flushed, Oliver's brother remarked, 'Julia was always a jolly good cook. Pity she can't be with us now.'

'She must have taken a great deal of trouble over this,' Mrs Craddock said, 'but I expect it was good for her, taking her mind off her sorrow. I'd like to take a little of it up to her and tell her how we've all been thinking of her, because with all the noise we've been making I'm sure she must be awake by now. I'll just pop up with a plateful, shall I, and perhaps a glass of wine?'

'That's the ticket,' Major Sowerby said, 'though whisky might do her more good. I took a good strong whisky up to my wife before I left for the church, and a sandwich. She said a sandwich was all she could face. Actually I had to insist on her staying in bed, she was so upset at not being able to make it to the funeral, but obviously she wasn't fit to go out. The fact is, you know, she thought a lot of Oliver. Sat for her portrait to him once, then made me buy the thing. Well, I didn't mind doing it really, because no one could guess it's Isobel, it's all squares and triangles and she says it's good and she knows far more about that sort of thing than I do.'

Mrs Craddock was spooning prawns and rice on to a plate, murmuring, 'I wonder if she likes cucumber – it disagrees with some people,' adding a slice of turkey, a small piece of ham and reaching for a bottle of wine to fill a glass for Julia.

Frightened beyond words and desperate, Frances snatched the plate and the glass from the woman's hands, said brusquely, 'I'll take them,' made for the door and while Mrs Craddock was still only looking startled at her rudeness, shot up the stairs and through the open door into Julia's bedroom.

In its silence she first began to feel the real horror of the situation. Here she was with food and wine in her hands for a woman who lay in a room downstairs with her body cooling and her head battered in. Her gaze held hypnotised by the sight of the empty bed with its dented pillows and its blankets thrown back, Frances gulped down the wine, wishing that it was something stronger, then went downstairs again and put down the plate of untouched food on the dining-table.

'She drank the wine, but she wouldn't eat anything,' she said to Mrs Craddock. 'I gave her another of the pills the doctor left for her. She's very sleepy. I really think it's best to leave her alone.'

Frustrated in her desire to do good, the vicar's wife soon left, sweeping her husband along with her, and after that, one by one, the other guests departed. At last the house was empty and quiet again.

Too quiet, too desolate. The last hour had been the worst nightmare that Frances had ever lived through, but at least the crowd of chattering people had been a defence against thought. Now she could not escape from it any longer. There was the problem of the photographs and the problem of the corpse in the studio. Looking at the table littered with china, wine glasses and left-overs, she had an absurd idea that she might do the washing-up before trying to cope with the murder, but recognizing this for the idiocy that it was, and that her motive was only to put off doing what she must, she poured out a glass of whisky, sat down at the head of the table and tried to concentrate.

The photographs came first. She must nerve herself to go back into the studio and search for them. What she did next would depend to some extent on whether or not she found them. She could hardly bear to face the possibility that she might not. With the dreadful things in his hands, Mark would certainly be able to obtain custody of the children when he went ahead with the divorce that he wanted, and she would never submit to that. For apart from the pleasure that she took in the two dear girls, it would be intolerable to let Mark triumph over her.

She thought of the photographs, of which Oliver had only once allowed her a glimpse, of how appallingly revealing they were, and of the bitter amusement with which Mark would view them. They were, in their way, superb photographs. Oliver might not have been an outstanding painter, but as a photographer he had been highly skilled, as well as incredibly ingenious. She had had no suspicion of the presence of the camera in the room at the time when he had taken the pictures, and when he had told her how he had done it, she had almost had to laugh, it had been so clever. But now she must get them back. That was what she must do before she thought of anything else.

She went back into the studio. It was easier than she had thought that it would be to disregard Julia's body, the darkening blood and the murderous hammer. Locking the door in case anyone, that well-meaning busybody, Mrs Craddock, for instance, should think of coming back, she began on a methodical search of the drawers and cupboards. To her surprise, she found the photographs almost at once, not merely prints, but the negatives too, in a box in a cupboard which she thought had not yet been opened by the previous searcher.

She found several other photographs of a similar character. Feeling dizzy with relief, close to bursting into tears as she had when she had first read of Oliver's death, she studied these, which were of three women, and wondered which of them was of Isobel Sowerby. Frances knew nothing about her except that her husband did not think that she looked as if she consisted of squares and triangles. But none of the women did. They all had more curves than angles. And two of them looked rather young to be married to Major Sowerby, though that was not the sort of thing about which it was ever possible to be sure. Men of sixty sometimes married girls in their teens. However, Frances thought that Julia's murderess was probably the third woman, who was about her own age, big, heavy-breasted, rather plump, with a look of passion and violence about her. In fact, a formidable-looking woman, surely capable of murder. After studying her face for some minutes, Frances put her photographs, the prints and the negatives, back into the cupboard, took those of herself and the two younger women to the sitting-room, put them down on the hearth and set fire to them.

The negatives spat, blazed briefly and disappeared, making a pungent smell in the room. The prints curled at the edges and caught fire more slowly, but as she prodded them with the poker, they flared up, then smouldered into ash. Watching them, sitting on her heels, she waited until there was not a spark left, then stood up and went to the telephone.

She had a plan now, a plan of sorts. It was a gamble, but then what could she do that was not? Picking up the directory, she looked up the Sowerbys' number and dialled it.

To her satisfaction, it was a woman's voice that answered. Frances did not introduce herself.

'I've found what you were looking for,' she said softly.

There was a silence. Frances suddenly became aware of how her heart was thudding. For this was the moment when she would discover whether or not her gamble had paid off. She might have guessed totally wrongly. Mrs Sowerby might be an innocent woman who had been in bed all day with flu, feeling very ill, and if that were so, Frances would have to start thinking all over again. It seemed to her lunacy now that she had not called the police as soon as she had found Julia's body. If only she had known how simple it was going to be to find the photographs, she would have done so, and would have had plenty of time to destroy them before the police arrived. But there was not much point in thinking on those lines now. It was too late. She waited.

At last an almost whispering voice said in her ear, 'Who are you?'

She drew a shuddering breath. So she had been right. Her plan was working.

'A friend of Julia's,' she said. 'I think you'd better come here as soon as possible.'

'What do you want?' the voice asked.

'Your help,' Frances said.

'I can't come. I'm ill.'

'I think it would be advisable to make a quick recovery.'

'But I can't. My husband wouldn't hear of my going out.'

'That's your problem. I'll wait here for a little, but not for long.'

There was another silence, then the voice said, 'All right, I'll see what I can do.'

The telephone at the other end was put down. Frances put down the one that she was holding, realising that the hand that had been gripping it was clammy with sweat and had left damp marks on the instrument. She wondered if that mattered, but decided that it did not. She would have another call to make presently, which would account for the fingerprints.

She waited an hour before there came a ring at the front door bell. The early dusk of the February afternoon was already dimming the daylight. She had spent some of the time while she had had to wait stripping Julia's body of the dressing gown and night-dress that she was wearing and re-dressing it in pants and bra, jeans and sweater. It had been a terrible undertaking. In the middle of it she had felt faint and had had to go back to the sitting-room to give herself a chance to recover her self-control. But she had been afraid to wait until the other woman arrived and could help her in case the body stiffened too much to make the undressing of it possible. She knew nothing about how long it took for rigor mortis to set in. The blood-stained clothes that she removed were a problem and so was the hammer. She had not thought about that until after she had started undressing Julia, but in the end she made a bundle of them, took them out to the garage and put them into the boot of the Darnells' car. Then she went back into the house to wait.

When the ring at the door came at last and she went to answer it, she found the woman whom she had been expecting on the doorstep. Her guess about the photographs had been correct. Isobel Sowerby was a middle-aged woman, tall and thick set, with thick dark hair to her shoulders, intense dark eyes and jutting lips. She was wearing slacks and a sheepskin jacket.

Staring at Frances with deep enmity, she said, 'What am I supposed to do now?'

'We're going to arrange a suicide,' Frances answered.

'I don't understand,' the other woman said. 'If you know so much, why haven't you turned me in?'

'Because I'm involved myself. I made the mistake of not calling the police as soon as I found the body. I wanted to find some photographs of me that Oliver had and I didn't think until it was too late how difficult it was going to be to explain how I'd managed not to find Julia as soon as I got back from the church. So I'm in almost as much trouble as you are. And I think the best thing for both of us to do is to put Julia into her car and send her over the cliffs into the sea. Suicide while the balance of her mind was disturbed by the death of her husband. I couldn't arrange it alone because she's too heavy for me to carry. I had to have help.'

'All right, whatever you say,' Isobel Sowerby said. 'But give me the photographs first.'

'Afterwards,' Frances said.

'No, now, or I won't help you.'

'Afterwards,' Frances repeated.

They looked at one another with wary antagonism, then Isobel Sowerby shrugged her shoulders.

'Let's get on with it then,' she said. 'I persuaded my husband to go to the golf club to get over the funeral, and he'll stay there for a time and have a few drinks, but he'll be home presently and it won't help us to have him asking me questions.'

'How did you get into the house this morning?' Frances asked. 'I've been wondering about that.'

'The back door was unlocked, as I knew it would be. We aren't particular about locking up round here.'

'And you left in a hurry when you heard me come in.'

'Yes. Now let's get on.'

It was almost dark by then and the garage doors could not be seen from the lane outside. There was no one to see them as they carried Julia's body from the house to the car, put it in the seat beside the driver's, covered it with a rug, got into the car themselves and with Isobel Sowerby driving, since she knew the roads, started towards the coast. She drove cautiously along the twisting lanes until at last they reached the cliff-top and saw the dark chasm of the sea ahead of them.

Stopping the car close to the edge of the cliff, she and Frances got out and between them moved Julia's body into the driving seat. After that it was only a case of turning on the engine again, putting the car into low gear, slamming the doors, and standing back while it went slowly forward to the brink, seemed to teeter there for an instant, then went plunging down, the sound of the crash that it made as it hit the rocks below carrying up to them with a loudness which it seemed to Frances must carry for miles.

But afterwards there was no sign that anyone else had heard it. The darkness around them was silent. They started the long walk back.

They did not talk to one another as they walked and had reached the Darnells' cottage before Isobel Sowerby said, 'I don't know what I'm going to say to my husband. He'll have got back from the golf club long ago.'

'You'll think of something,' Frances said. She did not think that Major Sowerby would be difficult to delude. 'You could always say you've been wandering around in a state of delirium.'

'Which is what I think I've been doing,' Isobel Sowerby said. 'Now give me the photographs.'

Frances took her into the sitting-room and showed her the heap of ashes in the grate.

'I burnt them.'

Isobel Sowerby stared at them incredulously, then broke suddenly into hysterical laughter.

'What a fool I am!' she cried. 'I've always been a fool. I needn't have come at all!'

'But I needed your help, so naturally I wasn't going to tell you that,' Frances replied.

'Are those really my photographs? You really destroyed them?'

'Along with some of my own. I'd get home now as soon as I could if I were you, because I'm going to telephone the police and tell them Julia's missing.'

Still laughing, Isobel Sowerby turned and plunged out into the darkness.

Frances went to the telephone, called the police and told them that she was very concerned because she had just discovered that Mrs Darnell, who was suffering from a high fever and was in a state of shock after the death of her husband, had disappeared. Her car was missing too. Frances said that she had only just discovered this, because after the lunch that had been held in the house after the funeral, she had felt so tired that she had gone to her room to lie down and had fallen asleep and had only just woken up, gone into Mrs Darnell's room to see how she was and found it empty. She said that she knew that Mrs Darnell had been in her room at about half past one, when she had taken some food and wine up to her and Mrs Darnell had drunk a little wine but had refused the food. But at what time she had got up and gone out Frances had no idea, because she had been so sound asleep. She had heard nothing. Anything might have happened in the house without her being aware of it.

The man who answered her call said that someone would be out to see her shortly. Putting the telephone down, Frances fetched a dustpan and brush, swept up the ashes in the grate and flushed them down the lavatory. Then in truth feeling as tired as she had told the policeman that she had felt earlier, she began to clear up the dining-room and had started on the washing-up when the police arrived.

After that everything went surprisingly smoothly. The police soon found the wreck of the car on the rocks at the foot of the cliffs and the hammer and the blood-stained nightdress and dressing-gown in the boot. They also found fingerprints on the steering-wheel which were later identified as Mrs Sowerby's and they found some highly obscene photographs of her in a cupboard in Oliver Darnell's studio. It had happened too that Major Sowerby, in a state of great anxiety at finding his wife missing when he returned from the golf club, had telephoned several friends to ask if she was with them, so without his intending it, he had destroyed any chance that she might have had of concocting an alibi. She told an absurd story about having been summoned by Mrs Liley to help her get rid of the body of Julia Darnell, whom she and not Isobel Sowerby had murdered, but the story was not believed. There was a little doubt as to whether she could have handled the body by herself, but she was a big, powerful woman and it was thought that she could and she was charged with the murder. Frances stayed on in the Darnells' cottage until after the inquest, then when her presence was no longer required, telephoned Mark and started for home.

As she drove, she fell into one of her rare moods of self-examination. She was not a nice person, she thought. Some people might even say of her that she was rather horrible. She did not really blame Mark for wanting to leave her and marry that little pudding of a woman who had been infatuated with him for the last five years. And if only he would give up his claim to the children, Frances would be quite willing to let him go. But they were the only people for whom she had ever felt any deep and lasting love. Or what she took to be love. It did not involve questioning whether it would be better for them to stay with her or with Mark, or which of their parents the girls themselves loved most. Even in her present mood of introspection, she did not ask herself that. She simply knew that they were hers, a possession from which it would be intolerable to be parted.

And horrible as perhaps she was, was she not an instrument of justice? Had she not arranged the arrest of Julia's murderess, without herself or those two foolish young women, whose photographs she had good-naturedly burnt, becoming involved? No mud would stick to any of them. None of it would splash devastatingly on to the children. Only the guilty would suffer. So why should anyone criticise her? In a state of quiet satisfaction, she drove homewards to Mark.

# DICK
# FRANCIS

## The Gift

When the breakfast-time Astrojet from La Guardia was still twenty minutes short of Louisville, Fred Collyer took out a block of printed forms and began to write his expenses.

*Cab fare to airport, fifteen dollars.*

No matter that a neighbour, working out on Long Island, had given a free ride door to door: a little imagination in the expense department earned him half as much again (untaxed as the *Manhattan Star* paid him for the facts he came up with every week in his Monday racing column).

*Refreshments on Journey,* he wrote. *Five dollars.*

*Entertaining for the purposes of obtaining information, six dollars fifty.*

To justify that little lot he ordered a second double Bourbon from the air hostess and lifted it in a silent good luck gesture to a man sleeping across the aisle, the owner of a third rate filly that had bucked her shins two weeks ago.

Another Kentucky Derby. His mind flickered like a scratched print of an old movie over the days ahead. The same old slog out to the barns in the mornings, the same endless raking over of past form, searching for a hint of the future. The same inconclusive work-outs on the track, the same slanderous rumours, same gossip, same stupid jocks, same stupid trainers, shooting their goddam stupid mouths off.

The bright burning enthusiasm which had carved out his syndicated by-line was long gone. The lift of the spirit to the big occasion, the flair for sensing a story where no one else did, the sharp instinct which sorted truth from camouflage, all these he had had. All had left him. In their place lay plains of boredom and perpetual cynical tiredness. Instead of exclusives he nowadays gave his paper rehashes of other turfwriters' ideas, and a couple of times recently he had failed to do even that.

He was forty-six.

He drank.

Back in his functional New York office the Sports Editor of the *Manhattan Star* pursed his lips over Fred Collyer's account of the Everglades at Hialeah and wondered if he had been wise to send him down as usual to the Derby.

That guy, he thought regretfully, was all washed up. Too bad. Too bad he couldn't stay off the liquor. No one could drink and write, not at one and the same time. Write first, drink after, sure. Drink to excess, to stupor, maybe. But *after*.

He thought that before long he would have to let Fred go, that probably he should have started looking around for a replacement that day months back when Fred first turned up in the office too fuddled to hit the right keys on his typewriter. But that bum had had everything, he thought. A true journalist's

182

nose for a story, and a gift for putting it across so vividly that the words jumped right off the page and kicked you in the brain.

Nowadays all that was left was a reputation and an echo: the technique still marched shakily on, but the personality behind it was drowning.

The Sports Editor shook his head over the Hialeah clipping and laid it aside. Twice in the past six weeks Fred had been incapable of writing a story at all. Each time when he had not phoned through they had fudged up a column in the office and stuck the Collyer name on it, but two missed deadlines were one more than forgivable. Three, and it would be all over. The management were grumbling louder than ever over the inflated expense accounts, and if they found out that in return they had twice received only sodden silence, no amount of for-old-times' sake would save him.

I did warn him, thought the Sports Editor uneasily. I told him to be sure to turn in a good one this time. A sizzler, like he used to. I told him to make this Derby one of his greats.

Fred Collyer checked into the motel room the newspaper had reserved for him and sank three quick mid-morning stiffeners from the bottle he had brought along in his briefcase. He shoved the Sports Editor's warning to the back of his mind because he was still sure that drunk or sober he could outwrite any other commentator in the business, given a story that was worth the trouble. There just weren't any good stories around any more.

He took a taxi out to Churchill Downs. (*Cab fare, four dollars fifty*, he wrote on the way; and paid the driver two seventy-five.)

With three days to go to the Derby the racecourse looked clean, fresh, and expectant. Bright red tulips in tidy columns pointed their petals uniformly to the blue sky, and patches of green grass glowed like shampooed rugs. Without noticing them Fred Collyer took the elevator to the roof and trudged up the last windy steps to the huge glass-fronted press room which ran along the top of the stands. Inside, a few men sat at the rows of typewriters knocking out the next day's news, and a few more stood outside on the balcony actually watching the first race, but most were engaged on the day's serious business, which was chat.

Fred Collyer bought himself a can of beer at the simple bar and carried it over to his named place, exchanging Hi-yahs with the faces he saw on the circuit from Saratoga to Hollywood Park. Living on the move in hotels, and altogether rootless since Sylvie got fed up with his absence and his drinking and took the kids back to Mom in Nebraska, he looked upon racecourse press rooms as his only real home. He felt relaxed there, assured of respect. He was unaware that the admiration he had once inspired was slowly fading into tolerant pity.

He sat easily in his chair reading one of the day's duplicated news releases.

'Trainer Harbourne Cressie reports no heat in Pincer Movement's near fore after breezing four furlongs on the track this morning.'

'No truth in rumour that Salad Bowl was running a temperature last evening, insists veterinarian John Brewer on behalf of owner Mrs L (Loretta) Hicks.'

Marvellous, he thought sarcastically. Negative news was no news, Derby runners included.

He stayed up in the press room all afternoon, drinking beer, discussing this, that and nothing with writers, photographers, publicists and radio newsmen, keeping an inattentive eye on the racing on the closed-circuit television, and occasionally going out onto the balcony to look down on the anthill crowd far beneath. There was no need to struggle around down there as he used to, he thought. No need to try to see people, to interview them privately. Everything and everyone of interest came up to the press room sometime, ladling out info in spoonfed dollops.

At the end of the day he accepted a ride back to town in a colleague's Hertz car (*cab fare, four dollars fifty*) and in the evening having laid substantial Bourbon foundations in his own room before setting out he attended the annual dinner of the Turfwriters' Association. The throng in the big reception room was pleased enough to see him, and he moved among the assortment of pressmen, trainers, jockeys, breeders, owners and wives and girlfriends like a fish in his own home pond. Automatically before dinner he put away four doubles on the rocks, and through the food and the lengthy speeches afterwards kept up a steady intake. At half after eleven, when he tried to leave the table, he couldn't control his legs.

It surprised him. Sitting down, he had not been aware of being drunk. His tongue still worked as well as most around him, and to himself his thoughts seemed perfectly well organised. But his legs buckled as he put his weight on them, and he returned to his seat with a thump. It was considerably later, when the huge room had almost emptied as the guests went home, that he managed to summon enough strength to stand up.

'Guess I took a skinful,' he murmured, smiling to himself in self-excuse.

Holding onto the backs of chairs and at intervals leaning against the wall, he weaved his way to the door. From there he blundered out into the passage and forward to the lobby, and from there, looking as if he were climbing imaginary steps, out into the night through the swinging glass doors.

The cool May evening air made things much worse. The earth seemed literally to be turning beneath his feet. He listed sideways into a half circle and instead of moving forwards towards the parked cars and waiting taxis, staggered head-on into the dark brick front of the wall flanking the entrance. The impact hurt him and confused him further. He put both his hands flat on the rough surface in front of him and laid his face on it, and couldn't work out where he was.

Marius Tollman and Piper Boles had not seen Fred Collyer leave ahead of them. They strolled together along the same route making the ordinary social phrases and gestures of people who had just come together by chance at the end of an evening, and gave no impression at all that they had been eyeing each other meaningfully across the room for hours, and thinking almost exclusively about the conversation which lay ahead.

In a country with legalised bookmaking Marius Tollman might have grown up a respectable law-abiding citizen. As it was, his natural aptitude and only talent had led him into a lifetime of quick footwork which would have done credit to Muhammad Ali. Through the simple expedient of standing bets for the future racing authorities while they were still young enough to be foolish, he remained unpersecuted by them once they reached status and power; and the one sort of winner old crafty Marius could spot better even than horses was the colt heading for the boardroom.

The two men went through the glass doors and stopped just outside with the light from the lobby shining full upon them. Marius never drew people into corners, believing it looked too suspicious.

'Did you get the boys to go along, then?' he asked, standing on his heels with his hands in his pockets and his paunch oozing over his belt.

Piper Boles slowly lit a cigarette, glanced around casually at the star dotted sky, and sucked comforting smoke into his lungs.

'Yeah,' he said.

'So who's elected?'

'Amberezzio.'

'No,' Marius protested. 'He's not good enough.'

Piper Boles drew deep on his cigarette. He was hungry. One eleven pounds to make tomorrow, and only a five ounce steak in his belly. He resented fat people, particularly rich fat people. He was putting away his own small store of fat in real estate and growth bonds, but at thirty-eight the physical struggle was near to defeating him. He couldn't face many more years of starvation, finding it worse as his body aged. A sense of urgency had lately led him to consider ways of making a quick ten thousand that once he would have sneered at.

He said, 'He's straight. It'll have to be him.'

Marius thought it over, not liking it, but finally nodded.

'All right, then. Amberezzio.'

Piper Boles nodded, and prepared to move away. It didn't do for a jockey to be seen too long with Marius Tollman, not if he wanted to go on riding second string for the prestigious Somerset Farms, which he most assuredly did.

Marius saw the impulse and said smoothly, 'Did you give any thought to a diversion on Crinkle Cut?'

Piper Boles hesitated.

'It'll cost you,' he said.

'Sure,' Marius agreed easily. 'How about another thousand, on top?'

'Used bills. Half before.'

'Sure.'

Piper Boles shrugged off his conscience, tossed out the last of his integrity.

'OK,' he said, and sauntered away to his car as if all his nerves weren't stretched and screaming.

Fred Collyer had heard every word, and he knew, without having to look, that one of the voices was Marius Tollman's. Impossible for anyone long in the racing game not to recognise that wheezy Boston accent. He understood that Marius had been fixing up a swindle and also that a good little swindle would fill his column nicely. He thought fuzzily that it was necessary to know who Marius had been talking to, and that as the voices had been behind him he had better turn round and find out.

Time however was disjointed for him, and when he pushed himself off the wall and made an effort to focus in the right direction, both men had gone.

'Bastards,' he said aloud to the empty night, and another late homegoer,

185

leaving the hotel, took him compassionately by the elbow and led him to a taxi. He made it safely back to his own room before he passed out.

Since leaving La Guardia that morning he had drunk six beers, four brandies, one double Scotch (by mistake), and nearly three fifths of Bourbon.

He woke at eleven the next morning, and couldn't believe it. He stared at the bedside clock.

Eleven.

He had missed the barns and the whole morning merry-go-round on the track. A shiver chilled him at that first realisation, but there was worse to come. When he tried to sit up the room whirled and his head thumped like a pile driver. When he stripped back the sheet he found he had been sleeping in bed fully clothed with his shoes on. When he tried to remember how he had returned the previous evening, he could not do so.

He tottered into the bathroom. His face looked back at him like a nightmare from the mirror, wrinkled and red-eyed, ten years older overnight. Hungover he had been any number of times, but this felt like no ordinary morning-after. A sense of irretrievable disaster hovered somewhere behind the acute physical misery of his head and stomach, but it was not until he had taken off his coat and shirt and pants, and scraped off his shoes, and lain down again weakly on the crumpled bed, that he discovered its nature.

Then he realised with a jolt that not only had he no recollection of the journey back to his motel, he could recall practically nothing of the entire evening. Snatches of conversation from the first hour came back to him, and he remembered sitting at table between a cross old writer from the *Baltimore Sun* and an earnest woman breeder from Lexington, neither of whom he liked; but an uninterrupted blank started from half-way through the fried chicken.

He had heard of alcoholic blackouts, but supposed they only happened to alcoholics; and he, Fred Collyer, was not one of those. Of course, he would concede that he did drink a little. Well, a lot, then. But he could stop any time he liked. Naturally he could.

He lay on the bed and sweated, facing the stark thought that one blackout might lead to another, until blackouts gave way to pink panthers climbing the walls. The Sports Editor's warning came back with a bang, and for the first time, uncomfortably remembering the twice he had missed his column, he felt a shade of anxiety about his job. Within five minutes he had reassured himself that they would never fire Fred Collyer, but all the same he would for the paper's sake lay off the drink until after he had written his piece on the Derby. This resolve gave him a glowing feeling of selfless virtue, which at least helped him through the shivering fits and pulsating headaches of an extremely wretched day.

Out at Churchill Downs three other men were just as worried. Piper Boles kicked his horse forward into the starting stalls and worried about what George Highbury, the Somerset Farms trainer, had said when he went to scale at two pounds overweight. George Highbury thought himself superior to all jocks and spoke to them curtly, win or lose.

'Don't give me that crap,' he said to Boles' excuses. 'You went to the

# The Gift

Turfwriters' dinner last night, what do you expect?'

Piper Boles looked bleakly back over his hungry evening with its single martini and said he'd had a session in the sweat box that morning.

Highbury scowled. 'You keep your fat ass away from the table tonight and tomorrow if you want to make Crinkle Cut in the Derby.'

Piper Boles badly needed to ride Crinkle Cut in the Derby. He nodded meekly to Highbury with downcast eyes, and swung unhappily into the saddle.

Instead of bracing him, the threat of losing the ride on Crinkle Cut took the edge off his concentration, so that he came out of the stalls slowly, streaked the first quarter too fast to reach third place, swung wide at the bend and lost his stride straightening out. He finished sixth. He was a totally experienced jockey of above average ability. It was not one of his days.

On the grandstand Marius Tollman put down his raceglasses shaking his head and clicking his tongue. If Piper Boles couldn't ride a better race than that when he was supposed to be trying to win, what sort of a goddam hash would he make of losing on Crinkle Cut?

Marius thought about the ten thousand he was staking on Saturday's little caper. He had not yet decided whether to tip off certain guys in organised crime, in which case they would cover the stake at no risk to himself, or to gamble on the bigger profit of going it alone. He lowered his wheezy bulk onto his seat and worried about the ease with which a fixed race could unfix itself.

Blisters Schultz worried about the state of his trade, which was suffering a severe recession.

Blisters Schultz picked pockets for a living, and was fed up with credit cards. In the old days, when he'd learned the skill at his grandfather's knee, men carried their billfolds in their rear pants' pockets, neatly outlined for all the world to see. Nowadays all these smash and grab muggers had ruined the market: few people carried more than a handful of dollars around with them, and those that did tended to divide it into two portions, with the heavy dough hidden away beneath zips.

Fifty-three years Blisters had survived: forty-five of them by stealing. Several shortish sessions behind bars had been regarded as bad luck, but not as a good reason for not nicking the first wallet he saw when he got out. He had tried to go straight once, but he hadn't liked it: couldn't face the regular hours and the awful feeling of working. After six weeks he had left his well paid job and gone back thankfully to insecurity. He felt happier stealing two dollars than earning ten.

For the best haul at racemeets you either had to spot the big wads before they were gambled away, or follow a big winner away from the pay-out window. In either case, it meant hanging around the pari-mutuel with your eyes open. The trouble was, too many racecourse cops had cottoned to this modus op, and were apt to stand around looking at people who were just standing there looking.

Blisters had had a bad week. The most promisingly fat wallet had proved, after half an hour's careful stalking, to contain little money but a lot of pornography. Blisters, having a weak sex drive, was disgusted on both counts.

For his first two days' labour he had only twenty-three dollars to show, and five of these he had found on a stairway. His meagre room in Louisville was

187

costing him eight a night, and with transport and eating to take into account, he reckoned he'd have to clear three hundred to make the trip worthwhile.

Always an optimist, he brightened at the thought of Derby Day. The pickings would certainly be easier once the real crowd arrived.

Fred Collyer's private Prohibition lasted intact through Friday. Feeling better when he awoke, he cabbed out to Churchill Downs at seven-thirty, writing his expenses on the way. They included many mythical items for the previous day, on the basis that it was better for the office not to know he had been paralytic on Wednesday night. He upped the inflated total a few more dollars: after all, Bourbon was expensive, and he would be off the wagon by Sunday.

The initial shock of the blackout had worn off, because during his day in bed he had remembered bits and pieces which he was certain were later in time than the fried chicken. The journey from dinner to bed was still a blank, but the blank had stopped frightening him. At times he felt there was something vital about it he ought to remember, but he persuaded himself that if it had been really important, he wouldn't have forgotten.

Out by the barns the groups of pressmen had already formed round the trainers of the most fancied Derby runners. Fred Collyer sauntered to the outskirts of Harbourne Cressie, and his colleagues made room for him with no reference to his previous day's absence. It reassured him: whatever he had done on Wednesday night, it couldn't have been scandalous.

The notebooks were out. Harbourne Cressie, long practised and fond of publicity, paused between every sentence to give time for all to be written down.

'Pincer Movement ate well last evening and is calm and cool this a.m. On the book we should hold Salad Bowl, unless the track is sloppy by Saturday.'

Smiles all round. The sky blue, the forecast fair.

Fred Collyer listened without attention. He'd heard it all before. They'd all heard it all before. And who the hell cared?

In a rival group two barns away the trainer of Salad Bowl was saying his colt had the beating of Pincer Movement on the Hialeah form, and could run on any going, sloppy or not.

George Highbury attracted fewer newsmen, as he hadn't much to say about Crinkle Cut. The three year old had been beaten by both Pincer Movement and Salad Bowl on separate occasions, and was not expected to reverse things.

On Friday afternoon Fred Collyer spent his time up in the press room and manfully refused a couple of free beers. (*Entertaining various owners at track, twenty-two dollars.*)

Piper Boles rode a hard finish in the sixth race, lost by a short head, and almost passed out from hunger-induced weakness in the jocks' room afterwards. George Highbury, unaware of this, merely noted sourly that Boles had made the weight, and confirmed that he would ride Crinkle Cut on the morrow.

Various friends of Piper Boles, supporting him towards a daybed, asked anxiously in his ear whether tomorrow's scheme was still on. Piper Boles nodded. 'Sure,' he said faintly. 'All the way.'

Marius Tollman was relieved to see Boles riding better, but decided anyway to hedge his bet by letting the syndicate in on the action.

Blisters Schultz lifted two billfolds, containing respectively fourteen and twenty-two dollars. He lost ten of them backing a certainty in the last race.

Pincer Movement, Salad Bowl and Crinkle Cut, guarded by uniformed men with guns at their waists, looked over the stable doors and with small quivers in their tuned-up muscles watched other horses go out to the track. All three would have chosen to go too. All three knew well enough what the trumpet was sounding for, on the other side.

Saturday morning, fine and clear.

Crowds in their thousands converged on Churchill Downs. Eager, expectant, chattering, dressed in bright colours and buying mint juleps in takeaway souvenir glasses, they poured through the gates and over the infield, reading the latest sports columns on Pincer Movement versus Salad Bowl, and dreaming of picking outsiders that came up at fifty to one.

Blisters Schultz had scraped together just enough to pay his motel bill, but self esteem depended on better luck with the hoists. His small lined face with its busy eyes wore a look near to desperation, and the long predatory fingers clenched and unclenched convulsively in his pockets.

Piper Boles, with one-twenty-six to do on Crinkle Cut, allowed himself an egg for breakfast and decided to buy property bonds with the five hundred in used notes which had been delivered by hand the previous evening, and with the gains (both legal and illegal) he should add to them that day. If he cleaned up safely that afternoon, he thought, there was no obvious reason why he shouldn't set up the same scheme again, even after he had retired from riding. He hardly noticed the shift in his mind from reluctant dishonesty to habitual fraud.

Marius Tollman spent the morning telephoning to various acquaintances, offering profit. His offers were accepted. Marius Tollman felt a load lift from his spirits and with a spring in his step took his two-sixty pounds downtown a few blocks, where a careful gentleman counted out ten thousand dollars in untraceable notes. Marius Tollman gave him a receipt, properly signed. Business was business.

Fred Collyer wanted a drink. One, he thought, wouldn't hurt. It would pep him up a bit, put him on his toes. One little drink in the morning would certainly not stop him writing a punchy piece that evening. The *Star* couldn't possibly frown on just *one* drink before he went to the races, especially not as he had managed to keep clear of the bar the previous evening by going to bed at nine. His abstinence had involved a great effort of will: it would be right to reward such virtue with just one drink.

He had however finished on Wednesday night the bottle he had brought with him to Louisville. He fished out his wallet to check how much he had in it: fifty-three dollars, plenty after expenses to cover a fresh bottle for later as well as a quick one in the bar before he left.

He went downstairs. In the lobby however his colleague Clay Petrovitch again offered a free ride in his Hertz car to Churchill Downs, so he decided he could postpone his one drink for half an hour. He gave himself little mental pats on the back all the way to the racecourse.

★     ★     ★

Blisters Schultz, circulating among the clusters of people at the rear of the grandstand, saw Marius Tollman going by in the sunshine, leaning backwards to support the weight in front and wheezing audibly in the growing heat.

Blisters Schultz licked his lips. He knew the fat man by sight: knew that somewhere around that gross body might be stacked enough lolly to see him through the summer. Marius Tollman would never come to the Derby with empty pockets.

Two thoughts made Blisters hesitate as he slid like an eel in the fat man's wake. The first was that Tollman was too old a hand to let himself be robbed. The second, that he was known to have friends in organised places, and if Tollman was carrying organisation money Blisters wasn't going to burn his fingers by stealing it, which was how he got his nickname in the first place.

Regretfully Blisters peeled off from the quarry, and returned to the throng in the comforting shadows under the grandstand.

At twelve-seventeen he infiltrated a close-packed bunch of people waiting for an elevator.

At twelve-eighteen he stole Fred Collyer's wallet.

Marius Tollman carried his money in cunning underarm pockets which he clamped to his sides in a crowd, for fear of pickpockets. When the time was due he would visit as many different selling windows as possible, inconspicuously distributing the stake. He would give Piper Boles almost half of the tickets (along with the second five hundred dollars in used notes), and keep the other half for himself.

A nice tidy little killing, he thought complacently. And no reason why he shouldn't set it up some time again.

He bought a mint julep and smiled kindly at a girl showing more bosom than bashfulness.

The sun stoked up the day. The preliminary contests rolled over one by one with waves of cheering, each hard ridden finish merely a sideshow attending on the big one, the Derby, the roses, the climax, the ninth race.

In the jocks' room Piper Boles had changed into the silks for Crinkle Cut and began to sweat. The nearer he came to the race the more he wished it was an ordinary Derby day like any other. He steadied his nerves by reading the *Financial Times.*

Fred Collyer discovered the loss of his wallet upstairs in the press room when he tried to pay for a beer. He cursed, searched all his pockets, turned the press room upside down, got the keys of the Hertz car from Clay Petrovitch and trailed all the way back to the car park. After a fruitless search there he strode furiously back to the grandstands, violently throttling in his mind the lousy stinking son of a bitch who had stolen his money. He guessed it had been an old hand, an old man, even. The new vicious young lot relied on muscle, not skill.

His practical problems were not too great. He needed little cash. Clay Petrovitch was taking him back to town, the motel bill was going direct to the *Manhattan Star,* and his plane ticket was safely lying on the chest of drawers in his bedroom. He could borrow twenty bucks or so, maybe, from Clay or others in the press room, to cover essentials.

Going up in the elevator he thought that the loss of his money was like a sign from heaven; no money, no drink.

Blisters Schultz kept Fred Collyer sober the whole afternoon.

Pincer Movement, Salad Bowl and Crinkle Cut were led from their barns, into the tunnel under the cars and crowd, and out again onto the track in front of the grandstands. They walked loosely, casually, used to the limelight but knowing from experience that this was only a foretaste. The first sight of the day's princes galvanised the crowds towards the pari-mutuel window like shoals of multi-coloured fish.

Piper Boles walked out with the other jockeys towards the wire-meshed enclosure where horses, trainers and owners stood in a group in each stall. He had begun to suffer from a feeling of detachment and unreality: he could not believe that he, a basically honest jockey, was about to make a hash of the Kentucky Derby.

George Highbury repeated for about the fortieth time the tactics they had agreed on. Piper Boles nodded seriously, as if he had every intention of carrying them out. He actually heard scarcely a word; and he was deaf also to the massed bands and the singing when the Derby runners were led out to the track. *My Old Kentucky Home* swelled the emotions of a multitude and brought out a flutter of eye-wiping handkerchiefs, but in Piper Boles they raised not a blink.

Through the parade, the canter down, the circling round, and even into the starting stalls, the detachment persisted. Only then, with the tension showing plain on the faces of the other riders, did he click back to realisation. His heart-rate nearly doubled and energy flooded into his brain.

Now, he thought. It is now, in the next half minute, that I earn myself one thousand dollars; and after that, the rest.

He pulled down his goggles and gathered his reins and his whip. He had Pincer Movement on his right and Salad Bowl on his left, and when the stalls sprang open he went out between them in a rush, tipping his weight instantly forward over the withers and standing in the stirrups with his head almost as far forward as Crinkle Cut's.

All along past the stands the first time he concentrated on staying in the centre of the main bunch, as unnoticeable as possible, and round the top bend he was still there, sitting quietly and doing nothing very much. But down the backstretch, lying about tenth in a field of twenty-six, he earned his thousand.

No one except Piper Boles ever knew what really happened; only he knew that he'd shortened his left rein with a sharp turn of his wrist and squeezed Crinkle Cut's ribs with his right foot. The fast galloping horse obeyed these directions, veered abruptly left, and crashed into the horse beside him.

The horse beside him was still Salad Bowl. Under the impact Salad Bowl cannoned into the horse on his own left, rocked back, stumbled, lost his footing entirely, and fell. The two horses on his tail fell over him.

Piper Boles didn't look back. The swerve and collision had lost him several places which Crinkle Cut at the best of times would have been unable to make up. He rode the rest of the race strictly according to his instructions, finishing flat out in twelfth place.

Of the one hundred and forty thousand spectators at Churchill Downs, only a handful had had a clear view of the disaster on the far side of the track. The buildings in the in-field, and the milling crowds filling all its furthest areas, had hidden the crash from nearly all standing at ground level and from most on the grandstands. Only the press, high up, had seen. They sent out urgent fact-finders and buzzed like a stirred up beehive.

Fred Collyer, out on the balcony, watched the photographers running to immortalise Pincer Movement and reflected sourly that none of them would have taken close-up pictures of the second favourite, Salad Bowl, down on the dirt. He watched the horseshoe of dark red roses being draped over the winner and the triumphal presentation of the trophies, and then went inside for the re-run of the race on television. They showed the Salad Bowl incident forwards, backwards and sideways, and then jerked it through slowly in a series of stills.

'See that,' said Clay Petrovitch, pointing at the screen over Fred Collyer's shoulder. 'It was Crinkle Cut caused it. You can see him crash into Salad Bowl . . . there! . . . Crinkle Cut, that's the joker in the pack.'

Fred Collyer strolled over to his place, sat down, and stared at his typewriter. Crinkle Cut. He knew something about Crinkle Cut. He thought intensely for five minutes, but couldn't remember what he knew.

Details and quotes came up to the press room. All fallen jocks shaken but unhurt, all horses ditto; stewards in a tizzy, making instant enquiries and re-running the patrol camera film over and over. Suspension for Piper Boles considered unlikely, as blind eye usually turned to rough riding in the Derby. Piper Boles had gone on record as saying 'Crinkle Cut just suddenly swerved. I didn't expect it, and couldn't prevent him bumping Salad Bowl.' Large numbers of people believed him.

Fred Collyer thought he might as well get a few pars down on paper: it would bring the first drink nearer, and boy how he needed that drink. With an ear open for fresher information he tapped out a blow-by-blow I-was-there account of an incident he had hardly seen. When he began to read it through, he saw the first words he had written were 'The diversion on Crinkle Cut stole the post-race scene. . . .'

*Diversion* on Crinkle Cut? He hadn't meant to write that . . . or not exactly. He frowned. And there were other words in his mind, just as stupid. He put his hands back on the keys and tapped them out.

'It'll cost you . . . a thousand in used notes . . . half before.'

He stared at what he had written. He had made it up, he must have. Or dreamed it. One or the other.

A dream. That was it. He remembered. He had had a dream about two men planning a fixed race, and one of them had been Marius Tollman, wheezing away about a diversion on Crinkle Cut.

Fred Collyer relaxed and smiled at the thought, and the next minute knew quite suddenly that it hadn't been a dream at all. He had heard Marius Tollman and Piper Boles planning a diversion on Crinkle Cut, and he had forgotten because he'd been drunk. Well, he reassured himself uneasily, no harm done, he had remembered now, hadn't he?

No, he hadn't. If Crinkle Cut was a diversion, what was he a diversion *from*? Perhaps if he waited a bit, he would find he knew that too.

Blisters Schultz spent Fred Collyer's money on two hot dogs, one mint julep, and five losing bets. On the winning side, he had harvested three more billfolds and a woman's purse: total haul, ninety-four bucks. Gloomily he decided to call it a day and not come back next year.

Marius Tollman lumbered busily from window to window of the pari-mutuel and the stewards asked to see the jockeys involved in the Salad Bowl pile-up.

The crowds, hot, tired and frayed at the edges, began to leave in the yellowing sunshine. The bands marched away. The stalls which sold souvenirs packed up their wares. Pincer Movement had his picture taken for the thousandth time, and the runners for the tenth, last, and least interesting race of the day walked over from the barns.

Piper Boles was waiting outside the stewards' room for a summons inside, but Marius Tollman used the highest class messengers, and the package he entrusted was safely delivered. Piper Boles nodded, slipped it into his pocket, and gave the stewards a performance worthy of Hollywood.

Fred Collyer put his head in his hands, trying to remember. A drink, he thought, might help. Diversion. Crinkle Cut. Amberezzio.

He sat up sharply. *Amberezzio.* And what the hell did that mean? *It has to be Amberezzio.*

'Clay,' he said, leaning back over his chair. 'Do you know of a horse called Amberezzio?'

Clay Petrovitch shook his bald head. 'Never heard of it.'

Fred Collyer called to several others through the hubbub, 'Know of a horse called Amberezzio?' And finally he got an answer. 'Amberezzio isn't a horse, he's an apprentice.'

*'It has to be Amberezzio. He's straight.'*

Fred Collyer knocked his chair over as he stood up. They had already called one minute to post time on the last race.

'Lend me twenty bucks, there's a pal,' he said to Clay.

Clay, knowing about the lost wallet, amiably agreed and slowly began to bring out his money.

'Hurry, for Chrissake,' Fred Collyer said urgently.

'OK, OK.' He handed over the twenty dollars and turned back to his own typewriter.

Fred Collyer grabbed his racecard and pushed through the post-Derby chatter to the pari-mutuel window further along the press floor. He flipped the pages . . . Tenth race, Homeward Bound, claiming race, eight runners. . . . His eye skimmed down the list, and found what he sought.

Phillip Amberezzio, riding a horse Fred Collyer had never heard of.

'Twenty on the nose, number six,' he said quickly, and received his ticket seconds before the window shut. Trembling slightly, he pushed back through the crowd, and out onto the balcony. He was the only pressman watching the race.

Those jocks did it beautifully, he thought in admiration. Artistic. You wouldn't have known if you hadn't known. They bunched him in and shepherded him along, and then at the perfect moment gave him a suddenly clear opening. Amberezzio won by half a length, with all the others waving their whips as if beating the last inch out of their mounts.

Fred Collyer laughed. That poor little so-and-so probably thought he was a hell of a fellow, bringing home a complete outsider with all the big boys baying at his heels.

He went back inside the press room and found everyone's attention directed towards Harbourne Cressie, who had brought with him the owner and jockey of Pincer Movement. Fred Collyer dutifully took down enough quotes to cover the subject, but his mind was on the other story, the big one, the gift.

It would need careful handling, he thought. It would need the very best he could do, as he would have to be careful not to make direct accusations while leaving it perfectly clear that an investigation was necessary. His old instincts partially re-awoke. He was even excited. He would write his piece in the quiet and privacy of his own room in the motel. Couldn't do it here on the racecourse, with every turfwriter in the world looking over his shoulder.

Down in the jockeys' changing room Piper Boles quietly distributed the pari-mutuel tickets which Marius Tollman had delivered: five hundred dollars' worth to each of the seven 'unsuccessful' riders in the tenth race, and one thousand dollars' worth to himself. Each jockey subsequently asked a wife or girlfriend to collect the winnings and several of these would have made easy prey for Blisters Schultz, had he not already started home.

Marius Tollman's money had shortened the odds on Amberezzio, but he was still returned at twelve to one. Marius Tollman wheezed and puffed from pay-out window to pay-out window, collecting his winnings bit by bit. He hadn't room for all the cash in the underarm pockets and finally stowed some casually in more accessible spots. Too bad about Blisters Schultz.

Fred Collyer collected a fistful of winnings and repaid the twenty to Clay Petrovitch.

'If you had a hot tip, you might have passed it on,' grumbled Petrovitch, thinking of all the expenses old Fred would undoubtedly claim for his free rides to the racecourse.

'It wasn't a tip, just a hunch.' He couldn't tell Clay what the hunch was, as he wrote for a rival paper. 'I'll buy you a drink on the way home.'

'I should damn well think so.'

Fred Collyer immediately regretted his offer, which had been instinctive. He remembered that he had not intended to drink until after he had written. Still, perhaps one . . . And he did need a drink very badly. It seemed a century since his last, on Wednesday night.

They left together, walking out with the remains of the crowd. The racecourse looked battered and bedraggled at the end of the day: the scarlet petals of the tulips lay on the ground, leaving rows of naked pistils sticking forlornly up, and the bright rugs of grass were dusty grey and covered with litter. Fred Collyer thought only of the dough in his pocket and the story in his head, and both of them gave him a nice warm glow.

A drink to celebrate, he thought. Buy Clay a thank-you drink, and maybe perhaps just one more to celebrate. It wasn't often, after all, that things fell his way so miraculously.

They stopped for the drink. The first double swept through Fred Collyer's veins like fire through a parched forest. The second made him feel great.

'Time to go,' he said to Clay. 'I've got my piece to write.'

'Just one more,' Clay said. 'This one's on me.'

'Better not.' He felt virtuous.

'Oh come on,' Clay said, and ordered. With the faintest of misgivings Fred Collyer sank his third: but couldn't he still outwrite every racing man in the business? Of course he could.

They left after the third. Fred Collyer bought a fifth of Bourbon for later, when he had finished his story. Back in his own room he took just the merest swig from it before he sat down to write.

The words wouldn't come. He screwed up six attempts and poured some Bourbon into a tooth glass.

Marius Tollman, Crinkle Cut, Piper Boles, Amberezzio . . . It wasn't all that simple.

He took a drink. He didn't seem to be able to help it.

The Sports Editor would give him a raise for a story like this, or at least there would be no more quibbling about expenses.

He took a drink.

Piper Boles had earned himself a thousand bucks for crashing into Salad Bowl. Now how the hell did you write that without being sued for libel?

He took a drink.

The jockeys in the tenth race had conspired together to let the only straight one among them win. How in hell could you say that?

He took a drink.

The stewards and the press had had all their attention channelled towards the crash in the Derby and had virtually ignored the tenth race. The stewards wouldn't thank him for pointing it out.

He took another drink. And another. And more.

His deadline for telephoning his story to the office was ten o'clock the following morning. When that hour struck he was asleep and snoring, fully dressed, on his bed. The empty Bourbon bottle lay on the floor beside him, and his winnings, which he had tried to count, lay scattered over his chest.

# ANTONIA FRASER

---

## Death Of An Old Dog

Paulina Gavin came back from the vet with a sweet expression on her heart-shaped face. The little crease which sometimes – just slightly – marred the smooth white skin between her brows was absent. Her eyes, grey yet soft, swept round the sitting room. Then they came to rest, lovingly, on Richard.

'Darling, I'm late! But supper won't be late. I've got it all planned.'

Widowerhood had made of Richard Gavin a good, as well as a quick cook. But Paulina had not seen fit to call on his talents before her visit to the vet: he found no note of instructions awaiting him. Now Paulina kissed him with delicious pressure on his cheek, just where his thick grizzled sideburn ended. It was her special place.

From this, Richard knew that Ibo was condemned to die.

Viewing the situation with detachment, as befitting a leading barrister, Richard was not the slightest bit surprised that the verdict should have gone against Ibo. The forces ranged against each other were simply not equal. On the one side, the vet, in his twenties, and Paulina, not much older. On the other side, Ibo. And Ibo was not merely old. He was a very old dog indeed.

He dated from the early days of Richard's first marriage, and that balmy period not only seemed a great while since, a long, long time ago (in the words of Richard's favourite quotation from Ford) but actually was. Even the origin of the nickname Ibo was lost in some private joke of his marriage to Grace: as far as he could remember the dog had begun as Hippolytus. Was it an allusion to his sympathies in the Nigerian Civil War? Based on the fact that Ibo, like the Biafrans, was always starving. . . . That too seemed a long, long time ago.

You could therefore say sentimentally that Ibo and Richard had grown old together. Except that it would not actually be true. For Richard had gingerly put out one toe towards middle age, only to be dragged backwards by Paulina's rounded arms, her curiously strong little hands. And having been rescued, Richard was obviously reposited in the prime of life, as though on a throne.

His past athletic prowess (including a really first-class tennis game which only pressure at the Bar had prevented him taking further) was easy to recall, looking at his tall, trim figure. If anything, he had lost weight recently. And it was not only the endearing Paulina but Richard's friends who generally described him as 'handsomer than ever'. It was as though the twenty-five-year age gap between Richard and his second wife had acted upon him as a rejuvenating injection.

The same miracle had not been performed for the master's dog. Casting his mind back, Richard could dimly recall embarrassing walks in the park with Ibo, portrait of a young dog at the evident height of his amorous powers. Now the most desirable spaniel bitch would flaunt herself in vain before him. Like Boxer in *Animal Farm*, where energy was concerned, Ibo was merely a shadow of his former self. And he did not even have Boxer's tragic dignity. Ibo by now was just a very shaggy and, to face the facts fully, a very smelly old dog.

Richard stirred in his chair. The topic must be raised. Besides, he had another important subject to discuss with Paulina, sooner or later.

'How did you get on at the vet, darling?' he called. She had after all not yet mentioned her visit.

But Paulina, having skipped into her kitchen, apparently did not hear. Pre-arranged odours were wafting from it. Richard guessed that she would soon emerge having removed her apron. He guessed that she would be bearing with her a bottle of red wine, already opened, and two glasses on a tray. There was, he suspected, a strong possibility that supper would be eaten by candle-light.

Both guesses were correct. The suspicion was confirmed when Paulina artlessly discovered some candles left over from Christmas and decided on impulse to use them up.

'Why not? Just for us,' she enquired to no one in particular, as she sat down at the now positively festive little table with its browny-red casserole, its red Beaujolais and scarlet candles. Then Paulina's manner quite changed.

'Poor Ibo,' sighed Paulina, 'I'm afraid the vet didn't hold out much hope.'

'Hope?' repeated Richard in a surprised voice. It was not surely a question of *hope* – what hope could there possibly be for a very old, very smelly dog? – but of life. It was the continuation of Ibo's life they were discussing, for that was all he had to expect, not the possibility of his magical rejuvenation.

'Well, *hope*,' repeated Paulina in her turn, sounding for the first time ruffled, as though the conversation had taken an unexpected and therefore unwelcome turn. 'Hope is so important, isn't it? Without hope, I don't see much point in any of us going on—'

But Richard's attention was distracted. There was an absence. He would have noticed it immediately had it not been for Paulina's charade with the dinner.

Where was Ibo? Obese, waddling, grey-muzzled, frequently flea-ridden, half-blind, where was Ibo? Normally his first action on entering the sitting room would have been to kiss, no, slobber over, Richard's hand. Then Ibo, an optimist, might have wagged his stumpy tail as though, despite the lateness of the hour and his incapacity, a walk was in the offing. Finally, convinced of his own absurdity, he would have made for the fire, pausing for a last lick of Richard's hand. None of this had happened. Where was Ibo?

Paulina began to speak quickly, muttering things about further tests, the young vet's kindness, the need to take a dispassionate decision, and so forth, which all seemed to add up to the fact that the vet had kept the dog in over-night. Once again Richard cut in.

'You do realise Toddie comes home from school tomorrow?'

This time an expression of sheer panic crossed Paulina's face. It was only too obvious she had quite forgotten.

'How can he be?' she began. 'He's only just gone there—' She stopped. She had remembered. Toddie, the strange silent ten-year-old son of Richard's first marriage, was returning the next day from school to have his new plate tightened. The dentist had emphasised that the appointments had to be regular, and had thus overruled protests from Richard who wanted Toddie to wait for half-term. At first Toddie had taken the news of his quick turn round with his usual imperturbability. But after a moment he had suddenly knelt down and flung his arms round Ibo, a mat of fur before the fire.

'Then I'll be seeing you very soon again, won't I, you good old boy? The best dog in the world.' It was a long speech for Toddie.

Toddie's embraces were reserved exclusively for Ibo. His father had tried a few grave kisses after Grace's death. Toddie held himself rigid as though under attack. Later they had settled for ritual handshakes. When Richard married Paulina he had advised her against any form of affectionate assault on Toddie, warned by his own experiences. For Paulina, the frequent light kiss was as natural a mode of communication as Richard's solemn handshake. Baulked of this, she had ended up deprived of any physical contact at all with Toddie. At first it worried her: a motherless boy. . . . Later, as her step-son remained taciturn, not so much a motherless boy as an inscrutable person, she was secretly glad she was not committed to hugging and kissing this enigma with his unsmiling lips, and disconcertingly expressionless eyes.

Only two things provoked any kind of visible reaction from Toddie. One was crime, murder to be precise. No doubt it was a natural concomitant to his father's career. But Paulina sometimes found the spectacle of Toddie poring over the newspapers in search of some gruesome trial rather distasteful. It was true that he concentrated on the law reports, showing, for example, considerable knowledge of appeal procedure, rather than on the horror stories in the popular press. Perhaps he would grow up to be a barrister like Richard. . . . In which case, where murder was concerned, he was making a flying start.

Toddie's other visible interest was of course Ibo.

Jolted by the prospect of the boy's return, Paulina now launched into a flood of explanation concerning the true nature of Ibo's condition. Ibo had a large growth, said the vet. Hadn't they noticed it? Richard clenched his hands. How long since he had brought himself to examine Ibo? Ibo simply existed. Or had simply existed up to the present time. Paulina went on to outline the case, extremely lucidly, for 'putting Ibo out of his misery' as she phrased it. Or rather, to be honest, sparing him the misery that was to come. Nobody pretended that Ibo was in violent misery now, a little discomfort perhaps. But he would shortly *be* in misery, that was the point. Richard listened calmly and without surprise. Had he not known since the moment that his wife pressed her lips to his cheek that Ibo was condemned to die?

What Richard Gavin had not realised, and did not realise until he conceded, judicially, regretfully, the case for Ibo's demise, was that the old dog was not actually condemned to die. He was already dead. Had been dead throughout all the fairly long discussion. Had been put to sleep by the vet that very afternoon on the authority, the sole authority, of Paulina Gavin. Who had then returned audaciously, almost flirtatiously, to argue her senior and distinguished husband round to her own point of view. . . .

The look on the face of Richard Gavin, QC, was for one instant quite terrible. But Paulina held up her own quite bravely. With patience – she was not nearly so frightened of Richard now as she had been when they first married – she pointed out to her husband the wisdom and even kindness of her strategy. Someone had to make the decision, and so she, Paulina, had made it. In so doing, she had removed from Richard the hideous, the painful necessity of condemning to death an old friend, a dear old friend. It was much easier for her – Richard had after all known Ibo for so much longer. Yet since Richard was such a rational man and loved to think every decision through, she had felt she owed it to him to argue it all out.

'Confident of course that you would make your case?'

Richard's voice sounded guarded, as his voice did sometimes in court, during a cross-examination. His expression was quite blank: for a moment he reminded Paulina uncomfortably of Toddie. But she stuck firmly to her last.

'I know I was right, darling,' she said, 'I acted for the best. You'll see. Someone had to decide.'

There remained the problem of Toddie's precipitate return, the one factor which, to be honest, Paulina had left out of her calculations. She had expected to be able to break the sad news at half-term, a decent interval away. But the next morning, Paulina, pretty as a picture in a gingham house-dress at breakfast, made it clear that she could cope with that too. With brightness she handed Richard his mail:

'*Personal and Confidential!* Is it the bank?'

With brightness she let it be understood that it was she, Paulina, who would sacrifice her day at the office – the designers' studio she ran with such *élan* – to ferry Toddie to and from school. Although she had already sacrificed an afternoon going to the vet. The only thing Richard was expected to do, Paulina rattled on, was to return from *his* office, in other words his chambers, in the afternoon and tell his son the news about the dog.

Richard continued to wear his habitual morning expression, a frown apparently produced by his mail:

'No, it's not the bank,' he said.

'Income Tax, then?' Paulina was determined to make conversation.

'No.'

'Some case, I suppose.'

'You could put it like that.'

'Why here? Why not to your chambers?' Paulina carried on chattily.

'Paulina,' said Richard, pushing back his chair and rising. 'You must understand that I don't exactly look forward to telling Toddie that Ibo is dead.'

'Oh God, darling,' cried Paulina, jumping up in her turn, her eyes starting with bright tears, 'I know, I know, I *know*.' She hugged all that was reachable of his imposing figure. 'But it was for *him*.'

'For Ibo?'

'Yes, for him. That poor dear old fellow. Poor, poor old Ibo. I know, I understand. It's the saddest thing in the world, the death of an old dog. But it is – somehow, isn't it, darling? – inevitable.'

The hugging came to an end, and then Paulina dried her tears. Richard went off to his study, the large book-lined room which Paulina had created for him above the garage. He indicated that he would telephone his clerk with a view to taking the whole day off from his chambers.

One of the features of the study was a large picture window which faced out at the back over the fields to the wood. To protect Richard's privacy, the study had no windows overlooking the house. There was merely a brick façade. This morning, Paulina suddenly felt that both the study and Richard were turning their back on her. But that was fanciful. She was overwrought on account of poor Toddie. And of course poor Ibo.

Paulina reminded herself that she too was not without her feelings, her own fondness for the wretched animal. It had been a brave and resolute thing she had done to spare Richard, something of which she would not have been capable a few years back. How much the studio had done for her self-confidence! Nerves calmed by the contemplation of her new wise maturity, Paulina got the car out of the garage and went off to fetch Toddie.

Of course Toddie knew something was wrong the moment he entered the empty house. He slipped out of the car and ran across the courtyard the moment they returned; although by re-parking the car in the garage immediately, Paulina had hoped to propel him straight into his father's care. As it was, she refused to answer Toddie's agitated question as to why Ibo did not come to greet him. She simply took him by the shoulder and led him back as fast as possible to the garage. Then it was up the stairs and into the study. Paulina did not intend to linger. She had no wish to witness the moment of Toddie's breakdown.

She had once asked Richard how Toddie took the news of his mother's death, so sudden, so appalling, in a road accident on the way to pick him up at kindergarten.

'He howled,' Richard replied.

'You mean, cried and cried.'

'No, howled. Howled once. One terrible howl, then nothing. Just as if someone had put their hand across his mouth to stop him. It was a howl like a dog.'

Paulina shuddered. It was a most distasteful comparison to recall at the present moment. She was by now at the head of the narrow staircase and thrusting Toddie into the big book-lined room with its vast window. But before she could leave, Richard was saying in that firm voice she recognised from the courts:

'Toddie, you know about the law, don't you?'

The boy nodded and stared.

'Well, I want you to know that there has been a trial here. The trial of Ibo.' Toddie continued to stare, his large round eyes almost fish-like. Paulina turned and fled away down the stairs. No doubt Richard knew his own business – and his own son – best. But to her it sounded a most ghoulish way of breaking the news.

A great deal of time passed; time enough for Paulina to speak several times to her office (pleasingly incapable of managing without her); time enough for Paulina to reflect how very unused she had become to a housewife's enforced idleness, waiting on the movements of the males of the family. She tried to fill the gap by making an interesting tea for Toddie, in case that might solace him. But it was in fact long past tea-time when Paulina finally received some signal from the study across the way. She was just thinking that if Richard did not emerge soon, she would be late returning Toddie to Graybanks (and that would hardly help him to recover) when the bleep-bleep of the intercom roused her.

'He's coming down,' said Richard's voice, slightly distorted by the wire which crackled. 'Naturally he doesn't want to talk about it, so would you take him straight back to school? As soon as possible. No, no tea, thank you. He'll be waiting for you in the car.' And that was all. The intercom clicked off.

Upset, in spite of herself, by Richard's brusqueness, Paulina hastily put away the interesting tea as best she could. Still fighting down her feelings, she hurried to put on her jacket and re-cross the courtyard. But she could not quite extinguish all resentment. It was lucky, she thought crossly, that as Richard grew older he would have a tactful young wife at his elbow; that should preserve him from those slight rigidities, or perhaps acidities was a better word, to which all successful men were prone after a certain age. For the second time that day she recalled with satisfaction the moral courage she had shown in having Ibo put down on her own initiative without distressing her husband; there was no doubt that Richard was relying on her already.

This consciousness of virtue enabled her – but only just – to stifle her irritation at the fact that Richard had not even bothered to open the big garage doors for her. Really, men were the most ungrateful creatures; it was she, not Richard, who was facing a cross-country journey in the dark; he might at least have shown his normal chivalry to ease her on her way – taking back his son, not hers, to school. Reliance was one thing, dependence and over-dependence quite another. Still in an oddly perturbed mood for one normally so calm and competent, Paulina slipped through the little door which led to the garage.

She went towards the car. She was surprised that the engine was already running. And Toddie was not in the passenger seat. In fact the car appeared to be empty. She tried the door. It was locked. Behind her was the noise of the little side-door shutting.

About the same time Richard Gavin was thinking that he would miss Paulina, he really would: her cooking, her pretty ways, her office gossip. Habit had even reconciled him to the last. In many ways she had been a delightful even a delicious wife for a successful man. The trouble was that she clearly would not make any sort of wife for an older man dying slowly and probably painfully of an incurable disease. This morning the doctors had finally given him no hope. He had been waiting for the last hope to vanish, putting off the moment, before sharing the fearful burden with her.

Really, her ruthless and overbearing behaviour over poor Ibo had been a blessing in disguise. For it had opened his eyes just in time. No, Paulina would certainly not be the kind of wife to solace her husband's protracted deathbed. She might even prove to be the dreadful sort of person who believed in euthanasia 'to put him out of his misery'. He corrected himself. Paulina might even *have* proved to be such a person.

Back in the garage, the smell of exhaust fumes soon began to fill the air. Still no one came to open the garage doors. Even the side-door was now apparently locked from the outside. Paulina's last conscious thought, fighting in vain to get the garage doors open, was that she would really have to arrange automatic openers one of these days – now that Richard was no longer as young as he was, no longer eager to help her.

A couple of fields away, in a copse, Toddie was showing his father the exact spot where he would like to have Ibo buried. Richard had been quite desperate, as he would tell the police later, to cheer the poor little chap up. It was a natural, if sentimental expedition for a father to make with his son. A son so bereft by the death of an old dog. A son so early traumatised by the death of his mother (a step-mother was not at all the same thing, alas).

And when the police came, as they surely would, to the regrettable conclusion that the second Mrs Gavin's death had not in fact been an accident, well, it really all added up, didn't it? Exactly the same factors came into play and would be ably, amply, interminably examined by the long list of child psychiatrists to whom Toddie would be inevitably subjected.

But Toddie, Richard reflected with a certain professional detachment, would be more than a match for them. What interested him most about his son was his burning desire to get on with the business of confessing his crime. He seemed to be positively looking forward to his involvement with the police and so forth. He was certainly very satisfied with the way he had compassed his step-mother's death.

Richard was also quite surprised at the extent of Toddie's knowledge of the law concerning murderers. You could almost say that Toddie had specialised in the subject. Whereas he himself had never had much to do with that line of country. Richard realised suddenly that it was the first time he had ever really felt interested by his son.

Under the circumstances, Toddie very much doubted that he would have to spend many years in prison. He intended to end up as a model prisoner. But there might have to be a bad patch from which he could be redeemed: otherwise he might not present an interesting enough case, and the interesting cases always got out first. No, Toddie really had it all worked out.

'Besides, Dad,' ended Toddie, no longer in the slightest bit taciturn, 'I'm proud of what I did. You told me how to do it. But I'd have done it somehow anyway. She deserved to die. She condemned Ibo to death without telling us. Behind our backs. No proper trial. And killed him. Ibo, the best dog in the world.'

# MICHAEL GILBERT

---

## Audited And Found Correct

At the offices of Messrs Maybury and Goodnight, Solicitors, the order of departure was an established ritual. It varied only when Mr Goodnight left early, as he usually did: in the summer for a game of golf or in the winter for a meeting of one of the many societies in which he was interested.

When he was not there Sal and Beth started at five o'clock packing up their typewriters and tidying their desks. They would be away by a quarter past five, closely followed and occasionally preceded by young Mr Manifold, the articled clerk. At five-thirty the litigation clerk, Mr Prince, and the conveyancing clerk, Mr Dallow, left, though not together since they had not been on speaking terms for two years.

There remained only Sergeant Pike, late of the Royal Marine Corps, who had the job of locking up; and Mr Prosper, the cashier.

As the girls hurried past on the pavement they could look down into the lighted semi-basement room where Mr Prosper sat at his work. They used to make jokes about him. He was a bachelor who lived by himself, so people said, in a small North London flat.

'Not much to go home to,' said Sal. 'No wonder he stays late.'

'When does he go home, anyway?' said Beth. 'I had to come back once, for something I'd left behind. It was after seven. He was still at it.'

'Perhaps he stays there all night,' said Sal.

They had a giggle about this.

'Poor old boy,' said Beth. She was the warmer-hearted of the two. 'What a life, eh? Adding up and subtracting and that sort of thing all day long.'

'He chose it,' said Sal. 'If he's bloody miserable, it's his own fault, isn't it?' Sal was the cynic.

They were both wrong.

Mr Prosper was not miserable. He was happy. He had a job which suited him precisely and he would have asked for no other.

Since childhood he had been fascinated by figures. He could add and subtract before he could spell. He liked arranging figures, setting them out in orderly columns, correcting and adjusting them, comparing the totals he arrived at. He compared primes and cube roots as another boy might have compared birds' eggs or stamps.

If his mind had been of a more theoretical bent he might have become a qualified accountant. It was a step he had considered more than once, but rejected. It was the figures themselves which interested him, not the intricacies of taxation and company law which he would have had to master to become an accountant. He was happy to be a bookkeeper and a cashier. That was his métier.

He had joined Messrs Maybury and Goodnight thirty-five years before, when Alfred Maybury was alive and Richard Goodnight was quite a young man. He had watched over its fortunes from the earliest days, when no one knew where the next week's wages were coming from, until the happy moment when they had acquired Sam Collard as a client. At that time Sam, who was now boss of the Collard Empire of shops and offices, had been at the beginning of *his* career. Richard Goodnight had done a job for him, and done it well. Their company work went, of course, to a large City firm, but all the conveyancing and much of the day-to-day contract work and debt collecting, inseparable from Collard enterprises, came to them.

Mr Prosper worried about it sometimes. He said to Sergeant Pike, who was his only confidant in such matters, 'We're a one-man firm with a one-man client.'

'Should last out our time,' said Pike. 'And old Goodnight's.'

'He'll take in young Manifold, as soon as he's qualified.'

'Don't care for him,' said Pike. 'Too much grease on his hair.'

They neither of them cared for Manifold, who had been to a famous public school, and wore the knowledge of it like a badge in the button-hole of his well-cut suit.

'Ought to be in some large outfit,' said Pike. 'Doesn't fit here.'

The smallness of the firm was an added attraction to Mr Prosper. In a larger organisation he would have had assistants. He would have been forced to delegate. Here, he could keep his eye on everything. Once a year a qualified accountant was called in to audit his books, for the satisfaction of the watchdogs at the Law Society. He had an easy task. 'I wish they were all like yours,' he used to say. 'Never a record mislaid or a penny missing.'

The early evening was Mr Prosper's favourite time. His papers, like good children, were all in bed, tucked up in their folders. Perhaps he might have, on the desk in front of him, a single sheet of foolscap ruled in double columns on which he would be making some last minute calculations, or he might be reconciling the client balances or adjusting the PAYE records. An adjustment and reconciliation which was entirely superfluous. But only part of his mind would be on the job. His real thoughts were running down other tracks.

It was his habit, during such moments of agreeable relaxation, to weigh up his colleagues and acquaintances, their achievements and failures, their gains and losses, just as though they were business enterprises, each with his own personal balance sheet, which he himself was charged with the job of inspecting.

How would Richard Goodnight come out of such an audit?

There were undeniable items on the debit side. He did a minimum of work to justify the profits of the firm which, since Mr Maybury's death, came into his hands alone. Mr Prosper knew little about his private life, but was aware that he had a flat near Sloane Square, a house in the country, and shares in a shooting syndicate in Kent and fishing in Scotland. He seemed to change his car every year.

Nor was his day an onerous one. His average time of arrival over the past six months had been 10.27. His average time of departure 4.59. Subtract from this an average lunch hour of one hour and fifty-two minutes, and this left a working day of four hours and forty minutes, during which he saw a few old clients and dictated a few letters.

The real work of the firm was done by Mr Prince and Mr Dallow.

On the credit side, Mr Prosper conceded, there were two balancing items. First, the fact that if anything did go really wrong – and the number of things which could go wrong with a one-man solicitor's firm were legion – the disaster would fall on Mr Goodnight alone. The rest of them would lose their jobs. He would lose all that he possessed. Again, credit had to be given for his share in setting up the firm, his part in the early struggles and the fact that Sam Collard's work, on which the firm depended, had come through him. Yes, his account was roughly in balance.

At the other end of the scale, take Sergeant Pike. There were substantial, if imponderable, assets on the credit side of *his* balance sheet. Twenty years of service in the Marines. The confidence which his record inspired. (Three firms had competed for him when he left the Service.) Excellent health. The financial security of his pension. Yes. A lot of pluses there and very few minuses.

In contrast, what could be said for young Manifold? Too much grease in his hair, Pike had said. Too much grease all round, thought Mr Prosper. He had been given his articles in the firm, in preference to a number of abler young men, because he was Sam Collard's nephew. He did the simplest work, and made mistakes which even the girls laughed at. All he seemed interested in was playing games. Indeed, thought Mr Prosper, he spent a great deal more time in squash and racquets courts than he did in the law courts; and for these inconsiderable services he was paid rather more than Sergeant Pike and almost as much as Mr Prosper himself. Moreover it was clear from his conduct and his manner that he already saw himself as future head of the firm.

It was at this point that the well-sharpened pencil in Mr Prosper's hand checked for a moment, moved on, checked again, and then went back.

The task to which he had been devoting himself that evening was his periodic check of disbursement books. These were records, kept by everyone in the firm, of the petty cash which they expended in the course of their duties: fares, searches, commissioners' fees and the like. They were operated on a simple in-and-out system. You paid the money out of your own pocket, noted it in your book, and recovered what was owing to you at the end of the week.

The disbursement book in front of him belonged to young Manifold, and the item at which his pencil had checked was dated September 20th. It said 'Collards. Purchase of shop 220 Holloway Road. Taxis £3.80.'

Mr Prosper climbed stiffly to his feet, went out into the passage, and made his way along to Manifold's room. Papers on the table, papers on the window ledge, papers on the floor.

'No idea of system and order,' said Mr Prosper. It took him some minutes to locate the file he wanted in the bottom drawer of one of the cabinets. He sat down to study it. The solicitors acting for the owners of that particular shop had been Blumfeldts, and it was at their offices, at the far end of Holborn, that the purchase would have been completed.

'Ten minutes' walk, five minutes in a bus,' said Mr Prosper.

The memory which had stopped him was of something he had overheard Sal saying to Beth. 'Guess what, I came back on the bus with Prince Andrew last Thursday, and he paid my fare.'

Last Thursday had been September 20th and Prince Andrew was the name which the girls had bestowed on young Manifold. It was possible, of course, that the bus trip had been unconnected with the completion of 220 Holloway Road, but in any event £3.80 was an incredible amount for a taxi fare to and from the end of Holborn.

Collards were always buying and selling small shop and office properties, and after the conveyancing work had been done by Mr Dallow it would have been normal for the routine job of completing the purchase, paying over the money and collecting the deeds to be entrusted to the articled clerk. There were a dozen files in the cabinet which related to such transactions.

Panting slightly with the exertion Mr Prosper gathered them up, and left the room.

In the passage he encountered Sergeant Pike, who said, 'Let me carry those for you.'

'Quite all right,' said Mr Prosper breathlessly. 'I can manage.'

It annoyed him that the slightest exertion made him puff and wheeze.

Back in his own room he spread the files on his desk and started to read them. From time to time he referred back from a file to the disbursement book. Now that his suspicions had been aroused it was only too easy to detect the signs of small but systematic cheating that had been going on.

In one case completion had been postponed at the last moment, from Friday in one week until Wednesday in the week following. Manifold had claimed taxi expenses for *both* occasions. Then there were the local search fees. Search fees had to be paid, of course, but there seemed to be altogether too many of them. An analysis of the transactions that Manifold had been engaged in over the last six months showed thirteen purchases, eleven sales and no fewer than sixty fees. Mr Prosper's pencil scurried across a fresh sheet of paper, analysing, computing, comparing.

Sergeant Pike pushed his head in and said, 'I'm off. I'll leave the front door on the latch. Bang it as you go out.' He spotted the pile of files and peered at the notes Mr Prosper was making.

'Has our golden boy been putting his foot in it again?'

'Yes,' said Mr Prosper. 'I really think he has.'

He was a man who liked to take his time and move slowly. He needed incontrovertible proof.

Next morning he had a word with Sal. He realised that one member of the staff would be unlikely to incriminate another, and he had to proceed with craft.

Fortunately, he had found, in the girl's own disbursement book, an item for a single bus fare to the Bank of England dated September 20th, and described, in her school-girl writing, as 'Documents by hand'.

He said to her, 'I've been checking these books. Surely you've been undercharging. Why only a single bus fare? Did you walk back?'

Sal thought about it, and said, 'No, that's quite right. Thursday afternoon, Mr Manifold paid my fare. He got on at St Paul's. We came back together.'

'Ah, that accounts for it,' said Mr Prosper, handing her back the book. It did, in fact, account for it. The completion had been that afternoon. Blumfeldt's office was within a stone's throw of St Paul's.

His next call was on Mr Dallow, a precise and solemn man with the air of an undertaker. He said, 'I've been looking through these disbursement books, and I've been puzzled by all these references to local search fees. Could you explain about that?'

'I usually get the articled clerk to do the local searches. Something wrong with them?'

'Nothing wrong, no. I wondered if you could explain. Just exactly what *are* local search fees? How many do you have to make?'

'That depends. Normally, one Borough Council and one County Council. If you're dealing with a County Borough, of course, you only have to make one search.'

'I see,' said Mr Prosper. He had been wondering whether it would be safe to take Mr Dallow fully into his confidence. He decided to do so. Mr Dallow was the soul of discretion.

He pushed the disbursement book across. Mr Dallow cast an eye down the entries, and uttered a series of 'tuts' and 'tchks' like an electric kettle coming to the boil.

He said, 'This is nonsense, absolute nonsense. Purchase of Malpas House. Three search fees! Why, that sale never went through at all. It was cancelled before it even started. And what's this? Six separate searches for 3, 5 and 7 Caxton House. They're all flats in the same block, and St Alban's is a County Borough. One search would have covered the lot. What's the boy playing at?'

'I should hardly describe it as "play",' said Mr Prosper coldly.

'And why wasn't it picked up in the bill?'

'It wasn't picked up,' said Mr Prosper, 'because they were all Collards transactions. Instead of sending them a separate bill for each one, as we should do, we debit them quarterly with all their costs for the last three months. I've often pointed out to Mr Goodnight that this was a slack and dangerous way of doing business and likely to lead to errors.'

'Which it has.'

'Not errors, Dallow. Systematic fraud.'

'We shall have to tell Mr Goodnight.'

'I'd rather you said nothing about it until I've had a word with Manifold. He might have some explanation.'

But Mr Prosper did not say this as though he believed it.

In the luncheon interval he left a note on Manifold's desk, *I would like to see you about your disbursement book. Please look in at 5.30 this evening. J.P.*

'Well,' said Manifold. 'So what's it all about? I hope it's not going to take too long. I've got a court booked for six o'clock.'

He indicated the handle of the squash racquet sticking out of the top of his briefcase. He did not seem at all apprehensive.

'How long it takes depends entirely on you,' said Mr Prosper. He had the offending disbursement book on the desk in front of him, and had marked a dozen places in it with slips of paper. 'I'd like an explanation, if there is an explanation, of some of these sums of money you've been claiming.'

'What do you mean, explanation? They're my petty cash expenses. Fares and so on.'

'Money you've actually spent.'

Manifold looked at him for a long moment, and then burst into laughter. It had quite a genuine ring about it. 'You've been snooping,' he said. He picked up the book and started to look at the entries which Mr Prosper had marked. Occasionally he chuckled. 'Quite a neat bit of detection,' he said, 'but you've missed one or two. Those commissioners' fees – four pound twenty. That was a bit of a try on. And a couple of extra taxi fares there.'

Mr Prosper was almost speechless. At last he managed to say, 'Do I understand that you admit it?'

'Fiddling the petty cash? Of course I admit it. Everyone does it.'

'I beg your pardon,' said Mr Prosper. 'Everyone does *not* do it. Not in a decent, honest, old-fashioned firm like this.'

'Old-fashioned is right,' said Manifold, looking round Mr Prosper's basement room, with its wooden cabinets, black deed-boxes and solid furniture. 'Dickensian' is the word that occurs to me. I think it's time we caught up with the twentieth century.'

Mr Prosper said, picking his words carefully, 'Nineteenth, twentieth or twenty-first century, it makes no difference. Honesty is still honesty, and dishonesty is dishonesty.'

'And realism is realism,' said Manifold. He had perched himself on the corner of the desk, and seemed to have forgotten the urgency of his appointment on the squash court. 'Have you ever worked out exactly what the effect of a transaction like that is?' He tapped the disbursement book. 'The effect on the client, I mean.'

'The effect is that, if he knew about it, he'd realise he was being cheated.'

'You're still not thinking about this realistically. Look. Suppose I help myself to a hundred pounds in this way. Everything I claim appears as an item in the Collard Company bill. Right?'

Mr Prosper said nothing.

'It's an expense, and allowable for tax in the accounts of the company. Corporation tax at fifty-two per cent. Then the profits of the company pay tax and surtax when they come into Uncle Sam's hands. Do you know, he once told me that for every hundred pounds that goes in at the bottom, he can only count on touching ten pounds when it comes out at the top?'

Mr Prosper still said nothing.

'Work it out for yourself. If I asked Uncle Sam for a hundred pounds – which I'm sure he'd be very happy to give me – it would cost him a thousand quid to raise it. Right? If, on the other hand, I work it this way, it costs him ten pounds, and the Chancellor of the Exchequer provides the other ninety, and loses nine hundred into the bargain.'

His face white, his mouth compressed to a thin line, Mr Prosper said, 'Fraud is fraud, however you wrap it up.'

Manifold got up off the desk. As he did so, Mr Prosper realised that he was a large and athletic young man, twice as big and twice as strong as he was himself. It also occurred to him that they might be alone in the building. Sergeant Pike sometimes got away early, leaving him to lock the street door. However, he had no intention of climbing down. He waited for Manifold's answer, which came in a very different way from the light and chaffing tone he had employed up to that point.

He said, 'What are you going to do about it?'

'I shall report it.'

'Who to?'

'Mr Goodnight.'

'And what do you suppose he'll do about it?'

'Inform the Law Society and have your articles cancelled.'

'He won't.'

'He'll have no option.'

'He won't do it, for two good reasons. The first is that, if he did, he'd lose all the Collard work. I'd guarantee that.'

Mr Prosper looked at him with loathing.

'The second reason is that, if old Goodnight starts stirring up trouble, he may find it bounces. Have you ever wondered why you don't look after his private tax? Why he handles it all himself?'

'What are you getting at?'

'How do you imagine he lives at the rate he does? Two houses, two cars, an expensive wife, shooting, fishing. He's been fiddling his tax for years. And the best of British luck to him.'

By this time Mr Prosper was profoundly shocked and almost speechless. If Manifold had cut short the interview at this point, the worst might not have occurred. Unfortunately, he changed gear, and said, with an unhappy assumption of bonhomie, 'Come along, old chap, don't be an ass. Forget the whole thing.'

Mr Prosper took a deep breath, and said, 'No.'

'You're determined to make a fuss?' Manifold's mouth hardened. 'You'd risk your job, and the jobs of everyone else here, for a few pounds that no one cares about, least of all the man who's paying it?'

'I won't be blackmailed into being accessory to a fraud.'

'I imagine,' said Manifold with calculated brutality, 'that other people here will be able to find themselves jobs. The typists and Sergeant Pike, and so on. But one thing I'm sure about, and that is that you won't.'

'Insolence won't help you.'

'You're not only stupid, you're old-fashioned. You're out of date. People like you aren't needed any more.'

Anger was having its way with Mr Prosper now. A red-hot, scalding anger that drove out fear.

'That job you're doing, counting on your fingers, it can be done by any school leaver with a pocket calculator. You're not just out of date. You're obsolete.'

Mr Prosper was on his feet now. His groping fingers touched the heavy round ruler on his desk and closed on it. He took two steps towards the astonished Manifold and swung a blow, downwards, at his head.

Manifold had no difficulty at all in avoiding it. His reactions were twice as fast as Mr Prosper's. He jumped back nimbly. The blow fell on thin air. Mr Prosper overbalanced and collapsed, hitting his head on the corner of the desk as he went down. As he did so the ruler shot out of his hand and hit Manifold on the shin.

Manifold laughed, picked up the ruler, and said, 'Watch it old boy. You'll be hurting someone.'

He was struck by the way Mr Prosper was lying and went down on to one knee beside him. He said, 'Come along, get up off the floor.'

The arm he was holding felt curiously limp.

A sound made him jerk his head round. Sergeant Pike was standing in the doorway. He said, 'You'd better get hold of a doctor, Sergeant. Mr Prosper's had a fall.'

Sergeant Pike came over, pushed Manifold roughly out of the way, and knelt beside Mr Prosper. After a long moment he got up, walked across the room, and locked the door, pocketing the key. Then he picked up the telephone and started to dial.

Manifold said, 'What are you doing.'

'I'm calling the police,' said Sergeant Pike.

Cosmo Franks deployed the case for the Crown with the dispassionate care which is expected of Senior Treasury Counsel.

In answer to his questions, Mr Dallow told the Court that the deceased had been on the point of exposing a systematic series of frauds by the accused. Sergeant Pike spoke of hearing a crash, coming into the room and finding the accused bending over the body. He had been holding a heavy wooden ruler in his hand and had put it down as the Sergeant came through the door. An officer from the Forensic Science Laboratory said that the fingerprints of the accused were on the ruler. The only surprise was the medical evidence.

Dr Summerson, the Home Office Pathologist who had carried out the autopsy, gave it as his opinion that although a blow from such a weapon might have been a contributory cause of death, it would not have killed a man of normal health. Mr Prosper, it appeared, was suffering from an advanced cardiac degeneration, a condition popularly known as fatty degeneration of the heart, probably the result of his life-long sedentary occupation.

'If it hadn't been for Summerson,' said Junior Counsel, as he and Franks walked back from Court, 'he'd have been booked for murder, that's for sure.'

'It was illogical, whichever way you look at it,' said Franks. 'If he meant to kill him, the fact that he didn't hit him hard enough to kill a healthy man, and only happened to kill him because he was unhealthy, shouldn't have reduced the charge from murder to manslaughter.'

'He was lucky,' said Junior Counsel.

'It's not the sort of luck I'd care for myself,' said Franks. 'A hardened criminal might laugh off a five-year sentence. Not Manifold. It'll crucify him.'

They walked on for some distance in silence. Franks said, 'And he's not the only person in trouble.'

This was true. When Sam Collard removed his work to another firm, Mr Goodnight had decided that it was time he retired. He had overlooked the fact that this step invited an automatic inspection of his affairs by the Revenue. He was now faced with criminal charges of tax evasion, the certainty of a crippling fine, and the possibility of imprisonment.

'When you think it through,' said Junior Counsel, 'really the only person who came well out of it was old Prosper. A quick death instead of months of hospital and misery.'

'I suppose that's right,' said Franks absently. He was already thinking about his next case, a multiple rape.

# WINSTON GRAHAM

## The Circus

It was Gareth Purdy's first visit for over twenty years and he was pleased to be back in the Old Country for a short time, even though he felt he owed it nothing either in sentiment or esteem. Everything he was and had become he owed to Australia, and that was where his family and his life were. Yet England, especially at this time of year when the trees were just budding, was an eye-catching place; he'd never realised how beautiful, how soft and gentle the countryside was, how warm the people were, how cultured the life. It had all looked different when you were a lad with no money and you stood shivering at a street corner – there wasn't much warmth then.

His first week-end he thought to spend in London looking round the old haunts but his business friend, Jock Munster, invited him down to his country house in Sussex, and when it came to the point this seemed so much more attractive a proposition that he accepted, and they drove to Fontain Manor on the Friday evening.

It was a lovely small manor house, weathered and mellowed by two hundred years and set in a few acres of ground in which beech trees were just unfolding elegant shot-silk feathery caterpillars of leaf. A level green lawn, bluebells, flowering cherries, daphnes, brooms and other plants he did not know gave a profusion of gentle colour which seemed far removed from the sub-tropical rigours of the district where he had made his life.

His host had a charming wife and two pretty daughters, the elder of whom willingly made a fourth at bridge for them, and they played till midnight, whereupon he retired to bed in a comfortable aura of well-cooked food, brandy and cigar smoke and slept for eight hours without stirring – something he had not done for many years. Soon after he woke a light breakfast was brought in for him by a maid, and he ate it, bathed, shaved and dressed and was up and walking about the house by nine-thirty. Jock had arranged a game of golf for eleven, but the only member of the family at present to be seen was the younger daughter, Phyllida, who chatted to him briskly about horses for a few minutes, and then he wandered out into the garden.

It was a superb morning. Remembering the drab, cheerless days of his youth, he cocked a suspicious eye at the palely cloudless sky and wondered if there was a catch somewhere. It was put on for his benefit, no doubt, just to convince him that all those sour memories were mistaken. He was not to be deceived; but in the meantime. . . .

In the far corner of the garden a gardener was planting out some bedding plants, and nearby a heated greenhouse was thick with tomatoes just beginning to ripen. These rich Englishmen, he thought, still did themselves well in a way it was more difficult to do back home. The tradition of employing servants, for instance; living-in servants too. The fact that you could still *find* them. They

218

were scarce here too, no doubt, but they were still *obtainable* and willing to do this work. Oh well, old feudal habits died hard. He'd seen nothing of this when *he* was in England – but it still persisted in spite of all.

He walked across the lawn, hands in pockets, confident, free, well-to-do, wondering if his swing would be in the groove this morning, wondering if the two men who were going to make up the foursome were anything in the same way of business as Jock and himself. As he passed the gardener he stopped a minute watching the man working, and his shadow fell across the soil. The gardener looked up and said: 'Good morning, sir.'

'Morning. Those wallflowers you're putting in?'

'No. Antirrhinums for – for summer . . . flowering . . .'

The man had straightened up, his voice hesitating, and he was staring. Fiftyish, tall, bony, thick upthrust greying hair, heavy jaw. They stared at each other. Gareth Purdy said:

'Good cripes! It's not . . . it's not Tom? . . .'

'Gareth? Is it Gareth? Yes, I can see it is! If there wasn't any other way I'd know. . . .'

'How?'

'By the scar on your chin! When you fell off that bike you borrowed from Bill Carter. . . .'

'Good *cripes*! . . . Tom!' Gareth held out his hand.

Tom wiped his hand down the side of his denims and they clasped hands.

'This is a bloody coincidence if ever there was one!' Gareth said. 'I'm only here for a couple of weeks and I thought I'd spend this week-end strolling round the old parts, maybe looking up one or two chums if I could find them; then Jock Munster invites me here for the week-end, and by God if I don't find my own brother digging his garden!'

Tom looked at the younger man, narrowing his eyes as if to see, but what he was trying to see was the boy whom he had not set eyes on for twenty-five years. 'I can't believe it,' he said. 'Mr Munster often has guests for the week-end, but I never thought . . . How *are* you, lad? You look well. Put on a bit of weight but it suits. Doing well? You look prosperous.'

'Yes . . . yes. I'm prosperous. And thanking God every day that I emigrated. I'm in the wool export business. Doing very nicely: wife and two kids; fine house outside Adelaide, drive a Cadillac, kids go to good schools. . . .' Gareth's round, high complexioned, energetic face clouded a little. 'You? This doesn't look too good. Pity we lost touch. . . .'

'Oh, I do well enough,' Tom said shortly. 'I was never the one with the brains. This suits me nicely—'

'Brains? I don't know about that! When I was a tiny kid I thought you knew everything – especially after Dad died. I know you found things a bit hard, but then we all did. You had Mum to consider – and you only eleven, was it?'

'Yes. Near twelve. And you six. Seems a long time ago.'

'Look, we must have a talk sometime. I'm playing golf later this morning, but after lunch – you'll be here then?'

'No, I knock off at twelve. But I'm just down the lane. First cottage. I'll be there all afternoon. Make some excuse—'

'Excuse hell! I'll tell them I'm going to meet my brother! It fair kills me, this meeting, out of the blue. It's a small world. I couldn't have believed it!'

Tom scraped some mud off his boot. 'Make an excuse. It's easier. And more comfortable all round.'

'What d'you mean? Why should I—?'

'I mean you're a guest of theirs. Business too, I expect: the Munsters are in wool. It would make 'em feel awkward to think they were employing your brother in their garden.'

'Hell! What do I care? There's too much bloody snobbery in the world, lad—'

'I care, Gareth.'

'What? What d'you mean?'

'I like this job. Had it for four years. Munster's a decent bloke – we get on very well. But we live in separate worlds. I never ask him personal questions – he never asks me. If you've been in Australia, maybe you don't understand this, but I'd rather it stayed that way. Maybe you think it's wrong to have a master – servant relationship in the seventies; but it *works*, see. It works for him and it works for me.'

Gareth stared. 'OK, Tom. Whatever you say. But it seems a pity— Anyway, I'll be along this afternoon. We can talk about old times. God damn it, it's a fantastic coincidence, I might have looked for you for weeks!'

'Would you?' Tom asked.

'Would I? I – don't know. Anyway, I wouldn't have had the *time*. I'm only here for fifteen days. Now we *have* met we must at least have an afternoon together!'

It was an easy foursome, for which Gareth Purdy was thankful because his swing didn't settle into its groove all morning. He developed a wicked hook which brought his normal length down by fifty yards and often landed him in the rough. His partner, tall and easy-going, was not at all put out, and they won by 2 and 1. But his idea of spending an hour or so in the cottage down the lane was frustrated by his host: they stayed at the golf club for lunch and played another round, then when they got home there were people in for drinks and dinner, so it was Sunday before the chance came. He walked round about eleven and found Tom in his small garden tying up some climbing thing.

'Sorry about yesterday, lad.' He explained. 'They've gone to church now. To *church*! I didn't believe anybody ever still did; but I said I'd rather take a walk and here I am.'

Tom took his pipe out of his mouth and looked at his younger brother quizzically. Indeed, they eyed each other. Tom was smart this morning, the smarter of the two, a good grey herringbone suit, white shirt, blue tie: a good looking bony, big man with a taut skin and light blue-grey eyes. Gareth had a flannel check shirt, a brown pull-over, fine quality wool slacks gone baggy with wear – half a head the shorter with a risk of becoming overweight. His face was as open as his shirt, Tom's inward-looking, reserved, brooding.

They went in. Gareth admired, saying Tom had done nicely for himself, while all the time seeing the tiny cottage, the restricted life. Gareth took out photographs: the wife, the kids, that's me at Rapid Bay; Joyce sunbathing; that's up in the Mount Lofty range. Did you ever marry, Tom?

'No . . . I never found the right one. Somehow I got put off early. Your wife – she's not a blonde? I never liked blondes.'

'No, brown hair. But blue eyes. You'd like her. Look. I've been thinking; why don't you come out there and join us? Make a new life. There's still plenty of opportunity.'

They talked about it while Tom made coffee. You're only forty-seven, Gareth said, forty-eight next month: I know. You could start something. I could set you up. They wrangled, but amiably. Tom said no. He was set here. It wouldn't do. It wouldn't work. I couldn't leave English gardens, been growing things on and off for years. Suppose it's been ever since we came down from Lancashire. Remember that time? Gareth shook his head.

'Well, you were only five. I was eleven. Dad was out of work – had been three years. More than two million unemployed in those days. Then he got this chance to move to London on a building site, so he jumped at it. Somehow he scraped together enough to bring the family. Remember the place in London?'

'Oh, yes. Top of the world. How long were we there? Two years? Three?'

'Three. I suppose it had been a rich merchant's house once, but when we were there there were different families living on each floor and one WC for the whole house. Remember the O'Haras?'

'That lot that made a kitchen of the bathroom? Yep. What went wrong with you there, Tom?'

Tom stared. 'Who said anything had? Did you notice?'

'Yep. I used to look up to you in those days. I noticed things. You kept getting into trouble. Was it because of Dad dying?'

'No . . . nothing to do with that. Anyway I never got into much trouble.'

'We had the probation officer round, I remember. Breaking and entering or something, wasn't it?'

Tom stirred the coffee. 'You remember too much. No, it was nothing to do with Dad. Did you know . . . ?'

'Know what?'

'Oh, never mind. Sugar?'

'Thanks.'

They sat and talked of domestic things, how their lives had gone since they had separated, Gareth of his early struggles in Australia, his marriage, the luck that seemed to bring: he'd never looked back; Tom of two years in the army – 'never did take much to discipline' – casual labour, factory work – 'you get so bored you'd do anything for a kick' – two brushes with the police but never inside, bound over, gardener in a London park, garage foreman in Brighton, then this job. 'Suits fine. I get a lot of fun. Shan't stay here all my life but maybe another couple of years. I've a fancy for Scotland – west coast. Good gardens there.'

Gareth said: 'What were you going to say just now?'

'When?'

'I thought you were going to say something about when we were kids in that top-floor flat.'

'Yes, I was. Well, yes, I was.'

Tom sipped his coffee and blew the steam away with his breath. Outside a bird was trilling as if it was early morning. He said: 'D'you remember that attic flat? D'you remember it looked out over the Common? It was quite a thrill to me, coming from a back-to-back in Gorton, coming from the provinces like that into the centre of the largest city in the world and – and you moved into the *country*! Houses and traffic all round, of course, but plane trees and beeches and Norway maples, and all the birds: robins, sparrows, finches. And thrushes singing just like that one now!'

'I remember the sloping ceiling,' Gareth said. 'From my bunk I could reach up and touch the rafters without even sitting up in bed.'

'Did you know,' Tom said, 'that I saw a murder?'

Gareth stared. 'What? When? In that house?'

Tom was silent for a while. 'Nay,' he said at length, 'not in the house. Outside . . I've never told anyone this before. . . . .'

'Good cripes! Why didn't you? When was it? Was I there?'

'You were there – asleep.'

There was another silence. 'Here, have one of mine,' Gareth said, as he saw his brother groping for his pipe.

Tom waved away the cheroots. 'Thanks, no.' He fumbled with his tobacco pouch. 'When we got to that house I tell you I was taken by being almost in the country, overlooking that Common. I'd often sit there after school – sit on a stool looking through the low window – watching the traffic and kids kicking a ball about on the worn grass, and courting couples, and young marrieds pushing prams, and dogs bounding about and lifting their legs, and birds fluttering and fighting, and once in a while an aeroplane in the sky. It was as good as a free entertainment.'

'Hadn't you been sick?'

'Oh, you remember that. Yes, I'd had polio – you'd never think it to look at me these days – but that time I was getting over it and my legs were weak. So I didn't play much. I used to sit and watch and dream. You know how kids dream – think they're going to be tops in some world: cricket or football, or a sea captain or a daring aviator. Those were the days when people still made records with solo flights. . . . I was a romantic. Remember the circus?'

Gareth narrowed his eyes. 'No.'

'That's where it began. The circus that came to the Common. Of course I'd seen the posters stuck on telegraph poles, and there'd been talk of it at school, but I hardly believed it until I saw it for real. It came every year, the lads said, sometimes oftener, and it was a big circus not just a little travelling job. I'd never seen a circus until then, not in real life, though I'd seen one once in the movies. It came twice while we were there. You don't remember it at all?'

'Think I have a vague recollection.' Gareth watched his brother's fingers, grown big and clumsy with their daily work, pushing the tobacco down into the old pipe.

'One day just before Christmas I came home from school and found they'd that moment arrived. I banged and clattered up three flights of stairs and saw them assembling right in the bare patch of ground among the trees almost just across the street from our house. It was great watching, that evening. The big smart caravans and decorated trailers crawling in one by one, making a circle like a – like a well-drilled army of snails. Then inside – in the centre of the circle – up went the big top, up it went, up and up. All through the night I stayed awake listening to the thump and bang of hammers, the beat of the engines, the rattle of chains, the shouts of men. Every now and then I'd slip out of bed and take another look. And sure enough there'd be something fresh to see, another pole up, another spread of canvas luffed out like a sail in the wind. . . .

'Dad had a proper pinched look – d'you remember it? I suppose you'd hardly remember *him*, would you?'

'Oh, yes, I do.'

'His look wasn't just from not eating enough but it was a sort of Labour Exchange look, a look a lot of men had in those days; of course he was a sick man then, and he hadn't much time for me and my enthusiasms. Going to the circus? We hadn't a penny to spare, let alone sixpence like the cheapest seats were.'

Tom struck a match. 'I didn't much care. Because I saw it all from the window – free. Once or twice I lifted you up, but usually you were too hungry to stay long – you had a rare appetite in those days. Mum said there was no filling you.'

'Just the same now. But now I have to watch it!'

'From that window I could see – see all the animals in their cages, and the horses, all the brown and white horses marked like maps. I used to think, if I could learn geography that way! . . .' Tom's face appeared out of a cloud of smoke. 'And there were four elephants standing in a line with chains on their feet; they were exercised daily, of course, and taken in for performances, but most of the time they stood there just rocking back and forth, all together. They never moved their feet much but just swayed in unison like, like four rubber dolls. Next to them, in the cages, were the lions and the tigers and the chimpanzees. Along the other side were the camels and the Shetland ponies and of course the seals. Even when it was dark you could still watch because of the lights they used. Sometimes early morning they'd put on an unrehearsed show – it might have been for my benefit. . . .'

Tom struck another match and held it to his pipe. His pale grey eyes were far gone in reminiscence.

'You were saying about a murder—'

'You could see the clowns, ready made up so far as the top half went, but still in sandals and grey flannel trousers. And the tightrope walker in her sequins emptying a pail of slops. And the cowboys playing cards. And when the show began all the piebald horses would come out and form into a line without a word and go into the tent as if they were soldiers at a drill. But the best thing of all, lad, was seeing the seals go in. They'd all come out of their cages, flopping down the wooden steps, and go hobbling across clapping their flippers. There was one always had to sing a song accompanied by the band, and I'd wait at night for the noise because you could hear it all over the place and this would be a sign their turn was over. And the very first night, lad, I fell in love.'

Gareth finished his coffee and waved away an offer of more. 'You, Tom? Then? Why—'

'Oh, I know it sounds daft, and daft it no doubt was, at my age then. But from the distance of our attic she looked hardly more than a kid herself. Her name was Tilly and she rode two of the piebald horses bareback. It was a turn called Rita and Tilly, and the other was much older; I thought it was probably mother and daughter. She was blonde, this girl, with long fair hair usually done in pigtails; but for her turn she wore it loose, and it fell almost to her waist and spread out like a fan when she swung on and off the horses. She'd got blue eyes and a short nose and long beautiful legs that made her look like a colt herself. Every day I watched her practising, and to me, you know, she was like a fairy out of another world, infinitely beautiful and infinitely remote. I got to see her in the end.'

'D'you mean in the ring?'

'Yes. I stole some sweets in Bray's sweetshop and sold 'em at school – I made ninepence altogether. I went the first Saturday – they stayed two weeks that time because of Christmas. When I actually saw her in the ring, doing the things I'd watched her practising – and a lot of other things besides, under the arc lights, twisting and turning and jumping and balancing – all my romantic notions were boosted to the limit. She really did look young, terribly young to have so much cleverness and poise; she was *very* pretty; she became a sort of dream girl. A dream girl. You all right here or shall we go back in the garden?'

'I'm OK.'

'Rita was nothing – did a few tricks but often as not just directed the horses for Tilly. Tilly was the star. And after watching for a few days from the window I changed my mind about Rita being the mother. Tilly had her own caravan. Rita lived in another caravan with the ringmaster and two little boys, so I reckoned they were a married family and Tilly was on her own. But that was where the trouble began. Two men were courting Tilly. At least two, but maybe more. It was two I noticed. But she was very popular, see, and everybody liked her. One or another would always be coming to talk at her doorway. She was always flitting around teasing or jollying people. But these two. One was a clown, big, heavy, clumsy, did a lot of falling about in the ring, but when he took the white off his face he wasn't a bad looking bloke, fair-haired, bit German looking. The other was one of the tightrope walkers, slim, dark, elegant like, fancied himself, you know. They'd been at odds more than once. Tilly didn't seem to have any preference, seemed to laugh at them both. But then she laughed at most things. Then this night, it was the second Monday, the show was over, everybody'd eaten and cleaned up and the arc lights were out and most of the lights were going out in the caravans, and I was just sitting at the window in my overcoat and thick stockings watching the single light in Tilly's caravan and wondering whether I should ever see her close to – I mean really close, because the sixpenny seats had been at the back. And suddenly there was this commotion in there.'

'In her caravan?'

'Yes. I think it was more a change in the light at first, more than actual noise. In fact, there wasn't really *ever* much noise, I suppose, but almost at once the door burst open and two men tumbled down the steps fighting. It was these two. And it was real fighting – to hurt, to kill – you hardly ever see that. And Tilly came to the door and stood there with her hand to her mouth watching them. It couldn't have lasted more than two, three minutes. If that. It was like an explosion, see. The big clown was winning, I thought, laying into the dark bloke, got him on the ground. Then they rolled over and a knife flashed, and suddenly it was over. And the clown was flat on his back, writhing like in slow motion, and the tightrope man got up with the knife still in his hand. And nothing moved for about twenty seconds, and then the clown lay still and the tightrope man dropped his knife and Tilly skimmed down the steps and into his arms. . . .'

Tom took his pipe out of his mouth and looked at the stem. Then he wiped either side of his hand with it and put the pipe back.

'In another half minute there were six or seven standing round – those that had been wakened by the struggle: the ringmaster, Rita, two clowns, a dwarf, the fat woman. A couple of them bent down looking at the clown. Pretty soon they straightened up; there was nothing to be done. The ringmaster took charge, just like he did in the ring. He turned on Tilly and the tightrope man, demanding an explanation. At least, that's what it looked like, and I could see Tilly defending the tightrope man, gesturing towards her caravan; you could almost see what she was saying: the clown forced himself in there, Tightrope came to protect me. They must have talked for an hour. Two others joined them – the lion tamer who'd been wakened because his lions were restless, the tightrope man's partner. There was a lot of angry talk one way or the other, angry accusations and angry denials, but you could see the ringmaster all the time holding up his hand to keep their voices down. He didn't want the whole circus roused. And now and then he'd glance up at the windows of the houses, wondering if anyone had seen. I'd no idea what he was going to do. At first I couldn't believe the clown was dead – it was too easy, killing someone like that – I expected him to sit up and join in the quarrel. Then when he didn't and I saw he really wasn't going to I waited for them to call the police. But they didn't do that either. It was cold in that bedroom and I was shivering, but maybe it wasn't all just the cold. I thought several times of waking you to come and look, but I knew you were too young and would only wail and whimper.' Tom stopped. 'Ah, well, it was a long time ago. Telling you brings it all back. What time is it?'

'Time? Now? Er, half-eleven.'

'Oh, there's plenty of time then. They'll not be back till after twelve. Sure you won't have more coffee?'

'Well, maybe, yes. Thanks. What did you do? What did they do?'

'The circus folk? With the clown? They buried him.'

'Where?'

'Right there. On the spot. It must have taken them another hour to decide and then to do it, but I couldn't leave that window. They dug a grave in the Common, right at the side of one of the caravans. The two clowns and the ringmaster and the tightrope walker. They dug a hole and put him in and filled the hole in again, and presently – it must have been near two in the morning – they cleared up the mess. The ringmaster took the knife, the tightrope man went off with his partner, Rita drove a weeping Tilly back into her caravan and stayed the night with her, the fat lady swilled water on the grass to make the blood less obvious. D'you know what they did next day? They moved the elephants. It was only a few yards, but they moved the elephants over the new dug grave. That way the ground was pressed down hard before they left. . . .'

Gareth took his second cup of coffee. 'You never told anybody?'

'Never till this minute. Not for thirty-five years. I don't know why I'm telling you now, except that you're my brother and we've not met for so long and may not meet for as long again.'

'Oh, come, that's not likely now we've made contact—'

'I *thought* of going to the police. I *thought* of telling Mum. After all, they might have pooh-poohed and said I'd dreamt it, but the proof was *there*. I only had to take them to the spot. But Tilly – I was still in love with Tilly. I knew if the police were once involved she would get dragged in, even though she was entirely innocent. Anyway, I wasn't too keen on the police in those days. . . . So I stayed quiet. . . . Of course you can see their point of view. I suppose everybody in the circus would have to know in the end – but no one outside. It's a closed community. Nobody'd miss one clown, see. But if they got the police in it meant not only a scandal, which would have been bad for them publicity-wise, but the loss of another man, and a very valuable one. So they all stayed quiet and just moved on. And I stayed quiet with them.'

'Well.' Gareth stretched his legs. They were a bit stiff from thirty-six holes yesterday. Getting out of condition. 'It's a queer tale. Fascinating. . . . And I suppose you never saw them again? You know—'

'Oh, yes, I did. They came back the following October.'

'Did they, by God? And was . . . ?'

'It's funny,' said Tom, staring out of the window with his pale absent eyes. 'All that year I hugged my secret. Once the circus had gone, of course, the Common was itself again. Kids kicking a ball, courting couples, young marrieds with prams, dogs sniffing and scratching. I used to wonder if some day a dog would scratch something up. But they'd been damned clever, they'd made sure of putting the clown just deep enough. I used to walk over in the long days and stare at the spot, wondering, wondering, thinking, "I know something nobody else knows". Hugging the thought to myself. Of course there wasn't any difficulty in picking out the spot; the grass grew during the summer, and it was that much thicker and greener where the clown was.'

'Good cripes. Because *he* was there?'

'Oh, yes. I wonder someone didn't tumble, but I suppose no one even thought.'

'Well, I wouldn't have *known*.'

'I think I grew up a lot that year, Gareth. You remember Dad died in the May. It wasn't so much what was wrong with him, I thought, as if he suddenly decided the whole thing was beyond him and he was opting out. It left us in a real mess. Public assistance and so on. Then Mum got evening work washing up at a hotel, and we were able to stay on, but I more or less had to look after things while she was out, like the head of the house. At twelve to be the head of the house. God help us all.'

'Well, He did in a way.'

'Not much, lad, not much. You got the best end. . . . Often during that year I dreamed about Tilly, wondering where she was, what she was thinking, wishing *I'd* been that tightrope walker so I could rescue her from a villainous clown who tried to take advantage of her. You know how it is when your mind feeds on dreams. . . .'

Gareth stared at his brother's taut shiny face. 'You saw *her* again?'

'Oh, yes. And how. In the October, coming home from school, there was a man pasting a bill round a telegraph post. I nearly got run over crossing the street to see because I'd recognised the blue and yellow notice.'

Tom said: 'As a matter of fact, though my thoughts ran on ahead of me, they didn't run quite far enough, you know, because seven days later when the circus arrived and pitched its big top again right under our windows there was something I absolutely hadn't bargained for. Never entered my head. The trees were all in leaf and I could hardly see a damned thing. . . .

'At the time it was a major tragedy – really was – something I'd never *dreamed* of. Although Rita and Tilly were billed and I knew they were there and caught tantalising glimpses of them, I couldn't really see Tilly at all – except by hanging round the gate like a lot of other kids, hoping to see her if she went in or out. The trees were everywhere, you know, dense. I could never see her practising or sitting on the steps of her caravan picking at a seam in her tights, I could never see her washing or brushing her hair or watch her riding into the tent to begin her act. And all the other things too: the clowns kicking a football about and sometimes clowning for the fun of the thing; the lions fed; the fat lady eating her supper, the elephants going for their daily walk.'

'I guess I remember that visit now. Vaguely. But I remember the elephants. I remember staring through the railings.'

'Yes, well, above all I wanted to know what they'd done, if anything, about the place where the clown had been buried. I watched as best I could, and I *thought* they'd pitched them in the same place, those elephants, over where they had been put before, but it was hard to be sure. And I couldn't see whether Tilly or anyone went and looked at the spot. I could only suppose they must have, just to make sure he was undisturbed. . . . The circus was only here for a week this second time, see, and so I had to make a big effort right away, and I got in with another lad from school on the Thursday matinée – sweets stolen from the same shop – second crime of my career. Tilly was just as marvellous as ever, and just as remote. The tightrope walker who'd done the deed was still performing. It was all wonderful – and unbearably frustrating. All Friday it was going over and over in my mind at school. Somehow I had to get nearer to her, perhaps even speak to her, even let her know if necessary that I knew her secret but that her secret was utterly safe with me. Mum had talked of going back North to live with Grandfather and Grandmother in Gorton, and I couldn't bear the thought that after Saturday I would never see Tilly ever in my life again. So the Friday evening. . . .'

'Did you go in?'

'Yes . . . yes, but it wasn't easy making up my mind. After all, I was only just going on thirteen, and in awe of the whole set-up. But it got to a stage of frustration where. . . . Mother never got back till half-eleven, so there was plenty of time, see. I heard the end of the show and heard the animals being fed, and presently I reckoned they'd be all settling down but not yet asleep. I left you asleep in bed and hoped you wouldn't wake up. The circus entrance was opposite Titus Street – you remember that – and at the side of it a big car park had been made so that people didn't block the roads in their cars (not much of a traffic problem in those days). A fence had been put up round the circus to keep out the non-paying public; but with all their hammerings and uprootings some of the stakes were pretty shaky, and the wire here and there was rusted and broken. So it wasn't too hard to climb through. But a couple of the lads from school had got in on the Monday and both had been caught and given a tanning, so it wasn't the sort of thing to try on just for fun.

'I wormed a way through in a dark patch at the back, and the farthest place from the big tent, and then I made for the elephants. I realised as soon as I got in that I'd left it a bit late, because most of the things had closed up for the night. Everybody'd eaten pretty quickly, and as it was a chilly night nearly everyone was indoors. Of course it made it safer for me – but it made it that much less likely I should catch a glimpse of Tilly.

'Anyway I went first for the elephants. They *had* been pitched over the grave, as before. The lush green grass was stamped down into a dusty desert. The elephants were still munching a few vegetables. You could hear the regular creak and rattle of the chains as they rocked on their feet all together. In a cage nearby some other animal was making a scuffling gobbling noise. Couldn't tell what. There wasn't anything more I could do. I made for Tilly's caravan.

Tom stopped and got up. His pipe had gone out and he knocked the burnt tobacco into the empty grate. Then he put the pipe in his pocket, frowned out of the window.

'I recall I had a couple of narrow escapes on the way. There were these two small dogs on the loose that I was afraid would latch on to me. Then I crawled on hands and knees round a corner made by two caravans and almost into a dwarf and a negro with tattoos on his face and a bearded woman, who were all sitting eating scrambled eggs or something. But I just ducked away in time. What I thought to do when I got to Tilly's caravan I never quite decided, but the door was shut and a light burned inside. So I just squatted down and looked and looked, hoping she might come out.

'But she didn't. And I sat. And a few people moved around here and there. And some monkeys chattered. And a lion coughed. And I began to get cold. So I went up to the caravan and crept up the three steps and looked in the window. She was in there all right. With a man. They were both naked. Their arms and legs were twined like they were an octopus or something. I suppose it was just the moment – the moment of completion. You hear about folk being rooted to the ground. Well, I was rooted. I could no more have moved away than gone in. Of course I wasn't exactly ignorant, but I'd never seen it before. This was a strange man – that slowly registered – and with my angel, my princess, my idol, see. I suppose I felt sick. I couldn't move. Then suddenly someone gripped me round the neck and by the arm and dragged me down the steps and started shouting and bashing into me.'

Tom's face was tight and grim. He had stopped sharply and seemed reluctant to go on. 'Ah, well, you see, it wasn't such a happy end to my circus.'

'Did you get a tanning?'

'Sort of. Sort of. But it was interrupted. It was this big dwarf who caught me – he was supposed to be a funny boy but he was a grown man when you saw him close to. We must have made too much noise because presently the caravan door opened and Tilly and the man put their heads out – discreet dressing-gowns by then. The dwarf said he'd caught a Peeping Tom. Tilly giggled. Let's see him, she said. The dwarf had been grinding my face in the dirt but when I stood up and she saw how young I was she laughed and said: "Reckon he's trying to pick up a few hints. . . ." '

A long silence followed. The sun had gone behind a cloud and the cottage room had become as grey and lifeless as Tom's voice.

'That the end?' Gareth asked, somehow knowing it wasn't.

'Yes. Well, I reckon so. It's enough for a fine morning. Let's go outside.'

They went out. With the cloud overhead there was a nip in the air.

'I was a big lad,' Tom said. 'Even then. Maybe you remember.'

'You always looked big to me.'

'Maybe I looked big to her. I expect she thought I was about sixteen. I know when her boy friend had gone grumbling off she just stood there looking at me, and she put her arms up to push back her hair and her dressing-gown sleeves fell back and her arms were like long pale swans. And she said to the dwarf: "Fetch him in. If he wants a lesson I'll give him one." '

They walked slowly round the small garden. Two riders in black coats and bowler hats were coming slowly up the hill.

'Cripes,' said Gareth. 'What a thing.'

'I wasn't right for it, not really,' said Tom. 'Being just that bit too young and still half scared.' His face was pale in the cloud and his lips very tight as if they would hardly open. 'She was – a lot older than I thought – twenty-eight or nine probably – beautiful, oh, I'll grant you, but a devil. You hear of an older woman and a young man being the right way for it to happen. But it has to be an understanding older woman, not a devil, sniggering, taunting. She was that all right. What a baby, she kept sniggering, what a baby. Try this way. Try this other way. And so on. When I left, when at last I got away I felt as if I'd been – befouled, dragged through filth, eternally corrupted, like. I was sick three times before I got home. Mum – I don't know what she thought but all her anger seemed to go when she saw my face. I was laid up for three or four days after that, in bed. D'you remember?'

'No.'

'I never saw the circus go. I heard the hammering and the shouts and the creaking of waggons, but I never saw it go and I never saw Tilly again. Maybe it was just as well. It's best not to see your temple after it's – after it's turned into a sewer. They didn't come again while we were there – and of course about nine months later Mum took me North, and you, lucky devil, went to live with Uncle Ted. . . .'

The riders had reached the cottage and as they passed Tom gave them a civil good morning. After they had passed Gareth said: 'Did you ever say anything to this Tilly about the clown you'd seen murdered?'

'No. . . . It wasn't – that sort of a meeting . . .'

'Just as well.'

'Why?'

'She might have tried to shut you up for good, her and her mates.'

'Oh, I don't know. . . .'

'Don't be too sure. After that night you might have been occupying a bit more of the Common. People *can* disappear, even those with proper homes to go to.'

'Oh, I know that too well. But I didn't think of it at the time. But maybe she did kill something in me – something, I don't know what, maybe a sense of the ideal – or – or a sense of love.'

They were silent. 'I remember well how difficult you were that last year in London. I do remember that. Think it triggered it off, like?'

'What off?'

'All that argy-bargy with the police. *I* could never please you either. Nor Mum. Like a dog that's sat on an ants' nest. It was chronic. So that when the family broke up I was desperate about losing her but glad enough I wouldn't have much more to do with you.'

'Nor did you.'

'Nor did I.' Gareth looked up at his brother, whose face, after the last confidences, had ominously closed up. 'But that's no reason why we shouldn't now. Think it over, man. There's a new life out there if you want to pick it up.'

Tom shook his head. 'I – make my own bed. And lie on it. It's time you were getting back, Gareth, they'll be out of church soon.'

'To hell with that. As if I cared.'

'I do. As I've told you.'

They talked for a few minutes more and then drifted to the gate. As he opened it Gareth said: 'I think you should have told the police. You know. After that bitch had treated you like that. What was stopping you?'

'I didn't care. I was too messed up to care. After they'd gone, when I'd got a bit better, I went and looked at the patch again. Often during the winter I often used to go and stare at it. It was like – looking at something of myself. That sound fanciful? Maybe. But it felt that way. Next summer the patch was green again. It taught me something about organic matter anyway – and too much about life, something maybe I've never been able to unlearn.'

Sunday lunch was finished and Jock Munster suggested they should go for a walk. This they did, the whole family, and a white terrier and a brown Airedale and a young man attaching himself to the elder of the girls. It was a pleasant outing for Gareth, though it was long years since he had done anything quite like it. After they returned they had tea, and he and Jock stood smoking at the open french window, talking business and arranging the deal that had almost been completed in London.

Out of the blue, his mind moving wilfully away from what they had been talking about, Gareth said suddenly: 'You've really got a great garden here. I met your gardener yesterday morning. Interesting bloke. He must be good.'

'Oh, Tom Preston. Yes. . . . He's more than good. Been here several years now. You ought to hear Eve talk about him. After the dismal procession we had before. Good gardeners are scarcer than gold.'

'Tom *Preston*, did you say?'

'Yes. He wins nearly all the prizes for us at the local show. The kitchen garden particularly *never* did anything before he came. Soil too clayey, they said. He gets fantastic results. Costs me a fortune in manures and fertilisers. Great believer in compost. What he puts in that heap of his is nobody's business. Look, Gareth, about forward dates, in the present climate, with rates of exchanges as they are. . . .'

Presently they went in as the air grew chilly, still talking business. The drawing-room was a happy family scene. The elder daughter had gone out with her boy friend but Eve Munster was sitting beside the small bright fire doing tapestry, Phyllida was lying on her stomach reading the Sunday papers; one dog curled beside her, the other slept asthmatically on the rug before the fire. Gareth had a moment's nostalgia for an England he had never known. Then he thrust it away from him.

'Have you had him long?' he said again irrelevantly.

'Who? Oh, Preston. Eve, I was telling Gareth what a find Preston was. Yes, we've had him over four years. Came along out of the blue, no particular references, but after all gardeners don't really need them. Very honest, we find him, a bit John Blunt, but nobody minds that these days. And *such* a good gardener.'

'Miracles, what he's done,' said Eve, staring at her pattern. 'Particularly the kitchen garden, but really almost everything. Everybody says what wonderful soil you must have, but we haven't really. I daren't tell them it's all Preston's doing for they might try to steal him.'

Gareth Purdy went to look at some coffee table books near the window. He turned over several of them without seeing the pictures.

Into the enduring, peaceful silence, Phyllida said:

'I see they haven't found that girl from Hailsham yet.'

'What girl?' asked her mother.

'Oh, that dizzy blonde, you remember. Went out the week-end before last and hasn't been seen since.'

Her mother said: 'Young people move around too much these days. They go off without even a hint to their parents.'

Phyllida said: 'The police are linking it with another girl, who disappeared from Eastbourne this time last year. And there was one the year before, the paper says, from Bexhill. They were all twenty-two and all blonde, but I don't know if there's any other connection.'

Gareth did not get eight hours' sleep that night. Nor even one. In the morning they left early to avoid the traffic, but he saw the tall figure of Tom Purdy bent over his border. He did not go to speak to him. When he reached London Gareth hurriedly tidied up a number of outstanding matters and then rang Jock Munster to thank him for a delightful week-end and to say that circumstances had arisen which made it necessary for him to return to Australia.

# PATRICIA HIGHSMITH

---

# Those Awful Dawns

Eddie's face looked angry and blank also, as if he might be thinking of something else. He was staring at his two-year-old daughter Francy who sat in a wailing heap beside the double bed. Francy had tottered to the bed, struck it, and collapsed.

'*You* take care of her,' Laura said. She was standing with the vacuum cleaner still in her hand. 'I've got things to do!'

'You hit her, f'Christ's sake, so *you* take care of her!' Eddie was shaving at the kitchen sink.

Laura dropped the vacuum cleaner, started to go to Francy whose cheek was bleeding, changed her mind and veered back to the vacuum cleaner, and unplugged it, began to wrap the cord to put it away. The place could stay a mess tonight for all she cared.

The other three children, Georgie nearly six, Helen four, Stevie three, stared with wet, faintly smiling mouths.

'That's a cut, goddammit!' Eddie put a towel under the baby's cheek. 'Swear to God, that'll need stitches. Look at it! How'd you do it?'

Laura was silent, at least as far as answering that question went. She felt exhausted. The boys – Eddie's pals – were coming tonight at nine to play poker, and she had to make at least twenty liverwurst and ham sandwiches for their midnight snack. Eddie had slept all day and was still only getting dressed at seven.

'You taking her to the hospital or what?' Eddie asked. His face was half covered with shaving cream.

'If I take her again, they'll think it's always *you* smacking her. Mostly it is, frankly.'

'Don't give me that crap, not this time,' Eddie said. 'And "they", who the hell're "they"? Shove 'em!'

Twenty minutes later, Laura was in the waiting hall of St Vincent's Hospital on West 11th Street. She leaned back in the straight chair and half closed her eyes. There were seven other people waiting, and the nurse had told her it might be half an hour, but she would try to make it sooner because the baby was bleeding slightly. Laura had her story ready: the baby had fallen against the vacuum cleaner, must've hit the connecting part where there was a sliding knob. Since this was what Laura had hit her with, swinging it suddenly to one side because Francy had been pulling at it, Laura supposed that the same injury could be caused by Francy's falling against it. That made sense.

It was the third time they'd brought Francy to St Vincent's, which was four blocks from where they lived on Hudson Street. Broken nose (Eddie's fault, Eddie's elbow), then another time a trickling of blood at the ear that wouldn't stop, then the third time, the one time they hadn't brought her on their own, was when Francy had had a broken arm. Neither Eddie nor Laura had known

Francy had a broken arm. How could they have known? You couldn't see it.
But around that time Francy had had a black eye, God knew how or why, and a
social worker had turned up. A neighbour must have put the social worker on
their tail, and Laura was ninety per cent sure it was old Mrs Covini on the
ground floor, damn her ass. Mrs Covini was one of those dumpy, black-dressed
Italian mommas who lived surrounded by kids all their lives. Nerves of steel,
who hugged and kissed the kids all day as if they were gifts from heaven and
very rare things on earth. That Mrs Covini didn't go out to work, Laura had
always noticed. Laura worked as a waitress five nights a week at a downtown
Sixth Avenue diner. That plus getting up at 6 a.m. to fix Eddie's bacon and eggs,
pack his lunchbox, feed the kids who were already up, and cope with them all
day was enough to make an ox tired, wasn't it? Anyway, Mrs Covini's spying
had brought this monster – she was five feet eleven if she was an inch – down on
their necks three times. Her name, appropriately enough, was Mrs Crabbe.
'Four children are a lot to handle. . . . Are you in the habit of using contracep-
tives, Mrs Regan?' Oh, crap. Laura moved her head from side to side on the
back of the straight chair and groaned, feeling exactly as she had felt in high
school when confronted by a problem in algebra that bored her stiff. She and
Eddie were practising Catholics. She might have been willing to go on the Pill
on her own, but Eddie wouldn't hear of it, and that was that. On her own, that
was funny, because on her own she wouldn't have needed it. Anyway, that had
shut old Crabbe up on the subject, and had given Laura a certain satisfaction. She
and Eddie had some rights and independence left, at least.

'Next?' The nurse beckoned, smiling.

The young intern whistled. 'How'd this happen?'

'A fall. Against the vacuum cleaner.'

The smell of disinfectant. Stitches. Francy, who had been nearly asleep in the
hall, had awakened at the anaesthetising needle and wailed through the whole
thing. The intern gave Francy what he called a mild sedative in a candy-covered
pill. He murmured something to a nurse.

'What're these bruises?' he asked Laura. 'On her arms.'

'Oh – just bumps. In the house. She bruises easily.' He wasn't the same intern,
was he, that Laura had seen three or four months ago?

'Can you wait just a minute?'

The nurse came back, and she and the intern looked at a card that the nurse
had.

The nurse said to Laura, 'I think one of our OPTs is visiting you now, Mrs
Regan?'

'Yes.'

'Have you an appointment with her?'

'Yes, I think so. It's written down at home.' Laura was lying.

Mrs Crabbe arrived at 7.45 p.m. the following Monday without warning.
Eddie had just got home and opened a can of beer. He was a construction
worker, doing overtime nearly every day in the summer months when the light
lasted. When he got home he always made for the sink, sponged himself down
with a towel, opened a can of beer, and sat down at the oilcloth-covered table in
the kitchen.

Laura had already fed the kids at 6 p.m., and had been trying to steer them to bed, when Mrs Crabbe arrived. Eddie had cursed on seeing her come in the door.

'I'm sorry to intrude . . .' Like hell. 'How have you been doing?'

Francy's face was still bandaged, and the bandage was damp and stained with egg. The hospital had said to leave the bandage on and not touch it. Eddie, Laura and Mrs Crabbe sat at the kitchen table, and it turned into quite a lecture.

'. . . You realise, don't you, that you both are using little Frances as an outlet for your bad temper? Some people might bang their fists against a wall or quarrel with each other, but you and your husband are apt to whack baby Frances. Isn't that true?' She smiled a phoney, friendly smile, looking from one to the other of them.

Eddie scowled and mashed a book of matches in his fingers. Laura squirmed and was silent. Laura knew what the woman meant. Before Francy had been born, they had used to smack Stevie maybe a little too often. They damned well hadn't wanted a third baby, especially in an apartment the size of this one, just as the woman was saying now. And Francy was the fourth.

'. . . but if you both can realise that Francy *is – here* . . .'

Laura was glad that she apparently wasn't going to bring up birth control again. Eddie looked about to explode, sipping his beer as if he was ashamed to have been caught with it, but as if he had a right to drink it if he wanted to, because it was his house.

'. . . a larger apartment, maybe? Bigger rooms. That would ease the strain on your nerves a lot . . .'

Eddie was obliged to speak about the economic situation. 'Yeah, I earn fine . . . Riveter-welder. Skilled. But we got expenses, y'know. I wouldn't wanta go looking for a bigger place. Not just now.'

Mrs Crabbe lifted her eyes and stared around her. Her black hair neatly waved, almost like a wig. 'That's a nice TV. You bought that?'

'Yeah, and we're still paying on it. That's *one* of the things,' Eddie said.

Laura was tense. There was also Eddie's hundred-and-fifty-dollar wristwatch they were paying on, and luckily Eddie wasn't wearing it now (he was wearing his cheap one), because he didn't wear the good one to work.

'And the sofa and the armchairs, aren't they new . . . You bought them?'

'Yeah,' Eddie said, hitching back in his chair. 'This place is furnished, y'know, but you shoulda seen that—' He made a derisive gesture in the direction of the sofa.

Laura had to support Eddie here. 'What they had here, it was an old red plastic thing. You couldn't even sit on it.' It hurt your ass, Laura might have added.

'When we move to a bigger place, at least we've got those,' Eddie said, nodding at the sofa and armchairs section.

The sofa and armchairs were covered with beige plush that had a floral pattern of pale pink and blue. Hardly three months in the house, and the kids had already spotted the seats with chocolate milk and orange juice. Laura found it impossible to keep the kids off the furniture. She was always yelling at them to play on the floor. But the point was the sofa and the armchairs weren't paid for yet, and that was what Mrs Crabbe was getting at, not people's comfort or the way the house looked, oh no.

'Nearly paid up. Finished next month,' Eddie said.

That wasn't true. It would be another four or five months, because they'd twice missed the payments, and the man at the 14th Street store had come near taking the things away.

Now there was a speech from the old bag about the cost of instalment-plan buying. Always pay the whole sum, because if you couldn't do that, you couldn't afford whatever it was, see? Laura smouldered, as angry as Eddie, but the important thing with these meddlers was to appear to agree with everything they said. Then they might not come back.

'. . . if this keeps up with little Frances, the law will have to step in and I'm sure you wouldn't want that. That would mean taking Frances to live somewhere else.'

The idea was quite pleasant to Laura.

'Where? Take 'er where?' Georgie asked. He was in pyjama pants, standing near the table.

Mrs Crabbe paid him no mind. She was ready to leave.

Eddie gave a curse when she was out of the door, and went to get another beer. '*Goddam invasion of privacy!*' He kicked the fridge door shut.

Laura burst out in a laugh. 'That old sofa! Remember? *Jesus!*'

'Too bad it wasn't here, she coulda broke her behind on it.'

That night around midnight, as Laura was carrying a heavy tray of four superburgers and four mugs of coffee, she remembered something that she had put out of her mind for five days. Incredible that she hadn't thought of it for five whole days. Now it was more than ever likely. Eddie would blow his stack.

The next morning on the dot of nine, Laura called up Dr Weebler from the newspaper store downstairs. She said it was urgent, and got an appointment for 11.15. As Laura left for the doctor's, Mrs Covini was in the hall, mopping the part of the white tiles directly in front of her door. Laura thought that was somehow bad luck, seeing Mrs Covini now. She and Mrs Covini didn't speak to each other any more.

'I can't give you an abortion just like that,' Dr Weebler said, shrugging and smiling his awful smile that seemed to say, 'It's you holding the bag. I'm a doctor, a man.' He said, 'These things can be prevented. Abortions shouldn't be necessary.'

I'll damn well go to another doctor, Laura thought with rising anger, but she kept a pleasant, polite expression on her face. 'Look, Dr Weebler, my husband and I are practising Catholics, I told you that. At least my husband is and – you know. So these things happen. But I've already got four. Have a heart.'

'Since when do practising Catholics want abortions? No, Mrs Regan, but I can refer you to another doctor.'

And abortions were supposed to be easy lately in New York. 'If I get the money together – how much is it?' Dr Weebler was cheap, that was why they went to him.

'It's not a matter of money.' The doctor was restless. He had other people waiting to see him.

Laura wasn't sure of herself, but she said, 'You do abortions on other women, so why not me?'

'*Who?* When there's a danger to a woman's health, that's different.'

Laura didn't get anywhere, and that useless expedition cost her $7.50, payable on the spot, except that she did get another prescription for half-grain Nembutals out of him. That night she told Eddie. Better to tell him right away than postpone it, because postponing it was hell, she knew from experience, with the damned subject crossing her mind every half hour.

'Oh, *Chr-r-rist!*' Eddie said, and fell back on the sofa, mashing the hand of Stevie who was on the sofa and had stuck out a hand just as Eddie plopped.

Stevie let out a wail.

'Oh, shut up, that didn't kill you!' Eddie said to Stevie. 'Well, now what? Now what?'

*Now what.* Laura was actually trying to think *now what.* What the hell ever was there to do except hope for a miscarriage, which never happened? Fall down the stairs, something like that, but she'd never had the guts to fall down the stairs. At least not so far. Stevie's wailing was like awful background music. Like in a horror film. 'Oh, can it, Stevie!'

Then Francy started yelling. Laura hadn't fed her yet.

'I'm gonna get drunk,' Eddie announced. 'I suppose there's no booze.'

He knew there wasn't. There never was any booze, it got drunk up too fast. Eddie was going to go out. 'Don't you want to eat first?' Laura asked.

'Naw.' He pulled on a sweater. 'I just want to forget the whole damned thing. Just forget it for a *little* while.'

Ten minutes later, after poking something at Francy (mashed potatoes, a nippled bottle because it made less mess than a cup) and leaving the other kids with a box of fig newtons, Laura did the same thing, but she went to a bar farther down Hudson where she knew he didn't go. Tonight was one of her two nights off from the diner, which was a piece of luck. She had two whisky sours with a bottle of beer as accompaniment, and then a rather nice man started talking with her, and bought her two more whisky sours. On the fourth, she was feeling quite wonderful, even rather decent and important sitting on the bar stool, glancing now and then at her reflection in the mirror behind the bottles. Wouldn't it be great to be starting over again? No marriage, no Eddie, no kids? Just something new, a clean slate.

'I asked you – are you married?'

'No,' Laura said.

But, apart from that, he talked about football. He had won a bet that day. Laura day-dreamed. Yes, she'd once had a marriage, love and all that. She'd known Eddie would never make a lot of dough, but there was such a thing as living decently, wasn't there, and God knew her tastes weren't madly expensive, so what took all the money? The kids. There was the drain. Too bad Eddie was a Catholic, and when you marry a Catholic—

'Hey, you're not listening!'

Laura dreamed on with determination. Above all, she'd *had a dream* once, a dream of love and happiness and of making a nice home for Eddie and herself. Now the outsiders were even attacking her *inside her house.* Mrs Crabbe. A lot

Mrs Crabbe knew about being woken up at five in the morning by a screaming kid, or being poked in the face by Stevie or Georgie when you'd been asleep only a couple of hours and your whole body ached. That was when she or Eddie was apt to swat them. In those awful dawns. Laura realised she was near tears, so she began to listen to the man who was still going on about football.

He wanted to walk her home, so she let him. She was so tipsy, she rather needed his arm. Then she said at the door that she lived with her mother, so she had to go up alone. He started getting fresh, but she gave him a shove and closed the front door, which locked. Laura hadn't quite reached the third floor when she heard feet on the stairs and thought the guy must've got in somehow, but it turned out to be Eddie.

'Well, how d'y'do?' said Eddie, feeling no pain.

The kids had got into the fridge. It was something they did about once a month. Eddie flung Georgie back and shut the fridge, then slipped on some spilled stringbeans and nearly fell.

'And lookit the *gas*, f'Christ's sake!' Eddie said.

Every burner was on, and as soon as Laura saw it, she smelled gas, gas everywhere. Eddie flipped all the burners shut and opened a window.

Georgie's wailing started all the others.

'Shut up, shut up!' Eddie yelled. 'What the hell's the matter, are they hungry? Didn't you feed 'em?'

'Of course I fed 'em!' Laura said.

Eddie bumped into the door jamb, his feet slipped sideways in a funny slow motion collapse, and he sat down heavily on the floor. Four-year-old Helen laughed and clapped her hands. Stevie was giggling. Eddie cursed the entire household, and flung his sweater at the sofa, missing it. Laura lit a cigarette. She still had her whisky sour buzz and she was enjoying it.

She heard the crash of a glass on the bathroom floor, and she merely raised her eyebrows and inhaled smoke. Got to tie Francy in her crib, Laura thought, and moved vaguely toward Francy to do it. Francy was sitting like a dirty rag doll in a corner. Her crib was in the bedroom, and so was the double bed in which the other three kids slept. Goddam bedroom certainly was a bedroom, Laura thought. Beds were all you could see in there. She pulled Francy up by her tied-around bib, and Francy just then burped, sending a curdled mess over Laura's wrist.

'Ugh!' Laura dropped the child and shook her hand with disgust.

Francy's head had bumped the floor, and now she let out a scream. Laura ran water over her hand at the sink, shoving aside Eddie who was already stripped to the waist, shaving. Eddie shaved at night so that he could sleep a little longer in the morning.

'You're pissed,' Eddie said.

'And so what?' Laura went back and shook Francy to make her hush. 'For God's sake, shut up! What've *you* got to cry about?'

'Give 'er an aspirin. Take some yourself,' Eddie said.

Laura told him what to do with himself. If Eddie came at her tonight, he could shove it. She'd go back to the bar. Sure. That place stayed open till three in the morning. Laura found herself pushing a pillow down on Francy's face to shut her up just for a minute, and Laura remembered what Mrs Crabbe had said: Francy had become the target – target? Outlet for both of them. Well, it was true, they did smack Francy more than the others, but Francy yelled more, too. Suiting action to the thought, Laura slapped Francy's face hard. That's what they did when people had hysterics, she thought. Francy did shut up, but only for a stunned couple of seconds, then yelled even louder.

The people below were thumping on their ceiling. Laura imagined them with a broom handle. Laura stamped three times on her floor in defiance.

'Listen, if you don't get that kid *quiet* . . .' Eddie said.

Laura stood at the closet undressing. She pulled on a nightgown, and pushed her feet into old brown loafers that served as house slippers. In the john, Eddie had broken the glass that they used when they brushed their teeth. Laura kicked some of the glass aside, too tired to sweep it up tonight. Aspirins. She took down a bottle and it slipped from her fingers before she got the top unscrewed. Crash, and pills all over the floor. Yellow pills. The Nembutals. That was a shame, but sweep it all up tomorrow. Save them, the pills. Laura took two aspirins.

Eddie was yelling, waving his arms, herding the kids toward the other double bed. Usually that was Laura's job, and she knew Eddie was doing it because he didn't want them roaming around the house all night, disturbing them.

'And if you don't stay in that bed, all of yuh, I'll *wham* yuh!'

*Thump–thump–thump* on the floor again.

Laura fell into bed, and awakened to the alarm clock. Eddie groaned and moved slowly, getting out of bed. Laura lay savouring the last few seconds of bed before she would hear the clunk that meant Eddie had put the kettle on. She did the rest, instant coffee, orange juice, bacon and eggs, instant hot cereal for the kids. She went over last night in her mind. How many whisky sours? Five, maybe, and only one beer. With the aspirins, that shouldn't be so bad.

'Hey, what's with Georgie?' Eddie yelled. 'Hey, what the hell's in the john?'

Laura crawled out of bed, remembering. 'I'll sweep it up.'

Georgie was lying on the floor in front of the john door, and Eddie was stooped beside him.

'Aren't those Nembutals?' Eddie said. 'Georgie musta ate some! And lookit Helen!'

Helen was in the bathroom, lying on the floor beside the shower.

Eddie shook Helen, yelling at her to wake up. 'Jesus, they're like in a coma!' He dragged Helen out by an arm, picked Georgie up and carried him to the sink. He held Georgie under his arm like a sack of flour, wet a dishtowel and sloshed it over Georgie's face and head. 'You think we oughta get a doctor? – F'Christ's sake, move, will yuh? Hand me Helen.'

Laura did. Then she pulled on a dress. She kept the loafers on. She must phone Weebler. No, St Vincent's, it was closer. 'Do you remember the number of St Vincent's?'

'No,' said Eddie. 'What d'y'do to make kids vomit? Anybody vomit? Mustard, isn't it?'

'Yeah, I think so.' Laura went out the door. She still felt tipsy, and almost tripped on the stairs. Good thing if she did, she thought, remembering she was pregnant, but of course it never worked until you were pretty far gone.

She hadn't a dime with her, but the newspaper-store man said he would trust her, and gave her a dime from his pocket. He was just opening, because it was early. Laura looked up the number, then in the booth she found that she had forgotten half of it. She'd have to look it up again. The newspaper-store man was watching her, because she had said it was an emergency and she had to call a hospital. Laura picked up the telephone and dialled the number as best she remembered it. Then she put the forefinger of her right hand on the hook (the man couldn't see the hook), because she knew it wasn't the right number, but because the man was watching her she started speaking. The dime was returned in the chute and she left it.

'Yes, please. An emergency.' She gave her name and address. 'Sleeping pills. I suppose we'll need a stomach pump . . . Thank you. Goodbye.'

Then she went back to the apartment.

'They're still out cold,' Eddie said. 'How many pills're gone, do you think? Take a look.'

Stevie was yelling for his breakfast. Francy was crying because she was still tied in her crib.

Laura took a look on the bathroom tiles, but she couldn't guess at all how many pills were gone. Ten? Fifteen? They were sugar-coated, that's why the kids had liked them. She felt blank, scared, and exhausted. Eddie had put the kettle on, and they had instant coffee, standing up. Eddie said there wasn't any mustard in the house (Laura remembered she had used the last of it for all those ham sandwiches), and now he tried to get some coffee down Georgie's and Helen's throats, but none seemed to go down, and it only spilled on their fronts.

'Sweep up that crap so Stevie won't get any,' Eddie said, nodding at the john. 'What time're they coming? I gotta get going. That foreman's a shit, I told you, he don't want nobody late.' He cursed, having picked up his lunch-box and found it empty, and he tossed the lunch-box with a clatter in the sink.

Still dazed, Laura fed Francy at the kitchen table (she had another black eye, where the hell did *that* come from?), started to feed cornflakes and milk to Stevie (he wouldn't eat hot cereal), then left it for Stevie to do, whereupon he turned the bowl over on the oilcloth table. Georgie and Helen were still asleep on the double bed where Eddie had put them. *Well, after all, St Vincent's is coming*, Laura thought. But they weren't coming. She turned on the little battery radio to some dance music. Then she changed Francy's diaper. That was what Francy was howling about, her wet diaper. Laura had barely heard the howling this morning. Stevie had toddled over to Georgie and Helen and was poking them, trying to wake them up. In the john, Laura emptied the kids' pot down the toilet, washed the pot out, swept up the broken glass and the pills, and picked the pills out of the dustpan. She put the pills on a bare place on one of the glass shelves in the medicine cabinet.

At ten, Laura went down to the newspaper store, paid the man back, and had to look up the St Vincent number again. This time she dialled it, got someone, told them what the matter and asked why no one had come yet.

'You phoned at seven? That's funny. I was on. We'll send an ambulance right away.'

Laura bought four quarts of milk and more baby food at the delicatessen, then went back upstairs. She felt a little less sleepy, but not much. Were Georgie and Helen still breathing? She absolutely didn't want to go and see. She heard the ambulance arriving. Laura was finishing her third cup of coffee. She glanced at herself in the mirror, but couldn't face that either. The more upset she looked, the better, maybe. Two men in white came up, and went at once to the two kids. They had stethoscopes. They murmured and exclaimed. One turned and asked: '*Wha'd* they take?'

'Sleeping pills. They got into the Nembutals.'

'This one's even cold. Didn't you notice that?'

He meant Georgie. One of the men wrapped the kids up in blankets from the bed, the other prepared a needle. He gave shots in the arm to both kids.

'No use telephoning us for another two, three hours,' one of them said.

The other said, 'Never mind, she's in a state of shock. Better have some hot tea, lady, and lie down.'

They hurried off. The ambulance whined towards St Vincent's.

The whine was taken up by Francy, who was standing with her fat little legs apart, but no more apart than usual, while pee dripped from the lump of diaper between them. All the rubber pants were still dirty in the pan under the sink. It was a chore she should have done last night. Laura went over and smacked her on the cheek, just to shut her up for a minute, and Francy fell on the floor. Then Laura gave her a kick in the stomach, something she'd never done before. Francy lay there, silent for once.

Stevie stared wide-eyed and gaping looking as if he didn't know whether to laugh or cry. Laura kicked her shoes off and went to get a beer. Naturally, there wasn't any. Laura combed her hair, then went down to the delicatessen. When she came back, Francy was sitting where she had lain before, and crying again. Change the diaper again? Stick a pair of dirty rubber pants on her? Laura opened a beer, drank some, then changed the diaper just to be doing something. Still with the beer beside her, she filled the sink with sudsy water and dumped the six pairs of rubber pants into it, and a couple of rinsed out but filthy diapers as well.

The doorbell rang at noon, and it was Mrs Crabbe, damn her eyes, just about as welcome as the cops.

This time Laura was insolent. She interrupted the old bitch every time she spoke. Mrs Crabbe was asking how the children came to get the sleeping pills. What time had they eaten them?

'I don't know why any human being has to put up with intrusions like this!' Laura yelled.

'Do you realise that your son is dead? He was bleeding internally from glass particles.'

Laura let fly one of Eddie's favourite curses.

Then the old bag left the house, and Laura drank her beer, three cans of it. She was thirsty. When the bell rang again, she didn't answer it, but soon there was a knocking on the door. After a few minutes, Laura got so tired of it, she opened the door. It was old Crabbe again with two men in white, one carrying a satchel. Laura put up a fight, but they got a straitjacket on her. They took her to another hospital, not St Vincent's. Here two people held her while a third person gave

242

her a needle. The needle nearly knocked her out, but not quite.

That was how, one month later, she got her abortion. The most blessed event that ever happened to her.

She had to stay in the place – Bellevue – all that time. When she told the shrinks she was really fed up with marriage, her marriage, they seemed to believe her and to understand, yet they admitted to her finally that all their treatment was designed to make her go back to that marriage. Meanwhile, the three kids, Helen had recovered, were in some kind of free nursery. Eddie had come to see her, but she didn't want to see him, and thank God they hadn't forced her to. Laura wanted a divorce, but she knew Eddie would never say yes to a divorce. He thought people just didn't get divorced. Laura wanted to be free, independent, and alone. She didn't want to see the kids, either.

'I want to make a new life,' she said to the psychiatrists, who had become as boring as Mrs Crabbe.

The only way to get out of the place was to fool them, Laura realised, so she began to humour them, gradually. She would be allowed to go, they said, on condition that she went back to Eddie. But she wrung from a doctor a signed statement – she insisted on having it in writing – that she was to have no more children, which effectively meant that she had a right to take the Pill.

Eddie didn't like that, even if it was a doctor's orders. 'That's not marriage,' Eddie said.

Eddie had found a girl friend while she was in Bellevue, and some nights he didn't come home, and went to work from wherever he was sleeping. Laura hired a detective for just one day, and discovered the woman's name and address. Then Laura sued for divorce on the grounds of adultery, no alimony asked, real Women's Lib. Eddie got the kids, which was fine with Laura because he wanted them more than she did. Laura got a full-time job in a department store, which was a bit tough, standing on her feet for so many hours, but all in all not so tough as what she had left. She was only twenty-five, and quite nice looking if she took the time to do her face and dress properly. There were good chances of advancement in her job, too.

'I feel peaceful now,' Laura said to a new friend to whom she had told her past. 'I feel different, as if I've lived a hundred years, and yet I'm still pretty young . . . Marriage? No, never again.'

She woke up and found it was all a dream. Well, not *all* a dream. The awakening was gradual, not a sudden awareness as in the morning when you open your eyes and see what's really in front of you. She'd been taking two kinds of pill on the doctor's orders. Now it seemed to her that the pills had been trick pills, to make the world seem rosy, to make her more cheerful – but really to get her to walk back into the same trap, liked a doped sheep. She found herself standing at the sink on Hudson Street with a dishtowel in her hands. It was morning. 10.22 by the clock by the bed. But she *had* been to Bellevue, hadn't she? And Georgie had died, because now in the apartment there were only Stevie and Helen and Francy. It was September, she saw by a newspaper that was lying on the kitchen table. And – and where was it? The piece of paper the doctor had signed.

Where did she keep it, in her billfold? She looked and it wasn't there. She unzipped the pocket in her handbag. Not there either. But she'd had it. Hadn't she? For an instant, she wondered if she was pregnant, but there wasn't a sign of it at her waistline. Then she went as if drawn by a mysterious force, a hypnotist's force, to a bruised brown leather box where she kept necklaces and bracelets. In this box was a tarnished old silver cigarette case big enough for only four cigarettes, and inside this was a folded piece of crisp white paper. That was it. She had it.

She went into the bathroom and looked into the medicine cabinet. What did they look like? There was something called Ovral. That must be it, it sounded sort of eggy. Well, at least she was taking them, the bottle was half empty. And Eddie was annoyed. She remembered now. But he had to put up with it, that was all.

But she hadn't tracked down his girl friend with a detective. She hadn't had the job in the department store. Funny, when it was all so clear, that job, selling bright scarves and hosiery, making up her face so she looked great, making new friends. Had Eddie had a girl friend? Laura simply wasn't sure. Anyway, he had to put up with the Pill now, which was one small triumph for her. But it didn't quite make up for what she had to put up with. Francy was crying. Maybe it was time to feed her.

Laura stood in the kitchen, biting her underlip, thinking she had to feed Francy now – food always shut her up a little – and thinking she'd have to start thinking hard, now that she could think, now that she was fully awake. Good God, life couldn't just go on like this, could it? She'd doubtless lost the job at the diner, so she'd have to find another, because they couldn't make it on Eddie's pay alone. *Feed Francy.*

The doorbell rang. Laura hesitated briefly, then pushed the release button. She had no idea who it was.

Francy yelled.

'All *right!*' Laura snapped, and headed for the fridge.

A knock on the door.

Laura opened the door. It was Mrs Crabbe.

# JANE AIKEN HODGE

Suicide, Or Murder

All night the wind had blown, savaging the house, tearing last leaves from the beech trees above it, slashing rain across the bedroom windows. Morning brought merely a slackening of darkness. 'I can't,' she said, when the alarm clock screamed on the far side of the bed.

'Again?' But he swung his legs out of bed and reached to turn on the overhead light.

'Don't. It hurts my eyes.'

James said something under his breath, picked up his clothes and vanished into the bathroom. Presently he would bring her a cup of tea, as he had on all the other mornings since her miscarriage, when she could not bring herself to get up, kiss her goodbye, and hurry down to get out the car for the drive to London. She ought to comb her hair, make herself presentable for him. But, 'I can't,' she told herself again, and pulled the bedclothes round her face.

When he brought the tea, she was half asleep, but pulled herself up reluctantly in the untidy bed. 'I didn't sleep all night,' she said. 'That wind. Put it on the table, would you?'

'Yes.' The saucer clicked sharply on the dusty table. 'Anything you'd like from town?'

'No thanks. What would I want? What shall I ever want?'

'God knows.' He picked up her old dressing-gown from the floor and dropped it on the bed. 'Have a good day. I'll be home about seven, I hope.'

'As late as that?' They had had this argument every day since she had left her job on doctor's orders and they had moved down here.

'I'm afraid so. Shall I take a run up to Smithfield at lunch time and get us a bit of steak?'

'Oh, no,' she shuddered. 'Too bloody. I'm sure there's something in the freezer.'

'Another TV snack? Oh, very well . . . Goodbye.' He was gone. It was a minute before she realised that he had forgotten to kiss her. She cried a little, sorry for herself, found the tea was cold, and dozed off again. Presently it would be eleven o'clock; time to get up and have her first drink of the day. Her mind was just comfortably blurring into sleep again when Ginger landed with a thud on the bed. Ginger was hungry. James must have forgotten to feed him. Characteristic. Thoughtless; inconsiderate . . . Ginger meant to be fed. He walked round and round her head, purring, and making little passes at her with gentle paws. In the end, at half-past ten, she gave in and got up.

The face in the bathroom mirror was smeared with sleep and misery. Her hair needed cutting, reconditioning, everything . . . Why should she care? James never noticed, never took her anywhere. What was the use, marooned down here in the country? 'Six months,' she told the dismal face in the glass. 'Six

247

months' hard.' When had she started talking to herself?

Downstairs, a chair was pushed back from the kitchen table, a half-empty coffee cup sat in a saucer full of cigarette ends. James knew she hated that. How could he? She started through to the telephone in the hall, meaning to call him up and complain, then thought better of it. The last few times she had telephoned there had been something odd about Miss Minton's voice. She had never liked Miss Minton. Disastrous to have her down for that week-end. House warming, indeed. To cheer her up. Miss Minton in one of her aprons being busy at the sink. Miss Minton oh so unobtrusively dusting the sitting-room. Miss Minton driving off with James to the Catholic church in the next village. Damn Miss Minton . . .

At least James had left some coffee in the pot. While it heated she opened a tin of cat-food and pacified Ginger. 'Cupboard love,' she grumbled at him. 'You don't care, so long as I feed you.' The cat glanced up nervously, then settled back to his food. He had taken to cringing away from her since that time she had kicked him on the stairs. Stupid.

The coffee was good, even if it had been reheated. She felt, for the moment, a little better. What had the doctor said? Make plans. Occupy herself. She reached for pad and pencil and made herself think about Christmas. But Christmas meant shopping, and shopping meant London, and how could she go to London? James would have to do the Christmas shopping. She must remember to make out a list for him at dinner tonight. He had been horrid about dinner. 'Another TV snack.' She got up and drifted over to the deep freeze. Steak in gravy. They had had that last night, and it had dried out because James was late. Fillets of cod in sauce. That was the night before. But down in the corner was one last packet of scampi. She would make her *scampi provençale*. James liked that.

Plan something. The doctor had been right. She felt better. She washed up the dishes, noticing that James seemed to have eaten nothing. Stupid. He would make himself ill, and then what would happen to her? She must speak to him about it. Call him up and urge him to have a proper lunch? This time she got half-way through dialling before she thought again and replaced the receiver. Anyway, it was after eleven o'clock. She went back to the kitchen, collected the sherry bottle and a glass and went through into the sitting-room.

It needed dusting. The roses James had bought for her birthday had dropped a trail of brown petals across the piano that she no longer played. Wind and rain lashed against the wide window. She shivered, went over to the thermostat, turned the heating up to seventy-four and listened with satisfaction as the boiler let out its willing roar in the cellar. James always turned the heat down when he got home. All right for him. He was out and about all day. Fresh air and exercise, the doctor had said. She looked down the rain-swept valley that showed no sign of human occupation. Not today, at all events.

It was well after eleven, and she had still not poured herself that life-saving first drink. Even after the coffee, her hand shook badly this morning, and when the telephone rang, she spilled the sherry and swore. James, no doubt: one of his anxious, boring calls. This time she would tell him he must do something about getting them twin beds. 'I can't stand it,' she told herself as she lifted the receiver.

But it was a woman's voice. Sally. Cheerful, stupid Sally from the magazine where she used to work. And she had left her sherry behind. How to cut her short? But Sally did not sound cheerful today. 'Look, love, I'm calling from home. Got the day off. Wanted a chance to talk to you. How are you, by the way?'

The casual question infuriated her. 'I wish I was dead.'

'You've got to snap out of it, love. Honestly! I tell you, I saw James the other day.'

'Well?'

'In a restaurant. A good one. With that pretty secretary of his. Miss Minton. I warn you . . .'

'God damn you.' She slammed the receiver down on its rest. 'Trouble-making bitch.' She said it aloud, reaching a shaking hand for the sherry glass. She had really been feeling better, ready to get started, do something . . . And now Sally had spoiled it all. Jealous of course. They had all been jealous when she had married James. And no wonder. The taste of lost happiness was sour in her mouth. She and James had been so happy. Brilliantly, greedily happy, cramming more into their days and most especially into their nights than days or nights could hold.

James's fault that they had lost it. He had been the one who wanted the baby. Or said he did. Catholic nonsense. Her glass was empty, and she refilled it automatically. Absurd of him to think she could keep on her job through those dreadful early months of pregnancy. Sick, and sick and sick again, retching her heart out in the ladies' loo. Horrible. Never again. If that doctor said once more that all she needed was another baby, she would leave him. Men. How should they understand? And as for pretending the miscarriage was her fault . . . 'Balls!' She put her sticky glass down on the marquetry table James's mother had given them and thought with satisfaction how furious the mark would make him. House proud, that was James. Always fussing about something.

The telephone rang. Not Sally again. If it was, she would give her a piece of her mind. But it was Miss Minton, putting James through. She rather thought Miss Minton listened when she and James were talking, and felt a wild temptation to tell him of Sally's call. But it was all spiteful nonsense. She would not lower herself by mentioning it. And James was in a hurry; he sounded actually breathless. 'I've got a brute of a day, darling, and the worst of it is, I've got to dine a client at the end of it. God knows how late I'll be. I thought I might put up at the club.'

'Oh.' She had longed to have the wide bed to herself, but now felt curiously depressed at the prospect. 'I'd been planning to do my *scampi provençale*,' she said.

'Pity.' What was wrong with his voice? 'I say,' he went on in a rush. 'I meant to tell you, but you were asleep when I left. I thought I smelled gas in the downstairs hall. Better get on to the gas board and have them come out and check the boiler. They'll come at once if you tell them it may be a leak.'

Fussing again. Just like James. 'I haven't smelled anything.' They both knew that she had lost almost all sense of smell after a childhood illness. 'If I call them, they'll keep me waiting round all day.'

'Were you thinking of going out?'

She looked through the glass pane of the front door down the windy valley. 'You know the doctor told me to. Down to the village and back every day, he said. Sludge, sludge, sludge through the mud . . .'

'Mr James . . .' Miss Minton's voice. 'I have a call for you on the other line.' Since when had she called him 'Mr James'?

'Damn,' he said. 'Promise you'll phone them, darling. For my sake. I'll be worrying.'

'Oh, very well. Enjoy yourself at your "business dinner".' With Miss Minton? Mr James, indeed. Perhaps Sally had been right after all. 'Anyone I know?' she asked now, with spurious interest.

'No.' Shortly. He must have caught her note of irony. And then, 'Must go, darling. Don't forget the gas board.' He rang off without giving her time to answer.

Rude. Boorish. Tears of self pity stood in her eyes as she thought of the time when they were engaged, and talked, every day, so long on the telephone that they were the laughing-stock of both their offices. Two years ago? Two centuries.

The day yawned before her. She had been going to marinate the scampi, and make her special rice dish to go with them. And before that, she had meant to walk down to the village and buy garlic. No need to do that now. A boiled egg for lunch. Another one for supper? And blessed early bed, with the women's magazines James sneered at. As for the gas board; it was his idea; let him call them himself.

The sherry was making her rather pleasantly drowsy. Tonight, with no James to come fumbling to bed in the small hours, she would sleep and sleep and sleep . . . He would never understand how badly she slept, maintaining cheerfully that she was always out like a light when he came to bed. Well, of course she was, or pretended to be. They would have twin beds for Christmas, or, better still, she could keep the double and put a single in James's study. After all, if he wanted to stay up till all hours working, the study was the place for him. She got up, half-empty glass in hand and walked slowly across the hall. When had James taken to keeping the study door shut? It was ages since she had been in here. James had told her, rather rudely, she had thought, after the last cleaning woman had left, that he would look after it himself.

He had done so, too. The room was a surprise compared with the rest of the house. Even James's work table, about which she used to tease him so, was comparatively tidy. But what she noticed first was the one red rose in a tall wine glass by the typewriter. Not a late one from the garden. A florist's rose. One of a dozen James had given someone? Kept here where he knew she never came; or flaunted here because he wanted her to find it?

Or all a lot of nonsense? She had always had too much imagination for her own comfort. It had been one of her virtues as an editor. But it was queer. There was something queer about the whole room, come to think of it. It felt – ridiculous, of course – but it felt hostile. Suddenly dizzy, she sat down with a bump in James's chair. Her sherry glass landed half on, half off a pile of papers, tipped and spilled. Now James really would be angry. Luckily, she had never taken off her apron. She untied it and dabbed at the sticky liquid, which was seeping in among the sheets. At least it was nothing finished, just notes for a speech or something of the kind.

She turned the pile over, to mop underneath. 'Chapter One,' she read. Good God, James was writing a book. Absurd. She was the one with literary talent in the family. It had been one of their jokes. Presently, she was going to write a best seller. She had actually started several, but there had always been so much else to do. Thinking this, she began idly to read poor James's attempt. 'Despair can be measured,' it began, 'by the quotient of lost happiness.' Oh, poor James indeed. He was trying to write one of those dreary modern novels he had taken to reading. He would never succeed, of course, not cheerful, extrovert James.

Cheerful? Well, they had neither of them been all that cheerful since the miscarriage. One must mourn one's dead. She had told him that when he tried to make a small festivity of her birthday. Pitiful, really. The champagne he had brought home had been warm, and half of it had fizzed out when the cork blew. And anyway, champagne with cod fillets. What a laugh. And, afterwards, inevitably, James's tentative, intolerable advances in bed. She looked about her. Plenty of room for a divan under the study window, and then, thank God, the argument would be over.

She did not think she wanted to read any more of James's depressing book. Besides, the dizziness was worse. She must be hungry. Just one more glass of sherry and she would boil herself two eggs. But first she must tidy up James's book. It was horrid of him to sit down here writing gloomy stuff like this, and pretending it was work he brought home from the office. No wonder she had felt the room hostile. And as for that rose . . . She felt a savage temptation to throw it away, but picked up her glass instead, and went through to refill it.

After lunch, she curled up on the sofa, and went off into a surprisingly heavy sleep, only to be awakened by Ginger, howling somewhere. 'What's the matter?' she called crossly, but he only howled louder, and finally she got sleepily up in her stockinged feet and found him sitting outside the cellar door. At sight of her he let out another banshee wail, almost as bad as the wind outside. 'Blast you.' She said it quite amiably. 'You woke me up. Think there's a mouse down there do you?' She opened the cellar door and heard the curious clicking, crackling noise the boiler made as it cooled off. But Ginger, who often went down to investigate this, had changed his mind, and backed away into the kitchen. 'Very well, then.' She shut the door with a bang and went back to the sofa.

This time her sleep was full of anxious dreams. She had watched a thriller on television a few nights before, where the bank robbers had been disguised as gas conversion crews. In her dream, she was one of them, on the run from the police, driving frantically down country lanes in her van with the gas board insignia. And all the time she knew, with that curious double vision of dreams, that the thing she was escaping was waiting for her at the end of the road. She heard the police siren . . . No, it was the front door bell. 'Blast!' She sat up, running hands through untidy hair. But why answer it? It would be one of those dreadful, dauntless tweeded ladies who prowled the lanes collecting for their favourite charities. Nobody else came to the house. Or, worse still, a political canvasser? The bell rang again, loud above the howling of the wind.

It was November dusk already, and no lights on in the house. In a moment, they would go away. She settled back in her corner of the sofa. Much better not answer it. A woman alone in the house. Ridiculous to come collecting for charity so late. How was she to know it wasn't a hippy, a mugger, a maniac? She had meant to have a chain put on the door, but forgotten all about it. Certainly she would not go. Too late now, anyway. Whoever it was must have gone. And thank God for that. If it had been one of the local good ladies, she would have had to ask her in, offer her tea. Nothing to eat and the house full of dust. Quite impossible. James would simply have to put his mind on finding a new cleaning woman. He was the one who was in touch with the village. He went to the pub every Saturday and Sunday, and knew all about everyone.

She would speak to him about it tonight. Oh – he was staying in town tonight. Stupid to be so forgetful. A little frightening? Perhaps she would ask the doctor for some different pills. God, if only that wind would stop. The whole house was working with it, like a ship at sea. And dark, too. She peered at her watch. Only four o'clock, but night time just the same. She reached out and switched on the reading lamp, then got up and drew heavy curtains across the windows. That was better. That gave her a feeling of safety. If it had been violence, ringing at her door, she had shut it out now. No one could see her. And James was not coming home. Early supper and early bed. None of that dreary keeping things hot while she waited for the sound of the car on the hill.

She still felt a little dizzy. What she needed was a drink. After all, she was going to have supper early . . . Crossing the hall without bothering to turn on the light, she tripped over the cat, and swore. He would kill her one of these days, getting under her feet. What was he doing sleeping in the hall anyway? Still watching for his cellar mouse? At least he had gone out now, with a frantic slam of his cat door. Good riddance.

She had not washed the lunch dishes, so the sherry glass was still sitting on the dresser. The bottle was almost empty. James must have been drinking it at night. She fetched another from the store room and paused for a moment to listen to rain slamming on the corrugated iron roof. Horrible house. Horrible weather. Horrible life.

Ginger came flapping back in, golden fur sleek with rain, and tried to dry himself on her ankles. 'Blast you,' she said without heat, the first sip of sherry going blandly down. But she had hardly settled on the sofa when he started howling again, out in the hall, the almost Siamese screech mixing eerily with the wail of the wind outside. The telephone, adding its note, was almost a relief. James again, fussing about the gas board? No; it was a strange, rather diffident male voice, and identified itself quickly as belonging to Paul Marchant, the young vicar. 'You're all right?' he asked. 'I do apologise for bothering you, but I called on you earlier this afternoon, and got no answer. I was a little worried. Yours is such a lonely house . . .' His voice trailed off, apologetic, inconclusive.

She wanted to laugh at him down the telephone. All right, indeed. But instinct warned her that it might sound more hysterical than she would like. So he had been her mugger, her maniac. The vicar. And doubtless had been afraid that she really had been attacked. Or – not such a nice thought – had he thought that she might have taken an overdose? She might be a lapsed catholic, but he ought to know she would never do that. 'Oh dear, I am so sorry.' She was pleased with the light note she achieved. 'I'm afraid I fell fast asleep this afternoon. It was such a brute of a night. I must have slept right through the door bell. I do apologise. I hope it wasn't anything important.'

'Oh, no,' he said. 'It just occurred to me that you might be lonely up there, on a day like this. No need to apologise; I enjoyed the walk. It's splendid out when you've got your teeth into it.'

'Rather you than me.' She was tired of the conversation now, and grateful when he rang off. Absent-mindedly, she reached for the sherry bottle and refilled her glass. Something odd about his calling? He had come when they first moved in, and she had given him a cup of tea and explained about being Catholics. Why come again? Did they get together, those men of religion, and compare notes? She doesn't come to my church, why don't you have a go? Or – she drank half a glass at one draught – had James said something to him? She knew they often met in the Four Feathers on Saturdays. Could James possibly have told that very young man that he was worried about her? Asked him to come and call? Involve her, perhaps, in some inspiring local activity? The Women's Institute, no doubt. Hardly the Mothers' Union.

She was crying again, hard tears that brought no comfort. If James had really done that to her; talked behind her back; betrayed her; she would . . . She would like to kill him. It would be the end of everything between them, except that it could not end, tied as they were by the iron bond of their Catholic marriage. Till death us do part. She had a sudden, horrible picture of herself, grinding up the sleeping pills the doctor handed out so lavishly, mixing them into . . . What would one mix them with?

Monstrous to be thinking like this. It was the wind, of course, and the loneliness, and the despair. Without James she would be lost, even more so than she was already. The thought brought her rather unsteadily to her feet. Memories of the red rose in the study had nagged at her all afternoon. Perhaps if she looked at more of that depressing book, it would tell her something about James. Because, suddenly, horribly, the thought of losing James had become a possibility, not remote, not hypothetical, but real.

Sally's telephone call. James lunching with Miss Minton. Giving her eleven red roses and keeping one for himself? Having an affair with her? Those late nights at the office? Not at the office at all? But – James? Pious, Catholic James, who had been so strait-laced before they were married? Impossible. Ludicrous. James and Miss Minton had gone to mass together, that week-end.

The bottle clicked against the glass as she crossed the hall to the study. Odd to be so unsteady on her feet. Something about her new lot of pills? She sat down in James's chair, put bottle and glass carefully on a sheet of rough notes, and picked up the typescript. Despair is the quotient of lost happiness. Blast James. What did he know about despair? He had not lain, all alone, crying with pain, crying with fright, losing their child. Compared with hers, his despair was simply childish. She did not want to read about it, and, besides, the words blurred queerly before her eyes. Too hard work.

Could she be sickening for something? If she was really ill, James would have to stay at home and look after her. Get her help. Move into the study. Make life possible again. Or would life ever be possible again? Reaching for the bottle, she knocked over the wine glass with its single, mocking red rose. Water seeped across the typescript, but this time she did not do anything about it. She was savagely busy, tearing the rose petals into shreds; scattering them across the table.

Hail rattled on the uncurtained window. This room was horrible. It hated her. And she hated it right back. James would know that when he saw what she had done to his rose. Destroy the book, too? Her child. His book. She tore the first page across. But her hands shook. It was too much trouble. Let him keep his childish book. Besides, she wanted to get out of his hateful room, with its bleak, black windows. She was ill. She would go to bed, and James, when he got back tomorrow night, would be sorry. But, first, she must get herself a new bottle of sherry. Defiantly, she threw the empty one into James's waste-paper basket. That would teach him to badger her about how much she drank. In the store-room, rain on the iron roof ground at her nerves. 'I shall go mad,' she said. 'It's too much. I can't bear it.' And, from the hall, the cat howled again. 'Too much.' Quite slowly, full bottle in hand, she moved through the kitchen into the hall, where the cat, lying across the cellar door, raised its head a little and howled again, horribly.

'God damn you.' She threw the bottle. Had she assumed that the cat would run for it, as it always had before when she threw things? If so, she was wrong. The bottle hit Ginger squarely on the head, then shattered on the cellar door.

'Puss?' But the cat lay still, blood seeping into the flood of sherry. Horrible. An accident. What would James say? She felt too ill to care. Too ill even to get upstairs to her room. She staggered into the sitting-room, subsided on the sofa, and let the tears come.

And outside, in the double-glazed hall, the gas went on seeping, as it had all day, up from the cellar, where James had loosened one vital connection before he left for work.

# P. M.
# HUBBARD

---

## Mary

The nastiest house I have ever been in was the Margesons' house at Marlow. It was not in Marlow, but Marlow was the address. It was on the river bank a bit downstream. There was nothing wrong with the position. For the matter of that, there was nothing seriously wrong with the house, not in itself. It was the Margesons who had made it so nasty.

Gerald Margeson had a mint of money, which he got from a manufacturing business at Slough. I never quite knew what he made, and it does not matter, though I cannot believe there was much taste involved. Whatever it was, it evidently sold well, and the company was a private one. I think he and his wife pretty well shared the profits between them. With all that money, if they had wanted to live on the river, they could have got themselves something really beautiful. Instead they bought a house called Riverlawns, which was a brick box built somewhere about 1920. Even that would not have mattered if they had left it alone. As I say, the house was harmless enough, and it had a garden down to the river. But having bought on the cheap – I mean by their sort of standards: it was a place I could not have come near buying myself – they set about making it into their idea of a tycoon's riverside residence.

They built patios and pergolas and sun-rooms and a garage on the road to take their three cars and a boathouse on the river to take their power-boat. The garage and boathouse had timber frames and fancy brick nogging, but they covered the honest brickwork of the house itself with pale pink cement paint. They filled most of the garden with a swimming pool surrounded by concrete amenities, including lavatories and a cocktail bar. One way and another, the lawns were pretty completely covered with concrete and crazy paving, and for all the picture windows you could hardly see the river, except from upstairs, where the windows were small.

It was just as bad inside. The house had little square rooms, which could at least have been cosy and comfortable, but they were got up as if they were something by Corbusier. Not that Gerald Margeson would ever have heard of Corbusier, but I expect Janet had, and the inside was her doing. The Margesons were not vulgarians. They were both middle-class people even before they started to make money. I had known them a long time, especially Janet, and I was fond of them. Also I had reason to be grateful to them. I was never very well off myself, and for all their odd way of going on, they were very kind. It was just that, having made the money, they had very little idea what to do with it. They were not even very happy.

They had nothing in particular to be unhappy about. Apart from their money, they were both obviously healthy, they had a son and a daughter and, since we are all Freudians nowadays, they had a satisfactory sex life. I know, because I

257

almost stepped on it one summer Sunday morning, when I had found no one in the house and gone through unannounced into the purlieus of the swimming pool. I managed to step back and out of sight before either of them, in their preoccupation of the moment, had seen me, but even from the other side of the screen Janet's satisfaction was audible. So there was nothing obviously wrong there, either. Maybe Gerald really preferred his secretary, but if he did, he was rich enough to afford her and man enough to have plenty left for Janet. I could see no reason why, within their terms of reference, they should not be happy, but I knew they were not.

I say 'within their terms of reference' because that is a proviso you have to make about anyone. To me, the life they lived and the place they lived in would have been quite insupportable, but it was very much of their choosing, and I thought they could have changed it if they liked. I was not so happy myself as to feel up to prescribing the means of happiness to other people, especially people who had as much of the raw material as the Margesons had. But at least I had a pretty clear idea what I wanted, whereas I do not think they had. They both at times had this look of slightly puzzled resentment, as if they could not make out why things were not better when everything was obviously as good as it was.

At least they did not, like other rich people I have known, try to achieve what they needed by going on diddling up the house. Riverlawns was saturated with diddle and could not take any more. They just went on living as they were in the house as it was. Perhaps they were both, in their ways, waiting for something to turn up, but if they were, neither of them knew what it was. I do not think they even knew they were waiting. The odd thing is that I was there when it did turn up, and I knew at once that it had.

A girl came up the paved path from the river. She was wearing a black one-piece bathing-dress, and I knew she was a girl from the shape of her bottom half. From the top half she might as well have been a boy, at least at that distance. She seemed very young, pretty well a child. Her skin was very white and her short hair very dark, and her eyes were wide open and very green. We were sitting out by the swimming pool having a drink before dinner. It was the middle of July, and warm. We all stopped talking and leant forward in our chairs, watching her. She came up the garden path quite slowly, looking at us each in turn. After a bit I took my eyes off her and looked at Gerald and Janet.

Gerald was a rubicund man with a round head and small gingery moustache. He was just beginning to lose a little hair on top and put on a little flesh in front, but he still looked very young because of the whole shape of his face. At times he looked so like a schoolboy that the moustache looked false. He looked at the girl with his head a bit thrust forward and his mouth a bit open. He was a man who always looked hot when he was hot, and now he looked hotter than ever.

Janet was his physical opposite, dark-haired and pale and slender. Their two children took after Gerald. Even the girl was gingery and solid. They were both away, the girl at school and the boy at a crammer's, having trouble with his 'A' Levels. The girl on the path could have been Janet's daughter, the dark, pale daughter she had never had. Janet looked at her with her eyebrows up and a small smile on her mouth. The girl came up to us and said, 'Hullo.' She said it three times, once to each of us, and each time differently. She was an odd little creature, and very wary.

Gerald said, 'Where have you come from?' He used the indulgent, rather bantering tone he had used to his own children before they got too big for it. He was good with children up to a certain age. After that they were too clever for him.

The girl said, 'From the river.' Her voice was very high and small, but somehow formed. I wondered whether she was as young as she looked.

Janet said, 'We can see that. How did you get into it?' She spoke very softly, and her voice wobbled a bit. I had never heard her talk like that to anyone.

The girl said, 'From the boat.' She did not look at me at all after that first hullo. She looked at Gerald and Janet. She looked at them both, her eyes going from one to the other, whichever one she was talking to.

Gerald got up from his chair and looked out over the river. Even from here you could not see the river unless you stood up. 'There isn't any boat,' he said.

'There was,' the girl said. 'It's gone on.'

Janet said, 'Do they know where you are?'

The girl hesitated. She rubbed one of her wet legs slightly against the other. She suddenly looked very forlorn. Then she said, 'I – I don't know. I don't think so. I hope not.' She shivered.

Gerald went into one of the changing rooms and came out with a towel. All this time none of us said anything. He wrapped the towel round her, and as he did so I saw the top of her body was, only just but unmistakably, a girl's. Then Janet got up and went to her. She put an arm round her and brought her over and sat her in a chair. Then she stood there, looking down at her. 'Run away?' she said, and the girl nodded.

'Why? Not happy?' The girl shook her head. Her head was all we could see of her except her feet. The rest of her seemed to have shrunk to nothing in the enveloping towel.

'Better tell us,' said Janet.

The girl looked at them both. They were both standing over her now, and she moved no more than her eyes. Then she looked, very briefly, at me. I was still sitting, and she looked at me out of the corner of her eye. Her face was solemn and expressionless. I knew she was thinking what to say. I do not mean that I thought that what she said would be untrue, but I thought she was calculating its effect on her audience. Of course children do this from a very early age. The only difference is that later they learn to make it less obvious.

She said, 'It's the school boat. It's our Summer Outing.' You could hear the capital letters, the way she said it. She was not consciously being sardonic about it, but the effect was extraordinarily desolate and disillusioned, as if spontaneous enjoyment was out of her ken.

Gerald said, 'They'll be worried about you.' He was smiling as he said it, because he was smiling all the time he looked at her. Just for a second she smiled back at him. It was the first time she had smiled at any of us. But she did not say anything. Even if she was only smiling at Gerald, it was clear that the school's worry did not worry her.

Janet said, 'Well, your parents will be, anyhow.'

The girl looked up at her. She was not smiling now. Nor was Janet. The girl shook her head. 'They're dead,' she said.

Janet's face crumpled with the horrifying suddenness of a pricked balloon. She bent and caught the girl in her arms, and the girl, muffled as she was in the towel, settled into them with a sort of instinctive satisfaction, as a kitten will when you pick it up. Gerald said, 'Poor kid.'

Janet's face had settled now. She looked almost unnaturally calm. Her face was very near the girl's, and the girl's face was calm, too. The likeness was really very extraordinary. Janet said, 'What's your name?'

'Mary.'

Janet stood up, lifting the girl with her. She still had both arms round her. When she spoke, her voice was quite cheerful and matter-of-fact. 'Well, Mary,' she said, 'I'm going to take you indoors and put you to bed. Then we'll decide what's to be done with you.'

They went off into the house together, walking naturally in step. One corner of the towel trailed behind the girl on the crazy paving as they went. Gerald said again, 'Poor kid.'

'Look,' I said, 'you'll have to get this sorted out, and you won't want me. I'll be off. Make my apologies to Janet. She'll understand.'

He looked at me a bit doubtfully. He was a bit out of his depth altogether. 'Well,' he said, 'all right, Bill. I'm sorry. Can you get yourself a meal?'

'Of course,' I said. 'Plenty of places.'

He said again, 'All right. I'm sorry.'

'Nothing to be sorry about,' I said. 'I'll look in tomorrow some time.'

He nodded and we went back towards the house. When we got there, he nodded again and went inside. I went round to the front and got my car. That was the way it started.

I did not go to the Margesons' until quite late the next evening. I had no time during the day, and I thought that if I went early in the evening they would feel bound to ask me to dinner, to make up for the dinner I had lost the day before. That was the sort of way their minds worked, Gerald's perhaps more than Janet's. He was very conscious of any obligation which could be reduced to terms of money. It was another warm evening. When I got there, they were both sitting in the sun-room, looking out through the picture window across the swimming pool to the gap in the landscape where they knew the river was. They had their coffee.

I came in, as I always did, and sat down between them. I said, 'Well, what did you do with our mysterious Mary?'

As soon as I said it, I knew it was wrong. They both looked at me and away again. Then they looked at each other. Gerald managed a chuckle, but there was more than a touch of embarrassment in it. He looked at me again, smiling a determined little smile. He looked like a small boy caught in some mild misdemeanour and braving it out. 'Mary's upstairs in bed,' he said.

I was more cautious now. I just raised my eyebrows and smiled back at him. 'Still here?' I said.

Janet said, 'Gerald made enquiries, but no one seems to be looking for her. And she doesn't want to go back to the school, wherever it is. So we let her stay another night. She's – I think she's happy here.'

I said, 'You don't know where the school is?' She shook her head, and I let it go at that. 'Well,' I said, 'it's very kind of you. I don't doubt you're making her happy here.'

Gerald said, 'We like having her here.' He said it a little stiffly, so that I felt in some way rebuked.

I never asked any more questions after that. I still do not know whether Gerald made any real effort to find out where the girl came from, and clearly she was not going to tell them. I suppose if she had come off one of the pleasure-steamers, the people in charge of her might not have missed her until it was miles upstream, perhaps Reading or somewhere. Of course they would have had to report it to the police, but if I had the picture right, they would not be courting publicity. Certainly her disappearance never made the national news, and if there were local press reports, there were none that I saw in Marlow. The river claims its victims every summer. Whatever the Margesons did, they never went to the police. I do not know how they reconciled it with their very respectable consciences to keep her. But they did keep her.

I did not see very much of them, and I never saw the girl. They did not even talk about her much when I did see them. But they both, in their different ways, gave the impression of people nursing some splendid secret. From what little they said, it was plain that their lives revolved round Mary, and I fancied that Mary had and did pretty well whatever she liked. So long as they were all happy and no one was breaking the law, I was glad to see it, though I must say it puzzled me. In any case, it was no business of mine. It was only after I met Mary again that I began to wonder.

This must have been a week or so after she had arrived. I had to see Gerald on business, and when I rang up his office, they told me he had already gone home. This was about half past three in the afternoon. I knew he pleased himself pretty much over the hours he kept. I suppose you can do that if you don't have shareholders on your back. Anyway, I still wanted to see him, so I drove to the house. I walked in, as usual. They kept no resident staff, and there would be no one on duty at this time of day in any case. The weather was still warm.

I went into the sitting-room, but there was no one there. The glazed doors into the sun-room were open, and as I walked towards them, someone called 'Hullo-oh' from just beyond them. It was the same voice I had heard in snatches that evening a week before, very high and small, but set. I said, 'Hullo, Mary,' and went through into the sun-room.

She was wearing the same black bathing-dress she had worn when I first saw her, but she gave the impression of filling it out more. I doubt if it was much more than an impression. She may have put on a little weight with a week of Janet's cooking, but it was not only that. She was more certain of herself. She was lolling in a long chair. Children do not often loll, it is a trick that comes with the inertia of adolescence, but that was the word for it. She had her face turned up and was looking at me, almost over the top of her head, as I came in. There was an expectant smile on her face, but when she saw me, it changed. She did not move, but her face changed, and as I came round to the front of her chair, first her eyes and then her face turned and followed me. There was the same sort of watchfulness in them as I had seen before. 'Oh, hullo,' she said.

I found myself in the ridiculous predicament of not knowing quite what to say. I wanted to ask her if Gerald was in, but I did not know what to call him, because I did not know what she called him. 'Mr Margeson' seemed absurdly formal with a child of that age, but 'Gerald' seemed wrong, too. I thought of saying 'Uncle Gerald', but I could not be certain she called him that. She said, 'Gerald's not back yet.'

I do not know why, but I did not like the sound of it. There was a craze some years back for children calling their parents by their Christian names, but it had always worried me, and in any case you do not hear it so much now. But there was more to it than that. She did not say it even as a nineteen–thirties child would have said it of her father. She said it like a grown-up. I was disconcerted, but I was too old to let myself be put out of countenance by a child. I said, 'Oh, never mind. I expect he'll be back soon. They said he was on the way.' I talked to her as if she was a grown-up, too. I did not like this, either, but I found myself doing it.

She was still watching me. She no longer lolled. She said, 'Do you want him?' There was a touch of resentment in it, very slight but quite unmistakable.

I said, 'Yes, I do rather.'

She said, 'Oh, well, he'll be in soon.' It was nothing to do with what I had told her. She seemed as certain of Gerald as she was of herself, even if it involved his leaving the office at half past three.

I sat there looking at her. I had no intention of treating her like a grown-up if I could help it. I wanted to have a good look at her, and I had it. She lay there in her long chair and stared back at me with her green eyes slightly narrowed. I have said she was no longer lolling. I do not mean that she had visibly changed her position at all, because she had not. But she was no longer limp. Her whole body was conscious of itself. It submitted itself consciously to my inspection while her mind watched me through those narrowed eyes. It struck me that her body was like her voice, very light and slight, but somehow formed. It meant nothing to me. I do not like very young girls. Her face was the face of a child, but then children have all sorts of faces. I said, 'Happy here?'

She opened her eyes then and screwed her face up into a slightly wistful little smile. She even wiggled a little in her chair. She was suddenly completely a child, and a very appealing one. 'Oh yes,' she said. 'It's lovely.'

I said, 'Good,' and meant it. I think I felt a little ashamed of myself. Then I heard Gerald's car stop in front of the house and Gerald himself come in at the front door. I got up. 'I'll go and have a word with Gerald,' I said. She nodded, and I went out and met him in the hall.

I was upset again almost at once, because Gerald was disconcerted to see me, too. He said, 'Oh – hullo, Bill,' staring at me with his rather round, prominent eyes, while his mouth pursed itself under his little moustache. He had a small parcel in his hand.

'Hullo,' I said. 'Can you spare me a minute or two? I phoned you at the office, but they said you were on your way home.'

'Oh?' he said. 'Yes, of course.' He hesitated for a moment, and then put his parcel on the hall table. 'Janet's out,' he said. 'Been talking to Mary?'

'That's right,' I said. 'But I've only just got here. She looks well.'

He turned and went into the room they called his study. 'Oh, yes,' he said, 'she's fine. Now – what can I do for you?' We discussed our business for a few minutes, and I took myself off. I did not see any of them again for another five days or so.

The next time I called at Riverlawns, I walked into some sort of upset. As I came into the hall, I heard the sound of crying in the sitting-room, and a moment later the door opened and Mary came out into the hall. She was wearing a very pretty cotton frock, but her face was set and her eyes shining. She checked when she saw me, and for a moment the green eyes included me in their wide, appraising stare. Then she put her handkerchief to her face, and turned and scuttled up the stairs. The handkerchief had been already in her hand when she came out of the sitting-room. I went in and found Janet sitting at one end of the sofa. She looked distressed, as if she had been crying a little, too, and still wanted to. Her head jerked up as I came in, and she said, 'Oh – Bill.'

'Hullo, Janet,' I said.

She looked at me, wondering. I have known Janet a very long time, longer than I have known Gerald. I had been very fond of her once, and now I was very sorry for her. I knew she wanted to talk to me, but could not quite make up her mind to it. I sat down at the other end of the sofa. I said nothing. At last she said, 'Did you see Mary?'

'Yes. Yes, she went upstairs as I came in.'

She took a breath and said, 'I'm – I'm worried, Bill.'

'What's the trouble?'

'I think – I think Gerald's being a bit unkind to Mary. And I'm so fond of her. It's not like him at all.'

I said very carefully, 'Have you spoken to him about it?'

She looked at me and shook her head. There was no disguising the distress now. 'That's the trouble,' she said, 'I don't seem able to. It's difficult to explain.'

'Well,' I said, 'have a try, now you've started.'

She was looking at her fingers now, twisting them in her lap. 'I don't know,' she said. 'I think in a sort of way he's jealous of her.'

'Why should he be that?'

She shook her head, still not looking at me. 'I don't know,' she said again. 'I am very fond of her. I have been, right from the start. As if' – she looked at me quickly and then away again – 'as if she belonged to me, somehow. And I think perhaps Gerald resents that.'

'I see,' I said. I did not see, at all, but it is the phrase one uses. 'Have you – I mean, is he unkind to her in front of you?'

'No, not really. He treats her just as he used to treat the children at that age. But I see him looking at her sometimes – I don't know. And the child herself is unhappy about it. I think she's afraid he'll send her away. She's just been having a bit of a cry about it. And it makes me feel terrible. I feel it's so – so wicked of him.'

I said again, 'I see,' and this time I thought I did see, at least more than I had. 'Look, Janet,' I said, 'why not send her away? You'll have to some time, won't you?'

She said, 'Oh no—' but I took no notice.

'I don't know what the legal position is,' I said, 'and it's no business of mine, anyway. But I don't imagine she can stay with you indefinitely. It's not worth having rows with Gerald about, surely?'

'There haven't been any rows,' she said.

'That's probably half the trouble. And the children will be home in a week or so. What are they going to make of it?'

She said, 'Why should they mind?' The way she said it was startling. It was as if I had suddenly seen the plain, puddingy Margeson children through their mother's eyes and found that they looked the same as they did through mine. No wonder I was startled.

I said very gently, 'I think they might a little, all the same. Especially if she makes trouble between you and Gerald.'

She jerked her head up and stared at me. There was a sort of fierce defensiveness in it. '*She's* not making trouble,' she said.

I said nothing because I did not know what to say. Then she said, 'Bill, will you speak to Gerald?'

'Janet,' I said, 'you're crazy. What would he think?'

'I don't mean on my behalf. I don't want him to know I've spoken to you about it – not at all. I mean – just talk to him and try to find out what his attitude is.'

'And then tell you?'

I meant it to shake her, and it did, but she did not give up. She said, 'Oh please, Bill. Thursday. That's the day after tomorrow. I shall be out that evening. It's my bridge. Come then and see if you can talk to Gerald. Please.'

'What about Mary?' I said.

'Oh, Gerald wouldn't talk in front of her. She'll be in bed, anyway.'

I got up. 'I'll see,' I said. 'But I've already told you what I think. Send her away, Janet.'

She shook her head. 'Please talk to Gerald first,' she said. I shrugged and left. I did not see anyone in the hall. The weather was really sultry now, as if the break was coming. It may have been partly the weather, but an oppression lay on me like lead.

During the next two days it got hotter than ever, but the break still did not come. On the Thursday I got to Riverlawns at about seven. The sun still slanted hot into the garden. There was not a sound anywhere. I went into the house and called, but no one answered.

I went through into the garden. I was just going to call when I heard voices from behind the screen by the swimming pool. I knew whose voices they were. I went on towards the opening in the screen. My feet made no sound at all on the paving. Just before I got there I heard Gerald say, 'Your back's just like a boy's.' His voice sounded throaty and a little breathless.

Mary laughed. It was a little tinkling sound. She said, 'My front's different, though, isn't it?'

I moved my head and looked at them round the edge of the screen. It was the place where I had once seen Gerald and Janet making love on a Sunday morning. Neither Gerald nor Mary was looking my way. Mary was standing up with her arms raised and her hands resting on top of her dark hair. Her bathing-dress was rolled down to her hips, and the upward pull of the arms threw up the little protuberances of soft flesh on her arching chest. Gerald was kneeling behind her. He had a tube of some sort of cream in his left hand, and his right hand moved up and down over Mary's back. It was not the way you handle a child. Every time it came to the bottom his hand touched the rolled edge of the bathing dress and pushed it a little farther down. He had nothing on but a pair of bathing trunks. His mouth was slightly open and in the silence I could hear his breathing. He said, 'I like all of you. Shall I put cream all over you?'

Mary laughed again, but she did not move. 'I don't mind,' she said. 'I don't mind what you do.'

I turned and started to walk back to the house. As I went, I heard Gerald say, 'Don't you?' as if he was saying it through his teeth, and Mary laughed again on a high, rising note. I went round to the front and started the car. I did not mind if anyone heard me, but I did not think anyone would. I was wondering what I was going to tell Janet when I saw her.

I never did see her, in fact, not till a lot later. I spoke to her once over the phone, but only very briefly. I saw Gerald again the same evening, but for the second time he did not see me. I drove away from Riverlawns with a dry mouth and a sick hollow in the pit of my stomach. I felt affronted, as if someone had made a homosexual pass at me. But mainly I was appalled at the mere practical situation and the fact that I was involved in it and could not get myself out. I turned into a pub on the other side of Marlow for a drink and something to eat. I did not take long over it. I came out and got into my car, and then Gerald drove into the car-park.

As I say, he never saw me. He got out of his car and went into the pub. He moved slowly. I only saw him sideways, but he looked dazed, as if his whole mind was occupied with something he could not quite come to terms with. He was frowning slightly, but more as if he was puzzled than as if he was worried or unhappy. As soon as he was inside, I ran my car out and drove straight back to Riverlawns.

I went round into the garden, but there was no one there. The sun was gone now, but the air was as hot and heavy as ever. There was not a sound anywhere. I went into the house from the back, and when I came into the hall, I saw Mary standing half-way up the stairs looking down at me. She had on some sort of flowery dressing-gown, very gay and expensive-looking, but she did not look gay at all. She stood quite still, and we looked at each other in the rather murky light, trying to make each other out. Then she said, 'Everyone's out. What do you want?'

I went a couple of steps up towards her, so that I could see her better. She did not move, but she seemed to draw in on herself. Her face had neither pleasure nor fear in it, only calculation. In a face of that age it was not nice to see. I spoke to her quite quietly, even gently. I said, 'When are you going to leave here, Mary? It's time you went. You'll have to go some time, you know.'

She shook her head. Now that she knew what I wanted, she was more sure of herself. She said, 'I don't want to go. I like it here. They don't want me to go, either.'

'Not now, perhaps,' I said. 'But I think they will.'

She was still watching me, trying to make out what I was at. She said, 'What did Mrs Margeson say?'

I said, 'What she said doesn't matter. You lied to her, and she believed you.'

Her eyes widened and she stared down at me. For quite a time she did not say anything. I suddenly saw that she was angry. It was a cold, venomous anger that had nothing childish in it. I stared back into those basilisk eyes, understanding for the first time what I was up against. She said, 'Why can't you leave me alone? I can tell lies about you, and they'll believe those, too. Gerald will. He doesn't know you're here, does he?'

I said, 'You can tell him what you like. I can talk to him, too, can't I? I think when I have, he'll want to send you away.'

She smiled. It was very sudden and unnerving. She went on looking down at me, still smiling at something in her own mind. She had not much amusement to spare on me, only a sort of contemptuous defiance. 'He can't,' she said. 'Not now. You ask him and see.'

She was no longer smiling. She seemed to have no expression on her face at all. I stared up at that small white mask for a moment or two. Then I nodded. I backed down the two stairs into the hall, turned and went out to my car. The one thing I did not know was whether she would tell Gerald I had been there. I did not think she would, but also I did not think it mattered much either way.

I spent a good deal of the night trying to think of any way out that would not involve almost total disaster. I had to do something, because to do nothing would only postpone the disaster, and I could not let disaster on this scale hit the Margesons. Mary herself I thought of as a sort of natural evil. I did not have any very personal feelings about her, but the sense of evil was very strong. There was no time now to find out where the evil had come from or to try to exorcise it. If you see people trapped in a burning house, you do not stop to establish the cause of the fire. I made my mind up somewhere in the small hours, and then slept on it. When I woke, I was startled by my decision, as one sometimes is, but could see no reason to change it.

I waited until I knew Gerald would have left, and then rang up Janet. She said, 'Oh, Bill. Bill, did you see Gerald?'

I said, 'Look, Janet, I've got to talk to you. But I can't manage it all day. Can you meet me this evening somewhere?'

'Well – yes, I suppose so. If it's not too far. What sort of time?'

'Ten, I'm afraid. I can't manage it earlier.'

She said, 'Oh dear, as late as that? It won't be easy.'

'It's necessary, Janet,' I said. 'Absolutely necessary.'

She hesitated, but not for long. 'All right,' she said. 'Where, then?'

'You know the pub called the Haywain? On the other side of Marlow. It's got a garden down to the river, with places to sit. In the garden, there. All right?'

She said again, 'Oh dear—' but I did not give her time to think about it.

'Ten, then,' I said, and rang off. I knew she would be there.

I left it until early in the afternoon before I rang Gerald. I rang him up at his office. He was still there. He said, 'Oh – hullo, Bill. What can I do for you?' He did not sound very glad to hear me.

I said, 'Gerald, I want to talk to you.'

*Mary*

He hesitated quite a long time. Then he said, 'I see. What about?'

'Mary,' I said.

The silence this time was so long that I wondered if he was still there. Then he said again, 'I see.' There was another pause. Then he said, 'Have you seen Mary?'

'Yes.'

When he spoke again, his voice was so low that I could hardly hear it. He said, 'Have you seen Janet?'

'No.'

He gave a sort of sigh. 'All right, Bill. Where do we meet?'

'The garden of the Haywain. Ten this evening. All right?'

He said, 'Bill—' Then he thought better of it. 'All right,' he said. I rang off.

The heat built up all day, and by sunset the whole sky was overcast. When I got to Riverlawns, you could hear the storm working down the river from the west, the way they do. I got there at a quarter to ten. I had left the car in a side road a quarter of a mile away. I went straight through to the swimming pool. I changed and left my clothes in one of the rooms. There was a black bathing-dress and a towel hanging on a hook. A small bathing-dress and a very large towel. I knew whose they were. It was a detail I had not thought of, but it might help. I took them and went into the house. It was dark now. The thunder rolled continuously and the whole sky to the west flickered with lightning. There was a wash of cold wet air moving up over the river. It would be raining soon.

I went straight upstairs to Mary's room. I knew which one it was. I opened the door and went in. There was no light on in the room, but I saw her at once, crouched against the window, looking out at the storm. For just a moment I wondered if she was frightened of it. If she had been, I do not know what I should have done. But she turned, quite slowly, and looked at me. She knew me all right. She was quite calm. She said, 'What do you want?'

'You, Mary,' I said.

Even then she was not quite sure what I meant. I went across the room to her, and she did not move at all. I threw the towel over her head and picked her up. She struggled a little and then lay limp in my arms. I think she knew then exactly what was happening. She knew too much altogether. That had been her trouble all along. As we went out of the house, there was a moment's tremendous glare of lightning, and then the storm broke over us. I went down through the garden in the flickering chaos, carrying Mary, by the way she had come, back to the river.

267

# P. D.
# JAMES

---

# The Girl Who Loved
# Graveyards

She couldn't remember anything about the day in the hot August of 1956 when they first brought her to live with her Aunt Gladys and Uncle Victor in the small east London house at 49 Alma Terrace. She knew that it was three days after her tenth birthday and that she was to be cared for by her only living relations now that her father and grandmother were dead, killed by influenza within a week of each other. But those were just facts which someone, at some time, had briefly told her. She could remember nothing of her previous life. Those first ten years were a void, insubstantial as a dream which had faded but which had left on her mind a scar of unarticulated childish anxiety and fear. For her, memory and childhood both began with that moment when, waking in the small unfamiliar bedroom with the kitten, Sambo, still curled asleep on a towel at the foot of her bed, she had walked bare-foot to the window and drawn back the curtain.

And there, stretched beneath her, lay the cemetery, luminous and mysterious in the early morning light, bounded by iron railings and separated from the rear of Alma Terrace only by a narrow path. It was to be another warm day, and over the serried rows of headstones there lay a thin haze pierced by the occasional obelisk and by the wing tips of marble angels whose disembodied heads seemed to be floating on particles of shimmering light. And as she watched, motionless in an absorbed enchantment, the mist began to rise and the whole cemetery was revealed to her, a miracle of stone and marble, bright grass and summer-laden trees, flower-bedecked graves and intersection paths stretching as far as her eyes could see. In the far distance she could just make out the top of the Victorian chapel gleaming like the spire of some magical castle in a long-forgotten fairy tale. In those moments of growing wonder she found herself shivering with delight, an emotion so rare that it stole through her thin body like a pain. And it was then, on that first morning of her new life with the past a void and the future unknown and frightening, that she made the cemetery her own. Throughout her childhood and youth it was to remain a place of delight and mystery, her habitation and her solace.

It was a childhood without love, almost without affection. Her uncle Victor was her father's elder half-brother; that, too, she had been told. He and her aunt weren't really her relations. Their small capacity for love was expended on each other, and even here it was less a positive emotion than a pact of mutual support and comfort against the threatening world which lay outside the trim curtains of their small claustrophobic sitting room.

But they cared for her as dutifully as she cared for the cat Sambo. It was a fiction in the household that she adored Sambo, her own cat, brought with her when she arrived, her one link with the past, almost her only possession. Only she knew that she disliked and feared him. But she brushed and fed him with conscientious care as she did everything and, in return, he gave her a slavish allegiance, hardly ever leaving her side, slinking through the cemetery at her heels and only turning back when they reached the main gate. But he wasn't her friend. He didn't love her and he knew that she didn't love him. He was a fellow conspirator, gazing at her through slits of azure light, relishing some secret knowledge which was her knowledge too. He ate voraciously yet he never grew fat. Instead his sleek black body lengthened until, stretched in the sunlight along her window sill, his sharp nose turned always to the cemetery, he looked as sinister and unnatural as a furred reptile.

It was lucky for her that there was a side gate to the cemetery from Alma Terrace and that she could take a short cut to and from school across the graveyard avoiding the dangers of the main road. On her first morning her uncle had said doubtfully: 'I suppose it's all right. But it seems wrong somehow, a child walking every day through rows of the dead.'

Her aunt had replied: 'The dead can't rise from their graves. They lay quiet. She's safe enough from the dead.'

Her voice had been unnaturally gruff and loud. The words had sounded like an assertion, almost a defiance. But the child knew that she was right. She did feel safe with the dead, safe and at home.

The years in Alma Terrace slipped by, bland and dull as her aunt's blanc-mange, a sensation rather than a taste. Had she been happy? It wasn't a question which it had ever occurred to her to ask. She wasn't unpopular at school, being neither pretty nor intelligent enough to provoke much interest either from the children or the staff; an ordinary child, unusual only because she was an orphan but unable to capitalize even on that sentimental advantage. Perhaps she might have found friends, quiet unenterprising children like herself who might have responded to her unthreatening mediocrity. But something about her repelled their timid advances, her self-sufficiency, the bland uncaring gaze, the refusal to give anything of herself even in casual friendship. She didn't need friends. She had the graveyard and its occupants.

She had her favourites. She knew them all, when they had died, how old they had been, sometimes how they had died. She knew their names and learned their memorials by heart. They were more real to her than the living, those rows of dearly loved wives and mothers, respected tradesmen, lamented fathers, deeply mourned children. The new graves hardly ever interested her although she would watch the funerals from a distance then creep up later to read the mourning cards. But what she like best were the old neglected oblongs of mounded earth or chipped stones, the tilted crosses, the carved words almost erased by time. It was round the names of the long dead that she wove her childish fantasies.

Even the seasons of the year she experienced in and through the cemetery. The gold and purple spears of the first crocuses thrusting through the hard earth. April with its tossing daffodils. The whole graveyard *en fête* in yellow and white as mourners dressed the graves for Easter. The smell of mown grass and the earthy tang of high summer as if the dead were breathing the flower-scented air and exuding their own mysterious miasma. The glare of sunlight on stone

271

and marble as the old women in their stained cotton dresses shuffled with their vases to fill them at the tap behind the chapel. Seeing the cemetery transformed by the first snow of winter, the marble angels grotesque in their high bonnets of glistening snow. Watching at her window for the thaw, hoping to catch that moment when the edifice would slip and the shrouded shapes become themselves again.

Only once had she asked about her father and then she had known as children do that this was a subject which, for some mysterious adult reason, it was better not to talk about. She had been sitting at the kitchen table with her homework while her aunt busied herself cooking supper. Looking up from her history book she had asked: 'Where is Daddy buried?'

The frying pan had clattered against the stove. The cooking fork dropped from her aunt's hand. It had taken her a long time to pick it up, wash it, clean the grease from the floor. The child had asked again: 'Where is Daddy buried?'

'Up north. At Creedon outside Nottingham with your mum and gran. Where else?'

'Can I go there? Can I visit him?'

'When you're older, maybe. No sense is there, hanging about graves. The dead aren't there.'

'Who looks after them?'

'The graves? The cemetery people. Now get on with your homework, do, child. I'll be wanting the table for supper.'

She hadn't asked about her mother, the mother who had died when she was born. That desertion had always seemed to her wilful, a source of secret guilt. 'You killed your mother.' Someone, some time, had spoken those words to her, had laid on her that burden. She wouldn't let herself think about her mother. But she knew that her father had stayed with her, had loved her, hadn't wanted to die and leave her. Some day, secretly, she would find his grave. She would visit it, not once but every week. She would tend it and plant flowers on it and clip the grass as the old ladies did in the cemetery. And if there wasn't a stone she would pay for one, not a cross but a gleaming obelisk, the tallest in the graveyard, bearing his name and an epitaph which she would choose. She would have to wait until she was older, until she could leave school and work, and save enough money. But one day she would find her father. She would have a grave of her own to visit and tend. There was a debt of love to be paid.

Four years after her arrival in Alma Terrace her aunt's only brother came to visit from Australia. Physically he and his sister were alike, the same stolid short-legged bodies, the same small eyes set in square pudgy faces. But Uncle Ned had a brash assurance, a cheerful geniality which was so alien to his sister's unconfident reserve that it was hard to believe that they were siblings. For the two weeks of his visit he dominated the little house with his strident alien voice and assertive masculinity. There were unfamiliar treats, dinners in the West End, a visit to a greyhound stadium, a show at Earls Court. He was kind to the child, tipping her lavishly, even walking through the cemetery with her one morning to buy his racing paper. And it was that evening, coming silently down the stairs to supper, that she overheard disjointed scraps of conversation, adult talk, incomprehensible at the time but taken into her mind and stored there.

First the harsh boom of her uncle's voice: 'We were looking at this grave stone together, see. Beloved husband and father. Taken from us suddenly on 14 March 1892. Something like that. Marble chips, cracked urn, bloody great angel pointing upwards. You know the kind of thing. Then the kid turned to me. "Daddy's death was sudden, too." That's what she said. Came out with it cool as you please. Now what in God's name made her say that? I mean, why then? Christ, it gave me a turn I can tell you. I didn't know where to put my face. And what a place to choose, the bloody cemetery. I'll say one thing for coming out to Sydney. You'll get a better view. I can promise you that.'

Creeping closer, she strained her ears vainly to catch the indistinct mutter of her aunt's reply.

Then came her uncle's voice again: 'That bitch never forgave him for getting Helen pregnant. No one was good enough for her precious only daughter. And then when Helen died having the kid she blamed him for that too. Poor sod, he bought a packet of trouble when he set eyes on that girl. Too soft, too romantic. That was always Martin's trouble.'

Again the murmur of indistinguishable voices, the sound of her aunt's footsteps moving from table to stove, the scrape of a chair. Then her Uncle Ned's voice again.

'Funny kid, isn't she? Old-fashioned. Morbid you might say. Seems to live in that bone yard, she and that damned cat. And the split image of her dad. Christ, it turned me up I can tell you. Looking at me with his eyes and then coming out with it. "Daddy's death was sudden, too." I'll say it was! Influenza? Well, it's as good a name for it as any if you can get away with it. Helps having such an ordinary name, I suppose. People don't catch on. How long ago is it now? Four years? It seems longer.'

Only one part of this half-heard, incomprehensible conversation had disturbed her. Uncle Ned was trying to persuade them to join him in Australia. She might be taken away from Alma Terrace, might never see the cemetery again, might have to wait for years before she could save enough money to return to England and find her father's grave. And how could she visit it regularly, how could she tend and care for it from the other side of the world? After Uncle Ned's visit ended it was months before she could see one of his rare letters with the Australian stamp drop through the letter box without the cold clutch of fear at the heart.

But she needn't have worried. It was October 1966 before they left England and they went alone. When they broke the news to her one Sunday morning at breakfast it was apparent that they had never even considered taking her with them. Dutiful as ever, they had waited to make their decision until she had left school and was earning her living as a shorthand typist with a local firm of estate agents. Her future was assured. They had done all that conscience required of them. Hesitant and a little shame-faced they justified their decision as if they believed that it was important to her, that she cared whether they left or stayed. Her aunt's arthritis was increasingly troublesome; they longed for the sun; Uncle Ned was their only close relation and none of them was getting any younger. Their plan, over which they had agonized for months in whispers behind closed doors, was to visit Sydney for six months and then, if they liked

Australia, to apply to emigrate. The house in Alma Terrace was to be sold to pay the air fare. It was already on the market. But they had made provision for her. When they told her what had been arranged, she had to bend her face low over her plate in case the flood of joy should be too apparent. Mrs Morgan, three doors down, would be glad to take her as a lodger if she didn't mind having the small bedroom at the back overlooking the cemetery. In the surging tumult of relief she hardly heard her aunt's next words. There was one small problem. Everyone knew how Mrs Morgan was about cats. Sambo would have to be put down.

She was to move into 43 Alma Terrace on the afternoon of the day on which her aunt and uncle flew from Heathrow. Her two cases, holding all that she possessed in the world, were already packed. In her handbag she carefully stowed the meagre official confirmations of her existence: her birth certificate, her medical card, her Post Office savings book showing the £103 painstakingly saved towards the cost of her father's memorial. And, the next day, she would begin her search. But first she took Sambo to the vet to be destroyed. She made a cat box from two cartons fitted together, pierced it with holes, then sat patiently in the waiting room with the box at her feet. The cat made no sound and this patient resignation touched her, evoking for the first time a spasm of pity and affection. But there was nothing she could do to save him. They both knew it. But then, he had always known what she was thinking, what was past and what was to come. There was something they shared, some knowledge, some common experience which she couldn't remember and he couldn't express. Now with his destruction even that tenuous link with her first ten years would go for ever.

When it was her turn to go into the surgery she said: 'I want him put down.'

The vet passed his strong experienced hands over the sleek fur. 'Are you sure? He seems quite healthy still. He's old, of course, but he's in remarkably good condition.'

'I'm sure. I want him put down.'

And she left him there without a glance or another word.

She had thought that she would be glad to be free of the pretence of loving him, free of those slitted accusing eyes. But as she walked back to Alma Terrace she found herself crying; tears, unbidden and unstoppable, ran like rain down her face.

There was no difficulty in getting a week's leave from her job. She had been husbanding her holiday entitlement. Her work, as always, was up to date. She had calculated how much money she would need for her train and bus fares and for a week's stay in modest hotels. Her plans had been made. They had been made for years. She would begin her search with the address on her birth certificate, Cranstoun House, Creedon, Nottingham, the house where she had been born. The present owners might remember her and her father. If not, there would be neighbours or older inhabitants of the village who would be able to recall her father's death, where he was buried. If that failed she would try the local undertakers. It was, after all, only ten years ago. Someone locally would remember. Somewhere in Nottingham there would be a record of burials. She told Mrs Morgan that she was taking a week's holiday to visit her father's old home, packed a hold-all with overnight necessities and, next morning, caught the earliest-possible fast train from St Pancras to Nottingham.

It was during the bus ride from Nottingham to Creedon that she felt the first stirrings of anxiety and mistrust. Until then she had travelled in calm confidence, but strangely without excitement, as if this long-planned journey was as natural and inevitable as her daily walk to work, an inescapable pilgrimage ordained from that moment when a bare-footed child in her white nightdress had drawn back her bedroom curtains and seen her kingdom spread beneath her. But now her mood changed. As the bus lurched through the suburbs she found herself shifting in her seat as if mental unease were provoking physical discomfort. She had expected green countryside, small churches guarding neat domestic graveyards patterned with yew trees. These were graveyards she had visited on holidays, had loved almost as much as she loved the one she had made her own. Surely it was in such bird-loud sanctified peace that her father lay. But Nottingham had spread during the past ten years and Creedon was now little more than an urban village separated from the city by a ribbon development of brash new houses, petrol stations and parades of shops. Nothing in the journey was familiar, and yet she knew that she had travelled this road before and travelled it in anxiety and pain.

But when, thirty minutes later, the bus stopped at its terminus at Creedon she knew at once where she was. The Dog and Whistle still stood at one corner of the dusty litter-strewn village green with the same bus shelter outside it. And with the sight of its graffiti-scrawled walls memory returned as easily as if nothing had ever been forgotten. Here her father used to leave her when he brought her to pay her regular Sunday visits to her grandmother. Here her grandmother's elderly cook would be waiting for her. Here she would look back for a final wave and see her father patiently waiting for the bus to begin its return journey. Here she would be brought at six-thirty when he arrived to collect her. Cranstoun House was where her grandmother lived. She herself had been born there but it had never been her home.

She had no need to ask her way to the house. And when, five minutes later, she stood gazing up at it in appalled fascination, no need to read the name painted on the shabby padlocked gate. It was a square built house of dark brick standing in incongruous and spurious grandeur at the end of a country lane. It was smaller than she now remembered, but it was still a dreadful house. How could she ever have forgotten those ornate overhanging gables, the high pitched roof, the secretive oriel windows, the single forbidding turret at the east end? There was an estate agent's board wired to the gate and it was apparent that the house was empty. The paint on the front door was peeling, the lawns were overgrown, the boughs of the rhododendron bushes were broken and the gravel path was studded with clumps of weed. There was no one here who could help her to find her father's grave. But she knew that she had to visit, had to make herself pass again through that intimidating front door. There was something the house knew and had to tell her, something that Sambo had known. She couldn't escape her next step. She must find the estate agent's office and get a permit to view.

She had missed the returning bus and by the time the next one had reached

Nottingham it was after three o'clock. She had eaten nothing since her early breakfast but she was too driven now to be aware of hunger. But she knew that it would be a long day and that she ought to eat. She turned into a coffee bar and bought a toasted cheese sandwich and a mug of coffee, grudging the few minutes which it took to gulp them down. The coffee was hot but almost tasteless. Flavour would have been wasted on her, but she realised as the hot liquid stung her throat how much she had needed it.

The girl at the cash desk was able to direct her to the house agent's office. It seemed to her a happy augury that it was within ten minutes' walk. She was received by a sharp featured young man in an over-tailored pin-stripe suit who, in one practised glance at her old blue tweed coat, the cheap hold-all and bag of synthetic leather, placed her precisely in his private category of client from whom little can be expected and to whom less need be given. But he found the particulars for her and his curiosity sharpened as she merely glanced at them, then folded the paper away in her bag. Her request to view that afternoon was received, as she expected, with politeness but without enthusiasm. But this was familiar territory and she knew why. The house was unoccupied. She would have to be escorted. There was nothing in her respectable drabness to suggest that she was a likely purchaser. And when he briefly excused himself to consult a colleague and returned to say that he could drive her to Creedon at once she knew the reason for that too. The office wasn't particularly busy and it was time that someone from the firm checked up on the property.

Neither of them spoke during the drive. But when they reached Creedon and he turned down the lane to the house the apprehension she had felt on her first visit returned, but deeper and stronger. Yet now it was more than the memory of an old wretchedness. This was childish misery and fear re-lived, but intensified by a dreadful adult foreboding. As the house agent parked his Morris on the grass verge she looked up at the blind windows and was seized by a spasm of terror so acute that, momentarily, she was unable to speak or move. She was aware of the man holding open the car door for her, of the smell of beer on his breath, of his face, uncomfortably close, bending on her a look of exasperated patience. She wanted to say that she had changed her mind, that the house was totally wrong for her, that there would be no point in viewing it, that she would wait for him in the car. But she willed herself to rise from the warm seat and scrambled out under his supercilious eyes, despising herself for her gracelessness. She waited in silence as he unlocked the padlock and swung open the gate.

They passed together between the neglected lawns and the spreading rhododendron bushes towards the front door. And suddenly the feet shuffling the gravel beside her were different feet and she knew that she was walking with her father as she had walked in childhood. She had only to stretch out her hand to feel the grasp of his fingers. Her companion was saying something about the house but she didn't hear. The meaningless chatter faded and she heard a different voice, her father's voice, heard for the first time in over ten years.

'It won't be for always, darling. Just until I've found a job. And I'll visit you every Sunday for lunch. Then, afterwards, we'll be able to go for a walk together, just the two of us. Granny has promised that. And I'll buy you a kitten. I'll bring it next weekend. I'm sure Granny won't mind when she sees him. A black kitten. You've always wanted a black kitten. What shall we call him? Little black Sambo? He'll remind you of me. And then, when I've found a job, I'll be able to rent a little house and we'll be together again. I'll look after you, my darling. We'll look after each other.'

She dared not look up in case she should see again those desperately pleading eyes, begging her to understand, to make things easy for him, not to despise him. She knew now that she ought to have helped him, to have told him that she understood, that she didn't mind living with Granny for a month or so, that everything would be all right. But she hadn't managed so adult a response. She remembered tears, desperate clingings to his coat, her grandmother's old cook, tight-lipped, pulling her away from him and bearing her up to bed. And the last memory was of watching him from her room above the porch, of his drooping defeated figure making its way down the lane to the bus stop.

As they reached the front door she looked up. The window was still there. But, of course, it was. She knew every room in this dark house.

The garden was bathed in a mellow October sunlight, but the hall struck cold and dim. The heavy mahogany staircase led up from gloom to a darkness which hung above them like a pall. The estate agent felt along the wall for the light switch. But she didn't wait. She felt again the huge brass door knob which her childish fingers had hardly encompassed and moved unerringly into the drawing room.

The smell of the room was different. Then there had been a scent of violets overlaid with furniture polish. Now the air smelt cold and musty. She stood in the darkness shivering but perfectly calm. It seemed to her that she had passed through a barrier of fear as a tortured victim might pass through a pain barrier into a kind of peace. She felt a shoulder brush against her as the man went across to the window and swung open the heavy curtains.

He said: 'The last owners have left it partly furnished. Looks better that way. Easier to get offers if the place looks lived in.'

'Has there been an offer?'

'Not yet. It's not everyone's cup of tea. Bit on the large size for a modern family. And then, there's the murder. Ten years ago, but people still talk in the neighbourhood. There's been four owners since then and none of them stayed long. It's bound to affect the price. No good thinking you can hush up murder.'

His voice was carefully nonchalant, but his gaze never left her face. Walking to the empty fire grate, he stretched one arm along the mantelpiece and followed her with his eyes as she moved as if in a trance about the room.

She heard herself asking: 'What murder?'

'A sixty-four-year-old woman. Battered to death by her son-in-law. The old cook came in from the back kitchen and found him with the poker in his hand. Come to think of it, it could have been one like that.'

He nodded down to a collection of brass fire-irons resting against the fender. He said: 'It happened right where you're standing now. She was sitting in that very chair.'

She said in a voice so gruff and harsh that she hardly recognized it: 'It wasn't this chair. It was bigger. Her chair had an embroidered seat and back and there were armrests edged with crochet and the feet were like lions' claws.'

His gaze sharpened. Then he laughed warily. The watchful eyes grew puzzled, then the look changed into something else. Could it have been contempt?

'So you know about it. You're one of those.'

'One of those?'

'They aren't really in the market for a place. Couldn't afford one this size anyway. They just want a thrill, want to see where it happened. You get all sorts in this game and I can usually tell. I can give you all the gory details if you're interested. Not that there was much gore. The skull was smashed but most of the bleeding was internal. They say there was just a trickle falling down her forehead and dripping on to her hands.'

It came out so pat that she knew that he had told it all before, that he enjoyed telling it, this small recital of horror to titillate his clients and relieve the boredom of his day. She wished that she wasn't so cold. If only she could get warm again her voice wouldn't sound so strange.

She said through her dry and swollen lips: 'And the kitten. Tell me about the kitten.'

'Now that was something! That was a touch of horror if you like. The kitten was on her lap, licking up the blood. But then you know, don't you? You've heard all about it.'

'Yes,' she lied. 'I've heard all about it.'

But she had done more than that. She knew. She had seen it. She had been there.

And then the outline of the chair altered. An amorphous black shape swam before her eyes, then took form and substance. Her grandmother was sitting there, squat as a toad, dressed in her Sunday black for morning service, gloved and hatted, prayer book in her lap. She saw again the glob of phlegm at the corner of the mouth, the thread of broken veins at the side of the sharp nose. She was waiting to inspect her grandchild before church, turning on her again that look of querulous discontent. The witch was sitting there. The witch who hated her and her daddy, who had told her that he was useless and feckless and no better than her mother's murderer. The witch who was threatening to have Sambo put down because he had torn her chair, because Daddy had given him to her. The witch who was planning to keep her from Daddy for ever.

And then she saw something else. The poker was there, too, just as she remembered it, the long rod of polished brass with its heavy knob.

She seized it as she had seized it then and, with a high scream of hatred and terror, brought it down on her grandmother's head. Again and again she struck, hearing the brass thudding against the leather, blow on splitting blow. And still she screamed. The room rang with the terror of it. But it was only when the frenzy passed and the dreadful noise stopped that she knew from the pain of her torn throat that the screaming had been hers.

She stood shaking, gasping for breath. Beads of sweat stood out on her forehead and she felt the stinging drops seeping into her eyes. Looking up she was aware of the man's eyes, wide with terror, staring into hers, of a muttered curse, of footsteps running to the door. And then the poker slid from her moist hands and she heard it thud softly on the rug.

He had been right, there was no blood. Only the grotesque hat knocked forward over the dead face. But as she watched a sluggish line of deep red rolled from under the brim, zig-zagged down the forehead, trickled along the creases of the cheeks and began to drop steadily on to the gloved hands. And then she heard a soft mew. A ball of black fur crept from behind the chair and the ghost of Sambo, azure eyes frantic, leapt as he had leapt ten years earlier delicately up to that unmoving lap.

She looked at her hands. Where were the gloves, the white cotton gloves which the witch had always insisted must be worn to church? But these hands, no longer the hands of a nine-year-old child, were naked. And the chair was empty. There was nothing but the split leather, the burst of horsehair stuffing, a faint smell of violets fading on the quiet air.

She walked out of the front door without closing it behind her as she had left it then. She walked as she had walked then, gloved and unsullied, down the gravel path between the rhododendrons, out of the ironwork gate and up the lane towards the church. The bell had only just started ringing; she would be in good time. In the distance she had glimpsed her father climbing a stile from the water meadow into the lane. So he must have set out early after breakfast and had walked to Creedon. And why so early? Had he needed that long walk to settle something in his mind? Had it been a pathetic attempt to propitiate the witch by coming with them to church? Or, blessed thought, had he come to take her away, to see that her few belongings were packed and ready by the time the service was over? Yes, that was what she had thought at the time. She remembered it now, that fountain of hope soaring and dancing into glorious certainty. When she got home all would be ready. They would stand there together and defy the witch, would tell her that they were leaving together, the two of them and Sambo, that she would never see them again. At the end of the road she looked back and saw for the last time the beloved ghost crossing the lane to the house towards that fatally open door.

And after that? The vision was fading now. She could remember nothing of the service except a blaze of red and blue shifting like a kaleidoscope then fusing into a stained glass window, the Good Shepherd gathering a lamb to his bosom. And afterwards? Surely there had been strangers waiting in the porch, grave concerned faces, whispers and sidelong glances, a woman in some kind of uniform, an official car. And after that, nothing. Memory was a blank.

But now, at last, she knew where her father was buried. And she knew why she would never be able to visit him, never make that pious pilgrimage to the place where he lay because of her, the shameful place where she had put him. There could be no flowers, no obelisk, no loving message carved in marble for those who lay in quicklime behind a prison wall. And then, unbidden, came the final memory. She saw again the open church door, the trickle of the congregation filing in, enquiring faces turning towards her as she arrived alone in the porch. She heard again that high childish voice speaking the words which more than any others had slipped that rope of hemp over his shrouded head.

'Granny? She isn't very well. She told me to come on my own. No, there's nothing to worry about. She's quite all right. Daddy's with her.'

# H. R. F. KEATING

---

# An Upright Woman

Mrs Prothero liked to keep an ordered Christmas. It meant a good deal to her that things should be done in the same way each year. So at precisely eleven o'clock in the morning on the day before Christmas Eve, a Saturday, she began putting up the simple decorations she and Mr Prothero liked. They neither of them wished for anything extravagant, but it was right that the season should be marked and so mark it they did.

She began by cutting out two silver angels to hang one on each side above the fireplace. In a few minutes Mr Prothero would come home with a small bunch of holly, just enough to put one sprig above each picture in the sitting-room.

Snip, snip went the big cutting-out scissors between Mrs Prothero's strong and somewhat work-roughened fingers. Piece by piece the unwanted edges of the sheet of tinfoil dropped to reveal the emerging figure of the angel – one figure only since both were cut at the same time from the folded sheet, thus ensuring a proper symmetry. Mrs Prothero had been making angels for a good many Christmases now, ever since foil became readily available and an article on 'Make Your Own Clever Xmas Decorations' had caught her eye in the church magazine. Soon the angels, long trumpets raised to their lips, angular and decisive, were released from the stiff foil.

Mrs Prothero put them on top of the bureau next to the telephone and glanced at the fob watch she had got into the habit of wearing in her nursing-sister days.

Arthur was a little late. But then with Christmas Day falling on a Monday there was bound to be an extra rush this morning. But thank goodness the bank did at least close on Saturdays leaving him free to go out into the hurly-burly of the town's shopping streets to get the last things that could not be bought earlier. It was good of him to do this each year, though no more than his duty.

However the angels had hardly begun to swing to and fro a little in the heat from the fire below when there came a scuffly sort of bump on the flat's front door and Mrs Prothero hurried out to the hallway.

She pictured Arthur standing outside, his arms – they were rather short – clutching an assortment of parcels, unable to get at the latch-key in his trouser pocket, fastened by a chain to one of his braces buttons. It happened every year.

A rare twinkle of pleasure lighting up her large grey eyes and quite transforming the helmet-severe face with its long straight nose and uncompromising lower jaw, she hastened across to the solid door and turned back the latch. And there he was, just as she had pictured.

'You poor dear,' she said. 'You must have had an awful time.'

She closed the heavy door firmly behind him.

'It was pretty rough,' her husband agreed, waddling forward and laying down the bundle of holly he had been clutching on the top of the bureau, the only clear space he could see.

Mrs Prothero quickly relieved him of the rest of his purchases and took them through into the spick-and-span kitchen she prided herself on.

'I tell you what,' she called while her husband went to hang his overcoat in the hall cupboard, 'we'll make a little change for once. Let's have our start-of-Christmas drink now, and I'll tidy these away while you put up the holly before luncheon.'

For a moment a really quite apprehensive look appeared on Mr Prothero's round, twinkling-eyed face at this departure from tradition. But then he gave a little squaring-up shrug of his shoulders under his black bank-manager's jacket.

'Right ho,' he called. 'Let's do that, and be damned.'

He strutted boldly over to the hanging corner-cupboard where he kept his cellar and poured two glasses of ginger wine, adding a tot of whisky to his own.

He held the latter bottle up after he had finished, and assessed the quantity remaining in it.

'The senior staff certainly punished this at our little do the other day,' he said as Mrs Prothero came back in.

She looked severe.

'It was Mr Perkins,' she said. 'Considering he's your second-in-command, he ought to be more restrained.'

Mr Prothero sighed. Then he brightened up.

'But I thought the whole affair went better than in some other years,' he said.

Mrs Prothero considered.

'Yes,' she said, 'the juniors behaved well. Especially young Smith. He spoke to me quite nicely, asking about our Christmas and so forth. Really showing an interest.'

Mr Prothero puffed out his pink cheeks dubiously.

'I try to like him,' he said. 'I feel I ought to. But he will dress in that provocative manner.'

'No,' said Mrs Prothero firmly. 'I was quite impressed. I shall revise my opinion of him.'

Her husband handed her her glass.

'Shall we drink to him?' he asked, only half in joke.

'No,' said Mrs Prothero decidedly, 'we'll drink to Christmas.'

'To Christmas,' said Mr Prothero, raising his glass.

'To three whole days of perfect peace,' his wife replied.

She took a modest sip and sat herself down in her customary chair to one side of the fire, her toes just resting on the black-leaded surround.

'Well,' she said, 'I do think it was one of the wisest things we ever did, to say we'd never go away for Christmas. This little spell of quiet means more to me than any amount of junketing.'

'Perfectly so,' agreed Mr Prothero, though it was hard, for all his pink benevolence of face, to conceive of him doing much in the way of junketing.

Mrs Prothero took another sip of her wine and gave an unexpected chuckle.

'Such a funny thing yesterday afternoon,' she said. 'I quite forgot to tell you last night what with all the rush.'

'What was that?'

'A man called. You know how they do sometimes, even though our door is so tucked away inside the flats. It's being on the ground floor, I think.'

'Yes, yes. I often feel something should be done about such people. Some sort of notice. Only chaps like that are just the kind to ignore notices.'

'Yes. Well, I tried to tell him I never deal with hawkers, but he had me answering all sorts of questions before I got rid of him. And can you guess how I did that?'

Mrs Prothero wore a look of mild triumph.

'No,' said Mr Prothero. 'Did you take a broom to him?'

He chuckled.

'Oh, I would if necessary,' Mrs Prothero answered. 'But nothing like that was needed. You see, in the end I got it out of him what he was meant to be selling. Insurance. And then I told him who you were. I've never seen a face fall so quickly. "Just my luck," he said, "think I'm interesting a client and it turns out to be the wife of the bank manager."'

But Mr Prothero appeared not to appreciate the joke to the full.

'Questions,' he said. 'You say he asked questions. What sort of questions?'

'Oh, dozens. And perfectly ridiculous some of them. Like were we going out to church late on Christmas Eve.'

'I don't like the sound of this,' said Mr Prothero, a look of almost pantomime shrewdness appearing on his round face.

'Oh, he had his reasons,' his wife replied. 'It was a dangerous time to be out in the cold, he said. What if one of us slipped and broke a leg?'

'You told him we weren't going out?' Mr Prothero asked.

'Oh, yes. But whatever makes you so serious?'

Mr Prothero gave a man-of-the-world shake of his head.

'Because I very much suspect,' he said, 'that your insurance salesman was nothing but a crook. That's an old dodge for spying out the lie of the land, you know. And these fellows often go about their business over the holiday period.'

Mrs Prothero took a moment or two to digest this example of duplicity.

'Well,' she said at last, 'he certainly learnt this flat wouldn't be empty over Christmas. Quite providential really.'

She looked comfortably over at her husband.

But he was not looking at her. Instead he was sitting open-mouthed in his cosy wing-chair staring at the door behind her.

Mrs Prothero turned to see what had transfixed him.

In the half-open doorway of the room a man was standing. He was aged about thirty, dressed in a trench-coat mackintosh in spite of the sharpness of the weather, hatless, and with a thin face from which two big brown eyes looked out with an uneasy mixture of bravado and pain. At his throat was the somewhat greasy knot of a striped club tie.

And now Mr Prothero found his tongue.

'Who the devil are you?' he demanded. 'And how did you get in here?'

But Mrs Prothero knew the man.

'Arthur,' she said, her voice suddenly hollow with unexamined fears. 'Arthur, this is the person I was telling you about.'

'That's right,' the intruder said with a jerk of brashness, 'I popped in yesterday. Mrs Prothero and I had a chat.'

'You know my name then?' Mr Prothero said, a small tremor of doubt taking away somewhat from the determination with which the question was meant to have been put.

The man smiled, almost ingratiatingly.

'We had to know all about you both,' he explained. 'Just the same as we had to pull your front-door key from your pocket last week and take an impression from it. It's all part of the job.'

The door beside him was pushed wide and a second man entered. He was older than the first, between forty-five and fifty, short, broad-shouldered and with a fat, aggressive belly pushing open his heavy overcoat.

'Keep your bloody mouth shut, Tony,' he said curtly.

'What is this?' Mr Prothero demanded again. 'Who are you?'

The self-confident newcomer ignored this pouter-pigeon question.

'Just listen to me, and do what you're told,' he said with a cheerful briskness that suited his bustling manner.

'I certainly will not. I don't even know your name.'

The small mouth in the mottled face split into a quick grin at this.

'Proper introductions, is it, mate? All right then. The name's Dawson. And I'm here to do your bank. We're going to go in underground. Tunnel beneath that alleyway to the building on the other side.'

'That won't get you anywhere,' Mr Prothero snapped back, ruffled but undaunted. 'You'll not find a penny piece that's not in the main safe, and you won't get into that in a hurry.'

Dawson grinned again, standing solidly on short legs.

'What about the deposit boxes, cock?' he said. 'You've got the key to the gate for them, ain't you?'

Mr Prothero's round pink face positively paled.

'How did you know that?' he asked petulantly.

Dawson turned and called out in a loud, larky voice.

'Here, Dennis boy, you'd better come and show your spotty face.'

A young man of nineteen or twenty entered the room a little sheepishly. Dawson was right: there was at least one blatantly inflamed pimple on his pale face, just below and to the left of the thin nose.

'Smith,' exclaimed Mr Prothero at the sight of him.

The boy gave him a belligerent look.

'Yes,' he said, 'that's how we know all about what goes on in the bank, sir.'

The last word was an open jeer.

Mr Prothero ignored it.

'You have betrayed your trust,' he said.

For all the schoolmasterishness of the remark there was a dignity to it. It was a condemnation.

For an instant Smith had nothing to answer. Then he gushed words.

'You bet I've betrayed my trust,' he said. 'What sort of trust do you think you bought for my measly so-called salary? I'm making some real money now, something to make a show with.'

It was a moment of triumph for him. A declaration of independence.

But he was not allowed to savour it. His new boss trampled on his fine thoughts just as unfeelingly as his old one had done.

'All right, lad,' he said, 'you'll get your cut.'

He turned to Mr Prothero.

'So we want your key to the safe-deposit gate, mate,' he said. 'Where do you keep it? Over here?'

He marched down on the well-polished dark-oak bureau.

Mr Prothero scuttled up behind him.

'Get out of here this instant,' he said.

Dawson turned and the two short men stood confronting one another. The indignant cock robin and the small, aggressive bird-of-prey.

'I'll give you till I count five,' Mr Prothero said. 'And then I ring for the police.'

He glared pointedly at the telephone on top of the bureau, magnificently ignoring the fact that Dawson stood, straddle-legged, between him and it with the salesman Tony and young Smith watching from in front of the cheerful little fire.

'One. Two. Three—'

'Arthur,' said Mrs Prothero, breaking in unsteadily. 'Arthur, there are three of them.'

'Leave this to me, Ellen.'

It was the Manager speaking.

'Four,' he counted. 'Five.'

He gave Dawson a push. He might as well have pushed at a solid stone statue.

'Phone's cut off anyhow,' Dawson said, 'so just let's have that key.'

His right hand dipped into the sagging pocket of his open overcoat and came out holding a strip of dulled brass.

'You know what this is?' he said. 'It's the brass knuckles.'

He slipped the vicious-looking instrument over his fingers.

'Arthur,' said Mrs Prothero urgently. 'It's no good trying to outfight a man like this.'

'Quite right, old lady,' Dawson said. 'So come on, cock.'

'No,' squawked Mr Prothero.

And he darted sideways to the end of the bureau, picked up the bunch of holly he had put there only a few minutes earlier and rammed it hard into Dawson's face.

Dawson gave a howl of agony and Mr Prothero swung sharply on his heel and headed for the open door of the room.

Only to come bang into collision with yet another intruder, a dark, curly-headed man in a white polo-necked sweater, broad as a barn-door. Mr Prothero was sent staggering backwards.

And then Dawson, his mottled face pinpointed with blood drops, caught him by the shoulder and swung him round.

The brass knuckles came up from below with terrible force.

The crack they made as they hit Mr Prothero's jaw was like a pistol-shot, clean and sharp. Mr Prothero fell as if he was was a tree under the axe. The back of his head struck the black-leaded fireplace surround with a sound that was quieter than Dawson's blow but as sickening.

Almost at once Mrs Prothero was on her knees beside him.

The man at the door spoke.

'What in the name of goodness did you do that for?' he asked Dawson in a strong Welsh accent.

'You never saw what the bastard did to me,' Dawson replied sharply. 'He jabbed that holly right in my face.'

'But you shouldn't have hit him like that, man,' the newcomer said.

The Welsh accent enabled him to voice a wealth of shocked dismay.

But Dawson was not easily put in the wrong.

'Listen, Morgan,' he said, 'when I want advice from you I'll ask for it.'

'Yes, but—'

'Get over to that desk and look for the key to the gate.'

Morgan gave one glowering look from his sombrely handsome Welsh face and then went over to the bureau, flapping the front down with unnecessary violence and starting to rummage.

'And where's the peterman?' Dawson snapped at him.

'Making himself at home in the bedroom, if you must know,' Morgan answered.

'Yes, I must know,' Dawson replied. 'He's the bloke who's going to blow the big safe. He's important.'

Morgan's white-sweatered back eloquently expressed his feelings at the implication that he himself was not important. But he said nothing.

Down on the floor beside the fireplace Mrs Prothero had been examining her husband with quiet competence. Now she looked up.

'He's badly hurt,' she said. 'He must on no account be disturbed till the doctor's seen him.'

'No doctor,' Dawson said.

It took Mrs Prothero, down on her knees on the floor, some two or three seconds to absorb this. Then she rose in two stiff movements.

'Listen to me,' she said to Dawson, 'I was a nursing sister for years. I can recognise a serious injury when I see one. My husband must be got to hospital.'

'You'll have to nurse him here,' Dawson said brutally. 'I know your sort. I've been in hospital. And right nasty bitches you are. Well, see what good it does him.'

He glanced down at the tubby little unconscious figure on the floor.

'Here, Morgan,' he said, 'you and Tony carry him into the bathroom. That's right it hasn't got an outside window?'

He flicked a look across at the boy Smith, standing where he had been ever since the sudden explosion of violence and looking paler than before.

'I told you,' the boy said hurriedly. 'I took a good look round during the party.'

'Then get him out,' Dawson said.

White-sweatered Morgan and Club-tie Tony exchanged glances, but seemed to find nothing to say. They moved over towards Mr Prothero.

'Don't jerk him,' his wife said. 'Whatever you do don't jerk.'

The two of them knelt almost with reverence and slowly lifted Mr Prothero up. Mrs Prothero followed them out, grim-faced.

Smith scuttled into the little hall of the flat and opened the bathroom door for them.

In the sitting-room Dawson went over to the bureau and tried to open the top drawer. He had just burst it open with the coal-shovel and had started into it like a gutsy hen with a dish of scraps when Tony came back in.

'She isn't liking it,' he said.

'And you'd want her to like it, eh?' Dawson answered, paying little attention. 'You'd like everyone to be merry and bright all the way along.'

Suddenly he swung round.

'Well, they ain't always merry and bright, not unless they bloody well make sure of it for themselves.'

In his hand there dangled a ring with two keys on it.

Tony's eyes lit up.

'Is that the one ?' he asked.

''Course it is. That and the front-door mortise here, by the look of it. But there's fifteen feet of solid earth between us and the bank, so get into that kitchen and get the boards up.'

At midnight the fire in the sitting-room was still burning well, something quite unprecedented. But the little fireplace was scattered with ash in a fashion which Mrs Prothero would never have tolerated. Above, the tinfoil angels swung in high perturbation.

But if the empty sitting-room was untidy, the kitchen beyond was chaos. The polished yellow-and-grey linoleum had been torn right across. Three floor-boards had been removed wholesale and lay piled beside Mrs Prothero's ironing-table. The corner of the room where normally the vegetable rack plumply held potatoes, carrots and onions was heaped with chunks of clay and dirt-encrusted brick from the foundations of the flats.

On the spotlessly kept kitchen table sat Dawson, swinging stubby legs and sipping coffee which Morgan, divested long since of his white sweater, had just made, neatly ranging cups, saucers and teaspoons in a fashion that did credit to his upbringing. Tony, his face dirt-streaked and unhappy, sat exhaustedly on one of Mrs Prothero's two kitchen chairs. Young Smith, his pimple inflamed to a yet angrier red by hours of hard work, sat on the other, elbows on knees, body slumped.

'Well,' Dawson barked abruptly, 'how much did you add just now?'

Tony looked up quickly.

'At least another foot,' he said.

'Nine inches,' said Morgan.

'Nine inches?' Dawson echoed with a touch of a snarl. 'Now listen, that's too bleeding slow.'

'We've been having to do a bit of shoring-up like,' Morgan explained, sulkily.

'Shoring-up? What the hell do you think you're making? The Channel Tunnel? Get back down and dig.'

'It isn't as if we're getting all that much help, is it?' Morgan answered.

'You'd like me down there, wouldn't you?' Dawson said. 'And what'd happen when some nosy neighbour came knocking at the door? That old bitch in the bathroom would start screaming, and we'd have a police-car outside in no time.'

Morgan glared at the grey and yellow checks of Mrs Prothero's desecrated lino.

'Well, what about the peterman?' he said. 'Playing bloody Patience in that bedroom. Not even coming out for his coffee. Why can't he take a turn?'

'Not in his contract, mate,' Dawson answered, with a return of his old cheerfulness. 'He comes to blow the safe, and he doesn't—'

He broke off.

From outside in the hallway there had come a tattoo of muffled knocks.

'It's them,' young Smith whispered hoarsely. 'The police.'

'It's the old bitch,' Dawson replied. 'Go and shut her up.'

'But last time . . .'

Dawson moved one stubby fist. Young Smith positively scuttled for the door.

He was not gone long.

'She wants to talk to you,' he said, putting his head shamefacedly only just back into the room.

'Did you tell her to stop that row?' Dawson said.

The boy looked as if he would have liked to have ducked his head back and stayed out of sight till things had calmed down. But plainly he did not dare.

'I told her it was no use asking to talk to you,' he offered.

A sharp grin flicked across Dawson's mouth.

'So you come and ask?' he said.

'But she said Mr Prothero's really bad,' Smith pleaded. 'She said something about a fracture of the skull. I don't know.'

'All right, so he's got a fractured skull,' Dawson said. 'Who cares?'

From behind Smith the thumping on the locked bathroom door began again. Smith stood where he was, half in, half out.

'All right,' Dawson said at last. 'Bring her in.'

Smith disappeared as quickly as a schoolboy let off a punishment. In a moment Mrs Prothero came marching into the kitchen ahead of him.

The hours locked away with her injured husband had worked on her. Her features had lost what feminine softness they had had. Her eyes were deep sunk. And they blazed.

'So,' she said, going straight up to Dawson, 'here you are quietly relaxing as you go about your money-grubbing moles' work. Well, here's a fact to slap into your dream of unending riches. Not three yards from where you sit lies a man facing his Maker. And it is at your hand he is dying.'

She got no reaction from Dawson, swinging his legs on the table. But she clearly had an effect on the others. Tony shifted on his neatly painted chair and darted a glance of entreaty at Morgan. And Morgan went stony-faced as a rock from his native mountains.

Soon enough Dawson answered her.

'OK, but I don't believe a word of it.'

He jumped down, forcing Mrs Prothero to take half a pace back.

'Now,' he said, 'back you get inside there, and don't let's have any more trouble.'

Mrs Prothero looked at him with conviction burning on her helmet-like features.

Dawson grinned.

'You can take a coffee,' he said. 'Or two, one each.'

'Coffee,' Mrs Prothero retorted. 'You are faced with a man who will be dead before Christmas Day is gone, and you offer him coffee.'

Suddenly she swung round to the others.

'No,' she said, 'I won't let you allow him to die. Isn't there one of you with the courage to speak up?'

But Dawson was undismayed.

'All right,' he said, 'let's see if anyone's chicken.'

He looked at them one by one. Then abruptly jerked back to stare at Tony.

'Do you believe the lady?' he asked. 'Come on, don't be scared to say. Do you believe the old geezer's dying?'

Tony reddened.

'Oh, shut up, for heaven's sake,' he said. 'Of course I don't believe it. He can't be.'

Behind Dawson young Smith's face registered almost comical relief to have escaped the dilemma.

Dawson turned to Morgan.

'Well, how about you, Welshie? Do you think he's dying?'

Morgan contrived to put on a judicial look.

'I expect the good lady's a bit hysterical like,' he said.

Dawson grinned his twisty little grin.

'Yes, hysterical,' he said. 'You can ignore her then, can't you, boy? Hysterical women are something a nice young man making his way in the world, with his own Health Club and all, doesn't have to have anything to do with.'

Morgan bit his lip.

'And ain't it a pity,' Dawson went on, 'that that Health Club got so rotten into debt that nice Mr Morgan has to rob a bank?'

Morgan started out of his chair, but thought better of it.

Now Dawson turned to young Smith.

'Well, do you believe your former employer'll never get his gold watch for fifty years' devoted service?' he said.

'No, no,' Smith almost shouted. 'No, I don't believe the stinking cow.'

But he was not going to escape so lightly.

Mrs Prothero marched up till her long implacable face was within inches of his.

'No,' she said. 'You have seen my husband. You are going to tell the truth.'

'I – I didn't get more than a glimpse.'

'You took your look. I was watching. Answer me.'

Young Smith had no answer.

'Come on, laddie,' Dawson said. 'Answer up.'

The boy tautened his whole body.

'No,' he flung out. 'No, I tell you. I don't believe a word she says. He's all right. Old Prothero's all right, I tell you.'

Dawson pushed his stocky frame behind him and Mrs Prothero.

'Too bad, Ma,' he said. 'It didn't come off. Now back inside.'

'I'm tired,' Morgan protested when Dawson woke the three of them next evening.

'Tired?' Dawson snapped. 'You've just had an hour's kip, haven't you? Do you think I have? Do you think I've closed a blessed eye since we've been here?'

'I don't see why you couldn't have done,' Morgan answered.

'Don't you? Well, I'll tell you why not. Because if I did Smithie here'd let that bitch out before anyone knew it. Anybody can see he's fallen for that story of hers.'

'I could have kept watch on him,' Morgan said.

Dawson darted him a look.

'Do you think the boy's scared of you?' he asked. 'He knows you're a sight too worried about what the neighbours'd think to belt him one. He'd get his little dander up and tell you to go to hell. And then where'd we all be?'

He turned away and studied the clock on the mantelpiece.

'Just gone half past six,' he said. 'We'll be in there by half-seven now. That gives the peterman all and more of his blessed three hours to muffle the safe and set his stuff right, and then we blow it just as the old church bells start going hammer and tongs. As planned.'

He stood there with his stumpy legs astraddle, and a gleam of something like visionary light in his eyes.

It was abruptly extinguished.

'Smithie,' he said, 'go and have a look in the bathroom.'

But young Smith jibbed.

'Me again. Why does it always have to be me?'

Dawson looked at him. Then he swiftly crossed the room to where his overcoat lay flung on a chair. He dipped his hand into a pocket and pulled out the knuckle-duster.

Young Smith needed no further hint.

But he was out of the room for only a few seconds before he came in again following Mrs Prothero.

'Christ,' said Dawson, 'you've not let her out again?'

Mrs Prothero ignored this.

'No,' she said harshly to Dawson, 'he is not dead. That's what you sent the boy to find out, isn't it?'

'If he was going to die,' Dawson replied, maintaining an appearance of calm, 'I might send to ask. But as he isn't, I don't.'

From the door Smith put in a word.

'He looks pretty rough now though.'

'Does he?' Dawson answered. 'Perhaps you're setting up as a doc, are you? Seeing you've given up a career in banking.'

'No,' said Smith, 'but he's rotten. You can see he is.'

Mrs Prothero pounced.

'Exactly,' she said. 'You can't get away from that face, can you? So you had better persuade your friends to let me go for help.'

'Don't be blasted silly,' Smith burst out at this. 'Do you think ambulance men are going to come and fetch him and leave us getting on with what we're doing?'

'Then you'll have to stop what you're doing, won't you?' returned Mrs Prothero implacably.

'We can't stop it, we can't,' Smith shouted. 'We're in sight of it now. More money than I ever dreamt of having. And then I'll show them. Out in South America I'm going to have cars by the garageful, and suits. And the dollies'll come crawling, you'll see.'

'Money,' retorted Mrs Prothero. 'A little money, and a human life. You've got to choose.'

'No,' the boy yelled. 'I tell you he isn't that bad. All I saw was a face with a lot of bandage round it. He might be fit as a fiddle for all I know.'

'You know he is not. And I am not budging from this spot till I've made you act on that.'

But now Dawson stepped in.

'Tony,' he said curtly, 'put her back.'

'Me?' Tony exclaimed, a look of hurt outrage beaming out of his liquid brown eyes.

'Yes, you,' Dawson said. 'I'm doing the telling now, and don't you forget.'

Tony went up to Mrs Prothero.

'You'll have to go, you know,' he said.

Mrs Prothero ignored him.

Tony offered her his arm in a gesture of slick over-politeness.

'Allow me to have the pleasure?'

Again she ignored him.

'Tony,' Dawson said.

A look of childish fury darkened Tony's face and he seized Mrs Prothero by the arm and dragged her out, slamming the door violently behind him. Out in the hallway, where quantities of dirty soil from the tunnel had by now encroached, he shouted loudly.

'For God's sake, stop all this.'

Then he abruptly lowered his voice.

'And anyhow it's no damn use. You don't know Dawson. He's got young Smith so scared he wouldn't do a thing, even if he wanted to. And I don't much suppose he wants. He's a nasty-minded little tick.'

Mrs Prothero whispered too. But it was a fierce whisper.

'And you're not nasty, are you? You'd like everyone to be nice and comfortable, wouldn't you? I know, you see.'

Tony shrugged his shoulders.

'Well, there's nothing wrong in wanting to have a good time and wanting others to have a good time, too,' he answered.

'And so you persuade yourself my husband is having a good time,' Mrs Prothero whispered sharply. 'A good time as he slips nearer and nearer the grave.'

'No,' said Tony, almost speaking aloud. 'But, I mean, all that's just a trick, isn't it? It's OK for keeping Dawson in his place, and I don't blame you. But you can tell me, you know.'

'All right, I will tell you. As a secret between the two of us.'

Mrs Prothero's grey eyes looked into his.

'My husband is dying,' she said. 'Get that into your head. Just one unpleasant fact. He is dying, and you are letting him die.'

'Listen,' answered Tony, casting a look desperately round. 'I'd like to help. But I can't. I'm just as much trapped as you are.'

'Pull yourself together, man,' Mrs Prothero snapped, with a glance of simple disgust. 'We're going back in there, and you are going to tell the others it's time my husband had help.'

'No,' Tony pleaded.

'Get in,' said Mrs Prothero.

She went over and jerked the sitting-room door open.

Tony went in, with Mrs Prothero close behind.

Dawson looked at him.

'I thought I told you to lock her up,' he said.

'Yes. Yes. Look, Mrs Proth—'

'Tell him,' Mrs Prothero said.

Tony turned to Dawson, almost all the way.

'For God's sake,' he suddenly burst out, 'she's right. We all know she is. The fellow's dying. We can't just let him.'

Now at last his eyes found Dawson's.

'You're going to let her go for help,' he said. 'Or I'll bloody shout out of this window.'

He swung away and began to make for the window. Dawson caught him by the elbow almost before he had moved. He spun him round and sent him smack back against the wall by the bureau. Then he stooped to the chair where he had let the knuckle-duster fall on top of his coat and picked up the little strip of heavy brass.

He stood in front of Tony and jabbed at his face until he fell to the floor.

Tony did not lie long where he had fallen. Dawson saw to that. He sent young Smith for water, splashed it over Tony, pulled him to his feet and sent him back down the tunnel, all within ten minutes.

But then something happened which had not at all entered Dawson's scheme of things. The tunnel fell in.

It fell partly on top of Smith, and Dawson himself went down and hauled the boy, who was in a dead faint, out by his wrists. Then he went down again and with the aid of one of Mrs Prothero's saucepans dug through the fall and got at Morgan.

When he eventually scrambled out Smith was still unconscious on the spoil-strewn kitchen floor with Tony, his spaniel face terribly distorted with bruises and cuts, sitting looking hopelessly down at him.

Dawson sent him to fetch Mrs Prothero.

'Get a look at the lad,' he said to her when Tony brought her in. 'Find out what's the matter with him. We've had a bit of trouble.'

Without a word Mrs Prothero knelt beside Smith, as earlier she had knelt beside her husband. She went to work with cool expertness and at the end of five minutes looked up.

'It's only his foot as far as I can tell,' she said. 'But that's badly crushed. It's impossible to tell how badly. Otherwise he's fainted, but he should come out of that soon enough. Poor lad.'

'All right,' Dawson said, 'do what you have to do for him.'

'What I have to do?' retorted Mrs Prothero, still kneeling on the earth-stained linoleum. 'It's not a question of what I can do. This boy must go to hospital.'

Dawson gave her one of his savage little grins.

'Hospital nothing,' he said. 'You told me he's just hurt his foot. You can deal with that. You missed your chance though, didn't you? You ought to have added him to your list of the dead and dying.'

Mrs Prothero had been busy with her patient. Now she gave Dawson a brief glance.

'Isn't it about time you stopped this nonsense of pretending my husband isn't as bad as I've said?' she asked.

Dawson made no reply. For a little while he walked about the kitchen, where he could for earth and rubble. Then he went and stood over Mrs Prothero again.

'Listen,' he said, 'you're going to get that boy patched up so we can leave here as planned with all our nice gift-wrapped parcels full of money as the crowds come out of the Midnight service at the church. If need be, we'll carry the lad and pretend he's drunk. But we're going then, and we're going with the money. Understand that.'

Mrs Prothero looked up.

'And what if I won't do as you say?'

Dawson's answer came without hesitation.

'You saw me deal with Tony here. You'll get the same. Woman or no woman.'

Mrs Prothero looked at him quite calmly.

'Then I shall have to help you,' she said.

Dawson glanced at Smith. He was, for all his youth, a full six feet tall and he occupied a lot of the kitchen floor.

'Here,' Dawson said, 'I'll dump him out in the hall. With the doorkey in my pocket you'll be as safe there as anywhere, and we can get on with the digging. There's a whole lot more earth to be shifted now. I'll have to take a hand myself.'

He left the kitchen and Mrs Prothero heard him with a sudden switch to considerable deference asking the man who all the while occupied the bedroom in solitary state whether he could as a special favour guard the bathroom key and 'keep an eye on the old bitch'. Apparently he agreed because Dawson came back in, unceremoniously picked up Smith's thin body and dumped him on the hall carpet next to the earthpile there. When she followed she caught a glimpse of the mysterious safe-blower. He was lying propped on one elbow on her bed, with his shoes on. And spread out on her husband's bed were two packs of playing-cards in an elaborate game of Patience.

Young Smith recovered consciousness soon after Dawson had gone back to the tunnel. Mrs Prothero wiped his forehead with the dampened tea-towel she had brought from the kitchen.

'Well,' she demanded briskly, 'and how are we feeling now?'

Smith admitted in a croaky voice to not feeling too bad. He demanded, querulously, to know what had happened and Mrs Prothero told him, right down to Dawson's instructions to her to get him well enough to leave with the money some three hours hence.

'It'll get better, my foot, in the end, won't it?' Smith asked.

'Provided you get proper attention,' said Mrs Prothero drily.

'I'll get that,' Smith assured her eagerly. 'They've got good hospitals in South America, same as anywhere else. And I'll be able to pay. I will, too. I want to be able to go about, hit the night-clubs, live it up.'

Mrs Prothero looked at him.

'You poor fish,' she said, very quietly and confidentially. 'They still won't care tuppence for you, the girls.'

Wide-eyed horror appeared on Smith's face. Blasphemy had been spoken.

'Look,' he whispered feverishly, 'when I've got money girls'll come running. Running.'

'To you? If you want that sort of success – and heaven knows that's pitiful enough – you've got to be the sort of person who earns some respect. And do you think that just because you've let that Dawson frighten you into committing a crime, and letting an innocent man die, you're any different?'

'I am. I am.'

'Don't be silly,' replied Mrs Prothero, as if she was in one of the children's wards. 'You're worth nothing, and you never will be.'

She looked him straight in the eyes.

'Not unless,' she added, 'when the time comes here you go the right way and go it hard.'

Smith looked away.

Mrs Prothero rose and went to the door of her bedroom. She addressed the man lying on her bed.

'I want to go and attend to my husband,' she said. 'Will you kindly unlock the bathroom door?'

The peterman gave her a stony look from little pale blue eyes. But he swung himself off the bed and did as she had asked.

In spite of the setback the tunnellers had suffered the church bells had been battering the night air with their clangour for only five minutes when Morgan unlocked the bathroom door and told Mrs Prothero the big safe was about to be blown.

'That peterman insisted on having a coffee first,' he said. 'It seems it's his right. So I brought you a couple of cups.'

Mrs Prothero looked at him.

'Do you still really believe my husband is fit enough to drink coffee?' she asked.

Morgan studied the hall carpet.

'You know, we're all very sorry that had to happen,' he said.

'Who's sorry?' Mrs Prothero countered. 'Do you think Dawson's sorry?'

Morgan bit his full lower lip.

'Well, not exactly.'

He looked up for an instant.

'In many ways,' he said, 'I wish I'd never got involved with that chap.'

'In many ways,' Mrs Prothero echoed ironically. 'But never in the way of doing anything about it. You're involved with him in what in a very few hours will be murder. The law says that you are equally guilty. And the law is right.'

Morgan looked pained.

'I wish you'd understand,' he said. 'There was a strict agreement there was to be no violence in this business. I said I wouldn't come in, unless. And he had to have me, you know, for my mining experience. Before I went in for the physical culture. It was only because that got in such a terrible jam that I had to consider this business at all.'

'And now you'll end up doing a life sentence,' Mrs Prothero capped him grimly.

But she failed to quench him.

'Oh, no,' he said. 'That's where you're wrong, see. What you haven't taken into account is how damn clever Dawson is. I've watched him, you know. And he's smart all right. He'll have us all off to South America before ever this business is known about.'

'Exactly,' said Mrs Prothero. 'Dawson is clever. Too clever for you.'

It took Morgan several seconds to absorb this. The thoughts crossing his mind could clearly be seen on his mobile Welsh face.

They had come to forming, almost aloud, the word 'Cheated' when from the tunnel in the kitchen there woofed up the sound of a single sharp boom.

'The safe,' Morgan said.

And the next moment faintly but shrilly through the tunnel there came the sound of a bell ringing and ringing.

Mrs Prothero was first to realise what must have happened.

'It looks as if your Mr Dawson is not so clever after all,' she said. 'There must have been an alarm bell he didn't neutralise.'

Morgan without a word tried to open the front door. But the mortise key was still in Dawson's pocket. He looked all round and then started off for the sitting-room and its windows. But he was not quick enough.

There was a thumping sound from the kitchen and Dawson himself came staggering out of the tunnel.

'Morgan,' he shouted. 'The bathroom key, quick. I've got to know where that bell is.'

In an instant Mrs Prothero ran across to the bathroom door and spreadeagled herself in front of it.

'You will not touch him,' she declared as Dawson came into the hall. 'Anything could be the end of him now.'

'Get out of my way.'

Dawson took a step forward, fist bunched.

And then the alarm stopped ringing.

Tony, coming in from the kitchen looking panic-stricken in every feature, stopped.

'The peterman,' he said. 'He must have found it. He was going round like a scalded rabbit when I left.'

Smith hobbled in from the kitchen, still holding an incongruously festive sheet of Christmas wrapping paper, and full of plaintive questions. Even when Dawson had tersely answered him they stood where they were, as if none of them could believe the alarm was over. And they had still scarcely shifted when the peterman came up out of the tunnel.

'Well,' he said, without ceremony to Dawson, 'what you going to do?'

Dawson thought.

'Wait here,' he said eventually. 'Give it a few minutes more to see if anyone heard. It must have been some old bell. We certainly did the one that rings at the police station.'

'All right,' the peterman said.

He went over to the front door and tried it.

'You'd better unlock this, mate,' he remarked. 'If we have to go, we'll have to go quick.'

Dawson took the mortise key from his pocket and turned it in the lock. Then, with an assumption of complete calm, he strolled into the sitting-room and plumped himself down in Mrs Prothero's armchair.

The others followed him in.

'Look,' Tony said, 'shouldn't we all wait round the corner somewhere? We could come back when we were sure it was all clear.'

'And have you scuttle off out of it?' Dawson said. 'We stay here, chum.'

He looked round the rest of them, coming to rest eventually on limping, white-faced Smith.

'Scared as hell, aren't you, lad?' he said.

'No, no, I'm not. Really, I'm not.'

It was plain that, however scared or not scared he might be of the police coming, he was frightened stiff of Dawson.

'Well,' Dawson said to him, 'you can calm down, sonny. No one's heard that bell. You can take it from me.'

From just inside the door Mrs Prothero intervened.

'It would have been better for you, far, if that bell had been heard.'

'I tell you it can't have been heard,' Dawson replied.

'And if it hasn't, and you carry out your plan and leave me here with Arthur when you go, they'll find a dead man in with me.'

Dawson's little grin returned.

'That's not going to worry me,' he said. 'I'll be far away.'

'And what then?' asked Mrs Prothero sternly.

'What then? Then I'll be up on the top side. Then it'll be my turn to rub faces in the dirt.'

He stuck out his muscled belly in defiance. But his boast had only confirmed Mrs Prothero in her diagnosis of him.

'Let me tell you something,' she said. 'Once I may not have understood a man like you. But there's some use to be made of long dark hours locked away with a dying man. I can see you now, right down to the very depths. And I'll tell you what you'll do when you get to South America and start living this life you've dreamt of so long. You'll curl up and die.'

Dawson jumped to his feet.

'You'll die,' Mrs Prothero continued unperturbed. 'You'll die because the only thing that's kept you going has been the thought of your turn to rub faces in the dirt. And when you feel you've got that, you'll be finished. I don't know what way it will take you. Gambling, I should say. You'll gamble yourself into the gutter, and then you'll creep into a hole and die.'

And it was clear then that Mrs Prothero had at last won her battle. Dawson stood without an atom of fight left in him. Above his head the trumpeting angels lazily swung.

'Well,' Mrs Prothero barked, turning to the others, 'are you going to take your chance now? Here's a decision you can make for yourself, Smith. And you, Tony, you can act in the real world for once. And, Morgan, do you still believe this creature's so clever?'

'I'm getting out of here,' Morgan announced.

He started towards the hall.

But a voice halted him.

Small, dry-faced and insignificant, the peterman stood there and uttered one word.

'Stop.'

Morgan turned.

'You're a lot of fools,' the peterman said. 'I've blown that safe for you. And you're running out just because of an old bitch's sharp tongue.'

'Yes,' said Morgan slowly, 'the money is there after all. It'd be stupid not to take it now.'

And Dawson was quick to scramble back into leadership.

'I should bloody well hope so,' he said. 'Not a soul's heard that bell. Inside again, quick.'

He hurried out into the earth-mounded hall, the others at his heels.

But not at his orders. Not all of them.

'No,' young Smith shouted suddenly at the back. 'I've seen you down, and I'm going.'

He was nearer the front door than any of them. He turned and got a hand to the Yale knob.

But Dawson was still formidable. He had wheeled round in an instant at Smith's hysterical shout and now he lunged.

And Smith, turning back, struck out. Blindly, but hard.

His fist connected with Dawson's face and stopped him. It stopped him just long enough for a frantic twist at the Yale knob, for the door to swing wide, for the boy to get out into the corridor.

'Help, help, police, help.'

The cries echoed loud, and the thump and thud of young Smith's lame run echoed too.

It was followed at once by a stampede of other running feet. Only the peterman stayed for a few seconds, stayed to deliver a parting valediction.

'You win, you hag,' he snarled at Mrs Prothero. 'You win, but I hope he does die. I hope he dies in agony.'

Then he too was off, at a fast, wary run.

Mrs Prothero turned to the bathroom door.

'Arthur,' she called, 'did you hear that? He hopes you'll die. You can come out now.'

# ANTHONY LEJEUNE

---

# Something On Everyone

John Deakin's voice, normally a controlled and confident instrument for speech-making, trembled on the verge of a stammer. 'As I told you on the telephone,' he said, 'I'm in rather a jam.'

'All right,' said Lord Frane, 'let's have the story.' It was lucky, he thought, that the Great British Public – the voting public – couldn't see Deakin now. The man was shaken and scared in a way that Frane had seen several times before in his long political experience; the way of hitherto unblemished success which suddenly hits trouble; the way of a much-praised rising politician before whose feet a gulf has opened which threatens to swallow up everything he has achieved and hoped to achieve.

Deakin's fears, whatever they were, might be exaggerated. People generally did manage to get out of their troubles somehow, particularly if they had sophisticated and powerful friends. But, of course, not always. Frane could remember one or two sad cases . . . He didn't really like John Deakin very much, but the Party had great hopes of him. He looked good on television – which is what mattered nowadays. If he came unstuck, it would be not only a personal tragedy but damaging: and Frane's job was to see that the Party didn't get damaged.

The other two people in his drawing-room were very old friends: George Liddle and Sir Peter Farmiloe, sound Party men both, who knew the world and knew Westminster. Frane had asked Deakin if he minded their being present; their advice might be useful, he'd said.

Deakin swallowed a little more whisky. 'I got this letter a month ago,' he said. 'It was from a man I once knew, called Derek Shee. You might have come across him. He was interested in politics. I think he was on the Candidates' List for a while. Anyway, this letter referred to something which once happened to me, and said that, if I wanted to talk about it, I was to put an advertisement in the personal column of *The Times*, consisting of just one word – 1968, the year 1968, which is when the thing happened.

'So I did that. I put the advertisement in. And late in the afternoon, when it appeared, Shee telephoned me at my office in the City. He wanted me to meet him at a pub that evening. I went there. And he asked me for money – to keep quiet, though I'm not sure he ever put it so crudely. But the implication was that, if I didn't pay, he would sell the story to a newspaper. He didn't ask for a great deal, only the equivalent, he said, of what a newspaper might pay him. Five hundred pounds. I agreed. I got the money out of the bank next morning, and delivered it to him at another pub.

'It's odd. I knew as well as anyone else that when you pay off a blackmailer you don't get rid of him. He's likely to come back for more. I've heard that, and read it, a dozen times. And yet I believed, or I convinced myself, that I was getting rid of him. He telephoned again this morning, wanting another five hundred. When I hesitated, he began putting on the pressure, hinting at what would happen to my career if the facts became known. Only hinting. He was obviously being careful not to say anything too explicit on the telephone. He told me to be at the same pub tomorrow evening at six-thirty. I said I'd think about it, and hung up.'

Deakin paused, and looked at the others for their reaction.

'Did you consider going to the police?' asked Frane.

'Of course I did. But I can't.'

'Because you don't want to tell them – whatever it is that Shee knows?'

'Partly that. And partly because it wouldn't be safe, would it? That's one of the things I wanted to ask your advice about. I mean, if there was a prosecution, I might appear as "Mr X", but surely the chances are it would leak? There would be gossip in the Temple or in Fleet Street, and then in the City and at Westminster. And I'd be done. Isn't that likely?'

Frane nodded. 'I must admit it is. At least, there would be a danger. And this is something you absolutely can't risk?'

Deakin took another drink of whisky. The only sound in the room was the soft ticking of a handsome clock on the chimneypiece and a faint murmur of traffic, deadened by good double glazing and heavy velvet curtains. At last Deakin said: 'I think I'd better tell you.' He glanced at Farmiloe and Liddle. 'I know I can trust all of you to keep quiet about it.'

From his inside pocket he produced an envelope. 'First,' he said, 'here's the original letter.'

The address on the envelope and the letter inside were typewritten, rather badly. Frane read it in silence, and then handed it to the others.

It said: *Dear Mr Deakin, It's a long time since you heard from me, but I've been hearing about you. As one of your supporters, I've been shocked by what I heard. It's about the poor little girl and the cover-up. At the moment I'm the only one who knows, apart from those who were involved. But if the facts were ever published, it would do great harm to the Cause we both believe in, and it would ruin you. I need reassurance. If you are willing to talk about it, please insert a small ad in The Times, just saying '1968'. Meanwhile I don't think you should tell anyone else about this letter. Yours very sincerely, Derek Shee.* There was no address or date.

Having read it, Farmiloe handed the letter back to Deakin. 'Quite clever,' Frane said. 'You couldn't exactly call it a blackmailing letter.'

'While making the intention fairly plain,' added Farmiloe.

Deakin took a deep breath. 'What he's referring to happened in my last year at London University. There was a girl. Not a student, just a girl I met at a party. She became pregnant – and that's when I found out she was only fifteen. Only fifteen! My God, in many ways she was far more sophisticated than me. My father and her father fixed it up between them. My father paid, quite a lot. I lived in a nightmare for several months, in case something went wrong. But nothing

303

did, and the girl kept quiet. I never saw her again, but a few years later I read about her in the papers. She'd killed herself. Sleeping pills and drink.

'I'm not proud of that story, but, looking back, I can't see myself as a villain. If it hadn't been me, it would have been someone else. The father was a drunk. Her mother was dead, and there were no brothers or sisters. That's how we were able to hush it up. Eventually I really had almost forgotten about it. It seems like something which happened to someone else.'

'How did Shee come to learn about it?' asked Liddle.

'From the girl's father, when he was in a maudlin condition one night. He swore Shee to secrecy, and said he was going to tell him a family secret he'd never told anyone before. Well, that's the size of it. What do you think?'

Frane poured whisky. 'It's not good. I've no idea if the police would prosecute after so long. Probably not, and I could make discreet enquiries about that. They might feel they had to if it became very public. But that's not entirely the point, is it? How do you think your Constituency Association would react?'

'Some of them might be sympathetic. But they'd sling me out. And then my job, which is really just a way for the bank to sponsor an MP, would go too.'

'So at all costs it must not become public. I think I agree; it would be too risky to go to the police. John, I'd like to mull this one over. Could you bear to go home now, and let Peter and George and me talk it out and see what we can come up with?'

Two hours later they hadn't come up with much. Farmiloe had begun by wondering if the matter was actually as serious as Deakin thought. 'It's a long time ago, and he wasn't responsible for the girl's death.'

'If that's all there is to it, I'm inclined to agree with you,' said Liddle. 'But is that all there is to it?'

Frane shook his head. 'I doubt it. You know Deakin's reputation. You've seen the gossip columns. He likes girls, and very young girls too. If once this can of worms is opened, who knows what may crawl out?'

'So you think that's really what's worrying him? Nice man, our promising young colleague.'

'We don't *know* there's anything else,' said Farmiloe.

'There's always something else,' replied Frane. 'He's not my favourite man, but nor am I inclined to throw first stones. The remarkable thing, surely, isn't when somebody gets found out but that most of us never do. If our lives and careers were extended indefinitely, we should all come a cropper sooner or later.'

'Speak for yourself.'

'Oh I am, I am. But the point is, we've all seen political scandals. Several in the past few years. And once they start to unravel, it's very difficult to stop them – particularly if the press has got wind of the story.'

'In most of the cases you're talking about, the best policy would have been to make a clean breast of it straight away. Trying to cover up was what did the real harm.'

'Making a clean breast of it might have been a very fine gesture,' said Liddle, 'but it usually wouldn't have saved the chap's career.'

'The art of covering up has always seemed to me an essential part of politics,' said Frane. 'The problem is to make the covering up stick. In Deakin's case, how do we persuade Mr Derek Shee to keep quiet permanently?'

'Threaten him with the police? I agree that an actual prosecution would be risky, but perhaps we could scare him.'

'We might scare him off demanding any more money, but that wouldn't prevent him from sending an anonymous letter to some newspaper. Rather the contrary indeed. He'd probably want to get his revenge.'

'Just think what Fearless Fred would do with it in the. *Daily News*,' said Farmiloe.

'I must confess I take that rag purely for Fred Mandeville's column,' said Liddle. 'He can be bloody funny.'

'"Scurrilous" is the old-fashioned word,' Farmiloe retorted.

'Well, a power in the land anyway,' agreed Frane. 'So we must keep his nose out of young Mr Deakin's past if we can. Any suggestions?'

'A private detective,' said Liddle, 'who might get something on Shee?'

'It's a thought, but I'm not very keen on bringing in someone else. We know where that sort of thing can lead, don't we?' Frane knocked the ash off his cigar, then said slowly: 'I think I might talk to Mr Shee myself.'

'Is that wise?' asked Farmiloe. 'Wouldn't it be exposing the Party, an admission of vulnerability?'

'Oh,' said Frane cheerfully, 'I'll go in disguise.'

And so, in a sense, he did. He arranged to go with Deakin to the rendezvous in the pub. 'Just introduce me as a friend. I can be Mr Robinson.'

'He's not going to say anything in front of a witness,' objected Deakin. 'He'll probably think you're a policeman.'

'If he believes that, he'll believe anything. My grey hairs should convince him I'm not. But let's see what happens. I want to size the fellow up myself.'

He indulged himself in the agreeable notion of disguise to the extent of wearing glasses, which he never normally did except for reading, wrapping a muffler round his neck and pulling an old tweed hat down over his eyes. 'Pretty sinister,' he said to his image in the looking-glass.

The pub was quite sinister too, in an alley off the Strand. Shee had probably chosen it because nobody could be watching the entrance without being seen, and the bar, at that time of the evening, contained only a couple of regulars – the stage doorkeeper from an adjacent theatre and a newspaper-seller who had just finished peddling his wares. Later there would be some theatregoers, fortifying themselves before the curtain went up and restoring themselves in the interval: but not yet.

Arriving at exactly six-thirty, Frane and Deakin bought drinks and took them to a table in the corner. Five minutes later Shee pushed open the door. He froze for a moment when he saw Frane, but then walked over to them grinning.

Neatly dressed, podgy, somehow too confident – Frane wondered if it was only knowing that he was a slippery villain which made him look like one.

'This is a friend of mine,' said Deakin, 'George Robinson.'

'I'm honoured,' said Shee. 'Don't I remember your friend from my political days? Not that we ever met. I was much too unimportant. But, of course, I've seen his picture in the papers. "George Robinson" – that's a good one.'

'I've heard about you too, Mr Shee,' replied Frane. 'Let me get you a drink.'

While he did so, Deakin and Shee sat in silence. When Frane had rejoined them, Shee said to Deakin: 'You decided to come then.'

'You asked me to.'

'So I did. Just for a friendly chat – since we have so many interests in common.'

'May I ask what those interests are?' said Frane.

'Oh, the good of the Party. And old times. I'm still very keen on politics, you know. I read the newspapers and I've a lot of friends in Fleet Street. I was thinking only today that I ought to get in touch with my friends in Fleet Street. Perhaps I will. Very soon.'

Deakin had already emptied his glass and was looking at it fiercely. 'For God's sake, man,' he muttered, 'say what you mean.'

'Mean? I don't mean anything in particular. But I had hoped for a quiet talk, just you and me. If you'd like that, perhaps you'd get in touch with me. The same way you did before. Shall we say within the next week? Now, if you gentlemen will excuse me. I'm afraid I can't afford to buy you a drink. I'm a little short of funds – temporarily: but that's a condition I hope to relieve. One way or another. Good night, Mr Deakin. Good night, Lord Frane.'

He grinned at them, and was gone.

'He thinks he's very clever,' said Lord Frane.

'Slimy bastard!'

'Oh yes. But a dangerous slimy bastard. I think we'll have to buy some more time.'

'You mean I'll have to buy some more time.'

'Insert that notice in the paper again. Say, two days from now. Then he'll presumably telephone you to arrange another meeting. Let me know. Meanwhile, I'll put my thinking cap back on, now that I've met him. Give me your glass. We need another drink.'

'Oh, let me,' said Deakin bitterly. 'It is my round.'

Frane was still sitting at his breakfast table, surrounded by newspapers, opened envelopes, coffee cup, marmalade and toast crumbs, when Liddle marched in, three days later.

'Richard,' he said, 'here's a turn-up for the books. I got a letter this morning.'

'Somebody loves you.'

'Somebody doesn't. Here, you'd better read it.'

Frane took the letter, examined the envelope, then the single sheet of paper inside. It was typewritten, rather badly. There was no address.

*Dear Mr Liddle*, it said. *You don't know me, but I have followed your political career with admiration for many years. It would be tragic – for you and for the Party – if anything were to damage your reputation now. I've recently learned certain facts which worry me very much, and if they were published I feel sure they would worry other people too. Need I say more than that they concern a house in St John's Wood? If you are willing to discuss this matter with me, please insert a small ad in* The Times, *just saying 'Thanks to St John'. Meanwhile I don't think you should tell anyone else about this letter. Yours very sincerely, A Well-wisher.*

'The style seems familiar,' observed Frane.

'Doesn't it? You know what he's talking about – the house in St John's Wood?'

'I remember there were rumours . . . '

'The point is, they were wrong. The Special Branch were watching that house, for reasons we all know, and they saw my car parked outside. But I was actually visiting a lady next door. I explained that to the Prime Minister at the time. I couldn't deny the rumours publicly without bringing her name into it, so we agreed to make no statement and just let the rumours die down. Which they did. But if any paper trotted that old story out now, I'd slap a writ on them quicker than you could say knife. The lady in question is divorced now, and it doesn't matter anyway. What Mr Shee seems to be doing is relying on out-of-date political gossip. With Deakin it worked. But he's picked the wrong man this time.'

'Two wrong men.' Frane picked up one of the opened letters from beside his plate and tossed it over to Liddle. 'Snap.'

Liddle glanced at it. 'You too?' he said with astonishment.

Frane nodded. 'Mr Shee appears to have launched on a new career. Or perhaps – more probably, come to think of it – Deakin wasn't the first, just the first we've heard of. Now he seems to be trawling, to see what he can catch. But I'm glad to say he's got my little affair slightly wrong too. I was used by those whizz-kids in the City, and the ice was thin. My fault; one shouldn't stray too far outside one's own territory. Anyway, I'm not worried now about what he's hinting at. The ice held, that's what matters.'

'So he hasn't really got anything on you either?'

'Not really. I can see why he might think he had, and I wouldn't be specially pleased to see the story revived in the City pages – or in Fearless Fred's column. But, like you, I wouldn't mind waving a few writs in the air.' He chuckled. 'Come to think of it, I wouldn't mind collecting some tax-free damages. At my time of life I'm quite willing to be libelled if the price is right.'

'It shouldn't come to that,' said Liddle. 'We're not as vulnerable as Deakin, so we should be able to nail Mr Shee. Shall we go to the police?'

'Not yet. We couldn't explain about Shee without telling them about Deakin. And the reasons for not doing that still apply. I'll tell you what – you give me a photostat of that letter, and I'll have a private word with my friend, the Assistant Commissioner. Then we'll see what we'll see.'

*     *     *

Later the same day, Deakin telephoned Frane to say that Shee had called, and that a new meeting had been arranged for the following evening in a different pub. 'He said I'd bloody well better not bring anyone with me this time. And he said – or rather implied – that I had better bring the money.'

'I'm afraid you'll have to pay him again,' said Frane. 'But cheer up. The US Marines may be on the way.'

'It's no joke to me,' said Deakin. 'And I can't say you've been much help so far.' He hung up.

Frane grimaced. No, decidedly he didn't like Deakin. He had made a note of the time and place of the new meeting with Shee. For a minute he was tempted by the notion of disguising himself properly – perhaps even a false beard? – and watching from a distance. Reluctantly he abandoned the idea and buzzed for his secretary. Her name was Carole. She was an inconspicuous sort of girl at first sight, but, Frane thought, distinctly attractive at second or third glance. He wouldn't have employed her otherwise.

The pub this time was in Earls Court. Again Shee arrived a few minutes after Deakin. He looked round suspiciously, making sure Deakin was alone before joining him.

'Left your friend at home?' he said.

'I came alone. That's what you told me to do. I've got some money.'

They both spoke quietly, and the room was noisy. No one could have overheard them. But Shee was wary. His eyes kept running round the room. 'How much?'

'Five hundred pounds.'

'In cash?'

'In ten-pound notes.'

'All right. This is what I want you to do. In a minute I'm going over to the bar to buy a drink. I'll leave this copy of the *Evening Standard* on the seat beside you. Slip the notes inside it and fold them in tightly. After I've come back, wait a minute, then say goodbye naturally and leave. Take the paper with you. There's a litter basket attached to the lamp-post immediately outside the door. Put the paper in that. Then go away.'

'I haven't told the police,' said Deakin. 'There's no one watching.'

'Just do it.'

He's nervous, thought Deakin while Shee was at the bar. I only wish he had more reason to be. He doesn't want anyone to be able to testify that he saw something pass between us.

His hand concealed by the table, Deakin carefully folded the paper so that the notes couldn't slip out. Shee returned. For a couple of minutes they made desultory conversation about the weather.

'All right,' said Shee. 'That's enough.' Obediently Deakin rose, nodded goodbye and went out, taking the paper with him. Shee watched through the window as Deakin deposited the folded paper in the litter-basket. He forced himself to wait another full minute, fearful that some passing tramp might fish the paper out of the basket. He felt reasonably sure, though, that Deakin had been speaking the truth, and that there was no one in the room who seemed in the least likely to be a detective.

Finally he put down his glass, left the pub and retrieved the newspaper, going through a little pantomime as though something in the headline which protruded from the basket had caught his eye. He walked away reading it.

He didn't notice the girl and her young man who came out of the pub almost on his heels. He had, after all, been quite right. They weren't detectives. But they followed him.

It was just about twenty-four hours later when Peter Farmiloe arrived at Frane's house in a state of some excitement. 'I've been at the club,' he said. 'Bill Broughton was there and that rather pompous City fellow, Wysard. They were talking to each other in the bar, and I gathered from what they were saying that they'd both received blackmailing letters during the past few days. Almost identical letters. And they sounded to me very like the letter which Shee sent to Deakin.'

'Oh really? Well, if they were talking about it in loud voices, they must have been rather less scared than Deakin was.'

'They were. Wysard had already been to the police. Actually, they were being slightly cagey about just what was in the letters – though I bet you I could guess in Wysard's case – but they both said that whoever wrote the letters seemed to know something about them but got his facts all wrong. You don't seem very surprised. Had you heard about this?'

'I know that George Liddle received a letter like that a couple of days ago. And so did I.'

'My God! The fellow's running amok. Has he got something on everyone?'

'Almost everyone. He's nothing on you, has he?'

'Certainly not.'

At that moment Frane's Filipino butler came in. 'Mr Mandeville here, sir.'

Farmiloe practically shot out of his seat. 'Fred Mandeville? Fearsome Fred? He's on to us. What are you going to say?'

'Calm yourself. I asked Fred Mandeville to come and see me.'

'You asked him? Why?'

'I thought I could put him straight about one or two things. A pre-emptive strike, you might say.'

'He'll bite your fingers off.'

'No, he won't. Journalists very rarely bite the hand that feeds them. Anyway, he's rather a nice boy. He was at school with my son. Do you want to meet him?'

Farmiloe didn't, though he glanced curiously at the soberly suited, bespectacled young man who was waiting in the hall.

Frane and Fred Mandeville were closeted together for nearly an hour. When Mandeville had gone, Frane looked at his watch and thought that, with a bit of luck, his friend the Assistant Commissioner (Crime) should be at home by now.

He telephoned him there, and they had a very private conversation. Afterwards he made another telephone call, no less private.

'Carole,' said Lord Frane around teatime the following day, 'I am now going to call on Mr Shee at that address to which you so kindly followed him. I shall take my swordstick.'

He didn't really think Shee was the dangerous type, but the swordstick made Lord Frane feel dangerous, which appealed to his romantic – or melodramatic – soul. A taxi deposited him outside a rather shabby Victorian house in South Kensington, which had been converted into flats. He pressed the buzzer beside the Entryphone.

Shee's voice said: 'Who is it?'

'Lord Frane. I want a word with you.'

'What about? I've nothing to say to you.' Frane was pleased to detect a note of panic.

'I've something to say to you. Let me in, unless you want another visit from the police.'

Silence. Then the door clicked open.

Frane walked up three flights of stairs. The door at the top was open. Shee was waiting there in his shirtsleeves, tie loose, hair unkempt, obviously a shaken man. Frane brushed past him into the sitting-room, then turned on him, standing rock-firm in front of the fireplace as though he owned the house.

Shee started to say something, but Frane cut him short. 'When the police came here this morning they took away a typewriter. Certain letters were typed on that machine.'

'That typewriter wasn't mine. And I never wrote the letters they were talking about. I'd never seen them before.'

'Of course you didn't,' said Frane cheerfully. 'I wrote them. And you might – I say you *might* – be able, eventually, to convince the police that you are innocent. Innocent of writing those letters. But in the process your little transaction with John Deakin is going to emerge, don't you think? And how are you going to explain that away? Are you with me so far?'

Shee tried to speak but proved literally speechless. Frane grasped his swordstick more tightly for a moment. It wasn't necessary though. Morally and even physically he felt in command, dominating the wretch who now sat down, almost collapsed, on to the sofa.

Frane was enjoying himself. He went on: 'The police came here today at my suggestion. They are presumably now examining the typewriter and the letters. The type-face will match. They will also examine them for fingerprints. They won't find your fingerprints, but I can assure you they won't find mine either. They haven't – yet – seen your letter to Mr Deakin, which of course was written on a different machine. But you can hardly tell them that, can you? There will, therefore, be an element of doubt. Further investigation will be needed. Somebody, I imagine, will come round again tomorrow to interview you. Very nasty, that sort of interview, very embarrassing. Now I might – mind you, I say

I might – be able to persuade my friends at Scotland Yard to take the matter no further, if, when the detectives come here tomorrow, they find that you've gone. Really gone. Left the country, without making any further nuisance of yourself. You've got funds – a thousand pounds which Mr Deakin gave you. I'm not asking for that back. You have a passport, I hope? Otherwise it'll have to be Ireland, to begin with. What do you say?'

'I really think we deserve this,' said Lord Frane, easing the cork out of the champagne bottle. He filled three glasses.

'How did you manage to plant the typewriter?' Liddle asked.

'I have useful friends in low places. I met this one long ago in the army. Locks speak to him: or rather he speaks to locks – and they open. It's his *métier*.'

'You mean he burgled Shee's flat?' said Farmiloe.

'I'm afraid so. Are you shocked? I've been wondering – purely as an academic question, you understand – whether I have actually committed any grave crimes. I caused that flat to be broken into – yes: but we didn't take anything, on the contrary we added something – *viz*, one typewriter. I issued a number of letters containing nasty insinuations: but I didn't demand any money. All round, I reckon I'm innocent. Pure as the driven snow.'

'While you were investigating nasty insinuations about me,' said Liddle, 'you might have invented something I could have let leak out publicly to please my constituents. You could have said I was the father of sixteen illegitimate children or something like that. I'd have increased my majority at the next election by thousands.'

'I hope some of your other victims don't find out who wrote those letters,' said Farmiloe, 'or you won't be at all popular.'

Frane chuckled. 'It was great fun. I'm tempted to go on and touch a few more of our friends and colleagues on sensitive spots – just to see them jump. One can do it to almost anybody. Except you, dear Peter. You're the unblackmailable man.'

'Hm. I wish I felt you intended that as a compliment. But what were you doing with Fred Mandeville the other day?'

'I was giving him a friendly tip. I told him that there was this man with a grudge against the Party who had been trying to blackmail several of its senior members. You may hear rumours, I said, about some of the stories he's got hold of. Somebody may even show you one of the letters. But be careful, I said. You'll be walking into a minefield of libel actions. This jolly blackmailer gets all his facts wrong. I suggested that, if Fearless Fred wanted a story, he might do one about The Incompetent Blackmailer.'

'You hid the leaf in the forest,' said Liddle. 'I hope friend Deakin is grateful.'

'I telephoned him. I just told him we'd got Shee off his back. He was moderately grateful. You know,' said Frane, emptying the bottle and starting to remove the wire from another, 'he really won't do. Not the right type at all. I must drop a word in a few ears . . .'

# MICHAEL Z. LEWIN

---

# The Reluctant Detective

It started as a tax fiddle. Well, paint on a little semantic gloss: call it a tax avoidance structurisation. Uncle Edward would have preferred that, I think.

It was Uncle Edward who was responsible for my coming to England in the first place. I am American by birth and by upbringing. So was he, but some time in his relative youth he moved over here – I don't know what brought him – and he stayed. That was a long time ago, his moving. Before I was born. I'm twenty-six now. And I never actually met him, though I wrote to him often. Not letters exactly, because what we did was play postal chess. We did that over a period of more than ten years, so while I didn't know him at all, I felt I knew him fairly well. You get a sense of people by their chess games. Look at Anatoly Karpov's style on the board and you'll see a map of his face. No expression in either.

But that's by the by. I was Uncle Edward's only child-age relative – he never had kids of his own – and from the time I was born he kept in contact. He was quite close to his sister – my mother – and I always got a present on my birthday and at Christmas. It added a certain cosmopolitan touch to these occasions. And then he wrote direct to me when he heard from Mom that I had begun to play with the chess set he sent. We took it from there, playing by post till he died. Even during my years in college we kept it up. And afterwards too, when I was realising I didn't want to be a lawyer, no matter what Dad said about it being useful to fall back on even if I didn't know what I *really* wanted to do.

When Uncle Edward died I was sad. He was one of my few fixed points, a focus for a little contemplative time no matter where I was or what a shambles I was making of the rest of my life.

When I learned that Uncle Edward had provided for me in his will, I was astonished.

What I inherited was a house over here. Also a small income to be sent to me every month from the States. Just about enough to live on.

At first I didn't know what to do. Sell the house, or what. But when I thought about it, it occurred to me that if I thought I could tell about Uncle Edward from our chess games, maybe he could tell about me. Perhaps he was suggesting that it would be good for me to live in England for a while. I'm sure he knew from Mom that I was kind of at loose ends anyway because they wrote to each other. Actual letters, I mean. She only ever quoted to me from one once. When I asked her why Uncle Edward lived in England. She said he had written, *Britain is the closest thing there is left to a civilised English-speaking country*. 'He was never very good at languages,' she said after. The more I thought about it the better an idea it seemed. So I decided to give it a try, and over I came.

\*     \*     \*

The tax fidd . . . tax avoidance structurisation didn't come up till I had been here a year or so. In fact, it was Dawn's idea, so in a way everything that's happened is down to her.

Dawn is the lady friend I've made. She is very civilised and if she is what Uncle Edward meant, I understand better why he spent his life here. It could happen to me, though that's not something I think about a lot.

Dawn agreed to move in after I'd been here about six months. We live in my house, and on my income. It gives us a lot of time to enjoy life. And think about things. We're not quite what they call drop-outs back home, because we intend to get into careers when we're sure what we want to do. But if we have no need to rush a decision . . . well, we didn't make the rules.

I see I'm already talking as if I am staying forever. Well, there are worse fates.

And, it turns out, we've already done something along a career line, even if it was strictly by accident. That's what this story is about.

OK, get the picture. I come over here to my house and an income. After six months Dawn and I are friends enough to live together. After six months we realise that comfortable as my income is, maybe there are things it would be nice to do if there were a little more money around.

Get a car for one. Nothing flash, but some wheels to see some of the rest of the country with.

Have I told you where I am? It's a little town in Somerset called Frome. (They pronounce it to rhyme with broom, by the way.) And it is pretty enough and in a lovely part of the country. But there are other places to see. Yes, it was considering getting a car that set us thinking in the first place.

Or set Dawn thinking, actually. She is the one who cooked it all up.

The idea was this. If I set up in business, as a self-employed person I could save money in taxes by deducting a lot of what we spent as necessary commercial expenses. Part of the house as an office; proportion of rates and heat and repairs and insurance; even a salary to Dawn as my secretary. And all the costs of my business vehicle.

Dawn worked it all out, and there was no question, it would pay for the car. And maybe a little bit more as we went along.

Then the question was what kind of business to supposedly set up in. That was Dawn's idea too. Well, not all ideas are necessarily bright.

I set up as a private detective. See, in Britain you don't need a licence of any kind. And, I have to admit, we yielded to a certain pleasant absurdity attached to the notion. I mean, a private detective, in Frome!

As well, the chances of anybody coming to us for business were, of course, nil.

Which was the idea. We didn't want the business to succeed, or, indeed, for there to be any work at all. What we wanted were the deductions. It was a tax fiddle. As I've mentioned.

So, I bought a notebook and pen, and a small sign to put on the front of the house. It gave my name and said under it *Private Inquiry Agent* which is what they call private detectives here.

And that was it.

No advertisements, no listing in the Yellow Pages.

And no business.

We bought a little yellow Mini. Life as planned. It worked like a charm.

For a while.

It was a Tuesday, I remember, because I was reading the basketball column in *The Guardian* – I try to keep up with some of my old interests from the USA – when the doorbell rang. It was about ten o'clock. I thought it might be the gas man. Dawn was out visiting her mother – she's got as many relatives here as I have none, so to speak. A lot is what I am saying.

At the door was a sallow-faced little man – well, I suppose he was about average height, but I am awkwardly tall, about 6′ 5″, so I have a distorted perspective on people. He had a jacket and tie on and he looked unhappy.

I thought, not the gas man but maybe a local government official.

'Are you Mr Herring?' he asked.

'Yes.'

'May I talk to you?'

'What about?' I asked.

He looked momentarily at the sign on the house by the door. It's so small you can hardly see it even if you know it's there. 'Are you the Mr Herring who is a private inquiry agent?'

And I suddenly realised he had come on business. I was stunned. I began to shake, though I don't know if he noticed.

'Yes, yes, of course,' I said. 'Fredrick Herring. Do come in.'

I led him to the living-room. It wasn't much to look at. Not for a detective's office. It was just a living-room, and lived in at that.

I sat him down. I didn't know what to say. But he made the running.

'My name is Goodrich,' he said.

'Hi.'

'I don't know whether I should even be here.'

'It's not a step to take lightly,' I said.

'I'm not,' he said. 'I'm not.'

'Oh.'

'I am a solicitor with Malley, Holmes and Asquith, but I need someone to make some inquiries for me on a private matter.'

'I see.'

'Well, you do that kind of thing, don't you?'

He looked at me. There was something devious in his eyes. And I had a sudden shock of suspicion.

You see, Dawn and I had talked about what to do if someone did actually come to us for work. We would just say that we were too busy to take the case on. But there was something about this man. The same thing that made me think he might be a council official. I got this idea that he was from one of the tax offices and that he was checking up on us.

It's just that on all these tax forms we'd been sending in we always had expenses listed, but never any income. It looked funny, of course. But economic times are hard and we assumed out amounts were so small, relatively, that nobody would notice.

But when you think you are being checked on, you suddenly feel the cold draught of accusation, prosecution.

'Of course,' I said.

Dawn was not pleased when she returned to the house and found that I had taken a case. But I explained my worries and she accepted the situation as a fact.

'It's about his brother-in-law, a guy named Chipperworth, who is a crook,' I said.

'Chipperworth . . .' Dawn said. She was thinking. She's lived in Frome all her life and knows a lot of people.

'He has a company that manufactures beds, up on the trading estate. The brand name is Rest Easy.'

'Ah.'

'You know it?'

'Rest Easy, yes.'

'And this man Goodrich says that Chipperworth set fire to a warehouse next to his factory up there and collected the insurance for it.'

'I read about the fire,' Dawn said. 'But not that it was on purpose. How does Goodrich know?'

'He says Chipperworth was bragging yesterday that he had just collected a cheque for over three hundred thousand pounds and it was for beds he wasn't going to be able to sell.'

'Good heavens,' Dawn said. 'But why doesn't Goodrich go to the police?'

'Because that's not what he's trying to sort out.'

'Oh.'

'What he's worried about is his sister. That Chipperworth is a crook, and he's dangerous. He wants his sister to divorce him.'

Dawn cocked her head.

'But his sister doesn't believe the stuff about the insurance fraud.'

'What are *we* supposed to do about that?'

'Goodrich wants us to prove Chipperworth has a woman on the side. If we can do that then the sister will divorce him and will be safe. Goodrich is sure that his sister will get a divorce in the end anyway, but if he precipitates it at least she'll be well off financially. If he waits till Chipperworth's activities catch up with him then it might ruin the sister too.'

'Oh,' Dawn said.

'I agreed to try.'

She nodded. Then she looked at me.

And I looked at her.

We were thinking the same thing.

I said, 'What the hell do we do now?'

Well, we had to go through the motions. The first motion was to find Chipperworth and identify him.

That wasn't hard. Mr Goodrich had given me a photograph and we decided to wait outside Rest Easy Beds toward the end of the work day. Rest Easy was not a big company. We counted about twenty people coming out after five-thirty. Chipperworth was the last and got into a new Sierra.

'OK,' Dawn said. 'There he is. What do we do now?'

'Drive along after him, I guess,' I said.

So we did. He went straight to a house on the Prowtings Estate. He pulled the car into the driveway. Got out. Went to the front door. Was met by a woman at 5.48 p.m. Then Chipperworth went into the house and closed the door.

That would have wrapped the case up if the woman hadn't been his wife.

Dawn and I sat.

'At least we know the registration number of his car now,' I said after ten minutes.

But we were both sinking fast.

After half an hour Dawn said, 'This is no good. What are we going to do, sit out here all night without any food or anything?'

And after some consideration of the situation, we decided to get fish and chips from Pangs. Even detectives have to eat.

When we got back, Chipperworth's car was gone.

Solicitor Goodrich rang up at nine the next morning. He seemed annoyed that I didn't have anything to report.

I explained that progress is not always rapid, that we'd had less than a day on the job.

But Goodrich knew that Chipperworth had been out the previous night. He'd called his sister and she told him.

'If you want to do the surveillance yourself,' I said, 'please say so. Otherwise, leave it to us.'

He took a breath, then apologised – rather unconvincingly I thought – and we hung up.

I told Dawn about the call.

'If we don't sort this out quickly,' she said, 'it's going to mess up our lives for weeks.'

'I know.'

'I'm going to see a couple of my cousins.'

I looked puzzled.

'Nigel is a telephone engineer,' she said. 'He's a nut case and would probably be willing to work out a way to tap the Chipperworths' telephone. And Paul works in the photographic section at Valets.' Valets was one of the local printing firms. 'He's a camera buff. He'll lend us a camera with a telephoto lens.'

'Right,' I said.

'We may have to borrow another car too, so we can cover Chipperworth the whole day. If it goes on for long we'll have to do shifts. I ought to be able to use Adele's Reliant. You remember Adele?'

'No.'

'She's the small one with the big—'

'I remember now,' I said.

Biggest feet I'd ever seen on a woman.

'I just wish I knew someone who could lend us a two-way radio.'

'There's your Uncle Mike,' I said.

'So there is,' she said. Then made a face. 'But he pinches and pokes whenever I get close enough and what he'd want for doing me a favour . . .'

'We'll get along without,' I said firmly.

In the end it only took a day.

It was the afternoon of my first shift. I was rigged up with a thermos, sandwiches and a radio. Even a specimen jar – from Dawn's friend Elaine, the nurse – in case time was short and need was great.

When Dawn and I get down to it, we're impressive.

I took the afternoon shift because Dawn had to see her Auntie Wendy who was having troubles with a neighbour's boy picking on her son Edgar.

The camera was one of those instant print jobs. We'd talked it over with Paul and he figured that would be best. No time waiting for the film to come back from the developers. 'And,' he said, 'considering what kind of pictures you may get, a commercial firm might not print them.' Does a great leer, does Paul.

He also gave us a foot-long lens for the thing. 'It'll put you in their pockets,' he said. 'If they're wearing pockets.'

Cousin Nigel jumped at the chance to plant a tape recorder up a telephone pole to tap the Chipperworths' home phone. He volunteered to do the company phone too. Well, you don't turn down offers like that.

It's always struck me that all of Dawn's family are just that little bit shady. I offer it as an observation, not a complaint.

Anyway, after an hour's lunch at home, Chipperworth didn't go back to his office. He drove instead to Marston Road and pulled into the driveway of a detached brick house just beyond the end of speed restrictions. I drove past but parked immediately. I left the car and got the camera aimed and focused just in time to see Chipperworth open the door to the house with a key.

The picture came out a treat.

I stood there in the road looking at it. And wondering what to do next.

But Dawn and I had talked it through. First I made a note of the time, date and location on the back of the photograph. Then I set about trying to find out who lived in the house.

I went next door and rang the bell and had a little luck.

A tiny old woman with big brown eyes answered it. I said, 'Excuse me. I have a registered letter for the people next door but nobody answers when I ring.'

'That's because Mrs Elmitt has her fancy man in,' the old woman said. 'And she wouldn't want to be disturbed now, would she? Some of the things I've seen! And they don't even bother to draw the curtains.'

Old women can do pretty good leers too, when they try.

Dawn was pleased as punch with me. I was pretty pleased myself. It meant that the wretched case would soon be over and we could get back to life as usual. I resolved to try to arrange for my income to arrive from America as some kind of retainer so that it looked like proceeds of the business. Then we wouldn't have to worry about being inspected by the tax people. Worry is a terrible thing.

But just about the time that we were getting ready to be pleased with each other, Cousin Nigel showed up at the front door.

He punched me on the shoulder as he came in, and gave Dawn a big kiss. A hearty type, Nigel.

'I've got your first tape,' he said jovially. 'Went up to see if it needed changing and blow me if there hadn't been a lot of calls. Thought you would want to hear them sooner rather than later, so I put another cassette in the machine and brought this one right over. Got any beer while we listen to it?' He dropped into our most comfortable chair. 'Hey Dawnie, how about something to eat? Egg and chips? Hungry work, bugging telephones.'

The tape was a revelation.

Right off, the very first phone call had things like the man saying, 'Darling, I can't wait until I see you again.'

And the woman: 'I don't know whether I'll be able to bear not being with you all the time for very much longer.'

'It will be soon. We'll be together, forever. Somewhere nice. Away from your wretched husband.'

'I don't know what will become of me if our plan doesn't work.'

'It will work. We'll make it work.'

'Oh darling, I hope so.'

And on and on, that kind of mushy stuff. There was a lot of slobbering sounds too. I would have been embarrassed if I hadn't been so upset.

'Wow!' Nigel said. 'All that kissy-kissy, and before lunch. They must have it bad.'

Dawn said, 'Isn't that great! We've got all we need now, Freddie, don't you think?'

But I was not happy, not even close.

Because, unlike my two colleagues, I had recognised one of the voices. The man's. The conversation was not between Mr Chipperworth and Mrs Elmitt. The man on the telephone was our client, Mr Goodrich, and the object of his affection was, presumably, Mrs Chipperworth, his 'sister'.

We got rid of Nigel before we talked it out.

'I guess this means that our client was not being completely open and frank with us,' Dawn said.

There was no law that a client had to tell us the truth. But neither of us liked it. 'But what do we do?'

We had a long chat about it.

What we did was go the next morning to Dawn's Uncle Steve, who is a police sergeant. We asked him about the fire in the Rest Easy Beds warehouse.

'Always knew it was arson,' Uncle Steve said. 'But we couldn't prove who did it. The owner was the only possible beneficiary, but he had an airtight alibi. Not quite as good as being out to dinner with the Chief Superintendent, but he was at a function with the Mayor and he was at a table, in full sight, the whole evening.'

'I see,' Dawn said.

'I interviewed Chipperworth myself,' Uncle Steve said, 'and he was quite open about being delighted about the fire. Business wasn't very good and he was having trouble moving the stock that was destroyed. Personally, I don't think he *did* have anything to do with it. I've been at this job long enough to get a good sense of people and that's the way he came across.'

'I see,' Dawn said.

'But we never got so much as a whiff of any other suspect. Checked through all current and past employees for someone with a grievance. Sounded out all our informants in town for a word about anybody who might have been hired to do the deed or who heard anything about it. But we didn't get so much as a whisper. It's very unusual for us not to get some kind of lead if something's bent and we try that hard. In the end, it was written off to kids. There are so many around with nothing to do these days that we're getting all sorts of vandalism.'

'Thanks, Uncle Steve,' Dawn said.

'Helps you, does that?' he asked.

'I think so.'

'If you know anything about the case, you must tell us. You know that, don't you?'

'Yes, Uncle Steve.'

He looked at her and shook his head. Then he said to me, 'Young man, there is a look in her eye that I don't like. There's something tricky about all her people. You watch yourself.'

He was right, of course. Dawn was cooking something up, and it wasn't chips.

When we got home we sat down over a nice cup of tea. She hadn't said a word during the whole drive.

I couldn't bear it any longer. I said, 'All right. What *is* the significance of that funny look?'

'I've decided we're going to get Mrs Chipperworth that divorce our client wants after all.'

'We are?'

'It's what we were hired to do, isn't it?'

★ ★ ★

I called Solicitor Goodrich to tell him that we had had success in our investigation and did he want our report.

He did. He was with us within twenty minutes.

I explained what I had seen the previous afternoon. I gave him the photographs I had taken of Chipperworth entering Mrs Elmitt's house with a key and, later, adjusting his flies as he came out. I reported what the neighbour had told me.

'She is willing to testify to what she's seen in court, or to swear out a statement,' I said. 'But she would like some money for it.'

'I think that can be arranged,' Goodrich said.

A little ready cash might help the old woman get some curtains for her own windows.

Goodrich wrote out a cheque for our fee and expenses on the spot.

'Of course, if *we* have to testify,' I said, 'there will be an additional bill.'

'I don't think it will come to that,' Goodrich said.

After he left I rang Rest Easy Beds.

I explained to Mr Chipperworth that we wanted to come over to speak to him.

'What is it that is so urgent, Mr Herring?' he said.

'We wanted to tell you about your wife's plans to sue you for divorce,' I said.

As soon as we arrived we were ushered into Chipperworth's office.

'But she's known about Madeleine for years,' he said when I explained what we'd been hired to do. 'It's an arrangement we have. She doesn't like *it*, you see. So Madeleine keeps me from making . . . demands.'

'She doesn't seem to mind the demands of her lover,' Dawn said.

'Her *what*?'

'Why don't you ask her about her telephone calls recently,' Dawn suggested. 'We have to be going now. Ta ta.'

We stopped at Nigel's and then we went on home.

We didn't have long to wait.

A few minutes after noon the bell rang. Before I could get to it, pounding started on the door. When I opened it I faced Solicitor Goodrich, in a fury. He swung fists at me.

For the most part being as tall as I am is an inconvenience. But at least I have long arms and could keep him out of reach. When he finished flailing, he started swearing. The rude language seemed particularly unseemly for a member of the legal profession. I would have been very embarrassed for Dawn if I hadn't heard as bad or worse from her family. But they are foul-mouthed in a friendly way. Goodrich was vicious.

Also defamatory. He claimed that we had sold information to Mr Chipperworth.

I was about to deny it when Dawn said, 'What if we did?'

'I'll have you for this,' Goodrich said. 'It's illegal. I can put you in gaol.'

'That's fine talk from somebody who set fire to a warehouse.'

Goodrich was suddenly still and attentive. 'What?'

'You're the arsonist responsible for the fire at Rest Easy Beds.'

'That's silly talk,' Goodrich said. But he wasn't laughing.

'The idea was that when Mr Chipperworth collected the insurance money Mrs Chipperworth would start divorce proceedings which would entitle her to claim half of it. With your help she could probably settle out of court and between the insurance cash and her share of the rest of the joint property, you and Mrs Chipperworth would have a nice little nest egg to run away on.'

'Prove it,' Goodrich said.

'Oh, I think it's a very clever plan,' Dawn said charmingly. 'I suppose you have an alibi for the night of the fire?'

'Why should I need one?'

'Well, if we went to the police . . .'

'Why the hell should you do that?' Goodrich burst out.

'Ah,' Dawn said. 'Now we're getting down to the serious questions.' She batted her eyelashes. 'We never actually gave our evidence to Mr Chipperworth, you know, and as long as Mrs Chipperworth has denied everything . . .'

'You want money, I suppose,' Goodrich said.

'Well, poor Freddie is terribly tall, and a bigger car would be so much easier for him to get in and out of.'

'All right,' Goodrich said. 'A car.'

'And there are so many little improvements that ought to be made on this house.'

'How about just getting to a bottom-line figure.'

'I think thirty thousand would come in very handy, don't you Freddie?'

'Oh, very handy.'

'Thirty thousand!' Goodrich said.

'Yes,' Dawn said. 'See how reasonable we are?'

When the trial came along it was plastered all over the local papers. Frome is not so big a town that we get serious court cases involving local people every week.

Especially not cases involving solicitors and arson, not cases with a little titillation in them. Goodrich pleaded guilty, but the local reporter, Scoop Wall, tracked down Mrs Elmitt's neighbour who was photographed pointing to some of the uncurtained windows through which she had been forced to witness indescribable acts. Well, the descriptions didn't make the papers anyway.

Uncle Steve was not pleased at first when he heard what we had done.

Heard is the operative word because we had tape-recorded the entire conversation with Goodrich on equipment we borrowed from Cousin Nigel.

But Dawn explained. After all this time the only way Goodrich's arson would be proved was if he confessed to it. But the police couldn't have used the threat of exposing his relationship to Mrs Chipperworth the way we did because that would have transgressed legal niceties. 'So it was up to Freddie and me,' Dawn said.

Eventually Uncle Steve laughed.

'I warned you about her,' he said to me.
But it worked out all right in the end.

Except . . . Scoop Wall tracked down Dawn and me too.
We begged her not to put anything about us in the paper.
But she refused. We were key figures in bringing a dangerous solicitor to justice. It was news. And besides, Dawn has good legs and photographs well.
It's not that we weren't proud of what we – or let's be fair – what Dawn had done.
But it meant that the Fredrick Herring Private Inquiry Agency burst from its quiet and planned total obscurity into the glare of public attention.
We started getting calls. We started getting visitors. We started getting letters. Find this, look for that, unravel the other.
And it wasn't actually the attention which was the problem.
The problem was that we found we quite liked it. See, some of the cases we were offered were pretty interesting. Rather like chess problems . . . So, we decided, maybe one more. Or two.

# AUDREY ERSKINE LINDOP

## The Mistaken Smile

When Laura first told me that she thought Robert was trying to murder her I laughed; the second time I repeated the story to Robert, but on the third occasion we both told her doctor. He advised a holiday, a wise if rather obvious prescription.

No woman likes to hear her husband say, 'My dear, I'm delighted you're leaving me. It'll save me pretending I want to sleep with you.' Much as she had come to detest Robert, it was not very flattering to know that she could not even satisfy a country parson.

As a solicitor I had acted for the Vinces for many years, and because I was their nearest neighbour I saw plenty of them.

I confess that I dreaded Laura consulting me professionally. Her absurd fears irritated me, almost as much as they seemed to irritate her; but Robert's personality had the opposite effect. It never failed to soothe me and bolster me up. Quite frankly I suspected Laura's complaints about him as being nothing but the ramblings of an over-excited mind. I still blame myself for my lack of perception. I have heard that there is no more cruel emotion than remorse and I have certainly had my share of it.

Laura Vince was a research worker and lecturer. She was a keen observer of life, and in spite of her apparent independence had a deep need for human company and affection.

Robert was an Anglican parson. They had met at Oxford and in the tumultuous unawareness of youth had thought themselves twin souls. But they were not, and it took marriage to prove the fact.

Laura was convinced that in his heart, Robert Vince knew himself to be a militant phoney – this he could at times hide from himself but he suspected that he could not hide it from Laura, no matter how hard she tried not to show it.

It was ironical, she always thought, how popular he was with both young and old parishioners. His was one of the few well-attended churches. He let the conventional believe him to be conventional, and the unconventional that he was 'way out'. Laura thought he should have been an actor. He gave an admirable daily performance and no one but she could have guessed at his narrow and hypocritical spirit. It was hard for her at times to sit and listen to his warm and entertaining sermons when she remembered the hours of rehearsal, the pauses for possible laughs, the studied effect of geniality expertly timed to switch into sincerity, humility and piety. Even his smile, the pitch of his voice and his gestures were worked out and timed. Nothing, she assured me, came from his heart. His easy charm was also practised in front of a looking-glass down to its smallest detail. She was sad because she had loved him once.

She was sure that he intended to become a bishop and she was also sure that she gave him a guilt complex. He felt that she would see through him and the mere sight of her sitting dutifully in a pew undermined his confidence.

What hurt her most was that even in their bitterest moments he could not forget the charm. It was as if he were trying to show her that however unlikeable she might be he was incapable of being objectionable. She would rather he had shouted his insults at her but he delivered them sulkily with the daily perfected smile. She might have been one of his parishioners.

Before they gave their dignified little sherry parties he would say, 'Don't forget, please, not to cap my stories – there's room for only one wit in this house, and don't try to entertain people by showing how greatly you've benefited from an academic education. Few things can be more boring.' And he said it as if he had paid her two loving little compliments.

It was the same when the party actually took place. Whilst warming the hearts of his glowing devotees he found time to pay chivalrous attention to his wife, sending her soft glances of affection and appreciation, apparently unaware that she received them stonily. She had few friends in Elstead. Everyone had come to see Robert and anyone who had not she rebuffed. She thought she was being patronised.

There were few women in their parish who did not envy lucky Mrs Vince, and they mistook her shyness for haughtiness.

I simply thought her dull and gauche but that, of course, was before I fell in love with her.

I am ashamed of my behaviour at those morbid little social gatherings at the Rectory with poor Laura circling stiffly round with cocktail snacks, hardly acknowledged by her guests whilst from her husband's corner there came nothing but warm laughter and obvious adulation.

Laura, failing in her efforts to hold anyone's attention for longer than strict politeness required, tended to attach herself fiercely to me. I did my utmost to shake her off and join the audience who were so appreciating Robert's witty anecdotes, but at the time I simply thought her a tiresomely neurotic woman and suspected that most of her troubles with Robert were due to jealousy over his popularity.

She was forever telling me how plain he made her feel and yet to me he praised her beauty. He said, 'Peter, don't you think Laura's got lovely features? They remind me of a Botticelli.'

'Why don't you tell her?' I snapped. 'It might make her less of a self-pitying bore.'

'I do,' he sighed. 'But it makes her worse. She simply thinks I'm making fun of her.'

'Did you,' I demanded, 'actually say to her that it would be a relief not to have to sleep with her?'

He sighed again. 'Yes, and it is. You've no idea what we go through on those occasions. She's moved to another room now. She's convinced I'm going to smother her in her sleep.'

I realise now that however ridiculous I might have thought it I should have shown Laura sympathy. Those fears were very real to her.

I told Robert that I would prefer Laura to get another lawyer, but he begged me to keep her on as a client. He said, 'For God's sake Peter, do let her come and let off steam. Please put up with her nonsense. I simply can't have a stranger listening to all that rubbish.'

Out of friendship for Robert I agreed, but I must confess that when I heard her shouting at my secretary in the outer office I felt like leaping out of the window.

'I *must* see Mr Cowles!' she was shrieking. 'It's terribly terribly urgent.'

My unfortunate secretary was doing her best to protect me, being well aware of my aversion to Laura and her lunatic suspicions, but she failed. Laura burst into my office.

'Peter, please help me! Something really frightening has happened!'

She pulled up a chair and sat panting in it. Oddly enough, it was at that moment that I realised that she had an eerie shell-like type of beauty. Her black eyes had a warm glow and her figure was really all that a man could ask for. But she was shouting at me as if I were in the spring-time of my senility and it was vital to catch me before I reached the autumn. I could have murdered her. Not a very happy thought in the circumstances.

I managed to calm her down with the aid of a spot of brandy out of my filing cabinet and said, as patiently as I could, '*What* has happened, Laura?'

She swallowed the rest of her brandy and said, 'Robert *smiled* at me.'

I laughed and she must have wept for a good five minutes whilst I sat and stared at her. Then she whimpered, 'You *must* believe me. I shall go mad if you don't. I simply have to get away from him. I tell you he actually smiled at me.'

'He smiles at everyone.'

'Yes, yes. Everyone but *me*. He's thought of something. He's thought of a way of getting rid of me. It wasn't his usual smile.'

'Which is notoriously charming.'

'I know, but this wasn't. This was sort of serious and dangerous – as if he had found himself out and wanted to dispose of anyone else who might have done the same.'

In desperation I said to Robert, 'For God's sake give us both a break and pack her off somewhere she can relax!'

He chose Provence and he rented a house called 'Le Bois des Papillons' in the village of Vallon. As its name suggested it stood in a wood full of butterflies. It was exceptionally cheap and the agent was completely honest about the reason. The house had once been the headquarters of members of the resistance and their chief had been tortured to death there. It was not everybody's idea of a happy villa. With true French logic no one suggested that it was haunted. Ghosts they said would keep away from a place like that with its sunny woods and gay butterflies and its fearful memories. But there was a persistent rumour that the resistance had buried their funds somewhere in the house. Now and again fools, chiefly foreigners, got wind of this little tale and broke into the house searching for the hidden treasure. None of the locals really believed there was any money there, but the agent suggested that it would be safer for Madame Vince to have a companion, just in case some bullion hunting enthusiast should break in again.

Laura was persuaded to take with her a friend called Ellen Cook. Miss Cook had a small mind and a narrow nature, but great physical strength. She would have been enough to frighten any treasure hunter.

But in spite of this Laura was not satisfied with the arrangements. She mistrusted anywhere Robert chose for her, and she wanted more than a holiday from him; she wanted a divorce. She told me that he could shatter her nerves to such an extent that she felt as if she was going out of her mind, but of course no one would take her word against his, not even her doctor who had only seen Robert as his charming self and apparently devoted to her.

I tried to be as patient as I could for Robert's sake and as he had asked I allowed her to 'let off steam' at me. She told me that during a quarrel he could remain reasonable and low voiced whilst she shrieked like a demented fishwife. When attacked in those soft clerical tones she lost all control. His constant taunt – 'My dear, you mustn't forget you're an intellectual. You have every advantage over a country parson. Please don't make a fool of yourself.'

Divorce, he told her, was out of the question. It would affect his career. He could afford no scandals.

He spoke in his most pleasing voice, 'If it will comfort you I can tell you that nothing would give me greater pleasure than to be rid of you. Your supercilious little face infuriates me – you're not the only woman to have obtained an MA or given lectures or done research work and written pamphlets – most women have done rather better and still remained feminine.'

She had to clench her fists to keep her nails out of his face. 'How could anyone be feminine with a megalomaniac like you? You're a Victorian sadist – you're such a master at it. But I'll divorce *you* – I'll divorce you for cruelty—'

His laugh was even more well-modulated than his voice. 'My *dear*! On what grounds?'

'I'll bring up mental cruelty.'

'Bring it up. Who in the world is going to believe you? My adoring parishioners? They all think I'm badly done by through my so-called intellectual little wife – with the only MA in the world after her undistinguished little name!'

In her temper she threatened him.

'You may despise my degree and hate me for it – but I'm still a woman and I have feelings. For you they cover every form of hatred. I shall follow no Christian ethic such as you're supposed to have. I'll do everything in my power to discredit you. I'll let your adoring flock know just what their beloved shepherd is really like. Every besotted spinster, every worshipping matron – they'll all know. I'll tell them that you're using the words of Jesus Christ to further your own ambitions.'

That was when he smiled at her and she came running in to me. I said, 'Yes, yes, yes. Now Laura, take the pills the doctor gave you and pack your things for France. Oh, and incidentally, "Le Bois des Papillons" is in mountainous country. Did you know? It's in the south of France, but Vallon is very high and can sometimes get as misty as Dartmoor, so put in some little woollies.'

She said, 'Oh, thank you,' and as she said it she reminded me of one of those forlorn little butterflies which get stuck in a house for the winter, and who creep out with faded wings and no hope of ever being able to fly happily in the outside world again.

She had nothing to thank me for and she knew it. I was just trying to get her out of the way for Robert's sake. It seemed so wrong that someone who was doing so much good for the Church as he was should be shackled by an hysterical wife who was verging on insanity.

'Le Bois des Papillons' due to everyone's understandable dislike of it was not immediately inhabitable. It rather resembled Miss Haversham's wedding chamber in *Great Expectations*. It needed 'doing up' and whilst it was being 'done up' I was stuck with Laura and her idiotic terror of Robert's smile. How wicked it is not to realise when someone is really frightened literally out of their life!

Wearily I told my loyal secretary to let her in whenever she came to see me. With any luck by the time they had swept 'Le Bois des Papillons' clean of cobwebs and goats' dung we should be rid of her and the unwinning Miss Cook.

In the meantime I had to put up with her theories on Robert's murderous intentions. She was not afraid that he would attack her *physically*. But there were so many other more subtle ways of disposing of a person. There was poison, tampering with car engines, unexplained domestic accidents, inexplicable 'assaults' on the way home, electrical faults in the bathroom, or electric blankets, garden steps made slippery, banisters weakened so that hers would be compared with the mystery fall of poor Amy Robsart. There were rat poisons, tisanes – there were a thousand ways in which he could get rid of her.

In her dreams she saw him as a mediaeval cardinal with a score of hired assassins to hack her down. She had threatened his precious career and everything he did or said confirmed her suspicions.

She hardly dared sleep at night in case he tried to suffocate her. She lost weight and came near to a breakdown. Finally whilst toying with an unwanted breakfast she burst out hysterically, 'Robert, I'm leaving you.'

It was then that he made his remark about being relieved not to have to try and sleep with an intellectual wife. For this pleasure he was willing to make her quite a handsome allowance. He had private money and was not dependent on a clerical living. But there was to be one condition. His parishioners were to be informed that she had gone away on a lengthy holiday to restore her health. There was to be no mention of a separation. Laura told me bitterly, 'The worshipping congregation must never know that his wife had the audacity to leave him.'

Finally I saw both her and the unwinning Miss Cook off at the station. It was hard to decide which of them I was glad to see the back of most: the mournful Laura constantly whimpering that this proved her failure as a person, or her immensely tall and sullen friend.

Miss Cook had that unhappy habit of spitting in one's face when she spoke;

another of her unlovable characteristics was her language. Every other word had four letters.

When they were safely on their way my secretary and I did a little caper of joy round the office.

But the joy did not last very long. A stream of letters started to arrive from Laura and Miss Cook. There had apparently been a series of attempts by unknown intruders to break into 'Le Bois des Papillons'. The police had been informed and seemed surprised that anyone should chance their luck at finding the legendary resistance gold when the house was occupied. When it was empty they could understand these fruitless attempts. Personally I suspected that what really surprised them was that anyone should have the temerity to risk being spat in the eye by that foul-mouthed Amazon Miss Cook.

But Laura was convinced that the intruders were Robert's 'hired assassins' trying to do away with her under cover of seeking the mythical treasure. No one would connect the crime with Robert preaching sweetness and light in England. She thought it ominous that the break-ins should have increased since she had taken up residence.

My secretary and I groaned together but we wrote back to say that I thought it extremely unsuspicious. The fact that anyone had been eccentric enough to take the dilapidated 'Le Bois des Papillons' must have convinced those who still believed in the existence of the gold that it really was hidden in the house. They probably thought that Laura had only taken the place in order to conduct a day and night search, and so they were determined to forestall her.

It was my secretary who first suspected that I was falling in love with Laura. When I laughed she said that she had noticed a change in my attitude. In the place of 'that blessed woman and her absurd obsessions' it was 'that poor woman and what she must have gone through'. Naturally I went on scoffing at the idea but I did become aware that I was thinking of Laura in a different way. It started as straightforward pity in place of exasperation. Then I began thinking of her as a beauty taunted into making herself feel plain. It made me dwell on her beauty. I remembered her when I had first met her when she was soft-eyed with love for Robert, glowing and witty and gay. Then I realised that I had been a witness to the slow strangulation of her heart, the garrotting of her spirit, and that I had done nothing to help, in spite of all her pleas.

It was not until Robert smiled at me that I acknowledged to myself that I was in love with her. I had gone to suggest to him that he should allow her to move to an address unknown to him. Her bank and my own firm would have the address but until she calmed down I thought it would be wiser if she felt that Robert and his 'hired assassins' should not know her whereabouts.

He shook his head and smiled at me. I put the same construction on that smile as Laura had done. I saw what she meant. It looked dangerous. It was so completely unlike Robert. There was not a vestige of charm in it. He had obviously not practised it. He seemed an utterly different man and I hated him on the spot and forever.

My secretary told me not to be a fool and to curb my imagination. She said, rather bitterly I thought, 'What has now become "that poor persecuted woman" has infected you with her own neurosis. Robert's no villain. You've just been taken in by Laura.'

I promptly accused her of falling into the common groove of Robert-worship and we quarrelled for the first time in ten years of working together.

Then we had a reconciliation over our common dislike of Miss Cook. We read in the paper that a false store of gold coins said to have been buried by the French resistance workers in a house called 'Le Bois des Papillons' in the village of Vallon had been found by a Miss Ellen Cook. She had discovered it in the side of an old well which she had been trying to clear of mosquito larvae. But it had been proved to be a little joke on the part of the resistance workers against the Nazis who had occupied the house and tortured their leader. They had spread the rumour that their funds were hidden on the premises so that the Nazis should spend their time looking for it. When they found it they would have seen what Ellen Cook saw: an insulting collection of tin circles cut in the shape of coins with 'MERDE' written very carefully in the middle of them. My secretary and I laughed at the irony of our foul-mouthed Amazon coming across this little nest of swear words.

That must have been the last time that I ever laughed. At first I was relieved because I felt that this 'treasure trove' discovery must have convinced even Laura that her intruders had been genuine bullion enthusiasts and nothing to do with Robert or hired assassins. But two weeks after the 'haul' the severely lacerated body of Ellen Cook was found in the sludge at the bottom of the old well in which she had been putting oil to kill off the mosquito larvae. She had thirty-six knife wounds and her head had been cleaved into a neat half. It was a crime of monstrous hatred. Unfond as I was of Miss Cook I was utterly baffled to think who could possibly have borne her such a grudge. She knew hardly anyone in Vallon. My secretary suggested spitefully that I probably thought it was Robert taking his revenge because Ellen had been Laura's bodyguard. I confess that she managed to sow that seed in my mind.

The Vallon police were much calmer and more correct. They thought that someone had believed Ellen's find to be a trick to disguise the real whereabouts of the resistance funds and had tried to beat the information out of her.

But Laura could not be persuaded that one of Robert's 'hired assassins' had not mistaken Ellen for herself.

In spite of my secretary reminding me that I had once thought of Laura as 'nothing but a thorough nuisance with a deranged mind', I made arrangements to fly out to Vallon. Without fully realising it at the time, I had become obsessed with Laura and her cause. My secretary repeated, 'This woman has made you as potty as she is.'

I cannot explain my sudden change of heart over Laura. It's possibly better not to try. I know from my professional experiences that these extraordinary emotional somersaults are inexplicable.

On the journey to Vallon I tried to work out my own somersault. Perhaps it was because I felt that she was the only person who really needed me. Perhaps I had suddenly realised her incredible beauty, and perhaps because I had become so outraged at the crippling of such a brilliant mind by a man who was obviously her inferior. Also I had seen Robert's unbelievable smile, and saw what Laura meant.

Long before we reached the airport, I had decided to ask her to live with me until we could make Robert see that a divorce would be more dignified for him. It would only bring him more sympathy and adoration from doting parishioners. He would be knitted more mufflers and baked more cakes than any other parson in history. 'Best friend runs away with good shepherd's wife' would bring him the kind of favourable publicity he worked so hard to achieve. Then Laura and I could be married.

I found Laura in the psychiatric ward of a hospital outside Vallon. The doctor said that the shock of Ellen's death and her fears for her own life had made it impossible for her to remain at 'Le Bois des Papillons' even with police protection.

In his opinion she was by no means insane but her health both mentally and physically had been so undermined that she had to be regarded as seriously unstable and in no position to care for herself. Any mention of her husband made matters so much worse that severe medical methods had had to be employed such as padded cells, injections, and special relaxing baths.

The whole thing made me feel quite ill myself and I thought if Robert ever treated me again to that poisonous, condescending smile, I would smash it right off his face.

At first Laura refused to allow me to visit her. She thought I was a spy for Robert. Then I sent her in a little note: 'Laura, I love you. Peter.'

She saw me then. She was nearly as pale as her pillow case but she managed to laugh. 'I couldn't believe your note . . . I thought you must have gone as mad as me. Robert said no one could love me. He said it embarrassed men to have to pretend they weren't bored by me and that no one was more bored than you.'

I said, 'Laura, Robert is an egotistical swine and I hate every gut in his body. We'll get rid of him and we'll marry.'

Then before she could answer I noticed the woman in the next bed. She was doing something very strange with her left arm, circling it round her nose like an elephant's trunk. Laura saw me staring at her and whispered urgently, 'Don't upset her. The poor soul thinks she's a teapot.'

'Thinks she's a teapot!!'

Laura said, 'Shush!' She was in earnest but she was not far off the giggles. 'It's wicked to make fun of her. She's had some emotional catastrophe and she thinks her arm is her spout and keeps on asking me to pour her out!'

I went straight off to have a severe word with the doctor. I said, 'How dare you put Madame Vince next door to a teapot.'

The doctor smiled, 'Madame de Saille is quite harmless and she will be cured. She is already responding to treatment. Besides, it is good for Madame Vince to have to look after her, it takes her mind off her own troubles.'

Nevertheless I argued with him that for a woman in Laura's nervous state to be next to an obvious lunatic could only have fatal results. I insisted that she should be put in a private room. He was very much against this. He said that she needed constant attention and supervision. She would get that far better in a public ward than in a private room. In the ward there were always nurses whereas in a private room there were sometimes long intervals before anyone might find time to pay the patient a visit, and he was adamant that Laura was not yet fit enough to be left alone. When she had made sufficient improvement and he could feel more confident he would certainly transfer her to a private room.

But I knew better, of course. I was absolutely determined that she should be spared the horrors of teapots and people under the impression that they were the Queen of Prussia. The doctor gave in but made it perfectly clear that he would accept no responsibility and neither would his staff if Laura suffered a relapse.

She was moved to a private room.

Two days later she was missing. The only clue as to the reason for her disappearance was that her husband had arrived in Vallon and had sent her a bunch of flowers saying that he had heard that she had been ill and wished to see her. This threw her into such a panic that the nurse rushed off to prepare a calming injection. During this interval Laura had managed to escape out of the window. Pinned to her husband's bunch of flowers was a note:

'*Dear Robert,*
*These will do for my grave. You had poor Ellen killed in mistake for me. But I'm going to save you any more errors of this kind.*
*Your once very, very loving wife,*

*Laura.*'

A big police search was instantly organised. The doctor and staff of the hospital put the blame squarely on me. Had I not insisted on having her transferred to a private room she would never had been left unguarded, and this would never have happened.

Robert apparently was questioned for hours, and so was I.

Before he knew that she was missing Robert had written her a letter. The police took charge of it and I did not know the contents until the trial.

Laura never even knew that it had been sent. Her body was found at 'Le Bois des Papillons' in the bottom of the old well in which Ellen Cook's gold hunting murderer had flung her. Laura had cut her throat before tipping herself down the well. Her blood tinged the green sludge and the mosquito larvae so that it looked in patches as if someone had been pouring in bottles of burgundy.

Robert and I were not allowed to leave the town. We were 'free' – but observed from every corner. Robert came to my hotel to ask my help. He said, 'Look, Peter, the police are suspicious of me. I sent my poor Laura a letter. It really was written from my heart but they think that it was a well-timed cover-up. It was nothing of the sort. I was trying to explain things to her and get her to see me. Now, you know the truth, Peter. You and I alone know what Laura was like – all this ridiculous assassin nonsense – for God's sake come and speak up for me.'

It is absolutely true to say that I forgot what happened. I certainly went for him. I remember that. But I forgot exactly what I did. I can only remember his smile and without any doubt I smashed it off his face.

At my trial they read out his letter to Laura.

It said:

*'My darling, and whatever you may think you are my darling. Please, please let the doctors and our good friend Peter Cowles get you over this fear that I am trying to kill you. I would rather kill myself. Your absence has made me realise what an abominable Christian I have been. In an odd way which I do not expect you to believe, my disgraceful behaviour was done for your sake. I felt that if I could impress my parishioners and make them like me it would impress you and make you like me. I have always felt so unworthy of you that it soured my whole nature.*

*If you had accused me of trying to murder your personality, your spirit or your soul, you would have been correct. I was frightened of you. I thought that your superior intellect would soon show me up for the cardboard prelate that I am, but quaintly enough I do love God and I should never have tried to shine at His cocktail parties in order to get my wife to admire me as much as my parishioners did. I doubt if He will forgive me for that! It is true that I tried to flatten you and make you frightened of me. I thought that that would keep you in lieu of love and respect. Please see me. My flowers are not poisoned. Get someone else to smell them! And if you will not see me please see our really great friend Peter Cowles. I really think that he will be the one to convince you that in spite of my appalling behaviour I really am devoted to you. Please put every faith in Peter Cowles. We have no greater friend. I promise to be a sincerely 'Good Shepherd' if you come back to me, but if you cannot forget everything and give me another chance I will give you your freedom and I strongly recommend you to put yourself in the hands of Peter Cowles. I think you would find much happiness with him.*

*Your loving and ever contrite husband,*

*Robert.'*

Whilst I was listening to this letter at my trial I was thinking of Robert's 'smile' – the one that both Laura and I had mistrusted.

It was his genuine smile.

It showed the true Robert for once trying not to hide his insecurity and his guilt. It was the only smile that had not been practised in the mirror. His real self and his sincerity had broken through. He had been asking our help on those occasions but because it was lacking its usual sickening charm we had mistaken that piteous smile.

He never had the chance to prove whether he could have made a really 'Good Shepherd'. He died from the wounds I inflicted upon him.

That is why I am in prison for life.

# ROGER LONGRIGG

## The Chair

'I selected, from the bill of fare, a cutlet,' replied Gregory Vardon to his friend's question. 'A lamb cutlet. Not without trepidation. I have known the chef to send up an underdone cutlet. It has occurred. But today's was excellent. And you, Charles?'

'My choice was comparable,' said Charles Corbishley, speaking with the gravity the subject demanded. 'Not at all dissimilar. My election, in a word, was a chump chop. With which I discussed a small carafe of the club claret.'

'A comfortable wine. Not distinguished but respectable.'

'Immature. But, at the price, what would you?'

Both men, who were very old, sighed in contemplation of the price of claret, which they frequently discussed, in this place, between themselves and with other members. Into the back morning-room of Blazon's Club the afternoon sun brought a wintry pretence of warmth. It gleamed on the coffee-urn, which dribbled on its table in the corner. It shamed the open fire, which nevertheless gave off a prodigious heat. It shone on Gregory Vardon's pink and well-scrubbed head; on Charles Corbishley's gold-rimmed bifocals it came and went, impertinently, as he wagged his ancient head.

'May I, Gregory,' said Charles, whose turn it was, 'summon a fellow and instruct him to bring you a glass of port wine?'

'I think that, of all things, a small glass of port is what I should most enjoy.'

'Good! Good!'

Charles was sitting at the end of the leather-covered sofa nearest to the wall by the fire. The bell was a yard away from him. He raised his rubber-tipped walking-stick and with it tried to stab the bell-push. He smote at the wall, leaving small circular marks on the wallpaper over a wide area surrounding the bell. He connected at last, and in triumph rang the bell for a long time.

A waiter appeared, a stunted Portuguese.

'A glass of vintage port, Gregory? Or shall we sustain ourselves more humbly with a beaker from the wood?'

Gregory appeared to reflect, to give the issue his full attention, to jump lightly to no ill-considered decision. 'A glass of the wood, I fancy,' he said at last.

Charles nodded with judicious approval. Had Gregory so far flown in the face of precedent (and invited Charles to spend so much more money) as to ask for vintage port, Charles would simply have disbelieved his own ears. They *offered* each other vintage port; the offer was not so much insincere as ritualistic.

'Be so good,' said Charles to the waiter, 'as to bring us two glasses of the wood port.'

Neither Charles nor Gregory talked, in any other place, in the orotund style

339

they adopted in the public rooms of Blazon's. Gregory seldom *was* in any other place: but if shown a menu in a restaurant he would not have called it a bill of fare. Charles elsewhere drank, rather than discussed, carafes of wine. But in the club they were clubmen; they were clubmen with a vengeance; they went at it thoroughly. It was not exactly a game, nor a conscious parody: but it lent a certain spacious stateliness to lives of rigorous budgeting, to lonely existences on pensions: it was harmless: it was fun: if it was time-consuming this was, if anything, a positive advantage.

The waiter subscribed to the ritual dutifully but without enthusiasm. He brought two small glasses of cheap port on a silver tray, and accepted payment.

The whole transaction was thus brought to a successful conclusion. Charles settled back in his corner of the sofa with a deep and fulfilled sigh; Gregory back in his with a gentler sigh expressive of gratitude, admiration, and delighted anticipation of his port. Tomorrow he would sit in the corner nearer the wall. The rubber tip of his walking-stick would (ultimately) activate the bell-push. In stately, well-rehearsed phrases he would offer Charles a glass of vintage port and buy him a glass of wood port. They would make their port last until half past three. Then there was only an hour to kill until tea-time. Charles would spend the hour where he was, in one or other corner of the sofa. On his lap, fetched with unimaginable labour, would be an open copy of *Country Life*: but his head would be back, his jaw loosened, his eyelids lowered, his breathing slow, his digestion proceeding with gentle diligence to prepare his stomach for Earl Grey and crumpets. Gregory, for his part, would ascend the stairs to the library, step by exhausting step, stick in one hand and banister in the other. There, solitary, he would hobble to the Trollope shelf between the all-unneeded signs requiring silence. He would take down the second volume of *The Small House at Allington*, and manage a page or two, in his special chair by the fire, before his own head went back, his jaw descended, and he had his forty winks before tea.

Nothing could be more civilised, nothing more delightful. No disaster more unpleasant could be imagined than the serious dislocation of this routine.

Gregory sipped his port (spinning it out) bought in proper sequence by Charles Corbishley. He was disagreeably surprised to see, crossing the morning-room to the table where the magazines were spread, the burly tweed-clad person of a member called Martyn, a brash and pop-eyed barfly in his early 60s.

Gregory had disliked Martyn before the latter was a member of the club, before he knew his name, before even he heard the fellow's braying and penetrating voice. He remembered his first sight of Martyn, quite a recent encounter, not a dozen years ago. He was a guest. Someone had asked him to lunch. He was waiting for his host in the hall. He was waiting in an ostentatious way, standing with his legs apart in front of the hall fire, patronising the club with his presence, staring pop-eyed at members who were decently hanging up their coats or drinking seemly drinks; he was looking condescendingly at the prints of Bay Middleton and Stockwell; he had a carnation in his buttonhole; there were veins all over his nose; his ginger moustache was an offence. He looked an abrasive personality, an irritant, a heavyweight gadfly, a bumptious bounder.

Once or twice a year thereafter, for perhaps four years, the man reappeared at lunchtime, guest of the same host. He had, or acquired, friends in the club. He greeted them boisterously. They were not visibly enraged. They bought him drinks. Groups, which his voice dominated, had several drinks and came late in to luncheon. They could be heard talking about salmon-fishing, pheasant-shooting, politics, the stock-market. The man's host, after lunch, bought him vintage port or brandy. Gregory's dislike increased with each visit, every one of which he witnessed, since he was always in the club, since he had nowhere else to go. The man was everything Gregory had always hated and feared. He was the jeering red-kneed boy at Gregory's private school who discovered that Gregory's mother had published poems (privately printed at her own expense) and led the cruel beagle-pack of future proconsuls which hunted him all across the playing-fields. He was the loud, confident footballer, the physical man, the swot-hater, the Flashman, the know-all. In every phase of his gentle life Gregory had known and detested such men. This man was the essence of their awfulness. He more than irritated Gregory: he made him feel ill. At least he came to the club only twice a year; and at least, as a guest, he was not allowed into the back morning-room.

Then came a shock which spoiled Gregory's sleep and his digestion for weeks.

In the bar one evil April day, when he was ordering the small dry sherry with which he anticipated luncheon, he was introduced to Martyn.

The man who always gave Martyn lunch said: 'Ah, Gregory, well met.'

'Good morning,' said Gregory, who could nowadays remember few names.

'Let me buy you a drink.'

'No thank you.'

'I want you to meet Barry Martyn.'

'Oh yes?'

Gregory looked, with nervous politeness, in the direction of the other's outstretched arm. There, grinning like a hyena, guzzling a glass of champagne, with a carnation in his filthy buttonhole, was the man whose face Gregory hated.

'Change your mind about that drink.'

'No thank you.'

'You two ought to get together. Lot in common.'

Gregory looked at the speaker with horrified incredulity.

'Fishing,' said the idiot. 'Both mad about fishing.'

'Aha,' brayed Martyn. 'A brother of the angle. The lordly salmon or the wily trout?'

'Trout,' said Gregory, fighting down his rage and nausea.

'A dryfly purist, for a monkey,' shouted Martyn. His bulging *faux-bonhomme* eyes goggled at Gregory like those of lordly salmon or wily trout.

'Actually,' said Gregory, 'I . . .'

'Where do you fish?'

'I have not, for many years, owing to failing health and imperfect vision—'

'Where *did* you fish?'

'I was so very fortunate as to enjoy, for a number of seasons, the hospitality of—'

'I've got two miles of the Test. About the best there is, though I say it as shouldn't. I wouldn't swap a yard of it for Leckford or the Houghton water. Four and five pounders. You'll bear me out, Derek. Not much mayfly. Good sport with the medium olive, iron blue, BWO, little red sedge. I can give you a day any time you like. I mean it. Always delighted to let a keen chap have a go.'

'You accept,' said the monster's host.

But Gregory managed, after ten minutes of unpleasant labour, to persuade them that his refusal was final.

Worse followed.

Martyn's host, a spindly industrialist from Staffordshire, drew Gregory aside as he went in to lunch.

'Awfully pleased you got on so well with Barry Martyn,' he murmured. 'Felt sure you would. Very good fellow indeed, most generous, everybody likes him. I expect you've twigged?'

'No,' said Gregory. But a terrible premonition gripped his bowels.

'I've put him up for membership here. Rallying support. Want plenty of signatures. You'll sign, I trust.'

Gregory was rescued from an appalling predicament, but in an unpleasant way. He fell over. The tip of his stick skidded on the marble of the hall floor and he crumpled gently at the industrialist's feet. Martyn helped him up. He was shaken and humiliated but not hurt. He was assisted into a chair in the morning-room. He stayed there, omitting lunch, and drank one of his rare glasses of brandy. The economy of missing lunch more than defrayed the cost of the brandy.

A *member*. Constantly about. Braying, buying drinks, rendering hideous the quiet places where Gregory spent nearly all his waking and some of his sleeping hours.

Gregory went home, after an early and miserable dinner, to the bed-sitter in Kensington in which he slept and made his tea in the morning: but he did not sleep, or enjoy his tea, or enjoy his port after lunch the next day.

There was a long waiting-list. Martyn would not be a member for two years. Something could be done in that time. The committee could be alerted. With tact, a word in season, the opening of a few eyes . . . After a few weeks Gregory recovered his confidence and his digestion.

He mentioned the matter to Charles.

Charles said: 'I know the chap you mean. He served with a nephew of mine in the Bushytails. He is stated, credibly enough, to have worn the king's uniform, as it then was, with some distinction. I have accorded his candidature the small benefit of my support.'

'You have *signed*?'

'My signature is inscribed on the appropriate leaf of the book, and may there, by the curious or doubtful, be inspected.'

Charles, misled by a family connection, fed with lies, could not be made to see that Martyn's election must be prevented. Gregory tried elsewhere. 'Rather a merry bird,' said one member. 'Not an intellectual, but a merry enough egg.' 'Kind,' said another man. 'Good war,' said a third.

The months passed. On Martyn's page of the Candidates' Book the signatures grew thick as autumn leaves in Vallombrosa. Gregory knew some of the names and they were *perfectly respectable members*.

Martyn's visits in this period grew more frequent. He was the guest of other hosts. To Gregory it seemed that his laughter was louder, his eyes more protuberant, his nose redder, his carnation more ostentatious, with each jocose tuck-in. It seemed, moreover, that he was working some dreadful magic on existing members of the club. Men Gregory believed to be sober and well-conducted spent longer in the bar before lunch, and laughed more loudly over lunch; there was more calling from table to table; there was more chat in the morning-room; there was more widely-audible talk of salmon and pheasant, of by-elections and race-meetings.

Charles said he noticed no change. 'The conversations,' he said, 'to which you animadvert, are, I fancy, endemic to this and to similar institutions. Many of our Georgian and Regency predecessors had the same preoccupations, Gregory.'

Somewhat less that two years later, the list went up on the notice-board of candidates for the next election. Major Barrington Martyn was among them.

A week later the Election Committee met. Gregory sat, feeling suffocated in the morning-room, knowing what horrible errors were being transacted above him.

The following day, on the notice-board, appeared the list of duly elected new members: and the day after that Major Barrington Martyn came, ebulliently gleeful, to lunch for the first time as a member. Came into the back morning-room, as of right. Greeted, as of right, Charles and Gregory, drinking ritual port on their sofa. Goggled, swaggered, brayed, sent for brandy, smoked a cigar, dominated a group, and gave Gregory an attack of indigestion which ruined the rest of his day.

One comfort remained in a situation otherwise comfortless. The man worked. He came from an office and returned to it. Though rendered hideous at lunchtime, the club returned to normal seemliness soon after 2.15. Nor did Martyn come in every day. Twice a week was his average. On these nasty days Gregory adjusted his routine, which he was far too old to enjoy doing, but which was far the lesser of evils. He lunched early and went straight to the library. Charles Corbishley was huffy.

So for six years. An imperfect life, but bearable.

And then, at 2.45, crossing the morning-room, Martyn. Going to the magazines. Taking one. Sitting down with it. Lighting a cigar. Set for the afternoon. *No office?*

'No indeed,' said Charles Corbishley softly. 'Released from the treadmill.

Well-earned retirement with effect, I am assured, from last week. We shall henceforth see much more of the gallant and popular Major Martyn.'

They did, much more: saw and heard. Gregory, always quiet, became quieter. Always solitary, he became eremitic. He spent less and less time in the morning-rooms front and back, the hall, bar, coffee-room, strangers' room, and other thronged areas in which, like disease or explosive, Martyn was apt to erupt; he spent more and more time in the library. He blessed the library. It was asylum, heaven-haven, the last refuge of civilised man on earth, unassailably quiet, almost always marvellously empty. There were the shelves; there was his chair. The chair was perfect. It was by the fire and out of the draught. It was deep. Yet, by dint of the shape and position of the arms, it was easy to get out of. It was wonderfully comfortable for sleeping and (new diversion) for extended reading. In daylight his book was served by the large window behind; at night it was illuminated by a handsome table-lamp at his elbow. He could reach a bell-push with his stick.

He was safe from Martyn. No intellectual. Illiterate, in effect. The last man to frequent the library.

On Tuesday the 6th of November, nine months after Martyn's retirement, Gregory lunched later than usual. The sound of Martyn's voice, on the landing outside the card-room, had imprisoned him mouse-quiet in the library. Until the incubus withdrew he would wait. He waited for twenty-five minutes, so interminable were Martyn's vainglorious anecdotes. The laughter that greeted them was, must be, that of idiots or sycophants. The hateful noise receded at last. Gregory emerged. He ate some saddle of lamb: a somewhat expensive dish, but one of which Trollope had that morning put him in mind. At the far end of the dining-room Martyn, also alone, was lunching. He had a magazine on a rack in front of him and a bottle of wine beside him. Gregory shifted his position so that he did not have to look at Martyn eating his lunch.

Martyn got up and left the dining-room. Soon his voice would be braying among the lustres of the morning-room chandeliers.

Gregory paid for his lunch. He started slowly, slowly crossing the dining-room. A waiter held the door for him as he went out into the hall; the rubber tip of his stick squeaked on the marble. He felt stiff and weak but pretty fit. His life was narrow, but his life had always been narrow. He preferred a narrow life, a few certainties, a small well-trodden area, no dubious adventures, no explorations and no risks.

Gregory embarked on the stairs; stick firmly grasped in his right hand, banister in his left. Both feet on each step, left-right left-right. The stairs were no problem. He went up them better than Charles did, although Charles was two years younger. Charles had almost given up bridge because of getting upstairs to the card-room. What Gregory could not do, of course, was hurry. It was no deprivation. There was no hurry. Going upstairs was something to do. It occupied a few minutes. It helped fill the day. It brought tea-time closer.

Gregory went along the landing to the library. He opened the enormous door. He went in and straight to the ranks of Trollope. He took *Phineas Finn* from the shelf. He turned and started slowly towards his chair.

Martyn was sitting in his chair.

Gregory did not cry out, nor froth at the mouth, nor shed scalding tears. He kept his rage and disgust under firm Anglo-Saxon control. He stopped and stared. This was, itself, unusual and *outré* behaviour. It betrayed feeling as no member of a gentleman's club should, on the club premises, betray feeling. But Gregory was no superman. He could restrain himself from Latin or Levantine excesses, but he could not help stopping and staring.

Martyn glanced up. He waved affably to Gregory with his cigar. He said nothing. He could, it seemed, read the word 'Silence'. Perhaps he could read a few words more, as a book lay open on the arm of his chair. Of Gregory's chair.

Gregory stood as though paralysed for a long moment. Martyn glanced at him again, with indulgent surprise. He gestured with his cigar, friendly but dismissive, and returned to his pretence of reading. His gesture said that Gregory was welcome to any other chair in the library. Gregory did not want any other chair. He did not want to share the library with Martyn. He did not want his life in ruins.

His life, his new life. The one he had made, fashioned out of adversity, built on the crumbling fragments of what had gone before. Martyn had driven him out of the haunts of men into this booksy hermitage. So be it. Old as he was he had adjusted. He had become a reader, an all-day reader in a library chair instead of an hour-long napper in that same chair, contentedly absorbed by the writings of good men long dead. A new way of life. Not better than the old (glasses of port, a cautious camaraderie) nor worse, but different, and his own courageous creation.

Now this was ended. His refuge was razed. Like Reynard the Fox he found his last earth stopped.

He was distraught. What could he do? What did the future hold? He was an old, old man on a small pension, living with frugal simplicity in his Kensington bed-sitter, living, in a truer sense, here in his club. Old friends long dead, except those few in the club. Family long dead. Colleagues (few intimate) long dead. It was little enough he asked of the world. One chair. And that was gone.

If a different man had usurped his chair, what then? A man with a kind of right to it, a learned man, a man who belonged in the library, a don (there were dons in the club) or a High Court judge or a retired cabinet minister? Then perhaps, another adjustment. Hard at his age: possible. A different chair in the library. Hard, at his age. But he would have acknowledged the suitability, the other's right. Or he might have framed an appeal: not of a broken and tragic but of an old and cantankerous man, a character. It could have been so phrased that no don, judge, or minister of the crown would refuse. A distasteful course, but possible.

But in this case! In the face of this! A different chair? Unbearable. An appeal, an old man's plea? To Martyn, the red-nosed, the pop-eyed, the show-off, the sport, the bon viveur, the bully? Never, never, never.

Then what?

Gregory got out of the library somehow, his old legs trembling, his stick insecurely held. He got out onto the landing and leaned against the wall. Unstoppably, to his infinite shame, the tears began to roll down his cheeks. He groped blindly to the lavatory that served the jovial elders of the card-room. It was occupied. He turned and hobbled along the passage that led to the bedroom-floor stairs. An Irish housemaid passed him, coming down the stairs at a run, girlish but massive, a healthy cow of a housemaid. She looked at Gregory with alarm and concern. He sniffed and gestured angrily with his cane.

'Are you all right, sir?'

'Yes!'

She went away slowly along the passage, casting glances back over her meaty shoulder.

His tear-ducts at last ran dry. He dabbed at his cheeks. He went back on a bus to Kensington. No tea in the club for him today, no dinner there tonight. He knew he would weep again, thinking of his chair and of his life.

For two days he moped at home in helpless, babyish rage. He wept from time to time. Then the thought struck him (why so long delayed?) that Martyn had been visiting the library for the first and only time. Why should he ever revisit it? What could be there to divert him? He was a creature of crowds, bars, drinks, the sound of his own voice. The library, any library, would bore and puzzle him. He had tried it, avid for new sensations; he would not return.

Gregory ventured to the club. The hall porter greeted him warmly, concerned about his health. Elderly gentlemen who lived alone in digs and lodgings could be ill, unnoticed for days; could die and lie unnoticed for weeks. But Gregory was neat as always, walking no worse, unaltered, dry-eyed.

He went upstairs to the library. He opened the door, frightened. The fine old room was empty. His chair was empty. The cushions had been plumped out by a servant, the ashtrays had been emptied and polished, the fire banked up. All was well. Sanity and safety had returned.

Gregory found his book and settled down, feeling deeply happy and slightly foolish. What a fuss about nothing. He was getting senile. He must fight it.

He lunched. He ate boiled silverside and pease pudding, and drank a glass of still cider.

Martyn was nowhere to be seen. He was away, or ill, or had fallen drunkenly under a bus.

Gregory had a glass of port with Charles Corbishley. Neither could remember whose turn it was; Charles insisted it was his.

They went upstairs together. Charles was playing bridge. Gregory opened the door of the library.

Martyn was in his chair.

It was then, the moment that he saw him, that Gregory decided upon murder. It was a brainwave: a solution of immediate and inescapable rightness. It would solve the problem as nothing else would solve it. Gregory had nothing to lose, even if caught; he had his chair to gain.

Gregory went into the strangers' room, empty and elegant but comfortless. He sat in a high backed chair and brooded about method. It was an area in which he recognised, and regretted, his inexperience. His career – forty years of concern with ancient buildings, in a financial and administrative role – gave him no basis for current planning. His private life, almost wholly without episode, provided no useful precedent. Even his reading was unhelpful. Trollope? Mrs Gaskell? Thackeray? There were beasts like Martyn in them all, and in Surtees and the Brontës and George Eliot. There was violence in these books. People were clubbed to the ground in lonely places. But there were no methods spelled out by any of these authors for killing usurpers in club libraries.

The strangers' room had a writing table. There was a dip-pen with a relief nib, a dutifully filled if unused inkwell, a clean blotter, and a selection of club writing paper in a variety of sizes. Administrative habit held. Gregory drew a sheet from the rack, dipped the pen into the ink, and wrote in capital letters:

POSSIBLE METHODS.

His writing was small and legible; the vertical strokes wavered a little because he made them slowly and his hand trembled.

He began to list methods as they occurred to him, attempting, at this stage, no order:

> *Shooting*
> *Stabbing*
> *Strangulation*
> *Suffocation*
> *Poison (in beverage, in food, or by venomous reptile or insect)*
> *Blunt instrument or bludgeon*
> *Fall down stairs (assisted)*
> *Ejection from windows, defenestration*
> *Injection of air into blood-vessel*
> *Burning (immolation)*
> *Drowning*
> *Electrocution*
> *Crushing by avalanche, falling building or similar*
> *Explosion, as of bomb or grenade*
> *Gas*
> *Pushing under car, train*

He paused and sucked his pen, which tasted of boot polish and snuff. Ancient memories of the early cinema enabled him to add:

> *Tying to railway lines in path of oncoming train*
> *Circular saw*
> *Introduction into den of wild beasts*
> *Lashing to log above large waterfall*
> *Trampling by stampeding herd of maddened steers*

Other memories produced:

> *Slingshot or catapult (stone through temple)*
> *Death ray*

> *Contact with fatal disease (Red Death or similar)*
> *Incarceration (cf. Amontillado), premature burial*

Further thought contributed:

> *Starvation*
> *Death by thirst (dehydration)*
> *Driving to suicide (query: by hint of blackmail)*
> *Inflation (compressed air)*
> *Deflation (vacuum-pump)*
> *Trampling by rogue elephants*

Gregory was pleased with his list, which was a great deal longer than he had expected.

He examined each entry, critically, dispassionately, considering the problems, logistic and other, intrinsic to each.

To his dismay this examination disposed, at once, of nearly all his possible methods. He had no gun, poison, asp or scorpion, hypodermic needle, bomb, gas-shell, circular saw, menagerie, slingshot, ray-gun, bacilli of the Red Death, niche in cellar with available trowel and mortar, air-pump, or elephant. He saw no way of travelling to, let alone inducing Martyn to travel to, the edge of a lake or the brow of a waterfall. There was no feasible method of killing by starvation or thirst a man who belonged to Blazon's and had plenty of money. He had not the physical strength to eject Martyn, who might be expected to resist, from an upper window, to smash his skull with a club, or to tie him to the rails in the path of an oncoming train.

Possibilities, however, survived this winnowing. Stabbing. Electrocution. Tripping at the top of the stairs. Burning. And blackmail leading to suicide.

Gregory pondered each of these, chilly in the strangers' room, while tea-time came and went.

The force of administrative habit, from which long years of retirement had not released him, induced Gregory to place his possibles in alphabetical order:

> *Blackmail*
> *Electrocution*
> *Fire*
> *Stabbing*
> *Tripping (top of stairs)*

After weeks of thought, intensive if not continuous, he decided to make his attempts in this order. If one failed he would proceed to the next; if one succeeded there would be no need to go on.

*Blackmail.* Gregory had left it in his list because it did not require, in a physical or mechanical sense, equipment he did not have, powers he could not summon. Gregory had heard that if you went up to no matter whom, approaching from behind, and whispered: 'All is known! Flee,' the archbishop himself would grab a suitcase and decamp, or (better) take a revolver from his cassock and shoot himself. Gregory tried to picture the scene, casting himself in the role of victim. He pictured a stranger, or indeed a person known to him, whispering with urgent menace that all was discovered. What was discovered? What was there to discover? Nothing in Gregory's life. He had secrets – his false teeth, the occasional malfunction of his waterworks, his use of the dictionary when doing the crossword – but they were not, Gregory thought, what was meant. As to Martyn? He was, surely, too crass to have guilty secrets. He would rather trumpet his conquests (sexual), proclaim his fiddles (tax-evasive), make comicheroic stories about his car accidents. His activities, his outrages, were of a public kind.

The conversation was lamentably predictable. 'All is discovered!' 'Yes, old boy, always has been.'

Four possibilities remained. Much reconnaissance was required. Gregory did the reconnaissance. He informed himself, in minutest detail, about Martyn's habits, his movements, the times he was here or there, the time he was alone in the library. It was agony to observe him in the chair, fat cigar to his fat lips, eyes fatly bulging over purple cheeks: but Gregory learned what he needed. The man's habits were regular. He was predictable. Things promised well for the four surviving possibilities.

*Electrocution.* The key was the table-lamp beside the chair. It was made of brass: a Doric column on a massive square base, the switch in the column three inches below the bulb. Gregory's knowledge of electricity was rudimentary, but he believed that, by de-earthing the plug and by re-routing the live wire to the brass, he could kill his enemy.

He was dissatisfied with his knowledge, and improved it. He spent some time with a courteous West Indian in a Kensington electrician's, enquiring (adroitly) after possible sources of *danger* in big brass table-lamps. He elicited wiring diagrams: wrong and right: how to be safe: how to kill.

He purchased a small screwdriver with a yellow insulated handle. He took screwdriver and diagrams to Blazon's. He waited his chance. What he required was an hour (an hour should suffice) during which Martyn was not in the library, but at the end of which he, and not some other, should come to the library: sit in the chair: require the table-lamp. A bright midday was useless. A dull sky, or a murky evening, would call the unsuspecting hand towards the brass. Many a promising occasion had to be passed up.

But the right occasion, after eleven weeks, arrived. The day was dark, heavy clouds moving sluggishly across the brown London sky. Martyn was in the club, not foul-hooking his fish or murdering tame pheasants. He had a guest for lunch, a pudgy financier, who would trundle in due course back to his extortions.

Between 1.30 and 2.30 Gregory could be sure of having the library to himself. All was planned. He would fix the lamp. Then he would lurk, innocently, feigning sleep, in a nearby chair. If by mischance some innocent should anticipate Martyn, make for the chair and lamp, Gregory could intervene and save him. It was unlikely. Martyn would come, cigar aglow, eyes abulge. Gregory would shrink back, so small and old as to be almost invisible. Pfft. A fault in the wiring. Gregory far elsewhere before Martyn was discovered, which might, indeed, be the following morning, when housemaids emptied ashtrays.

Gregory crept into the penumbrous library. He set to work on the plug. He knew what to do. Urgency lent deftness to his old fingers. The screws were hard to undo but he undid them. Crouching was hard on his knees but he compelled his knees to obedience. Plug done, earthless, its safety factor removed. He thrust it back into its socket. He addressed himself to the next, the crucial part. His screwdriver whirled. Flex snaked out at him. He consulted his diagrams. Wrong, right. The right now wrong, the wrong now right. With his left hand he grasped the brazen column of the lamp, with his right he groped among the bright-tipped wires which spiralled up its gut—

*Bam.* A great blow knocked the lamp out of his hands, knocked him into the chair (*the chair*), knocked him out.

Got a shock, they said. Lucky to be alive. Trying to mend the lamp, misguided old gentleman. Fancy him having a screwdriver.

His pulse was taken by a distinguished elderly physician (a member) who was dragged protesting from his Irish stew. All was well. Brandy was pressed to Gregory's lips. He drank the brandy. It ran like a fire down his gullet, reviving him wonderfully. He sat up, quite recovered.

Martyn, it appeared, had brought the brandy; his hand had held it to Gregory's bloodless old lips.

Many weeks passed before Gregory recovered strength and resolution to proceed. But his intention, during convalescence, never wavered.

Electricity, he concluded, had been beyond him. It was too technical, too modern. He had thought to understand but he had not understood. It took younger men. Better to rely on the natural, the elemental killers, the weapons of the cavemen and the ancient gods.

*Fire.*

The plan was simple but it took a great deal of careful and exhausting preparation. Gregory procured a gallon can. He caused it to be filled with petrol. He procured another. This was also filled. He tried to take both, in a suitcase, to Blazon's, but the suitcase was too heavy. He took one, wrapped in brown paper; he smuggled it, smiling with false brightness, past the hall-porter's box, and struggled with it up to the library. He hoped it would be taken for a bundle of books. He hid it on a floor-level shelf behind volumes of German pastoral literature. He imported the second gallon the same way, varying the wrapping in order to deceive. No one looked at him or at his shabby bundle.

Above the bookshelves, all round the library, stood urns of Attic character, gifts of a Victorian bishop. One of them, indecently decorated with paintings of Spartan athletes, stood above *the chair*.

The next phase took all that Gregory had of strength and resolution. He moved the library ladder all the length of the library. He climbed it, with one of his gallon cans. He hoisted the can from shelf to shelf, displacing books, until it rested by the urn on the top. With infinite difficulty he poured most of the petrol from the can into the urn. Some dribbled onto the books below, some onto Gregory. The place reeked of petrol. Time, and Martyn's cigars, would cure that.

Ten days later (he needed the rest) he added the second can. It was neither easier nor more difficult. He spilled less, but it seemed heavier. He was, to be sure, ten days older.

Gregory disinterred, that night, a spool of nylon from the elderly tangle of his fishing-gear. It was twenty-pound test; he had unlimited yards of it. It lived in his pocket for three weeks.

After three weeks opportunity again occurred. He put the ladder under the urn, and a loop of nylon about the urn. He let the nylon drop invisibly down the front of the bookshelf, trail invisibly across the floor, and finish in his hand, twenty feet away, in a small armchair in the semi-darkness.

Martyn came. He sat down. He lit his cigar. He opened his book. He never saw Gregory.

Gregory took up the slack of his nylon line. It rose from the floor and the bookcase; it was a visible silver thread, behind Martyn, between Gregory's hand and the death-laden urn.

Now! All worked to perfection. The thread tipped the urn. The urn upended over the chair. Flood of petrol, to be ignited by the cigar, to shroud Martyn in flames, to give him a noble, a Viking death which he did not deserve? No petrol. The urn tumbled, dry. Martyn sprang from his chair with a shout. He glanced at the urn, unbroken on the carpet beside him. He glanced up at the bookshelf. He shrugged and settled back to his book.

Gregory never moved.

An hour later Martyn went away. Gregory hobbled forward, to remove his telltale nylon and to examine the urn. The urn had a hole in the bottom. Not a new one, occasioned by its fall, but an old one, original, part of the design. The urn had, no doubt, been intended for plants.

Too elaborate, thought Gregory sadly. Too dependant on the treacherous and delusive gifts of Victorian bishops. He must be simpler, more basic, more primitive. He must rely upon a tool he could trust.

*Stabbing*.

He bought, in a Kensington ironmonger's, a kitchen knife, razor-sharp, needle-pointed, its blade a wicked eleven inches long.

Observation assured him that Martyn, in his gross way, unbuttoned his waistcoat when he sat in the library chair (*whose chair?*) to pretend to read his book. Penetration of tweed or worsted was therefore needless; only silk or poplin need be pierced. Great force was not needed, not with so sharp an instrument.

The placement was important. Gregory studied anatomical drawings in books in the public library. He required to hit the heart, avoid ribs. He practised, nightly for some weeks, on a dummy he constructed from a bolster, dressed in coat and waistcoat of his own. He drilled himself in the position he must adopt, given the position he knew Martyn adopted.

Nothing, nothing was this time left to chance.

Martyn came to the library. He sat down, waving to Gregory with his cigar, waving with the voiceless freemasonry of a fellow-user of the library.

Gregory went to the French section. He drew forth a book, long identified. He leafed through the pages. With a start of surprise, and a somewhat overplayed grunt of displeasure, he affected to discover that the pages were uncut. He went to a drawer in a writing-table. He took from the drawer a knife: not the heavy brass paper-cutter which lived there, but his Kensington kitchen knife. He began to cut the pages of the book. The light was bad where he stood. He hobbled, grumbling, to the window. He stood behind the chair.

Martyn glanced at him, sympathetic, preoccupied.

Trr, trr. The razor-sharp knife slit the pages of a forgotten French novel.

Gregory moved closer to the chair. Martyn's waistcoat was unbuttoned. His rib-cage was outlined, rib on rib, against the pink and white stripes of his shirt. Gregory examined his target. He picked his spot. It was an inch and a half to the left of a stripe in Martyn's Old Harrovian tie, an inch to the right of the buckle of his braces. Between ribs, straight to heart.

Gregory gulped. Could he do this? Plunge cold steel into the breast of an unsuspecting man? Yes! Martyn smelled of cigar-smoke and sandalwood hair-lotion. Gregory remembered Martyn; he remembered all the Martyns in his life; he looked at his chair. He could do it.

He kept up his camouflage, trr trr, cutting the pages, but looking at the triangle of pink and white shirt.

There was a sudden and shocking pain in his thumb. He looked down, aghast. Blood welled. He had cut himself. He cried out, unnerved by the redness and wetness of his blood. It was all over the book. His thumb hurt shockingly. He staggered, faint. An arm gripped him. He was lowered into a chair. His thumb was bound with a clean cotton handkerchief. Brandy was summoned and carried to his lips.

Martyn had caught him. Martyn had bandaged his thumb. Martyn had paid for the brandy.

A final possibility remained.

*Tripping (top of stairs)*. Nylon again. Nylon had given satisfaction before; in the failure of attempt number two the fault had not been nylon's.

The stairs were broad, curved, and made of stone. There were posts each side at the top, between which a trip-wire could be stretched.

Thought convinced Gregory that he could not rig his trip-wire and leave it unattended, in the expectation of Martyn descending before anyone else descended. Someone was apt to come out of the card-room and go down the stairs. Not only would Gregory's ruse be discovered, and Martyn saved, but some bluff bridge-player would have his skull split and his back broken.

What Gregory had to do was to station himself at the top of the stairs, out of sight or innocently employed, holding one end of his nylon. At the approach of Martyn, but of no other, he would tighten. In the hurly-burly which would follow the death of Martyn, Gregory could, assuredly, detach his nylon. The method was so greatly simpler and surer than the others that it was, as now emerged, a pity that Gregory had not listed his ideas in reverse alphabetical order.

What had to be established was his own station. Undoubtedly the place was the card-room lavatory. No doubt of it. It chose itself. The nylon must be secured (with knots that, as a fisherman, Gregory had known and could relearn) to the further newel-post at the head of the stairs; it would lie, harmless and invisible, along the top step; it would loop round the nearer newel-post; at a slight angle it would cross the passage to the keyhole of the lavatory, and to Gregory's hand inside the lavatory door. When the door stood slightly ajar Gregory established that he could, through the crack, see the top of the stairs.

One further preparation remained.

Gregory obtained drawing-pins.

He went to the strangers' room. On a sheet of the largest club writing-paper he wrote OUT OF ORDER in ink, with the dip-pen. The letters wavered but were clearly legible. He blotted his work carefully. The message, in mirror-writing, glared from the blotting-paper. Gregory burned the blotting-paper in the fire in the strangers' room.

Some days later he lunched on a fillet of excellent haddock. He watched Martyn lunching alone. Martyn lunched heavily. Gregory joined Charles Corbishley for a glass of port. Charles paid for the port. Gregory then, for the first time in a dozen years, suggested a second glass of port. He astonished himself as much as he astonished Charles.

The port drunk, more quickly than usual, he went upstairs, also more quickly than usual. Excitement accelerated both his drinking and his ascent. He confirmed that Martyn was in the library, fatly occupying the chair. There were voices from the card-room. No one else was about. Gregory threaded the end of his nylon through the keyhole of the lavatory door. He led it across the passage, round the nearer newel-post, along the top of the stairs, and to the further newel-post. There he secured it with his relearned knot. He went back to the lavatory. He took his OUT OF ORDER notice from his pocket, and pinned it to the lavatory door with his drawing-pin.

He went into the lavatory, leaving the door ajar. He sat on the seat and watched.

After a very long time a bridge-player stumped from the card-room to the lavatory. He grunted with chagrin when he saw the notice. He stumped away to try elsewhere.

More time passed. It was very quiet. There was very little noise from the card-room, hardly more than a murmur, agricultural in quality, rather soothing than otherwise. The club was almost empty, before tea on a week-day. The sound of traffic hardly reached this central point of the solid old building.

Gregory faithfully gripped the plastic spool of his nylon. It seemed to him that he was transported backwards, seventy or more years in time, to the bows of a dinghy off the West Coast of Scotland: that he was fishing for mackerel with a hand-line; his cousin Maud was there in a tam-o'-shanter, and old Dougal the boatman . . .

'Good God, what are you doing there?'

'Fishing,' said Gregory thickly, emerging slowly from deep sleep, stupid and heavy-lidded from his second glass of port.

Martyn peered into the lavatory. He saw Gregory sitting, a little frail hunched figure, on the lavatory seat. He saw the spool in Gregory's hand, and the nylon line going from the spool through the keyhole.

Martyn said: 'What are you trying to catch?'

Then he began to laugh. His face purpled. Tears streamed down his cheeks. He tried to speak. The effort turned his laughter to coughing. He coughed helplessly, dangerously. His face went from scarlet to black. He staggered. He collapsed against the lavatory door, fighting, coughing, struggling for breath, a hand clutching his heart.

They said he died on his way to hospital. His heart failed owing to a paroxysm brought on by coughing, itself the result of mirth. He died of laughing.

'Scrutiny,' said Gregory solemnly, 'revealed the availability of ox-tail. Which I allowed myself to accompany with a dish of spinach. Now, my dear Charles, may I request a steward to carry us a glass of vintage port?'

'Wood-port, I thank you,' said Charles Corbishley.

'So be it.'

At half past three Gregory went up to the library. He read a page of *The Eustace Diamonds*; in his chair by the fire, before falling gently asleep until tea-time.

*This story was originally published under the pseudonym of Ivor Drummond.*

# PETER LOVESEY

## The Secret Lover

'Pam.'

'Yes?'

'Will you see him this weekend?'

Pam Meredith drew a long breath and stifled the impulse to scream. She knew exactly what was coming. 'See who?'

'Your secret lover.'

She summoned a coy smile, said, 'Give over!' and everyone giggled.

For some reason, that last session of the working week regularly turned three efficient medical receptionists into overgrown schoolgirls. They were all over thirty, too. As soon as they arrived at the health centre on Saturday morning, they were into their routine. After flexing their imaginations with stories of what the doctors had been getting up to with the patients, they started on each other. Then it was never long before Pam's secret lover came up.

He was an inoffensive, harassed-looking man in his late thirties who had happened to walk into the centre one afternoon to ask for help. A piece of grit had lodged under his left eyelid. Not one of the doctors or the district nurse had been in the building at the time, so Pam had dealt with it herself. From her own experiences with contact lenses, she had a fair idea how to persuade the eye to eject a foreign body, and she had succeeded very quickly, without causing the patient any serious discomfort. He had thanked her and left in a rush, as if the episode had embarrassed him. Pam had thought no more about him until a fortnight later, when she came on duty and was told that a man had been asking for her personally and would be calling back at lunchtime. This, understandably, created some lively interest in Reception, particularly when he arrived at five minutes to one carrying a bunch of daffodils.

At thirty-three, Pam was the second youngest of the medical receptionists. She exercised, dieted and tinted her hair blonde and she was popular with many of the men who came in to collect their prescriptions, but she was not used to floral tributes. In her white overall she thought of herself as clinical and efficient. She had a pale, oval face with brown eyes and a small, neat mouth that she had been told projected refinement rather than sensuality. Lately, she had noticed some incipient wrinkles on her neck and taken to wearing polo-necked sweaters.

Under the amused and frankly envious observation of her colleagues, Pam had blushingly accepted the flowers, trying to explain that such a tribute was not necessary, charming as it was. However, when the giver followed it up by asking her to allow him to buy her a drink at the Green Dragon, she had found him difficult to refuse. She had stuttered something about being on duty after lunch, so he had suggested tomato juice or bitter lemon, and one of the other girls had given her an unseen nudge and planted her handbag in her hand.

That was the start of the long-running joke about Pam's secret lover.

Really the joke was on the others. They hadn't guessed it in their wildest fantasies, but things had developed to the extent that Pam now slept with him regularly.

Do not assume too much about the relationship. In the common understanding of the word, he was not her lover. Sleeping together and making love are not of necessity the same thing. The possibility was not excluded, yet it was not taken as the automatic consequence of sharing a bed, and that accorded well with Pam's innate refinement.

So it wasn't entirely as the girls in the health centre might have imagined it. Pam had learned over the first tomato juice in the Green Dragon that Cliff had a job in the cider industry which entailed calling on various producers in the West Midlands and South-West, and visiting Hereford for an overnight stay once a fortnight. He liked travelling, yet he admitted that the nights away from home had been instrumental in the failure of his marriage. He had not been unfaithful, but, as he altruistically put it, anyone who read the accounts of rapes and muggings in the papers couldn't really blame a wife who sought companionship elsewhere when her husband spent every other week away on business.

Responding to his candour, Pam had found herself admitting that she, too, was divorced. The nights, she agreed, were the worst. Even in the old cathedral city of Hereford, which had no reputation for violence, she avoided going out alone after dark and she often lay awake listening acutely in case someone was tampering with the locks downstairs.

That first lunchtime drink had led to another when Cliff was next in the city. The fortnight after, Pam had invited him to the house for a 'spot of supper', explaining that it was no trouble, because you could do much more interesting things cooking for two than alone. Cliff had heaped praise on her chicken *cordon bleu*, and after that the evening meal had become a fortnightly fixture. On the first occasion, he had quite properly returned to his hotel at the end of the evening, but the following time he had introduced Pam to the old-fashioned game of cribbage, and they had both got so engrossed that neither of them had noticed the time until it was well after midnight. By then, Pam felt so relaxed and safe with Cliff that it had seemed the most natural thing in the world to make up the spare bed for him and invite him to stay the night. There had been no suggestion on either side of a more intimate arrangement. That was what she liked about Cliff. He wasn't one of those predatory males. He was enough of a gentleman to suppress his natural physical instincts. And one night six weeks after in a thunderstorm, when she had tapped on his bedroom door and said she was feeling frightened, he had offered in the same gentlemanly spirit to come to her room until the storm abated. As it happened, Pam still slept in the king-size double bed she had got used to when she was married, so there was room for Cliff without any embarrassment about inadvertent touching. They had fallen asleep listening for the thunder. By then it was the season of summer storms so, next time he had come to the house, they had each agreed it was a sensible precaution to sleep together even when the sky was clear. You could never be certain when a storm might blow up during the night. And when the first chill nights of autumn arrived, neither of them liked the prospect of sleeping apart between cool sheets. Besides, as Cliff considerately mentioned, using one bed was less expensive on the laundry.

Speaking of laundry, Pam took to washing out his shirts, underclothes and pyjamas. She had bought him a special pair of bottle-green French pyjamas without buttons and with an elasticated waistband. They were waiting on his pillow, washed and ironed, each time he came. He was very appreciative. He never failed to arrive without a bottle of cider that they drank with the meal. Once or twice he mentioned that he would have taken her out to a restaurant if her cooking had not been so excellent that it would have shown up the cook. He particularly relished the cooked breakfast on a large oval plate that she supplied before he went on his way in the morning.

So Pam staunchly tolerated the teasing in the health centre, encouraged by the certainty that it was all fantasy on their part; she had been careful never to let them know that she had invited Cliff home. She was in a better frame of mind as she walked home that lunchtime. It was always a relief to get through Saturday morning.

As she turned the corner of her street, she saw a small car, a red Mini, outside her house, with someone sitting inside it. She wasn't expecting a visitor. She strolled towards her gate, noticing that it was a woman who made no move to get out, and whom she didn't recognise, so she passed the car and let herself indoors.

There was a letter on the floor, a greetings card by the look of it. She had quite forgotten that her birthday was on Sunday. Living alone, with no family to speak of, she tended to ignore such occasions. However, someone had evidently decided that this one should not go by unremarked. She didn't recognise the handwriting, and the postmark was too faint to read. She opened it and smiled. A print of a single daffodil, and inside, under the printed birthday greeting, the handwritten letter C.

The reason why she hadn't recognised Cliff's writing was that this was the first time she had seen it. He wasn't one for sending letters. And the postmark wouldn't have given Pam a clue, even if she had deciphered it, because she didn't know where he lived. He was vague or dismissive when it came to personal information, so she hadn't pressed him. He was entitled to his privacy. She couldn't help wondering sometimes, and her best guess was that since the failure of his marriage he had tended to neglect himself and his home and devoted himself to his job. He lived for the travelling, and, Pam was encouraged to believe, his fortnightly visit to Hereford.

Presently the doorbell chimed. Pam opened the door to the woman she had seen in the car, dark-haired, about her own age or a little older, good-looking, with one of those long, elegant faces with high cheekbones that you see in foreign films. She was wearing a dark blue suit and white blouse buttoned to the neck as if she were attending an interview for a job. Mainly, Pam was made aware of the woman's grey-green eyes that scrutinised her with an interest unusual in people who called casually at the door.

'Hello,' said Pam.

'Mrs Pamela Meredith?'

'Yes.'

The look became even more intense. 'We haven't met. You may not even know that I exist. I'm Tracey Gibbons.' She paused for a reaction.

Pam smiled faintly. 'You're right. I haven't heard your name before.'

Tracey Gibbons sighed and shook her head. 'I'm not surprised. I don't know what you're going to think of me, coming to your home like this, but it's reached the point when something has to be done. It's about your husband.'

Pam frowned. 'My husband?' She hadn't heard from David in six years.

'May I come in?'

'I suppose you'd better.'

As she showed the woman into her front room, Pam couldn't help wondering if this was a confidence trick. The woman's eyes blatantly surveyed the room, the furniture, the ornaments, everything.

Pam said sharply, 'I think you'd better come to the point, Miss Gibbons.'

'Mrs, actually. Not that it matters. I'm waiting for my divorce to come through.' Suddenly the woman sounded nervous and defensive. 'I'm not promiscuous. I want you to understand that, Mrs Meredith, whatever you may think of me. And I'm not deceitful, either, or I wouldn't be here. I want to get things straight between us. I've driven over from Worcester this morning to talk to you.'

Pam was beginning to fathom what this was about. Mrs Gibbons was having an affair with David, and for some obscure reason she felt obliged to confess it to his ex-wife. Clearly the poor woman was in a state of nerves, so it was kindest to let her say her piece before gently showing her the door.

'You probably wonder how I got your address,' Mrs Gibbons went on. 'He doesn't know I'm here, I promise you. It's only over the last few weeks that I began to suspect he had a wife. Certain things you notice, like his freshly ironed shirts. He left his suitcase open the last time he came, and I happened to see the birthday card he addressed to you. That's how I got your address.'

Pam's skin prickled. 'Which card?'

'The daffodil. I looked inside, I'm ashamed to admit. I had to know.'

Pam closed her eyes. The woman wasn't talking about David at all. It was Cliff, *her* Cliff. Her head was spinning. She thought she was going to faint. She said, 'I think I need some brandy.'

Mrs Gibbons nodded. 'I'll join you, if I may.'

When she handed over the glass, Pam said in a subdued voice, 'You *are* talking about a man named Cliff?'

'Of course.'

'He is not my husband.'

'What?' Mrs Gibbons stared at her in disbelief.

'He visits me sometimes.'

'And you wash his shirts?'

'Usually.'

'The bastard!' said Mrs Gibbons, her eyes brimming. 'The rotten, two-timing bastard! I knew there was someone else, but I thought it was his wife he was so secretive about. I persuaded myself he was unhappily married and I came here to plead with you to let him go. I could kill him!'

'How do you think I feel?' Pam blurted out. 'I didn't know there was anyone else in his life.'

'Does he keep a toothbrush and razor in your bathroom?'

'A face-flannel as well.'

'And I suppose you bought him some expensive aftershave?'

Pam confirmed it bitterly. In her outraged state, she needed to talk, and sharing the trouble seemed likely to dull the pain. She related how she and Cliff had met and how she had invited him home.

'And one thing led to another?' speculated Mrs Gibbons. 'When I think of what I was induced to do in the belief that I was the love of his life . . . ' She finished her brandy in a gulp.

Pam nodded. 'It was expensive, too.'

'Expensive?'

'Preparing three-course dinners and large cooked breakfasts.'

'I wasn't talking about cooking,' said Mrs Gibbons, giving Pam a penetrating look.

'Ah,' said Pam, with a slow dip of the head, in an attempt to convey that she understood exactly what Mrs Gibbons *was* talking about.

'Things I didn't get up to in ten years of marriage to a very athletic man,' Mrs Gibbons further confided, looking modestly away. 'But you know all about it. Casanova was a boy scout compared to Cliff. God, I feel so humiliated.'

'Would you like a spot more brandy, Mrs Gibbons?'

'Why don't you call me Tracey?' suggested Mrs Gibbons, holding out her glass. 'We're just his playthings, you and I. How many others are there, do you suppose?'

'Who knows?' said Pam, seizing on the appalling possibility and speaking her thoughts aloud. 'There are plenty of divorced women like you and me, living in relative comfort in what was once the marital home, pathetically grateful for any attention that comes our way. Let's face it: we're secondhand goods.'

After a sobering interval, Tracey Gibbons pushed her empty glass towards the brandy bottle again, and asked, 'What are we going to do about him?'

'Kick him out with his toothbrush and face-flannel, I suppose,' Pam answered inadequately.

'So that he finds other deluded women to prey on?' said Tracey. 'That's not the treatment for the kind of animal we're dealing with. Personally, I feel so angry and abused that I could kill him if I knew how to get away with it. Wouldn't you?'

Pam stared at her. 'Are you serious?'

'Totally. He's ruined my hopes and every atom of self-respect I had left. What was I to him? His bit in Worcester, his Monday night amusement.'

'And I was Tuesday night in Hereford,' Pam added bleakly, suddenly given a cruel and vivid understanding of the way she had been used. Sex was Monday, supper Tuesday. In her own way, she felt as violated as Tracey. An arrangement that had seemed to be considerate and beautiful was revealed as cynically expedient. The reason why he had never touched her was that he was always sated after his night of unbridled passion in Worcester. 'Tracey, if you know of a way to kill him,' she stated with the calm that comes when a crucial decision is made, 'I know how to get away with it.'

Tracey's eyes opened very wide.

Pam made black coffee and sandwiches and explained her plan. To describe it as a plan is perhaps misleading, because it had only leapt to mind as they were talking. She wasn't given to thinking much about murder. Yet as she spoke, she sensed excitedly that it could work. It was simple, tidy and within her capability.

The two women talked until late in the afternoon. For the plan to work, they had to devise a way of killing without mess. The body should not be marked by violence. They solemnly debated various methods of despatching a man. Whether the intention was serious or not, Pam found that just talking about it was a balm for the pain that Cliff had inflicted on her. She and Tracey sensibly agreed to take no action until they had each had time to adjust to the shock, but they were adamant that they would meet again.

On the following Monday evening, Pam received a phone call from Tracey. 'Have you thought any more about what we were discussing?'

'On and off, yes,' Pam answered guardedly.

'Well, I've been doing some research,' Tracey told her with the excitement obvious in her voice. 'I'd better not be too specific over the phone, but I know where to get some stuff that will do the job. Do you understand me?'

'I think so.'

'It's simple, quick and very effective, and the best thing about it is that I can get it at work.'

Pam recalled that Tracey had said she worked for a firm that manufactured agricultural fertilisers. She supposed she was talking about some chemical substance.

Poison.

'The thing is,' Tracey was saying, 'if I get some, are you willing to do your part? You said it would be no problem.'

'That's true, but—'

'By the weekend? He's due to visit me on Monday.'

The reminder of Cliff's Monday assignations in Worcester was like a stab of pain to Pam. 'By the weekend,' she confirmed emphatically. 'Come over about the same time on Saturday. I'll do my part, I promise you, Tracey.'

The part Pam had to play in the killing of Cliff was to obtain a blank death certificate from one of the doctors at the centre. She had often noticed how careless Dr Holt-Wagstaff was with his paperwork. He was the oldest of the five practitioners and his desk was always in disorder. She waited for her opportunity for most of the week. On Friday morning she had to go into his surgery to ask him to clarify his handwriting on a prescription form. The death certificate pad was there on the desk. At twelve-fifteen, when he went out on his rounds, and Pam was on duty with one other girl, she slipped back into the surgery. No one saw her.

Saturday was a testing morning for Pam. The time dragged and the teasing about her secret lover was difficult to take without snapping back at the others. She kept wondering whether Dr Holt-Wagstaff had noticed anything. She need not have worried. He left at noon, wishing everyone a pleasant weekend. At twelve-thirty, the girls locked up and left.

When Pam got home, Tracey was waiting on her doorstep. 'I came by train,' she explained. 'Didn't want to leave my car outside again. It's surprising how much people notice.'

'Sensible,' said Pam, with approval, as she opened the door. 'Now I want to hear about the stuff you've got. Is it really going to work?'

Tracey put her hand on Pam's arm. 'Darling, it's foolproof. Do you want to see it?' She opened her handbag and took out a small brown glass bottle. 'Pure nicotine. We use it at work.'

Pam held the bottle in her palm. 'Nicotine? Is it a poison?'

'Deadly.'

'There isn't much here.'

'The fatal dose is measured in milligrams, Pam. A few drops will do the trick.'

'How can we get him to take it?'

'I've thought of that.' Tracey smiled. 'You're going to like this. In a glass of his own buckshee cider. Nicotine goes yellow on exposure to light and air, and there's a bitter taste which the sweet cider will mask.'

'How does it work?'

'It acts as a massive stimulant. The vital organs simply can't withstand it. He'll die of cardiac arrest in a very short time. Did you get the death certificate?'

Pam placed the poison bottle on the kitchen table and opened one of her cookbooks. The certificate was inside.

'You're careful, too,' Tracey said with a conspiratorial smile. She delved into her handbag again. 'I brought a prescription from my doctor to copy the signature, as you suggested. What else do we have to fill in here? *Name of Deceased*. What shall we call him?'

'Anything but Cliff,' said Pam. 'How above Clive? Clive Jones.'

'All right. Clive Jones it is. *Date of death*. I'd better fill that in after the event. What shall we put as the cause of death? Cardiac failure?'

'No, that's likely to be a sudden death,' said Pam, thinking of post-mortems. 'Broncho-pneumonia is better.'

'Suits me,' said Tracey, writing it down. 'After he's dead, I take this to the Registry of Births, Marriages and Deaths in Worcester, and tell them that Clive Jones was my brother, is that right?'

'Yes, it's very straightforward. They'll want his date of birth and one or two other details that you can invent. Then they issue you with another certificate that you show to the undertaker. He takes over after that.'

'I ask for a cremation, of course. Will it cost much?'

'Don't worry,' said Pam. 'He can afford it.'

'Too true!' said Tracey. 'His wallet is always stuffed with notes.'

'He never has to spend much,' Pam pointed out. 'The way he runs his life, he gets everything he wants for nothing.'

'The bastard,' said Tracey with a shudder.

'You really mean to do it, don't you?'

Tracey stood up and look steadily at Pam with her grey-green eyes. 'On Monday evening when he comes to me. I'll phone you when it's done.'

Pam linked her arm in Tracey's. 'The first thing I'm going to do is burn those pyjamas.'

Tracey remarked, 'He never wore pyjamas with me.'

'Really?' Pam hesitated, her curiosity aroused. 'What exactly did he do with you? Are you able to talk about it?'

'I don't believe I could,' answered Tracey with eyes lowered.

'If I poured you a brandy? We *are* in this together now.'

'All right,' said Tracey with a sigh.

Sunday seemed like the longest day of Pam's life, but she finally got through it. On Monday she didn't go in to work. That evening, she waited nervously by the phone from six-thirty onwards.

The call came at a few minutes after seven. Pam snatched up the phone.

'Hello, darling.' *The voice was Cliff's.*

'Cliff?'

'Yes. Not like me to call you on a Monday, is it? The fact is, I happen to be in Worcester on my travels, and it occurred to me that I could get over to you in Hereford in half an hour if you're free this evening.'

'Has something happened?' asked Pam.

'No, my darling. Just a change of plans. I won't expect much of a meal.'

'That's good, because I haven't got one for you,' Pam candidly told him.

There was a moment's hesitation before he said, 'Are you all right, dear? You don't sound quite yourself.'

'Don't I?' said Pam flatly. 'Well, I've had a bit of a shock. My sister died here on Saturday. It wasn't entirely unexpected. Broncho-pneumonia. I've had to do everything myself. She's being cremated on Wednesday.'

'Your sister? Pam, darling, I'm terribly sorry. I didn't even know you had a sister.'

'Her name was Olive. Olive Jones,' said Pam, and she couldn't help smiling at her own resourcefulness. After she had poisoned Tracey with a drop of nicotine in her brandy, all it had wanted on the death certificate was a touch of the pen. 'We weren't close. I'm not too distressed. Yes, why don't you come over?'

'You're sure you want me?'

'Oh, I want you,' answered Pam. 'Yes, I definitely want you.'

When she had put down the phone, she didn't go to the fridge to see what food she had in there. She went upstairs to the bedroom and changed into a black lace *négligé*.

# DESMOND LOWDEN

# The Old Mob

Satchel Anderson got up at four that morning. He got his Merc out of the garage and drove off through the suburbs. By half-past four he'd reached the motorway, and by five was approaching the new spur where he was to meet the Geordie. Satchel parked on the hard shoulder and looked across at the floodlights of the twenty-four hour shift. He saw the timber claddings of the piles they were constructing, saw the thick wet cement they were pouring down inside. And then the gravel track he could reverse down, meaning he could get the body out of the boot without getting mud on his Merc.

He drove down to the site hut and got out. But it was then that the first thing went wrong. The Geordie wasn't there. Only his side-kick, the Irishman.

They went inside the hut. The Irishman, bent, cold in his bones and not yet forty-five. He wore a hand-stitched suit covered in white mud. And he had that squint of long eyelids, long upper lip, that came from smoking fags down to the stub.

'Noa, de Geordie, he boggered off,' he told Satchel. 'Boggered off two days back.'

'You're joking,' Satchel said.

'Noa, he went to de ski-ing.'

'Again?'

'Had dis call from him last noit. Cortina di Ampezzo. De *piste* is piss poor, he says, piss poor.' The man took a packet of Balkan Sobranies from his pocket. 'Me, oi doan't loik de ski-ing. Not de *apray*, de *avong*, or de *pondong* . . . Noa, oi cruises. Moastly oi cruises.'

'Get away,' Satchel said.

'Now, about dis consignment.' The Irishman put his hand out.

But Satchel shook his head. He knew all about Irishmen in hand-stitched suits, smoking Balkan Sobranies. Irishmen with their hands out. He went away to phone.

London told him to travel east, keep travelling east, and phone in every hour. 'Every *hour*?' Satchel asked. 'Listen, in three hours I'll hit the bleeding sea.'

That was all right, they told him. They wanted him there. What they were working on now was a burial at sea.

The coast bothered Satchel when he arrived. It was flat, grey, with not a dent, not a prick out at sea. The only pricks were on the marshy foreshore, bird-watching pricks maybe, with khaki anoraks and cameras. Satchel drove on, but later he came across more of them, standing in a car park by the road. And the cars behind them all had Press labels. Press, Jesus, that was all he needed with a stiff in the boot.

Satchel drove quicker, putting a lot of miles between himself and the car park. Until, that was, he had the shock that made him swerve off the road. Shock? Series of shocks. Warplanes, huge and spiky, came at him low, about ten feet off the deck. Each one a clap of thunder that flattened the marsh-reeds. Satchel, his hand shaking, switched on the radio, expecting to hear war was declared. But then he remembered East Anglia, and all that low-level flying. They were on his side.

He started the car again and came to low flat hills. His map told him he was nearing journey's end, the head of an estuary that wound up from the sea. Ten minutes later he got there. It was a small village. Most of it was mud. And what wasn't mud was little round stones made up into houses, a hotel, a shop, and a yacht chandler's. Stones also made up a wall that went up on the low hill and disappeared over the horizon. Satchel looked at it. He reckoned it had taken a hundred men a hundred years to build that wall.

He parked. In the hotel he found they served six different kinds of malt. In the shop he found paperbacks without any tits on the covers, and Eucryl tooth-powder. And going back outside, he saw something else that exactly fitted into the landscape. Down on the quay a detachment of the green welly brigade arrived in their Volvo. They stood in a line in their bright green wellingtons. They stared palely down at the mud, told Fiona to stop throwing stones. Then they pissed orf.

And Satchel should have been warned, but he wasn't. He followed instructions and went out on the marshes, driving carefully on a pot-holed track. Then a mast rose ahead of him, just as he'd been told it would, a massive mast, followed by massive spars, and a massive curving deck. It was one of those Thames barges with the wooden flipper things on the sides. And sitting waiting near the gang-plank was the man he'd come here to meet, Darcy.

As soon as he heard Darcy speak, the warning came back. That warning that was ten per cent green welly brigade, ten per cent Eucryl tooth-powder, and eighty per cent stone wall going up over the hill. Because Darcy, he knew in a flash, was no more no less than D'arcy, bl'eeding de'ath with a capital D'. He was as massive as his boat. His sweater, torn and fluffed, went up to a torn and fluffed face. And beneath his taut angry skin was bile that had bubbled since the Middle Ages.

And why, Satchel asked himself, why in God's name had three phone calls to London got him involved with this? The old mob? The real Mafia? The *real* wild boys?

But he knew the answer when Darcy crooked a finger and led him below. It was simple. They were saving money in London. Darcy was poor. He sat like some flaking figurehead against the huge barge timbers, and around him was poverty. There was the paraffin smell from the beat-up Aladdin stoves. There was the damp of the frayed straw-matting. There was junk furniture, and an old portable record-player with the ringmarks of glasses.

Darcy poured himself a tumbler of Scotch and gave Satchel none. 'Ship's captain,' he said then in a voice like a spadeful of gravel, 'used to be able to marry people, outside territorial waters. And bury them, of course. Legally allowed to dispose of troublesome stiffs. Had high hopes of founding the East Anglian Burial Service once. Considerable undercutting.'

Satchel nodded, trying to kick away a long black dog that was nosing at his crutch.

'Nowadays, different story, of course, I mean . . . *marriage*?' A bark of laughter. 'Always tell people they can surrender to uncontrollable urges on my ship. But the burial part . . . ' He sucked in his breath. ' . . . Only for a *vast* consideration.'

Vast, don't make me laugh, Satchel thought. He fingered the tight roll of twenties in his pocket, the Geordie's pay-packet, the two grand folding which he'd never handed over. It wasn't going to be anything like that here. Casually, Satchel dropped five hundred quid into the talk.

They sparred. Darcy sucking in his breath all the time, and shaking his head. Satchel upped it by fifties. But when he reached seven-fifty, the man started pouring him Scotches.

The sparring went on. The black dog went out, and a woman came in. She was lean and stooping. She had red hair, the kind that shone almost white. And she moved like a ghost, keeping behind Darcy all the time. Suddenly he turned. He shouted at her as soon as he saw her, and went on shouting. Satchel watched her. It was her eyes that bothered him. They shivered, like those old servant-discs used to shiver, in those big old houses when buttons were pressed. Because she was a servant, or Darcy treated her like one. She brought mugs of tea when they had tea-and-Scotch. Gentleman's Relish when they had sandwiches-and-Scotch. Brought them and said nothing.

Satchel got tired of sparring. He thought a moment, then he went up to eight-fifty. His last offer, he said.

'Call it a thou,' Darcy said. 'Extras come into it. I mean, I could say a few words, get out the old union jack.'

'Not for this one.' Satchel nodded in the direction of the bankside, the Merc. 'This one's not British.'

'Oh?' Darcy's eyes were sharp. 'Not your Arab. Your Arab's trouble.'

'No. Black.'

'Blackie, eh?'

'Well, it wasn't really us that handled it,' Satchel said apologetically. 'More like a sub-contract.'

'Blackie,' Darcy repeated. 'Natural sense of rhythm, the Blackie. What about funeral music? What if I played some jazz on my clarinet?' He got up then and went past the record-player, showing a clarinet on a stand.

'No.' Satchel spread out his hands. 'No music. Eight-fifty it is, or I go elsewhere.'

'Eight-fifty.' Darcy glanced across to where the woman was standing. 'All right. Game's on.'

The woman spoke, for the first time. 'Game's on, is it?' she asked, a hopeless shrug to her shoulders. 'Loonies, Nil. The Rest Of The World, Nil.'

Satchel didn't understand her. He went to the porthole that looked out on the bankside. And suddenly he stiffened. The black dog was at the boot of the Merc, up on the bumper, sniffing.

'Listen.' He turned. 'Listen, we could have trouble. I mean, it's mild, isn't it? The papers keep on about what a mild winter we're having . . . And that stiff, it should have been in concrete hours ago.'

'Good thinking,' Darcy said. He turned to the woman. 'Get it in the freezer.'

She moved away. Satchel offered to help her, but Darcy said, no, she was your yeoman stock. And she was. Through the porthole they watched her get out the long polythene bundle wound round with insulating tape. She got it up on her shoulder, and, swaying, brought it in over the gangplank.

They followed her, dark ahead of them through the tunnel of the ship. At one point there was a tight corner. A length of the insulating tape came unstuck, and a hand poked out.

Darcy looked at it. 'Thought you said he was black.'

'Well, more coffee-coloured,' Satchel said. 'More Gold Blend.'

The woman made no sound, showed no effort on her face as she rested the body finally by a long chest-freezer.

'Granny-size,' Darcy said darkly, and opened the lid.

He made room, shifting a forequarter of beef and a loin of lamb. Then the woman flipped the body in. Its hand came to rest, scooping up frozen peas.

'Could do with a cutlet,' Darcy said, rummaging around. 'Couple of good lean cutlets and some broccoli tips. How about you?'

Satchell pushed the hand back inside the polythene, restuck the tape. 'Don't fancy it myself,' he said.

Half-an-hour later Darcy pushed his empty plate to one side. Lamb-fat glistened on his chin. 'You know, my mother, God rest her soul, always used to make a cock-up of the French language,' he said. 'Lived in France half her life, yet every time she went to a butcher's shop she asked for *culottes d'agneau*. Lamb's knickers.'

'That so?' Satchel stared at him.

'Fact. Though maybe she knew about it. Certain amount of cunning in our family.' Darcy waved a fork in the air. 'Take her Georgian silver. At the end of her life she had no room for it. She knew we wanted it. She knew she didn't want us to have it. So she solved the whole problem with a stroke of genius. Sent the stuff over from France in the train. Two packing-cases, and she labelled them both Georgian silver.'

Satchel frowned. It wasn't the sort of story he liked to hear, it went against everything he stood for. Then his frown deepened. Suddenly he caught sight of his watch. Four o'clock, Jesus, how many Scotches to the bad was he?

He leaned forward. 'Listen,' he said, 'a couple of hours ago I gave you four hundred and twenty-five quid. The other half to come when you finish. Which I thought was going to be this evening.'

Darcy shook his head. 'Not a chance.'

'*Not?*'

'Tide's all wrong.'

'That right? When's High Tide then?'

'Oh nine thirty-four.'

And it was too quick. He was lying. Satchel looked across at the Scotch bottle, now nearing the end of its natural life.

'You're telling me it's tomorrow then?'

'Tomorrow as ever is.'

Satchel stood up, needing fresh air. 'Where do I go to get a slash?' he asked.

'Out there. First on the right.'

Starting away, Satchel suddenly heard a crash behind him. He turned. Darcy's food-plate lay smashed on the floor. The man had got up too quickly, was coming at Satchel now, reaching out for his pockets. 'Haven't got any Andrex, have you?'

'*What?*'

'Andrex. That tissue stuff. Jams up a ship's loo.' Darcy patted his pockets in turn. 'Surprising the number of people who try to smuggle Andrex in here.'

Satchel went off. He should have been warned, he told himself, should have been bleeding warned.

When he got back, the woman was there, picking up pieces of plate. Darcy had the record-player on, traditional jazz, and was playing along on his clarinet. And it wasn't that he was out of tune, wasn't even that it was all rasping breath and squeaks. It was that he was lurching around, his ears and neck red, and every time he lurched the record missed a groove.

He stopped, and swung round on the woman. 'Keep bloody still,' he shouted.

The woman froze where she was, hand halfway towards a piece of china. Darcy played on, lurched on. The record missed another groove.

Suddenly he went over and clouted her.

She didn't look up at him. 'Loonies, One. The Rest Of The World, Nil,' she said quietly.

He clouted her again.

'Loonies, Two. The Rest Of The World, Nil,' she said.

His arm went back once more.

Satchel looked at him. He looked on at the empty Scotch bottle. Jesus, he thought, the *energy* of the man. Then he left.

It was getting dark outside, and he was surprised by that. Even more surprised, as he drove back to the hotel in the village, to hear the sounds of drinking, the bar going in and out.

Satchel thought about it. There was only one kind of people could get a drink after hours, he knew. Only one kind of people could raise a large Scotch in a Temperance House in Llanelli. And then he saw them, the Press cars, parked by the hotel. The cars he'd seen earlier out on the marshes, just before the warplanes had come.

Going into the bar, it suddenly all came together. Because the word was, the shouted word, that it was Nato manoeuvres. The word was, that in the next war the West would last two days. That on the third day the only paper to file with would be *Pravda*.

And the word was, there were more manoeuvres tomorrow. Combined manoeuvres, at sea.

The barge-deck throbbed to the sound of the wheezy engine. Darcy spun the wheel and glowered out at the morning. He had his sailor hat on, the black dog was crouching beside him. It was his act, hungover, but still his act.

''Preciate your concern, m'dear feller, really do,' he said, unrolling a long tube of cardboard. 'But, see here. We go out in a straight line to the Territorial Limit thingy. And your war-johnnies fart around here. Always do. To the right. The right as you look at the map.'

Satchel had some idea it should be 'starboard', and 'chart', but he said nothing. They got out of the river without hitting anything. The marsh-reeds fell back behind them, and they wheezed out on a wide silver sea. Darcy got the woman to bring a bottle up on deck. He stoked up on his hangover, overtook it, then got attacks of Charles Laughton and Robert Newton, alternately.

They lasted until he looked at his watch, checked the chart, and cut the engine. The barge slowed up, and fell to slapping and rattling. Darcy moved into the centre of the deck. He looked at the woman and at Satchel. 'There,' he swung an arm round the empty horizon, 'miles and miles of bugger-all.'

Which was when the black tower, the size of four double-decker buses, followed by the black hull the length of two Inter-Cities, suddenly surfaced, close to their right.

'*Piss orf!*' Darcy shouted at the nuclear sub.

A huge metal voice came across from the black shape. 'You are in violation of restricted war-zone number six-four-three-stroke . . . '

Men appeared on the deck of the sub, ratings, with rifles.

'Loonies, Three. The Rest Of The World, Five,' the woman said to Darcy.

He swung round and got a large fat-barrelled pistol from a locker. Satchel went for him, but he wasn't at his best, not with the barrel of that pistol by his cheek. He ducked as it went off. A Verey light fizzed up into the air, stuck in the ratlines above, and rained red fire down on them. The dog howled.

Then there was a new sound. A metal launch had come from the sub. It bumped against the barge, and an officer and two ratings held it there. One rating came up over the side. He took the Verey pistol away from Darcy kindly, then hit him kindly, twice, on the face.

Darcy sat down.

The rating moved on to the woman. His voice was conversational. ''kin-ell,' he said ''kin-Icelandic, is he?'

The woman started to laugh. A slow, strange sound.

The rating came on. 'Not 'kin-Icelandic?' he asked Satchel.

'No. Not that.'

''kin-ecological then? 'kin-Greenpeace?'

'That's it,' Satchel said. 'Greenpeace.'

The rating offered him a Navy-issue fag. ''kin-save the whale,' he said. ''kin-know what you mean. 'kin-Jane Fonda, she's all tied up with your mob, isn't she?'

He lit Satchel's fag and went away to the bows of the barge. He took a line from the Navy launch and made it fast. Then they were towed, the sub keeping station behind them.

It went on for quite some time. Until there was the sound of a siren, and the tow-line slackened. The rating stubbed out his fag. ''kin-shame about Jane Fonda,' he said. 'Always reckoned she had such a good 'kin-body on her.'

He went back to the bows, untied the line, waved at Satchel, and disappeared over the side. The launch disappeared. The sub disappeared. The sea was suddenly flat and grey again, as if nothing had happened.

Darcy, two angry bruises on his face, crawled across the deck to the Scotch bottle.

Satchel kicked it away. 'No,' he said. 'No bleeding more of that. What we do now is wait ten minutes, then we get this stiff out of the freezer and chuck it over . . .'

Three strikes of combat-planes crashed over at mast-height. Satchel threw himself flat. The planes swung in towards the land. White smoke trails ziggered away from them. They did real damage to two hundred square yards of sand, then they swung away and disappeared.

Satchel picked himself up. But suddenly there was another sound, a drone, from out at sea. He turned. The horizon was full of square blocks, black square blocks, with huge bow-waves.

'Start the engine,' he shouted at Darcy. 'Will you just start that bleeding thing?'

But Darcy had got hold of the Scotch bottle again. He was drinking hard. And huffy.

'No,' he said.

'*No?*'

'Put it like this,' the man drank two fingers, then another two fingers, 'can *you* start it?'

Satchel turned towards the engine-hatch, the rusty pipes that were inside it, held together with wire.

''xactly,' Darcy said. He capped the Scotch bottle, hugged it to him. Then he turned. 'Things to settle here.'

He was looking at the woman. And she was crouching on the deck, frightened.

The drone from the sea was now a roar. The black boxes, maybe fifty of them in a line, swept past. Landing-craft, with rows of steel helmets inside them.

Darcy stood huge and mottled in the centre of the deck. 'She *laughed* when that war-johnny called me Icelandic,' he said.

'Oh, come on,' Satchel said. 'I mean. Jesus . . .'

But Darcy went to the woman, stood over her. 'I may have picked you up in some North London ghetto,' he shouted. 'But I've told you, I will not, repeat *not* put up with your Tulse Hill tendencies.'

He swung his arm back, clouted her. 'Loonies, *Four*. The Rest Of The World, Nine,' he screamed. 'Loonies, *Five*. The Rest Of The World, Five . . . '

Satchel turned away. He saw the landing-craft hit the beach. He saw the assault troops leap out into the surf. They did tricky things with hooks and nylon lines. They swarmed up the sand-cliff and captured the bus shelter at the top. Then they sat down.

'. . . Loonies, *Fourteen*. The Rest Of The World, Five. Loonies, *Fifteen* . . . '

Satchel went over and stopped it. The woman was clutching her left arm, it had bad bruises on it. Turning, Satchel found a bit of old canvas on a hatch-cover. He made her a sling, and she seemed more comfortable. But it wasn't her arm that bothered him, it was her eyes. There wasn't that flicker of yesterday, that nervousness. They just stared at Darcy with a slow burning hate.

Satchel walked towards him. 'Satisfied?' he asked.

Darcy shrugged.

'So what do we do now?'

'Now,' Darcy said. 'Now I have luncheon.'

'You're joking.'

'Twelve noon.' The man looked at his watch. 'I have a rump steak, I have mushrooms, and . . . ' he raised his voice for the woman's benefit, ' . . . and I have chips.'

'Chips?' she shouted back at him. 'I can't peel potatoes with one hand.'

'Course you can!' he bellowed. '*Course* you can peel potatoes with one bloody hand!'

She went below. More boats came up . . . but by now Satchel was expecting them, the Press boats, with their cameras at the ready. Darcy posed. And Satchel, crouching out of sight, let him. Jesus, he thought, in another second it'd be David bleeding Dimbleby. In another second it'd be Darcy leaning over the side, shouting, 'War-johnny called me Icelandic. Do I *look* Icelandic? And would you like to see the blackie in the freezer?'

The Press boats went away. Darcy drank Scotch, and gradually mellowed. 'Sorry about that little thingy with the good lady just now,' he said. 'Landlub-bers don't know about these things. Different camps set up aboard ship, you see, always two different camps. Something to do with being out at sea. Strain, you know, the loneliness.' He pointed to the maybe two thousand people on the beach.

The rump steak, the mushrooms, and the chips arrived. Darcy ate them cross-legged on the hatch. He drank a little Scotch, played a little clarinet, drank a little more Scotch. Finally he sighed, and went over and started the rusty engine. 'Another day, another dollar,' he said.

And he earned his dollar. Two hours later, with a tiny *plop*, the polythene-wrapped bundle, chained to a forty-pound ballast weight, sank beneath the sea. Satchel paid over the second instalment of £425, and Darcy spun the wheel, heading for home.

There was mist, twilight over the marshes as they drew level with Satchel's parked Merc. Darcy got the woman to jump on to the bank with a line. She jumped, but then dropped the line, ran off among the reeds, and disappeared. The tide caught the long hull of the barge. It swung out across the estuary. The engine coughed and died.

Satchel expected Darcy to start shouting again. But he didn't. It was the last straw. 'M'dear feller,' he took Satchel's arm, 'don't ever, *ever* go to Tulse Hill.'

Darkness was on them by the time they'd unshipped the dinghy, by the time Darcy had rowed a line across to the mooring-post and back and started the winch. They edged in. Then Satchel looked up.

And saw the two flat-hats getting out of the police car on the bank.

'Nothing to worry about,' Darcy said. 'Dog licence, or some such lunacy. Always these damn creditors turning up. Usually I move on, and they just find these two holes in the bank. I change the ship's name, of course. Make a couple of subtle changes to the superstruct . . .'

But Satchel wasn't listening. Jesus, he thought, it'd better be those war-johnnies, sending someone round to complain.

But it wasn't. The flat-hats led the way below, to the freezer.

'Information laid, Sir,' the tall one said. 'Woman's voice.'

Satchel edged towards the door.

The flat-hat opened the freezer, removed a few plastic bags. And there, where the forequarter of beef should have been, was a dark hand, clutching frozen peas.

Satchel edged further away.

'Arabic gentleman, sir,' the flat-hat said.

'*Blast!*' from Darcy.

'Seems to be some signs of mutilation, sir,' the flat-hat said. 'This slice, cut out of the rump.'

Satchel's mouth dropped open.

'And some sort of note, sir. What's it say? "Loonies, Fifteen? The Rest Of The World, Ninety-Three?"'

Satchel ran.

# JAMES McCLURE

---

## The Last Place On Earth

The building breathed you in. You were wheeled down a ramp by the ambulance men, passing rockeries and lily ponds, and then across a patio of crazy-paving the colour of cornflakes. You peered over your toes, which gave twin peaks to the grey blanket covering you, and saw the huge glass doors marked clearly IN. The other set of doors did not have OUT on them.

You approached the IN doors. They remained closed. Then, with a loud and sudden sound, like a swimmer's gasp for air, they opened inwards, leaving you no time to think before the sky overhead vanished. You saw a pine ceiling, had a glimpse of a tropical fish tank, and the doors wheezed slowly shut again, clenching their jaws.

The visitor arrived at the wrong moment. His aunt had just had a suppository inserted. So he went through to the lounge of the hospice and sat down in front of the television set. The early evening news was on.

'Forty-three people are believed to have died today,' said the newscaster, as a film clip began, 'when a gas leak caused an explosion in this block of flats in South London.'

The dying, seated on either side of the visitor, shook their heads and tut-tutted and one said, 'Now, isn't that terrible? What is the world coming to?'

They had forgotten.

But one old man sat with his back to the television set, and toyed with his lighter, cigarette packet and a thick glass ashtray, while his urine dripped steadily down a tube into the clear plastic bag at his side. This old man looked angry and more interesting than the others.

So the visitor rose, wandered into the adjoining chapel, where magazines and paperbacks were kept beside the hymnals, and chose himself something that would serve as an excuse for changing seats. It was a May 1976 copy of Country Life.

'Evening,' said the visitor, as he sat down opposite the old man's wheelchair. 'You don't mind?'

The old man seemed to ignore him.

The visitor dipped the magazine each time he turned a page, sneaking quick glances across the low coffee table. He noted a middling mottled brow, dense brown hair protruding from each ear like mattress stuffing, full lips that were pale and striated, with gleams of scarlet in the cracks. He studied the weathered hands and their chipped fingernails, the ragged scar across the back of the right wrist such as barbed wire might make. He wondered where, in that heavy-limbed body, a dread thing was growing.

379

If one wanted to picture cancer cells, his aunt's doctor had said, then simply imagine a handful of thistle seeds tossed into a bed of poppies, and these thistles thrusting upwards, flourishing.

'What I mind,' said the old man, 'was not stopping.'

The visitor glanced up. 'Not stopping?' he said. 'Smoking, you mean?'

'Not stopping at home, more like!'

'You don't like it here?'

'Bah!'

'Oh, I don't know. When you compare it with—'

'I should've stopped outside and taken one more look.'

The visitor put down the magazine and leaned forward. 'I'm sorry,' he said, 'not quite with you.'

'The universe,' snapped the old man, pointing to the top of the coffee table. 'Right? And here, what they calls the solar system. Big ashtray's the sun, ciggie packet is this bleedin' planet, and that's me, a cheeky little blighter of a lighter, comin' in between! That's how we were, three score and more, with me shadow on the ground to prove it.'

The visitor nodded.

'Got bugger-all shadow now,' said the old man.

There was a soft bubbling from the tank of tropical fish over on the left. The visitor glanced that way, and then round the room. It was large and warm and very unhospitalish. The walls and ceiling were lined with pine in the Swedish manner, and the furnishings suggested the lounge of a comfortable if modest hotel. In one corner, there was a small alcove where hot and cold drinks were always available; in another, was the television set with its huge screen, and, to the right of it, hung a neat rack holding brochures that gave some idea of local scenic attractions, concerts, plays and exhibitions. Some stuffed toys, made under the guidance of the hospice's occupational therapist, lolled glassy-eyed on a wide shelf, sharing it with two boxes of Monopoly. Crocheted cushions abounded, so did big-leaved pot plants. The lighting was low, shadowless, and its sources invisible.

'Comfy enough,' said the old man, shrugging as he gave his own glance around. 'But still a bit of a disappointment – y'know, when it comes home to yer, this is the last place on earth.'

Then a grey-haired woman, wearing a chequered smock over drab street clothes, came up to the visitor and said, 'So sorry you wait, but your aunt she is ready for you now.'

The visitor's aunt waved a greeting at his reflection in the window as he entered the room behind her back. She had to lie on her right side most of the time, what with the oozing on her left.

'My sweet,' she said. 'Goodness, are those for me?'

He held out the bouquet in its flower-shop wrapping and wondered why her eyes darted aside before taking a second look.

'Oh, *carnations*,' she said. 'How lovely! So very, very red . . . '

'They come with Chloe's love, too, Aunt Judith.'

'See you give her mine, Richard, and tell her how pleased I am with them. Be a dear, won't you, and see if you can find that volunteer lady to have them popped in a vase right away.'

'The foreign one in the smock?'

His aunt nodded. 'Not *so* foreign,' she chided, knowing her nephew's prejudices of old. 'Mrs Daventry has been in England since only a few years after the war. Hasn't she the most marvellous, deep brown eyes?'

'She looks—' he began, then stopped himself.

You lay there and wanted to cry out, but the crab had you by the throat.

A new terror seemed impossible, after all you had gone through since the initial, mumbled diagnosis. That moment when a very young doctor, her lower lip trembling prettily, had pushed an X-ray plate into your hands and asked you, as a man of science, to take a look at it. One glance had been enough, and ahead of time your voice had failed. Not even a croak.

Yet there was indeed this new terror, far more terrible than any before, and what was worse, you didn't know the reason for it.

Or even what you had seen to make you so fearful.

'This is my nephew, Richard,' said the visitor's aunt, when Sister Braithwaite came in, as quietly as a nun. 'He brought me the carnations.'

'Gorgeous,' said Sister Braithwaite, sniffing them.

The visitor had to suppress a laugh. There was only one smell in that room, nothing else could compete with it, and nobody could possibly mistake it for the scent of carnations.

'And how is Mr Joliffe today?' said his aunt. 'I do miss our little chats together.'

Sister Braithwaite looked her very straight in the eye.

'Oh, dear, has he?' said his aunt. 'Then is there someone new in his room?'

'Yes, a professor.'

'Oh, really? Not from Oxford, by any chance? My late husband—'

'Leicester University, I believe,' said Sister Braithwaite, retreating to the doorway. 'Well, it's almost time for the drugs round.'

The visitor took this as his cue to look at his wristwatch. 'Half seven already! Chloe will—'

'Off you go, my sweet,' said his aunt. 'We've had a lovely natter, but I must confess I'm feeling a little tired now.' And she looked at him most accusingly.

'Mrs Daventry has told the voluntary help organiser that she wants to resign,' Staff Nurse Pam Clement remarked to Sister Braithwaite in the day wing, to which they had retreated for a quick cigarette apiece. 'I overheard her ringing her at home only about five minutes ago.'

'That's a bit out of the blue!' said Sister Braithwaite, undoing her silver belt buckle. 'Seemed as happy as a lark at tea time – and of all the volunteers, she's the only one I'd really miss around here.'

Staff Nurse Clement nodded. 'Not a trace of bloody do-gooder in her.'

'Empathy. I know sweet FA about Mrs Daventry, but one thing sticks out a mile: that woman's seen a *lot* of suffering in her time.'

'Making it stranger she should want to chuck it all of a sudden.'

'But don't we all? I'm forever writing out my resignation!'

The two women laughed, and shared the match flame.

'I'll try and have a word with her,' Sister Braithwaite said. 'Perhaps she could do with the support of our stress group. I don't see why it should be restricted to trained staff.'

'God,' sighed Staff Nurse Clement, running a hand over her freckled face. 'I can guess what the talk's going to be about at the next one.'

'Paraplegic, carcinoma larynx, spinal secondaries, no next of kin, eyes that bore holes in you, terrified out of his wits . . .?'

'Uhuh, Prof Thingy.'

'But it shouldn't be for long. Have you seen the whopping morphine dosage he's on?'

You swallowed your morphine and dreamed great swirling, chaotic dreams with moments of shrill clarity.

Faces.

Thousands of faces, each with an open mouth.

If there were screams, you did not hear them.

One face keeps returning, spinning by, smiling.

Then a huge empty beach and a great stillness, except down at the sea's edge, where a crab has its claws deep in the neck of a thrashing eagle.

That one face.

You awake, and it's looking at you.

But not quite.

The next night, the visitor called at eight to see his aunt again, but first detoured into the lounge. 'And how did today go?' he asked the old man in the wheelchair.

'Boring,' said the old man. 'No flowers?'

'Chocolates. "Boring" in what way?'

'Dead boring,' said the old man, and cackled at the visitor's expression. 'You remind us,' he added, 'of that smarmy doctor what comes round, sort of rubbing his hands like he was soapin' 'em, and says to me, "Well, William and how are we today?" So I says, "I'm dyin' to get out of here, doc!" You should've seen the face on *him* by the time I was finished.'

The visitor laughed. 'You're a character,' he said.

'No, I'm not, I'm a dying man, son. And different to you, I know what I'm going to die of, no scope for the old imagination.'

'And that's what bores you?'

'Aye, a bit.' The old man nodded at the group around the television set. 'With most of them, it's quite a relief, really, this knowin'. Frightens yer, gets yer dander up, can ruin yer religion if you're that way inclined, but it's still a weight off your mind – y'know, being certain it won't be no car crash, all trapped screamin' in the wreckage, or Flight Bing-bong to sunny Spain goin' smack into a mountain. Personally, I'd high hopes of another kind.'

The visitor noticed a flare of yesterday's anger return, twisting the striated lips slightly. 'And what were these hopes?' he asked.

'Same as yours, son! Goin' hammer and tongs till the old ticker can't take any more, but the lass with her legs around yer keeps cheerin' you on!'

Beginning to colour, the visitor gave a crooked smile. 'For a moment there, I thought you could read minds,' he said.

'Not just the chocolates.'

'Sorry . . . ?'

'You've also,' said the old man, with a gleam in his rheumy eye, 'brung along a bit o' paper for the old lady to sign . . . '

The visitor stared at him, turned about and walked away, his cheeks burning.

'I spoke to Mrs Daventry this morning,' said the voluntary help organiser, telephoning from home, 'and I think she must just have become over-tired the other day. She tells me she's carrying on as a volunteer as per usual.'

'Are you sure that's all it was?' said Sister Braithwaite, watching Mrs Daventry pass her desk in the corridor.

'I can't imagine any other reason, Sister.'

'Fine. And by the way, one of your volunteer drivers left a day patient stranded here this afternoon.'

'*Not* that wretched vicar's wife again! Was the patient Mr Gibb?'

You knew what the new terror was. For weeks, you had been preparing to die a particular natural death, and as *unnatural* as that had seemed, it was at least something a man could adjust to. Nobody had a right to so many years, only to live out his allotted span, and this was what, with the help of the hospice, you had expected to do. Yet now you knew you couldn't count on even that any longer.

Your dreams told you so.

'Professor,' a nurse was saying, leaning over so you could look up at her. 'See? I've brought your morphine.'

You shut your mouth tightly.

'You're being very silly, you know! We have got to control the pain. You don't want more pain, do you?'

You nodded.

'You *don't* want your morphine?'

You nodded again.

The ward sister came and gave you your morphine, not by mouth but with an injection. She threw the syringe away. The pain subsided and the dreams began. There was no way of stopping them.

\*       \*       \*

'What has the house to do with my being in here?' demanded Aunt Judith.

The visitor hastily changed the subject: 'Oh, by the way, how is your new neighbour getting on?'

'The professor?' she said, brightening.

'That's right. Has he been across to see you, like Mr Joliffe?'

'Heavens, no. Quite immobile, Madge tells me, and unable to speak as part of his condition. What's fascinating is, he's apparently spent his life in medical research trying to find a cure for you-know-what.'

The visitor felt strongly that his aunt should face up to the word. 'You mean cancer?'

She helped herself to another chocolate.

'Yes, ironic,' said the visitor. 'Must make things a lot worse, too, if you're a medic and know all the options, symptoms, et cetera, what can be done for you and what can't. I know I'd be happier being left in the dark.'

'I won't be left in the dark,' said his aunt, with a sudden show of strong feeling. 'I was very cross last night when that little nurse tried to put the lights off before I—'

'Hello, my duck!' said a broad, homely woman, wheeling in the drinks trolley. 'Cocoa, two sugars, in a beaker? Or is it your night for a drop of something a bit stronger?' And she winked like a barmaid.

'Madge, you really are naughty!' said Aunt Judith, delighted. 'Whatever will my nephew think I get up to in here?'

Something wasn't right. Sister Braithwaite had experienced this sense of unease once before as a young VSO nurse in a mission hospital in Africa, and the next morning a one-eyed orderly and two orphans were reported missing – he'd stolen the babes to sell for witchdoctor's medicine, the black auxiliaries had said.

'A penny for them, Sue,' whispered Staff Nurse Clement, pausing at the desk in the corridor.

'Sorry?' said Sister Braithwaite, brusquely.

'Be like that . . .' said Staff Nurse Clement with a shrug, walking off.

Annoyed with herself for her rudeness and for giving way to a ridiculous mood she couldn't define, Sister Braithwaite rose and moved with a brisk step, hoping to make amends by seeing to one of the external tumours herself. Pam Clement had admitted in the stress group to finding them particularly distressing.

An unexpected smell coming from the staff changing room made her pause and look in. Staff Nurse Wong was dabbing at a mark on her overcoat with cotton wool soaked in a dry-cleaning fluid.

'Ah, so that's it!' said Sister Braithwaite.

'Sister? My bike chain came off and I ended up with grease everywhere. I noticed this bottle of—'

'Have you managed to fix the bike? If not, ring Security and Max—'

'It's fine now, thank you, Sister.'

Sister Braithwaite remained in the doorway, wishing she could avoid the stereotype but seeing Theresa Wong as inscrutable. That lovely, heart-shaped face, with its neat-as-a-button nose and cherry-pink mouth, never gave one any idea of what was going on in her head. And she politely declined every invitation to join the stress group.

'I noticed when I came on tonight,' said Sister Braithwaite, 'that your Kardexes on the professor were – well, a bit skimpy. Those notes are there to help us pick up the threads, Staff.'

'So sorry, Sister.'

'Why were they like that? Do you have difficulty with that patient?'

'He's—'

'Yes? Go on, dear . . . '

'He is unusual, Sister,' said Staff Nurse Wong, very evenly and inscrutably.

Again, Sister Braithwaite was aware of her sense of unease.

You dreamed of wards and of operating theatres, of great pain and suffering.

You felt nothing.

The crab, in the head-dress of eagle feathers, sat on its rock.

The visitor made for the exit, thinking how like a spaceship the inside of the hospice could appear at times. It had the same sort of passages in the ward area, the hum of hidden machinery, a small kitchen like a galley, tiny storerooms with everything from bed sheets to ginger ale, neatly stowed, and outside its windows, all eternity.

He glanced into a room and saw the old man there, moving his hand back and forth in front of the bulb in his reading light. The old man looked round.

'Er, popped by to say good night,' said the visitor.

'Thought you was Mrs Daventry.'

'Yes, the volunteer lady.'

'Smasher, she is,' said the old man. 'Funny habits, mind.'

The visitor stepped into the room. 'Such as?' he said, intrigued.

'Writes phone numbers on herself.'

Disappointed, the visitor said with a grudging laugh, 'But I do that sometimes!' And he mimed a quick scribble on the back of his left hand.

'That's never where she puts it,' said the old man. 'Good night.'

'The remarkable thing, Sister,' said Dr Murphy-Jones, the consultant, the next evening, 'is that the professor seems to have rallied, to be fighting tooth and nail to stay alive.'

She sighed. 'It often amazes me, the will to live.'

'Yet, when I saw him on admission, he appeared totally resigned. Has he had a visitor, someone who has—'

'No visitors, not one. The professor hasn't any kith and kin either, as you know.'

'And he hasn't been making any use of his pad to write on?'

'Hasn't touched it. We literally haven't had a word out of him.'

'Odd, very odd. And a bit of an embarrassment, between ourselves. I thought we'd have that bed free by the weekend.'

'His quality of life isn't . . .'

'Quite. Perhaps we could increase the dosage a fraction.'

You were so cold. Drenched in your sweat and shivering. As cold as a naked man left out in the snow on a stretcher.

You remembered the letter. 'I am very curious about the experiments with animal heat. Personally I believe these experiments may bring the best and most sustained results.'

You remembered the letter because you could feel the heat.

Seeping into you.

The visitor brought his wife, Chloe, his other aunt, and a distant cousin. They had been told by the hospice that a sudden relapse had occurred.

Sister Braithwaite, the one who moved like a nun and had peppermint on her breath, met them outside the lounge. 'It could be tonight,' she said. 'If anyone would like a bed, we do have a guest room – and more beds can be put up in the chapel.'

They nodded their thanks.

'Then if you'll come along with me,' said Sister Braithwaite.

The old man was watching them from in front of the tropical fish tank. He raised his scarred hand in greeting, and the visitor smiled. God knows why, but it was good to see him.

As the visitor reached his aunt's room, he glanced across into the room almost opposite it. A gaunt, bone-coloured man was shivering in his sleep and making movements that were shocking.

'It's going to be one of those nights, Pam,' said Sister Braithwaite, too much canteen food distending her again, making her silver buckle bite.

Staff Nurse Clement snorted. 'Christ, don't tell me! Mrs Grosvenor, the new admission, lung, has started deliriums.'

'I'd better get Dr Murphy-Jones down.'

'He'll have to be here sooner or later, so you might as well.'

'I've not had a moment since coming on to go through the Kardex properly – any special problems?'

'No, not really,' replied Staff Nurse Clement. 'That dozy OT has gone and upset old William. Thought Tess Wong's notes on the professor were a bit weird.'

'Yes, I talked to her about that last night.'

'Oh?'

'They were skimped.'

'No, *weird* weird, Sue.'

'In what way?'

'I've never – well, I don't know what to think.'

*     *     *

Aunt Judith, although greatly weakened, had adopted an imperious manner. With a limp wave of her hand, she dismissed the attention being paid her by close members of her family and demanded that Madge fetch Mrs Daventry.

'I've got a feeling she's probably off home by now, my duck,' said Madge. 'But I'll go and look in the changing room, see if we can catch her.'

Mrs Daventry came in, dressed in her street clothes and carrying her handbag. She nodded pleasantly, then went and took Aunt Judith's hand. Nothing was said, but the face of the dying woman became tranquil and she smiled. The visitor found Mrs Daventry a chair.

Then he studied her, covertly. The woman was probably in her mid-fifties, slightly-built, a little bowed in the legs like someone once poorly nourished, and had raven black hair that set off her pale, high-cheeked face. Her brown eyes, it was true, were remarkable; large and luminous, as deep as wells. Wells filled with tears, he added as an afterthought, before scorning such mawkish sentiment.

But he couldn't see where she wrote telephone numbers on herself, no matter how hard he looked.

Sister Braithwaite sat at her desk in the corridor and stared at the notes made on the professor by Staff Nurse Wong.

The notes were indeed far more comprehensive than those of the previous day. They gave a very good idea of how the professor had spent the last eight hours, both as a person and as an organism under attack. They said, in short that he'd displayed signs of great agitation, but was physically no worse.

What Pam Clement had called the 'weird' part had been placed in brackets at the end:

*(Observation: On looking in on the patient at 4.20 p.m., I found him asleep on his right side, facing the door, and shivering. I felt his arm but it was not cold. I still took his temperature but it was normal. I noticed an indentation in his bed on the far side. The coverlet had been crushed and creased from the level of his shoulders to his feet. I smoothed out his coverlet and left.)*

You were freezing.

You had been taken from the water with a rectal temperature of 86 degrees Fahrenheit.

You were on a wide bed.

Between two naked women.

And the crab was writing in the sand.

It wrote: 'Once the test persons regained consciousness, they never lost it again, quickly grasping their situation and nestling close to the naked bodies of the women. The rise of body temperature then proceeded at approximately the same speed as with test persons swathed in blankets.'

You read and approved what had been written, but pointed out certain exceptions to the rule.

'An exception,' scrawled the crab with its pincer, 'was formed by four test persons who practised sexual intercourse between eighty-six and eighty-nine point five degrees. In these persons, after coitus, a very swift temperature rise ensued, comparable to that achieved by means of a hot-water bath.'

*Ja, ja*, you agreed, yet there was another exception more extraordinary than that, Dr Rascher – whereupon, a thousand fighter pilots, downed in the icy North Sea in special suits designed by you, applauded.

'Chloe, this is the old gentleman I've told you about,' said the visitor. 'Mr William – er, I'm sorry, I'm not sure I know your last name.'

'Atkins, son – same as Tommy, and no better off than 'e was at the Somme!'

'Pleased to meet you, Mr Atkins,' said the visitor's wife, pale behind the cosmetics on a plain, hard face. 'May I sit down?'

'Fancy plonking yourself in me lap, luv?'

But she declined with an awkward laugh, taking the seat opposite his wheelchair. 'I had to get out of there for a while,' she said, fanning herself with a copy of *Woman's Own*. 'It's so . . . well, depressing.'

'I see the others what come with you have hopped it already,' said the old man. 'Wasn't it that what the taxi came for?'

The visitor nodded. 'Even worse for them, the same generation,' he explained. 'Can I get you both a drink of some sort from the corner? Coffee, perhaps? Tea?'

'No, I'll see to that, Richard,' said Chloe. 'You'd better get back to poor Aunt Judith.'

'Mrs Daventry's with her, so I don't see—'

'Off you go, Richard,' she said softly in that special tone of hers.

He went. His aunt was alone.

'Mrs Daventry has gone to tell Sister I've asked her to spend the night,' said Aunt Judith. 'She's a widow, you see, so it won't make any difference.'

Close to wakening, your dreams changed.

You were in a snow-filled ditch with a dead horse and greasy black smoke was rising in the sky behind the barbed wire. It was the first time you had ever felt such cold. You were freezing.

Then fleeing.

Killing.

You had another man's clothes, another man's name.

Soon, if you were careful, only you would know the difference.

And you were careful, you were welcomed in, given another man's life to begin. Leicester University. Unbelievable.

Yet always fleeing.

Never far enough.

On second thoughts, Sister Braithwaite decided to ask Mrs Daventry if she really had the strength to make a night of it, having already spent much of the day in the hospice.

So she left her desk and hurried after her, seeing Mrs Daventry stop outside the professor's room, hesitate, and then go in. When she reached the room itself, Mrs Daventry was standing at the foot of the bed, rubbing her arm, and the professor was gazing at her, his eyes huge in their sunken sockets.

'So we're awake again?' said Sister Braithwaite, walking in. 'I suppose you've met Mrs Daventry before?'

To her surprise, he shook his head violently.

'Yes, wide awake,' said Mrs Daventry. 'It is what I noticed.'

'You've more than enough on your plate across the way,' said Sister Braithwaite. 'Are you sure that family isn't imposing on you too much? I'd pack anybody else off home, you know that!'

'No, I have the strength, Sister. If you will excuse me . . . '

Sister Braithwaite remarked to the patient when they were alone, 'She's a saint that woman – I never thought I'd live to say that of anyone.'

The professor turned his head away and stared out of his window at the night, so dark and empty out there.

'I'll close your curtains,' said Sister Braithwaite.

The visitor glanced up and was shaken to see the expression on his wife's face. 'Good God, Chloe,' he whispered, 'whatever's happened—?'

'Richard, take me home this instant.'

'But Aunt Ju—'

'Damn and blast Aunt Judith!' she hissed, her face very white. 'Get – me – out – of – here.'

So he scrambled to his feet in a fluster, to be calmed by Mrs Daventry laying a hand on his arm.

'You can return later,' Mrs Daventry said, 'or maybe not, as circumstances they are permitting. Your aunt will altogether be safe in my keeping.'

'Thank you,' he said, 'thank you very much.' And wanted to hug her, his emotions were in such a turmoil.

Chloe dug her long nails into his hand as he led her away up the short passage, to the right and then to the left, heading towards the lounge and the exit.

'No!' said Chloe, stopping. 'I won't go *near* there, not near that horrible old man again!'

'But I don't know another way out, so be sensible! And what do you mean by—'

'Richard!'

He turned and hurried her in the opposite direction, still very confused. Then, passing two empty wheelchairs beside some other equipment, a sudden insight made him laugh. A cruel laugh, but what the hell, Chloe's cold blood had been a bitter disappointment to him.

\*     \*     \*

You were awake and the crab had you by the throat and still the dreaming went on. But it wasn't dreaming, it was remembering.

That final, fascinating exception being, Dr Rascher, as you yourself wrote and I endorsed, one woman was able to warm a frozen man faster than two women. Your report read: 'I attribute this to the fact that in warming by means of one woman personal inhibitions are avoided and the woman clings more closely to the chilled person. Here, too, return of full consciousness was notably rapid.'

'There,' said the ward sister, 'all nice and clean again, and time for your medicine, professor.'

You shook your head.

The prick of a needle.

*Bzzzzzzzt – bzzzzzzzt – bzzzzzzzt . . .*

Once a patient pressed that button, that heavy droning device buzzed and buzzed until someone had hurried in to switch if off and enquire what the matter was. Sometimes the matter was all too self-evident.

Sister Braithwaite, hastening in one direction, heard the sound stop and then begin again. This meant a second patient needed attention, so she spun on her heel and set off to see who this could be. She passed a doorway and saw Mrs Daventry sitting quietly, holding the old woman's hand.

No more than a quick glimpse, it left an odd impression: Mrs Daventry's face had seemed set very hard and those luminous eyes were as cold as ice. Some trick of the lighting.

The crab had made a quill of one of the eagle feathers. It started pricking out numbers. Blue numbers. Sets of numbers.

Then scurried across the beach, digging and scattering the pebbles to expose experimental bone grafts and gas gangrene wounds, all fascinating. In the rock pools, poison bullets grew in clusters, ready for testing, and here a sea anemone was swallowing a lethal dose of typhus. Down at the bright arc of sparkling surf, gypsies were being made to see how long they could live on salt water.

'Crab!' you cried. 'Crab, I never noticed you at Ravensbrück!'

*Bzzzzzzzt – bzzzzzzzt – bzzzzzzzt . . .*

There it was, going again!

'I'm dying for a quick puff,' muttered Staff Nurse Clement.

'Not tonight, Josephine,' Sister Braithwaite muttered back, pushing the dressings trolley. 'How is Mrs Daventry faring over on the other side?'

'I've not had a moment.'

'She'll ring if she needs us.'

'Where *is* Dr Murphy-bloody-Jones?'

'Hush, Staff! That's no way to speak of God.'

'It is, when you're left to do his dirty work for him!'

\* \* \*

Now the ravens were circling and the crab was lying low.

A winter landscape, with the snow outside striking a white light up through the barred windows and brightening the whole room, making it a bridal suite. On the bed, fresh from the snow, with a rectal temperature of 86 degrees Fahrenheit, a brutish young Pole. Pressed against him, a skinny female with black shining hair, naked and shivering, too. He warmed slowly. There was time to see the female was of poor background, a sufferer from rickets. There was time to study her face, and find in it evidence of the sub-human. There was even time to memorise its every line and hollow, if need be.

There was no need, but it must have happened.

'My God!' Dr Rascher exploded with a laugh. 'The animal thinks he's woken up in Heaven! Just look . . . '

Everyone was looking, smirking. The Pole, mumbling, had clutched the female to him, and now wept as he suckled at her flat breast, his loins already slowly heaving.

'Temperature reading?' said Dr Rascher.

You glanced at the dial, calling out: 'Eighty-eight and rising!'

'*And* rising . . . ' echoed Dr Rascher, giggling.

The brute rolled over on to the female. She whispered softly, kissed his ear and opened her legs, welcoming him.

Dr Rascher gaped. 'What is this?' he said. 'Even here, she can enjoy it?'

'I think,' said the cameraman, 'she is sorry for him, that's all. She knows he gets his benzine injection when this is over.'

'Degenerate!' snapped Dr Rascher, then giggled again. 'These Poles . . . ! See this rabbit is kept for me, she excites certain possibilities.'

'Ninety degrees!' you reported.

'Yes, she must be kept and fed well,' declared Rascher. 'In nineteen forty-six, I propose beginning a series of experiments which . . . '

He talked on, but you were no longer listening. You were watching. As the Pole bucked harder and harder, moving to his climax, the female submitted herself totally to him, throwing back her arms and grasping the bedposts. Her limbs were thin but beautiful, marred only by her concentration-camp number, tattooed in blue on the left inner arm.

Then they cried out together.

'What was that?' asked Sister Braithwaite, pausing with the flame an inch from her cigarette.

'Didn't hear a sound,' said Staff Nurse Clement.

Sister Braithwaite was trembling like on that night in Africa. 'It was—' she began, then swallowed. 'Look, I can't explain, I just think we'd better get back.'

They left the day wing and went first to the six-bed ward, found everyone asleep and started checking on the one-bed side wards.

'Funny smell down this way,' said Staff Nurse Clement.

'Oh, that's Staff Wong and her blessed greasy coat.'

'Pardon?'

'You're right, that was two days—'

'Oops!' said Staff Nurse Clement, coming to a sudden halt in a doorway. 'Guess who's . . . ' And she tiptoed in. 'Yes, he has – the professor's gone,' she said, reaching out to close an eyelid. 'A bit sudden.'

'And look at the way he's arched back, Pam! That really isn't natural.'

'What isn't natural? asked Dr Murphy-Jones, wandering in amiably. 'I say, quite a spasm. I hope you're not suggesting foul play, are you, Sister? This is surely the last place on—'

'No, no, it's simply I—'

'Excellent! You've someone you'd like me to take a look at!'

'Yer-yes, please,' said Sister Braithwaite, trying to get a grip on herself. 'If you'll just come this way, doctor.'

As she turned out into the corridor, she caught a glimpse of Mrs Daventry holding the old woman's hand, which was clenched tightly now. The light was playing another of its tricks, for when Mrs Daventry glanced round to give a quick, gentle smile, she looked absolutely beautiful, a young girl.

*Both Dr Sigmund Rascher's own fate and his reports to Heinrich Himmler, the letter writer, are dealt with in detail in* The Rise and Fall of the Third Reich *by William L. Shirer.*

# ELLIS
# PETERS

---

# A Light On The Road
# To Woodstock

The King's court was in no hurry to return to England, that late autumn of 1120, even though the fighting, somewhat desultory in these last stages, was long over, and the enforced peace sealed by a royal marriage. King Henry had brought to a successful conclusion his sixteen years of patient, cunning, relentless plotting, fighting and manipulating, and could now sit back in high content, master not only of England but of Normandy, too. What the Conqueror had misguidedly dealt out in two separate parcels to his two elder sons, his youngest son had now put together again and clamped into one. Not without a hand in removing from the light of day, some said, both of his brothers, one of whom had been shoveled into a hasty grave under the tower at Winchester, while the other was now a prisoner in Devizes, and unlikely ever to be seen again by the outer world.

The court could well afford to linger to enjoy victory, while Henry trimmed into neatness the last loose edges still to be made secure. But his fleet was already preparing at Barfleur for the voyage back to England, and he would be home before the month ended. Meantime, many of his barons and knights who had fought his battles were withdrawing their contingents and making for home, among them one Roger Mauduit, who had a young and handsome wife waiting for him, certain legal business on his mind, and twenty-five men to ship back to England, most of them to be paid off on landing.

There were one or two among the miscellaneous riff-raff he had recruited here in Normandy on his lord's behalf whom it might be worth keeping on in his own service, along with the few men of his household, at least until he was safely home. The vagabond clerk turned soldier, let him be unfrocked priest or what he might, was an excellent copyist and a sound Latin scholar, and could put legal documents in their best and most presentable form, in good time for the King's court at Woodstock. And the Welsh man-at-arms, blunt and insubordinate as he was, was also experienced and accomplished in arms, a man of his word, once given, and utterly reliable in whatever situation on land or sea, for in both elements he had long practice behind him. Roger was well aware that he was not greatly loved, and had little faith in either the valour or the loyalty of his own men. But this Welshman from Gwynedd, by way of Antioch and Jerusalem and only God knew where else, had imbibed the code of arms and wore it as a second nature. With or without love, such service as he pledged, that he would provide.

Roger put it to them both as his men were embarking at Barfleur, in the middle of a deceptively placid November, and upon a calm sea.

'I would have you two accompany me to my manor of Sutton Mauduit by Northampton, when we disembark, and stay in my pay until a certain lawsuit I have against the abbey of Shrewsbury is resolved. The King intends to come to Woodstock when he arrives in England, and will be there to preside over my case on the twenty-third day of this month. Will you remain in my service until that day?'

The Welshman said that he would, until that day or until the case was resolved. He said it indifferently, as one who has no business of any importance anywhere in the world to pull him in another direction. As well Northampton as anywhere else. As well Woodstock. And after Woodstock? Why anywhere in particular? There was no identifiable light beckoning him anywhere, along any road. The world was wide, fair and full of savour, but without signposts.

Alard, the tatterdemalion clerk, hesitated, scratched his thick thatch of grizzled red hair, and finally also said yes, but as if some vague regret drew him in another direction. It meant pay for some days more, he could not afford to say no.

'I would have gone with him with better heart,' he said later, when they were leaning on the rail together, watching the low blue line of the English shore rise out of a placid sea, 'if he had been taking a more westerly road.'

'Why that?' asked Cadfael ap Meilyr ap Dafydd. 'Have you kin in the west?'

'I had once. I have not now.'

'Dead?'

'I am the one who died.' Alard heaved lean shoulders in a helpless shrug, and grinned. 'Fifty-seven brothers I had, and now I'm brotherless. I begin to miss my kin, now I'm past forty. I never valued them when I was young.' He slanted a rueful glance at his companion and shook his head. 'I was a monk of Evesham, an *oblatus*, given to God by my father when I was five years old. When I was fifteen I could no longer abide to live my life in one place, and I ran. Stability is one of the vows we take – to be content in one stay, and go abroad only when ordered. That was not for me, not then. My sort they call *vagus* – frivolous minds that must wander. Well, I've wandered far enough, God knows, in my time. I begin to fear I can never stand still again.'

The Welshman drew his cloak about him against the chill of the wind. 'Are you hankering for a return?'

'Even you seamen must drop anchor somewhere at last,' said Alard. 'They'd have my hide if I went back, that I know. But there's this about penance, it pays all debts, and leaves the record clear. They'd find a place for me, once I'd paid. But I don't know . . . I don't know . . . The *vagus* is still in me. I'm torn two ways.'

'After twenty-five years,' said Cadfael, 'a month or two more for quiet thinking can do no harm. Copy his papers for him and take your ease until his business is settled.'

They were much of an age, though the renegade monk looked the elder by ten years, and much knocked about by the world he had coveted from within the cloister. It had never paid him well in goods or gear, for he went threadbare and thin, but in wisdom he might have got his fair wages. A little soldiering, a little clerking, some horse-tending, any labour that came to hand, until he could turn his hand to almost anything a hale man can do. He had seen, he said, Italy as far south as Rome, served once for a time under the Count of Flanders, crossed the mountains into Spain, never abiding anywhere for long. His feet still served him, but his mind grew weary of the road.

'And you?' he said, eyeing his companion, whom he had known now for a year in this last campaign. 'You're something of a *vagus* yourself, by your own account. All those years crusading and battling corsairs in the midland sea, and still you have not enough of it, but must cross the sea again to get buffeted about Normandy. Had you no better business of your own, once you got back to England, but you must enlist again in this muddled mêlée of a war? No woman to take your mind off fighting?'

'What of yourself? Free of the cloister, free of the vows!'

'Somehow,' said Alard, himself puzzled, 'I never saw it so. A woman here and there, yes, when the heat was on me, and there was a woman by and willing, but marriage and wiving . . . it never seemed to me I had the right.'

The Welshman braced his feet on the gently swaying deck and watched the distant shore draw nearer. A broad-set, sturdy, muscular man in his healthy prime, brown-haired and brown-skinned from eastern suns and outdoor living, well-provided in leather coat and good cloth, and well-armed with sword and dagger. A comely enough face, strongly featured, with the bold bones of his race – there had been women, in his time, who had found him handsome.

'I had a girl,' he said meditatively, 'years back, before ever I went crusading. But I left her when I took the Cross, left her for three years and stayed away seventeen. The truth is, in the east I forgot her, and in the west she, thanks be to God, had forgotten me. I did enquire, when I got back. She'd made a better bargain, and married a decent, solid man who had nothing of the *vagus* in him. A guildsman and counsellor of the town of Shrewsbury, no less. So I shed the load from my conscience and went back to what I knew, soldiering. With no regrets,' he said simply. 'It was all over and done, years since. I doubt if I should have known her again, or she me.' There had been other women's faces in the years between, still vivid in his memory, while hers had faded into mist.

'And what will you do,' asked Alard, 'now the King's got everything he wanted, married his son to Anjou and Maine, and made an end of fighting? Go back to the east? There's never any want of squabbles there to keep a man busy.'

'No,' said Cadfael, eyes fixed on the shore that began to show the solidity of land and the undulations of cliff and down. For that, too, was over and done, years since, and not as well done as once he had hoped. This desultory campaigning in Normandy was little more than a postscriptum, an afterthought, a means of filling in the interim between what was past and what was to come, and as yet unrevealed. All he knew of it was that it must be something new and momentous, a door opening into another room. 'It seems we have both a few days' grace, you and I, to find out where we are going. We'd best make good use of the time.'

There was stir enough before night to keep them from wondering beyond the next moment, or troubling their minds about what was past or what was to come. Their ship put into the roads with a steady and favourable wind, and made course into Southampton before the light faded, and there was work for Alard checking the gear as it was unloaded, and for Cadfael disembarking the horses. A night's sleep in lodgings and stables in the town, and they would be on their way with the dawn.

'So the King's due in Woodstock,' said Alard, rustling sleepily in his straw in a warm loft over the horses, 'in time to sit in judgement on the twenty-third of the month. He makes his forest lodges the hub of his kingdom, there's more statecraft talked at Woodstock, so they say, than ever at Westminster. And he keeps his beasts there – lions and leopards – even camels. Did you ever see camels, Cadfael? There in the east?'

'Saw them and rode them. Common as horses there, hard-working and serviceable, but uncomfortable riding, and foul-tempered. Thank God it's horses we'll be mounting in the morning.' And after a long silence, on the edge of sleep, he asked curiously into the straw-scented darkness: 'If ever you do go back, what is it you want of Evesham?'

'Do I know?' responded Alard drowsily, and followed that with a sudden sharpening sigh, again fully awake. 'The silence, it might be . . . or the stillness. To have no more running to do . . . to have arrived, and have no more need to run. The appetite changes. Now I think it would be a beautiful thing to be still.'

The manor which was the head of Roger Mauduit's scattered and substantial honour lay somewhat south-east of Northampton, comfortably under the lee of the long ridge of wooded hills where the King had a chase, and spreading its extensive fields over the rich lowland between. The house was of stone, and ample, over a deep undercroft, and with a low tower providing two small chambers at the eastern end, and the array of sturdy byres, barns and stables that lined the containing walls was impressive. Someone had proved a good steward while the lord was away about King Henry's business.

The furnishings of the hall were no less eloquent of good management, and the men and maids of the household went about their work with a brisk wariness that showed they went in some awe of whoever presided over their labours. It needed only a single day of watching the Lady Eadwina in action to show who ruled the roost here. Roger Mauduit had married a wife not only handsome, but also efficient and masterful. She had had her own way here for three years, and by all the signs had enjoyed her dominance. She might, even, be none too glad to resign her charge now, however glad she might be to have her lord home again.

She was a tall, graceful woman, ten years younger than Roger, with an abundance of fair hair, and large blue eyes that went discreetly half-veiled by absurdly long lashes most of the time, but flashed a bright and steely challenge when she opened them fully. Her smile was likewise discreet and almost constant, concealing rather than revealing whatever went on in her mind; and though her welcome to her returning lord left nothing to be desired, but lavished on him every possible tribute of ceremony and affection from the moment his horse entered at the gate, Cadfael could not but wonder whether she was not, at the same time taking stock of every man he brought in with him, and every article of gear or harness or weaponry in their equipment, as one taking jealous inventory of his goods and resolved to make sure nothing was lacking.

She had her little son by the hand, a boy of about seven years old, and the child had the same fair colouring, the same contained and almost supercilious smile, and was as spruce and fine as his mother.

The lady received Alard with a sweeping glance that deprecated his tatterdemalion appearance and doubted his morality, but nevertheless was willing to accept and make use of his abilities. The clerk who kept the manor roll and the accounts was efficient enough, but had no Latin, and could not write a good court hand. Alard was whisked away to a small table set in the angle of the great hearth, and kept hard at work copying certain charters and letters, and preparing them for presentation.

'This suit of his is against the abbey of Shrewsbury,' said Alard, freed of his labours after supper in hall. 'I recall you said that girl of yours had married a merchant in that town. Shrewsbury is a Benedictine house, like mine of Evesham.' His, he called it still, after so many years of abandoning it; or his again, after time had brushed away whatever division there had ever been. 'You must know it, if you come from there.'

'I was born in Trefriw, in Gwynedd,' said Cadfael, 'but I took service early with an English wool-merchant, and came to Shrewsbury with his household. Fourteen, I was then – in Wales fourteen is manhood, and as I was a good lad with the short bow, and took kindly to the sword, I suppose I was worth my keep. The best of my following years were spent in Shrewsbury, I know it like my own palm, abbey and all. My master sent me there a year and more, to get my letters. But I quit that service when he died. I'd pledged nothing to the son, and he was a poor shadow of his father. That was when I took the Cross. So did many like me, all afire. I won't say what followed was all ash, but it burned very low at times.'

'It's Mauduit who holds this disputed land,' said Alard, 'and the abbey that sues to recover it, and the thing's been going on four years without a settlement, ever since the old man here died. From what I know of the Benedictines, I'd rate their honesty above our Roger's, I tell you straight. And yet his charters seem to be genuine, as far as I can tell.'

'Where is this land they're fighting over?' asked Cadfael.

'It's a manor by the name of Rotesley, near Stretton, demesne, village, advowson of the church and all. It seems when the great earl was just dead and his abbey still building, Roger's father gave Rotesley to the abbey. No dispute about that, the charter's there to show it. But the abbey granted it back to him as tenant for life, to live out his latter years there undisturbed, Roger being then married and installed here at Sutton. That's where the dispute starts. The abbey claims it was clearly agreed the tenancy ended with the old man's death, that he himself understood it so, and intended it should be restored to the abbey as soon as he was out of it. While Roger says there was no such agreement to restore it unconditionally, but the tenancy was granted to the Mauduits, and ought to be hereditary. And so far he's hung on to it tooth and claw. After several hearings they remitted it to the King himself. And that's why you and I, my friend, will be off with his lordship to Woodstock the day after tomorrow.'

'And how do you rate his chances of success? He seems none too sure himself,' said Cadfael, 'to judge by his short temper and nail-biting this last day or so.'

'Why, the charter could have been worded better. It says simply that the village is granted back in tenancy during the old man's lifetime, but fails to say anything about what shall happen afterwards, whatever may have been intended. From what I hear, they were on very good terms, Abbot Fulchered and the old lord, agreements between them on other matters in the manor book are worded as between men who trusted each other. The witnesses are all of them dead, as Abbot Fulchered is dead. It's one Godefrid now. But for all I know the abbey may hold letters that have passed between the two, and a letter is witness of intent, no less than a formal charter. All in good time we shall see.'

The nobility still sat at the high table, in no haste to retire, Roger brooding over his wine, of which he had already drunk his fair share and more. Cadfael eyed them with interest, seen thus in a family setting. The boy had gone to his bed, hauled away by an elderly nurse, but the Lady Eadwina sat in close attendance at her lord's left hand, and kept his cup well filled, smiling her faint, demure smile. On her left sat a very fine young squire of about twenty-five years, deferential and discreet, with a smile somehow the male reflection of her own. The source of both was secret, the spring of their pleasure or amusement, or whatever caused them so to smile, remained private and slightly unnerving, like the carved stone smiles of certain very old statues Cadfael had seen in Greece, long ago. For all his mild, amiable and ornamental appearance, combed and curled and courtly, he was a big, well-set-up young fellow, with a set to his smooth jaw. Cadfael studied him with interest, for he was plainly privileged here.

'Goscelin,' said Alard by way of explanation, following his friend's glance. 'Her right-hand man while Roger was away.'

Her left-hand man now, by the look of it, thought Cadfael. For her left hand and Goscelin's right were private under the table, while she spoke winningly into her husband's ear; and if those two hands were not paddling palms at this moment Cadfael was very much deceived. Above and below the drapings of the board were two different worlds. 'I wonder,' he said thoughtfully, 'what she's breathing into Roger's ear now.'

What the lady was breathing into her husband's ear was, in fact: 'You fret over nothing, my lord. What does it matter how strong his proofs, if he never reaches Woodstock in time to present them? You know the law: if one party fails to

appear, judgement is given for the other. The assize judges may allow more than
one default if they please, but do you think King Henry will? Whoever fails of
keeping tryst with him will be felled on the spot. And you know the road by
which Prior Heribert must come.' Her voice was a silken purr in his ear. 'And
have you not a hunting-lodge in the forest north of Woodstock, through which
that road passes?'

Roger's hand had stiffened round the stem of his wine cup. He was not so
drunk but he was listening intently.

'Shrewsbury to Woodstock will be a two- or three-day journey to such a
rider. All you need do is have a watcher on the road north of you, to give
warning. The woods are thick enough, masterless men have been known to
haunt there. Even if he comes by daylight, your part need never be known. Hide
him but a few days, it will be long enough. Then turn him loose by night, and
who's ever to know what footpads held and robbed him? You need not even
touch his parchments – robbers would count them worthless. Take what
common thieves would take, and theirs will be the blame.'

Roger opened his tight-shut mouth to say in a doubtful growl: 'He'll not be
travelling alone.'

'Hah! Two or three abbey servants – they'll run like hares. You need not
trouble yourself over them. Three stout, silent men of your own will be more
than enough.'

He brooded, and began to think so, too, and to review in his mind the men of
his household, seeking the right hands for such work. Not the Welshman and
the clerk, the strangers here; their part was to be the honest onlookers, in case
there should ever be questions asked.

They left Sutton Mauduit on the twentieth day of November, which seemed
unnecessarily early, though as Roger had decreed that they should settle in his
hunting-lodge in the forest close by Woodstock, which meant conveying stores
with them to make the house habitable and provision it for a party for,
presumably, a stay of three nights at least, it was perhaps a wise precaution.
Roger was taking no chances in his suit, he said; he meant to be established on
the ground in good time, and have all his proofs in order.

'But so he has,' said Alard, pricked in his professional pride, 'for I've gone
over everything with him, and the case, if open in default of specific instructions, is plain enough and will stand up. What the abbey can muster, who
knows? They say the abbot is not well, which is why his prior comes in his
place. My work is done.'

He had the faraway look in his eye, as the party rode out and faced westward,
of one either penned and longing to be where he could but see, or loose and
weary and being drawn home. Either a *vagus* escaping outward, or a penitent
flying back in haste before the doors should close against him. There must
indeed be something desirable and lovely to cause a man to look towards it with
that look on his face.

Three men-at-arms and two grooms accompanied Roger, in addition to

Alard and Cadfael, whose term of service would end with the session in court, after which they might go where they would, Cadfael horsed, since he owned his own mount, Alard afoot, since the pony he rode belonged to Roger. It came as something of a surprise to Cadfael that the squire Goscelin should also saddle up and ride with the party, very debonair and well-armed with sword and dagger.

'I marvel,' said Cadfael drily, 'that the lady doesn't need him at home for her own protection, while her lord's absent.'

The Lady Eadwina, however, bade farewell to the whole party with the greatest serenity, and to her husband with demonstrative affection, putting forward her little son to be embraced and kissed. Perhaps, thought Cadfael, relenting, I do her wrong, simply because I feel chilled by that smile of hers. For all I know she may be the truest wife living.

They set out early, and before Buckingham made a halt at the small and penurious priory of Bradwell, where Roger elected to spend the night, keeping his three men-at-arms with him, while Goscelin with the rest of the party rode on to the hunting-lodge to make all ready for their lord's reception the following day. It was growing dark by the time they arrived, and the bustle of kindling fire and torches, and unloading the bed-linen and stores from the sumpter ponies went on into the night. The lodge was small, stockaded, well-furnished with stabling and mews, and in thick woodland, a place comfortable enough once they had a roaring fire on the hearth and food on the table.

'The road the prior of Shrewsbury will be coming by,' said Alard, warming himself by the fire after supper, 'passes through Evesham. As like as not they'll stay the last night there.' With every mile west Cadfael had seen him straining forward with mounting eagerness. 'The road cannot be far away from us here, it passes through this forest.'

'It must be nearly thirty miles to Evesham,' said Cadfael. 'A long day's riding for a clerical party. It will be night by the time they ride past into Woodstock. If you're set on going, stay at least to get your pay, for you'll need it before the thirty miles is done.'

They went to their slumber in the warmth of the hall without a word more said. But he would go, Alard, whether he himself knew it yet or not. Cadfael knew it. His friend was a tired horse with the scent of the stable in his nostrils; nothing would stop him now until he reached it.

It was well into the middle of the day when Roger and his escort arrived, and they approached not directly as the advance party had done, but from the woods to the north, as though they had been indulging in a little hunting or hawking by the way, except that they had neither hawk nor hound with them. A fine, clear, cool day for riding, there was no reason in the world why they should not go roundabout for the pure pleasure of it – and indeed, they seemed to come in high content! – but that Roger's mind had been so preoccupied and so anxious concerning his lawsuit that distractions seemed unlikely. Cadfael was given to thinking about unlikely developments, which from old campaigns he knew to prove significant in most cases. Goscelin, who was out at the gate to welcome them in, was apparently oblivious to the direction from which they came. That way lay Alard's highway to his rest. But what meaning ought it to have for Roger Mauduit?

The table was lavish that night, and lord and squire drank well and ate well, and gave no sign of any care, though they might, Cadfael thought, watching them from his lower place, seem a little tight and knife-edged. Well, the King's court could account for that. Shrewsbury's prior was drawing steadily nearer, with whatever weapons he had for the battle. But it seemed rather an exultant tension than an anxious one. Was Roger counting his chickens already?

The morning of the twenty-second of November dawned, and the noon passed, and with every moment Alard's restlessness and abstraction grew, until with evening it possessed him utterly, and he could no longer resist. He presented himself before Roger after supper, when his mood might be mellow from good food and wine.

'My lord, with the morrow my service to you is completed. You need me no longer, and with your goodwill I would set forth now for where I am going. I go afoot and need provision for the road. If you have been content with my work, pay me what is due, and let me go.'

It seemed that Roger had been startled out of some equally absorbing preoccupation of his own, and was in haste to return to it, for he made no demur, but paid at once. To do him justice, he had never been a grudging paymaster. He drove as hard a bargain as he could at the outset, but once the agreement was made, he kept it.

'Go when you please,' he said. 'Fill your bag from the kitchen for the journey when you leave. You did good work, I give you that.'

And he returned to whatever it was that so engrossed his thoughts, and Alard went to collect the proffered largesse and his own meagre possessions.

'I am going,' he said, meeting Cadfael in the hall doorway. 'I must go.' There was no more doubt in voice or face. 'They will take me back, though in the lowest place. From that there's no falling. The blessed Benedict wrote in the Rule that even to the third time of straying a man may be received again if he promise full amendment.'

It was a dark night, without moon or stars but in fleeting moments when the wind ripped apart the cloud covering to let through a brief gleam of moonlight. The weather had grown gusty and wild in the last two days, the King's fleet must have had a rough crossing from Barfleur.

'You'd do better,' urged Cadfael, 'to wait for morning, and go by daylight. Here's a safe bed, and the King's peace, however well enforced, hardly covers every mile of the King's highroads.'

But Alard would not wait. The yearning was on him too strongly, and a penniless vagabond who had ventured all the roads of Christendom by day or night was hardly likely to flinch from the last thirty miles of his wanderings.

'Then I'll go with you as far as the road, and see you on your way,' said Cadfael.

There was a mile or so of track through thick forest between them and the highroad that bore away west-north-west on the upland journey to Evesham. The ribbon of open highway, hemmed on both sides by trees, was hardly less dark than the forest itself. King Henry had fenced in his private park at Woodstock to house his wild beasts, but maintained also his hunting chase here, many miles in extent. At the road they parted, and Cadfael stood to watch his friend march steadily away towards the west, eyes fixed ahead, upon his penance and his absolution, a tired man with a rest assured.

Cadfael turned back towards the lodge as soon as the receding shadow had melted into the night. He was in no haste to go in, for the night, though blustery, was not cold, and he was in no mind to seek the company of others of the party now that one best known to him was gone, and gone in so mysteriously rapt a fashion. He walked on among the trees, turning his back on his bed for a while.

The constant thrashing of branches in the wind all but drowned the scuffling and shouting that suddenly broke out behind him, at some distance among the trees, until a horse's shrill whinny brought him about with a jerk, and set him running through the underbrush towards the spot where confused voices yelled alarm and broken bushes thrashed. The clamour seemed some little way off, and he was startled as he shouldered his way headlong though a thicket to collide heavily with two entangled bodies, send them spinning apart, and himself fall a-sprawl upon one of them in the flattened grass. The man under him uttered a scared and angry cry, and the voice was Roger's. The other man had made no sound at all, but slid away very rapidly and lightly to vanish among the trees, a tall shadow swallowed in shadows.

Cadfael drew off in haste, reaching an arm to hoist the winded man. 'My lord, are you hurt? What, in God's name, is to do here?' The sleeve he clutched slid warm and wet under his hand. 'You're injured! Hold fast, let's see what harm's done before you move . . . '

Then there was the voice of Goscelin, for once loud and vehement in alarm, shouting for his lord and crashing headlong through bush and brake to fall on his knees beside Roger, lamenting and raging.

'My lord, my lord, what happened here? What rogues were those, loose in the woods? Dared they waylay travellers so close to the King's highway? You're hurt – here's blood . . . '

Roger got his breath back and sat up, feeling at his left arm below the shoulder, and wincing. 'A scratch. My arm . . . God curse him, whoever he may be, the fellow struck for my heart. Man, if you had not come charging like a bull, I might have been dead. You hurled me off the point of his dagger. Thank God, there's no great harm, but I bleed . . . Help me back home!'

'That a man may not walk by night in his own woods,' fumed Goscelin, hoisting his lord carefully to his feet, 'without being set upon by outlaws! Help here, you, Cadfael, take his other arm . . . . Footpads so close to Woodstock! Tomorrow we must turn out the watch to comb these tracks and hunt them out of cover, before they kill . . . '

'Get me withindoors,' snapped Roger, 'and have this coat and shirt off me, and let's staunch this bleeding. I'm alive, that's the main!'

They helped him back between them, through the more open ways towards the lodge. It dawned on Cadfael, as they went, that the clamour of furtive battle had ceased completely, even the wind had abated, and somewhere on the road, distantly, he caught the rhythm of galloping hooves, very fast and light, as of a riderless horse in panic flight.

The gash in Roger Mauduit's left arm, just below the shoulder, was long but not deep, and grew shallower as it descended. The stroke that marked him thus could well have been meant for his heart. Cadfael's hurtling impact, at the very moment the attack was launched, had been the means of averting murder. The shadow that had melted into the night had no form, nothing about it rendered it human or recognisable. He had heard an outcry and run towards it, a projectile to strike attacked and attacker apart; questioned, that was all he could say.

For which, said Roger, bandaged and resting and warmed with mulled wine, he was heartily thankful. And indeed, Roger was behaving with remarkable fortitude and calm for a man who had just escaped death. By the time he had demonstrated to his dismayed grooms and men-at-arms that he was alive and not much the worse, appointed the hour when they should set out for Woodstock in the morning, and been helped to his bed by Goscelin, there was even a suggestion of complacency about him, as though a gash in the arm was a small price to pay for the successful retention of a valuable property and the defeat of his clerical opponents.

In the court of the palace of Woodstock the King's chamberlains, clerks and judges were fluttering about in a curiously distracted manner, or so it seemed to Cadfael, standing apart among the commoners to observe their antics. They gathered in small groups, conversing in low voices and with anxious faces, broke apart to regroup with others of their kind, hurried in and out among the litigants, avoiding or brushing off all questions, exchanged documents, hurried to the door to peer out, as if looking for some late arrival. And there was indeed one litigant who had not kept to his time, for there was no sign of a Benedictine prior among those assembled, nor had anyone appeared to explain or justify his absence. And Roger Mauduit, in spite of his stiff and painful arm, continued to relax, with ever-increasing assurance, into shining complacency.

The appointed hour was already some minutes past when four agitated fellows, two of them Benedictine brothers, made a hasty entrance, and accosted the presiding clerk.

'Sir,' bleated the leader, loud in nervous dismay, 'we here are come from the abbey of Shrewsbury, escort to our prior, who was on his way to plead a case at law here. Sir, you must hold him excused, for it is not his blame nor ours that he cannot appear. In the forest some two miles north, as we rode hither last night in the dark, we were attacked by a band of lawless robbers, and they have seized our prior and dragged him away . . .'

The spokesman's voice had risen shrilly in his agitation, he had the attention of every man in the hall by this time. Certainly he had Cadfael's. Masterless men some two miles out of Woodstock, plying their trade last night, could only be the same who had happened upon Roger Mauduit and all but been the death of him. Any such gang, so close to the court, was astonishing enough, there could hardly be two. The clerk was outraged at the very idea.

'Seized and captured him? And you four were with him? Can this be true? How many were they who attacked you?'

'We could not tell for certain. Three at least – but they were lying in ambush, we had no chance to stand them off. They pulled him from his horse and were off into the trees with him. They knew the woods, and we did not. Sir, we did go after them, but they beat us off.'

It was evident they had done their best, for two of them showed bruised and scratched, and all were soiled and torn as to their clothing.

'We have hunted through the night, but found no trace, only we caught his horse a mile down the highway as we came hither. So we plead here that our prior's absence be not seen as a default, for indeed he would have been here in the town last night if all had gone as it should.'

'Hush, wait!' said the clerk peremptorily.

All heads had turned towards the door of the hall, where a great flurry of officials had suddenly surged into view, cleaving through the press with fixed and ominous haste, to take the centre of the floor below the King's empty dais. A chamberlain, elderly and authoritative, struck the floor loudly with his staff and commanded silence. And at sight of his face silence fell like a stone.

'My lords, gentlemen, all who have pleas here this day, and all others present, you are bidden to disperse, for there will be no hearings today. All suits that should be heard here must be postponed three days, and will be heard by his Grace's judges. His Grace the King cannot appear.'

This time the silence fell again like a heavy curtain, muffling even thought or conjecture.

'The court is in mourning from this hour. We have received news of desolating import. His Grace with the greater part of his fleet made the crossing to England safely, as is known, but the *Blanche Nef*, in which his Grace's son and heir, Prince William, with all his companions and many other noble souls were embarked, put to sea late, and was caught in gales before ever clearing Barfleur. The ship is lost, split upon a rock, foundered with all hands, not a soul is come safe to land. Go hence quietly, and pray for the souls of the flower of this realm.'

So that was the end of one man's year of triumph, an empty achievement, a ruinous victory, Normandy won, his enemies routed, and now everything swept aside, broken apart upon an obstinate rock, washed away in a malicious sea. His only lawful son, recently married in splendour, now denied even a coffin and a grave, for if ever they found those royal bodies it would be by the relenting grace of God, for the sea seldom put its winnings ashore by Barfleur. Even some of his unlawful sons, of whom there were many, gone down with their royal brother, no one left but the one legal daughter to inherit a barren empire.

Cadfael walked alone in a corner of the King's park and considered the foolishness of mortal vainglory, that was paid for with such a bitter price. But also he thought of the affairs of little men, to whom even a luckless King owed justice. For somewhere there was still to be sought the lost prior of Shrewsbury, carried off by masterless men in the forest, a litigant who might still be lost three days hence, when his suit came up again for hearing, unless someone in the meantime knew where to look for him.

He was in little doubt now. A lawless gang at liberty so close to a royal palace was in any case unlikely enough, and Cadfael was liable to brood on the unlikely. But that there should be two – no, that was impossible. And if one only, then that same one whose ambush he had overheard at some distance, yet close enough, too close for comfort, to Roger Mauduit's hunting-lodge.

Probably the unhappy brothers from Shrewsbury were off beating the wilds of the forest afresh. Cadfael knew better where to look. No doubt Roger was biting his nails in some anxiety over the delay, but he had no reason to suppose that three days would release the captive to appear against him, nor was he paying much attention to what his Welsh man-at-arms was doing with his time.

Cadfael took his horse and rode back without haste towards the hunting-lodge. He left in the early dusk, as soon as the evening meal was over in Mauduit's lodging. No one was paying any heed to him by that time of day. All Roger had to do was hold his tongue and keep his wits about him for three days, and the disputed manor would still be adjudged to him. Everything was beautifully in hand, after all.

Two of the men-at-arms and one groom had been left behind at the hunting-lodge. Cadfael doubted if the man they guarded was to be found in the house itself, for unless he was blindfolded he would be able to gather far too much knowledge of his surroundings, and the fable of the masterless men would be tossed into the rubbish-heap. No, he would be held in darkness, or dim light at best, even during the day, in straw or the rush flooring of a common hut, fed adequately but plainly and roughly, as wild men might keep a prisoner they were too cautious to kill, or too superstitious, until they turned him loose in some remote place, stripped of everything he had of value. On the other hand, he must be somewhere securely inside the boundary fence, otherwise there would be too high a risk of his being found. Between the gate and the house there were trees enough to obscure the large holding of a man of consequence. Somewhere among the stables and barns, or the now empty kennels, there he must be held.

Cadfael tethered his horse in cover well aside from the lodge and found himself a perch in a tall oak tree, from which vantage point he could see over the fence into the courtyard.

He was in luck. The three within fed themselves at leisure before they fed their prisoner, preferring to wait for dark. By the time the groom emerged from the hall with a pitcher and a bowl in his hands, Cadfael had his night eyes. They were quite easy about their charge, expecting no interference from any man. The groom vanished momentarily between the trees within the enclosure, but

407

appeared again at one of the low buildings tucked under the fence, set down his pitcher for a moment while he hoisted clear a heavy wooden bar that held the door fast shut, and vanished within. The door thudded to after him, as though he had slammed it shut with his back braced against it, taking no chances even with an elderly monastic. In a few minutes he emerged again empty-handed, hauled the bar into place again, and returned, whistling, to the hall and the enjoyment of Mauduit's ale.

Not the stables nor the kennels, but a small stout hay store built on short wooden piles raised from the ground. At least the prior would have fairly snug lying.

Cadfael let the last of the light fade before he made a move. The wooden wall was stout and high, but more than one of the old trees outside leaned a branch over it, and it was no great labour to climb without and drop into the deep grass within. He made first for the gate, and quietly unbarred the narrow wicket set into it. Faint threads of torchlight filtered through the chinks in the hall shutters, but nothing else stirred. Cadfael laid hold of the heavy bar of the storehouse door, and eased it silently out of its socket, opening the door by cautious inches, and whispering through the chink: 'Father . . . ?'

There was a sharp rustling of hay within, but no immediate reply.

'Father Prior, is it you? Softly . . . Are you bound?'

A hesitant and slightly timorous voice said, 'No.' And in a moment, with better assurance: 'My son, you are not one of these sinful men?'

'Sinful man I am, but not of their company. Hush, quietly now! I have a horse close by. I came from Woodstock to find you. Reach me your hand, Father, and come forth.'

A hand came wavering out of the hay-scented darkness to clutch convulsively at Cadfael's hand. The pale patch of a tonsured crown gleamed faintly, and a small, rounded figure crept forth and stepped into the thick grass. He had the wit to waste no breath then on questions, but stood docile and silent while Cadfael re-barred the door on emptiness and, taking him by the hand, led him softly along the fence to the unfastened wicket in the great gate. Only when the door was closed as softly behind them did he heave a great, thankful sigh.

They were out, it was done, and no one would be likely to learn of the escape until morning. Cadfael led the way to where he had left his horse tethered. The forest lay serene and quiet about them.

'You ride, Father, and I'll walk with you. It's no more than two miles into Woodstock. We're safe enough now.'

Bewildered and confused by so sudden a reversal, the prior confided and obeyed like a child. Not until they were out on the silent highroad did he say sadly, 'I have failed of my mission. Son, may God bless you for this kindness which is beyond my understanding. For how did you know of me, and how could you divine where to find me? I understand nothing of what has been happening to me. And I am not a very brave man . . . But my failure is no fault of yours, and my blessing I owe you without stint.'

'You have not failed, Father,' said Cadfael simply. 'The suit is still unheard, and will be for three days more. All your companions are safe in Woodstock, except that they fret and search for you. And if you know where they will be lodging, I would recommend that you join them now, by night, and stay well out of sight until the day the case is heard. For if this trap was designed to keep you from appearing in the King's court, some further attempt might yet be made. Have you your evidences safe? They did not take them?'

'Brother Orderic, my clerk, was carrying the documents, but he could not conduct the case in court. I only am accredited to represent my abbot.' But, my son, how is it that the case still goes unheard? The King keeps strict day and time, it's well known. How comes it that God and you have saved me from disgrace and loss?'

'Father, for all too bitter reason the King could not be present.'

Cadfael told him the whole of it, how half the young chivalry of England had been wiped out in one blow, and the King left without an heir. Prior Heribert, shocked and dismayed, fell to praying in a grieving whisper for both dead and living, and Cadfael walked beside the horse in silence, for what more was there to be said? Except that King Henry, even in this shattering hour, willed that his justice should still prevail, and that was virtue in any monarch. Only when they came into the sleeping town did Cadfael again interrupt the prior's fervent prayers with a strange question.

'Father, was any man of your escort carrying steel? A dagger, or any such weapon?'

'No, no, God forbid!' said the prior, shocked. 'We have no use for arms. We trust in God's peace, and after it in the King's'

'So I thought,' said Cadfael, nodding. 'It is another discipline, for another venture.'

By the change in Mauduit's countenance Cadfael knew the hour of the following day when the news reached him that his prisoner was flown. All the rest of that day he went about with nerves at stretch and ears pricked for any sensational rumours being bandied around the town, and eyes roving anxiously in dread of the sight of Prior Heribert in court or street, braced to pour out his complaint to the King's officers. But as the hours passed and still there was no sign, he began to be a little eased in his mind, and to hope still for a miraculous deliverance. The Benedictine brothers were seen here and there, mute and sombre-faced; surely they could have had no word of their superior. There was nothing to be done but set his teeth, keep his countenance, wait and hope.

The second day passed, and the third day came, and Mauduit's hopes had soared again, for still there was no word. He made his appearance before the King's judge confidently, his charters in hand. The abbey was the suitor. If all went well, Roger would not even have to state his case, for the plea would fail of itself when the pleader failed to appear.

It came as a shattering shock when a sudden stir at the door, prompt to the hour appointed, blew into the hall a small, round, unimpressive person in the Benedictine habit, hugging to him an armful of vellum rolls, and followed by

his black-gowned brothers in close attendance. Cadfael, too, was observing him
with interest, for it was the first time he had seen him clearly. A modest man of
comfortable figure and amiable countenance, rosy and mild. Not so old as that
night journey had suggested, perhaps forty-five, with a shining innocence about
him. But to Roger Mauduit it might have been a fire-breathing dragon entering
the hall.

And who would have expected, from that gentle, even deprecating presence,
the clarity and expertise with which that small man deployed his original
charter, punctiliously identical to Roger's according to the account Alard had
given, and omitting any specific mention of what should follow Arnulf
Mauduit's death – how scrupulously he pointed out the omission and the
arguments to which it might give rise, and followed it up with two letters
written by that same Arnulf Mauduit to Abbot Fulchered, referring in plain
terms to the obligatory return of the manor and village after his death, and
pledging his son's loyal observance of the obligation.

It might have been want of proofs that caused Roger to make so poor a job of
refuting the evidence, or it might have been craven conscience. Whatever the
cause, judgement was given for the abbey.

Cadfael presented himself before the lord he was leaving barely an hour after the
verdict was given.

'My lord, your suit is concluded, and my service with it. I have done what I
pledged, here I part from you.'

Roger sat sunk in gloom and rage, and lifted upon him a glare that should
have felled him, but failed of its impact.

'I misdoubt me,' said Roger, smouldering, 'how you have observed your
loyalty to me. Who else could know . . .' He bit his tongue in time, for as long
as it remained unsaid no accusation had been made, and no rebuttal was needed.
He would have liked to ask: How *did* you know? But he thought better of it.
'Go, then, if you have nothing more to say.'

'As to that,' said Cadfael meaningly, 'nothing more need be said. It's over.'
And that was recognisable as a promise, but with uneasy implications, for
plainly on some other matter he still had a thing to say.

'My lord, give some thought to this, for I was until now in your service, and
wish you no harm. Of those four who attended Prior Heribert on his way here,
not one carried arms. There was neither sword nor dagger nor knife of any kind
among the five of them.'

He saw the significance of that go home, slowly but with bitter force. The
masterless men had been nothing but a children's tale, but until now Roger had
thought, as he had been meant to think, that that dagger-stroke in the forest had
been a bold attempt by an abbey servant to defend his prior. He blinked and
swallowed and stared, and began to sweat, beholding a perilous gulf into which
he had all but stumbled.

'There were none there who bore arms,' said Cadfael, 'but your own.'

A double-edged ambush that had been, to have him out in the forest by night, all unsuspecting. And there were as many miles between Woodstock and Sutton Mauduit returning as coming, and there would be other nights as dark on the way.

'Who?' asked Roger in a grating whisper. 'Which of them? Give him a name!'

'No,' said Cadfael simply. 'Do your own divining. I am no longer in your service, I have said all I mean to say.'

Roger's face had turned grey. He was hearing again the plan unfolded so seductively in his ear. 'You cannot leave me so! If you know so much, for God's sake return with me, see me safely home, at least. You I could trust!'

'No,' said Cadfael again. 'You are warned, now guard yourself.'

It was fair, he considered; it was enough. He turned and went away without another word. He went, just as he was, to Vespers in the parish church, for no better reason – or so he thought then – than that the dimness within the open doorway beckoned him as he turned his back on a duty completed, inviting him to quietness and thought, and the bell was just sounding. The little prior was there, ardent in thanksgiving, one more creature who had fumbled his way to the completion of a task, and the turning of a leaf in the book of his life.

Cadfael watched out the office, and stood mute and still for some time after priest and worshippers had departed. The silence after their going was deeper than the ocean and more secure than the earth. Cadfael breathed and consumed it like new bread. It was the light touch of a small hand on the hilt of his sword that startled him out of that profound isolation. He looked down to see a little acolyte, no higher than his elbow, regarding him gravely from great round eyes of blinding blue, intent and challenging, as solemn as ever was angelic messenger.

'Sir,' said the child in stern treble reproof, tapping the hilt with an infant finger, 'should not all weapons of war be laid aside here?'

'Sir,' said Cadfael hardly less gravely, though he was smiling, 'you may very well be right.' And slowly he unbuckled the sword from his belt, and went and laid it down, flatlings, on the lowest step under the altar. It looked strangely appropriate and at peace there. The hilt, after all, was a cross.

Prior Heribert was at a frugal supper with his happy brothers in the parish priest's house when Cadfael asked audience with him. The little man came out graciously to welcome a stranger, and knew him for an acquaintance at least, and now at a breath certainly a friend.

'You, my son! And surely it was you at Vespers? I felt that I should know the shape of you. You are the most welcome of guests here, and if there is anything I and mine can do to repay you for what you did for us, you need but name it.'

'Father,' said Cadfael, briskly Welsh in his asking, 'do you ride for home tomorrow?'

'Surely, my son, we leave after Prime. Abbot Godefrid will be waiting to hear how we have fared.'

'Then, Father, here am I at the turning of my life, free of one master's service, and finished with arms. Take me with you!'

# ANTHONY PRICE

---

## The Boudicca Killing

A foolish boy throws a stone at his brother on the mountainside, and starts an avalanche – that is how it begins. Not by accident, but not by deliberate intent either.

A syndicate of City financiers complains that it has been cheated over certain military and civilian contracts in Britain.

The complaint is unofficial (which it has to be, for no actual law has been broken), but the complainants are determined to make trouble for the man who has beaten them at their own game. So they maintain piously that, just as their lost investment in the new province was originally undertaken for patriotic rather than commercial reasons, now their sole concern is for the welfare of the state, that first and highest duty of every citizen.

Thus is the stone cast, and the avalanche set in motion.

At first, however, it is no more than a shiver on the loose scree of the hillside. For if the syndicate has indirectly sustained a great loss over its British investment, many others have also lost their money – and directly – as a result of the terrible insurrection in that unhappy province.

Two colonies of veterans have been destroyed; vast quantities of military stores and private goods have gone up in smoke during the sack of Londinium; many thousands of persons, both citizens and freemen, not to mention valuable slaves, have been massacred – in effect, both debtors and their property; and many other debtors among the native aristocracy are now proscribed rebels, whose wealth (such as remains of it) is the legitimate booty of the armed forces, which not even Caesar himself may safely appropriate.

Yet once in motion, an avalanche may not be hindered – and a fiscal investigation is inexorable.

This is not because the fiscal inspectors set any store whatsoever by the syndicate's patriotism; nor are they usually very interested, all things being equal, in the particular identity of contract-holders, provided such men pay their taxes.

Yet they are also by nature intensely suspicious men, and Gnaeus Alfrenius Cotta is a new name in their files.

Gn. Alfrenius Cotta, recently in a modest way of business in Ostia, but now a major financial power in the City.

Gn. Alfrenius Cotta, who has made a fortune out of Britain, where everyone else had lost money.

Gn. Alfrenius Cotta, who (so it transpires) knows how the dice will fall before they have been thrown.

I: *In the City*

The Colonel of *Arcani* goes to that office between the Capitoline and the Palatine where such briefings are held, under orders to proceed without delay to that Province.

There are present three senior fiscal clerks, together with the Sub-prefect of the Imperial Courier Service, and a freedman from the Palace (whom the Colonel instantly identifies as one of Caesar's principal secretaries-of-state).

One of the clerks speaks first.

He sketches the course of the late British insurrection; which the Colonel understands better than any fiscal clerk, not only because such things are his business but also because he has served in Britain, which (he surmises) is why he is now under orders for the island, and not Hierosolyma (where there is also trouble, as usual).

The clerk concludes: 'Colonel, it amounts to this: after the despatches of the late Decianus Catus, Procurator of the Province, we received the first true account of the situation from the noble Governor, Gaius Suetonius Paulinus.'

That is good, thinks the Colonel. Caesar's justice has made Decianus 'the late' and Suetonius 'the noble' – which is as things should be.

'By that time the *colonia* at Camulodunum has been destroyed—'

'And one whole battlegroup of the Ninth Legion, says the second clerk, the one with rabbit's teeth. 'Three regular cohorts of the line – *obliterated*!'

He makes it sound like an entry on the wrong side of one of his ledgers. Which for him no doubt it is, thinks the Colonel bitterly. The best footsloggers in the world are . . . expensive – to a clerk.

'They were ambushed on the march, in wooded country,' adds Rabbit's-teeth. 'It's a situation the legions have never learned to handle. Varus couldn't – and they still can't.'

So Rabbit's-teeth is an amateur tactician. And the nearest thing Rabbit's-teeth has seen to 'wooded country' is the Garden of Lucullus.

The Sub-prefect, who has served in Germany, has the grace to look uncomfortable; the Colonel, who has served in Britain and knows that hell is a dank, dripping, trackless undergrowth without end, merely smiles politely and asks to see the Governor's despatch.

It is short, and to the point.

And, although it is from the noble Governor himself, who one week later won the greatest victory of the reign, over a British horde outnumbering his army ten-to-one, it smells unmistakably of Roman defeat, disaster and death.

Decianus Catus, Procurator of Britain, has fled the Province. The Twentieth Legion has disobeyed orders, failing to march to the Governor's aid, and the Second is too far away; the Ninth (what is left of it) is closely besieged in its camp. Consequently, the Governor must abandon Londinium and Verulamium, which are now indefensible, and retire to his field army in the north-west – one tired Legion with its auxiliary regiments.

If Queen Boudicca and her savages catch him on the road, or if she ambushes his army (shades of Rabbit's-teeth!) before he can conduct that army to his chosen battle-ground, or if she waits ten days until his supplies are exhausted, then Rome in Britain is finished. That must be faced, and plans laid accordingly by Caesar.

Alternatively, within seven days, if the Gods favour Rome, the Governor will have the honour of laying a great victory at the feet of Caesar.

So . . . the Governor writes of victory, but expects defeat, like a gambler throwing against a Venus. It is a dead man's despatch, with expectation overshadowing hope.

'Is that clear, Colonel?' says the first clerk.

The room is cooler now. In his youth the Colonel has seen (as the clerks and the freedmen have not seen, though the Sub-prefect may have seen) what the savages do to their prisoners. And, remembering a grove on the high chalk downs, he recalls particularly how ingenious the British women were in impaling a young officer of the Batavians, who was his special friend, who was still alive when—

No! That is not a proper memory for a Colonel of the *Arcani*.

The Colonel nods.

'Very well.' The first clerk accepts the nod. 'When the syndicate heard the contents of that despatch, which they did within an hour of its receipt—'

Now the Colonel understands more: one of Caesar's chief ministers is in the syndicate.

'—they commenced to offer their contracts on the open market in the City. And their provincial debts.'

'At a reduced rate?' asks the Colonel, deliberately insulting.

'Not initially . . . You must remember, Colonel, that Decianus Catus had made light of the rising in *his* despatches. Rather, he emphasised the number of slaves taken during the Governor's campaign in the north-west – and the gold mines of the new territories . . . The syndicate made it sound as though they were putting new shares on the market, with new areas for capital development.'

The Colonel nods again, dutifully. High finance isn't so very different from betting on the races: the biggest wins are always to be made on outsiders.

But this race has to be different – and the Sub-prefect is looking decidedly uncomfortable.

'Someone talked?'

Even the first clerk looks uncomfortable. Imperial couriers who talk only talk once – or twice, the second time being when they admit that they talked. Which is positively the last time that they ever talk.

'And then the market fell – and Cotta started to buy?' The Colonel is beginning to enjoy himself, and to like Gn. Alfrenius Cotta, who has evidently beaten the official odds.

'Not immediately . . . The market was nervous – Decianus Catus has a bad name—'

'Nobody bought.' It is the third clerk who speaks, a goat-faced man who has been silent hitherto. 'British investments have never been attractive. The slaves are unsatisfactory, and the cost of mineral extraction is high unless it's under local control. And the loan repayments from the local aristocracies have been unreliable. We should never had invaded the island.'

Rabbit's-teeth nods to that. 'So the syndicate dropped its prices. And then the details of that despatch leaked out—'

'The bottom dropped out of the market,' says Goat-face. 'On the second day – in the afternoon.'

'And then Cotta bought?'

'No,' says Goat-face. 'Then he started to *borrow*.'

'To – borrow?'

'Yes, Colonel. You see – you must understand – this man Cotta is . . . was . . . nothing special, financially speaking . . . Mostly import-export, Massilia-Ostia. Plus a few contracts the bigger groups had missed – only four in Britain—'

'His agent there is his nephew, his sister's son,' supplements Rabbit's-teeth eagerly. 'The youth has – *had* – a minor post on the staff of the Procurator, Decianus Catus—'

'The *late* Decianus Catus,' murmurs Goat-face. 'But . . . the point is, he had no cash on hand. He had to borrow in order to buy.'

'More than borrow,' amends Rabbit's-teeth. 'He called in all his debts – he mortgaged all his property . . . And then he took out second mortgages. He sold his villa at Praenestina—'

'At a loss,' says the first clerk.

'At a loss. And then he mortgaged his sister's property,' says Rabbit's-teeth. 'And *then* he borrowed on the open market!'

Goat-face gestures abruptly. 'He went beyond all reason and prudence – he borrowed on risk-cargoes in transit, even. And he has a reputation in Ostia for good sense – sharp, but sensible—'

'Which helped his credit in Ostia.' Rabbit's-teeth nods.

'He even borrowed from the syndicate—' Goat-face smiles. 'Short-term, high interest – they took him for a stupid provincial, and he took *them*—'

'But he didn't buy openly,' says Rabbit's-teeth. 'It was all through nominees – more provincials.'

'He bought everything they had, including that palace we're building for the client-king in the south,' says Goat-face. 'By the eighth day – all signed, sealed and delivered. Plus a dozen other contracts from . . . other groups.'

The Prince's ministers had sold out too, naturally.

'He owns half the Province now,' says Rabbit's-teeth. 'If he had a son he'd have to call the child "Britannicus".'

'But he has no son. Only that nephew, whom he exiled to Britain because they mistrusted each other,' murmurs the first clerk. 'Tiberius Alfrenius Martinus . . . Britannicus . . .'

It adds up to one conclusion, and one only. They have been at pains to make that clear.

'So – he knew,' says the Colonel.

'He knew,' Goat-face nods. '*And he knew before we did.*'

It is Goat-face who is the senior clerk, the Colonel decides. It irritates him that he did not guess that more quickly.

But now he does not wish to compound that error.

The despatch he has seen was not the latest despatch, there has to be another— *Queen Boudicca dead, her Army destroyed, the Province saved!*

The noble Governor, Gaius Suetonius Paulinus, would have sent that despatch no less quickly than its predecessor. It would have taken maybe a day or two longer, travelling from the battlefield, but it would have taken the same route, under the same absolute priority of the imperial Governor's seal – courier, and fast galley, and courier; relay after relay, the best men on the fastest horses, along the imperial highways. Ever since the Varus disaster, fifty years before, when there had been disgraceful scenes of panic in the City, bad news had always been brought to Caesar first, before being released to the Senate; and even good news, travelling on its own fair wind, is supposed to reach the Palatine Hill first.

But if that has been compromised then the Sub-prefect should be looking more unhappy . . .

Which he is not. (And Caesar's freedman hasn't spoken a word either, yet; but then his job is to listen and report back, no more, of course.)

So the Colonel says nothing. And for a moment or two no one else wishes to speak, either.

'And that is the sum of our problem,' says Goat-face finally. (Naturally, it must be Goat-face.) 'He knew – but he could not have known.'

Rabbit's-teeth surreptitiously signs himself against evil.

The first clerk speaks: 'It is the time factor, Colonel . . . No one in his right mind would have risked what Alfrenius Cotta did, unless he was certain. Because he pledged himself, and his freedom, and his life . . . and his family—'

'Three times over,' cuts in Rabbit's-teeth, actuarially.

'But he is in his right mind,' says Goat-face. 'Yet he started raising money *before* Boudicca was defeated. And he began buying *before* the victory despatch had crossed the Narrow Sea to Gaul—'

'Which leaves us with only two explanations,' says Rabbit's-teeth. 'First . . . sorcery – of the worst kind!'

'Um . . . present knowledge of a future event, that is,' says the first clerk. 'The supernatural.'

'Of which there have been cases – well-authenticated cases—' Rabbit's-teeth is cut off by a look from Goat-face.

'Well-authenticated cases . . . *after* the event.' Goat-face looks at the Colonel dispassionately. 'But there has *never* been a case where the immortal Gods have helped a small businessman to make a large fortune while Caesar himself is sacrificing on the Altar of Victory in the hope of a sign from heaven.'

Rabbit's-teeth is crestfallen. Caesar's freedman begins to look interested.

Goat-face continues to observe the Colonel. 'The noble Governor's despatch foreshadowed a great defeat. But someone else evidently knew better – and what is more, he knew better enough to convince Gnaeus Alfrenius Cotta, who is certainly nobody's fool, that he knew better, Colonel.'

No one rejects this reasoning.

'Now . . . I think I know *who*, Colonel . . . since there is only one person who could have known.'

The Colonel begins to understand what is required of him.

'What I need to know is *how*—'

The imbecile innocence of the Sub-prefect's expression confirms the understanding: his service has not failed twice.

'—and I want to know quickly.' Goat-face's voice is like marble. 'So . . . this day you will leave the City, carrying Caesar's formal congratulations to the noble Governor, Gaius Suetonius Paulinus—'

## II: *In the Province*

Britain is different from Germany in the early autumn. In a few weeks it will be bare, and every gutter will be choked with fallen leaves, but now it is a riot of red and yellow and gold, where Germany is an eternal dark green.

These are the colours which the Colonel remembers, when the world was young and he was a junior staff officer of auxiliaries.

But now it is different in a different way, with the fresh scars of hastily dug ditches and the raw wood of new palisades around every halt on the road to Londinium; and the town itself a burnt-out horror smelling of damp ash and rotting flesh, in which he sleeps under canvas for one night only, thankful to obey the letter of his orders to the last syllable.

Except that what follows, as he moves on towards the noble Governor's field headquarters, is worse, even allowing for the satisfaction of the crowded prison camps in which the women and children are held (there are no male adult prisoners in the forward areas; the Gallic irregular cavalry are spearheading the mopping-up operations, and they are head-hunters by both inclination and religion, and they are earning their bounty-money; so . . . satisfaction and yet death and devastation are always depressing, even when justly imposed on the guilty – and these natives are undeniably guilty).

But tonight he is dining with the Governor himself, as befits his Praetorian rank and his status as Caesar's honoured messenger, carrying greetings from the Roman Senate and People.

(What the Governor does not know is that his is a political mission: Caesar has no use for governors who win victories which take the imagination of the Roman Senate and People, such men must be cut down to smaller size – Goat-face has made that abundantly clear in private, with the freedman's nod.

(And that makes his task both distasteful and difficult; distasteful, because he admires the noble Governor's brilliant victory over odds; and difficult . . .

(Difficult, because there is not one shred of evidence so far that the noble Governor has conspired with Tiberius Alfrenius Martinus – and Gnaeus Alfrenius Cotta – to execute a gigantic fraud on Caesar and the City . . .

(Difficult, because the dates check out – the noble Governor was still fighting when Gn. Alfrenius Cotta was borrowing . . .

(Difficult, because when the noble Governor abandoned Londinium nobody, but *nobody*, knew which way Boudicca was marching; indeed, if anything, the consensus was that she would destroy the Governor and his army first, and the town afterwards, for which very sensible reason ten thousand Roman settlers and friendly tribesmen remained there, hoping for the best, and died there very unpleasantly when she stormed the decaying ramparts before chasing the Governor . . .

(*So* difficult that the Colonel is almost of a mind to agree with Rabbit's-teeth on the matter of sorcery . . .

(Almost, but not quite. For Tiberius Alfrenius Martinus, nephew to Gnaeus Alfrenius Cotta and formerly a tax accountant with the late, unlamented Procurator, Decianus Catus, is now the trusted military secretary of the noble Governor. And that, in the circumstances of the Procurator's behaviour, is a very curious promotion, which makes no sense at all . . .

(And which, therefore, requires investigation.)

So . . . now the Colonel is dining with the noble Governor, and the last of the food has been removed, and the small talk, though it is apparently continuing, is in fact over—

'Wasn't that young Alfrenius Martinus I saw taking notes at your briefing this afternoon, my lord?' enquires the Colonel conversationally.

'My secretary?' The noble Governor is mellowed by the wine and the day's gratifying head-count. 'You know him?'

'I know his uncle slightly – one of the coming men in the City . . . But I thought young Martinus was on Catus's staff?'

The Governor frowns momentarily, and then smiles in quick succession, no doubt thinking first of his former procurator, whose crass stupidity caused the insurrection, and then of the fate of both procurator and insurrectionists.

'Yes, so he was. But . . . '

The Colonel listens as the Governor, wine-mellowed, talks—

It had been just after the news had been confirmed that the Twentieth Legion hadn't marched: what had already become a serious tribal uprising was something far worse now – it had a Varus-disaster premonition about it now.

The Governor was desperately tired, quite drained by bad news; and, what was worse, he knew he was beginning to despair. Also, the last of the galleys was waiting to slip its moorings, and he had a despatch (which he now believed would be the last of his career) to send aboard, but he had no one to take it down in writing for him.

'Who?' he snapped at the Guards sergeant.

'Alfrenius Martinus – Tiberius Alfrenius Martinus, my lord.'

He didn't want to see anyone, and the name meant nothing to him. But he knew that fear was infectious, and he must not let it spread from him.

'Very well – I'll see him.'

He turned away, waiting until the sergeant had made himself scarce.

Tiberius what-was-his-name was youngish and short and rather fat, and he wore an ill-fitting uniform, and the smell of the infection was already on him.

'Yes?'

Martinus saluted self-consciously and badly, and began to explain what he was, rather than who. Which was a mistake, because at the mention of the Procurator's name the Governor cut him off brutally.

'You are too late. Your master has run for it – and I'm damned if I'm giving you a place on the despatches galley. Get out!' It was a measure of the Governor's weariness that this death sentence gave him no special satisfaction.

But Martinus stood firm. 'I wasn't too late. I chose to stay, sir.'

'Oh?' The words registered only partially. 'Then that was very foolish of you.'

Martinus swayed, as though embarrassed. 'My . . . my father was a soldier. A-and his father – my grandfather – was a soldier.' He blinked. 'It would have been . . . dishonourable.'

The Governor discovered that he could still be surprised. The fellow was sweating with fright, and he was also ridiculous. But he was nevertheless volunteering to die with his betters – a bloody tax-man – and *that* wasn't ridiculous.

'I know I'm no soldier' – Martinus blinked again – 'but they said . . . in the Officers' Mess . . . that your secretary had run away. So I thought—' He stopped suddenly, and seemed to take his fear, if not his courage, in both hands. 'They said, if the army is to have a chance, then Boudicca must attack Londinium first. But they don't think she will . . . But I think there's a way, sir . . .'

The Governor nodded, speechlessly. It would be stupid, whatever it was, it would be stupid. But he mustn't laugh, because this man's 'honour' was like a flower on a dunghill – and his fear was something they possessed in common. So he mustn't laugh.

'Sir – if Boudicca believes that the Procurator is still here in the town . . . They say he had her flogged under her own roof – if she thought he was still here—'

The Governor felt a pang of disappointment. In spite of himself, in spite of instinct and appearances, he had hoped for a miracle.

'Martinus . . .' He edited out the sharpness. 'Martinus, this city – this town – is full of spies. He's gone, the bastard – and they saw him go, Martinus.'

'Yes, sir.' Martinus nodded. 'But not all of them – and the ones who didn't will want to report that he's still here. If we give them something to report – if we give them rumours even . . . We could say the galley grounded in the estuary, and you'd had him brought back – and we could put guards on his house . . . Just a rumour, sir – that might be enough to decide her . . . Just the outside chance of taking him *alive*—'

Plainly ridiculous. Boudicca knew well enough that Catus had run away, and even if she didn't then the obvious military logic of attacking the army first was the only thing that made sense.

And yet—

'Just the chance, sir.' Martinus bared his teeth. 'If she could lay her hands on him . . . '

Yet there was something about this little fellow which lent force to his words.

Suddenly the Governor caught the undertone of anger beneath the fear.

So that was it, then: if Tiberius Something Martinus had Decianus Catus in his hands now, the bastard would die as slowly as if he'd fallen to Boudicca, Queen of the Iceni!

It had never occurred to him to take such elemental passions into the reckoning, to be weighed against the better strategy. Yet if the image of Decianus Catus impaled living on a sharpened stake could fire a snivelling tax-man, how much more might a well-placed rumour distort Boudicca's judgement?

He was clutching at straws. But they were all he had.

He was also staring poor little Martinus out of countenance.

But he felt better—

'I have a despatch to send. Can you take dictation?'

'Sir?' Martinus stiffened. 'Yes, sir!'

'After that . . . we'll see what we can do with your rumours.' Absurdly, the Governor felt much better. The thought of Martinus drawing his rusty sword against a great hairy Briton might be laughable, but he had seven thousand heavy infantry up the road from this doomed town – Roman infantry, the true Rome – who knew how to use their swords. And Martinus could meanwhile draw his pen to good effect to settle Decianus Catus, whatever the outcome.

The little man was trying to speak again.

'Yes?'

'I was wondering, sir . . . Might I send a private letter – two private letters – with your despatch?' He fumbled beneath the armour. 'I have them here, sir.'

'What?' The Governor found he had accepted the letters.

'To my mother, sir. I – I am her only son . . . And – and to my uncle, sir. She is a widow.'

The Governor read the two letters, and as he read them the last of his tiredness and fear fell away from him.

This – *this* – was also the true Rome, here in this unprepossessing little pen-pusher, as surely as in his unbeatable footsloggers.

And these were words he would never forget.

'Very well – send them.' He returned the letters. 'But now–'

Now they were going to beat that damned woman Boudicca.

And that, says the noble Governor, was what they did.

III: *In the Forward Headquarters*

The Colonel is still following the noble Governor into the newly pacified – totally devastated – territory of the Iceni two days later (with that damned woman only a dark memory now), and it is raining. (And that is another thing the Colonel recalls from '96 – the rain.) Off the log corduroys of the camp the lines are already halfway to quagmires.

But the tent of Tiberius Alfrenius Martinus, with its charcoal brazier and its plank floor, is snug and warm – as befits that of the Governor's chief secretary, whom the Governor has been pleased to honour with the rank of acting-colonel for the duration of the emergency.

The chief secretary/acting-colonel is busy drafting tomorrow's operational orders when the Colonel enters the tent.

(The chief secretary/acting-colonel is also still in uniform too, which seems to support the camp joke – that he is so proud of his armour that he sleeps in it. But then it is better-fitting now, the Colonel notes.)

He looks up at his visitor, clearly a little irritated at this interruption of his work. He is a world away – a great victory away, and the Governor's favour away, and a private fortune away – from the frightened tax-man of former days.

So shock tactics are called for: the Colonel tosses his Imperial warrant on to the table, with its seal of life and death uppermost.

To the slave at Martinus's shoulder he says: 'Get out.'

The slave has never seen that seal, and perhaps Martinus hasn't either. But he has heard of it.

'Leave us,' he orders his slave. Then: 'Can I help you, Colonel?'

'You can. And you will.' The Colonel looks round for a seat. There is a stool piled with papers – quartermaster's reports, muster rolls, casualty lists and head-count tallies. He tips them on to the floor and sits down opposite Martinus.

'I don't know how you did it, Tiberius Alfrenius Martinus. But I know you did it somehow.'

Martinus says nothing.

'And I know that you are a liar.'

Still nothing.

'A considerable liar. Not an only son, for example. And your father was a tally-clerk. And his father was also a tally-clerk. For a start – a considerable liar, Tiberius Alfrenius Martinus.'

Martinus smiles . . . as if to say that these are minor matters now.

'Very well!' The stool is uncomfortable. 'Then I'll tell you a story, Tiberius Alfrenius Martinus . . .

'There was once a tax official – a *junior* tax official – who was sent to the south coast of Britain, to Noviomagus, to collect the Procurator's share of the palace contractors' bribes. But when he got back to Londinium – not without difficulty – he found that a revolt had broken out—'

Martinus stirs suddenly, as though he wants to speak.

'No! Don't spoil my story!' The Colonel cuts him off. 'This *very junior* tax official also finds that his master, the Procurator, has already run away. And there is only one galley left . . . and when he tries to bribe his way aboard – with the Noviomagus gold – he is turned away with a sharp sword. Because the last galley is reserved for the Governor's last despatch . . . and no one – no one else – and least of all a damned tax official – is going aboard, at any price.

'So *he* – our minor cog in the broken wheel of Decianus Catus – *he* then goes in despair to the Governor's headquarters, to see if his gold will buy safety there.

'But it won't. Because gold has lost its value in Londinium. It won't buy a berth on the last galley. And all the roads are cut now, anyway. And the Governor himself is about to abandon the town and march to almost certain defeat, if Boudicca keeps her head and does the right thing. And then the town will fall.

'So when he offers his gold to the officers they just laugh at him – and offer him a breast-plate two sizes too big and a nasty sharp sword – No! Don't deny it, Tiberius Alfrenius Martinus – I've talked to them, and I know what happened!'

The stool is quite excruciating, really.

'But now it becomes interesting, because we come to what I don't know . . . Because you went to the Governor, and you suggested to him how he might lure Boudicca to Londinium while he chose his battlefield – very good!

'And you sent two letters by his courier – two Roman letters to warm the heart of a Roman general on the eve of battle—

' "*Mother – I write to you on the eve of battle. I hope to serve with honour, fighting beside my General and Governor, the noble Gaius Suetonius Paulinus. Know that I shall not disgrace Father's memory, and that, should I fall, my last thought but one will be of you, and my last of Rome, the Great Mother of us all.*

*Your loving and dutiful son,*

*Tiberius*"

' "*Uncle – I write to you on the eve of the battle. The odds are against us. If I should fall, I charge you by the glorious memory of my father, your brother, who also gave his life for Rome, to comfort and sustain my dear mother.*

*Your dutiful nephew,*

*Tiberius*"

'—letters engraved on that general's heart,' continues the Colonel, gazing on Martinus not without admiration.

'But what is engraved on my heart is . . . that you are a most ingenious and absolute liar, Tiberius Alfrenius Martinus – and I want to know *what was in the letters you actually sent*, not in those which you showed to the Governor.'

He leans forward and taps the seal on the warrant to emphasise this request. But now there is a cast of obstinacy in Martinus's expression: on the strength of his acting-rank, and the Governor's favour, and his new wealth, he is still inclined to cover his dice with his cup and bet on them.

'Pardon me, Colonel – I know of no letters – a few small . . . inaccuracies, perhaps – slips of the tongue made in a moment of enthusiasm, no more. But the Governor will forgive them, Colonel. And I know that I have committed no crime' – his eyes flick for an instant to the seal – 'no crime whatsoever, Colonel.'

No crime. And he has the Governor nicely calculated: the noble Gaius Suetonius Paulinus will never admit being taken for a fool by this man, it will be against the dignity of his great victory.

Martinus knows that. He strokes his breast-plate as if to emphasise his knowledge. Nothing can be proved, and the past will bury the past. He is guilty, but safe.

'So, Colonel—?' The pudgy little hand continues to massage the gilded bronze, which no gentleman would wear at such an hour – certainly no officer—

In that moment the Colonel sees his way, towards which that hand has pointed.

Under his bronze, Martinus must be frightened, because everyone is frightened by that seal.

Under that bronze is a man who knows his law and his rights as a citizen. But not his miliary law, for a guess—

And under that bronze is a snob, a parvenu and a social climber – as might be expected of a junior tax official—

So . . . the stick and the carrot.

'No crime?' The Colonel pretends to be comfortable. 'It is our belief, as the facts indicate, that you entered into direct communication with the woman Boudicca, without your commander's knowledge or consent . . . whereby you obtained details of her plans, on which you acted—'

'No—'

'*And*, under military law in the field, and in uniform – and with your rank – on my authority alone I can have you flogged and crucified, Tiberius Alfrenius Martinus. Which will get you conveniently out of the Governor's way—'

'*No*—'

The stick has landed squarely on those white buttocks. The man doesn't know his military law – but he has seen what the scourge and the cross-tree can do to a man.

'*But*. . . Caesar is merciful.' Now for the carrot: the Colonel balances himself carefully. 'And he is also grateful—'

Martinus's battle line is bending: surprise has joined fear in the frontal assault.

'Grateful. For it was *you* who put backbone into the noble Governor, Tiberius Alfrenius Martinus – it was you who saved Britain with your treason!'

One last reinforcement is needed. The Colonel calls it up.

'Your uncle is a crude person – rich now, but still crude. Your family's influence requires proper representation in the City . . . In the equestrian order at once . . . and, in due time, in the Senate itself.' By a miracle the words do not choke their speaker. 'All we need to know, before your equestrian sponsors are nominated, is . . . exactly how you knew what Boudicca was going to do, sir.'

The line is shattered. Dreams of gentility are too much for it.

'But . . . that is to say . . . I didn't actually *know* . . . '

It is a moment to hold one's breath. And to smile, as one colonel to another, encouragingly.

'You are right – I came back, and *he* had gone—' There is the flare of anger which the Governor saw. 'He had gone, and they laughed at me. I could have crucified him—'

So the Governor had been right, too!

'And I could have crucified my uncle with him – for sending me to this filthy place!'

But the Governor had also been quite wrong too, evidently.

'Then . . . one of the officers said . . . he said I needn't worry. Because in a few days' time we'd all be heroes – or we'd all be dead . . . if we were lucky . . . He said the Governor needed a secretary, and if he took me on at least it would be quick – win or lose – when *she* caught up with us. *Aut Caesar, aut nihil* – one way or the other—'

'So I wrote the letters – the real ones—'

'"*Mother – Do exactly what I order, no more and no less. In two days' time take the enclosed letter to my uncle, Alfrenius Cotta, together with all the monies I have remitted to you to hold for me. Tell him you have just received the letter and instruction from a stranger. Do not tell him of the delay. Do not fail me. Destroy this letter at once.*

*Your loving son,*

*Tiberius.*"'

'"*Uncle – In haste. The Army has won a great victory. Londinium and the two veterans' colonies have been destroyed, but the rest of the Province is substantially undamaged. I am acting as the Governor's secretary and will delay his victory despatch for six days. I send this letter in advance by a secure messenger. My mother brings it to you with my savings to invest in Britain at your discretion. Act quickly to make us rich.*

*Your dutiful nephew,*

*Tiberius.*"'

The Colonel looks at Martinus incredulously. 'You didn't know?'

Martinus spreads his hands. 'Nobody knew, Colonel. But they all said – all the officers said – that these savages only have one big battle in them. We couldn't get away . . . so they'd either wipe us out completely, like Varus. Or we'd smash them to pieces—'

'*But you didn't know, man*—'

'I knew it would be one way or the other. And if I was wrong, then I bloody well wouldn't be there to admit it. But if I was right – I'd be rich, Colonel.'

'So you gave him your money?'

Martinus smiles. 'I had to make him believe me – and if there's one thing my dear uncle believes, it's money. So I bought his belief with my savings, Colonel – it was an investment, you might say.'

'But you could have ruined him—?'

'Yes. And that was also part of the investment.' Another, colder memory freezes the smile. 'He would have been ruined – and I would have been dead—'

Martinus pauses for a moment to listen to the incessant sound of the rain on the canvas above him.

'—Dead. But also avenged on him for condemning me to death on this frightful island, Colonel.'

Beyond the downpour there is the distant noise of the Gallic irregulars celebrating drunkenly over the day's trophies.

Martinus brightens. 'But I was right. And now we're both rich . . . And being right and rich isn't yet a crime in the City – is it, Colonel?'

# RUTH RENDELL

## The Irony Of Hate

I murdered Brenda Goring for what I suppose is the most unusual of motives. She came between me and my wife. By that I don't mean to say that there was anything abnormal in their relationship. They were merely close friends, though 'merely' is hardly the word to use in connection with a relationship which alienates and excludes a once-loved husband. I murdered her to get my wife to myself once more, but instead I have parted us perhaps for ever, and I await with dread, with impotent panic, with the most awful helplessness I have ever known, the coming trial.

By setting down the facts – and the irony, the awful irony that runs through them like a sharp glittering thread – I may come to see things more clearly. I may find some way to convince those inexorable powers that be of how it really was; to make Defending Counsel believe me and not raise his eyebrows and shake his head; to ensure, at any rate, that if Laura and I must be separated she will know as she sees me taken from the court to my long imprisonment, that the truth is known and justice done.

Alone here with nothing else to do, with nothing to wait for but that trial, I could write reams about the character, the appearance, the neuroses, of Brenda Goring. I could write the great hate novel of all time. In this context, though, much of it would be irrelevant, and I shall be as brief as I can.

Some character in Shakespeare says of a woman, 'Would I had never seen her!' And the reply is: 'Then you would have left unseen a very wonderful piece of work.' Well, would indeed I had never seen Brenda. As for her being a wonderful piece of work, I suppose I would agree with that too. Once she had had a husband. To be rid of her for ever, no doubt, he paid her enormous alimony and had settled on her a lump sum with which she bought the cottage up the lane from our house. On our village she made the impact one would expect of such a newcomer. Wonderful she was, an amazing refreshment to all those retired couples and cautious weekenders, with her clothes, her long blonde hair, her sports car, her talents and her jet-set past. For a while, that is. Until she got too much for them to take.

From the first she fastened on to Laura. Understandable in a way, since my wife was the only woman in the locality who was of comparable age, who lived there all the time and who had no job. But surely – or so I thought at first – she would never have singled out Laura if she had had a wider choice. To me my wife is lovely, all I could ever want, the only woman I have ever really cared for, but I know that to others she appears shy, colourless, a simple and quiet little housewife. What, then, had she to offer to that extrovert, that bright bejewelled butterfly? She gave me the beginning of the answer herself.

'Haven't you noticed the way people are starting to shun her darling? The Goldsmiths didn't ask her to their party last week and Mary Williamson refuses to have her on the fête committee.'

'I can't say I'm surprised,' I said. 'The way she talks and the things she talks about.'

'You mean her love affairs and all that sort of thing? But, darling, she's lived in the sort of society where that's quite normal. It's natural for her to talk like that, it's just that she's open and honest.'

'She's not living in that sort of society now,' I said, 'and she'll have to adapt if she wants to be accepted. Did you notice Isabel Goldsmith's face when Brenda told that story about going off for a weekend with some chap she'd picked up in a bar? I tried to stop her going on about all the men her husband named in his divorce action, but I couldn't. And then she's always saying, "When I was living with so-and-so" and "That was the time of my affair with what's-his-name". Elderly people find that a bit upsetting, you know.'

'Well, we're not elderly,' said Laura, 'and I hope we can be a bit more broad-minded. You do like her, don't you?'

I was always very gentle with my wife. The daughter of clever domineering parents who belittled her, she grew up with an ineradicable sense of her own inferiority. She is a born victim, an inviter of bullying, and therefore I have tried never to bully her, never even to cross her. So all I said was that Brenda was all right and that I was glad, since I was out all day, that she had found a friend and companion of her own age.

And if Brenda had befriended and companioned her only during the day, I daresay I shouldn't have objected. I should have got used to the knowledge that Laura was listening, day in and day out, to stories of a world she had never known, to hearing illicit sex and duplicity glorified, and I should have been safe in the conviction that she was incorruptible. But I had to put up with Brenda myself in the evenings when I got home from my long commuting. There she would be, lounging on our sofa, in her silk trousers or long skirt and high boots, chain-smoking. Or she would arrive with a bottle of wine just as we had sat down to dinner and involve us in one of those favourite debates of hers on the lines of 'Is marriage a dying institution?' or 'Are parents necessary?' And to illustrate some specious point of hers she would come out with some personal experience of the kind that had so upset our elderly friends.

Of course I was not obliged to stay with them. Ours is quite a big house, and I could go off into the dining room or the room Laura called my study. But all I wanted was what I had once had, to be alone in the evenings with my wife. And it was even worse when we were summoned to coffee or drinks with Brenda, there in her lavishly furnished, over-ornate cottage to be shown the latest thing she had made – she was always embroidering and weaving and potting and messing about with water colours – and shown too the gifts she had received at some time or another from Mark and Larry and Paul and all the dozens of other men there had been in her life. When I refused to go Laura would become nervous and depressed, then pathetically elated if, after a couple of blissful

431

Brenda-less evenings, I suggested for the sake of pleasing her that I supposed we might as well drop in on old Brenda.

What sustained me was the certainty that sooner or later any woman so apparently popular with the opposite sex would find herself a boy friend and have less or no time for my wife. I couldn't understand why this hadn't happened already and I said so to Laura.

'She does see her men friends when she goes up to London,' said my wife.

'She never has any of them down here,' I said, and that evening when Brenda was treating us to a highly coloured account of some painter she knew called Laszlo who was terribly attractive and who adored her, I said I'd like to meet him and why didn't she invite him down for the weekend?

Brenda flashed her long green-painted fingernails about and gave Laura a conspiratorial woman-to-woman look. 'And what would all the old fuddy-duddies have to say about that, I wonder?'

'Surely you can rise above all that sort of thing, Brenda,' I said.

'Of course I can. Give them something to talk about. I'm quite well aware it's only sour grapes. I'd have Laszlo here like a shot, only he wouldn't come. He hates the country, he'd be bored stiff.'

Apparently Richard and Jonathan and Stephen also hated the country or would be bored or couldn't spare the time. It was much better for Brenda to go up and see them in town, and I noticed that after my probing about Laszlo, Brenda seemed to go to London more often and that the tales of her escapades after these visits became more and more sensational. I think I am quite a perceptive man and soon there began to form in my mind an idea so fantastic that for a while I refused to admit it even to myself. But I put it to the test. Instead of just listening to Brenda and throwing in the occasional rather sour rejoinder, I started asking her questions. I took her up on names and dates. 'I thought you said you met Mark in America?' I would say, or 'But surely you didn't have that holiday with Richard until after your divorce?' I tied her up in knots without her realising it, and the idea began to seem not so fantastic after all. The final test came at Christmas.

I had noticed that Brenda was a very different woman when she was alone with me than when Laura was with us. If, for example, Laura was out in the kitchen making coffee or, as sometimes happened at the weekends, Brenda dropped in when Laura was out, she was rather cool and shy with me. Gone then were the flamboyant gestures and the provocative remarks, and Brenda would chat about village matters as mundanely as Isabel Goldsmith. Not quite the behaviour one would expect from a self-styled Messalina alone with a young and reasonably personable man. It struck me then that in the days when Brenda had been invited to village parties, and now when she still met neighbours at our parties, she never once attempted a flirtation. Were all the men too old for her to bother with? Was a slim, handsome man of going on fifty too ancient to be considered fair game for a woman who would never see thirty again? Of course they were all married, but so were her Paul and her Stephen, and, if she were to be believed, she had had no compunction about taking them away from their wives.

If she were to be believed. That was the crux of it. Not one of them wanted to spend Christmas with her. No London lover invited her to a party or offered to take her away. She would be with us, of course, for Christmas lunch, for the whole of the day, and at our Boxing Day gathering of friends and relatives. I had hung a bunch of mistletoe in our hall, and on Christmas morning I admitted her to the house myself, Laura being busy in the kitchen.

'Merry Christmas,' I said. 'Give us a kiss, Brenda,' and I took her in my arms under that mistletoe and kissed her on the mouth. She stiffened. I swear a shudder ran through her. She was as awkward, as apprehensive, as repelled as a sheltered twelve-year-old. And then I knew. Married she may have been – and it was not hard now to guess the cause of her divorce – but she had never had a lover or enjoyed an embrace or even been alone with a man longer than she could help. She was frigid. A good-looking, vivacious, healthy girl, she nevertheless had that particular disability. She was as cold as a nun. But because she couldn't bear the humiliation of admitting it, she had created for herself a fantasy life, a fantasy past, in which she queened it as a fantasy nymphomaniac.

At first I thought it a huge joke and I couldn't wait to tell Laura. But I wasn't alone with her till two in the morning and then she was asleep when I came to bed. I didn't sleep much. My elation dwindled as I realised I hadn't any real proof and that if I told Laura what I'd been up to, probing and questioning and testing, she would only be bitterly hurt and resentful. How could I tell her I'd kissed her best friend and got an icy response? That, in her absence, I'd tried flirting with her best friend and been repulsed? And then, as I thought about it, I understood what I really had discovered, that Brenda hated men, that no man would ever come and take her away or marry her and live here with her and absorb all her time. For ever she would stay here alone, living a stone's throw from us, in and out of our house daily, she and Laura growing old together.

I could have moved house, of course. I could have taken Laura away. From her friends? From the house and the countryside she loved? And what guarantee would I have had that Brenda wouldn't have moved too to be near us still? For I knew now what Brenda saw in my wife, a gullible innocent, a trusting everlastingly credulous audience whose own inexperience kept her from seeing the holes and discrepancies in those farragos of nonsense and whose pathetic determination to be worldly prevented her from showing distaste. As the dawn came and I looked with love and sorrow at Laura sleeping beside me, I knew what I must do, the only thing I could do. At the season of peace and goodwill, I decided to kill Brenda Goring for my own and Laura's good and peace.

Easier decided than done. I was buoyed up and strengthened by knowing that in everyone's eyes I would have no motive. Our neighbours thought us wonderfully charitable and tolerant to put up with Brenda at all. I resolved to be positively nice to her instead of just negatively easy-going, and as the New Year came in I took to dropping in on Brenda on my way back from the post or the village shop, and if I got home from work to find Laura alone I asked where

Brenda was and suggested we should phone her at once and ask her to dinner or for a drink. This pleased Laura enormously.

'I always felt you didn't really like Brenda, darling,' she said, 'and it made me feel rather guilty. It's marvellous that you're beginning to see how nice she really is.'

What I was actually beginning to see was how I could kill her and get away with it, for something happened which seemed to deliver her into my hands. On the outskirts of the village, in an isolated cottage, lived an elderly unmarried woman called Peggy Daley, and during the last week of January the cottage was broken into and Peggy stabbed to death with her own kitchen knife. The work of some psychopath, the police seemed to believe, for nothing had been stolen or damaged. When it appeared likely that they weren't going to find the killer, I began thinking of how I could kill Brenda in the same way so that the killing could look like the work of the same perpetrator. Just as I was working this out Laura went down with a 'flu bug she caught from Mary Williamson.

Brenda, of course, came in to nurse her, cooked my dinner for me and cleaned the house. Because everyone believed that Peggy Daley's murderer was still stalking the village, I walked Brenda home at night, even though her cottage was only a few yards up the lane or narrow path that skirted the end of our garden. It was pitch dark there as we had all strenuously opposed the installation of street lighting, and it brought me an ironical amusement to notice how Brenda flinched and recoiled when on these occasions I made her take my arm. I always made a point of going into the house with her and putting all the lights on. When Laura began to get better and all she wanted in the evenings was to sleep I sometimes went earlier to Brenda's, had a nightcap with her, and once, on leaving, I gave her a comradely kiss on the doorstep to show any observing neighbour what friends we were and how much I appreciated all Brenda's kindness to my sick wife.

Then I got the 'flu myself. At first this seemed to upset my plans, for I couldn't afford to delay too long. Already people were beginning to be less apprehensive about our marauding murderer and were getting back to their old habits of leaving their back doors unlocked. But then I saw how I could turn my illness to my advantage. On the Monday, when I had been confined to bed for three days and that ministering angel Brenda was fussing about me nearly as much as my own wife was, Laura remarked that she wouldn't go across to the Goldsmiths that evening as she had promised because it seemed wrong to leave me. Instead, if I was better by then, she would go on the Wednesday, her purpose being to help Isabel cut out a dress. Brenda, of course, might have offered to stay with me instead, and I think Laura was a little surprised that she didn't. I knew the reason and had a little quiet laugh to myself about it. It was one thing for Brenda to flaunt about, regaling us with stories of all the men she had nursed in the past, quite another to find herself alone with a not very sick man in that man's bedroom.

So I had to be sick enough to provide myself with an alibi but not sick enough to keep Laura at home. On the Wednesday morning I was feeling a good deal better. Dr Lawson looked in on his way back from his rounds in the afternoon and pronounced, after a thorough examination, that I still had phlegm on my chest. While he was in the bathroom washing his hands and doing something with his stethoscope, I held the thermometer he had stuck in my mouth against the radiator at the back of the bed. This worked better than I had hoped, worked, in fact, almost too well. The mercury went up to a hundred and three, and I played up to it by saying in a feeble voice that I felt dizzy and kept alternating between the sweats and the shivers.

'Keep him in bed,' Dr Lawson said, 'and give him plenty of warm drinks. I doubt if he could get up if he tried.'

I said rather shamefacedly that I had tried and I couldn't and that my legs felt like jelly. Immediately Laura said she wouldn't go out that night, and I blessed Lawson when he told her not to be silly. All I needed was rest and to be allowed to sleep. After a good deal of fussing and self-reproach and promises not to be gone more than two hours at the most, she finally went off at seven.

As soon as the car had departed, I got up. Brenda's house could be seen from my bedroom window, and I saw that she had lights on but no porch light. The night was dark, moonless and starless. I put trousers and a sweater on over my pyjamas and made my way downstairs.

By the time I was halfway down I knew that I needn't have pretended to be ill or bothered with the thermometer ploy. I *was* ill. I was shivering and swaying, great waves of dizziness kept coming over me, and I had to hang on to the banisters for support. That wasn't the only thing that had gone wrong. I had intended, when the deed was done and I was back home again, to cut up my coat and gloves with Laura's electric scissors and burn the pieces on our living room fire. But I couldn't find the scissors and I realised Laura must have taken them with her to her dressmaking session. Worse than that, there was no fire alight. Our central heating was very efficient and we only had an open fire for the pleasure and cosiness of it, but Laura hadn't troubled to light one while I was upstairs ill. At that moment I nearly gave up. But it was then or never. I would never again have such circumstances and such an alibi. Either kill her now, I thought, or live in an odious *ménage à trois* for the rest of my life.

We kept the raincoats and gloves we used for gardening in a cupboard in the kitchen by the back door. Laura had left only the hall light on, and I didn't think it would be wise to switch on any more. In the semi-darkness I fumbled about in the cupboard for my raincoat, found it and put it on. It seemed tight on me, my body was so stiff and sweaty, but I managed to button it up, and then I put on the gloves. I took with me one of our kitchen knives and let myself out by the back door. It wasn't a frosty night, but raw and cold and damp.

I went down the garden, up the lane and into the garden of Brenda's cottage. I had to feel my way round the side of the house, for there was no light there at all. But the kitchen light was on and the back door unlocked. I tapped and let myself in without waiting to be asked. Brenda, in full evening rig, glittery sweater, gilt necklace, long skirt, was cooking her solitary supper. And then, for the first time ever, when it didn't matter any more, when it was too late, I felt pity for her. There she was, a handsome, rich, gifted woman with the reputation of a seductress, but in reality as destitute of people who really cared for her as poor old Peggy Daley had been; there she was, dressed for a party, heating up tinned spaghetti in a cottage kitchen at the back of beyond.

She turned round, looking apprehensive, but only, I think, because she was always afraid when we were alone that I would try to make love to her.

'What are you doing out of bed?' she said, and then, 'Why are you wearing those clothes?'

I didn't answer her. I stabbed her in the chest again and again. She made no sound but a little choking moan and she crumpled up on the floor. Although I had known how it would be, had hoped for it, the shock was so great and I had already been feeling so swimmy and strange, that all I wanted was to throw myself down too and close my eyes and sleep. That was impossible. I turned off the cooker. I checked that there was no blood on my trousers and my shoes, though of course there was plenty on the raincoat, and then I staggered out, switching off the light behind me.

I don't know how I found my way back, it was so dark and by then I was light-headed and my heart was drumming. I just had the presence of mind to strip off the raincoat and the gloves and push them into our garden incinerator. In the morning I would have to get up enough strength to burn them before Brenda's body was found. The knife I washed and put back in the drawer.

Laura came back about five minutes after I had got myself to bed. She had been gone less than half an hour. I turned over and managed to raise myself up to ask her why she was back so soon. It seemed to me that she had a strange distraught look about her.

'What's the matter?' I mumbled. 'Were you worried about me?'

'No,' she said, 'no,' but she didn't come up close to me or put her hand on my forehead. 'It was – Isabel Goldsmith told me something – I was upset – I . . . It's no use talking about it now, you're too ill.' She said in a sharper tone than I had ever heard her use, 'Can I get you anything?'

'I just want to sleep,' I said.

'I shall sleep in the spare room. Good night.'

That was reasonable enough, but we had never slept apart before during the whole of our marriage, and she could hardly have been afraid of catching the 'flu, having only just got over it herself. But I was in no state to worry about that, and I fell into the troubled nightmare-ridden sleep of fever. I remember one of those dreams. It was of Laura finding Brenda's body herself, a not unlikely eventuality.

However, she didn't find it. Brenda's cleaner did. I knew what must have happened because I saw the police car arrive from my window. An hour or so later Laura came in to tell me the news which she had got from Jack Williamson.

'It must have been the same man who killed Peggy,' she said.

I felt better already. Things were going well. 'My poor darling,' I said, 'you must feel terrible, you were such close friends.'

She said nothing. She straightened my bedclothes and left the room. I knew I should have to get up and burn the contents of the incinerator, but I couldn't get up. I put my feet out and reached for the floor, but it was as if the floor came up to meet me and threw me back again. I wasn't over-worried. The police would think what Laura thought, what everyone must think.

That afternoon they came, a chief inspector and a sergeant. Laura brought them up to our bedroom and they talked to us together. The chief inspector said he understood we were close friends of the dead woman, wanted to know when we had last seen her and what we had been doing on the previous evening. Then he asked if we had any idea at all as to who had killed her.

'That maniac who murdered the other woman, of course,' said Laura.

'I can see you don't read the papers,' he said.

Usually we did. It was my habit to read a morning paper in the office and to bring an evening paper home with me. But I had been at home ill. It turned out that a man had been arrested on the previous morning for the murder of Peggy Daley. The shock made me flinch and I'm sure I turned pale. But the policemen didn't seem to notice. They thanked us for our co-operation, apologised for disturbing a sick man, and left. When they had gone I asked Laura what Isabel had said to upset her the night before. She came up to me and put her arms round me.

'It doesn't matter now,' she said. 'Poor Brenda's dead and it was a horrible way to die, but – well, I must be very wicked – but I'm not sorry. Don't look at me like that, darling. I love you and I know you love me, and we must forget her and be as we used to be. You know what I mean.'

I didn't, but I was glad whatever it was had blown over. I had enough on my plate without a coldness between me and my wife. Even though Laura was beside me that night, I hardly slept for worrying about the stuff in that incinerator. In the morning I put up the best show I could of being much better. I dressed and announced, in spite of Laura's expostulations, that I was going into the garden. The police were there already, searching all our gardens, actually digging up Brenda's.

They left me alone that day and the next, but they came in once and interviewed Laura on her own. I asked her what they had said, but she passed it off quite lightly. I supposed she didn't think I was well enough to be told they had been enquiring about my movements and my attitude towards Brenda.

'Just a lot of routine questions, darling,' she said, but I was sure she was afraid for me, and a barrier of her fear for me and mine for myself came up between us. It seems incredible but that Sunday we hardly spoke to each other and when we did Brenda's name wasn't mentioned. In the evening we sat in silence my arm round Laura, her head on my shoulder, waiting, waiting . . .

The morning brought the police with a search warrant. They asked Laura to go into the living room and me to wait in the study. I knew then that it was only a matter of time. They would find the knife, and of course they would find Brenda's blood on it. I had been feeling so ill when I cleaned it that now I could no longer remember whether I had scrubbed it or simply rinsed it under the tap.

After a long while the chief inspector came in alone.

'You told us you were a close friend of Miss Goring's.'

'I was friendly with her,' I said, trying to keep my voice steady. 'She was my wife's friend.'

He took no notice of this. 'You didn't tell us you were on intimate terms with her, that you were, in point of fact, having a sexual relationship with her.'

Nothing he could have said would have astounded me more.

'That's absolute rubbish!'

'Is it? We have it on sound authority.'

'What authority?' I said. 'Or is that the sort of thing you're not allowed to say?'

'I see no harm in telling you,' he said easily. 'Miss Goring herself informed two women friends of hers in London of the fact. She told one of your neighbours she met at a party in your house. You were seen to spend evenings alone with Miss Goring while your wife was ill, and we have a witness who saw you kissing her good night.'

Now I knew what it was that Isabel Goldsmith had told Laura which had so distressed her. The irony of it, the irony . . . Why hadn't I, knowing Brenda's reputation and knowing Brenda's fantasies, suspected what construction would be put on my assumed friendship with her? Here was motive, the lack of which I had relied on as my last resort. Men do kill their mistresses, from jealousy, from frustration, from fear of discovery.

But surely I could turn Brenda's fantasies to my own use?

'She had dozens of men friends, lovers, whatever you like to call them. Any of them could have killed her.'

'On the contrary,' said the chief inspector, 'apart from her ex-husband who is in Australia, we have been able to discover no man in her life but yourself.'

I cried out desperately, 'I didn't kill her! I swear I didn't.'

He looked surprised. 'Oh, we know that.' For the first time he called me sir. 'We know that, sir. No one is accusing you of anything. We have Dr Lawson's word for it that you were physically incapable of leaving your bed that night, and the raincoat and gloves we found in your incinerator are not your property.'

Fumbling in the dark, swaying, the sleeves of the raincoat too short, the shoulders too tight . . . 'Why are you wearing those clothes?' she had asked before I stabbed her.

'I want you to try and keep calm, sir,' he said very gently. But I have never been calm since. I have confessed again and again, I have written statements, I have expostulated, raved, gone over with them every detail of what I did that night, I have wept. Then I said nothing. I could only stare at him. 'I came in here to you, sir,' he said, 'simply to confirm a fact of which we were already certain, and to ask you if you would care to accompany your wife to the police station where she will be charged with the murder of Miss Brenda Goring.'

# MAURICE
# RICHARDSON

---

## Tower Of Silence

I'm fond of my club. There is something deliciously reassuring in its leathery eunuchoid cosiness and all-male meals. Yes, I know waitresses have taken over; but ours are the right type, respectable old nannies, not those menopausal Medusas wafting scent over your game pie.

Of course it has its defects. One of them is a convention of mateyness that makes it difficult to escape bores; but it's extremely comfortable and has a good library. I only wish I could spend more time in it but as a budding psychiatrist, registrar at a large suburban mental hospital, I'm lucky to get half a day a fortnight.

This day I was cosseting myself. I'd just shaken off an attack of 'flu and felt I deserved a treat. I lunched alone, an invalid's lunch of foie gras, chicken fricassee, and claret. Then I retired with a large glass of tawny port and coffee to the red leather sofa in the bow window of the smoking room which is the most euphoric sofa I know.

There are several doctors among the members. We've quite a medical tradition. I was once told this was the only club in London where you could find two venerealogists giving the under-porter a free consultation on the billiard table. And we include a sprinkling of psychiatrists, among them two analysts who started as Freudian and Jungian enemies and have now become bosom chums in some nebulous doctrinal half-way house, and are rumoured to exchange patients every leap year. All of us refrain from talking shop, all of us with one exception. And now, as I opened my eyes from my postprandial coma, I found him sitting beside me: the one and only Dr Gilhooley, the Ancient of Days, or as some call him the Ancient Mariner. He's certainly the oldest member, but it's incorrect to call him the Club Bore because he can be extremely interesting. However he likes to take his time over it, and unless I've got an afternoon off I prefer not to be the one of three that he stoppeth.

He is a small well-proportioned man of the type whose heart doesn't have to do too much work. His face has wizened into a faintly reptilian cast but his hazel eyes still shine and his movements have a lizard-like agility. He always wears comfortable looking, well-cut flannel suits and soft silk shirts with flapping collars.

'I was hoping you would wake,' he said. 'I wanted to congratulate you on your DPM.'

The Diploma of Psychological Medicine is a compulsory hurdle in the career of the budding psychiatrist. It was cute of him to know that I'd passed it.

'I hope,' he said, with an old man's cackle which was meant to signal a joke,

441

'that you haven't overstrained your cerebral cortex. You remember Batty Tuke's hypothesis?'

'I'm afraid I don't,' I said. 'I think he was a bit before my time.'

'He was indeed. Sir J Batty Tuke. That was his real name. He was a big noise in Edwardian psychiatry. He held that over-exertion of the brain was a frequent cause of insanity. One of his ideas was – whisper it – that many a young doctor never recovered from passing his examinations.'

I ordered two more glasses of port. Dr Gilhooley approved of tawny as less onerous on arteries and alimentary canal than vintage, and I sat back at ease, ready for more curiosities of Edwardian psychiatry. But with the liability of old age his mood changed abruptly. He was off on a detailed description, not far short of total recall, of the film of *Murder on the Orient Express*.

'Now tell me,' he said, 'would you say that a situation, in which a dozen people conspire together to murder one individual in such a way that suspicion cannot fall on any one of them, is likely to be found in real life?'

I said I thought it must be very rare, though I supposed you might find it in a closed institution like a prison or a ship or a barracks.

'But not, you would think, in a mental hospital?'

'Good heavens no. At least I should hope not.'

'And yet such a murder was committed in Wendover which, if I mistake not, is where you are at present a registrar.'

'Is that really true? It must have been a very long time ago.'

'It was. Considerably before you were born. Would you like to hear the story? Of course if one were telling it to a lay audience one would set the scene. For you that's not necessary . . .'

Wendover is one of those huge mental hospitals, like Hanwell and Friern which were built in the middle of the last century. It's a Betjemanic architect's nightmare in greyish yellow brick. Only in the last fifteen years or so has it become decongested and even partly modernised. It still leaves an enormous amount to be desired but compared to what it was I daresay it's a demi-paradise.

Dr Gilhooley took a large swig of port and licked his lips which I noticed were bluish and faintly mottled like some rare orchid. 'I will now proceed with this atrocious history,' he said. 'The period is about the turn of the century. The hospital looked much the same then as it does now. But there was one feature you will not have seen because it has been pulled down. That was the tower, which commanded a view of the entire hospital grounds. It was a watch tower. In those days nearly all patients were certified and the authorities were obsessed with escapes. Bear this tower in mind . . . I hardly know how to convey to you the difference between mental hospitals then and now. Let me see, when did you qualify?'

'Seven years ago.'

'In that case you've never experienced a male refractory ward in the days before the chlorpromazine revolution. There were fights and tussles the whole day long. Patients in states of acute catatonic excitement would be confined to the padded rooms. Hypomanics would pester and incite the others until trouble started . . .'

'Of course,' I said, 'only a small proportion of patients were excitable at the same time.'

'True enough. But the role of the staff, both doctors and nurses, was largely custodial. Bless my soul, why when I was a young man the male nurses wore dark blue uniforms and peaked caps like prison warders. And a lot of them ate their dinners off newspapers. Not that they were any the worse for that. Some of the unlettered types made good nurses. They had a kind of natural animal sympathy.'

I said I wondered what they would have thought of a really modern mental hospital run on therapeutic community lines with daily group meetings of doctors, patients and nurses.

'They'd have had a fit,' Dr Gilhooley said.

'Mind you,' I said, 'even in our enlightened days you sometimes get a lot of opposition. When ward community methods were first introduced there was often bitterness among the staff. They felt insecure, not so much afraid, if you follow me, but anxious lest their authority was going to be taken away from them.'

Dr Gilhooley pressed his lips together. 'Do you know what a bear-pit is?' he said. 'I don't mean what the Elizabethans had instead of television. A bear-pit in old fashioned mental hospital parlance was a field about a hundred yards square surrounded by high wooden palings. There might be a few trees growing in it and there would certainly be some seats. Every fine afternoon some two hundred of the more severely ill male patients would be turned loose in the bear-pit for their daily exercise. You might see a young man writing on a tree with a stick, like Orlando in *As You Like It* only he would be chasing his writing round the trunk. There would be catatonics standing about in odd stereotyped positions. Some would be stalking round and round at a furious pace. Nobody spoke to anybody. Nurses in uniform sat on the seats. Bear-pits were not uncommon until right up to the last war. That gives you some idea of conditions. Of course there was a lot of variation between hospitals. But they were hopelessly understaffed. You hear a lot about that today, but when Wendover held two thousand six hundred patients there was one Medical Superintendent and four medical officers. The Superintendent was a law unto himself. If he was slack, and the atmosphere flaccid, the MOs might degenerate. In one or two hospitals I've known they did nothing but drink and play snooker all round the clock.'

'Booze and billiards,' I said. 'The occupational diseases of primitive psychiatry. But aren't you laying it on a bit thick, Dr Gilhooley?'

'No, my dear boy, I promise you I'm not. There were foci of enlightenment here and there. But as I say everything depended on the Superintendents. These had their eccentricities. There was one I served under who was mad about cricket and believed it had special therapeutic virtues. When he advertised for an MO he used to put, "Only keen cricketers need apply. Slow bowler preferred." Then there was dear old Chesney who was Superintendent at Coverdale. He was crazy about hydrotherapy. The continuous bath. It used to be very popular at one time especially for manic-depressives. If you look up "Baths" in the standard English Dictionary of Psychological Medicine for eighteen ninety-two you'll find sixteen different varieties. That's as true as I'm sitting here. Of course, facilities were extremely limited so Chesney had a gigantic shallow tank constructed . . .'

I looked at my watch. Nearly time for strong tea and anchovy toast. Dr Gilhooley was delighted at having a captive audience for so long. He snapped his fingers with pleasure. Still fully wound up, he unreeled a string of bizarre anecdotes. At a mental hospital in the Channel Islands there had been a schizophrenic, a man of no education, who, if you handed him a fossil, would give you a most vivid description of the landscape of its period. The Superintendent used to show him off to visitors. At another hospital a Scandinavian sailor had passed at one single evacuation a pound and three quarters of pebbles. In nineteen thirty-one Dr Alexander Cannon, a medical officer on the staff of Colney Hatch had been requested to resign his appointment because he had written a book called *The Invisible Influence* in which he claimed to have levitated, together with eighteen pieces of luggage, across a chasm in Tibet . . .

'But I am digressing,' Gilhooley said. 'Senility, of course. Now I was going to tell you a horrible story, wasn't I? What was it about?'

'It happened at Wendover in the old days. Something to do with a tower.'

'Of course. Of course. Well, now, it all began with the reign of a new Superintendent. Wantage, the old Superintendent who retired had been one of the passive custodial type. "Let's have a quiet peaceful hospital," he used to say. There was always a strong smell of paraldehyde in his wards. He was bone lazy. He was a member of the Garrick and used to play bridge there a lot. It got so that when they wanted him to attend to hospital business they would telephone the club and say: "Urgent message for Dr Wantage. Patient's escaped." When he got back, breathless, to Wendover they'd greet him with: "It's all right, doctor. Patient's been recovered. But while you're here would you mind signing these forms?"

'Well, the new Superintendent, Dr Makins, was the exact opposite of old Wantage, burning with reformist zeal. And of course all his reforms meant more work for the staff. He insisted that terminal schizophrenics, who had been left to vegetate, should be taken for walks by two nurses every day. He stalked through the hospital regrading patients, unlocking locked wards. In no time he had the staff loathing his guts.'

'What about the medical staff?' I asked.

'They had to toe the line, of course. They didn't like it, but there was nothing they could do about it. Anyway they weren't so far gone in sloth that they couldn't respond to Makins's therapeutic enthusiasms. All might have been well if it hadn't been for the tragedy, which I'm just coming to.'

Dr Gilhooley broke off to offer me a fat Turkish cigarette from an elderly but still posh-looking leather case. He followed up with a history of cigarette-smoking in England from the Crimean War onwards, with special reference to the virtues of Macedonian as opposed to Virginian tobaccos. I steered him back to Wendover by tapping the glass of my watch.

'You are eager for the denouement, what I believe is known as the pay-off. Very well. I shan't keep you waiting any longer. Now among the patients Dr Makins had upgraded was a man named Beavis. When Makins first examined him he was in the Refractory Ward. He'd been diagnosed as manic–depressive, manic phase with distinct paranoid tendencies. This, as you know, is not an uncommom combination, and it can lead to very uncertain and aggressive behaviour. Beavis was a middle-aged man of some intelligence and education. He made a favourable impression on Makins, was quiet and orderly and free from any signs of delusions. He complained that he was being kept strictly confined to the ward and not allowed to go out or occupy himself in any way. Makins asked him if he had any particular occupation in mind and he said: "Yes, carpentry." Makins discussed his case with the Medical Officer in charge of the male side, and the Ward Charge, who were both in attendance. He told them in his opinion Beavis had recovered from his manic attack and should be upgraded with a view to possible discharge in a matter of weeks. The Ward Charge begged to differ. He said Beavis was a very tricky patient, given to sudden fits of violence when you least expected them. "I warn you, Doctor Makins, sir," he said respectfully, "he's very deceptive. He'll be good as gold for days at a time and then without any warning he'll turn nasty. And of course when the moon's at the full there's no holding him."

'Makins wasn't standing for this. "Don't give me that superstitious rubbish, my man," he snapped. "It's not surprising if a patient of his intelligence gets irritable when he's kept cooped up like this. I'm regrading him to Ward Three as from today until further notice. See that he's taken over there before dinner time."

'So Beavis was upgraded to Ward Three, and there was more muttering among the male nurses. I always say that if you take your hospital nursing staff by and large you'll find a small proportion of saints, a more or less average collection of people who'll be both nice and nasty, and a small proportion of bullies. Among the average bunch there may be not a few who'll swing one way or the other, nice or nasty, all according to the general tone of the place. And that comes from the top.'

Dr Gilhooley darted me one of his bright lacertilian glances to make sure I was listening and poured us out two cupfuls of dark brown tea strong enough to induce an attack of anxiety neurosis. 'Of course,' he said, 'it must be admitted that Makins was not a tactful man. Reformers seldom are. He was a congenital fusspot and he had a genius for putting people's backs up. But he is not to be blamed for what happened. No he is not to be blamed. For a little while all went well. Beavis's equilibrium remained undisturbed. He worked long hours in the carpenter's shop, making a model of a Roman galley, and gave no trouble in the ward. And then the precipitating factor arrived on the scene. You may say that with psychotics there is always a precipitating factor ready to hand. That may or may not be so. It doesn't alter the fact that this was a piece of damned bad luck. In the course of his reforms Dr Makins, as well as regrading patients, had been shifting some of the nurses around, for he thought, rightly no doubt in some cases, that several of them had been too long in the same ward. The changes were made after a confabulation between Makins and the Head Male Attendant, Tunstall. This official, equivalent to the Matron on the Women's side, was a very powerful figure in the hospital hierarchy of those days. He was allowed the dignity of wearing a swallow tail coat at hospital functions. Tunstall was very jealous of his own personal authority, and opposed to any libertarian reforms on principle; but being a Pecksniffian hypocrite, as well as a man of considerable natural organising ability, he'd managed to keep up a suitable façade of co-operation in front of the new Superintendent. Now one nurse who had been moved from the Refractory Ward was a certain Birkbeck, a youngish man from the north. A bit of a rough diamond. Like not a few male nurses he'd been a soldier. He was genial on the surface and popular with his colleagues but he was inclined to be rather a bully. And between him and Beavis there was a long standing feud. Beavis had sneered at him and touched him on the raw with that intuitive feeling for the weak spot which paranoid manics possess. There had been one rough house between them and the Ward Charge had accepted Birkbeck's version. And now Birkbeck was moved to Ward Three and the first patient he saw was Beavis.

'You might think that the appearance of his deadly enemy would depress Beavis, like a prisoner who's been recaptured; and that at first was what it seemed to do; but only at first. You can imagine the tension that was generated between these two: the intelligent educated imaginative patient and the ignorant loutish male nurse. It was like a thunderstorm piling up in stages. One stage was when Birkbeck persuaded Oakes, the Ward Charge in Three, that Beavis should be searched every time he came back from his carpentry.'

'Not,' I said, 'an altogether unreasonable suggestion, surely?'

'Possibly not. But the searching, I understand, was carried out by Birkbeck with the maximum of indignity. Beavis retaliated by compiling a notebook which he called 'Crimes of the Male Nurse Henry Birkbeck'. It was found afterwards in his locker. The final stage was reached when a mischievous patient told Beavis that Birkbeck, and the Ward Charge, and the Head Male Attendant, and the Medical Officer responsible for the Ward were all petitioning the Superintendent to have Beavis sent back to the Refractory Ward.

'That afternoon the storm burst. Beavis comes in from the carpenter's shop and stands meekly in front of Birkbeck waiting to be searched. Birkbeck bends forward a little as he runs his hands over him. Beavis whips out a small chisel which he's been hiding up the sleeve of his overalls and drives it into Birkbeck's neck, slap into the carotid. Blood spouts. Birkbeck collapses and is dead in a matter of seconds.

'Staff come running. Beavis is taken to the Refractory Ward and locked up alone in a full padded room nearest the entrance to the ward. So that's your first murder for you.'

'No mystery there,' I said.

'No indeed. And not much about the next either. Well, as you may imagine

446

the shock was felt right through the hospital. Beavis, of course, as a certified patient, was outside the law. However, there were demands for a detailed investigation from several quarters: the Commissioners, the local police and coroner's office, the Asylum Workers Federation, and not least from the Superintendent himself. He didn't exactly improve matters by calling meetings of the male nursing staff, in relays, and telling them that they mustn't imagine that what had happened was going to make the slightest difference to his policy of reform. It was very late that night before everyone settled down to sleep, and there was a big run on the chloral. And next morning what do you think they found? Surely you can guess?'

'Oh come, now,' I said. 'Even if I could, which I can't, I wouldn't want to spoil your pleasure in telling me.'

Dr Gilhooley rubbed his aged mottled hands. 'Next morning,' he croaked dramatically, 'on the concrete flooring at the foot of the tower, they found the body of Beavis. His skull was fractured. There were no marks of violence upon him. Now what do you make of that?'

'I suppose,' I said sportingly, trying to keep up the mystery, 'it could have been suicide.'

'Suicide my stethoscope! It was murder, carried out with the precision of a military operation. Motive? Partly vengeance but mainly a demonstration to intimidate the Superintendent, a warning to him to drop his reforms. Tunstall, the Head Male Attendant, was the organising genius behind it all. The killing of Birkbeck brought to a head the trouble that had been brewing between him and the Superintendent. Tunstall called a meeting of twelve of the male nurses whom he thought were most incensed. There was some stump oratory on the lines of: "Our colleague has been foully murdered with deliberate malice aforethought by one who, though he is a certified patient, knew full well what he did, and all because of the new and perilous system of licence and misrule which has been imposed upon us. If we do not take action now, and drastic action at that, our lives will no longer be safe." And so on and so forth. They then put it to the vote and solemnly announced that Beavis was guilty of murder . . .

'They stole quietly along to the Refractory Ward where Beavis was asleep. They put a strait-jacket on him, and told him he had been tried in his absence and found guilty of the wilful murder of Birkbeck. They were taking the law into their own hands and were going to execute just sentence upon him. Then they gagged him and carried him out of the ward and up the steps of the tower. They removed the strait-jacket and the gag and slung him over.'

'But what about the MO on night duty?'

'They hadn't forgotten him. They'd laced his cocoa. They'd thought of everything, even to removing any traces of the gag.'

'But wasn't there a frightful row? You don't mean to say they got away with it?'

'There was hell to pay. But there was absolutely no evidence to show that Beavis hadn't chucked himself off the top of the tower. They'd been very careful how they'd handled him and they'd planted on him a master key which opened all locks in the hospital, making sure it had his fingerprints on it and no one else's. The suggested explanation was that Beavis had somehow managed to pinch a key from the Head Male Attendant's office. It could neither be proved nor disproved. So the Coroner's jury brought in an open verdict. The Superintendent swore they were a lot of murdering blackguards. The men threatened an action for slander. The atmosphere got so strained that the authorities transferred the Superintendent and appointed a new one.

'Tell me,' I said, 'were you yourself on the staff at the time? Surely not?'

'Indeed I was not,' said Gilhooley. 'That would make me a centenarian. I was told the story when I first joined the hospital staff as a very junior MO just qualified. I was told it over cocoa on night duty by an elderly ward charge who had been a young nurse at the time. He took no part in it himself, but he heard all about it . . . Well, there you are. It's not a very nice story but we're not a very nice species.'

I heaved a deep sententious sigh. 'Ah well,' I said. 'In the great global therapeutic community of the future which is our only salvation . . . .'

Dr Gilhooley interrupted me sharply. 'Good gracious! Is that your idea of the millennium? It's not mine . . .'

'What is?' I asked.

'A nice snug club and a captive audience.'

# GEORGE SIMS

## Family Butcher

Pasterne is arguably the prettiest village in the Hambleden valley. Skirmett, Frieth, Fingest and Ibstone all have their attractions as does Hambleden itself, and Turville is surmounted by a delightful windmill perched on a hill-top, a rarity indeed in the Chilterns, but Pasterne most conforms to a picture-postcard village. There is the large green, immaculately trimmed, known as Pasterne Pound, with carefully preserved oak stocks, and a dozen brick and flint cottages grouped round the green just as if some Edwardian water colourist had placed them there for a painting. The village pond is a fine example too, kept fresh by a spring, with white ducks and mallards, and occasionally a nesting pair of swans. Postcards on sale in the village stores-cum-Post Office sell well in the summer months, particularly those featuring the pond and the rather eccentrically placed Norman church which appears to have turned its back on Pasterne due to its being the sole relic of an even earlier settlement. But people in picture-postcard villages live lives much the same as the rest of us.

Another popular view of the village shows a northern aspect of the Pound with Daniel Patchin's butcher shop centrally placed, together with his Pound Cottage and the copse which hides Lord Benningworth's Manor House. Patchin's shop was originally an Elizabethan cottage that has been a good deal refurbished over the centuries, but the exterior, apart from the small shop window, must appear much as it did originally with its massive black oak beams and the plaster walls that are freshly white-washed each year. The name Daniel Patchin is in large white italic letters on the black façade, together with the trade description Family Butcher in smaller capitals.

Patchin's ancient establishment and the Post Office Stores are the only village shops: both are attractive and 'quaint', looking rather like the toy shops favoured by children of less sophisticated epochs. And Patchin's shop too is a model one for he is fanatical about personal cleanliness and hygiene: he wears a fresh apron twice a day, and the wash-basin at the rear of the shop is much used but kept spotless as are the display area and the large bench where Patchin works, 'looking more like a surgeon than a butcher', as Lord Benningworth once described him to some friends. Patchin's shop window always has a sparse display: a brace of pheasants, which he may well have shot himself, a hare, a local chicken or two, and one specimen of the prime meat he has for sale. Inside the shop there is a similarly small amount of meat on show: very likely just a side of Scotch beef hanging up with a Welsh shoulder of lamb. Under the impeccable refrigerated display counter there will be some of the famous Patchin sausages. Anything else that is required Daniel Patchin will have to fetch from the large cold room which takes up most of the rear portion of the shop.

The same shop when run by Daniel's father Gabriel was well known throughout the Chilterns in the 1930s, as was Reuben Patchin's before that: Daniel Patchin has an equally enviable reputation. Though the population of the village is not large enough to support such a thriving business, and Lord Benningworth who owns most of the village and the surrounding land is against more houses being built locally, callers come regularly from High Wycombe, Henley and Marlow for their meat. The Patchin sausages are still made exactly as detailed in Reuben's 1912 recipe with generous amounts of pork, herbs, spices and freshly ground black pepper; they bear no resemblance at all to the products churned out in factories, and they attract customers from as far away as Slough and Oxford.

Daniel Patchin, a quiet, sometimes taciturn man, is widely respected. He seems to live for his work and is busy throughout a long day for five and a half days each week. Wednesday is early closing and that afternoon he devotes to either fishing or shooting according to the season. When he returned from the Korean war Daniel Patchin came to an amicable unwritten agreement with Lord Benningworth that on Sundays he would act as an unpaid forester for the estate, keeping Benningworth's copses and woodland in good order, felling all diseased treees and clearing undergrowth, in return for which service he was allowed to keep all the timber he wanted. Every Sunday is devoted to this occupation and Patchin has a wood-yard at the back of his cottage where villagers can purchase logs and firewood.

The Patchin family has lived in Pasterne for centuries but the Benningworth connection with the locality is even more ancient: Lord Benningworth can trace his ancestry back in this country to a Baron Will de Benningworth in 1220, and there are stone effigies of another Benningworth Knight and his Lady installed in the church in 1290. The churchyard also houses many Patchin graves, but the earliest is dated 1695 with the epitaph:

> *Good people all as you*
> *Pas by looke round*
> *See how Corpes' do lye*
> *For as you are som time Ware We*
> *And as we are so must you be*

Occasionally in an evening Daniel Patchin may stroll round the churchyard, eyeing the graves, particularly those of his own family. He likes those epitaphs which hint of un-Christian attitudes for he has a cynical, mordant sense of humour; he is not a church-goer. During his army service in Korea he found out that human life there was as cheap as that of turkeys at Christmas and he adopted a stoic's attitude to life and death. Serving as an infantryman he was awarded the Military Medal for his bravery in hand-to-hand fighting and won the nick-name 'Pig-sticker' from his comrades for his skill with the bayonet.

Daniel Patchin leads a very quiet life, devoted to work and country pursuits including gardening in the evenings. Lord Benningworth will sometimes stroll to the edge of his copse with a friend to point out Patchin's garden with its fine rose-beds and lines of potatoes, peas and beans as straight as guardsmen on parade. Patchin's wife Angela is ten years younger than him and before the marriage was known as a pretty, jolly and slightly flighty girl in Skirmett where she was brought up in a large farming family. The Patchins have no children as Angela proved to be barren, and over the ten years of marriage she has taken on the Patchin family's traits of seriousness and quiet outward mildness. She is a natural blonde with very fair, clear skin who blushes easily: any compliment from Benningworth's son and heir before he left to work in America would always make her change colour. She works behind the till in a cubicle-like office in the shop on Patchin's busiest days, always on Friday and Saturday, and occasionally on Thursday. Patchin employs a boy who makes himself generally useful on Friday evenings and Saturday mornings, otherwise he does all the work himself. He is a stocky man with massive muscles, enormously strong. Behind the shop there is a large shed which was used for all the slaughtering for the business up till about twenty years ago, and that is where Patchin despatches local poultry and scores of turkeys and geese at Christmas.

It was on a glorious late May afternoon that Daniel Patchin first became suspicious of his wife. It was a Monday and at lunch she had said that she would go for a walk in the afternoon. Returning at five she looked in at the shop to ask if he would like a cup of tea. He nodded and asked if she had enjoyed the walk. She hesitated and he looked up from the mincing machine to see that she had blushed and was nervously fiddling with the buttons on her blouse as if to make sure they were all fastened. It would be difficult to imagine a more observant man than Daniel Patchin: his whole life both at work and during his time away from the shop had sharpened his perceptions. He had made a life-time study of his customers and of nature; it was his sole inactive hobby. The slightest change in a pensioner's expression, even the movement of an eye, was enough to tell Patchin that he was proffering a too expensive piece of meat; the faintest ripple at the end of a roach 'swim' caught his notice as did the sound of a twig snapping. When she did not reply about the obvious pleasures of a country walk on a perfect May afternoon, Patchin covered his wife's loss for words with a quick comment about an old woman who always called in for broth bones on a Monday.

When Angela left the shop Patchin gave her back an intense look, noticing that she had changed completely from the clothes she had worn at lunch. When she returned with the tray of tea, she had covered her pretty white blouse with an old brown cardigan. She was still nervous, restless, very slightly ill at ease. Patchin knew that she was a hopeless liar but did not ask any more questions. There was a fresh smell of lemon soap and Patchin knew she had washed her face, probably plunging it repeatedly into cold water to get rid of the faint, pink flush. Again he covered her silence with talk of how he might go down to the river that evening. The season for coarse-fishing did not start till mid-June but it was something he occasionally did out of season, inspecting favourite angling haunts to see how they had been affected by the high level of the Thames in winter.

During the next few weeks he added to his short list of pastimes the one of observing his wife: nothing that she did escaped him, even the merest hint of exasperation or frustration was filed away silently in his head – but nothing unusual ever attracted a comment from him.

It would not have required special ability as an observer to note Angela Patchin's revived interest in her clothes; even on Monday mornings when she did her weekly wash and on Wednesdays when she usually cleaned Pound Cottage from top to bottom she stopped wearing her old navy skirt and blossomed out in a new green one worn with a pretty apron, or jeans. She went to the Marks and Spencer store in Reading ostensibly to buy a summer frock but returned with several packages.

One Monday afternoon when Angela had gone for another walk Patchin closed the shop for a quarter of an hour and thoroughly inspected her chest of drawers. He took meticulous care in moving and replacing the various things; he found several new items of underwear including a particularly skimpy pair of knickers and a brassière designed to thrust size thirty-six breasts up and outwards as if proffering them to some lusty lad in a Restoration play. But which lusty lad? – that was the question that teased Daniel Patchin's brain, taking his attention away from his work so that he tended for the first time in his life to become a little absent-minded and not quite the usual model of efficiency. It was immediately noted by the villagers – 'Seems more human somehow', was the general verdict though expressed in different ways.

For a while Patchin speculated as to whether Lord Benningworth's son had returned to Pasterne and was again flattering Angela: if so it seemed a more serious matter than before, now apparently extending to her amply filled blouse. But an inquiry, casually phrased, to the Benningworths' housekeeper informed Patchin that the heir to the estate was still working happily in New York and did not plan to return home before Christmas.

Patchin's reaction to Angela's unusual behaviour varied considerably. At times he became quite fascinated by his secret observation in a detached way, as he had once studied an elusive old pike in a pool near Hambleden Mill: for weeks throughout one autumn he had tried various baits to entice the wily monster until he realised that the pike could be stirred into action only by a fish with fresh blood on it; so Patchin had served up a dace, liberally doused in blood, and the pike had succumbed. At other times Patchin experienced a feeling of cold fury that someone was stealing his wife from him – he was quite certain that it was happening. Once he woke with a horrid start in the middle of the night convinced that the telephone had rung just once, and then lay awake consumed with feelings of jealousy and twisted lust – he did not fall asleep till just before the alarm bell rang at six.

Perhaps Angela's changed attitude to sex was the most obvious give-away. Before the Monday afternoon walks and the new clothes she seemed to have regarded it as a rather boring routine matter to be managed as quickly as possible before turning away to sleep. Now she never turned away and was always ready for sex, keener than he could ever remember her being. Her kisses were open-mouthed and lingering, her embraces passionate and urgent – as he brooded on this he realised that 'urgent' was the key word – that was it, she was urging him on to more effort so that he resembled, when her eyes were closed, her other, very passionate lover. Even after an orgasm she was unsatisfied, longing for something else. It would be impossible to describe the various feelings Patchin experienced as his wife became ever more knowing in bed, with wanton behaviour and explicit movements trying to get him to obtain the results she enjoyed elsewhere. One night she wanted him to make love in a new position and as she determinedly pushed him into place he could see the grim joke of it so clearly that he nearly laughed. Nothing could make it more plain that Angela had a very virile, enthusiastic lover, much more skilled at the amatory arts than he would ever be; a lover who liked first to be inflamed by skimpy knickers and a 'display' brassière, and then performed perfectly.

It was not until a Friday in the middle of June that Patchin was able to indentify his cuckold enemy. He disturbed Angela while she was making a phone call when he entered Pound Cottage that lunch time a few minutes earlier than usual. As he opened the door the telephone was slammed down and Angela ran upstairs to cover her confusion. That afternoon Ray Johnson, the youngest postman in the area, called in at the shop ostensibly for a pound of sausages and some bacon. Johnson grinned over at Angela in the little office, calling out: 'Afternoon Mrs Patchin.' Angela did not reply but just nodded, flushing very slightly. Apart from that tell-tale flush there was something subtle about the way Johnson addressed her, with just an inflection of the 'Mrs Patchin', as though the formal mode of address was something of a joke between the pair. Daniel Patchin took his time in the cold storage room to give them a chance for a few words. The moment he opened the door Ray Johnson stopped talking and grinned foolishly as though he had forgotten what he was going to say.

Idiot, Patchin thought, you young idiot, but passed over the momentary awkwardness for Johnson by commenting on the sausages: 'Cook's specials this lot. Part of a batch I made up for the Manor. The old man likes just an extra pinch of pepper.'

Having once seen his wife with Johnson there was no longer any doubt in Patchin's mind, for it seemed to him as if there was some invisible but subtly tangible connection between them, an unspoken intimacy born of their long afternoons together, probably in Calcot Wood where there were some idyllic glades. As he did up the bacon and sausages and the embarrassed couple said nothing Patchin could visualise them on a green sward in a patch of dappled sunlight – the flimsy knickers being removed together with the trick brassière – and then Angela's urgent movements as the mutual madness began. Patchin felt as though his obsessive thoughts might show on his usually phlegmatic face so he cleared his throat loudly and shook his head, saying, 'Sorry. Throat's a bit sore. Hope it's not a summer cold.'

Ray Johnson gave Patchin an unusually serious, not altogether friendly look as he replied, 'Yes. Let's hope not.' The look negated the banal response and Patchin thought: Liar. It would please you if I came down with pneumonia. For the first time it struck him that the feeling of jealousy might not all be on one side. Probably Johnson was also jealous, of the nights when Patchin slept with Angela; possibly Johnson was coming to hate him as he had hated the unknown lover.

Later that afternoon, when Angela had gone back to the cottage to make some tea, Daniel Patchin stood at the open door of the shop staring at the pond where a pair of Canada geese had alighted and were being harried and made unwelcome by the aggressive though small coots which dashed in and out of the reeds, making proprietorial noises. And indeed Patchin did not miss anything that happened on the pond, noting how the mallards vanished and the white ducks kept out of the noisy quarrel like only faintly interested spectators. But Patchin's mind was elsewhere, brooding on his predicament: it was the first time since the Korean war that Patchin felt he was faced with a problem he did not know how to handle. Ray Johnson was a tall slight lad with curly black hair and a mouth that always seemed to be open, either grinning or laughing to show very white teeth. Johnson was easily the most popular of the local postmen; he was extremely cheerful, full of banter and old jokes. Patchin had always found that slightly irritating – but now the trifling feeling of irritation was replaced by the strong one of implacable enmity. Patchin had no intention of confronting Angela with his suspicions or of trying to surprise the lovers in the act, even though he thought it could be arranged one Monday afternoon in Calcot Wood. For all he knew Angela might then decide to leave him – he did not know how heavily their reasonably prosperous and comfortable life together weighed against the hours of passion spent with Lothario Johnson. No, the only answer was to get rid of him as the coots would undoubtedly rid themselves of the intruding Canada geese.

After the break for tea Patchin got down to work again. Friday evening was one of his busiest times as dozens of joints had to be prepared for the weekend – he had some particularly choosy customers who liked to have their meat prepared in the finicky French manner and he was quite willing to cater to their tastes. A great deal of beef had been ordered for that weekend and his young assistant was not up to preparing it, being capable of carrying out only the humblest jobs. Patchin set the boy to mincing pork and then began butchering two sides of beef, attacking the carcase with relish.

Once supper was finished he could hardly wait to get Angela to bed: knowing that she was the young man's mistress had the strange, unexpected effect of doubling his lust for her. And she semed equally ready for sex, falling back on the bed and raising her knees, smiling at him in a new way, a smile that contained a hint of amusement at his fumbling efforts to please her. This time it was his turn to be left feeling unsatisfied and empty even though he took her twice, as if possessing her half a dozen times would not be enough to assuage his restless yearning.

From mid-June Daniel Patchin spent most of his Sundays in Calcot Wood – it was by far the largest area of woodland owned by Lord Benningworth. One Sunday he decided to devote to searching for clues as to the lovers' meeting-place and did come on a bed of crushed ferns with a strange sensation that left him feeling slightly sick. From the improvised bed he made his way down to a deserted cottage in the remotest part of the wood, a spot that never seemed to be reached by the sun as it stood in the shadow of Calcot Hill. It had been a game-keeper's cottage up to 1939 but the pre-war Benningworth regime of having a game-keeper had been dropped and the remote, unattractive cottage was let, when Patchin was a youth, to a strange old man called Ted Ames, then left to rot. Lord Benningworth was a true conservative in that he was against change of any kind, even that of having a wreck of a building knocked down. The old widower Ames had eventually gone off his head and been taken away to a mental hospital in 1948, where he died. Since then the cottage had been stripped of its gutters and drain-pipes; most of the roof was still sound but rain had dripped in through a few missing tiles and some of the rafters were rotten, covered in mould: even on the warmest summer day the old cotttage smelt of dank decay. There was fungus on the kitchen walls and weeds were gradually invading the ground floor rooms, sprouting up from the cracks in the brick floors.

Daniel Patchin stood absolutely still for a long while staring at the ruined building which some villagers claimed was haunted by Ted Ames. Patchin did not believe in ghosts, spirits, Heaven or Hell: he believed that the Universe was incomprehensible and absolutely indifferent to mankind. Suddenly he said aloud: 'What a waste. Pity not to make some use of the old place.' The second sentence, spoken in a particularly mild voice, ended on a faintly questioning note and for the first time he moved his head as though he were talking to someone and waiting for a comment on his suggestion. Then he gave the idea engendered by his memory of a certain feature of the ancient fireplace in Ames's kitchen a mirthless smile and turned on his heel.

Throughout Calcot Wood there were piles of logs that Patchin built till he was ready to remove a truckload. There was also a hut where he kept a chain-saw, tins of petrol, axes and bags of wood chips and sawdust. He looked around to make sure that there was no one about, and began to carry sacks of sawdust and chippings over to the cottage; he felt a great satisfaction in commencing work on his plan.

On succeeding Sundays Daniel Patchin spent a good deal of time in transport-ing dry branches and brushwood; he also used his van to move cans of paraffin, half-empty tins of paint, plastic bags that had contained dripping, sacks of fat, soiled rags and other rubbish. These he carefully planted throughout the cottage, gradually turning it into a massive bonfire.

While the preparations in Calcot Wood were proceeding satisfactorily Patchin made a study of Ray Johnson's working life. By casual questions to the village Postmistress, who delighted in gossip, he wormed out the routine of Johnson and other postmen in the area. One of his discoveries was that Johnson often had either Monday or Wednesday afternoon off, and this was confirmed for him on the first Wednesday in July when Angela took a surprising interest in his fishing plans for that afternoon. Usually she was bored by angling so he answered these questions with concealed, wry humour. Then, prompted by a whim, he took more time than usual in his preparation for the weekly expedition to the Thames. His fishing equipment was the simplest that could be devised – he despised the 'London crowd' who invaded the river at weekends weighed down with paraphernalia. He had an all-purpose rod, a few hooks and floats and one reel carried in an army haversack. As he pretended to fuss over these things, and to take an unusually long time in making the flour paste for bait, he could see that Angela was very much on edge, nervous and yet pleasurably excited at the same time. She had not mentioned going out so he suspected that there might be a plan for Johnson to visit Pound Cottage while he was away: 'While the cat's away the mice will play,' he said over and over in his mind as he rolled the ball of dough between his strong, dry fingers.

When he at last set off in the van he was again ironically amused that Angela came out to wave goodbye as though to be certain of his departure. Patchin spent an hour on the river-bank but was not in the mood for fishing. The reeds were haunted by colourful dragon-flies and there was a brief darting visit from a kingfisher – sights that usually pleased him, but on this occasion he was hardly aware of anything about him, feeling rather like a ghost returned to haunt the scene of past pleasures.

Patchin drove back from the Thames with not much heart for what lay immediately ahead, but he now felt it was essential to make quite sure of the situation. In Pasterne he parked his van by the pond and appeared to stare down into its clear water for a while. Such behaviour on his part would not excite comment for he had been known to catch stickle-backs and frogs there to use as bait when angling for pike.

After some minutes of staring with unseeing eyes Patchin ambled back to his closed shop, then walked through it into the garden that led up to Pound Cottage. He trod noiselessly over the lawn and entered the side door very quietly. Within a minute his suspicions were dramatically confirmed: through the board ceiling that separated the living-roon from the bedroom he heard the squeaking springs of his double bed, squeaking so loudly that it seemed as if the springs were protesting at the extraordinary behaviour of the adulterous couple. Then there began a peculiar rhythmical grunting noise and his wife called out something incomprehensible in a strange voice.

Patchin retreated noiselessly, got back into his car and returned to Hambleden Mill. He fished stolidly for three hours with a dour expression on his face – an expression that some North Korean soldiers had probably glimpsed before he killed them with his bayonet. Usually he returned small fish to the river but on that afternoon he just ripped them off the hook and threw them on the bank.

Returning home again at about his usual time, Patchin found his wife in an excellent mood. Fornication seemed to be good for her health as she appeared blooming. A delicious supper had been prepared for him and Angela had popped over to the village stores to buy a bottle of the dry cider he favoured. She looked quite fetching with her flushed cheeks, her curly blonde hair freshly washed, and the two top buttons of a new pink blouse left undone, but Patchin could not respond at all; momentarily he found it difficult to keep up the pretence of not knowing about her affair and felt as though an expression of suspicion and cold contempt must appear on his face. When he went to wash he stared in the mirror and was surprised to find the usual phlegmatic expression reflected.

After supper Angela wanted to stroll around in the garden. It was something Patchin normally enjoyed, seeing the results of all his hard work, for in July the garden looked at its best with the rose-beds 'a picture' as Angela said, and usually it was very satisfactory to inspect the neat rows of vegetables. Instead he experienced a most unusual mood of emptiness and frustration – everything seemed hollow and meaningless.

While his wife bent down to smell a rose Daniel Patchin stared up at the clear evening sky. He knew his enjoyment of life was temporarily lost, and that it would not return until he was rid of the man who threatened his marriage. Angela came and stood by him, took his hand and placed it on her firm round breast, an action that would have been quite out of character a few months before; but her new sensuality did not move him at all, and when they went to bed making love to her was like a ritual, quite spoilt by his memory of the protesting bed-springs.

Patchin decided to try to put his plan of murder into effect on the second Wednesday in July. Angela went for a walk again on the Monday of that week, so according to his understanding of the postman's routine it seemed probable that Ray Johnson would be working on the Wednesday afternoon. If so he would then be driving down the narrow lane that skirted Calcot Wood to clear a remote, little-used post-box at about 3 p.m.

On the Wednesday Patchin felt quite calm and confident that everything would go as he devised. He set off from Pound Cottage promptly at 2 p.m. after an excellent lunch of roast loin of pork with the first new potatoes from the garden and a large helping of broad beans. His haversack had been got ready on the previous evening: it now contained some other things as well as fishing tackle – rubber gloves, matches, a ball of extremely tough cord, sticking plasters and a foot-long piece of iron pipe.

Parking his van just off the lane by the wood in a cunningly chosen spot where it would not be seen, Patchin took his haversack and walked quickly through the wood to Ames's cottage. He experienced pleasurable excitement in doing so and in inspecting the fire he had laid in the kitchen grate. It consisted of three fire-lighters, paper spills and wood chippings, a few sticks and numerous small pieces of coal. It had been constructed with the care that a chaffinch gives to making its nest, and he estimated that it would burn intensely for an hour or two. 'Quite long enough to roast a joint,' he said in an expressionless voice as he got up from his crouching position in front of the grate.

After inspecting the trails of wood chippings soaked in paraffin which he had laid throughout the cottage like long fuses to explosive charges, he glanced round the wildly overgrown plot that had once been a garden. Rank grass a foot high contended with massive clumps of nettles, giant docks and cow parsley.

He did not think that it would be possible to trace foot-prints on such a terrain, but also he did not expect his enterprise to be risk-free. There were bound to be risks in a life governed by mere chance.

It was 2.45 p.m. when he walked back through the wood to the narrow, twisting lane. He wore the rubber gloves with his left hand in his old fishing-jacket pocket and the other plunged into the haversack that hung from his right shoulder. He positioned himself in the lane so that he would be on the driver's side of the van when it approached him. The oppressive mood which had dogged him for so many weeks lifted and he whistled as he waited – a rather tuneless version of *As time goes by* which he repeated over and over again.

At 3 p.m. precisely he heard a motor engine in the lane and got ready to wave the van down if it was driven by Johnson. For the first time that afternoon excitement seized him, with a thumping of his heart and a sudden tremor of fear such as he had always experienced before hand-to-hand fighting in Korea. He had once said to another soldier there: 'Everyone's afraid at times. Anyone who says he isn't is either a liar or a fool.'

As the Post Office van came round the corner Patchin waved it down, first tentatively then more vigorously as he spotted Johnson's head of black curly hair. Johnson stopped the van, rolled its window further down and called out, 'What's up?'

Patchin walked slowly across to the van, limping very slightly and holding himself as though he was in pain. 'Sorry, sorry,' he said. 'Bit of trouble.' He came close to the van door and stood silent, with his eyes half-closed and swaying slightly as though he was going to faint.

With a puzzled expression in which there was just the faintest hint of suspicion Johnson opened the van door and began to get out – his height made doing so a rather awkward business. Patchin took out the iron pipe and hit Johnson on the head, a measured blow by someone who had considerable experience in stunning animals. Johnson lurched forward and then fell in a heap, just like a poleaxed bullock. Patchin bundled him back into the van, got into the driving seat and drove off down the lane, whistling the same tune again. After a hundred yards he turned off on to a track which led in the direction of the gamekeeper's cottage. Before leaving the red van he pressed Johnson's fingers on the steering-wheel, then bundled the body up and carried it on his shoulder as easily as he managed a side of beef.

He also paused in the decaying doorway to impress Johnson's fingerprints on two empty paraffin cans, and carried him through to the kitchen. The tall man was still inert, but as Patchin dropped his burden on to the cement floor Johnson's eyelids flickered. Patchin sat him up like a ventriloquist's dummy and then knocked him out with a blow to the jaw that would have floored most boxers.

Patchin put sticky plasters over Johnson's large mouth, then worked on the unconscious man with the skill he always showed in preparing joints. He put his legs neatly together and bound them tightly from above the knee to the ankles, using the same binding technique he used in repairing his fishing rod, pulling the cord so tight that the legs became immobile; he left a loop by the ankles. He repeated the process with the limp arms. Then came the part that gave him most satisfaction: lifting the two loops on to the hooks that had once supported a turnspit in front of the fire. Immediately Johnson was suspended like an animal carcase ready to be roasted. Patchin lit the fire in the grate and left the cottage.

Before taking off his rubber gloves Patchin picked up the empty paraffin cans and left them near the old garden gate which was half hanging off its hinges, then strode off to the place where he had hidden his own van. The time was 3.30 and everything had gone exactly as he had hoped. There was always blind chance of course – for instance the remote possibility that another pair of lovers might be trespassing in the woods and see him striding along so purposefully, but there was nothing he could do about it.

Driving to the Thames, Patchin mentally examined his plan again and formulated one or two more things to be done. As soon as he had parked the van near Hambleden Mill he assembled his rod and line right down to putting on the bait, a thing he never did till he was actually on the river bank, so that anyone seeing him might think he had already been fishing and was trying another spot. Then, carrying the assembled rod, he walked along the gravel path and over the complicated series of weirs which cross the Thames at Hambleden Mill. As he approached the lock he watched to see whether the keeper there might be in sight and was relieved to be able to cross unseen.

Patchin threw his piece of iron pipe into the river before spending an hour angling: he fished like a young boy, close in to the bank where there were more bites to be had but the fish were always small. He caught a tiny roach and three gudgeon but was quite satisfied with them, leaving the last gudgeon on the hook as he walked back to the lock. Good fortune was still with him for the lock-keeper was now at work opening the gates for a motor cruiser. The keeper, who knew Patchin well, called out, 'Any luck Dan?'

'Not much. Just tiddlers,' Patchin called out, shaking his rod so that the suspended gudgeon twisted about at the end of the line. 'Think I'll use them to try for a pike in the pool by the mill. See you.'

'Yes, see you. Will you keep me a nice small chicken for the weekend?'

'Yes. Right.' Patchin walked off just fractionally quicker than he did normally. With excitement working in him at the prospect of revisiting Ames's cottage it was not easy to appear just as usual. For once he was grateful that he had a rather expressionless face.

His mind on other things, he mechanically dismantled the fishing rod and line as quickly as he could. 'Yes, all going to plan,' he said aloud though there was no one within a hundred yards of him.

Driving back to the lane once more he experienced a suprising feeling of letdown and anti-climax. It was true that it had all gone without a hitch as far as he could tell, but somehow it seemed a bit too easy. There would have been more satisfaction if he could have allowed the tall but puny Johnson a chance to fight, some ludicrous attempt at self-defence which he would have brushed away derisively, as easily as a tom-cat deals with a rat.

Once in Calcot Wood again Patchin's nose twitched. There was a faint aroma like that of roast pork which had greeted him at lunch time at Pound Cottage. It grew stronger at every step he took. Desultory grey fumes struggled up from the ancient chimney. The smell was very strong in the hall and unpleasantly so in the kitchen which reeked of cooking odours and where a blackened, twisted carcase was still roasting and dripping fat into a dying fire.

Despite the smell Patchin stayed there looking at the object which bore no resemblance to the once garrulous postman. Patchin's hatred of the man had quite disappeared now that there was no longer any need for it – he was not gloating over his victim, but musing on the quintessential evanescence of man. How easily was man humbled, how soon was he changed into rotting meat! It had been just the same in Korea: one minute his friend 'Dusty' Seddon had been telling a dirty joke, the next moment lying mute with most of his face blown off.

Pausing in the hall, Patchin set light to a pile of paraffin-soaked sawdust and then lit the trails of wood-chips and retreated to the sagging front door, throwing the box of matches behind him.

The fire had taken a firm grip on the cottage before Patchin had even left the garden: he could hear it raging and roaring unseen until a sheet of flame sprang up at one of the diamond-leaded windows. For the second time that day Patchin experienced a slight attack of nerves; momentarily his right hand shook and for a few minutes he seemed to be walking on lifeless legs, having to make an extraordinary amount of effort just to propel himself along.

Seated in his van Patchin took out a large handkerchief and wiped his forehead which was sweating profusely, and allowed himself a few minutes rest before driving off in his customary careful manner. Was there something he had overlooked – perhaps a trifling slip which might lead the police to his door in a few days' time? As he navigated a series of lanes and minor roads that would put him once again on the main road from Hambleden to Pasterne, his mind was exercised by the nagging suspicion that he might have made one vital mistake.

Calm gradually returned as he drove slowly along, and he began to think of the possible effect of the fire on the Benningworth estate. The large garden of rank grass and weeds should act as a barrier between the fire and Calcot Wood, but even if it did spread then Lord Benningworth owed him a favour for all the hard work he had put in there as amateur forester for twenty-five years. A sudden thought made Patchin smile. The Benningworth family motto, *Esse quam videri*, 'To be rather than to seem to be', was well known in the locality; it was a pity that Ray Johnson had not known that Daniel Patchin also had a motto: 'What I have I hold.'

When Patchin arrived in Pasterne he felt completely normal. His pleasant life had been momentarily threatened with an upheaval but that was now all over. The village looked particularly lovely in the late afternoon sunlight. The white ducks were sedulously paddling to and fro as though they were paid to do so, and swifts were skimming over the clear pond's mirror-like surface, occasionally dipping down to it, hunting midges. The Postmistress's black and white cat moved carefully over the neatly clipped grass as if it might be stalking a newt and sat down at the edge of the pond. 'Pretty as a picture,' Patchin said.

Walking along to Pound Cottage Daniel Patchin thought of what he should say when he saw Angela. It was essential to appear absolutely as normal so that when she heard of the perplexing tragedy in Calcot Wood nothing about his behaviour should prompt suspicion in her mind. Then he understood Angela's difficulty in appearing quite normal or saying anything about that walk she had taken on the glorious May afternoon because phrases that he went over in his mind seemed artificial and suspicious. 'Nice afternoon, but I didn't catch anything' – false. 'I enjoyed it, but not good fishing weather' – unnatural.

But Patchin need not have worried, for as soon as he opened the side door he heard the squeak of protesting bed-springs and Angela calling out in a voice that sounded false and unnatural.

# JEAN STUBBS

## The Belvedere

The memory of cousin Fanny troubles me so greatly that I wake crying in the night. There is a candle burning against the dark, and Nanny sleeps in an adjoining room with her door open so that she can come to me quickly. Mamma must have her sleep, they say, but she sits with me during the day and sews rows of lace onto the baby's clothes and tells me fairy-tales. They shaved my head when the fever began and I wear a little linen cap bordered by a frill. Mamma says my hair will grow again, and when I am better she will send me to Aunt Dith who lives by the sea. But just yet I am not strong enough to travel, and hardly strong enough to support a nightmare I can in no way convey to them. They changed my room so that I should not see the belvedere at the end of the garden, but it shimmers pale and terrible in my dreams. Cousin Fanny stands at the foot of my bed and smiles and smiles. Sometimes she begins to glide towards me with her arms outstretched: a phantom walking in its phantom sleep. And then I scream myself back to a reality hardly less fearful than the things that haunt me.

Our house in Blackheath was large enough for a dozen children, standing in its own garden, and we thought ourselves a fortunate family. Papa worked in the City and wore a black silk top-hat and a black frock-coat. But in the evenings he donned a plum-coloured velvet jacket and an embroidered cap with a silk tassel. Mamma stayed at home, arranging the life of everyone and the proper state of everything from attic to basement. She discussed the day's menus with Cook and our lessons with the governess, and the flowers and vegetables with the gardener. And in the afternoons, unless she was resting on the sofa, she visited or received ladies like herself.

We should indeed have been nine children, but four of us had died in infancy and lay at rest in the churchyard under two weeping cherubs and a stone urn. We visited their grave every Sunday after morning service to contemplate the bliss that was our sorrow, and to garland them with flowers. And on the anniversary of each death we spent the day quietly at home, and remembered them in our evening prayers. Mamma told us they had gone to a better place and it was wrong to grieve. Yet she wore black for a year after their decease, and the boys had crêpe bands sewn on their left sleeves, and all the joys of heaven could not stop her mourning them.

After baby Rachel died of diphtheria Papa took Mamma to Italy for her health, and she returned full of delightful and impractical fancies. At least, Papa said they were impractical, and when the orange trees refused to grow – proving him right – he advised her to mark the Italian tour with a more tangible and durable memento. She had loved the churches built delicately upon hills, through whose campanile one glimpsed the blue skies and feathers of cloud, and she mentioned this in her pretty, beseeching manner during breakfast.

'I cannot build you a church, my love,' said Papa, smiling, 'that is too great an undertaking. But we shall build a belvedere at the end of the garden if you wish, and fashion it after the Italian style.'

Mamma clasped her hands and cried that she would treasure that above all things.

'And what *is* a belvedere, James?' Papa asked, seeing that he was not attending to the conversation and improving his knowledge. 'Define it, if you please.'

James, concealing a pet white mouse in the pocket of his Norfolk jacket, replied that he thought a belvedere was a very *little* church.

'Your thought is an erroneous one, James,' said Papa, taking his gold watch from his waistcoat pocket. 'If you do not know something you should always say so, and ask permission to look up the word in the dictionary. I believe I have five minutes to spare. Bring me the dictionary.'

'This is exceeding kind of Papa,' said Mamma automatically. 'For he is a very important man with a great deal to do, and every minute is precious to him.'

James mumbled his thanks, stumbled out of his chair, concealed the mouse in a drawer on his way to the study (from which it would later leap onto a shrieking housemaid) and returned with a heavy volume in very small print. He stood pink and upright but one could tell he was no lexicographer, and I could see Mamma praying that he would not drop the book or wrinkle the pages. And with Papa's watch ticking away in his right hand like an accuser, and Papa's eyes fixed first on it and then on him, James made a clumsy job of finding the right place.

'A belvedere is a raised turret,' he said at last, and Mamma breathed out, 'from which one views the scenery. It is formed from the Italian *bel*, meaning *beautiful*, and the verb *vedere*, meaning *to see*.'

'Very well, James. Remember that definition. A word remembered is a word gained, and an extensive vocabulary is the mark of a cultivated person.'

Then he put back his watch, folded *The Times* in three and went off to that mysterious temple in the City, from which flowed the means to keep a wife and five children, a staff of eight and an establishment whose conservatory alone was a matter of envy to all who saw it.

Richard and Edward were being trained for life at a public school, so that left James and me to the tuition of our governess, and baby Frederick was scarcely in breeches. Mamma lay on the sofa after breakfast, and though I should not have dared mention it I guessed why. It meant a great many nods and winks between the women servants, frequent injunctions not to make a noise and disturb poor Mamma, and in due time a new baby in the nursery. I have never understood why Mamma was ill for months, since babies are found in an instant lying under currant bushes or flown in by a stork or produced like a conjuror's rabbit from Dr Fogg's bag. But that was an adult mystery which one seemed destined never to unravel.

I think I may say, without excessive pride, that before cousin Fanny came I used to be a good child. I had long learned, in my ten years, that to please Mamma I must be pretty and loving, and to gratify Papa modest and docile. I could not please my three elder brothers except by staying out of their way, but I kissed and petted little Frederick – who was not old enough to dislike girls, and indeed preferred me to anyone. But I was never a clever child, and though Nanny said, 'Better to be good than clever,' I noticed that goodness was treated as a dull quality whatever anyone said. None of the servants made a favourite of me as Cook made of James (in spite of his mice), or Nanny of her first-born Richard (now a stalwart fifteen and naughty at Marlborough), or Nora, the housemaid, of Edward (who coaxed macaroons from her in the holidays). And everyone loved Frederick though goodness could hardly be reckoned as his forte. Perhaps I was something of a favourite with Papa whom I longed to charm as Mamma did. She would laugh and glance sideways at him, and lift her hands gracefully to her crown of black hair to touch it into perfection. My hair had long since been abandoned, except for a torment of curl-papers before parties, and hung down my back: brown and neat and without distinction. Neither were music and needlework my accomplishments as they were hers. I produced samplers in a misery of pricked fingers and sorry tears, and they had to be washed and ironed before presentation in the parlour. Whereas Mamma's *petit point* graced chairs and stools and fire-screens. I had not struck half a dozen wrong notes on the piano before the penny on the back of each hand fell down, proving that I did not even arch them properly let alone play accurately. But Mamma could play and sing like an angel. I used to creep down and sit on the stairs when she had a Musical Evening, hoping she would sing a song called *Somewhere a Voice is Calling*. Now I am afraid of it, because it seems to beckon to the realm where cousin Fanny lies; and I pray that I, at least, might live for ever so that I do not have to join her there. And then I remember that I, above all others, am least fitted to pray to God – Who Sees and Knows All Things. So I drift into a limbo of sleep, and watch the belvedere stand in ghostly beauty, and watch cousin Fanny walk in ghostly horror.

The belvedere came first. Papa, who is as Miss Wilder our governess says 'a most cultivated gentleman', designed the turret from numerous Italian models. So that, though it belonged to no particular school or style, it appeared to be the essence of every belvedere created. Mamma sat smiling and sewing with an air about her that I envied and could not fathom. Now, from the depths of my separateness, I know it was the air of the well-beloved. In my envy I tried to attract Papa's attention and made him spill a bottle of Indian ink on the parlour carpet, which I suppose was my just desert – only I should not have been envious had I been well-beloved too. He was exceedingly angry.

My papa's taste was impeccable, as Mamma always said, but I felt considerably disappointed by the size of the belvedere. I had imagined a tower twenty feet high and it was not above ten: very slender and beautiful in a pale stone, with its narrow steps leading to a view that perhaps the Italians would not have pronounced perfect, but nevertheless extremely pleasant. From the garden side it held no awe, but ours was sloping ground so that a drop, calculated to inspire a delightful terror, lay on the other side. Mamma and Papa might gaze when and as they liked, and the two elder boys were cautioned to be careful, but James and I were only allowed to ascend in the company of a responsible adult. Little Frederick was not permitted at all, and spent his days attempting to reach the forbidden area and scale what must have appeared a veritable Babel. Visitors exclaimed over its splendour and originality, though Papa's business friends chaffed him for such a display of useless loveliness.

'You must be a warm man to put up a piece of feminine foolery!' said Mr Bullock, and Papa laughed and said it was a present to Mamma.

I asked him what 'warm' meant, and he told me that it was a slang word, on no account to be used by any of us, which suggested that he had a great deal of money. I was proud to think that my papa could be important enough to spend as he pleased.

The belvedere came first, and cousin Fanny came second. We had not heard of Mamma's sister Eleanor before the envelope arrived bordered in black. And her explanation was so worded as to confuse me further.

'We have not spoken of Eleanor, your aunt Eleanor, for many years. What she did is of no matter now, but between herself and her Maker. Suffice it to say that she sinned, she suffered, and by the grace of God is now in heaven. She has left behind her one child, a daughter of thirteen whom she calls Fanny – I suppose she was christened Frances after my dear mother . . .'

'If she was christened at all,' said Papa.

'Why should she not be christened?' I asked. 'Is not every child christened? I thought it must be the law, Papa.'

'Your dear papa was joking. He merely refers to the fact that Aunt Eleanor and Frances lived for many years abroad where things are very different from here. Most certainly the child was christened, Mr Brook.'

She never addressed my papa as 'Mr Brook' except on very formal occasions, and I felt he had erred.

'My sister begs me to look after the child,' said Mamma hurriedly, but his momentary indiscretion had given her strength. She moved closer to him so that I should not hear, and said something about money in trust.

'Money of what complexion?' Papa said sternly.

I crawled under the table and sat there, hidden by the chenille cloth with its tawny silk tassels.

'The letter has been written by a nun, my dear Charles. My sister would hardly deceive *her*. Perhaps the – perhaps her – Mr Marechale settled something on the child quite legitimately. We cannot punish the daughter for the mother's transgressions. No one claims her. She is at present being cared for in the convent where my sister died.'

'Popish nonsense. I'll have no rag, tag and bobtail in my house.'

For the first time since I had known her Mamma set up her will against Papa's. A child was involved. A child of mature years, certainly, of obscure background and strange origins. But one of those blessed creatures who are admitted to the

Gates of Heaven, being innocent of heart and mind.

'My sister had a sound Protestant upbringing, Mr Brook. In France, as you know even better than myself . . .' A marital sop. '. . . the national religion is that of the Roman Church. The nuns possibly took her in out of kindness because she had neither friends nor relatives. We are all equal in the sight of God. The child cannot be blamed.'

In the end Papa agreed that Fanny should live with us for a few months, with the proviso that she should also be sent to a suitable boarding school if she showed signs of contaminating us. She had not been in the house a fortnight before she established herself as another favourite.

'Eleanor was always the family beauty,' said Mamma fondly, 'and Fanny is the image of her mother.'

Her beauty was undoubted, even in that transitory stage between childhood and womanhood where awkwardness reigns. Her hair curled black and glossy down her back, she held herself like a queen, her manners were faultless, her gratitude immense without being embarrassing. Mamma had Miss Briggs, the dressmaker, in the house for a month sewing new clothes.

'Since these – though most elegant, my dear Fanny – are a little unsuitable for your years.'

Fanny agreed humbly, anxious not to offend, but asked if she might keep her French wardrobe in memory of her own mamma. Since no other solution occurred to my own mother (one can hardly pass finery on to the poor and deserving) she allowed this. Indeed, as I hung jealously and uncertainly about the fringes of this new relationship, I discovered that Fanny was allowed a great deal, and by the means of seeming to give in to authority. It was an attitude I had been neither clever enough nor ruthless enough to adopt myself, and I hated her for her strategies.

Somewhere in that past which will never, I imagine, come to light, Fanny had learned how to deceive. She was a mistress of deception: subtle, plausible and intuitive. She had found that people could be manipulated through their own weaknesses, and she sought out those weaknesses with a frightening degree of perception. My family were revealed to me for what they were not, and they will never seem the same again. It is not only Fanny's ghost and the pale belvedere which haunt me now. It is the awakening to something even more terrible: the knowledge that the people who comfort and care for me are strangers, victims even frailer than myself. I wake, not safe and whole with my feet on that daisy-field of innocence, but shrieking on the edge of a long drop. And those who seek to save me tread the same precipice and do not know it for what it is. Where Fanny is now I cannot tell, but we shall never be safe from her, being no better. She deceived others, but we deceive ourselves.

Take Nanny, who arrived in our happy household to nurse Richard: a rosy-faced wholesome girl from Clapham. Fifteen years here taught her nothing more than the homely threats and axioms she employed when she came. They have robbed her of her freshness, perhaps of marriage to some honest man who might have made her contented. When she used to warn us that the bogey-man came for disobedient children, or promise us that to eat our crusts would make our hair curl, we believed her. The facts that no bogey ever appeared, even when we were naughtiest, that my poor hair never altered from its straight and stubborn fall, seemed due only to one's good fortune or personal sinfulness. I know her now to be both powerless and untruthful because Fanny found her out, and found her out for a purpose.

The new baby, another boy, was at first fretful, then quiet, and then listless. The doctor prescribed a month at the sea.

'How *I* should like a month at the sea,' said Fanny wistfully.

'If wishes were horses, then beggars would ride!' Nanny replied sharply, because rumours of Fanny's background had been hot gossip among the servants and she regarded Fanny as being less than her self and more fortunate.

'I feel that the sea air would benefit me,' said Fanny gently. 'Dear Nanny, may I hold baby for a few minutes?'

'No, Miss. He'll be better presently. He wants his Nanny, don't you, my lamb? Go you downstairs, Miss, and take Miss Helen with you. Children should be seen and not heard.'

Fanny gave her a peculiar look, but took my hand and led me into the parlour, where I presently heard her treading softly round the subject of the seaside. But it appeared that Papa's expenses were heavy enough, and the cost of Mamma, Nanny and the baby were all he was prepared to afford. Not that Fanny asked him outright, merely tried out the ground.

She made her first night excursion shortly afterwards. I woke to see her gliding from our bedroom into the nursery next door, where little William was crying persistently. My curiosity was too strong to permit me to remain, and I followed her, much as Adam must have followed Eve in that first bite of the forbidden fruit. My fault was a secondary one, it was to taste equally bitter.

William's cries ceased and on that instant Fanny pushed open the door. I crept in after her and saw a frozen tableau, a moment of time captured and delineated. Nanny, her hair plaited, her usual severity softened by a dressing-jacket, stood mouth open with the baby in her arms. A little bottle was on the table beside her.

'I *thought* you were giving him laudanum,' said Fanny, soft and triumphant, and her fingers closed on the bottle.

'Put that down at once, Miss!' said Nanny, low and fierce. 'You've got a nasty mind from those foreign parts. That's good wholesome drops, that is. The doctor left them for Master William.'

Coolly, Fanny unstoppered the bottle and smelled it.

'Laudanum,' she said, and smiled.

Nanny stowed the baby in his bassinette and made a snatch for the evidence. I had never seen her before, except as a pillar of authority, and her terror sickened me. Fanny held the bottle high.

'If you come any nearer,' she said quietly, 'I shall smash the bottle and fetch Mrs Brook to smell it.'

There was a long and dreadful silence. Then Nanny began, in a voice I had not heard, to coax her to give it up.

'Come, Miss,' she said, placating. 'You're a good clever young lady. You know as well as me that it isn't good for Master William to cry so. Give it to me like a kind young lady.'

Fanny said softly, 'I need a month at the seaside, Nanny. I have been deeply disturbed since my mamma's death. I walk in my sleep.'

I saw cunning come into Nanny's round red face and little black eyes.

'Do you, Miss?'

'I might have been walking in my sleep tonight,' said Fanny gently. 'And you know that sleep-walkers see nothing. Only they should not be wakened and frightened. They need rest. You know that, Nanny.'

'Yes, Miss,' said Nanny, and she trembled so much that she was forced to sit down. But she never took her eyes from Fanny's face. They were sending each other instructions in the silence.

'I had a brother that walked in his sleep,' said Nanny, after a pause. '*He* needed a rest and a change, but we were a poor family. And your mamma's death upset you, I don't doubt, Miss. Poor young lamb,' she added automatically.

Fanny held the bottle out, smiling.

'You must tell Mrs Brook that you found me sleep-walking,' she said.

'Yes, Miss. I shall, Miss. Perhaps you should come with us, to take your mind off your trouble. Mrs Brook will see the sense of that, I'm sure.'

She took the proffered bottle and her manner changed instantly.

'And now get you back to bed,' she said. 'I'll have no wicked liars in *my* nursery. I've been fifteen years in this household and never a word of complaint from anybody. If I tell Mrs Brook anything it will be that you're a bad influence. Don't think we don't know about *you*, Miss, belowstairs. I'll make it hot for you with the master, too. *He* had his doubts, but the mistress won't say no to an act of charity. And don't think as you're the only clever one round here. I can play a few tricks equal to any of yours! Off with you!'

Fanny's smile never faltered.

Very evenly, she said, 'I know you drink, too, though you *are* clever about it. I have a bottle of gin to show my aunt.'

Nanny's hand went to her mouth, confronted by a personal bogey.

'Did you think I should be so stupid as to take your word?' said Fanny wondering. 'Now you do exactly as you are told. And goodnight to you.'

She turned serenely away and found me behind the door, watching.

'Here endeth the first lesson,' she said, unperturbed.

'Miss Helen,' Nanny whispered. 'You don't believe a word she says, I know. You've always been a *good* girl. You'll not let her make trouble between me and your dear mamma, will you?'

I was terrified to find myself a witness, and even more afraid when Fanny put her arms about me.

'Dear cousin Helen,' she said persuasively, 'we all have our faults. You have seen Nanny's and mine tonight. Do you want to see your own?' And she shook me gently, playfully. 'Tell me,' she said, 'what will you say to your mamma tomorrow?'

As though I had been taught I said, 'You have been walking in your sleep and need a rest and change, Fanny.'

'Now we are truly sisters. Closer than sisters usually are, since we *know* each other.'

'But are you going to let Nanny give William laudanum?' I asked.

'That is Nanny's business. Nanny knows best.'

I showed the first and last spark of courage.

'*I* could tell Mamma,' I said.

Fanny laughed.

'Mamma would not find anything if you did. And I know nothing. I was walking in my sleep.'

These two, then, understood each other and had wiped the incident from their minds. I stood on the outside of a drama which I was to watch over and over again: a fearful little play in which the victim acquiesced and Fanny forgot to accuse. I had thought our family a model of domestic perfection, and myself a model of unobtrusive goodness. Fanny showed me what we truly were, and the revelation was terrible.

Our governess, Miss Wilder, became her next victim. No one knew her age, except perhaps Mamma, but she was elderly and certainly unmarriageable: the sixth and insignificant daughter of a poor parson, who had picked up sufficient knowledge to be entrusted with a girl's education. It was she who kindly washed and ironed my samplers before they could be shown. She who placed the pennies on the back of my hands so that I should arch them properly over the keyboard. She who made me sit upright for an hour, with a ruler tied to my spine, to learn deportment. She who struggled to lodge the names and dates of kings, French irregular verbs, the art of sketching and a few simple mathematical essentials, into my muddled head. James's curriculum was slightly different but he showed no more signs of brilliance than I did, and she welcomed Fanny, who from the first was quick, obedient and adaptable.

Our life at home was restricted, our outings infrequent and educational, and only Miss Wilder could be entrusted with the choice and guardianship of these excursions into the world. Fanny, accustomed to a broader canvas, intended to use the governess as a passport by gaining her approbation, undermining her confidence, and at last showing her who was mistress of the situation. She began by using her superior knowledge of the French language.

Miss Wilder had learned the tongue painstakingly, never venturing farther than the bounds prescribed, and she was flustered by Fanny's fluency and ease of idiom. Her early estimate, that this would be a pupil in whom she could feel pride and show off as an ornament to her teaching, survived a number of quiet impertinencies. But the day that Fanny had instructed us first in her choice of epithets, and then applied them to the bewildered governess, sent us into covert grins and then open laughter.

Miss Wilder, sensing rebellion, asked Fanny sharply to remember her manners.

'I owe my knowledge of your native tongue merely to *industry*, my dear

Fanny. I cannot compete with you in *argot*!'

Unshaken, Fanny begged her pardon, but I felt Miss Wilder had been unwise to indulge in that little slap. Fanny had made her less important in our eyes, certainly, and hurt her self-esteem, but the governess was not Nanny and not so easily routed. Fanny discovered that Miss Wilder was devoted to her family, and encouraged her to recount their many excellencies, drawing her out and leading her on until the simple woman betrayed herself.

'My papa was, and is still, a particularly fine classical scholar. Indeed, it was he who taught me Latin, though Greek – I fear – was always beyond me. Why, I have seen my papa sit at his desk, in the brief time that his duties allowed him, and translate passages from William Shakespeare into both languages. It was he who first gave me an insight into Greek and Roman history. Ah! How can Richard and Edward call them *dry*? They were people, even as ourselves, though in widely different times and circumstances. I can remember the winter afternoon when he related the tale of the Trojan Wars and they came alive to me. I saw the plumes nodding on those stern helms, the dust at the chariot wheels, the devotion of brave Menelaus forgiving his erring Helen – how fortunate you are, dear Helen, to be the possessor of that lovely name! – and Troy burning.'

She was alive now. Plain and poor and absurd, and alive. I looked at her amazed, and Fanny looked at her with calculation.

'But, Miss Wilder,' she said, with a soft urgency, 'you have inherited your papa's own gift – that of making history seem here and now. Do, I beg of you, tell us something more.'

'Helen should be mastering her French verbs,' said Miss Wilder, recalled to the cold rice pudding of duty. 'I know that you may amuse yourself by reading the plays of Racine, but Helen has much to learn.'

'And learn she shall! Dear Miss Wilder, I shall help her when we are together, and so relieve you of a dull task. Do not be distressed, Helen dear, that I call it dull. Miss Wilder has your interests at heart, but when one knows a language through and through it is hard to turn back to the beginning. And if I help Helen – and you shall judge the results for yourself, Miss Wilder, you shall see I am no idle boaster – will you not, just for half an hour or so, instruct us in a wider, subject?'

'There is no need . . . indeed, I am not sure it is *proper*,' said poor Miss Wilder, 'to instruct you in classical history. If you were boys that would be different – though their instruction should come later when they are at school. It is sufficient that you know your *own* history. That is all I am supposed to impart.'

'Not *proper*?' cried Fanny, astonished. 'Not proper, when your own papa – who should best know how a young lady may be educated – thought fit to instruct *you*, dear Miss Wilder?'

She had her there, and the governess hesitated.

'Dear Helen, would you not rather have two lessons than one?' Fanny persisted. 'Would you not rather work at your French with me, in our own time, and have the inestimable value of Miss Wilder's insight into classical history in the schoolroom?'

I was long since lost in the thicket of her intentions, and promised that I would work hard if only the magic of the Trojan Wars was unfolded. Fanny kept my word for me and added a private torment of her own: waking me at all times of the night and forcing me to chant irregular verbs until I begged for sleep. She was wonderfully clever in that way, keeping her promises, keeping her counsel, leaving no loophole in her schemes, no place where an accusing finger might point.

And Miss Wilder, flattered by her interest and attention, made history come alive. Even I, though Hector and Achilles and Paris and Helen and Menelaus might pillage and fight and betray four Troys for all I cared, even I was captured. I look back in a double pity for the governess: a pity for what became of her and for what she had not become. Trapped in that undistinguished body, cramped in that rigorous background, was a great romantic. Her vocabulary broadened under the impact of old wars and passions and encompassed them with love. Flames leaped and crackled, the horse loomed wooden and impelling upon the shore, the body of Hector rode its sorry way through the dust, fierce plumes nodded on bronze helmets, and Helen was once more beautiful.

Fanny waited until they were a part of our daily life before she crushed them and Miss Wilder.

'I wonder what our dear Queen would think of such things?' she observed.

Miss Wilder paused, at a loss between Troy and respectable Windsor.

'Is it not strange,' Fanny continued, in her most speculative voice, 'that a Christian gentleman such as your dear papa, Miss Wilder, should set such store by pagan violence?'

Miss Wilder said stoutly that one must take a broad view, but she had been made uncertain.

'Well, I am very sorry, Fanny, if you regret asking me. I did mention – when you were so insistent – that I wondered if such history was proper for a young lady,' said Miss Wilder stiffly.

'But you are in charge of *us*. We are not in charge of *you*, dear Miss Wilder,' said Fanny, appearing puzzled by a vast discrepancy. 'If you had truly thought it improper you would surely not have told us at all.'

She sighed to herself, brooding.

'You have made so many improvements in my education, dear Miss Wilder. Encouraging me to read the plays of Racine, extending my knowledge in so many spheres. And I have worked hard. You said yourself I was a great credit to you. It would be such a pity if my aunt and uncle felt it necessary to send me to a boarding school for young ladies. And, of course, with Helen old enough to be my companion, she would go too. And I had so hoped that we three should be together for a few more years – which would bring little Frederick into your excellent charge, and perhaps other dear children too in good time.'

I sat very small and tight and sick in my chair. Miss Wilder sat small and upright in hers, amid the smoking ruins of Troy. And I prayed, for I knew she was a good woman, that she could conquer Fanny.

I had reckoned, in my innocence that I now see as ignorance, without

# Jean Stubbs

*Jean Stubbs*

domestic economy. Out of her salary Miss Wilder sent home money to support an ailing mother and an aged father. If she could hold on to her position for even another five years she might merit a little pension. But with a hint of improperness attached to her references, with the improbable chance of finding another place at her age, with the near-impossibility of achieving a position half so comfortable, she was defeated. Still, she waged one more campaign: a very brief one.

'Do I understand that you intend to complain to your uncle and aunt?' she asked, very dignified.

'Oh no, dear Miss Wilder. I was but drawing a picture of two different societies, and wondering if you might be good enough to take me and James and dear Helen to such places as would continue to broaden our minds? Do you not find the present education of young ladies a little narrow? In your charge we should discover more than any boarding school could offer.' She cast up her eyes. 'Paintings, sculptures, manuscripts. All the spiritual wealth of London would be ours.'

I think that the governess, like the rest of us, could draw a veil between what she knew to be true and what she preferred to believe. Pinched by her circumstances, Miss Wilder chose to forget the threat (which, of course, Fanny then forgot as well) and regard this plea as a genuine desire for self-improvement. Fanny had other plans, and an ally in James who had always found the governess dull and myself duller. Together they pressed their advantage, lengthening the time allowed in the new museums, losing themselves by walking away while she explained some educational point to me, asking questions she could not – or did not wish – to answer. And everything was done so subtly, with Fanny as leader (for James was simply a brash twelve-year-old boy who would soon go to Marlborough and thought it all a tremendous lark) that Miss Wilder could never put her finger on what was wrong. Her reprimands were met with an immediate and solemn apology, her suggestions ignored, her authority flouted. And lest she attempt to curtail our expeditions Fanny had tutored James in conversations which he had with Papa. So that Papa praised the governess for bringing him out and was ready for him to be brought out still further.

It was a dark November afternoon, with a hint of fog, when Fanny asked Miss Wilder to give us a little discourse on Renaissance paintings and drew us aside as she launched upon a long praise of Raphael's Madonna.

'I have got some money from Miss Wilder's purse,' she said, flushed with triumph, 'and James and I are going to see London on top of a bus. Will you come with us? We can slip out when she reaches the next room.'

'That's *stealing*! James, that's *stealing*!' I whispered.

He was shaken, but only for a moment. Fanny was masterly in argument.

'Certainly it is not stealing. The money is not Miss Wilder's. It is your papa's and he meant it for us. Think of all the sights we shall see. Buckingham Palace and St Paul's Cathedral. The Tower and Lambeth Palace. And there will be enough for us to have a cup of coffee at a stall and a penny slab of Nelson cake afterwards.'

I could see it all. The knifeboard buses were splendid contraptions, with rooftop seats and a legion of advertisements on their sides and back: Horlick's Malted Milk, Zebra Grate Polish, Pears Soap, Coleman's Mustard, Heinz 57 Varieties, Sanitas Non-Poisonous and Fragrant Disinfectant. The winding stair to the top was an adventure in itself. And then to take a seat which set all London before one's eyes; and to look down on the driver, wrapped against the cold and flicking his two great horses to a jolting trot; was nothing short of perfection.

'But what shall we tell Papa?' I asked, sorely tempted.

'We shall say we were lost. I shall ask a policeman to direct us when we have done with sight-seeing. And, of course, I shall apologise to Miss Wilder and make sure she is not blamed.'

'Are you children attending to me?' cried Miss Wilder, aware of the whispers and no doubt fearing they were directed at her.

'Yes, indeed, Miss Wilder,' said Fanny promptly. 'Helen was inquiring of me whether Raphael used the same model for all his madonnas. For are not the faces very like?' As the governess hesitated and consulted her catalogue Fanny whispered, 'Are you coming with us, Helen?'

I shook my head and she pinched my arm.

'Stay here then, Miss! And hold your tongue!' And she nodded so meaningfully in warning that I should not have dared do otherwise.

When we reached the next room they had gone. But even Fanny could not cajole, blackmail or bully the weather, and a London pea-souper brought her plans into disrepute.

It was eleven o'clock at night when a policeman brought James and Fanny home. James seemed genuinely afraid, but she merely worried lest she was unable to talk her way out of the escapade. She had also miscalculated a Puritan conscience, for Miss Wilder, seeking the safety of her soul rather than her position, had confessed all. I saw simple goodness and honesty made into a weapon of defeat, for in her anxiety the governess had painted a picture of herself which showed her as a monster of depravity: unfitted to instruct or care for tender minds and bodies. She was upstairs, packing her trunk and weeping fit to put out all the flames of Troy, when the policeman knocked at our imperial front door.

Had I, who knew far more than Miss Wilder, attempted to set matters right? Had I exposed cousin Fanny as a liar, a spy and a thief? The fears that really gnaw one's courage are nameless ones, and I feared my cousin more than the eye of God. My feeble props of truth would be kicked contemptuously away, my accusations proved unfounded, myself branded as an envious mischief-maker, if I faced Fanny. So I said nothing, and was praised for being a good child who stayed close to my governess, and she praised me too – dropping a tear on my head, and begging me to persevere with my music and needlework. And Fanny, once the situation cleared and she was confined to her room for two days with a scolding and no puddings, knew my sin of omission and played upon it. And there again all my beliefs were shattered, for James threw off the escapade with ease, showing no sorrow once his punishment was over, merely saying, 'Poor old Wilder' with a lack of respect that relegated her to the shadows for ever. It was I who *cared* – for all my weaknesses – who took the burden of her dismissal upon myself. The other two, uncaring, were freed from remorse.

Lest she be thought wicked and hard-hearted, Fanny took upon herself to walk in her sleep and be found weeping silently in corners. So that my parents forgave her, and wooed her back to her normal self.

'Do not, on any account, waken poor Fanny suddenly, if you should find her walking again!' my mamma urged. 'It is highly injurious to the mind. You may recollect that we had to take her to the sea for a month when she first came, on that account.'

I recollected more than my mamma would ever know, for poor William lay on my conscience still, though he was now a fine and sturdy little child, beginning to walk.

Forbidden pleasures were Fanny's driving force, and for a long time the belvedere had attracted her, but because of the long fall on the other side we children never found the opportunity to mount it without an adult companion. There she would stand, demurely away from the edge, and admire the view with a peculiar glint in her eyes. So far its position had confounded her, for my papa built it not only for its view but for its location. The belvedere was under observation from the back of the house at all times. My mamma's escritoire faced it from the window, the servants faced it from the kitchen, the gardener and the gardener's boy were given strict instructions to see it untenanted except on specified occasions. So only at night could it beckon, pale and tall and beautiful, from the end of the lawn, and only at night did Fanny attempt it at last. She did not intend to enjoy it alone, and chose her companion carefully. James would regard it as another lark, which did not interest her. She needed someone with her who did not want to go, who was afraid of heights and disobedience, who could suffer as an accomplice and a victim in one. She chose me.

I woke to find her dressed in one of her French gowns: a delicious affair of pleats and bows and swathed green taffeta, tucked up at the back to show four formal frills below. Her little heeled *glacé* kid boots were buttoned. The art of a French milliner had created the be-ribboned and be-flowered hat. Tormeline drops hung from her small pierced lobes. She looked far older than her fourteen years.

'Some time,' said Fanny softly, 'you must try my clothes on. Though we must take care your mamma does not see you.'

The future threat hung over my head, as though the present threat were not enough.

'Put on your wrapper,' Fanny ordered. 'We are going to climb the belvedere. And if you so much as creak a stair, Miss, I shall see you are blamed for it!'

Trembling, I followed her obediently: a lost soul, losing itself further. I had long since ceased to pray to God, since apparently He did not hear.

The night was a diamond of moonlight and frost, and the tower rose still and pure at the end of the garden. Ahead of me stalked Fanny, aware of her fashionable dress even though she had but one slave to observe it. We mounted the stone steps and the chill struck through my slippers, but Fanny's boots clicked nimbly up and she drew a deep breath of fulfilment as we reached the top. She meant to enjoy herself to the utmost and to annihilate me.

'Do you believe in God, dear Helen?' she asked idly, running her fingers along the parapet.

I said I did, though I was no longer sure. I knew that the Devil existed and was abroad, but his heavenly opponent seemed to have suffered a decline.

'And do you believe that good will prevail?' she asked.

I mumbled an assent and she laughed.

'Then you have learned nothing,' she said. 'Do you believe that you are a good child, Helen?'

I said, on the edge of tears, that I feared I was not. She smiled at me, amused and confident and beautiful.

'You are even more wicked than you know,' she said. 'For you are like all these good people, you see what you want to see and act only if it serves. You could have gone to your mamma, with Nanny's laudanum, and though Nanny would have lost her position she would not have left without harming me – and you could have told your mamma how I behaved. You did not speak for Miss Wilder, nor tell your papa that the money in her purse was not lost but stolen – and by me. You have stood by a hundred times, dear Helen, and watched me do what you would call wrong. And you will watch a thousand times, and still say nothing.

'For you are not good, you are weak. You are not obedient, you are a coward. You do not love the truth, you are a hypocrite. And however hard you pray it will make no difference, for you are not honest.'

I cried, through my tears, 'God forgives sinners. He does. He does. I shall tell my papa and my mamma everything.'

'You had better be careful,' she said quietly, 'for you are not clever, and they might think you had lost your mind. You are easily influenced, dear Helen, and things prey upon you. I shall be with you, night and day. I shall tell your mamma that someone should be with you. Someone who loves you as a sister and will watch over you. Night and day, until you go mad. Don't make a noise or I shall rouse the house and say I found you sleep-walking in the garden!'

I pressed both hands over my mouth and the tears ran from my fingers.

'And now,' said Fanny briskly, 'I am going to walk the parapet. And then *you* are going to walk it. Do not tell me otherwise. I can make you. You know that.'

'But if I fall?' I whispered. 'What if I should fall?'

She looked at me, dark and beautiful, and said, 'Then you would go to Hell.'

She had taught me deception over the last year. I was not clever enough to reach ahead of her to forestall what she might do, but the past was rich with examples of what she had done. As I watched her, arms outstretched for balance, little boots pointed delicately, face absorbed in the sweet terror of daring, I formed a deception of my own and rehearsed it in my mind.

'I heard Fanny walking in her sleep, Mamma. Poor poor Fanny. Her dreams must have transported her to those happy days she spent with her own mamma. For when I opened my door – softly, so that I should not startle her, for you have ever told me that sudden awakening injures the brain – there was poor dear Fanny dressed in her fine clothes. I followed her at a distance – like a *mouse*, Mamma, truly – to see she came to no harm.

'Oh, Mamma, Mamma, she walked through the house and into the garden – I did not think she would have dared, for was she not always obedient, and fearful of heights? Mamma, she began to mount the belvedere!

'Should I leave her, unconscious as she was, and rouse you? Should I follow her as rapidly and silently as I could, and fetch her down again? I did not know. Even as I hesitated she climbed upon the parapet! And then, Mamma, I could not *help* it, I cried, "*Fanny!*"'

I had become her mind, and to savour the full extent of my iniquity I said, 'Fanny?' very softly, so that she should know what I meant to do. And in that moment of becoming her I knew the headiness of supreme power. She turned and saw what was written in my face. Her own reflected mortal terror. So she was human after all, and could be overthrown. Her fear was luxury to me. I screamed '*Fanny!*' as though I would warn her – and pushed. Her shriek matched my own while she fell.

I have even told them, again and again, what really happened, but they hush and cradle me, and Dr Fogg shakes his head and says that the shock has temporarily disturbed my mind. For they know we were the best of friends, walking always with our arms about each other, smiling. And they know that Fanny is safe in heaven with her mamma, and that in time I shall be glad for her eternal bliss.

So she lies with the other children beneath the weeping cherubs and their urn, and when I am better I shall visit the grave after morning service each Sunday. And once a year we shall remember the anniversary of her untimely and unlucky death, and mention her in our evening prayers. And her memory will remain with us until we join her.

Now and for a long time hence I shall see the belvedere rise in my dreams, and Fanny will smile upon me from the foot of my bed, and no one will ever be the same again. She has taught me that nothing is what it seems, that the innocent may be judged guilty, that God turns His face away from the penniless and the helpless, that the betrayed may suffer more than the betrayer. I wonder whether her suggestions are true or false. *Does* my mamma tell lies about her household accounts so that she may have more money for dress? *Does* my papa visit another lady near the city? *Was* Richard almost expelled for gambling at Marlborough? *Did* Edward crouch at the housemaid's door to watch her undress, and *did* Nora see him and merely call him a saucy wretch? *Could* James have stolen those grapes from the greenhouse and let the gardener's boy be whipped for it? All these, and many more thoughts trouble me. And when I turn to Him who is without spot or stain, and beg His Mercy, there is no help to be found there either. I see Him point an accusing finger and pronounce that judgement which will live with me all my days.

'Thou shalt not kill.'

# JULIAN SYMONS

---

# The Flaw

1

'Drink your coffee.'

Celia sat feet up on the sofa reading a fashion magazine, the coffee cup on the table beside her. 'What's that?'

'I said drink your coffee. You know you like it to be piping hot.'

She contemplated the coffee, stirred it with a spoon, then put the spoon back in the saucer. 'I'm not sure it's hot enough now.'

'I poured it only a couple of minutes ago.'

'Yes, but still. I don't know that I feel like coffee tonight. But I do want a brandy.' She swung her legs off the sofa and went across to the drinks tray. 'A celebratory brandy. Can I pour one for you?'

'What are we celebrating?'

'Me, Giles, not you. I'm celebrating. But you want me to drink my coffee, don't you? All right.' She went swiftly back, lifted the coffee cup, drank the contents in two gulps and made a face. 'Not very hot. Now may I have my brandy?'

'Of course. Let me pour it for you.'

'Oh no, I'll do it myself. After all, you poured the coffee.' She smiled sweetly.

'What do you mean?'

'Just that we've both had coffee. And you poured it. But I gave it to you on the tray, remember?'

Sir Giles got up, put a hand to his throat. 'What are you trying to say?'

'Only that if I turned the tray round you'll have got my cup and I shall have got yours. But it wouldn't matter. Or would it?'

He made for the door and turned the handle, but it did not open. 'It's locked. What have you done with the key?'

'I can't imagine.' As he lumbered towards her, swaying a little, she easily evaded him. 'You think I'm a fool, Giles, don't you? I'm not, that's your mistake. So this is a celebration.'

'Celia.' His hand was at his throat again. He choked, collapsed on to the carpet and lay still.

Celia looked at him thoughtfully, finished her brandy, prodded him with her foot and said, 'Now, what to do about the body?'

The curtain came down. The first act of *Villain* was over.

2

'I enjoyed it enormously,' Duncan George said. 'Is it all right if I smoke?'

484

'Of course.' Oliver Glass was busy at the dressing-table, removing the make-up that had turned him into Sir Giles. In the glass he saw Dunc packing his pipe and lighting it. Good old Dunc, he thought, reliable dull old Dunc, his reactions are always predictable. 'Pour yourself a drink.'

'Not coffee, I hope.' Oliver's laugh was perfunctory. 'I thought the play was really clever. All those twists and turns in the plot. And you enjoy being the chief actor as well as the writer, don't you, it gives you an extra kick?'

'My dear fellow, you're a psychologist as well as a crime writer yourself, you should know. But after all, who can interpret one's own writing better than oneself? The play – well, between these four walls, it's a collection of tricks. The supreme trick is to make the audience accept it, to deceive them not once or twice but half a dozen times, to make them leave the theatre gasping at the cleverness of it all. And if that's to be done, Sir Giles has to be played on just the right note, so that we're never quite certain whether he's fooling everybody else or being fooled himself, never quite sure whether he's the villain or the hero. And who knows that better than the author? So if he happens to be an actor too, he must be perfect for the part.'

'Excellent special pleading. I'll tell you one thing, though. When the curtain comes down at the end of the first act, nobody really believes you're dead. Oliver Glass is the star, and if you're dead they've been cheated. So they're just waiting for you to come out of that cupboard.'

'But think of the tension that's building while they wait. Ready, Dunc.'

He clapped the other on the shoulder, and they walked out into the London night. Oliver Glass was a slim, elegant man in his fifties, successful both as actor and dramatist, so successful that he could afford to laugh at the critic who said that he had perfected the art of over-acting, and the other critic who remarked that after seeing an Oliver Glass play he was always reminded of the line that said life is mostly froth and bubble. Whether Oliver did laugh was another matter, for he disliked any adverse view of his abilities. He had a flat in the heart of the West End, a small house in Sussex, and a beautiful wife named Elizabeth who was fifteen years his junior.

Duncan George looked insignificant by his side. He was short and square, a practising psychiatrist who also wrote crime stories, and he had known Oliver for some years. He was typified for Oliver by the abbreviation of his first name, *Dunc*. He was exactly the kind of person Oliver could imagine dunking a doughnut into a cup of coffee, or doing something equally vulgar. With all that, however, Duncan was a good fellow. Oliver tolerated him as a companion.

They made their way through the West End to a street off Leicester Square where the Criminologists' Club met once a quarter, to eat a late supper followed by a talk on a subject of criminal interest. The members were all writers about real or fictitious crime, and on this evening Oliver Glass was to speak to them on 'The Romance of Crime', with Duncan George as his chairman. When he rose and looked around, with that gracious look in which there was just a touch of contempt, the buzz of conversation ceased.

## Julian Symons

'Gentlemen,' he began, 'criminologists – fellow crime writers – perhaps fellow criminals, I have come tonight to plead for romance in the world of crime, for the locked room murder, the impossible theft, the crime committed by the invisible man. I have come to plead that you should bring wit and style and complexity to your writings about crime, that you should remember Stevenson's view that life is a bazaar of dangerous and smiling chances, and the remark of Thomas Griffiths Wainewright when he confessed to poisoning his pretty sister-in-law: "It was a terrible thing to do, but she had thick ankles." I beseech you not to forget those thick ankles as a motive, and to abandon the dreary books some of you write concerned with examining the psychology of two equally dull people to decide which destroyed the other, or looking at bits of intestines under a microscope to determine whether a tedious husband killed his boring wife. Your sights should be set instead on the Perfect Crime . . .'

Oliver Glass spoke, as always, without notes, fluently and with style, admiring the fluency and stylishness as the words issued from his mouth. Afterwards he was challenged by some members, Duncan George among them, about the conjectural Perfect Crime. Wasn't it out of date? Not at all, Oliver said, Sir Giles in *Villain* attempted it.

'Yes, but as you remarked yourself, *Villain's* a mass of clever tricks,' Dunc said. 'Sir Giles wants to kill Celia as a kind of trick, just to prove that he can get away with it. Or at least, we think he does. Then you play all sorts of variations on the idea, is the poison really a sleeping draught, does she know about it, that kind of thing. Splendid to watch, but nobody would actually try it. In every perfect murder, so called, there is actually a flaw.' There was a chorus of agreement, by which Oliver found himself a little irritated.

'How do you know that? The Perfect Crime is one in which the criminal never puts himself within reach of the law. Perhaps, even, no crime is known to have taken place, although that is a little short of perfection. But how do we know, gentlemen, what variations on the Perfect Crime any of us may be planning, may even have carried out? "The desires of the heart are as crooked as corkscrews," as the poet says, and I'm sure Dunc can bear that out from his psychiatric experience.'

'Any of us is capable of violence under certain circumstances, if that's what you mean. But to set out to commit a Perfect Crime without a motive is the mark of a psychopath.'

'I didn't say without motive. A good motive for one man may be trivial to another.'

'Tell us when you're going to commit the Perfect Crime, and we'll see if we can solve it,' somebody said. There was a murmur of laughter.

Upon this note he left, and strolled home to Everley Court, passing the drunks on the pavements, the blacks and yellows and all conditions of foreigners, who jostled each other or stood gaping outside the sex cinemas. He made a slight detour to pass by the theatre, and saw with a customary glow of pleasure the poster: *Oliver Glass in* Villain. *The Mystery Play by Oliver Glass.* Was he really planning the Perfect Crime? There can be no doubt, he said to himself,

486

that the idea is in your mind. And the elements are there, Elizabeth and deliciously unpredictable Evelyn, and above all the indispensable Eustace. But is it more than a whim? Do I really dislike Elizabeth enough? The answer to that, of course, was that it was not a question of hatred but of playing a game, the game of Oliver Glass versus Society, even Oliver Glass versus the World.

And so home. And to Elizabeth.

A nod to Tyler, the night porter at the block of flats. Up in the lift to the third floor. Key in the door.

From the entrance hall the apartment stretched left and right. To the left Elizabeth's bedroom and bathroom. Almost directly in front of him the living-room, further to the right dining-room and kitchen, at the extreme right Oliver's bedroom and bathroom. He went into the living-room, switched on the light. On the mantelpiece there was a note in Elizabeth's scrawl: *O. Please come to see me if back before 2 a.m. E.*

For two years now they had communicated largely by means of such notes. It had begun – how had it begun? – because she was so infuriatingly talkative when he wanted to concentrate. 'I am an artist,' he had said. 'The artist needs isolation, if the fruits of genius are to ripen on the bough of inspiration.' The time had been when Elizabeth listened open-eyed to such words, but those days had gone. For a long while now she had made comments suggesting that his qualities as actor and writer fell short of genius, or had pointed out that last night he had happily stayed late at a party. She did not understand the artistic temperament. Her nagging criticism had become, quite simply, a bore.

There was, he admitted as he turned the note in his fingers, something else. There were the girls needed by the artist as part of his inspiration, the human clay turned by him into something better. Elizabeth had never understood about them, and in particular had failed to understand when she had returned to find one of them with him on the living-room carpet. She had spoken of divorce, but he knew the words to be idle. Elizabeth had extravagant tastes, and divorce would hardly allow her to indulge them. So the notes developed. They lived separate lives, with occasional evenings when she acted as hostess, or came in and chatted amiably enough to friends. For the most part the arrangement suited him rather well, although just at present his absorption with Evelyn was such . . .

He went in to see Elizabeth.

She was sitting on a small sofa, reading. Although he valued youth above all things he conceded, as he looked appraisingly at her, that she was still attractive. Her figure was slim (no children, he could not have endured the messy noisy things), legs elegant, dainty feet. She had kept her figure, as – he confirmed, looking at himself in the glass – he had kept his. How curious that he no longer found her desirable.

'Oliver.' He turned. 'Stop looking at yourself.'

'Was I doing that?'

'You know you were. Stop acting.'

'But I am an actor.'

'Acting off stage, I mean. You don't know anybody exists outside yourself.'

'There is a respectable philosophical theory maintaining that very proposition. I have invented you, you have invented me. A charming idea.'

'A very silly idea. Oliver, why don't you divorce me?'

'Have you given me cause?'

'You know how easily it can be arranged.'

He answered with a weary, a world-weary sigh. She exclaimed angrily and he gave her a look of pure dislike, so that she exclaimed again.

'You *do* dislike me, don't you? A touch of genuine feeling. So why not?' She went over to her dressing-table, sat down, took out a pot of cream.

He placed a hand on his heart. 'I was—'

'I know. You were born a Catholic. But when did you last go to church?'

'Very well. Say simply that I don't care to divorce you. It would be too vulgar.'

'You've got a new girl. I can always tell.'

'Is there anything more tedious than feminine intuition?'

'Let me tell you something. This time I shall have you followed. And *I* shall divorce *you*. What do you think of that?'

'Very little.' And indeed, who would pay her charge account at Harrods, provide the jewellery she loved, above all where would she get the money she gambled away at casinos and race meetings? She had made similar threats before, and he knew them to be empty ones.

'You want me as a kind of butterfly you've stuck with a pin, nothing more.'

She was at work with the cream. She used one cream on her face, another on her neck, a third on her legs. Then she covered her face with a black mask, which was supposed to increase the effectiveness of the cream. She often kept this mask on all night.

There had been a time when he found it exciting to make love to a woman whose face was not visible, but in her case that time had gone long ago. What was she saying now?

'Nothing gets through to you, does it? You have a sort of armour of conceit. But you have the right name, do you know that? *Glass* – if one could see through you there would be nothing, absolutely nothing there. Oliver Glass, *you don't exist.*'

Very well, he thought, very well, I am an invisible man. I accept the challenge. Elizabeth, you have signed your death warrant.


3

The idea, then, was settled. Plans had to be made. But they were still uncertain, moving around in what he knew to be his marvellously ingenious mind, when he went to visit Evelyn after lunch on the following day. Evelyn was in her early twenties, young enough – oh yes, he acknowledged it – to be his daughter, young enough also to be pleased by the company of a famous actor. But beyond that, Evelyn fascinated him by her unpredictability. She was a photographer's

# The Flaw

model much in demand, and he did not doubt that she had other lovers. There were times when she said that she was too busy to see him, or simply that she wanted to be alone, and he accepted these refusals as part of the excitement of the chase. There was a perversity about Evelyn, an abandonment to the whim of the moment, that reached out to something in his own nature. He felt sometimes that there was no suggestion so outrageous that she would refuse to consider it. She had once opened the door of her flat naked, and asked him to strip and accompany her down to the street.

Her flat was off Baker Street, and when he rang the bell there was no reply. At the third ring he felt annoyance. He had telephoned in advance, as always, and she had said she would be there. He pushed the door in a tentative way, and it swung open. In the hall he called her name. There was no reply.

The flat was not large. He went into the living-room, which was untidy as usual, glanced into the small kitchen, then went into the bedroom with its unmade bed. What had happened to her, where was she? He entered the bathroom, and recoiled from what he saw.

Evelyn lay face down, half in and half out of the bath. One arm hung over the side of the bath, the other trailed in the water. Her head rested on the side of the bath as though her neck was broken.

He went across to her, touched the arm outside the bath. It was warm. He bent down to feel the pulse. As he did so the arm moved, the body turned, and Evelyn was laughing at him.

'You frightened me. You bitch.' But he was excited, not angry.

'The author of *Villain* should be used to tricks.' She got out, handed him a towel. 'Dry me.'

Their lovemaking afterwards had the frantic, paroxysmic quality that he had found in few women. It was as though he were bringing her back from the dead. A thought struck him. 'Have you done that with anybody else?'

'Does it matter?'

'Perhaps not. I should still like to know.'

'Nobody else.'

'It was as though you were another person.'

'Good. I'd like to be a different person every time.'

He was following his own train of thought. 'My wife puts on a black mask after creaming her face at night. That should be exciting, but it isn't.'

Evelyn was insatiably curious about the details of sex, and he had told her a good deal about Elizabeth.

'I'm good for you,' she said now. 'You get a kick each time, don't you?'

'Yes. And you?'

She considered this. She had a similar figure to Elizabeth's but her features were very different, the nose snub instead of aquiline, the eyes blue and wide apart. 'In a way. Being who you are gives me a kick.'

'Is that all?'

'What do you mean?'

'Don't you like me?'

489

'It's wet to ask things like that. I never thought you were wet.' She looked at him directly with her large, slightly vacant blue eyes. 'If you want to know, I get a kick out of you because you're acting all the time. It's the acting you like, not the act. And then I get a kick out of you being an old man.'

He was so angry that he slapped her face. She said calmly, 'Yes, I like that too.'

By the time that night's performance was over his plan was made.

## 4

In the next two weeks Tyler, the night porter at Everley Court, was approached three times by a tall, bulky man wearing horn-rimmed spectacles. The man asked for Mrs Glass, and seemed upset to learn on every occasion that she was out. Once he handed a note to Tyler and then took it back, saying it wouldn't do to leave a letter lying around. Twice he left messages, to say that Charles had called and wanted to talk to Mrs Glass. On his third visit the man smelled of drink, and his manner was belligerent. 'You tell her I must talk to her,' he said in an accent that Tyler could not place, except that the man definitely came from somewhere up north.

'Yes, sir. And the name is—'

'Charles. She'll know.'

Tyler coughed. 'Begging your pardon, sir, but wouldn't it be better to telephone?'

The man glared at him. 'Do you think I haven't tried? You tell her to get in touch. If she doesn't I won't answer for the consequences.'

'Charles?' Elizabeth said when Tyler rather hesitantly told her this. 'I know two or three people named Charles, but this doesn't seem to fit any of them. What sort of age?'

'Perhaps about forty, Mrs Glass. Smartly dressed. A gentleman. Comes from the north, maybe Scotland, if that's any help.'

'No doubt it should be, but it isn't.'

'He seemed—' Tyler hesitated. 'Very concerned.'

On the following day Oliver left a note for her. '*E. Man rang while you were out, wouldn't leave message. O.*' She questioned him about the call.

'He wouldn't say what he wanted. Just rang off when I said you weren't here.'

'It must be the same man.' She explained about him. 'Tyler said he had a northern accent, probably Scottish.'

'What Scots do you know named Charles?'

'Charles Rothsey, but I haven't seen him for years. I wish he'd ring when I'm here.'

A couple of evenings later the wish was granted, although she did not speak to the man. Oliver had asked her to give a little supper party after the show for three members of the cast, and because two of them were women Duncan was invited to even up the numbers. Elizabeth was serving the cold salmon when the telephone rang in the living-room. Oliver went to answer it. He came back almost at once, looking thoughtful. When Elizabeth said it had been a quick call, he looked sharply at her. 'It was your friend Charles. He rang off. Just announced himself, then rang off when he heard my voice.'

'Who's Charles?' one of the women asked. 'He sounds interesting.'

'You'd better ask Elizabeth.'

She told the story of the man who had called, and it caused general amusement. Only Oliver remained serious. When the guests were going he asked Duncan to stay behind.

'I just wanted your opinion, Dunc. This man has called three times and now he's telephoning. What sort of man would do this kind of thing, and what can we do about it?'

'What sort of man? Hard to say.' Duncan took out his pipe, filled and lit it with maddening deliberation. 'Could be a practical joker, harmless enough. Or it could be somebody – well, not so harmless. But I don't see that you can do much about it. Obscene and threatening phone calls are ten a penny, as the police will tell you. Of course if he does show up again Elizabeth could see him, but I'd recommend having somebody else here.'

This was, Oliver considered, adequate preparation of the ground. It had been established that Elizabeth was being pursued by a character named Charles. There was no doubt about Charles's existence. He obviously existed independently of Oliver Glass, since Tyler had seen him and Oliver himself had spoken to him on the telephone. If Elizabeth was killed, the mysterious Charles would be the first suspect.

Charles had been created as somebody separate from Oliver by that simplicity which is the essence of all fine art. Oliver, like Sir Giles in *Villain*, was a master of disguise. He had in particular the ability possessed by the great Vidocq, of varying his height by twelve inches or more. Charles had been devised from a variety of props like cheek pads, body cushions and false eyebrows, plus the indispensable platform heels. He would make one more appearance, and then vanish from the scene. He would never have to meet anybody who knew Oliver well, something which he slightly regretted. And Charles on the telephone had been an actor whom Oliver had asked to ring during the evening. Oliver had merely said he couldn't talk now but would call him tomorrow, and then put down the receiver.

In the next few days he noticed with amusement tinged with annoyance that Elizabeth had fulfilled her threat of putting a private enquiry agent on his track. He spotted the man hailing a taxi just after he had got one himself, and then getting out a few yards behind him when he stopped outside Evelyn's flat. Later he pointed out the man to Evelyn, standing in a door-way opposite. She giggled, and suggested that they should ask him up.

'I believe you would,' he said admiringly. 'Is there anything you wouldn't do?'

'If I felt like it, nothing.' She was high on some drug or other. 'What about you?'

'A lot of things.'

'*Careful* old Oliver.' What would she say if she knew what he was planning? He was tempted to say something but resisted, although so far as he could tell nothing would shock her. She suddenly threw up the window, leaned out and gave a piercing whistle. When the man looked up she beckoned. He turned his head and then began to walk away. Oliver was angry, but what was the use of saying anything? It was her recklessness that fascinated him.

His annoyance was reflected in a note left for Elizabeth. '*E. This kind of spying is degrading. O.*' He found a reply that night when he came back from the theatre. '*O. Your conduct is degrading. Your present fancy is public property. E.*'

## 5

That Oliver Glass had charm was acknowledged even by those not susceptible to it. In the days after the call from Charles he exerted this charm upon Elizabeth. She went out a good deal in the afternoons, where or with whom he really didn't care, and this gave him the chance to leave little notes. One of them ran: '*E. You simply MUST be waiting here for me after the theatre. I have a small surprise for you. O.*,' and another: '*E. Would supper at Wheeler's amuse you this evening? Remembrance of things past . . . O.*' On the first occasion he gave her a pretty ruby ring set with pearls, and the reference in the second note was to the fact that they had often eaten at Wheeler's in the early months after marriage. On these evenings he set out to dazzle and amuse her as he had done in the past, and she responded. Perhaps the response was unwilling, but that no doubt was because of Evelyn. He noticed, however, that the man following him was no longer to be seen, and at their Wheeler's supper mentioned this to her.

'I know who she is. I know you've always been like that. Perhaps I have to accept it.' Her eyes flashed. 'Although if I want to get divorce evidence it won't be difficult.'

'An artist needs more than one woman,' Oliver said. 'But you must not think that I can do without you. I need you. You are a fixed point in a shifting world.'

'What nonsense I do talk,' he said to himself indulgently. The truth was that contact with her nowadays was distasteful to him. By the side of Evelyn she was insipid. A great actor, however, can play any part, and this one would not be maintained for long.

Only one faintly disconcerting thing happened in this, as he thought of it, second honeymoon period. He came back to the flat unexpectedly early one afternoon, and heard Elizabeth's voice on the telephone. She replaced the receiver as he entered the room. Her face was flushed. When he asked who she had been speaking to, she said, 'Charles.'

'Charles?' For a moment he could not think who she was talking about. Then he stared at her. Nobody knew better than he that she could not have been speaking to Charles, but of course he could not say that.

'What did he say?'

'Beastly things. I put down the receiver.'

Why was she lying? How absurd, how deliciously absurd, if she had a lover. Or was it possible that somebody at the supper party was playing a practical joke? He brushed aside such conjectures because they did not matter now. Nothing could interfere with the enactment of the supreme drama of his life.

## 6

Celia's intention in *Villain* was to explain Sir Giles's absence by saying that he had gone away on a trip, something he did from time to time. Hence the remark about disposition of the body at the end of Act One. Just after the beginning of the second act the body was revealed by Celia to her lover shoved into a cupboard, a shape hidden in a sack. A few minutes later the cupboard was opened again, and the shape was seen by the audience, although not by Celia, to move slightly. Then, after twenty-five minutes of the second act, there was a brief blackout on stage. When the lights went up Sir Giles emerged from the cupboard, not dead but drugged.

To be enclosed within a sack for that length of time is no pleasure, and in any ordinary theatrical company the body in the sack would have been that of the understudy, with the leading man changing over only a couple of minutes before he was due to emerge from the cupboard. But Oliver believed in what he called the theatre of the actual. In another play he had insisted that the voice of an actress shut up for some time in a trunk must be real and not a recording, so that the actress herself had to be in the trunk. In *Villain* he maintained that the experience of being actually in the sack was emotionally valuable, so that he always stayed in it for the whole length of time it was in the cupboard.

The body in the sack was to provide Oliver with an unbreakable alibi. The interval after Act One lasted fifteen minutes, so that he had nearly forty minutes free. Everley Court was seven minutes' walk from the theatre, and he did not expect to need much more than twenty minutes all told. The body in the sack would be seen to twitch by hundreds of people, and who could be in it but Oliver?

In fact Useful Eustace would be the sack's occupant. Eustace was a dummy used by stage magicians who wanted to achieve very much the effect at which Oliver aimed, of persuading an audience that there was a human being inside a container. He was made of plastic, and inflated to the size of a small man. You then switched on a mechanism which made Eustace kick out arms and legs in a galvanic manner. A battery-operated timer in his back could be set to operate at intervals ranging from thirty seconds to five minutes. When deflated, Eustace folded up neatly, into a size no larger than a plastic mackintosh.

Eustace was the perfect accomplice, Useful Eustace indeed. Oliver had tried him out half a dozen times inside a sack of similar size, and he looked most convincing.

On the afternoon of The Day he rested. Elizabeth was out, but said that she would be back before seven. His carefully worded note was left on her mantelpiece. '*E. I want you at the flat ALL this evening. A truly sensational surprise for you. All the evening, mind, not just after the show. O.*' Her curiosity would not, he felt sure, be able to resist such a note.

During Act One he admired, with the detachment of the artist, his own performance. He was cynical, ironic, dramatic – in a word, superb. When it was over he went unobtrusively to his dressing room. He had no fear of visitors, for he was known to detest any interruption during the interval.

And now came what in advance he felt to be the only ticklish part of the operation. The cupboard with the sack in it opened on to the back of the stage. The danger of carrying out an inflated Eustace from dressing-room to stage was too great – he must be inflated on site, as it were, and it was possible although unlikely that a wandering stage hand might see him at work. The Perfect Crime does not depend upon chance or upon the taking of risks, and if the worst happened, if he was seen obviously inflating a dummy, the project must be abandoned for the present time. But fortune favours the creative artist, or did so on this occasion. Inflation of Eustace by pump took only a few moments as he knelt by the cupboard, and nobody came near. The timer had been set for movement every thirty seconds. He put Eustace into the sack, waited to see him twitch, closed the cupboard's false back, and strolled away.

He left the theatre by an unobtrusive exit used by those who wanted to avoid the autograph hunters outside the stage door, and walked along head down until he reached the nearest Underground station, one of the few in London equipped with lockers and lavatories. Unhurriedly he took Charles's clothes and shoes from the locker, went into a lavatory, changed, put his acting clothes back in the locker. Spectacles and revolver were in his jacket pocket. He had bought the revolver years ago, when he had been playing a part in which he was supposed to be an expert shot. By practice in a shooting range he had in fact become a quite reasonable one.

As he left the station he looked at his watch. Six minutes. Very good.

Charles put on a pair of grey gloves from another jacket pocket. Three minutes brought him to Everley Court. He walked straight across to the lift, something he could not do without being observed by Tyler. The man came over, and in Charles's husky voice, with its distinctive accent, he said: 'Going up to Mrs Glass. Expecting me.'

'I'll ring, sir. It's Mr Charles, isn't it?'

'No need. I said, she's expecting me.'

Perfectly, admirably calm. But in the lift he felt, quite suddenly, that he would be unable to do it. To allow Elizabeth to divorce him and then to marry or live with Evelyn until they tired of each other, wouldn't that after all be the sensible, obvious thing? But to be *sensible*, to be *obvious*, were such things worthy of Oliver Glass? Wasn't the whole point that by this death, which in a practical sense was needless, he would show the character of a great artist and a great actor, a truly superior man?

The lift stopped. He got out. The door confronted him. Put key in lock, turn. Enter.

The flat was in darkness, no light in the hall. No sound. 'Elizabeth,' he called, in a voice that did not seem his own. He had difficulty in not turning and leaving the flat.

He opened the door of the living-room. This also was in darkness. Was

Elizabeth not there after all, had she ignored his note or failed to return? He felt a wave of relief at the thought, but still there was the bedroom. He must look in the bedroom.

The door was open, a glimmer of light showed within. He did not remember taking the revolver from his pocket, but it was in his gloved hand.

He took two steps into the room. Her dimmed bedside light was switched on. She lay on the bed naked, the black mask over her face. He called out something and she sat up, stretched out arms to him. His reaction was one of disgust and horror. He was not conscious of squeezing the trigger, but the revolver in his hand spoke three times.

She did not call out but gave a kind of gasp. A patch of darkness showed between her breasts. She sank back on the bed.

With the action taken, certainty returned to him. Everything he did now was efficient, exact. He got into the lift, took it down to the basement and walked out through the garage down there, meeting nobody. Tyler would be able to say when Mr Charles had arrived, but not when he left.

Back to the Underground lavatory, clothes changed, Charles's clothing and revolver returned to locker for later disposal, locker key put in handkerchief pocket of jacket. Return to the theatre, head down to avoid recognition. A quick glance at his watch as he opened the back door and moved silently up the stairs. Nearly thirty minutes had passed.

He knelt at the back of the cupboard and listened to a few lines of dialogue. The moment at which the body was due to give its twitch had gone, and Eustace proved his lasting twitching capacity by giving another shudder, of course not seen by the audience because the cupboard door was closed. Eustace had served his purpose. Oliver withdrew him from the sack and switched him off. With slight pressure to get out the air he was quickly reduced and folded into a bundle. Oliver slipped the bundle inside his trousers, and secured it with a safety pin. The slight bulge might have been apparent on close examination, but who would carry out such an examination upon stage?

Beautiful, he thought, as he wriggled into the sack for the few minutes before he. had to appear on stage. Oliver Glass, I congratulate you in the name of Thomas de Quincey and Thomas Griffiths Wainewright. You have committed the Perfect Crime.


7

The euphoria lasted through the curtain calls and his customary few casual words with the audience, in which he congratulated them on being able to appreciate an intelligent mystery. It lasted – oh, how he was savouring the only real achievement of his life – while he leisurely removed Sir Giles's make-up, said goodnight, and left the theatre still with Eustace pinned to him. He made one further visit to the Underground, as a result of which Eustace joined Charles's clothes in the locker. The key back in the handkerchief pocket.

As he was walking back to Everley Court, however, he realised with a shock

that something had been forgotten. The note! The note which said positively
that he would be at the flat during the interval, a note which if the police saw it
would certainly lead to uncomfortable questions, perhaps even to a search, and
discovery of the locker key. The note was somewhere in the flat, perhaps in
Elizabeth's bag. It must be destroyed before he rang the police.

He nodded to Tyler, took the lift up. Key in door again. The door open. Then
he stopped.

Light gleamed under the living-room door.

Impossible, he thought, impossible. I know that I did not switch on the light
when I opened that door. But then who could be inside the room? He took two
steps forward, turned the handle, and when the door was open sprang back with
a cry.

'Why, Oliver. What's the matter?' Elizabeth said. She sat on the sofa. Duncan
stood beside her.

He pulled at his collar, feeling as though he was about to choke, then tried to
ask a question but could not utter words.

'Come and see,' Duncan said. He approached and took Oliver by the arm.
Oliver shook his head, resisted, but in the end let himself be led to the bedroom.
The body still lay there, the patch of red between the breasts.

'You even told her about Elizabeth's bedtime habits,' Dunc said. 'She must
have thought you'd have some fun.' He lifted the black mask. Evelyn looked up
at him.

Back in the living-room he poured himself brandy and said to Elizabeth, 'You
knew?'

'Of course. *Would supper at Wheeler's amuse you this evening?* Do you think I
didn't know you were acting as you always are, making some crazy plan.
Though I could never have believed it – it was Dunc who guessed how crazy it
was.'

He looked from one of them to the other. 'You're lovers?' Duncan nodded.
'My dreary wife and my dull old friend Dunc – a perfect pair.'

Duncan took out his pipe, looked at it, put it back in his pocket. 'Liz had kept
me in touch with what was going on, naturally. It seemed that you must be
going to do something or other tonight. So Liz spent the evening with me.'

'Why was Evelyn here?' His mind moved frantically from one point to
another to see where he had gone wrong.

'We knew about her from having you watched, and all that nonsense about
Charles made me think that Elizabeth must be in some sort of danger. So it
seemed a good idea to send your note to Evelyn, so that she could be here to
greet you. We put the flat key in the envelope.'

'The initials were the same.'

'Just so,' Dunc said placidly.

'You planned for me to kill her.'

'I wouldn't say that. Of course if you happened to mistake her for Liz – but we
couldn't guess that she'd put on Liz's mask. We just wanted to warn you that
playing games is dangerous.'

'You can't prove anything.'

'Oh, I think so,' Dunc said sagely. 'I don't know how you managed to get away from the theatre, some sort of dummy in the sack I suppose? No doubt the police will soon find out. But the important thing is that note. It's in Evelyn's handbag. Shows you arranged to meet her here. Jealous of some younger lover, I suppose.'

'But I *wasn't* jealous, I didn't arrange—' He stopped.

'Can't very well say it was for Liz, can you? Not when Evelyn turned up.' The door bell rang. 'Oh, I forgot to say we called the police when we found the body. Our duty, you know.' He looked at Oliver and said reflectively, 'You remember I said there was always a flaw in the Perfect Crime? Perhaps I was wrong. I suppose you might say the Perfect Crime is one you benefit from but don't commit yourself, so that nobody can say you're responsible. Do you see what I mean?' Oliver saw what he meant. 'And now it's time to let in the police.'

# MILES TRIPP

## Fixation

It was Freddie, my oldest friend, who dragged me out of a sinking spiral of depression following my mother's death. He wouldn't accept my refusal to go out for a drink and when we were sitting in a pub he asked what the trouble was. I told him there was no trouble. He didn't reply. He simply rested his hand on the sleeve of my coat for a few seconds and then removed it. He still didn't speak. It was obvious he didn't intend to speak. 'I'm beginning to wonder if I'm quite normal,' I burst out.

He didn't laugh. He didn't look surprised. He said, 'Don't we all sometimes wonder whether we're normal?' and took a long drink.

It was difficult to believe the implication of his remark. What worries could Freddie have? He was happily married, he had three daughters, a splendid home and he was senior partner in a well-established legal firm. To all appearances he lived a full and successful life. 'You are certainly normal,' I stated.

'Am I? What is normal?'

'That's not easy. Not in a few words.'

'What is abnormal then?' he asked.

'Isn't it a bit abnormal,' I asked, 'for a man of forty-two to have spent all his life with his mother and when she has gone to realise that his life has been devoted to performing for her, to winning praise and approval? Is that abnormal or normal?'

'I'll answer that,' he said, 'by telling you of the time when I wondered whether I was normal.' And he told me of a period when he had quarrelled violently, and every day, with one of his daughters until the stage was reached when he felt unsafe to be alone with her in case he strangled her. Fortunately one of his clients was a psychiatrist who had told him the border between normality and abnormality would only be crossed if, once the daughter started going out with boy-friends, Freddie still continued the warfare. It was a certainty that the girl wouldn't continue once she had a boy-friend.

Freddie gave me a quick glance. 'It seems that fathers and daughters can have pretty complicated relationships under the surface, but these are quite normal. I was normal.'

It was astute of him to make the observation about fathers and daughters because there had been times when I had wondered – never very coherently and with thoughts quickly suppressed – about mothers and sons. References in books and newspaper articles to the Oedipus complex have always made me feel uncomfortable, particularly since my father's death was inadvertently caused by me when I was a small boy. I fell off a pier into the sea. My father, who couldn't really swim, jumped after me and was drowned. I was saved by a local lifeguard.

'So you see,' Freddie continued, 'we all get these times of doubt. You are as normal as the next man but I'd like to give you a bit of advice. It's free. No professional charge.'

'I know. I need a holiday. No thanks, Freddie.'

'Get married.'

I had to laugh. I know it was impolite, but I couldn't help it. What woman would look twice at a man of my age, whose face had never been his fortune, and who held a humdrum job as an executive in a firm of chartered accountants.

'I know of a marriage bureau,' he said, 'where they interview you very carefully and then get a computer to work out what sort of partner is likely to be compatible. I'm told it works very well.'

Sometimes, in the quiet of my flat, I had wondered about consulting a marriage bureau but could never nerve myself to take the plunge.

'Don't forget,' he said, 'you'll not only be doing yourself a good turn, you'll be doing someone else a good turn. Someone who at this very moment is probably sitting alone wondering whether her loneliness will ever end.'

Although it was a busy pub and there was noise and movement all around I felt as though I was sitting in a sealed capsule. I was an astronaut on a launch pad and it was for me, and only me, to decide whether the infinite sky should be explored.

'All systems go,' I said.

He grinned. 'That's more like it. I'll arrange the interview for you. Can't do more than that, I'm afraid.'

I had a snatch of awful hesitation. 'Not this week,' I said.

'I'll arrange it tomorrow and don't tell me you can't take a couple of hours away from adjusting other people's tax returns, because I know you can . . . Have another?'

'It's not Dutch courage I need at this moment.'

'You'll be all right. Damn it, what have you got to lose?'

I had no answer.

'You can only gain,' he said.

I was interviewed, documented, tabulated, coded and programmed into a computer.

Two weeks later I was looking at a photograph of Kay. A little white triangle of a face with big, staring eyes, and hair torn back from temples and forehead. I remember thinking, 'She looks quite pretty,' and then, 'Why has she found it hard to get married?'

She was thirty-five, an audio-typist in the personnel department of a London store, and her interests were reading, crocheting and walking. She liked to go on day trips to the country and would try to identify and name all the wild flowers and grasses she saw. She enjoyed listening to classical music, and cooking French regional dishes. She usually took her holidays in France.

The computer had done its work well.

We could have met in the bureau's office but it was suggested that I should ring her for a date for an evening meal. A particular restaurant was recommended where the service and food were excellent, and we could be sure of special attention if I mentioned the bureau when making the reservation. It was important that slow service or indifferent waiting should not spoil the evening.

A timid voice answered the telephone and when I announced my name and asked if we could have a meal together the voice became slightly breathless, but the date was made and two evenings later we met.

She was small and fragile and looked like a sparrow that might dart into flight if anyone came too close.

We shook hands and I asked if she would like a drink or whether she would prefer to go straight in for a meal.

'I'd like a gin and tonic,' she said.

We sat opposite each other at a small table. A waiter swooped and was an attentive parrot to my order. I began to feel more confident.

'It looks like rain,' I said.

'I listened to the forecast before I came out.' She paused and gathered breath. 'They expect a cold front bringing rain to reach London during the night.'

'The farmers need rain.'

'Yes.'

'Not that there are many farmers in London,' I said. It was meant as a little joke, but she gave the futile remark a sort of strained and serious attention.

'No,' she said, after a pause.

'What I mean is that the rain tonight in London won't mean much to farming communities.' Although the tiny joke was dead I was parading its corpse. And even as I spoke I realised the phrase 'farming communities' was one I had never used before. Hearing my own voice was rather like overhearing a pedantic stranger talking about the most boring triviality imaginable. And then my mind went utterly blank. All the conversational gambits I had rehearsed were scattered to the four corners of my unconscious mind. If she didn't speak we should sit here for ever, figures trapped in an engraving of embarrassment.

'Have you had a holiday this year?' she asked.

She had produced one of my lost gambits.

'Not yet. I suppose I should plan something but since my mother's death . . . We used to go on a cruise each August . . . How about you?'

'I used to go away with a girl-friend. But the last of my single girl-friends got married in March and . . . I don't fancy going on my own.'

The waiter arrived with our drinks.

I lifted my glass to her. 'Cheers.'

'Cheers,' she replied, and her hand was shaking so much as she raised her glass that she had to use the other hand to steady it. When she drank it was as though she was holding a chalice.

Then she put down the glass and said, 'Look, if you would sooner finish these drinks and say goodbye, we can. The meal hasn't been ordered.'

I felt as breathless as she sounded. Had she decided against me, having met and seen me? A voice which I scarcely recognised as my own said, 'I'm in no hurry to go. But how about you?'

She smiled for the first time, and if smiles were electrical discharges I should have become a pile of bemused ash. And when the enchanting, stunning smile faded, she said, 'I don't want to go. I like the view from where I'm sitting.' And she directed another smile at me.

It was at this moment we fell in love.

The following weeks were a dream but as the wedding date drew near I had misgivings, not about the marriage but about my competence. I was inexperienced.

Because this subject has some bearing on what follows I cannot gloss over it, but briefly, I had a word with Freddie about my fears and his advice was, 'For God's sake don't leave it to the first night of the honeymoon unless there's no alternative. Start now, and start slowly. Get to know each other gently. Don't worry if nothing happens on the first or second nights. It will. Leave it to Mother Nature, but don't try to push the old girl. Nothing good ever came of trying to push Mother Nature.'

Freddie's advice was absolutely right. What a splendid lawyer the man is.

By the time we went on honeymoon – to a little French village near the Pyrenees where the scent of flowers is so strong that it seems to pervade food and drink and even the pores of one's body – we were lovers, and completely attuned.

That was seven years ago.

Marriage didn't alter our lives. I continued to work in an accountant's office and Kay, after a six-month period of housekeeping, decided she preferred to be a working girl and went back to being an audio-typist. We changed physically, however. My scant hair accelerated its departure and within a year I was completely bald, and within two years I had a disgraceful paunch. Kay's appearance changed more dramatically. 'I used to be an undersized weakling,' she laughed. 'Now look at me!'

In her own words she was 'a tub on two match-sticks', and although this was a slur on her beautiful legs, she had certainly put on weight. Her face had filled out too; but I love her face and every surplus ounce on her. To someone looking at her objectively she would be a plump, ordinary, middle-aged woman, but I cannot be objective about her although, in retrospect, I can see that when the trouble started I did act with admirable objectivity.

She would usually come home to our flat an hour before me and prepare the evening meal. It was on a perfect June evening as we were clearing away the plates that she said, 'Have I ever mentioned Wilson to you?'

'No. Who's Wilson?'

'He's fairly new. In the Buying Department. He's only about twenty.' She hesitated. 'He seems to have a ridiculous sort of crush on me.'

I asked what she meant and I felt mildly amused.

'He makes all sorts of excuses to come into our room. And he hangs about looking at me. Josie and Pat pull my leg about it.'

'He hasn't asked you for a date, then?' I asked jokingly.

'No. He seems too shy for that. He just stands. And looks. It's getting quite unnerving.'

'It's your fatal fascination,' I said.

Kay wasn't amused. 'It's absurd,' she said. 'I'm old enough to be his mother. There are dozens of young attractive girls around the place. Why pick on me to make sheep's eyes at?'

'If it bothers you, you can tell him to shove off,' I said, but immediately I had spoken I knew this would be difficult. Kay is incapable of being rude to anyone.

'Oh well,' she said, 'I expect he'll get tired of it when he sees he's getting nowhere.' And that, so far as I was concerned, was the end of Wilson.

But one evening during the next week, just after we had switched off the television and were preparing to go to bed, she said, 'There's something I must tell you.'

An anxious note in her voice made me stop whatever I was doing and look at her.

'It's been on my mind all evening,' she said.

'What has?'

'You remember I told you about Denis Wilson?'

I had to think. The name 'Denis' wasn't familiar.

'You know,' Kay said. 'The boy at our office.'

'Oh yes. What's he been up to now?'

'On Monday he was waiting for me at the main entrance when we were all leaving. I know it was me he was waiting for. He said, "Goodnight." It was the same yesterday, Tuesday. Today he came across and said, "May I speak to you?"'

'What did you say?'

'I asked what he wanted. Do you know what he said?'

How could I know? 'I've no idea,' I said rather brusquely.

'He asked if I'd have a drink with him in the lunch hour tomorrow.'

This jolted me. 'And what did you say?'

'I said, "No thank you," and hurried off. He didn't try to follow, but I felt very upset. I know it sounds stupid but when I stopped at the Underground to get a ticket my legs were shaking.'

I put my arms round her. 'Don't think anything more about it, darling. He probably had to get it out of his system and now that you've given him the brush-off he won't bother you any more.'

'I hope he doesn't,' she said. 'There's nothing wrong with him. To look at, I mean. But there's something about him that frightens me. Josie says I'm an idiot to worry about it. She says he'll soon get tired.'

'I'm sure she's right.'

'But I think even Josie and Pat are a bit puzzled by it. There are so many young and pretty girls he could choose from but he doesn't seem interested in any of them. I'm twice his age and not a beauty by any stretch of the imagination.'

I told her my imagination didn't need to stretch an inch to find her beautiful.

She nestled against me. 'You're different,' she said, and she added softly, 'Thank God.'

The following evening I asked whether the young fellow had troubled her. She said she hadn't seen him. But the next day, Friday, she told me she had seen a medical certificate for Wilson on the Personnel Manager's desk. He was suffering from gastric enteritis but expected to return to work early next week.

'No doubt caused by frustrated calf-love,' I said, trying to make a joke of it.

Kay said, 'I hope not,' and I was surprised to see that she had taken my remark seriously. 'I'd hate to be the cause of anyone's – pain,' she said.

'He's probably eaten too many green apples,' I said, but this time, although I meant it to sound reassuring, I had the first intimation, or perhaps it was an intuition, that I should take the Wilson business more seriously.

I suppose it was about two weeks later when we were walking home from the cinema that I asked, 'How's the Wilson boy these days?'

We had been walking slowly side by side, enjoying the mild evening, but she quickened her step. 'He's all right.'

'Not giving any trouble?'

'Not here,' she said. 'Wait till we get home.'

Ten minutes later, as she was making coffee, she said, 'It seems to be getting worse.'

'How do you mean?'

'He hangs round the main entrance to see me arrive in the morning, he comes into our room on the most feeble pretexts and he hangs around in the evening to say "Goodnight".'

'He hasn't asked you out for a drink again?'

'No. But I think he might have tonight only I had Pat with me and I sensed he was disappointed. He gave her a sort of look.'

'What sort of look?'

'I can't describe it. But she noticed it too. She said it made her feel like a gooseberry.'

She passed a mug of coffee. 'He makes me nervous,' she said. 'I get a terrible feeling of panic inside me when I see him. And then I tell myself he can't help what he's doing. I ought to feel sorry for him.'

I snorted into my coffee. 'Don't waste your emotions on him. He isn't worth it.'

'But if he's . . . I mean . . . People do get fixations, don't they?'

I don't know why this question, and the use of the word 'fixation' should have made me suddenly very annoyed, but it did. 'Is that what you think this is?' I said. 'A fixation?'

She lowered her eyes. 'Josie said she read a letter in a woman's magazine some time ago about a similar sort of situation and the reply was that young men sometimes get fixations on older women. The thing is for the woman to give absolutely no encouragement. Eventually it fades or he gets fixated elsewhere.'

'You don't encourage him?'

She lifted her eyes, and to my dismay I saw they were filled with tears. 'Of course I don't,' she said. 'What sort of woman do you think I am?'

Rather unhappily we went to bed. That night our love-making lacked something, not in technique (to use the textbook word) but in mental harmony. Afterwards we lay silent. Then, out of the darkness Kay said, 'I wonder if he thinks about me all the time or just when he's at work.'

I didn't reply but her words stabbed me with an arrow of anxiety. Kay soon went to sleep but dawn was creeping into the eastern sky before I drifted into a shallow loss of wakefulness.

It was on the following night that the telephone calls started. Kay answered, and I turned down the sound of television.

'It is,' she said.

'Yes,' she said.

'What do you want?' she asked.

'Certainly not,' she said.

She hung up the receiver without saying goodbye.

'Not him,' I said incredulously.

'He must be mad,' she said. 'Ringing me here. He must know you'll be home.'

'What did he want?'

'I asked him.'

'I heard you. What did he say?'

Kay flushed. 'He said, "You know what I want. Will you come out with me?"'

'Well, your reply should have given him the message. You sounded very firm.'

'I need a drink,' she said.

I got her a drink without question but it worried me that she should be so upset by the call that her first thought was for alcohol to steady her nerves.

The telephone rang again the next evening and I answered.

The caller rang off.

He rang again an hour later. Again I answered. Again he rang off.

The third time he rang Kay answered and I stood beside her.

'Yes,' she said.

'It's me,' said a man's voice.

'What do you want?' she asked, and I took the phone from her.

'Please come out with me. Just for a drink. I need to talk to you.'

'Look here,' I said. 'If you don't stop troubling my wife I shall call the police.'

He rang off when I reached the word 'wife'.

Kay gave me an agonised look. 'We can't go on like this,' she said. 'Every time the phone goes my heart seems to lurch.'

I thought for a few moments. 'Tomorrow I'll come with you to the store,' I said, 'and if he's there I shall tell him in no uncertian terms what I shall do if he persists in his conduct.'

I don't know what reaction I expected from Kay. A look of gratitude perhaps. I didn't expect her to groan, 'Oh no!'

'Why not?'

'I'm sure he can't help himself. It's something out of his control.'

'But not out of my bloody control,' I replied.

That night we didn't make love.

Kay's store is in Oxford Street. At nine in the morning the street is a rush of workers scurrying from buses and trains, most of them looking as though they are late for an urgent, but somewhat unpleasant, appointment. At least, the older ones look like this; the younger ones are more casual. They wander and seem to get in the way of the dedicated clockers-in.

'That's him,' whispered Kay.

She was gazing at a tall, thin youth. His pale face was fringed with dark hair which fell in curls to his shoulders. He had what used to be called 'poetic good looks' and I felt a twinge of jealousy.

'Please don't be unkind to him,' said Kay.

She had tried to dissuade me from coming along, and this final plea was very annoying. Why shouldn't I be unkind to him? He had been unkind to us.

'You go along,' I said. 'I'll see you tonight.' Later I realised that this was the first time we had ever parted without a kiss.

I made straight for the young man and said, 'Your name is Denis Wilson?'

He looked startled. 'That's right.'

'And you have been pestering my wife. Asking her to go out with you.'

'I only want to talk with her,' he said.

'She doesn't want to talk with you.'

He flinched. 'I'm sorry,' he said.

'I'm sorry too. This thing is becoming a nuisance to both of us. My wife and me.'

'I'm sorry,' he repeated.

'So you've already said. It's got to stop. If you bother her any more, hang around for her, speak to her or ring us up, I shall report this to your manager and to the police. Is that clear?'

He nodded, and I felt a sense of relief. All he needed was a straight talking to.

'I have your promise that you won't cause any more trouble?' I asked.

'What do you mean? Trouble?'

He looked at me with soft brown eyes.

'You know exactly what I mean.'

He gave a sigh. 'I love Kay,' he said.

What I did was incxcusable, but I don't regret it. I grabbed his shirt collar intending to shake him as one might shake a naughty pup, but as I tugged the collar his tie, a scarlet bow tie, came away in my hand. I gazed at it feeling somehow off-balance.

'If you like it, you can keep it,' he said, and before I could give him back the tie he turned and ran into the building.

Kay was standing on the steps. Our eyes met, and then she followed him inside.

That evening she said she had felt humiliated when she saw me grab at his collar. I asked whether he had been waiting for her when she left, and she said, 'No.'

'In that case,' I said, 'your humiliation was worth it. He's obviously seen the error of his ways.'

A few minutes later the telephone rang. I picked it up. 'Yes?'

'This is Denis,' said a voice.

'I warned you this morning to stop this nonsense.'

'May I speak to Kay? Just for a moment?'

'You may not,' I said and slammed down the phone. Turning to Kay I said, 'He's asking for it.'

She was apprehensive. 'What are you going to do?'

'There's no point in making threats if one isn't prepared to carry them out.'

'No. Please, no!'

'I'm sorry, Kay. I've had enough. I'm involved in this too.'

'Please, please!'

There is no point in relating word by word, phrase by phrase, how I slowly weakened. Nor how our love-making reached a new height that night. It is sufficient to say that at this stage I did nothing more than fix an appointment to see Freddie. I didn't tell Kay.

As ever, Freddie was the cheery, solicitous friend. 'What can I do for you, old chap?' he asked. 'By the look on your face it's not advice on a fortune you've inherited.'

He listened patiently to my account of the absurd infatuation of Denis Wilson for Kay. And yet it wasn't a resigned patience. Once or twice (it might have been my imagination) I thought he was on the verge of smiling. When I had finished he said, 'All this is a great compliment to Kay, and indirectly a compliment to you for choosing Kay.' He seemed to be speaking with perfect seriousness. 'I can understand that you might be aggravated,' he said, and then qualified this statement by adding, 'In a way, I can see it.'

'Wouldn't you be annoyed, Freddie?'

He picked up his pen and began to peck at the blotting pad on his desk. 'Perhaps I should,' he said. 'But you know Cynthia.'

I did know his wife but the implication escaped me.

'How do you mean?'

'Obviously Kay and Cynthia aren't the same. We're all different. But Cynthia would have frozen him off within ten seconds.'

'Kay finds it difficult to be – cold.'

'I know. I appreciate that. And I'm not saying that she's actively encouraging him . . .'

'I should hope not!'

'But a woman of Kay's years . . . How old is she?'

'Forty-two.'

'Women of forty-two usually know how to handle these situations.'

'Kay doesn't,' I said doggedly. 'And I want it to stop. How do I go about it?'

Freddie frowned slightly. 'My advice is – do nothing. You've already done enough. Technically you committed an assault on him. Tell Kay not to speak to him if he speaks to her, and if she's always with another woman he's bound to give up in the end. No man can persist against endless snubs.'

'Wilson can. What about reporting it to the police?'

He shook his head. 'What can they do? He isn't guilty of threatening behaviour. There's been no breach of the peace. The police will dismiss it as a domestic matter.'

'I'm sorry, Freddie. I want some action. What about suing him for invasion of privacy?'

He continued to prod the blotting pad with his pen. 'Not in this country, old chap,' he said. 'It might be different in the States, but the courts over here don't recognise what you call "invasion of privacy".'

'Can't you do anything?' I asked.

He put down the pen and looked me straight in the eyes. 'The fellow is obviously a bit of a pest but I wouldn't be optimistic about obtaining an injunction to restrain him from molesting Kay. And that's your only legal remedy. Look at the facts. He has hung around for her at her place of employment – but it is his place of employment too. He has telephoned your flat a few times, and these are admittedly annoyances. But would they amount to a nuisance in a court of law. I doubt it. This isn't a case of obscene calls. He's been quite well-mannered and polite, as I understand it. Apart from anything else an action on the grounds of nuisance – which I don't think this is – happens to be a lengthy and expensive process.'

'In other words, you don't want to act for me.' I said huffily.

To Freddie's credit he didn't greet this remark with the chill it deserved. He said, 'You can always count on me, old chap, but you said something earlier about not making threats unless you were prepared to carry them out. I feel the same. I could easily write to this man and say that my client has instructed me with regard to the unwelcome attention being paid to my client's wife, and unless these attentions cease we shall reluctantly be compelled to institute proceedings against him. I can say that, but I wouldn't want to carry it through. I don't think you've got a case. However, if you're not satisfied with my opinion, I could take counsel's opinion.'

I felt as though I were banging my head against a brick wall. I knew and respected Freddie well enough to realise that he was giving good advice.

'Try to treat the whole thing as a joke,' he said, 'even if it's a joke in rather bad taste.'

I stood up. 'I doubt if I can do that. I'm a bit old-fashioned. But thanks for the advice, Freddie.'

'Now don't go doing anything silly, will you? And for God's sake don't grab hold of him again. If you can treat it as a joke you'll find that it's become a joke. And I'll bet, six months from now, you'll have forgotten his name.'

Looking back, I can see that the sensible course would have been for Kay to leave the store and find a job elsewhere. But she liked the work and I felt that for her to resign would be a sort of defeat. Too often in life the innocent suffer through the actions of irrational and selfish people. Why should Kay be another victim?

I decided to take advantage of the Personnel Department summer party to approach Kay's boss about Wilson. These parties, sociable without being exciting, were normally held in the private bar of a pub to the rear of the store. The formula was the same this year. Members of the staff were each allowed to bring one guest. I was Kay's guest.

Her boss was an extrovert who answered to the name of 'Mr Forbes'. He was in his early fifties and with erect bearing and trim moustache he looked like a retired army officer.

When Kay was busy elsewhere I went across to him.

'Hello there,' he said. 'No spot prizes today!'

This was a reference to a prize Kay and I had won during a waltz at the Christmas dance.

'I wonder if I could speak to you for a few moments, Mr Forbes. Off the record, as it were.'

His smile vanished and he assumed the air of a man accustomed to being entrusted with important confidences. 'Somthing to do with Kay?' he asked.

'Yes.'

'Happy here, isn't she? We're all very fond of Kay.' He was annulling in advance any complaint that she was unhappy through neglect.

'Oh yes. She enjoys her work and likes her colleagues in Personnel. But there is a fly in the ointment.'

He listened to the story of Wilson. At first his forehead was furrowed with concern but gradually this expression changed to one of slight hostility.

'Sounds like a storm in a teacup,' he said when I had finished. 'Wilson's a very good man. Excellent progress reports.'

'I was hoping you might have a word with him.'

He shook his head. 'Let's be men of the world,' he said, and paused.

I had no objection to being a man of the world. If I am not a man of this world, of what world am I a man? I said I didn't understand what he was driving at.

'A young lad finds your wife attractive. Nothing criminal in that. Flattering, if anything. He asks her out for a drink. Nothing criminal in that either.' He lowered his voice. 'There are hundreds of friendships made in office hours. You know that. I know that. Nothing harmful. Just a couple of people who get along well having a drink or a meal together in the lunch hour. They may be married to other parties, but what's the harm? Anyway, where's the opportunity, even if harm crossed their minds?'

'That isn't the point.'

Forbes straightened his shoulders and looked very military. 'This is not a departmental problem,' he said. 'I'm sure Kay, or one of her friends, is capable of treading on Wilson's toes if he goes beyond the bounds. And, as I say, he has an excellent record here. The sort of man we don't want to lose.'

He meant, 'I don't give a damn how many married women Wilson seduces so long as his work is first-class.'

'So you won't do anything about it,' I asked.

He made an impatient gesture with his hand. 'It's nothing to do with me. We're not living in the reign of Queen Victoria now, you know.'

That was the end of the conversation. Later, Kay said, 'What were you and Mr Forbes talking about?'

I knew the truth would upset her and, feeling a curious mixture of cowardice and kindness, I told her we were discussing London's transport problems.

'How dull,' she commented and mercifully the subject was dropped.

I doubt if Forbes said anything to Wilson, or to Kay, but from that night things began to improve. When I asked Kay if she had been bothered by Wilson she would say, 'I didn't see him at all today,' or 'He was around when I left but I'm not sure whether he saw me.'

There was a change in her which was probably due to the ending of a period of tension. She had lost some weight and this made her look younger. Her eyes regained their sparkle and her skin looked softer. But although she seemed happy, the memory of the ridiculous affair lingered in my mind and was reinforced by practically everything I saw or read.

Articles in newspapers and magazines which presumably I had sub-consciously avoided reading after my eyes had skated across the heading seemed preoccupied with 'the permissive society'. One couldn't turn a page without finding some reference to adultery, pregnant schoolgirls or 'the Pill'. I began to read the articles I had formerly ignored and when I was travelling I found myself examining posters on Underground platforms and escalators. Why hadn't I noticed before that everywhere there were invitations to the vacant-minded passer-by to think about sex. Had I been travelling in blinkers for the last decade?

And I began noticing the name 'Wilson'. It was on shop fronts, in references to the Labour leader, and most frequently of all in my local library. Whenever I glanced through the rack of recently returned books there seemed to be a work by one of the Wilson trinity – Angus, Colin and Edmund.

Sex and Wilson were inescapable. I began to wonder for the first time since my mother's death whether I was normal. I disliked what I saw and yet was strangely compelled to contemplate it. I was out of step with the times, but was I also out of step with normal behaviour? From what I read nobody seemed to care much if his wife committed adultery. Parties were even arranged where wives could be swapped like used postage stamps. It was commonplace for wives to conduct affairs under their husbands' noses and with their husbands' consent. This was inevitably referred to as 'civilised behaviour'.

And then I read a passage in a book which gave me comfort. It is from Aldous Huxley's *Brave New World Revisited*:

*The really hopeless victims of mental illness are to be found among those who appear to be most normal . . . They are normal not in what may be called the absolute sense of the word; they are normal only in relation to a profoundly abnormal society. Their perfect adjustment to that society is a measure of their mental sickness.*

I didn't fit in with modern society but this wasn't evidence of abnormality on my part. The abnormal ones were those who swapped wives because it was fashionable to swap wives, and who regarded the Pill as mankind's salvation. They were those who advocated promiscuity as a norm and found it necessary to sell cars, chocolate and even kitchen utensils by blatantly sexual advertisements. They were men like Forbes who said, 'What's the harm?' and like Wilson who with fantastic impudence could say 'I love Kay' to Kay's husband. These were the new sick born of the permissive society. Thank God I was normal.

And then there occurred the incident of the carnations.

Many months before, we had booked to go on a cruise in August. It was to be my first holiday afloat since my mother's death and the boat, a luxury liner, was scheduled to make calls at Lisbon, Madeira, the Canaries and Casablanca. A week before sailing we decided to catch an early morning train on Saturday and go for a tramp on the Sussex downs. Unfortunately when we woke it was raining heavily and the forecast was for continuing rain. Even so, we almost went, but Kay eventually decided the issue by saying, 'What if we catch colds? It would ruin the start of the holiday.'

So we stayed in the flat. If we hadn't been at home we shouldn't have heard the bell ring during the morning and answered it to find a messenger boy on the doorstep with a dozen deep red carnations.

'Who on earth would send me these?' asked Kay when the boy had gone.

I said it must be a mistake.

'It can't be,' she replied. 'It's my name and address. And here's a card.' Her eyes were shining and I wished I had sent the flowers.

She read the card. 'Oh,' she said.

I took it from her.

'TO KAY, WITH DEEPEST RESPECT AND ADMIRATION – DENIS'

'The bastard,' I said.

'Aren't they lovely?'

I wondered for a split second if she had gone insane and then I took the sheaf of carnations from her and hurried outside to the dustbin.

She ran after me calling, 'Have you gone mad?'

'I thought you had gone mad,' I said.

'What do you think you're doing,' she asked, retrieving the carnations from the dustbin. 'These are *flowers!*'

Dear Kay. She is so sensitive and sympathetic towards flowers. To her they are as much creatures as animals are. What I had done was almost equivalent to putting a child in the dustbin.

'I'll put them in water,' she said, and I followed her back into the flat.

'I'd prefer not to be reminded of their provenance,' I said. 'If you must keep them, would you mind keeping them in the spare room?'

'Why? They're lovely to look at.'

'They have come from a young fool who would, if he could, wreck our marriage. It's not asking too much to have them kept out of sight.'

She looked at me in a way I shall never forget. It is said that one remembers only the pleasant things in life and forgets all else. I can only remark that this may be true for the majority but it is not true for me. Kay's disdainfully cold look was photographed on my memory. 'Very well,' she said. 'We'll keep them in the spare room.'

'You do understand?' I asked.

'I understand,' she said. 'Perfectly,' she added.

And she put them in a cut-glass vase in the spare room. I didn't know whether to be angry at her disregard for my feelings or to find her love of flowers so endearing as to erase my annoyance.

The carnations remained in the spare room until we sailed.

On boarding at Southampton we were shown to our cabin. It was compactly designed with separate berths covered in green and blue tartan overlays and with a wide dressing table between the bed-heads. Piped music drifted into the cabin and we had a choice of different radio channels so that, if we wished, we could listen to non-stop classical music instead of the pop which was playing on our arrival. The cabin had its own small bathroom. Kay peeped out of the porthole by her berth and said, 'This is going to be fun.'

After unpacking some luggage we went up to the restaurant to obtain a table number from the manager. Then we went aft to enjoy the sunshine on the quarter deck. The first meal was tea which could be taken in one of the lounges. As we sipped from our cups we watched the shore of the Isle of Wight slide slowly past.

I am a fairly good sailor but on my advice Kay had been inoculated against sea-sickness and although by dinner time there was a moderately heavy swell in the Channel we went to the restaurant, happy and hungry.

It is said that one never realises when one *is* happy only that one *was* happy. Happiness is in the wake. As we entered the restaurant I wasn't conscious of being happy (although at that moment I was happy) but the moment we sat down I was acutely aware of being suddenly unhappy. Directly across the aisle and gazing at a menu was Wilson.

I said, 'Good God,' and the words emerged aloud although I had meant to keep them under my breath.

'What's the matter?' asked Kay.

'Look!'

She had been slightly flushed but the blood faded from her cheeks. 'I can't believe it,' she said.

At that moment he looked up from the menu, saw us staring aghast at him and gave a timorous half smile.

'Did you know he would be on board,' I asked in a lowered voice.

'No. How could I?'

'He must have known you'd be on board.'

'Well, lots of people at the office know about this trip. He could easily have heard about it.'

I said I was going to get our table changed.

'Please don't make a fuss,' she said. Kay dislikes fuss and scenes. 'Please!' she begged.

I looked around. Every table was full. It was unlikely that we could change now.

'Let's see what delicacies they have for us,' she said, trying to sound bright. 'I'm famished.'

My appetite had gone. I was thinking, 'Twelve days . . . Twelve days on the same ship with him!'

This was only the beginning. We should see him in the bars, as we moved around the decks, as we lay sunbathing, as we ate, as we danced, as we debouched at each port of call; we were all captives in the same prison and my only escape was in the cell of our cabin.

I was glad Kay wanted to turn in early. I could hear her breathing in sleep on the far side of the cabin as a succession of furious thoughts tumbled through my mind. If Wilson had walked in through the cabin door I am certain I should have strangled him with my bare hands.

If he spoke to us, even to say 'Good morning', I should have to restrain myself. And there were twelve days of this accumulating tension.

Eventually my immediate fury burned itself out and I resolved to exercise iron self-control and to ignore the fellow if he spoke to us. If you discipline yourself to ignore an unpleasant fact of life it can sometimes happen that, except when your nose is rubbed in it, you can succeed in ignoring it.

At first it wasn't quite as bad as I expected; we managed to eat at different times from him and although we saw him about the ship he made no attempt to speak to us.

'Why the devil doesn't he get a girl,' I said. 'There are enough around for a thousand and one shipboard romances.'

'I feel rather sorry for him,' said Kay. 'He looks awfully lonely.' She adjusted her sun-glasses and lay back on a reclining chair. 'Isn't this wonderful,' she said. 'I'm going to get as brown as a berry.'

In the distance I could see Wilson leaning forlornly on the rail gazing out at a blue expanse of water and sky.

At Lisbon we didn't join an organised shore excursion but took a taxi to the top of Parque Eduardo VII and then strolled down past the little bird sanctuary with its splendid peacocks towards the main part of town. The day was warm without being too hot and we wandered along pavements that were diapered in black and white stones observing the lottery ticket sellers, the plethora of policemen, country-women with panniers on their heads, the numerous blind, the numerous shoe-shiners, the well-stocked shops; and thus idling we reached the Praco Rossio Don Pedro IV in time for lunch. In the afternoon we went to look at the castle district with its warren of narrow streets and ancient buildings. It was a delightful day and I hardly thought about Wilson whom we had seen earlier departing, glum-faced, on a coach tour bound for Estoril via Quelez and Sintra.

Kay and I are used to walking long distances without tiring and although we must have covered more than a dozen miles we walked all the way back from the castle district to the dock where our ship was berthed passing through fish and fruit markets on the way. Kay hugged my arm. 'Not a tourist in sight,' she said. 'We really are away from it all.'

The ship pulled out while we were having dinner and we watched the Salazar Bridge and the illuminated statue of Christ glide past as we sampled *espalada*, a fish caught off the Portuguese coast. There was no sign of Wilson. Perhaps he had got lost at Estoril, Quelez or Sintra. I hoped so.

'There's a dance tonight,' said Kay. 'Let's go, or are you too tired?'

A Spanish proverb has it that a gentleman is never tired and I quoted it to her.

'Good,' she said. 'I'll wear my long red dress.'

But, a couple of hours later, we were no sooner on the dance floor than I saw Wilson standing on his own at the bar. His face matched the colour of Kay's dress and he was wearing an orange kipper tie on a bilious yellow shirt. His suit was bright emerald green and he looked like a garish advertisement for poster paints.

'Look who's here,' said Kay, fashioning her body to the rhythm of a quickstep. 'Hasn't his face caught the sun?'

'I've seen him. A walking Joseph's coat of many colours.'

We danced, and we sat out, and we danced again, and then we were in a waltz with spotlights dappling the dancers. Wilson had disappeared. Perhaps he'd gone to bed.

'Excuse me,' said a voice. I felt a tap on my shoulder.

The dance was a gentleman's excuse-me. I turned to see who had requested the pleasure of taking my place and before I could protest (or 'make a scene' as Kay would say) Wilson had whisked her into the splashes of moving light.

My first reaction was to re-excuse him, but I decided to ignore his unwanted intervention. I had planned to ignore him, and ignore him I would.

The dance seemed to last a long time. When Kay rejoined me she looked tense and I wondered what had upset her.

'Let me sit down,' she said. 'My feet are ruined. I don't think he's ever danced a waltz in his life.'

Shortly after this we left the dance, and while we were undressing in the cabin I asked what Wilson had talked about.

'He kept apologising for his steps. He needed to.' She gave a brief smile. 'He said, "They call me the octopus of the Buying Department – I've got four times the usual number of feet."' She gazed down at her own small and pretty feet. 'They don't look too bruised and battered, do they?'

515

I moved towards her but she turned away. 'I'm dog-tired, darling. And we've been on our feet all day.'

I shrugged. 'All right . . . What else did you talk about?'

She scrambled into her bed. 'Nothing really.'

'He just kept saying that he was an octopus?'

'I'm too tired to remember,' she said and she switched off the bed-head light.

I suppose a normal man by the standards of the permissive society would have dropped the subject, or even said, 'You were slow, dear. Why didn't you go to his cabin?' but I am not normal by the standards of a sick society.

I got into my bunk and persisted with the question. 'He must have done more than apologise for bad dancing. You were a full three minutes together.'

'Three minutes!'

'What do you mean,' I asked, 'saying "three minutes" like that?'

She didn't reply.

'Kay. What did he say to you?'

'Please. I'm dreadfully tired.'

I switched off my light. The cabin was in darkness.

'Kay?'

'What?'

'Answer my question.'

She sighed loudly. 'How do you expect me to remember anything when you were sitting glowering at us?'

'I wasn't glowering. I was ignoring the whole thing.'

She gave a laugh.

'What's so funny?' I asked.

She gave no answer.

'I was watching,' I said. 'Not glowering. And he was talking a lot. What did he say?'

'What does it matter?'

'It matters to me.'

'You just want an excuse to make a scene with him.'

'Look, Kay, I swear I won't make a scene. I shall ignore the whole thing, but I do want to know what he said.'

She gave another sigh. 'We talked about Madeira. He asked what plans I had for the day ashore.'

'What did you say?'

'I said I left the planning to you.'

'What did he say to that?'

'Oh, please, can't we stop this? I really am whacked out.'

'What did he say, Kay?'

'I don't remember.'

'Of course you do. What did he say?'

'It was a joke.'

'Tell me the joke, Kay.'

'It was just a joke. He asked me to ditch you.'

'He asked you to ditch me?'

'Can I go to sleep – please?'

'What did you say? Did you say, "Well, I don't like making scenes so you can take me out if you like."'

Suddenly she was furious. Her voice came across the cabin like a whiplash. 'Yes, that's what I said. And I told him I'd do my best to ditch you. Now are you satisfied? Can I go to sleep?'

It was my turn to make no reply.

Within seconds she was snoring.

As I lay miserably awake in the darkened cabin I realised that Kay would not have said this, and she was only pretending to have said it to stop my incessant questions. I didn't hold her snappish reply against her, but I did hold Wilson responsible for an argument between man and wife, and I couldn't forgive the suggestion he had made to her. No wonder she had looked tense and distressed after dancing with him.

What else would happen in the days ahead? It was plain that Wilson would never give up his obsessive quest for Kay and I was beginning to wonder if his obsession might not, in the end, win the day. How does one fight a man who is utterly preoccupied with obtaining a woman's affections? How do you deal with a man whose *idée fixe* is far beyond reason, persuasion, threats of bodily violence or (provided he doesn't overstep certain bounds) the reach of the law?

Wilson would pursue his objective ruthlessly, never doing enough to condemn him in a legal tribunal, but he would erode my marriage by gifts of flowers, unstinted devotion and indelicate suggestions. Kay would gradually be attracted to him against her will and she would begin to regard me, and not him, as the enemy. Kay is gentle; Kay is kind. She can't even refuse a street flag-seller. Her life has been sheltered and she doesn't know how to cope with the harsher realities. How long would she be able to stand Wilson's pernicious pressures? One day a situation would arise when her fidelity would be tested beyond the limit. It might happen at her office. Pat and Josie would be out at lunch and Wilson would walk in. He would lock the door. Only a typewriter on a desk would be between them. Silently he would push the typewriter aside, vault the desk, and she would succumb to his overwhelming desires.

It is said by some philosophers that to understand a problem is also to know its solution. I understood the problem and the solution was obvious.

On the following day Kay seemed very subdued and all my efforts to cheer her failed.

There is no point in charting the various twists and turns of my mind on that unhappy day; it is sufficient to say that I wrote a note in a fair imitation of Kay's hand and slipped it under Wilson's cabin door, having first obtained the cabin number from the ship's telephone operator.

The note said: 'Meet me at 1.30 a.m. tomorrow morning at Station 5 on the Boat Deck. Urgent. Kay.'

She was asleep when I slid, fully dressed, off my bed and stole out of the cabin.

The long narrow corridor was empty. I hurried to the elevator and ascended to the Boat Deck. As I stepped out, I looked around. Nobody in sight. I went to the door which opened on to the deck. It swung open silently. A cool salt breeze was blowing and the sky was milky with millions of stars. I walked to Station 5. I could see Wilson's outline. He was leaning on the rail and characteristically gazing out across the moon-washed sea.

I should never have a better opportunity. I crept up behind him. He didn't move. I bent down, pushed both arms between his thighs and bundled him over the rail. He let out a piercing, blood-curdling scream as he fell.

I heard the splash and was about to run away when I noticed a sandal on the deck. Somehow, one of his sandals had fallen off. It is very odd but that lone sandal looked more human than Wilson. I picked it up and tossed it over the side, but I knew I should always remember its shape and its feel.

Then I scampered back to the elevator, descended to our deck, ran along the empty corridor, tip-toed into our cabin, undressed and climbed into bed. The sheets were still warm. A moment later the ship's siren blew a long powerful blast.

I could feel a faint vibration running through the panels of the cabin. Was the ship stopping?

Kay woke and called my name. I gave a sleepy grunt.

'The siren's just gone,' she said. 'It woke me up. What do you think is happening?'

'Didn't hear it,' I mumbled.

A few minutes later she kneeled on her bunk, drew the curtain aside and peered out of the porthole. 'We've stopped,' she said.

'Stopped?'

'Come and look.'

She was right. The water around us was still. The ship might have been moored to a quay.

For half an hour we conjectured why the ship should have stopped in mid-ocean; then the engines started and we were on our way.

When the steward woke us with early morning tea I asked, 'Why did we stop in the night?'

He pulled a grim face. 'Man overboard, sir.'

'Good God. Was he saved?'

'They got a boat out to him with the ship's surgeon on board but he failed to respond to artificial respiration.'

'How did he fall?' I asked.

'No idea, sir.'

'Who saw him?'

'Someone on watch heard a scream, I think, sir. He looked over and saw what appeared to be a person in the water.' The steward edged towards the door. 'Very interesting manoeuvre the first officer made. Slowed the engines and did what we call a "Williamson Turn". Brings the ship back on a reciprocal course.' He left before I could ask more questions.

# Fixation

The day in Madeira was in contrast to the carefree day in Lisbon. Kay seemed unhappy and she didn't care for Funchal. She begged me to go sight-seeing without her; but I had to pretend Wilson was still alive and I said jocularly, 'Can't leave you alone with that young wolf around.'

She took a couple of aspirins and lay down on her bed. After a while she fell asleep and I went off to the coffee bar. I wanted to be on my own. Nobody could have seen me bundle Wilson overboard but they might find the note signed 'Kay'. But even if it was traced to us a hand-writing expert would confirm it wasn't in Kay's writing. There was nothing to fear. Wilson's death could not be attributed to me.

I felt no guilt or remorse. I had been provoked beyond endurance by a young man obsessively interested in my wife. I had acted as any normal man would. Only a permissive society could suggest that my action had been abnormal. Strangely, the single sandal worried me for a while. I knew Oedipus was a name meaning 'swollen foot' and I had an idea that this damned myth was haunting me. Did the oracle say that Oedipus would enter Thebes wearing one sandal? Luckily, the ship's library had a book on mythology and I soon realised I had been confusing Oedipus with Jason. It was Jason who lost a sandal in a muddy river and thereby began the fulfilment of an oracle.

To hell with Wilson; I had regained peace of mind.

If Kay hadn't been feeling so seedy I would have turned cartwheels all over the deck.

When she learned that Wilson had been the 'man overboard' she cried. I could understand her reaction. After all, she is a very sensitive woman and he was an office colleague.

Back in England her health did not improve. She went to a doctor who told her she had a mild depression and gave her drugs. The depression persisted. Physically she melted away and became an undersized weakling again.

I was at my wits' end wondering how to help her when, after a fit of crying, she let slip the cause of her depression. She had convinced herself that Wilson had committed suicide.

'What if he did,' I asked. 'That's not your fault.'

'But it is,' she cried. 'That night at the dance when he asked me to ditch you, I steeled myself and told him I wouldn't look at him if he was the last man on earth.'

I was amazed. 'That isn't what you told me.'

'I only said what I did because I was fed up with all your questions. I wanted to be left alone. I knew if I told you the truth you'd want to make love to me, and I couldn't bear the thought of being touched. Can't you understand?'

I shook my head. 'Not really . . . And you didn't make him commit suicide.'

She looked at me with tear-filled eyes. 'I finished by telling him he could jump overboard for all I cared!'

Kay's health is slowly improving. I couldn't let her suffer for my actions and so I told her the truth. When the shock wore off she said we couldn't live the rest of

519

our lives together with this secret between us. But if I gave myself up and took my punishment, she would wait for me, and one day we would start afresh.

Freddie has briefed counsel and has impressed on me that if we can make out that I was suffering from a temporary abnormality of mind the sentence should be less and the reunion with Kay will be speedier.

I can see the force of his argument, but it goes against the grain that I, a man who has given the extreme proof of his normality, should have to parade himself to the world as a specimen of abnormality.

Wilson was the one with an abnormal fixation, not me.

# MICHAEL UNDERWOOD

## OK For Murder

'You will try and get home a bit early this evening, won't you, love?' Oscar said as he watched Oliver making his preparations to leave the house that morning. 'It *is* our anniversary,' he added as though Oliver needed the further reminder.

Oliver smiled. 'Of course. And don't *you* forget to book a table! Better make it eight-thirty.'

Oscar nodded. 'That'll give us time to have a little celebration here first. I'll put a couple of bottles of champagne on ice.' He opened the front door and gave Oliver an almost wistful look as he went out. 'Six years ago today, it was,' he murmured.

Oliver paused and glanced back. 'Wonder what we'll be doing in another six years,' he said with a faintly quizzical smile.

'One thing for sure, I'll still be the same age as I am now,' Oscar remarked. 'As from today I'm not getting any older.' He held up his left wrist from which hung the twenty-two carat gold chain Oliver had given him as an anniversary present. 'It's beautiful and I love it,' he said.

'Good, because it cost enough.' Then observing Oscar's suddenly clouded expression Oliver said, 'Don't get all sentimental, it's too early in the day. Save it for this evening.' With a final wave he got into his car and started the engine.

Oscar watched him out of sight before going back into the cottage. If everything went according to plan, it was the last time he would see Oliver alive.

The day was indeed the sixth anniversary of their first meeting which had taken place on the upper deck of a number 14 bus as it was passing Harrods. That in itself, they later agreed, had been a sort of omen.

Oscar had been casting interested glances at Oliver for two or three minutes before Oliver became aware of the fact. His return glance when it came, though less brazen, was sufficient for Oscar to get up and move into the seat next to him. By the time the bus reached Hyde Park Corner, they had exchanged telephone numbers and discovered, to Oscar's entrancement, that they had the same initials. Oliver Knight and Oscar Knudsen. To Oscar, who sought omens everywhere, this was the clearest possible indication that they were meant for each other. It was Oliver, however, who phoned that evening and suggested dinner the next day.

They met at a small Italian restaurant in South Kensington, not far from where Oliver had a flat. Oscar, at the time, had a bedsit in less fashionable West Kensington.

In the course of dinner Oscar learned that Oliver was thirty-two and therefore six years older than himself, that he still carried the scars of a failed marriage, and that he was the director of a firm of travel agents.

In turn Oliver learned that Oscar was of Danish extraction though he had been born and brought up in England and that he worked in the publicity department of a magazine where he was underpaid and generally miserable.

One week later Oscar moved into Oliver's flat and they had lived together ever since, moving to Maple Cottage, five miles from Dorking, two years ago.

Oscar had long since given up his job, leaving Oliver as the bread-winner. Not that there was any shortage of bread for the travel agent business had prospered, in addition to which Oliver had inherited £100,000 from his grandmother.

For a time it had been a perfect match, the temperamental, fickle and passionate Oscar and the good looking Oliver behind whose relaxed appearance lurked an acreage of insecurity. But whereas Oliver seemed prepared to condone his friend's infidelities, Oscar was apt to work himself up into a jealous rage every time he suspected Oliver of being unfaithful to him. And suspicion came as naturally to Oscar as rainfall to the western isles. Oliver had always accepted that Oscar's philandering involved no more than ships that passed in the night, except that mid-afternoon was their more usual time, when Oscar had the cottage to himself. When 'business' kept Oliver late in town he was careful to conceal from Oscar what he had been up to. Anything, but anything, to prevent his sinking into one of his foul moods.

As yet Oliver had not met Keith, the new lad who came twice a week to help in the garden. Oscar always referred to him in an off-hand tone and said he smelt strongly of compost.

'Thank goodness he doesn't work inside,' he would add disdainfully.

Thereafter, whenever Oliver enquired after him, Oscar was dismissive.

Nevertheless, it was Keith who filled Oscar's thoughts as he turned back into the cottage after waving Oliver goodbye that morning. Keith, with whom he had fallen head-over-heels in love. Keith, who was the pivot of the carefully laid plan that was to result in Oliver's death.

Oscar glanced at his watch. The morning, hardly begun, was already dragging. He felt anxious and ill-at-ease as he closed the front door and went upstairs to the bedroom. A quick shake of the pale mauve duvet and matching pillows and the bed was made. Oliver's pillow smelt of the Vidal Sassoon almond shampoo he always used and he buried his face in it for a sentimental moment. He was still very fond of Oliver and didn't want to hurt him; that's why a quick drastic solution was best. He was almost able to persuade himself that Oliver wouldn't mind being removed from life in such a good cause. And this time next year there would be a new anniversary in his calendar. That of Oliver's death.

Oscar reckoned that eleven o'clock was the earliest Keith would be back, but that lunchtime was a more realistic hour. After all, the logistics of the plan were formidable, involving the disposal of Oliver and the abandonment of his car, followed by Keith retrieving his own car and getting back to Maple Cottage.

In its essence, the plan was simple enough. Keith, his cropped blond hair hidden under a dark wig and with a matching moustache to complete his disguise, was to be waiting to thumb a lift as Oliver came along on his way to work. A rucksack on his back and a stout pair of boots on his feet would reinforce the impression of a genuine hitchhiker and exploit Oliver's weakness for offering lifts to lonely young men at the roadside. On a usually deserted stretch of the road where it passed through a dark wood Keith was to feign an urgent call of nature. When Oliver drew up he would be overpowered by the physically much stronger Keith and strangled. His body would be dumped in the back of the car and covered by a blanket, after which Keith would drive eight miles along by-roads to a disused gravel pit where he would dump the body in deep water. The car was to be abandoned elsewhere. Thereafter Keith would retrieve the bicycle he had hidden in advance and make his way back to where he had left his own car. After which he would be ready to make his way to Maple Cottage and report 'mission accomplished' to a nervously waiting Oscar.

That was the plan which Oscar reviewed in his mind as he moved restlessly about the kitchen. At one stage he had thought to ask their cleaning woman to change her day and come that Thursday to provide him with an alibi, but on subsequent reflection he decided this might arouse suspicion on the part of those investigating Oliver's mysterious disappearance. Moreover, the fact he had never learnt to drive a car himself was alibi enough in the circumstances.

He sat down at the table in the breakfast alcove with another cup of coffee and reached for his cigarettes. He glanced idly at the front page of the *Mirror* (Oliver always took the *Daily Telegraph* with him), but found it impossible to concentrate. His mind was too full of other thoughts. Thoughts of life with Keith. Sturdy, muscular, twenty-two-year-old Keith who had already served a sentence for GBH and to whom the prospect of committing murder was a normal progression – provided the rewards were sufficient. Oscar had not been slow to tell him that he and Oliver had made wills in each other's favour which meant that he, Oscar, would inherit a considerable fortune on Oliver's demise.

'If I die first, all Oliver will get will be a few old T-shirts,' he was fond of saying to their friends with a slight moue.

Obviously he and Keith would need to behave with circumspection at the outset, but once everything was settled and Oliver's estate was legally his, they would be able to make a proper life together. Meanwhile, there was no reason why he shouldn't dream about the day that lay ahead . . . Why, there was even a portent to be found in Keith's own initials. KO for Keith Offingham, and he was certainly a knock-out. Though Keith had shown no patience with Oscar when he purported to find special significance in their initials.

'For Chrissake,' he had said the last time Oscar had referred to it, 'who cares a bugger what your initials are as long as they don't spell bum or shit!'

Meanwhile Oscar lit another cigarette and continued to dream of Keith.

Around ten-thirty he decided to call Oliver's office. Oliver wouldn't be there, of course, but it would give him an opportunity to express concern and anxiety.

His car broken down? Or a pile-up on the Kingston by-pass? He didn't often call Oliver at work as Oliver had made it plain he should only do so in the event of urgency. But he and Ruth, Oliver's secretary, knew each other's voices and always exchanged pleasantries when they spoke.

As Oliver wouldn't be there, he didn't really have to think of an excuse for phoning, but, if necessary, he'd tell Ruth it was about their arrangements that evening. He dialled the number and waited.

'Suntravel,' a voice announced with a briskness that was apt to leave callers floundering.

'May I speak to Mr Knight, please?'

'Mr Knight's secretary, can I help you?' Ruth answered a moment later.

'Hello, Ruth, it's Oscar Knudsen.'

'Good morning, Mr Knudsen.'

'May I have a quick word with Oliver, please?'

'I'm afraid Mr Knight's not in.'

Oscar smiled into the receiver. 'I suppose he must have been held up in the traffic. It seems to get worse every day.'

'He's not expected in at all today,' Ruth remarked.

'Not expected in at all?' Oscar said in a voice that trembled.

'No, he's not been in since Tuesday and won't be back in the office till next Monday.'

Oscar's mind reeled, but after what seemed to him like several minutes of paralysed silence, he managed to stammer something about having obviously misunderstood what Oliver had told him and rang off, falling back into an armchair in a state of collapse.

If Oliver had not been at his office yesterday either, where had he been? He'd left home at the usual hour and returned in the evening as if he'd spent an ordinary working day. Oscar tried to recall whether he had said anything in particular about the day, but couldn't remember anything. He had been too eager to find out what Oliver had bought him as an anniversary present to ask him what sort of a day he'd had. And this morning he had again set off as usual, but where was he going? Oscar felt a sudden constriction of his throat muscles. Supposing Oliver had not taken his normal route. After all, if he was not going to work, was he necessarily making for London? But if not, where? Where? Might Keith still be waiting futilely at the roadside? No, that at least could be ruled out, for if their plan had been aborted that early on, he would surely know by now. Keith would have been on the phone.

It was now two and a half hours since Oliver had left home and Oscar felt suddenly angry and outraged. How devious and deceitful Oliver had become! He'd always believed he could read him like an open book, but after this morning's shock . . . The more his mind pored over events, the wilder became his speculation and the greater grew his anxiety.

He wondered whether to call Ruth again and see if she had any notion where Oliver was, but even as he reached for the phone he saw it as a rash move and shrank back.

All he could do was wait. Wait until Keith turned up. Pray God that he would – and soon! Albeit that it was now too much to hope that their carefully thought-out plan had succeeded. Indeed, such was his mental turmoil, it would hardly surprise him if Oliver came through the front door.

But as the minutes ticked laboriously away neither Oliver nor yet Keith appeared and one morbid thought chased another through Oscar's aching head. Supposing Oliver had somehow managed to kill Keith, instead of the other way about? Or, even worse, supposing the two of them had gone off together leaving Oscar high and dry and totally deserted? Oscar felt he had to do something to relieve the tension, but what? His nerves were in shreds and he'd already smoked more cigarettes that morning than he normally did in the course of the day.

And then just when he was about to surrender to a full-blooded bout of hysterics, a car pulled up in the lane outside and Keith got out. Oscar flew to the front door and flung it open, undecided whether to upbraid the approaching figure or fling his arms round his neck.

'Everything OK?' he asked tensely. Keith nodded. 'I've been worried out of my wits,' he went on. Then in a choked voice he said, 'Am I relieved to see you, love! I was expecting you much sooner.'

'I don't know why. This is my usual time for coming, isn't it?'

'Yes, but . . .'

'It'd have looked funny if I'd come earlier.'

'Yes, yes, of course. I didn't think of that,' Oscar burbled in his relief.

'Well, I did.'

'Come in and I'll make you a cup of coffee and you can tell me everything.' As he closed the door behind them, he wrapped his arms around Keith and hugged him tightly. Keith accepted the embrace without any show of enthusiasm, but then he never was one for overt emotion. His forte was the bedroom where he could be vigorous and physically exciting.

'Did everything go according to plan?' Oscar asked when they were in the kitchen.

'Without a hitch.'

'Oliver, where is he?' Oscar asked with a slight catch in his voice.

'In thirty feet of dirty water.'

'And his car?'

'Where we decided.'

'No problem getting him to stop and offer you a lift?'

'None.'

'What did you talk about before . . . while you were in the car?' Oscar enquired tremulously.

'He just asked me where I came from and where I was heading for.'

'He didn't try and make a pass at you?' Oscar said with a nervous giggle.

'At eight o'clock in the morning? He's not as randy as you are.'

'So it all went according to plan?'

'Like I've already said.'

'And you got rid of your disguise and rucksack without any difficulty?'

Keith gave a big nod. 'I keep on telling you, there were no hitches anywhere along the line.'

'I don't mind telling *you*, love, I almost had kittens at one stage. I phoned Oliver's office.' When he had told Keith what had transpired, he added, 'Did Oliver mention where he was going?'

'He said London.'

'Did he say he was going to work or anything like that?'

Keith shook his head. 'He said he was a travel agent, but that was all.'

'I'm still puzzled as to what he's been up to.'

'Whatever it was, he's not up to it now.' Keith drained his coffee mug and put it down.

'Shall we go upstairs for a little while?' Oscar asked hopefully.

'I'm here to do some gardening, remember? Your nosey neighbour will be wondering what I'm doing indoors all this time.'

'It's all right. She's away.'

'Even so.'

'Later then?'

'Perhaps,' Keith said with a wink that made Oscar's heart skip a beat. Observing Oscar's reaction he suddenly grinned, revealing a row of beautifully even, white teeth. Oscar felt he was going to swoon with anticipation. The day was only half over, but it was already one he would never forget for as long as he lived.

As soon as Suntravel opened the next morning, Oscar was on the phone, speaking to Ruth.

'I'm terribly worried about Oliver,' he said in an anxious voice. 'He never came home yesterday evening and I've not heard a word. Have you any idea where he can be?'

'I'm afraid not, Mr Knudsen. As I said when you called yesterday, he's not expected back in the office until Monday.'

'But didn't he leave any clue as to what he'd be doing?'

'No, he didn't. He simply said he had some private business to attend to and was taking three days off.'

'Where on earth can he be?' Oscar said in the agonized tone he had been rehearsing. 'We were meant to be going out to dinner last night. It was a special occasion and he just never came back. I'm sure something dreadful has happened.'

'It's certainly very strange.' Ruth said warily. 'Let me have a word round the office and see if anyone knew his plans. He may have said something to one of the other directors. I'll call you back in a few minutes.'

'I'd be most grateful if you'd do that as I'm getting frantic.'

'I'm sure there'll turn out to be some innocent explanation, Mr Knudsen.'

'I wish I could think so,' Oscar replied.

Ten minutes later the phone rang. Oscar answered it immediately so that Ruth would be aware he'd been waiting anxiously for her return call.

'No news at all I'm afraid, Mr Knudsen. I've spoken to both Mr Parker and Miss Satchell, but it doesn't appear that Mr Knight told either of them where he was going. Mr Parker suggests that, if you've had no news by tomorrow, you should inform the police. Mr Parker also said not to hesitate to contact him at home over the weekend if you wish.'

'Please tell him I'm going to get in touch with the police immediately. I can't go through another twenty-four hours not doing anything. Obviously something terrible must have happened . . . ' Oscar's voice trailed away.

'I'm sure there'll be a happy ending,' Ruth said stoutly.

'It was all Oscar could do not to giggle. It was in a small sad tone, however, that he thanked her for her help.

Later he telephoned the police and said he wanted to report a missing person. The officer at the other end of the line took down the necessary particulars, including the registration number of Oliver's car and assured Oscar they'd be in touch with him as soon as they had any news. Oscar thanked the officer profusely and repeated how worried he was for his friend's well-being.

That evening Keith picked him up after dark and they drove to a secluded spot where he parked the car.

'It's driving me mad only being able to see you in this furtive way,' Oscar remarked petulantly.

'No point in running unnecessary risks. We oughtn't to be seen out together until the dust has settled,' Keith said matter-of-factly.

'I'll go and see the solicitor on Monday and tell him to get things moving.'

'Not much he can do until the body's been found.'

'Surely the police'll have started dredging all the ponds and quarries in the area by then. Failing which, Oliver's death will just have to be presumed.' He rested his head against Keith's shoulder. 'Tell me you love me!'

'Don't say such daft things!'

'What do you mean?' Oscar asked in an offended voice.

'I'd hardly have gone through all that hassle yesterday if I didn't like you, would I! Commit bloody murder and you ask me if I love you.'

'But do you? Not just like me, but love me?'

'Oh, for Heaven's sake, stuff it!'

Oscar sat back sulkily. At the very moment he longed for a display of affection, Keith was in one of his funny moods. He quickly cheered up, however, when Keith suggested he should put in an extra afternoon's gardening the next day, Saturday.

The following afternoon Keith dug a flower bed while Oscar pretended to do a little weeding nearby, though his attention was more on Keith's rippling muscles than on the removal of any weeds.

Keith suddenly paused and glanced in Oscar's direction.

'The phone's ringing,' he said.

'Oh, I didn't hear it,' Oscar said, coming out of his reverie.

'It's still ringing.'

Oscar hurried indoors and picked up the receiver.

'Is that Mr Knudsen?' a male voice enquired.

'Speaking.'

'This is Detective Sergeant Claymore. You phoned yesterday about a missing person. A Mr Knight. I believe he lived at your address.'

'That's right. We've been at Maple Cottage two years.'

'We've found his car, but there's no trace of him.'

'Where was his car?' Oscar asked with the right note of anxiety.

'It was up a track in Effingham Forest. It was locked and my guess would be that it hadn't been touched since being abandoned there.'

'Was his briefcase still in the car?'

There was a slight pause while Sergeant Claymore apparently consulted a piece of paper.

'There wasn't a briefcase in the car.'

'Oh!'

'Presumably he took it with him which makes it look as if he's still alive and well. If he'd intended taking his life, he'd hardly have bothered to remove his briefcase.'

'He might have,' Oscar said tentatively.

'Most unlikely. Anyway, for the moment there's no indication that he's met a sudden end.'

'But what on earth can have happened to him?' Oscar burst out in an anguished voice.

'You're in a better position to answer that than I am, Mr Knudsen. You knew him, I didn't.'

'I'm sure something awful's happened. I mean, he left here to drive to work but never arrives and the next thing is his car's found abandoned off his normal route.'

'It's a not unknown pattern.'

'But it's totally unlike Oliver. He's the most orderly and systematic person you could meet.'

'Well, there's not much the police can do for the moment other than post him as a missing person.'

'Surely you'll initiate a search?'

'Not until there's some evidence of foul play. And there's none, I'm happy to say.'

Sergeant Claymore might have been happy to say it, but Oscar was anything but happy to hear it. He returned to the garden and reported to Keith.

'What did you do with his briefcase?' he asked.

'Weighted it and threw it in after the body.'

'It might have been better to leave it in the car. Also to have left signs of a struggle.'

'Bit late in the day to think of that now,' Keith observed in a not too friendly tone.

'I'm not criticising you,' Oscar said hastily. 'Somehow we've got to get the police to dredge that quarry. At the moment they obviously think Oliver's just walked out on me. I could tell from the officer's voice. Though goodness knows why he should have abandoned his car if that were the case! It may make sense to the police, but it won't to anyone else.'

'Go and put the kettle on,' Keith said after a pause, 'I'm ready for a cup of tea.'

'Perhaps you'll be ready for something else as well,' Oscar remarked with a leer.

'Perhaps.'

But as soon as Keith had departed later that afternoon, all Oscar's anxieties returned. Why couldn't everything work out as smoothly as he had envisaged?

Sunday was every bit as wearisome and frustrating as Oscar had expected. He felt it was never going to reach an end as he paced restlessly about the cottage, smoking endless cigarettes and drinking countless cups of black coffee, while his nerves became more taut by the minute.

Keith had driven down to the coast to visit his grandmother, who was his closest relative and who had brought him up. He had never known his father and his mother had abandoned him and gone off with an American airman when he was only a few months old. He had moved into the Dorking area after his release from prison and now lived at a hostel, earning his living as an odd-job man and casual gardener.

Oscar had suggested he should accompany him on the drive, saying that he would go and look at the sea while Keith was with his gran. But Keith had vetoed the idea and Oscar had to be content with his promise to phone him on his return.

The call came around eight o'clock, by which time Oscar's nerves had become so raw-edged he was ready to scream.

'Thank God it's you love,' he exclaimed with a small strangulated sound. 'I was going mad. It's been the worst day of my life.'

'Why? What's up?'

'It's just that I've had nothing to do all day. I've talked to nobody and I've missed you terribly.'

'Oh, is that all?'

'Isn't it enough?'

'I thought you'd have been phoning round your friends telling them of Oliver's disappearance.'

'I did try and call Desmond and Tony, also Patrick and Ian, but everyone seems to have gone away for the weekend.'

'Nothing further from the police?'

'Not a word.' Aware that Keith would ring off in a moment if he didn't keep the conversation going, Oscar said desperately, 'How did you find your grandmother?'

'Fine.'

'Pleased to see you, was she?'

'Yep.'

'What was the traffic like?'

'Not bad.'

'When will I see you next?' Oscar asked frantically.

'I'll call you tomorrow evening.'

'Why don't you come round for supper? You can park away from the cottage, so nobody'll know you're here.'

'It's a possibility.'

'I'll cook your favourite. Steak and kidney pie followed by chocolate mousse.'

'OK, but make it a steak, I had pie at my gran's today.'

'Anything you want, love.'

'A nice fillet steak with all the trimmings.'

Oscar purred with delight. 'It shall be done. When we're living together you'll be able to have steak three times a day.'

Keith chuckled. 'Let's hope Oliver's money holds out!'

The next morning Oscar phoned a solicitor friend. This seemed better than calling the London lawyer who looked after his and Oliver's affairs.

'It's Oscar, Peter. I'm turning to you for advice as a friend who's also a lawyer. I'm desperately worried about Oliver, he's disappeared. Went off to work last Thursday, never arrived and hasn't been heard of since. The police have found his car which had been abandoned, but there's no trace of Oliver. I'm certain something terrible has happened.'

'You mean, you're afraid he's dead.'

'Yes,' Oscar said in a faltering tone.

'Are the police making a search?'

'No, because they say there's no evidence of foul play,' Oscar said indignantly.

'So what advice do you want from me?'

'How long will it be before Oliver is presumed dead?'

'Seven years. The odds are, however, that if he *is* dead, his body'll be discovered before then.'

'But if it's not?'

'Then seven years is the period that must elapse before you can apply for a presumption of death.'

It was a stunned Oscar who put down the receiver and lit a cigarette with a trembling hand.

There was only one thing for it, Oliver's body had got to be found. And soon.

Four cigarettes and two cups of coffee later, Oscar decided to phone the police. He had conjured up a picture of a quite young Detective Sergeant Claymore, clean-limbed and dark-haired. This on the evidence of his crisp telephone manner. When Sergeant Claymore answered the phone, Oscar was jolted out of his reverie.

'I was wondering if you'd had any news over the weekend?'

'Nothing, I'm afraid.'

'I can't remember if I told you that apparently Oliver wasn't expected at his office the day he disappeared. In fact he'd not been in the previous day, either.'

'No, you didn't tell me that, Mr Knudsen,' Sergeant Claymore said more crisply than usual. 'But I found out when I spoke to one of his fellow directors.'

'Oh! I hadn't realised you'd been in touch with his office.'

'But naturally. It was a routine enquiry.'

'I believe I did mention that he'd been rather depressed of late,' Oscar went on.

'No, you didn't tell me that, either.'

Oscar let out a nervous laugh. 'I've been so worried about him, I don't know what I've said and what I haven't said. But it's one of the reasons why I think he may have . . . may have done something drastic.'

'Killed himself, you mean?'

'That's what I'm afraid of.'

'He'd hardly have needed his passport for that.'

'His passport?' Oscar echoed foolishly.

'Yes, didn't I tell you? His fellow director to whom I spoke said he must have taken his passport from the desk drawer in which he kept it when he left his office last Tuesday, because it was no longer there.'

'How strange!' Oscar said, feeling as if he had trodden on a missing floorboard.

'Strange or not, it doesn't look as if he was intending to do away with himself. Seems more likely he was planning a trip. But I gather he never mentioned that to you?'

'No, never.' Oscar gulped and wished the conversation could be brought quickly to an end, but Sergeant Claymore hadn't finished.

'I've also been in touch with his solicitor,' he now went on. 'It seems that Mr Knight had recently re-arranged his affairs. Made a new will, that sort of thing. Are you still there, Mr Knudsen?'

'Yes, I'm listening,' Oscar said, his head swimming.

'I gather you didn't know about that?'

'No.'

'All of which leads one to believe that Mr Knight is somewhere alive and well. So I shouldn't worry too much if I were you. I expect I'll be talking to you again before long.'

With which Sergeant Claymore rang off leaving Oscar feeling as if he'd been mugged.

'Now what's happened?' Keith asked when he arrived that evening.

The question was quite superfluous as nothing was going to stop Oscar giving him a blow-by-blow account of what he had been through that day.

While Oscar talked, Keith helped himself to a Scotch and dry ginger and sat down.

'Sounds like a right cock-up,' he said, when Oscar reached the end. 'And what's all this about his changing his will?'

Oscar gave a helpless shrug. 'I wish I knew. I can hardly ring the solicitor and ask him.'

'Why not?'

'Because he wouldn't tell me. It'd be a breach of professional confidence.'

'Even though you and Oliver were like husband and wife?'

'He still wouldn't.'

'Pity you didn't think of that earlier. Come to that, pity you didn't think of a lot of things, such as this presumption of death business. One thing for sure, we don't want the police finding his body.'

'But they must.'

'And see he's been murdered? You must be mad.'

'But there'll be nothing to connect either of us with it. And anyway it may look like suicide.'

'With marks on his throat and a load of hard rock in his pockets!'

'I could say he once told me that if he ever committed suicide, he'd drown himself.'

'The police would be on to you in no time. They'd squeeze you as if you were a tube of toothpaste.'

'They certainly wouldn't get anything out of me.'

'They would if they put enough pressure on. They're experts at it. Anyway, you'd be tempted to put it all on me.'

Oscar gave a cry of dismay. 'How can you say such a thing when all I want is to spend the rest of my life with you! Haven't I done all this just for you?'

'What about me? I'm the fall guy. I'm the one who's taken the risks.'

'We mustn't quarrel, love,' Oscar said in a tone of suppressed hysteria. 'It's all going to be all right, I promise you. It's no more than a hiccup in our plans.'

'More like a bloody great belch, if you ask me,' Keith observed as he got up and went across to pour himself another drink.

The meal that followed was not one of the most successful. In his distracted state Oscar overcooked the steaks and the chocolate mousse turned out lumpy, both an indication of the stress he had been through earlier in the day.

After dinner, Keith remained impervious to all Oscar's blandishments and the evening concluded on a generally unsatisfactory note.

After a restless night, Oscar drifted into a stuporous sleep around five o'clock. He was brought out of it by the insistent ringing of the front-door bell. He peered bleary-eyed out of the bedroom window and saw a blue saloon car parked outside the gate. Hurriedly combing his hair and putting on his kimono dressing-gown, he went downstairs and opened the door.

'Mr Knudsen? I'm Detective Sergeant Claymore, we've spoken on the phone a few times. It looks as if I've woken you up.'

'I don't even know what time it is,' Oscar said numbly.

'Just turned ten o'clock. May I come in?' Without waiting for an answer he entered and Oscar closed the door behind him. 'Why don't you go and get dressed and, if you'll show me where the things are, I'll make us a cup of coffee.'

Oscar nodded. Sergeant Claymore was almost exactly as he had pictured him, trim-figured and friendly in a detached sort of way. Maybe they could get on first name terms. That would make for ease, as well as being propitious.

Ten minutes later Oscar returned to the kitchen, dressed in a white roll-top sweater and a pair of purple cords.

'I've even had a quick shave,' he said, giving Sergeant Claymore a hopeful smile. 'If you don't mind my saying so you're exactly as I'd pictured you would be.'

'Oh!' Sergeant Claymore sounded momentarily nonplussed, but quickly recovered and said, 'I thought you'd prefer me to come and see you, Mr Knudsen, rather than get you along to the station.'

There was a touch of steel in his tone that had not been there before. Picking up the tray of coffee things, on which he had placed a plate of fancy French biscuits, Oscar led the way into the sitting-room.

'I'll come to the point straight away, Mr Knudsen,' Sergeant Claymore said while Oscar assumed an air of polite interest. 'I wonder why you're so certain Mr Knight is dead?'

Oscar blinked. 'It's just that when somebody with whom you've lived for six years suddenly vanishes, you're apt to assume the worst. I'm still stunned by what's happened. I can't believe he'd leave just like that.'

'It wouldn't be because you had some part in his disappearance?'

'Some part? I . . . I don't follow you,' Oscar replied, swallowing hard.

'That you'd planned his death, shall I say?'

'You can't be serious,' Oscar exclaimed, quickly putting down his cup which had begun to rattle in its saucer. 'I loved Oliver. You mayn't understand that, but I assure you that gay people are capable of the same sort of love as ordinary married couples.'

'And the same sort of rows and deceits, too, I've no doubt,' Sergeant Claymore remarked equably.

'Oliver and I never rowed.'

'But to get back to my original point, why are you so keen to persuade me that your friend must be dead?'

'It's just that I have this sense of foreboding.'

'Of the two of you, he was the one with the money?'

'Yes.'

'To put it crudely, Mr Knudsen, he kept you?'

'Only in the sense that a man keeps his wife. In every other respect our life together was one of total sharing.'

'What do you think has really happened to him? It's obvious you believe he's dead, but how do you suppose he came by his death?'

'As I mentioned on the phone yesterday he'd recently been depressed . . .'

535

'And so he decided to take his life, is that it?' Oscar nodded. 'How would you expect him to have done it?'

'He once told me he'd drown himself, as that would be the simplest and least painful way, should he ever be driven to suicide.'

'So he sets off as usual last Thursday morning, abandons his car in Effingham Forest and looks for a suitable stretch of water in which to drown himself. Is that how you see it?'

'Of course, we now know he wasn't intending to go to his office that day.'

'Naturally not, if he had suicide in mind.'

'And he'd not been in the previous day.'

'Maybe he spent it doing a recce!'

'It doesn't seem to me that the police are taking the matter very seriously,' Oscar said stiffly.

'Oh, but you're wrong, Mr Knudsen, I'm deadly serious. But forget suicide for the moment, what else do you think may have befallen him?'

'I suppose he could have been murdered,' Oscar said with a shudder.

'In what sort of circumstances?'

'He used to pick up people in his car. Young men thumbing a lift. I'd told him it was a risky thing to do as you never knew when one of them mightn't attack you and steal your wallet, but he continued despite my warning. He used to say that they were often interesting company and a change from the radio.'

'So you believe he may have been murdered by a hitchhiker?'

'It seems a possibility.'

'You think we ought to explore that line?' Sergeant Claymore said thoughtfully.

'I most certainly do.'

'Do you think it's more likely than the suicide theory?'

'Yes, I think it probably is,' Oscar said with a frowning nod.

'Would you see it something like this? Hitchhiker persuades him to stop for some reason or another, they both leave the car and walk off together, hitchhiker attacks and kills Mr Knight and disposes of his body, doubtless stealing any money he had on him . . .'

'Oliver never had less than two hundred pounds in his wallet,' Oscar broke in.

'There you are then!'

'I think it could easily have happened just like that,' Oscar observed, trying not to sound complacent.

'There is, of course, the alternative,' Sergeant Claymore said, fixing Oscar with a steady stare.

'What alternative?'

'The one I mentioned earlier on. The one that has you playing a part in his disappearance. In his murder, in fact.'

The room seemed to give a sudden lurch and Oscar gripped the arms of the chair. He stared disbelievingly at his questioner, but words refused to come.

'The police are not as simple as some people think,' Sergeant Claymore went on. 'We don't just accept everything we're told without question. We look around, then probe here and there.'

'You're making a monstrous . . . outrageous suggestion,' Oscar managed to say at last. 'What possible motive could I have had for murdering Oliver?'

'You've already told me that.' He glanced around the room. 'You inherit all this and more besides.'

'Incidentally, I have an alibi for the whole of last Thursday morning. I was here at home.' His tone was coldly defiant.

'I never said *you* murdered Mr Knight. I'm sure you *didn't* do the actual deed, but you certainly had a part in it. A big part. The major part.' Oscar tried to look scornfully dismissive, but his expression had become one of frozen panic. Sergeant Claymore went on, 'In the language of the law, Mr Knudsen, you conspired to murder Mr Knight.'

'Conspired? Conspired with whom, may I ask?'

Sergeant Claymore looked at him pityingly. 'You don't really want me to answer that, do you? You see, we picked up Keith Offingham when he left here last night. We've had a long chat with him and he's told us everything.'

'I don't believe you. Anyway, he probably told you lies.'

'Lies? How you worked out a plan which involved him disguising his appearance and thumbing a lift in Mr Knight's car. How you and he were going to set up home together once you'd got your hands on Mr Knight's estate. Lies?'

'He's just a little money-grabber,' Oscar shouted hysterically. 'Anything he did was his idea.'

'That'll be for a jury to decide, Mr Knudsen.'

At this point, Oscar covered his face with his hands and surrendered himself to a bout of noisy and uncontrolled sobbing, while Sergeant Claymore observed him impassively.

In the days that followed Oscar's prevailing mood was one of obsessive self-pity and vicious resentment, which was transformed into a destructive fury when he learned that Keith had turned Queen's evidence against him and would be a witness for the crown instead of standing at his side in the dock.

It was during this period that he received a letter. It bore a Florence postmark and read:

*'Dear Oscar,*

*You were certainly right about one thing, Keith does smell strongly of compost. I noticed it as soon as he got into the car. Whatever his qualifications as a lover, he has few as a potential murderer. Admittedly I held all the cards once I'd rumbled him and he was astute enough to realise just how vulnerable his situation was. Even so he accepted my counter-plan with a readiness that was hardly flattering to yourself. I would 'vanish' for a short while and he would pretend to you that he had done the deed. As a matter of fact I'd realised several weeks ago that he meant more to you than a mere tiller of soil. You were always devious, Oscar, but on this occasion you were incredibly naïve as well. Your elaborate plan showed little attention to detail, but then you were always inclined to be slapdash in your eagerness to reach a goal. Anyway, I won't go on other than to say that my death would not have brought you the anticipated goodies as I had recently made a fresh will in which you're not mentioned.*

*I'll be back in England before your trial.*

*Yours still alive,*
**OK'**

# JOHN WAINWRIGHT

## A Wise Child

It is almost a year, now, since I decided to kill my father. To murder him, as retribution for re-marrying after the death of my mother.

I knew what I was doing. Let that be clearly understood. A modern fifteen-year-old, with a good education, can never claim 'ignorance' on moral issues. I knew I contemplated murder. Patricide, in fact. And, because I was capable of appreciating the moral issues I was, equally, capable of reaching a moral conclusion.

He didn't deserve to live.

Until my mother's death we had been a happy enough family. Just the three of us. Mother had doted on me a little; allowed me the occasional excess while he, in turn, had frowned mild disapproval without openly objecting. Long before I reached my teens, I realised he was a weak man. Mother was the dominating partner and, if sides had to be taken, she was always on my side.

On the other hand, I cannot remember seriously misbehaving myself. Sometimes a schoolboy prank that went a little wrong, or was taken beyond the point of moderation. Now and again, the deliberate playing of one against the other, in order to get my own way. Those were the limits. In the main, I was happy enough to obey my parents, because I loved them and because I respected them.

They, in turn, loved me . . . I make no Freudian excuse of being a 'misunderstood' child.

Perhaps we were too close. Perhaps we were too interdependent. Other than when he was at work, they were always in each other's company. For myself, I was a solitary person and wanted it that way. I read a great deal. Books on every subject under the sun. Travel books and history books; biographies and autobiographies. I read fiction, too – even crime fiction – but always, at the back of my mind, there was the knowledge that fiction was merely the out-pourings of an over-active imagination. The concocted murders were too involved. The alibis were too easily broken. The culprit was far too obvious – or, if not obvious, far too ridiculous.

Most of all, I enjoyed reading about trials. Real trials. Real murderers, who were stupid men, because they'd been caught.

I think the Seddon trial fascinated me more than any of the others. Frederick Seddon. He was called 'the meanest murderer of them all', but I could never understand that. To suggest *that* implies a price on human life. A cash value. I read and re-read various accounts of the Seddon trial and, to this day, I can't accept the proposition that he poisoned Miss Barrow for her money. She had so little. More than that, she was as valuable to him alive as she was dead.

There was just no case to answer. Edward Marshall Hall knew that. So, I'm sure, did Rufus Isaacs, who was prosecuting. Oh, no – the man who put the noose around Seddon's neck was Seddon himself. He was too clever by half. Too fond of the limelight. Had he *not* given evidence – had he declined to take the stand – he'd have walked away from court a free man.

As it was . . .

We were a happy enough family. (*We*, I mean, not the Seddons.) Mother was no raving beauty, but she was pretty enough, in her own way. A somewhat middle-class way, I suppose, but that's what we were – *very* middle class. Father worked in a solicitor's office. He wasn't a solicitor, of course, but he worked in the closed environment of parchment and law books. He was, I think, something to do with the conveyancing side. Something dreary, and not too technical. It must have been a very boring job, but that didn't worry him. He was a very boring man. Not deliberately unkind. Merely monotonous – and *very* boring.

He had jokes and witticisms. An amazingly limited repertoire of jokes and witticisms. He would trot them out with a regularity warranted to make me cringe. Something would be said – some remark a comedian might have described as a 'feed line' – and I'd know *exactly* what that dull-dog of a father would say next. Mother would dutifully laugh. A quick, obliging touch of laughter, which never reached her eyes. And, sometimes, she would glance at me, almost appealingly, as if to say, 'Can't we *do* something to stop this irritating man from *always* saying the same ridiculous things?'

We couldn't. We could only tolerate him. I think that, tacitly, we both accepted the burden of toleration until such time as nature took its course.

Odd . . . there was an unspoken assumption that he'd go first.

I rather think the same applies in all families, large or small. In some subtle way, one member is earmarked as being the first to die. Nothing to do with age. Nothing to do with illness. A sort of herd-instinct which prepares the rest for the first shock of close-range bereavement.

I suspect life-style has something to do with it. Father, for instance, was never fully *alive*. Whenever you caught him in an attitude of complete relaxation, the first thing you noticed was that his mouth corners drooped. His natural expression was that of a sad man. An everlastingly serious man. Even a sombre man. Which was quite ridiculous. A fiddling little clerk in the office of some unimportant solicitor, and his attitude suggested that he carried an impossible burden across his shoulders.

Young as I am, I have seen many men of father's ilk. Grey, vaguely unhappy men, without even a splash of colour. And most of them (like father) suffer slight pangs of indigestion. The first signs of quite unnecessary ulcers.

Mother, on the other hand, was quite charming – or would have been, had she not had the millstone of father around her neck. She had a certain spontaneous gaiety which bubbled beneath the surface. On the few occasions when just she and I went out together – to a show, to a cinema, to a concert – she fairly sparkled. She was a changed woman, without him around. She was a delightful companion and (a couple of times, no more) I suspected her of mildly flirting with some man sitting next to her. Nothing serious. Nothing objectionable. Just a happy exchange of pleasantries, accompanied by the sort of smile she so rarely had the chance of using at home.

Then, she died.

I truly couldn't believe it, at first. The head sent for me, from the chemical lab. He made me sit down in his study, then told me. He did his best – but I suspect there's no *easy* way.

'I have some bad news for you, my boy.'

'Yes, sir.'

'Your mother collapsed in the supermarket, earlier today.'

'Oh!'

'It's serious, I'm afraid.'

'How serious, sir? Is she in hospital?'

'I'm afraid she's dead. They think it was a heart attack.'

There was an inquest, and there was a funeral, and not once did I weep. Nor, come to that, did father. With me, it was a hurt too deep for tears. With him, it was – nothing.

I had difficulty in bringing myself to believe she was dead. I think he had equal difficulty in remembering that she'd ever been alive.

In bed, at night, I used to stare into the darkness and wonder what sort of man he was. What sort of a human being. He wasn't evil . . . God knows, he wasn't *evil*. He wasn't even hard. I could have understood, had he been one of the 'manly' types, to whom tears are a sign of weakness. Had he been like me, with a grief too savage for mere tears. But, he wasn't that. He wasn't that, at all. He had simply erased her from his life. From his memory. Like a misspelled word on a page. She wasn't there any more . . . period.

I once took him to task.

'Don't you miss her?' I asked.

'Of course I miss her.' But, he mouthed the words – he didn't *mean* them.

'You don't show it,' I accused.

'I'm not very demonstrative,' he said, gently. Then, with a quick, half-smile, 'One day you'll know. There's nothing more lonely than a double bed.'

'Not *that*!' The quick spat of disgust made me almost shout the words.

'Not *only* that,' he corrected me. 'You're young, yet. You don't . . . ' He stopped, mid-way through the sentence and looked awkward and embarrassed.

'I don't "know".' I ended the sentence for him, then added, 'But one thing I *do* know. One thing I'm certain of. I miss her. I miss her terribly. Far more than you miss her . . . and in a different way.'

He didn't argue, and that was the end of the conversation. Nor did we touch on the subject again. There was this distance between us – this gap – and it couldn't be bridged. He was kind enough. He refused me nothing, within reason, and he gave me freedom which I, in turn, didn't abuse. There was a certain deference between us. But not love. Not even real respect, at least, not on my part.

I had no aunts, no uncles, no grandparents. My parents had been only children and I, too, was an only child. But that didn't matter too much. I was given a key to the house, let myself in when I arrived from school and often prepared our meal for when father got back from the solicitor's office.

I was quite able to live a satisfactory life, without the help of adults. Without the companionship of people of my own age. I counted myself in no way odd. In no way peculiar. I had no real interest in sport, I could see no merit in pop music, I found the bulk of television facile, but having completed my homework each evening, I had my books.

The woman was called Angelica. *Angelica!* Botany lessons had taught me that angelica was a garden plant whose leaf-stalks and mid-ribs were candied for use in Christmas cakes. A sweetmeat. A nothing. I think she had a most appropriate name.

I don't know how or when they met. Neither of them ever saw fit to tell me. They became far too besotted with each other ever to give much thought to simple civilities.

I recall (it was little more than a year after mother's death) that father arrived home from the solicitor's office and announced that he was going to a concert that evening. Some string quartet was performing at the local hall. Part of the local musical society's programme, I think. After the concert, he was having supper with some friends. I remember that quite well. *Friends* – plural – not *a* friend.

I was surprised. It was so out of character. I admit, I was not displeased. My preference was to be alone; to do what I wanted to do, without the slightly strained atmosphere which had gradually built up between us.

Just before he left, he said, 'Don't wait up. I may be a little late.'

Again, there was some slight astonishment on my part, but no complaint. As far as I was able, while still being dependent upon him for a home, I lived my own life.

Nevertheless, and although I was in bed, I heard him return. It was past midnight, and he was humming quietly to himself.

That became the pattern. Twice a week. Sometimes three times a week. A concert. The cinema. Some amateur Gilbert and Sullivan production. That sort of thing. There was always an excuse – always a reason – and always 'supper with friends'.

His character gradually changed, although not towards me. He became less serious. Less hangdog. His choice of ties, while not being flamboyant, became less drab, and he didn't *always* wear a white shirt. In a way difficult to explain, he became 'different'. Not flash – he could never have become in any way flash – but 'different'.

Then, about six months after that first concert, he brought her home, after one more concert. No 'supper with friends' this time. They arrived at about half past nine – shortly after I'd settled down to read one of the *Famous Trials* series –

and I heard the key in the lock and the door open and close without taking much notice.

I was a little surprised and a little disgusted, when he brought her into the front room and introduced us. But, in honesty, I kept my distaste to myself because (I told myself) he was a weak man. A basically stupid man. A contemptuous little man living his own contemptuous little life and, for a few more years, I'd have to tolerate him.

But, *after* those few more years . . .

Then, he said, 'I've asked Angelica to be my wife, and she's done me the honour of accepting.'

It caught me completely flat-footed. I was so unready for the remark. So unprepared.

I think the shock showed itself, because she gave a saccharine smile, and said, 'You don't mind, dear, do you?'

'Mind?' I struggled to regain control of myself.

'You see, dear, we don't want to . . .'

'Why should *I* mind?' I closed my book, then repeated the question, but with a different emphasis. 'Why *should* I mind?'

'Of course you don't mind.' The pompous little man thought that, because I was able to hide my outrage, I approved. 'You'll have a mother again . . . won't you?'

He married her two months later.

It was a quiet enough wedding. The registrar was a paunchy, fussy little man, with loose dentures. The two witnesses were complete strangers to me. I think one came from the office where father worked, and the other was a woman friend of 'the bride'. Everybody dutifully kissed each other, after the ceremony – but nobody kissed me!

'He's at that awkward age.' This, from the 'Angelica' woman, when I backed away from the female witness. 'He thinks it's weak to show any outward signs of emotion. Don't you, dear?'

That was another thing. She would insist upon calling me 'dear'. I didn't want to be her 'dear'. I didn't even want to *know* her.

They went away for a fortnight's honeymoon. Somewhere near Southport. They gave me the address, before they left, but I didn't write. They, in turn, sent me two 'wish you were here' postcards.

Perhaps they did, too – wish I was with them, I mean. They must have been very boring company for each other. The gushing, simpering woman, and the pathetic little man with his limited stock of funny remarks. Two weeks of each other's company must have almost driven them mad. Perhaps they spent most of the time going to 'concerts'. Or having 'supper with friends'.

I never asked, and they never told me.

While they were away, I planned the murder.

I decided upon arsenic. What was good enough for the Borgias seemed good enough for me. I also felt that it had a certain 'romantic' connotation. It is reputed to have aphrodisiac properties. I think some cosmetic preparations include it in their formula. In a typically cynical Continental expression, it is known as the Inheritance Powder, the *poudre de succession*.

Definitely arsenic.

It wasn't difficult to come by. It was there, for the careful filching, at the school lab. I called in at the reference section of the local library, and checked in Glaister's *Medical Jurisprudence and Toxicology*. Three hundred grains was more than enough. Much less than an ounce. I didn't steal it all at once. Four times, and nobody missed it.

Then I stored it in an empty pill box, and hid the box at the back of my books, on a shelf in my bedroom. Then I waited.

The waiting was the worst part. I knew him to be a worrying man, and I knew the worrying brought on the indigestion and the stomach pains. Strangely, his guts seemed not to be causing him as much trouble as they had done previously. He remained the same apology for a man, but seemed not to carry his petty concerns around so heavily. Or, come to that, so obviously.

Perhaps this new wife of his was good for him. If so, she was only going to be good for him for a limited period, and I loathed both of them that little bit more for that fact. He had no *business* being content. Mother had been his wife – morally, was *still* his wife – not this giggling, empty-headed female with a ridiculous name.

In retrospect, the waiting period worked in my favour. I'd stolen the arsenic from the school lab, and the science master was more than a little lackadaisical in his checking of equipment and materials. Nevertheless, three hundred grains *had* been 'lost'. When a new supply arrived and was added to the little left in the container, I breathed more freely. I had the poison. Nobody knew I had it. And now, nobody would *ever* know I'd taken it. I was quite safe.

Thereafter, Lady Luck walked alongside me.

He came home on the Friday evening holding his middle.

'What is it, dear?' She sounded quite distressed. 'Are you ill?'

'Indigestion. That's all. I've had quite a day.'

'Should I send for the doctor.'

'No, no.' He played the part of the brave little sufferer. 'It comes on, periodically. I have some capsules the doctor gave me. I'll take them for a day or two. They always do the trick.'

I knew those capsules. They were part of the plan. As much a part as the arsenic itself.

The GP was a busy man; too busy to be forever examining a patient with recurring belly-ache. There was a 'repeat prescription' arrangement. Added to which, father was the sort of man who hoards medicines. The bathroom cabinet bulged with bottles and boxes and, amongst them, there was a fine supply of capsules from past bouts of indigestion.

He said, 'Four a day. They'll put me right.'

He went to bed early and, privately, I determined to make sure he would never get up again.

The next morning, the woman Angelica said, 'I have the weekend shopping to do. I've given your father his capsule. You're not going out, are you?'

'Later. About noon.'

'I should be back by then. He's asleep at the moment. I'll give him his second capsule when I get back.'

That left me two hours, and I didn't need two hours.

I gave her time enough to ensure she wasn't returning for something she might have forgotten, then I moved cautiously into the bedroom. He was still fast asleep. I took the bottle of capsules and returned downstairs. I spread a newspaper on the kitchen worktop, then began the substitution. I did it, one capsule at a time. Emptying the contents down the sink, under a running tap, then carefully substituting arsenic. The capsules were green, and when the two halves were replaced they looked no different from when they'd held whatever it was they'd originally held. As I filled each with arsenic I dropped it back into the bottle. There must have been forty capsules – at least forty – and I doctored every one.

Then, I returned upstairs. Father was still asleep, and I returned the bottle to the bedside table.

On an impulse – a quite imaginative brainwave – I sought, and found, the woman's work-basket. It contained reels of cotton, needles, thimbles (the usual junk) and I pulled the stuff to one side and carefully scattered the barest hint of arsenic in one corner of the silk-lined interior. Then I returned the work-basket, folded what was left of the arsenic into the sheet of newspaper, took it out into the garden, stuffed it into the fire-basket and lighted it.

When the woman, Angelica, returned she said, 'How is he?'

'The last time I looked in he was asleep.'

'Good.' She dumped her basket. 'I'd better go up. It's time he took another capsule.'

It took him all weekend to die. It was very painful and very messy. All the classic symptoms of arsenic poisoning were there. A burning pain in the stomach. Severe vomiting and diarrhoea. The fools thought it was a worse-than-usual attack of indigestion and, because it was the weekend, hesitated about sending for a doctor.

Having been up all Saturday night, on Sunday morning she said, 'He has it bad, this time.'

'Really?'

She described the night's activity, then said, 'Go up and see him, dear.'

'It wouldn't do any good.'

'No. Probably not. He doesn't like to be disturbed.' She frowned, then added, 'I think I'll double the dosage of his capsules.'

'That might help,' I agreed.

I borrowed five pounds from her, took a bus into the country and walked a little. It was a beautiful day. I enjoyed a quiet lunch at an out-of-the-way café, walked a little more, then took the bus back home.

She was in something of a panic when I walked into the house.

'He's getting worse. I'm sure he's getting worse.'

'Indigestion?' I smiled.

'He's in pain. Terrible pain.'

'The capsules have worked before,' I murmured.

'I know,' she wailed. 'He keeps asking for them, and I keep giving them to him.'

'Do you think you should call a doctor?'

The suggestion had to be made, if only for the sake of appearances.

'I keep saying so.' She sighed, heavily. 'He won't have it. He doesn't want to be a nuisance. But if he's no better tomorrow . . .'

It was a 'tomorrow' that never came.

Because he hadn't attended him, the doctor couldn't issue a death certificate. Because there wasn't a death certificate, there had to be an inquest. Because there was an inquest, there was a post mortem examination.

It was all rather like The House That Jack Built.

The pathologist found traces of arsenic. The police took possession of the remaining capsules. Later that same day the police returned and made a clinical search of the house. Among the things they took away was the workbasket.

Early next morning, they arrested the woman Angelica.

Although I was questioned, and gave the appropriate answers, I discovered that I could watch all this with complete detachment. It was, of course, what I'd planned, and it went as smooth as silk.

I found myself thinking how like the Seddon case it all was.

The same poison. The same lack of real, or obvious, motive. The same outpourings of indignation when the suspected murderer was arrested, and the same continuation of that indignation at the trial. In so many ways, a perfect parallel to the Seddon case.

Like Seddon, she was convicted.

For myself, I tried to out-do *Mrs* Seddon – and succeeded.

That fine lady (if you recall) was jointly charged, with her husband but, unlike that husband, she made herself as inconspicuous as possible. She allowed her husband to hog the limelight and, from the shadows, defied the prosecution to overturn the Presumption of Innocence. Every scrap of evidence that convicted her husband *could* have convicted her. But it didn't. Figuratively speaking, she crept from the stage, while Frederick Henry made a fool of himself, and was hanged for his trouble. She was acquitted!

I built upon Mrs Seddon's wisdom. My profile was so low, they didn't even charge me. They asked a few questions and, as was becoming in the circumstances, I bravely fought back crocodile tears and answered quietly, but vaguely. They were satisfied.

Even the woman Angelica didn't suspect. She ranted on about 'mistakes'. She raved about the incompetence of the pharmacist. She screamed abuse at the police, and accused them of cooking the evidence.

Like Seddon, she virtually convicted herself.

She was convicted, of course, and, within the first month of her prison sentence, managed to commit suicide.

For myself, I managed quite well. I could (still can) live alone, without any real difficulty. I taught myself to cook simple meals and carefully organised the housework to ensure that keeping the place moderately clean was moderately easy. I had money, of course – not a fortune, but enough – and could take an occasional meal out when I felt like it.

I congratulated myself upon a remarkably efficient removal of certain annoyances. I assure you, I didn't suffer a single bad dream, nor yet the hint of a prick of conscience.

Then, some few weeks ago, the man from the office where father had worked called. He was obviously embarrassed, as he handed me a well-sealed envelope.

'We – er – we all liked your father,' he muttered.

'Thank you.'

'He left this with us. The envelope I mean. To be given to you, in the event of the death of himself and his wife.'

'What is it?'

'I'm sorry. I don't know. Just that he asked for it to be kept, and when – *if* – you were ever left alone . . . '

His voice trailed off, miserably.

'That's very kind of you,' I smiled.

'Just that – y'know – with all the upset of the trial, and such. We thought it better to wait until you'd had time to settle down a bit.'

'That's very thoughtful of you.'

Then, he left, and I opened the envelope.

I have the letter in front of me. It's from the man I'd called 'father' all my life. He *wasn't* my father . . . and, to be honest, I wasn't too surprised. A little taken aback, that I'd poisoned the wrong man, I think, but not really *shocked*. My mother had been pregnant when he'd married her. He'd 'made her respectable' – his words, not mine. So like him. So much the action of a strait-laced ninny.

Mother had told him who the father was. My *real* father, that is. But the man hadn't known he'd impregnated her. That word – 'impregnated' – was his way of putting it. He was never told.

The name of my real father was there in the letter. And his address.

I made a few enquiries. It wasn't difficult. He'd moved house, and he's now happily married. He doesn't know, of course. He doesn't know how much I hate him, how much I've already learned about him. He certainly doesn't know what's going to happen to him.

I went up to London for the day. Talked to people in the offices of Macmillan Publishers. Convinced them that I had the germ of an idea for a short crime

549

story. They agreed to read it, to 'consider' it. Publish it, if it was good enough.

This is it. You've just read it. My father – my *real* father – likes anthologies of crime stories. That's something else I learned about him.

Hopefully, he'll read this anthology – read this story – then he'll know . . . won't he?

# TED
# WILLIS

---

# The Man From
# The White Mountains

In one sense, of course, murder may be measured in moments. It takes only a split second after the squeezing of a trigger for a bullet to enter the brain or the heart, and only a fraction longer for a knife to slice into the soft flesh of the throat or penetrate a breast.

But to say this is to say little or nothing, the equivalent of asserting that love is no more than the fleeting moment of sexual climax.

A murderer – and, for that matter, his victim – is not made in a moment. He is the product of a long process, a combination of genes, background, upbringing, circumstances; in short, of his or her entire life. Luck can also play a vital part. There are many people, living innocent, respectable lives, who, in certain conditions, could and would commit murder, but who probably never will. It is their good fortune to escape the sequence of events which could drive them to kill. Others are not so lucky.

If, for example, we are to understand why a man called Marcos Kolomenos committed murder in Adelaide, South Australia, on March 17, 1972, it will be necessary to go back over forty years in time. The actual crime took only a few seconds, its preparation was a matter of careful planning over a period of months. But the seed of murder was planted in Marcos Kolomenos many years before, and ten thousand miles away, in the high White Mountains of Sphakia, to the west of the island of Crete.

It was there in the tiny village of Nigrita, on October 8, 1931, that a married woman named Lilika Kollias was taken, with her lover, in the act of adultery.

In accordance with the age-old custom of the mountain people, the woman was driven from the village with stones and left to fend for herself. In the weeks which followed she was seen from time to time on the outskirts of the village, a pathetic, starving, half-mad creature, trying desperately to get a glimpse of her children. No one spoke to her, no one fed her, no one lifted a little finger to help her. Eventually she was seen no more, but it was strongly rumoured that she had found her way to Athens and was working there in a hundred-drachma whore-house.

The man, Angelos, with whom she had sinned was left, according to custom, to the mercy of the husband and the brothers of the husband. For such a man castration was normally considered to be an apt punishment, but there was a complication. Angelos was a relative of the husband, a first cousin on the maternal side, and this made his betrayal of the unwritten code all the more serious.

The husband and the brothers sought the advice of Stavros Kontas, the oldest and wisest man in Nigrita. It was, after all, a question of the honour of the family. Stavros had to think for a long time and search his memory before he could give them an answer, for the problem was an unusual one. In his long lifetime there had only been two instances of adultery in Nigrita, and since relatives were not involved, the customary punishment had been meted out. Expulsion for the woman, castration for the man.

And then Stavros remembered that his grandfather had once told him of a case in which a wife had betrayed her husband with his own brother. In such severe circumstances, the code decreed that the man should be put to death. It was a savage and primitive judgement but some deep instinct, centuries old, told the people that without such strict moral sanctions their isolated communities would degenerate and perish.

The following morning, as the sun was rising, Angelos was taken from the village into the mountains. He was stripped naked and while the three brothers held him, the husband castrated him. He was still screaming in agony as they carried him to a ledge and threw him on to the rocks eight hundred feet below. Then the husband broke Angelos' knife on a rock and threw the pieces after him. They left the body for twenty-four hours and then covered it with stones.

Marcos Kolomenos was five years old at this time. He heard the outcry in the village when the lovers were first discovered, and he realised from the behaviour of his elders that something of great importance and seriousness had taken place. Although he had been ordered to remain indoors, he crept out and from a discreet hiding-place watched the grim-faced women, his own mother among them, as they stoned Lilika Kollias and drove her away. He was appalled, yet excited by this strange game.

The next morning he saw four men leave the village with a fifth man, whose arms were tied behind his back. He recognised this man as Angelos, a person whom he had always admired. Angelos was tall and handsome, with white flashing teeth and a fierce, manly expression. At first, Marcos had been afraid of him, but once Angelos had carried him on his shoulders up into the mountains for a long, long way and shown him the hidden entrance to a wonderful, secret cave; and on another occasion Angelos had made him a wooden knife, shaped just like the sharp, steel knife he carried in his own belt.

Marcos wondered what his friend had done to have his hands tied thus, and why he was being taken away. He wanted to call out to him but he was too frightened to do so. He was puzzled to see that Angelos was wearing his best clothes, just as though it were a Sunday or a feast-day, and to see the knife with its decorated handle in his belt. Angelos walked proudly, with his head high, looking neither to left nor right and Marcos watched until he was out of sight.

Marcos never saw Angelos again, but the incidents made a deep impression upon him. His life changed with the years, he became a different person, but there were times when the memory of Lilika and her lover echoed and surged in him like the sound of distant bells. Whenever he saw a man carrying a small boy on his shoulders, he would remember his friend. At such moments he imagined that he could smell, across the years, the strong, masculine scent – a blend of wine and old leather – which was his first experience of Angelos.

It wasn't until he was twelve years old that the full significance of what had happened was revealed to him. He did not question the judgement or the sentence. Both were just, they followed naturally from the unwritten code of the Cretan mountain people.

It was, after all, a simple question. Every man had the right and the duty to defend his honour. If he failed to do so he betrayed not only a code which had lasted a thousand years, but himself. Such a man was not fit to live.

In May, 1941, when Marcos Kolomenos was almost fifteen years of age, the Germans carried out a massive airborne invasion of the island and succeeded in occupying the main towns and the coastal plains. But the Cretans, helped by remnants of the British army, retreated to the mountains and carried on the resistance. The Germans turned in fury against village after village, but they were never able to break the spirit of a people for whom honour was more important than life.

This was a crucial time for Marcos. In a few weeks, even a few days, he became a man; with his father and his uncles, he joined the partisan forces. He saw many of his comrades die, and there were times when death brushed his own shoulder. He learned the art of survival the hard way. Older men came to admire and respect not his courage, for that in a Cretan was taken for granted, but his cunning, resourcefulness and adaptability.

He learned, also, that there was another world beyond the White Mountains and his village. He became friends with an Australian sergeant, a former schoolmaster, and in the long intervals between engagements the sergeant taught Marcos English and the elements of arithmetic. He talked to him for hours of other lands and other peoples, but most of all, he spoke of his native Australia, holding the boy fascinated with his tales of that immense brown country. By a strange coincidence, they spent most of their time together in the big, secret cave which Angelos had shown Marcos years before.

'When the war is over, you must leave,' the sergeant told Marcos. 'There is nothing for you here. Australia is the world's last frontier, it's a young man's country. You could make your mark there.' He said it time and time again.

The idea of leaving Crete shocked and frightened Marcos at first. He could not imagine himself living in any other place. In the event, it was the Germans who, inadvertently, settled the issue for him.

His mother was caught by an enemy patrol in the act of smuggling ammunition to the Resistance. She was stripped naked and hanged on a gallows in the village square as a deterrent to any others who might be tempted to follow her example.

The death of his wife changed Marcos' father. Normally a careful, slow-thinking man, he allowed anger and grief to overcome caution. At noon one day he went down to the nearest town with a British Sten gun concealed under his cloak. He sat on a bench in the little square and waited in the hot sun until a detachment of German soldiers came marching by on the way to the local barracks; then, quite calmly, he opened fire. Fourteen of the enemy were killed and seven wounded before the father was himself cut down.

From that point onwards, his comrades noted a new depth of ruthlessness in Marcos. It was as though all human pity had been drained from his soul. He rarely took prisoners, and those few enemy soldiers who did fall into his hands longed for death.

When the war was over, there was nothing to keep him in Crete. He had a brother, Alexander, who was seventeen years his junior, but there was no one else towards whom he felt any responsibility. In March, 1946, at the age of twenty, he emigrated to Australia. He left Alex with an aunt, promising to send for him as soon as he had settled in the new land.

He was still only twenty years of age, but he had the look and bearing of a man fifteen years older.

Marcos settled in South Australia, near the city of Adelaide, at a place called Paradise. The name appealed to him. But for the first year, his life was something less than Elysian.

He was employed as a labourer by a farmer named George Smith, a harsh, humourless man, who had a contempt for 'New Australians' and regarded them as a source of cheap labour. He worked Marcos as one would work an ox, housed and fed him little better than an animal. The young Cretan seemed to accept this patiently, even willingly; but underneath the resignation his spirit glowed fiercely, waiting like a fire which has been momentarily dampened but remains unquenched.

During those twelve months Marcos learned another valuable lesson – that patience can also be a weapon, that there are times when a man must simply wait and watch and learn. He perfected his knowledge of English (though he never completely lost his accent or the Cretan rhythm of speech) and he took the measure of this country in which he had decided to make his home. He saw that it was, indeed, a land of opportunity, and he knew, after only three months, that he could and would succeed there. This inner knowledge fortified him as the days of back-breaking labour passed; he had no doubts, his self-confidence was complete.

Quite suddenly, one morning, he decided he was ready. He had been into Adelaide the day before and seen the opportunity for which he had been waiting. He packed his few belongings, told Smith that he was leaving immediately and waited for the reaction. He did not wish to go quietly, he had a debt to pay and he was hoping that the farmer would give him an honourable opportunity to settle it. He was not disappointed. Smith began to rant and rave, piling the old familiar insults one on the other. He was a heavy man of formidable strength, but Marcos was confident.

He dropped his worldly possessions to the ground, stripped off his shirt and faced the astonished Smith. His right fist thudded into the farmer's beer-ripened belly, and as the big man gasped in anguish and doubled-up, Marcos linked his hands together and chopped down with pulverising force on Smith's neck. Smith fell to the ground, tried desperately to raise himself, and rolled over on his back. Marcos was angry that it had been so swift and easy a victory. He felt cheated of his revenge. He looked down at the farmer and, for a moment, he felt himself back in the White Mountains, standing over a fallen enemy, his hand reaching automatically for the knife in his belt. Smith must have read the intent in the Cretan's face, for he rolled his blue eyes imploringly and cried in fear, 'No, Marcos, no! No, no!'

Marcos steadied himself. He was not in Sphakia, there was no knife in his belt, the blubbering man at his feet was not a Nazi. He lifted a heavy boot and Smith whimpered in fear, then screamed as the boot crunched home. Marcos gave a grunt of contempt and spat at Smith; the spittle rolled slowly down the farmer's cheek, but he did not attempt to wipe it away.

Mrs Smith, a thin, scrawny woman in a shapeless dress, stood watching the scene from the homestead, her face like a sallow moon in the dark shade of the verandah. She made no move towards her husband, her eyes looked at Marcos without expression.

He picked up his things and walked away from Paradise without regret, and without once looking back.

The first thing Marcos did after this was to buy himself a hole in the ground. It was about two miles from the centre of Adelaide, a stretch of derelict and neglected earth, just over an acre in size, almost entirely made up of this huge, yawning hole. He bought the site for £90, which was half of what he had saved, and the man who sold it to him thought he was mad. But Marcos had seen, with the fresh eyes of a stranger, that Adelaide was growing, and that trucks, loaded with rubble from the demolition of old buildings, were being driven each day to tips on the city outskirts. He posted a notice inviting the demolition companies to dump their rubble on his site. Since, by so doing, the companies saved themselves time and mileage, they were quite happy to pay Marcos the nominal charge of £1 per truck-load which he imposed.

Within six months the hole was full and the site more or less levelled. Marcos sold it to a developer for £2,500, and with most of this capital he bought a half-share in a small building and construction company. His partner was Andy Byers, a small, genial, happy-go-lucky Australian who knew a great deal about building but very little about business. Marcos waited again, learning all he could from Byers, and at the end of two years he bought him out. Byers was drunk when he signed the contract of sale and on the following morning his wife tried to get Marcos to tear it up. He listened without emotion to her frantic pleading.

'Your husband is a good bricklayer, Mrs Byers,' he said. 'If he wishes to come back and work for me as a bricklayer, I will find him a place. But the business is mine. From now on, it is mine, please understand this.'

'You cheated him!' she screamed. 'He didn't know what he was doing, he was drunk. You made him drunk.'

'He has no head for drink and no head for business,' said Marcos calmly. 'Take my advice. Keep him away from both these things.'

A few months later, when he had run through his money, Andy Byers swallowed his pride and came back to Marcos for a job. He was made foreman-bricklayer on a big new development in the suburb of Springfield, a position which he accepted gratefully and humbly, and in which he served Marcos well.

It gave Marcos no satisfaction to take back his old partner on these terms. He valued pride in a man above all things, and the servile attitude of Byers offended him. Whenever they met – something he tried to avoid – Marcos found it difficult to conceal his contempt.

Shortly after taking over the construction firm Marcos Kolómenos changed his name to Mark Coleman. It was a difficult step to take, and one which he regretted, but he decided that it was essential to the success of the business. In any case, this was his country now, he knew he could never go back to the old life in Crete. When he had lived the statutory five years in Australia, he applied for and was granted naturalisation. He felt a surge of pride as he swore the oath of allegiance to the Queen and to his new country. He had left his old life behind forever, he was now an Australian, a man of substance.

In 1955 he built himself a new, modern house in Springfield, and sent for his younger brother, Alex, and his aunt, Amalia. He longed for their arrival, he wanted to have his own family around him, to show them what he had achieved. He had no interests outside the business, his one concession to his own nature was a weekly visit to a brothel in the port area of the town; but these cold encounters only served to sharpen his growing feeling of loneliness.

In the event, Aunt Amalia refused to leave Crete, and Alex, now a sturdy lad of twelve, travelled to Adelaide alone. He knew little or nothing of life outside Nigrita and the White Mountains and he was astonished by the sophistication and luxury which he saw around him. Most of all, he was enthralled by his brother, who seemed to be so much a part of this new environment, to be so confident, rich and successful. The house, the car, his bedroom with its own bathroom – the sheer space, the grandeur of it all took his breath away, it was like a dream.

But it wasn't a dream, it was astonishingly real. On that first evening Marcos said: 'All this is ours, Alex. Yours and mine. And believe me, it is only the beginning.'

Only the beginning? Alex was amazed. What could be better than this, how could a man want or have more? But he said nothing, only watched his brother with big, dark, wondering eyes.

'You will become an Australian like me,' Marcos continued. 'First, you will learn to speak the language. I've arranged all that. Then school, real school. And after that, university.' He spoke proudly.

'University?' It was a new word to Alex, he had never heard it before.

'You are tired. We will speak of it tomorrow – we shall have time enough to talk.' At the door, Marcos paused and looked back at his brother. 'Alex. Do you know what a millionaire is?'

'A rich man?'

'A very rich man. Like Onassis. I am going to be a millionaire, that is my plan. I shall achieve this in ten years.'

'Why do you want this?'

'Because it is important. Money is important.'

'But in this country it seems to me that everyone has money.'

'Not everyone. You will learn that. And it is the same here as it is back home. The rich give the orders and the poor obey. The greater the riches, the greater the power.' He moved in closer to the boy and put a hand on his shoulder. 'This is the way I see it, Alex. Our mother and our father did not die so that we should live for the rest of our lives taking orders from other people. I did not fight in the mountains for that either. Do you understand?'

Alex nodded, although he did not properly follow what Marcos was saying.

'The important thing is that you are now with me. We shall do well together.' Marcos embraced his brother and kissed him in the Cretan style. The boy was very near to tears but he held them back, knowing that it was unmanly to weep and that Marcos would not approve such weakness.

Marcos was as good as and better than his word. These were the lush, plush years when half the world seemed to be set on a course of endless growth, and whole nations nourished themselves on greed. Money made money and more money; the quick-witted and the corrupt fattened themselves on their easy killings. It was a time tailor-made for Marcos, a time for which all his background and experience had prepared him.

Within ten years he had expanded into real estate and mineral development; he had extensive interests in the wine districts of the Barossa Valley, he owned a television station in Adelaide, two radio stations in the country, and he was a major shareholder in several newspapers and leading industrial companies. He was a millionaire three times over, a powerful and influential figure, to whose views politicians and businessmen listened with respect, and even fear. Such was his reputation that he figured prominently in news stories and press cartoons; one satirical television programme (not on his own station) lampooned him at regular intervals.

This programme was to play an important part in later events.

What his critics did not understand was that Marcos seemed to take no joy from his success, no satisfaction from his conquests. Though few doors were closed to him, he found no pleasure in social life; he remained an enigma, a grim, solitary person for whom there was no existence outside his business. His one relaxation was an occasional weekend flight in his private plane to a small station he owned near Townsville, in North Queensland; but even on these occasions he took his working papers with him, and he was invariably alone.

This weekend hide-out was also destined to feature prominently in the unfolding pattern of the drama that was to come.

The force that continued to drive Marcos forward was disappointment. As Alex grew older it became clear that he shared none of his brother's character or ambition. The simple truth was that he had been spoiled. Marcos had pampered the boy, giving him all he asked – and more – without question. Content to enjoy the fruits of the harvest, Alex gave nothing in return. He became notorious as a rich dilettante who was only protected from the consequences of his irresponsibility by the power and influence of his older brother. He developed artistic and literary pretensions, and openly mocked Marcos, making no secret of the fact that he regarded him as an uncultured moron whose horizons were bounded by balance-sheets. He returned cynicism for affection, coldness for warmth. The two men reached a point where they could hardly exchange a civil word and Alex left home.

Marcos continued to pay him an allowance, for to do otherwise would have been to deny his own roots. He was the eldest brother, he was still responsible. But beyond this there was nothing, only the business, into which he sank his energy and his bitter sense of loss.

And then fate or luck (aren't they, after all, the same thing?) made the final move in its long, remorseless build-up to inevitable tragedy.

It was as though Kristina Ayres had been kept waiting in the wings until the stage was set, and the other protagonists in position.

Marcos met her at one of his rare social engagements, a dinner party given by the Premier of South Australia to honour a group of visiting businessmen. The hostess paired her with Marcos and within a few minutes he was completely captivated by his dark-haired, vivacious and beautiful partner.

'Kristina?' he asked. 'It is a Greek name. Are you Greek?'

'I am Australian,' she answered with a smile. 'My father was English and mother Greek. I am called after her.'

He nodded with approval. Throughout the evening he watched her, noting her poise and sophistication, her humour and bright intelligence; above all, the odd, shy moments of innocence which showed in her big, dark expressive eyes. For the first time he felt his own lack of the social graces, his awkwardness. In her presence he felt like a thick-fingered peasant.

In a sense, it was for him a rebound from the crushing disappointment he had experienced with Alex. He needed someone as the centrepiece of his life, someone to show off his glittering wealth and thus give it purpose and meaning. And there was something more. She could give him a replacement for Alex, she could give him children, the sons he yearned for. Alex had been a sort of son, but that was ended, Marcos could take no pride in his brother. But with Kristina he could be proud again; to possess such a woman would make him the envy of other men, she would be a magnificent confirmation of his success and position.

What he felt for her could hardly be described as love, though he admired her body and desired to take her. It was as though he had seen something of extraordinary beauty and value in a shop-window and was desperate to own it. But this was the man he had become and he could think in no other terms. It was the nearest approach he could make to the concept of love; sadly he knew no other way.

For weeks he laid siege to her, bombarding her with invitations and presents. She liked him, he amused her, and she was flattered to be courted by such a rich and famous man. And she was intrigued to find that, unlike other men, he made no sexual advances, there was no attempt to get her into bed. There were times when she wanted this herself, for she found him physically attractive; and she felt that only in this way, naked and in the act of love, would she discover the true Marcos, the man behind the image. But she held back, sensing that this would cheapen her in his eyes, that she was, in a sense, on trial.

Day by day, she saw herself coming more and more under the spell of his forceful personality. He wanted her, he was determined to have her, and any obstacles she erected were swept aside like so much chaff. He surrounded her, overwhelmed her, and she was helpless to resist.

They were married on August 2, 1970, a wedding of such magnificence that it made headlines in all the newspapers and was featured on television. Alex attended the reception, even putting on a suit for the occasion, and met Kristina for the first time.

'So you are his latest possession,' he said mockingly. 'Not bad, not bad. I've known him make worse bargains.'

She turned away from him in anger and distress, but she was to remember the words later, when the bitter truth they carried was stamped into her consciousness. Perhaps, in her heart, she had recognised some part of this truth from the beginning.

For truth it was. She was deeply fond of Marcos, she admired and respected him, and she told herself that this was enough, that she could build on this foundation and draw from him the response which would make her truly love him.

But it was a response of which he was incapable. He was generous and affectionate, proud of her, but that was all. She was, indeed, a possession, treasured as such and treated as such. And if the possession, at times, tried to assert her own individuality, to move beyond the mechanical role allotted to her, he rode over her with a ruthlessness which was frightening.

There was warmth between them, at least during the first year, but little tenderness. In bed, any veneer of sensitivity which he had acquired was left outside the sheets with his clothes; he coupled her as he had coupled the girls in the brothel, as though it was his right to do so, and he was only collecting what he had paid for. It was then that she felt most strongly that to him she was an ornament, an object, a possession.

Many women have suffered as much or more and have come to terms with their lives, content to accept half a loaf. It is possible that Kristina would have followed this path, for she was by nature an honest person with a strong dislike of intrigue or of anything that smacked of the underhand. Had she met and fallen in love with a stranger, her first instinct would have been to face Marcos with the fact, and to brave his inevitable wrath.

But almost inevitably, the man who came into her life was Alex. He began to call at the big house in Springfield again, it seemed that he was prepared to make some sort of peace with Marcos. Kristina was forced to amend her first impression of Alex; as time went on she found his company amusing and relaxing. Marcos was pleased that this should be so and encouraged them to see more of each other; it relieved him of certain social duties which he found irksome.

He liked to see them laughing happily together, like children. In a way, that was how he looked upon them both. The change in Alex made him happy also; for the first time in months he began to feel something of the old warmth for his younger brother.

This was a time of deep content for Marcos. His business affairs were thriving, there was some talk that he might be recommended for a knighthood; his marriage, though not perfect, seemed to have settled into a secure pattern, and Alex was once more back in the family circle. The one disappointment was that Kristina had so far failed to produce the sons he wanted, but there was time for that, he told himself.

The contentment did not last long. One evening, working in his study on the first floor, he happened quite by chance to get up and look out of the window towards the large flood-lit swimming-pool. He smiled as he saw Alex and Kristina sporting together in the blue water, and he felt a touch of envy also. Kristina was seldom as relaxed and carefree with him. Perhaps it was his fault? He used the pool for exercise only, grimly swimming a statutory ten lengths each morning; to him it was a tool, useful for toning the muscles, not a playground.

The trouble was that he had gone from boyhood to manhood in one step. He had missed his youth – the best time of all. He was forty-five years of age, almost old enough to be their father – and at that moment, he felt the weight of the years that separated them. He would try to relax more. There was the yacht, moored in the harbour, idle for most of the year. He would take time off, he would take Kristina and Alex away for a long cruise, he would show them that he, too, knew how to enjoy life.

It was then that the incident occurred.

Alex was helping Kristina from the pool, pulling her up out of the water. He could see them clearly in the amber light, their bodies striking long shadows on the paved surface behind them. As Kristina straightened up, she stood close to Alex, and he put up a hand and held it against her cheek. It was more than a gesture, it was a caress as intimate and full of meaning as if he had touched her breast. They stood there motionless for a moment, not smiling, simply looking into each other's eyes, his hand still resting gently on her cheek. Then she pulled away abruptly and threw a warning look towards the house.

It was no more than that, a small, trivial thing. But watching them, Marcos felt a sudden, inexplicable apprehension of danger, manifested as in the old partisan days in the mountains, by a chill stiffening of his neck and spine.

He tried to set the thought aside, telling himself that the gesture was no more than a sign of friendship, that they were children, that it meant nothing, but it was useless. Fear and suspicion filled his mind, spreading like a virus in the bloodstream. He dared not watch Kristina too closely, lest she in turn should suspect, but as the days passed his torment grew. He feared to learn the truth but he knew that without it he would find no peace of mind.

At the end of a week, he hired a private detective agency to keep observation on his wife and Alex. They came back in five days with their report. She had visited Alex in his studio-apartment in South Adelaide three times during that period, and each visit had lasted for two hours or more. On one of those occasions she had told Marcos that she was visiting her dressmaker; and on another that she had driven up to Elizabeth to visit a girl-friend.

He put the issue to a further test. That weekend he flew up to the house in Queensland on one of his regular visits. On his return, a new report awaited him. Kristina visited Alex at his apartment on the Saturday evening. They went out to dinner and then returned to his place. She left him at 5 a.m. the next morning.

Marcos paid off the detective and dismissed him. His instinct had proved to be right – Kristina had lied to him, she was deceiving him with Alex, his own brother.

He instructed his secretary to block all calls and cancel his appointments. He was surprised at his own outward calmness; in that sense, at least, the truth had brought a certain peace. It was only later, as he sat at the big desk, with the light fading behind him, that the anger and bitterness crowded in on him. From that moment on, it could be said that the balance of his mind was disturbed, that he ceased to be a rational person.

Or perhaps it would be more accurate to say that Mark Coleman became more truly himself, the new Australian became once again the old Cretan, Marcos Kolomenos. Centuries of history, age-old instincts and concepts of honour stirred in his blood. He remembered Angelos and Lilika, he saw again as in a film, his own mother as she hurled a stone at the guilty woman, he saw Angelos being led from the village. The sharp scent of leather and wine came back to him across the years.

But this was not Sphakia, he knew that; there vengeance could be simple and direct, everyone would expect him to redeem his honour, they would see it as something obvious and inevitable, as natural as breathing. It was different in this new land; here they would not understand his motives; quite simply they would call it murder and instead of being honoured for the deed he would be hunted down as if he were the guilty party.

It would have to be done, there was no question about that, but it would have to be done in a different way. For why should he suffer, why should he throw away all he had worked for and achieved? He had done nothing wrong, he had been a faithful husband and brother. It was they, Kristina and Alex, who had brought dishonour to the family, not he.

And now all the sharp cunning and talent for organisation which Marcos had acquired over the years came to his aid. When he left the office it was quite dark, but the main outline of a plan was already clear in his mind.

It was not until one weekend, almost three months later, when all the pieces were in position, that he began to put the plan into operation.

It was nothing new for Marcos to fly to Queensland to spend a weekend alone with his papers, but Kristina was worried, on edge. During the past few weeks she had sensed a new tension in her husband and it frightened her. There was nothing she could put a finger on, no positive evidence; it was simply that he seemed to be burning with some secret, inner fierceness.

Nino and Faustina Silone, the Italian couple who looked after them, had gone to Melbourne and would not be back until Monday. There was nothing unusual in that, they had relations there whom they visited regularly, but their absence added to Kristina's foreboding. Even the air was heavy and oppressive, it weighed on her skin, as though warning that a storm was about to break. At least, it seemed so to her.

Alex laughed at her fears. He saw in the absence of Marcos and the servants a wonderful opportunity for them to be together. He wanted to spend the night with Kristina in the house, under his brother's roof: the thought of it gave him a peculiar satisfaction.

'Oh, come on, Kris,' he said petulantly. 'What's wrong?'

'I don't know. I wish I did. It's just this feeling. I can't explain it.' She moved around restlessly. 'It's just – just that it is all too convenient. I mean – Marcos has a cold, a terrible cold, but he insisted on going. And then there's Nino and Faustina – they offered to cancel their trip, but he insisted they should go. He has been strange lately, Alex, he really has. I'm not imagining that.'

'You are! It's all in your mind!' Her attitude was making him irritable. 'Look, the main thing is – did he go or didn't he?'

'Yes,' she said listlessly. 'He left here at nine o'clock this morning.'

'Well, then!' he said as though that settled it. He tried to take her in his arms, but she eluded him with a frown.

'Yesterday,' she said thoughtfully, as though Alex hadn't spoken. 'Yesterday I was checking my make-up in the bedroom. Marcos came in, and I caught a glimpse of him in the mirror. It was only a flash, a moment, but the look in his eyes – it was terrible, Alex. I can't describe it – hate, madness, despair – all those things, but mainly hate.'

'Why should he suddenly hate you?'

'It could only be for one reason.'

'No,' he said firmly. 'Now you are imagining things. He trusts us. He goes out of his way to throw us together. This weekend is an example. He wouldn't go away if he suspected anything. Why, he even asked me to keep an eye on you! Which, of course, I said I would do with pleasure.'

He kissed her, but her response was cool. 'OK,' he said angrily, 'OK. If that's how it's going to be, there's not much point in my staying!' He moved to the door, and she made no effort to stop him. 'Listen,' he said, from the doorway, 'is that place in Queensland on the telephone?'

'Of course.'

'Then ring Marcos. Put your mind at rest. Speak to him. Find out once and for all if he is there.'

'What shall I say?'

'God, you're his wife. Ask him about his cold – say you're worried – anything.' He went to the phone and picked it up. 'What's the number?'

'Greenvale, North Queensland 274. Area Code 032.'

He dialled the operator, gave her the area code and number, and asked for a personal call to Mr Mark Coleman. She took the phone from him, and he kissed her lightly on the cheek. 'Don't be frightened,' he said.

Relief showed in her eyes as she heard Marcos answer. She nodded towards Alex, who spread his hands as if to say, 'I told you so.'

'Marcos, it's Kristina. I – I just thought I'd ring to find how you were feeling. How's the cold?'

'It's much the same,' he answered abruptly. She could hear the slight hoarseness in his voice. 'Is everything all right at your end?' he continued.

'Yes, oh, yes. I was only concerned about you.'

'There is no need. I'm not going to die. I shall be back tomorrow as arranged. Goodbye.' There was a note of irritation in his tone.

She put the telephone down slowly. 'Yes,' she said, 'he's there. He's there, all right. His usual polite courteous self.' She went to Alex. 'Come on, let's go to bed.'

She spoke with bitterness, it was as if the need to spite Marcos was uppermost in her mind. They went up to the main bedroom.

She found little enjoyment in their love-making. She felt ill-at-ease lying in the bed which she had so often shared with Marcos and regretted the bitter impulse which had led her to take Alex there. And there was something in his attitude which disturbed her. He had taken her fiercely, swiftly, and when it was over he lay back smiling as though in triumph.

'That was the best ever,' he said with a deep sigh, 'the best ever. Great! In this bed, in this room! Great!'

'In his room, in his bed. Isn't that what you mean?'

'You've got to admit, it adds an edge to the situation. A certain flavour.'

There was a smugness in his voice which angered her. A sense of disgust, as much for herself as for him, rose in her throat like bile. She got out of bed and put on a robe.

'Oh, stay here, Kris,' he pleaded and his voice sounded like that of a spoiled child. 'Come back to bed.'

'Alex,' she said quietly, 'when Marcos comes back, I am going to tell him.'

'Oh, yes,' he said with a smile, 'I can just see you doing that.'

'I mean it. I shall tell him everything, and then I shall leave him.'

'You're out of your mind!' He sat up in the bed. 'You don't know Marcos. He won't just sit back and accept it. Kristina, come back to bed and don't be foolish.'

'Alex,' she said quietly, 'what is more important to you? Your love of me or your hatred of your brother?'

'What the hell are you talking about? Kris, for heaven's sake, what's wrong?'

'Nothing. Only, perhaps, that I don't like being used.'

'Used?'

'By Marcos. And by you against Marcos. Because that's what you've been doing, isn't it? Oh, I daresay you love me well enough in your spoiled, little-boy way, but that's not really what drives you, is it? You're using me to get back at Marcos. I'm just a—'

She stopped suddenly, holding her breath, listening. 'What was that?' she whispered.

'What?'

'I heard something. A door. Someone's in the house, Alex.'

'Oh, rubbish!' he said. But fear showed in his eyes and he rose from the bed quickly, reaching for his clothes.

'Listen! Listen!' she said urgently. He paused in the act of pulling on his shirt. Nothing at first, no sound, and then they heard it; the quiet, measured tread of someone mounting the stairs. Each step seemed to crack the silence like a footfall on ice.

Alex scrambled in panic for his jeans. 'Help me, help me, for Christ's sake!' he croaked. But Kristina was standing still and calm, as though she had anticipated this moment and was almost relieved that it had come.

The sounds stopped outside the door. A century passed, and then the handle began to turn. Alex, holding his jeans around his waist, his shirt flapping, snatched up the rest of his clothes and rushed for the bathroom, as the door opened.

'Marcos!' said Kristina, trying to keep the fear out of her voice. 'What is going on? I thought you were in Greenvale – I spoke to you on the phone only a half-hour ago. What are you up to?'

He looked at her in contempt and past her with the same contempt to the soiled and rumpled bed. His dark eyes glowed, he was breathing heavily; she caught in her nostrils a sour scent, as of an animal, and then he hit her. She cried out and fell across the bed. He looked down at her for a moment.

'Whore!' He ground out the word from behind his clenched white teeth.

'Marcos, please,' she whispered. 'Let me explain.'

'Explain? How do you explain this? And this?' He ripped the robe from her shoulder, tearing it to the waist; he plucked the blue sheet from the bed and tore at it with his great hands as though it were tissue. As he did so he kept repeating: 'Whore! Whore! Whore!'

He pulled her up, hit her again, and caught her as she fell unconscious into his arms.

In the darkness that surrounded her, Kristina heard the shot. It seemed to come from a long way off, and it took her a full minute to work out what it could be. She opened her eyes and saw that she was in one of the spare rooms. The full realisation of what had happened came as she looked at her tattered robe. She struggled painfully to her feet and stumbled to the door. It was locked on the outside; she wrenched at the handle, hammered feebly on the door-panels.

Quite suddenly it opened and she saw Marcos standing there. He seemed very calm now and when he put a hand on her arm his touch was gentle. She dimly registered the fact that he was wearing gloves.

'Now, Kristina,' he said evenly. 'Let us talk together for a moment or two.'

'Alex,' she said hoarsely, 'where is Alex?'

'Alex and I have reached an understanding,' he said, smiling. 'It was quite simple really. I offered him fifty thousand dollars if he would clear off. He stuck out for double, and I agreed. After all, he is my brother. He left you a farewell note.'

Still dazed, she took the piece of paper he held out to her. 'Dear Kris,' she read, 'It is impossible for us to go on like this, so for your sake, I am doing the only thing possible in the circumstances. Please understand, and try to forget me. Goodbye, darling.' It was signed *Alex* and she knew that it was his handwriting.

'No, no,' she moaned, 'it isn't possible.' Her head cleared suddenly and she remembered the shot; pushing past Marcos, she ran to the bedroom. The door was open, the bitter smell of gun-fire hung in the air, and Alex was lying on the floor at the foot of the bed. There was a spreading crimson stain on the white carpet and half his face and head was missing. She turned on Marcos in horror and began to beat at him with her clenched fists, but he held her easily.

'I wasn't lying, Kristina,' he said. 'I told you the truth. He agreed to take a hundred thousand dollars and go to South America. That was your price. That was how much he loved you. He was a coward, he was a cheat. He had no true feeling for you.'

She wrenched herself free and ran like a mad thing, trying to reach the telephone at the side of the bed, but he was too quick for her. She stared past him towards the body; he took her chin and pulled her face close to his own. A trickle of sweat ran down his cheek.

'It had to be done, Kristina!' he shouted. 'Listen to me, listen! He should have respected and cherished you as a sister, as if you were of the same seed. Instead, he lay with you, he took you into my bed, he did this – this – dirty thing with you. He had to die, there was no other way.'

'They'll hang you!' she cried. 'They'll hang you or lock you up in a cell for the rest of your life!'

'Oh, no!' he said smoothly. 'That is not the way I have planned it. You see, I am not here. Have you forgotten so soon? You spoke to me on the telephone. I am in Queensland.'

'Who was that? Who did I speak to?'

'An actor. A drunken out-of-work actor. Very good at impersonation. He took me off several times on TV – do you remember? He is in my debt – and we agreed that this would be a good way to pay it off. Please Kristina, you surely know me by now. I like to organise things properly, thoroughly. You think I am standing here – but I am not. It is an illusion.' He glanced at his watch. 'As a matter of fact, at this moment, I am on my way into Greenvale to collect some supplies. I shall be seen by several people – it is what they call establishing an alibi, I believe.'

'They know you up there! They'll know it isn't you.'

'You under-estimate the acting ability of my friend. He really is very good. I took care to put on a cold to help him with the voice. As for the locals – well –

they know I prefer to be alone. On my recent visits I've taken care to develop a reputation for surliness. Oh, I have no fears about that part of it, Kristina.'

She remembered the actor now although she couldn't put a name to him. His impersonation of Marcos on TV had been stunningly convincing, he had got the voice and the mannerisms exactly right. And he had managed to look so much like Marcos.

'The pilot!' she said suddenly. 'He knows you too well! You couldn't fool him!'

'Lockstey? Oh, he wasn't on duty today. He's on leave. I hired a temporary pilot. I went to the airport this morning. I met my actor friend in the gentlemen's lavatory, I gave him my coat and bag, and he took off in the plane while I stayed behind. All he had to do was pick up the car I keep at the Townsville airfield and drive to the house. He'll look after himself there as I always do. Tomorrow he'll drive back to Townsville, and take the plane back. I'll meet him as before, he'll hand back my identity and then disappear.'

'Suppose he decides to talk?'

'He won't,' he said blithely. 'I have, shall we say, strong reasons for believing that.'

'You blackmailed him!'

'It's a word. I prefer to think I persuaded him. So there you are, Kristina. It took weeks to perfect, but it was worth it. A good plan – I'm rather proud of it.'

'You haven't yet told me how I fit into it,' she said. 'I'm sure you can't have overlooked that.'

'Oh, not at all. The – what is the word they use? – scenario. The scenario runs as follows. You and Alex have been having an affair. You are madly in love with each other. Alex, my dear brother, is overcome by conscience. He feels that he can no longer go on betraying me. This fit of remorse comes upon him after he has made love to you in this room on his brother's bed. He tells you that the affair must be broken off. You argue, even fight – that will explain those bruises on your face. But you make up – and then go downstairs. He takes a sheet of paper from the drawer – there – a sheet of my paper and writes you a farewell letter.' He held up the note. 'It isn't a forgery, he really did write it – to my dictation. He thought it was a ticket to freedom and a hundred thousand dollars. To catch a jackal it is necessary to bait the trap, you understand. So – to continue – he writes this letter, then he takes your pistol from another drawer, and blows his brains out. Yes, it is your pistol, Kristina – the snake-pistol I bought you two years ago.'

He took it from his pocket and weighed it in his gloved hand.

'Then what happens?' he continued. 'Isn't it obvious? You hear the shot and come running upstairs. You see your dead lover, you read the note. You are overcome, you cannot bear the thought of life without him so you turn the pistol on yourself. Very romantic – like a lovers' suicide pact. And while all this is going on, I am quietly working on my papers in Queensland. I shall come home tomorrow afternoon and discover the tragedy. I shall weep for my dead wife and mourn for my dead brother. End of scenario.'

There was a long silence. Then in a small voice she said: 'Don't you ever frighten yourself? Don't you ever wonder if one day the luck will turn against you?'

'I don't believe in luck,' he said shortly. 'A man makes his own fate. Alex chose his own path, he knew where it must lead.'

'The Cretan code,' she said.

'Yes. A man is nothing without honour.'

'You call this honourable? This act of bloody murder! Oh, no, Marcos. That I will not take. You killed him meanly, for revenge, to satisfy your own vanity. There is no honour in it.'

'If this had happened in Sphakia,' he said coldly, 'you would have been stoned out of the village and left to die. The women would have done it. That is their way with an adulteress. It is not a pleasant thing. I shall be more merciful.'

'I don't think I want your mercy,' she said. 'In any case, it is too late. Think about that, Marcos. If you'd shown a little mercy, a little tenderness at the beginning, even after the beginning, we might have made it. I was prepared to love you, to be a good wife. But it wasn't in you. What happened to your human feelings? Did you leave them behind in the White Mountains?'

'I loved Alex, I cared for him. I loved you and cared for you also.'

'As you love this house, your position, your business. And that isn't enough, Marcos, it really isn't.' She was suddenly weary of it all. 'Give me the gun then. Let me get it over with. That's what you want, isn't it?'

She held out her hand, and at that moment the telephone rang, startling them both. It rang for a long time, shrill and angry.

'Aren't you going to answer it?' she mocked. 'Oh I forgot, you can't. You are not here, are you?'

He seized her arm and dragged her to the bedside table. He held the gun against her bare breast. 'Answer it!' he shouted. 'Answer it – and watch what you say!'

She picked up the telephone. 'Mrs Coleman speaking. Who is that, please? Police?' She felt him tighten at her side; the gun was pressed hard against her flesh. She listened for a long time, looking up at Marcos, her eyes widening. 'Yes. You're positive? Yes – yes – I understand. Yes – all the evening. Thank you. Yes, I'll be all right. Goodbye.'

She lowered the phone on to its cradle, sat down on the bed and a smile grew on her face like a flower opening; then came laughter, soft at first, but growing louder and crackling with hysteria. The tears ran down her face as he shook her fiercely.

'What did they want? What was that about!'

Her whole body was shaking and she got the words out only with difficulty. 'The Queensland police. Calling from Townsville. You're dead, Marcos.' She laughed again. 'Didn't you know? I thought you knew everything. You took the car out this evening for a drive. You'd had rather a lot to drink. You went off the road, and crashed into a brick wall. The car burned out, with you in it.'

'You're lying!'

She picked up the phone, and held it towards him. 'Want to check? Come to think of it, why don't you call them and say it was all a mistake – just some drunken actor who took your place so that you could do a little murder on the side. Chalk up another death, Marcos.' She crossed herself. 'Poor devil. I shouldn't laugh. God have mercy on his soul.'

Marcos knocked the phone from her hand and it fell on to the crumpled pillow, the dialling tone purring steadily. He lifted the gun and shot Kristina, the bullet entering the forehead between her eyes.

Once before in his life, when he had heard of the death of his mother, Marcos had howled like an animal in pain. The same cry swelled in his lungs now and burst from his throat.

He turned the gun on himself and fired.

# P. B. YUILL

# Hazell And The Patriot

On the Tube to Dot Wilmington's office that August morning I'd read over somebody's shoulder in the *Mirror* where another of our pop geniuses was moving out to dodge tax.

Reluctantly, of course.

'No, I'm not desperate for work,' I said to the short, dumpy woman with the dyed blonde hair. 'I got at least eighty quid in the iron tank and the garage only wants ninety for clutch work. Plus I got about a hundred and fifty owing to me on a job I did . . .'

'All right, you're desperate,' Dot said.

We stared at each other across her desk. The window behind her was open to let in a cool breeze but any air moving outside was hotter than three in a bed.

'Business is terrible all round,' she said. 'That was your mistake, not becoming a brewer or a bureaucrat.'

'Or a rocker.'

'There's an electrical wholesaler in Acton – somebody's weeding out the stock. How's your double-entry bookkeeping?'

'Nine times nine is . . . ninety-nine?'

'Didn't you make two grand out of the crook you saved from the heavies?'

'Paid off the motor, didn't I? A week in Jersey . . . soon goes. Anyway, it was you phoned me, remember.'

Outside on the ledge two pigeons muttered among themselves about the drought. It did just cross my mind that Dot was enjoying all this. I'd once been on the staff of her security consultancy, seventy-five quid a week on the muck and bullet line.

Then she brought up a file from the carpet.

'Bad debts,' she said, shoving it across the desk. 'I usually bung 'em to a smart cookie called Vinnie Rae on a split-commission basis. Penny ante stuff most of it, not even worth the small-claims court. As a favour to me she might let you take a couple – twenty per cent of anything you recover. I'll ring and tell her you're coming over . . .'

'Her?'

'Yeah – and a word of warning, lover boy. Karate was her best subject at Roedean.'

'All go with you women nowadays, innit?'

Sicilian Avenue is an arched passage off Southampton Row in the no-man's land west of Tottenham Court Road. Little businesses, a stamp-collectors' shop, a restaurant with outside tables, a touch of the Continongs if you didn't look too hard. Naturally the developers had wanted to destroy it a couple of years back.

One good thing about the country being bust – you can count on seeing the same buildings two weeks in a row.

Vinnie Rae had told Dot she'd be having coffee outside.

I spotted her partner first.

Jason. Black mostly, with a bit of brown, very sleek and shiny. Bit of a gay dog judging by the way his big eyes said hello.

She was cream mostly, what you might call a biggish girl, very healthy, in a pale blue denim suit and white shoes.

'Vinnie Rae?' I said standing well away from the hound. 'James Hazell . . .'

'Ah yes.' She squinted up at me. The dog checked my credit-rating and decided I wasn't worth burying for later. 'Do have a seat . . . it's all right, Jason only goes for the throat if I raise a finger.'

'What does he go for if you raise two fingers?'

'A lady never raises two fingers.'

I sat down and put the folder on the table.

'Had any experience of debt-collecting?'

'Collecting new ones every day.'

She smiled.

Up to the table came this second hound, mostly black, very sleek, very shiny. Only this one had a dry nose. And big shades.

'All hail,' he said dramatically, clicking his heels and sliding into a seat. He was wearing a black shirt open to the navel, with a gold ornament on a chain dangling down his hairy chest. From his flared jeans he brought out a bundle of readies, which he slapped down beside her coffee-cup.

'Four hundred and twenty-five, full settlement!'

'Well *done*, Roger,' she said. 'Never thought you'd crack it.'

'I knew it would take something special,' he said modestly, with a little wave of his hand. 'I steam into his reception . . .' He held both hands behind his back . . . 'I steam past his plush secretary and there he is behind his desk. "You again?" he says sarcastically. "Yes, me again, Mr Slippery" . . . then I go *whoosh*!' He brought his right hand down smack on the table. 'First axe – smack into polished cedar! "Better give me the doings or this one"' – he brought his left hand up – '"is for your *skull*!" Paid up like a lamb!'

'Poetry in motion,' Vinnie murmured, starting to thumb notes off the bundle. She slung him around seventy or eighty fives and oncers. The way they disappeared into his skyrocket his jeans might have had jaws.

'And I had to buy two axes,' he said, quite reasonably I thought. Vinnie wasn't impressed.

'Deduct them.'

'*Tax*?' He stood up and gave her a clenched fist salute. 'Those about to die of Socialism salute you!'

His slimline buttocks jigged away through the tables. 'Roger's an out-of-

work actor – he can make a bad debt seem like a death warrant.'
    Then she came back to me. 'Oh yes.' She opened the file. 'All right – here's an old friend you can have a beginner's bash at.' She handed me the sheet of paper. 'A mere two hundred and thirty pounds but you only have to go as far as Oxford Street . . .'
    'What's the . . . er . . . form?'
    'Question of psychology really. No violence.'
    'Yeah? What do you call smashing axes into desks?'
    She smiled and touched the hound's chin. 'We call that applied psychology, don't we, Jason?'
    I got away without being retrieved . . .

You'll find a lot of buildings like it in the West End, tucked away in odd corners. The notice-board listed everything from escort agencies to cut-rate carpets, cheap fares to Australia, palms read (crystal ball by special arrangement), a yoga health clinic, several secretarial agencies . . . and Mr Dornford's little conglomerate.
    I went up to the fourth floor. On the way I passed three or four silent Indians. The businessman sort. Most of the doors looked a bit damaged – it's a safe bet any building like that in the pulsating West End echoes at night to the traditional sounds of splintering panels and jemmied hinges.
    Mr Dornford was in Thirty-Nine. Judging by the number of companies with notices on his door his office had to be slightly bigger than the Vickers building. Travel and insurance mostly.
    I knocked.
    He was about sixty-five, dark suit, white hair combed back with a strict parting, a moustache the colour of old piano keys, a regimental tie with the kind of knot that makes fingernails yell for help.
    A gentleman of the old school, no doubt about it.
    'Mr Dornford?'
    'He's gone. What's it about?'
    Two silent Indians came along the corridor. He gave them a bit of a glare. They slid past me.
    'Gone?'
    'Knew what he was doing,' he said, quite viciously, staring at the disappearing Indians. 'I bought his businesses—'
    'Gresham's office equipment reckon he owes them—'
    'Sorry, can't help you.'
    He was going to shut the door. For twenty per cent of two hundred and thirty quid I was willing to risk causing offence. I put my hand on the door.
    'Where is he then?'
    'He drops in occasionally to collect his mail – write to him. Now, unfashionable as it may seem, I have work to do.'
    'They've tried writing – he never replies.'
    'Can't blame him, postage rates these days. Now . . .'

'If you bought the business you'd be legally responsible . . .'

'I bought only the goodwill – the ill-will as it turned out.'

Behind him in the office a phone rang. He turned to look at it. On the wall I caught a glimpse of a framed photograph of a young geezer in uniform.

'If he comes in I'll ask him for his address – best I can do,' he said . . .

Half an hour later I was going into Vinnie Rae's office on the third floor above Sicilian Avenue. She was on the phone. The Dobermann was on the floor. The bundle of notes was on her desk.

I was on edge.

But the hound gave me the benefit of the doubt.

'Funny how people never complain about our forty per cent until the money's been recovered,' she was saying. She gave me a little wave, pointing me in the direction of a small purple sofa with wooden arms.

They say animals can smell fear.

Maybe Jason had a cold in the nose.

'Well, I have two hundred and fifty-five pounds here for you,' she said, thumbing the notes. I reached the sofa without provoking Jason. Vinnie laughed. 'Oh no no no no,' she said, giving me a wink, 'we deduct at source. Cash business, no cheques – and *no* bad debts . . . very good.'

She rang off.

'Well?'

'Bit hot.'

She stretched her arms. Her denim suit seemed a bit tight.

I dunno why, I looked quickly at Jason.

Oh yeah, he knew what I was thinking. He sort of sneered. There was only one dirty dog in the room and it wasn't him.

'Dornford's sold out to an old geezer called Telford,' I said. 'Telford's getting me an address for Dornford.'

She managed to frown and smile at the same time.

'And what're you going to do while you're waiting for the address?'

'I dunno . . . maybe try another one . . .'

She sighed. 'Dot did say you needed a bit of help.'

'I'll register as a charity I expect.'

'I *hate* to tamper with masculine pride and all that but . . . Telford – one of the old brigade? Seedy but a certain air of previous distinction? Pushing seventy perhaps? Moustache, white hair?'

It was paper-hat time. The kind with a big D.

She smiled ever so sweetly.

'We don't have time for looking and learning in this racket,' she said.

So back I went to Oxford Street.

This time it was Plan B . . . steam in like a fist with a smile on its face.

Knock knock.

'Who is it?'

'Hazell.'

'You're beginning to be a nuisance.'

I got down in a crouch and looked through his letter-box. He was on the other side of the room, looking at me over a desk.

'You going to let me in, Mr Dornford?'

'I told you – my name's Telford.'

'And mine's Lawrence of Bethnal Green.'

'Oh . . . oh very well.'

As he opened the door a teenage person came along the corridor. Hard to say what sex, pale face, green hair.

'Did you see that?' Dornford let his head fall. I closed the door. 'What *is* the country coming to?'

'To a halt. Anyway, this debt of yours . . .'

He snorted as if I'd made a bad joke. He went to the window. 'When I think of all the wonderful men I saw dying around me in the desert – the lifeblood of a proud nation seeping into the sand . . . *now*? Has it ever occurred to you – who would fly the Spitfires today?'

'Look . . .'

'Long-haired layabouts. Poofs. Hermaprodites with green hair. Thieves – in this rat-hole they'd steal the paint off the woodwork. The only ones that will work are these dusky devils – place is full of 'em. Is this the Britain we fought and died for?'

'You owe Greshams two hundred and thirty quid.'

He waved a gentlemanly hand. 'Is that the only motivation we have left – money, money, money?'

'Let me put it this way. You pay your debt and I'll buy British.'

'Haven't got it, old boy. Business is abominable.'

'You had an electric typewriter out of them . . .'

'Stolen. Burglars. Kicked the door down.'

'The insurance . . .'

'I insured with my own company.' He heaved with silent laughter. 'My insurance company's gone bust!'

I decided to cut out the social niceties.

'I think you're an old bleeding fraudsman,' I said heavily. 'Don't give me all that dying in the desert crap . . .'

He nodded and walked to his desk. He sat down, folded his arms and closed his eyes.

'Well, get on with it,' he said.

'Get on with what?'

'The rough stuff. That's what they pay you for, isn't it? Go on – you represent the new morality. Kick an old man whose only crime was to fall behind with his payments.'

'Fall behind? You never got under starters' orders!'

'They should never have encouraged a man of my age to incur such a debt. That's how they make their money, you know – tempting people into commitments with seductive blandishments and then . . .' He opened his eyes. 'Does your work make you feel *proud*?'

I walked across to his desk and thumped my fist down. It was supposed to make him . . . well, not exactly putting the frighteners in but letting him know. I hurt my knuckles as it happened.

'Can't you pay *anything*?' I said.

He brought a wallet out from his hip-pocket and opened it wide. 'My daily entitlement,' he said, sliding out a solitary pound note. 'My own fault – I should've packed in years ago, but when you have a sick wife . . .'

I had the pound out of his hand.

'Let's talk about the balance.'

'I *could* break into a small building society account that my wife and I hoped would see us through . . . very bleak at our age . . . you young chaps never think it will happen to you . . .'

'Look, mate,' I said, wagging my finger at him, 'I want the money.'

He had a bright idea.

'Man in your line – how are you off for insurance?'

Honest to God. He was trying to sell me insurance.

'I'll act as broker – you pay me the initial premium and I'll give you back my commission – it won't cover the whole debt but it's a start, isn't it?'

The phone rang. He picked it up, still looking at me with his small blue eyes. His hand had blue veins and looked slightly warped. It shook a bit. His eyes were watery.

'Oh hello,' he said into the phone, 'how is my wife?' He listened. 'Oh . . . confirmed, is it? . . . Well yes, one has had to prepare oneself for the worst . . . yes, thank you very much for phoning.'

He put down the phone. Somebody knocked at the door. He motioned at me to keep quiet.

'Mr Dornford? It's Captain McInnes.'

'The block manager,' Dornford said, going to the door.

They'd have made a fine pair of book-ends, only the Captain was fatter.

'Just thought I'd tell you, old chap – two offices done over last night. I'm chucking out this damned security mob – oh, busy are you?'

'It's all right ./. .'

The Captain gave me a look. 'No, won't disturb you, Dornford. You seem to be the only other white man in this teeming bazaar. May drop by later.'

Dornford shut the door. He shook his head. 'In a way I'm glad my time's about over,' he said cheerfully, 'this isn't what I was used to. Oh well . . .'

He went to the window.

He looked much older, standing there against the sunshine. Call me a naïve sentimental fool but there was something stopping me from putting the boot in.

I did have a spin through his wallet. Didn't even have a credit card, just junk.

'No, I don't envy you your youth,' he said. 'I had my best days in a much better world. Different class.'

'Oh ballocks.'

I got up and went to the door. I wasn't put in this world to terrorise old geezers with shaky hands, was I?

'Going?'

'Yeah.'

We looked at each other. I don't know why, I found myself laughing.
I went back to his desk and put the pound note down.

He nodded wisely.

'Thank you.'

I left with that good deed feeling. Sort of clean, you know what I mean?

'You got *what*?' Vinnie demanded.

She was back outside having coffee and a pastry.

'One sov.'

'One pound?'

'Yup.'

'Very good . . . you've earned twenty pee.'

'No I haven't. I gave it back.'

'What?'

'I don't think I got the stomach for this debt-gathering caper. Better send him, the old axe trick.'

'Dot said you were a bit of a romantic but . . . a debt-collector giving the money *back*? You might get in the *Guinness Book of Records*.'

I raised my hand. The waiter came over. I ordered a cup of tea. Jason was on the deck, tongue hanging out. A girl passed in a white summer dress. One thing about all this heat, legs were coming out of hiding.

'I like to think of myself as a professional,' I said. 'Enquiry agent I suppose you'd call it. You know – missing poodles, missing husbands, who stole the priceless eggcups? Some old guy living in a dream world . . .? I mean, he actually expected me to whack him about.'

'Drink your tea,' she said, 'we're going for a little walk. You can tell me about these lofty ideals of yours.'

Oxford Street on a hot August afternoon. All your foreigners and that, come to sunny Britain for a bargain. She had Jason on a chain. People do tend to dodge a Dobermann. Vinnie seemed amused by something.

I was sweating a bit by the time we turned into Dornford's building. On the stairs we met these two way-out characters, Indians – but something else. White surgeons' masks, white robes, little white mops over their shoulders.

'Jains,' Vinnie said.

'Who's Jane?'

'No it's a religious sect. They believe in the sanctity of life. The masks are to stop flies getting into their mouths. The mops are to wipe the ground in front of each step in case they tramp on an ant.'

'You'd learn that kind of stuff at Roedean I expect.'

'My father was Indian Army.'

'He could come here for a reunion.'

'He's having it in Heaven.'

'Sorry about that.'

'I'm not.'

When Dornford saw the hound he tried to close the door. Jason didn't exactly knock him down and trot all over him but he wasn't standing any nonsense.

'What's all this?' Dornford demanded, getting the desk between himself and our four-legged friend.

'I believe you've been giving our Mr Hazell a hard time,' Vinnie said.

'I explained to Mr Hazell . . .'

'I'm afraid Mr Hazell is learning our business. You can take this as a compliment.'

'Compliment?'

'I am the final sanction. Vinnie and the Dobermann.' She cocked a finger at Jason. 'Good dog.'

Jason did his imitation of the MGM lion. Dornford looked ready to get up on the desk.

'I appeal to you – as a man of reason,' he stammered.

'You don't appeal to me,' Vinnie said. 'Now – can we settle this matter once and for all?'

'I told Mr Hazell – I'm in no position to . . .'

'What a lovely view of dirty walls,' she said, looking out at the well behind the building. 'Are we going to be here long enough to get to like it?'

'I daresay I could make some kind of proposal . . .'

Vinnie took a deep breath, shaking her head.

'It's too late for proposals, Mr Dornford. I'm instructed to collect the whole amount. It's not the principle, it's the money. Do you like Dobermann pinschers? They have a bad reputation but by and large they're quite sensible. Jason can count up to ten. Talk, Jason, talk.'

The hound barked.

'This is outright intimidation,' Dornford said. There was a note of complaint in his voice. I began to think this Vinnie was a bit strong.

It took them long enough but once women find the way in . . . look out.

'No, it has to be a lot worse than this before it's intimidation, Mr Dornford,' Vinnie said.

'Bringing a brute like that in here? That's bad enough in my book. Are you willing to get yourself involved in this sort of thing, Mr Hazell?'

I shrugged. 'Better give the dog a bone, Mr Dornford.'

'Let me make two things quite clear, young woman. I am not paying you a penny and I'm also going to make sure Gresham's pay heavily for this gross intrusion . . . demanding money with menaces is the legal description.'

'False pretences is the legal description for assuming a false name,' Vinnie said.

The old geezer was beat.

Vinnie didn't wait till he was down.

'There's also an electric typewriter bought on hire-purchase . . .'

'The burglar took it.'

'Why didn't you tell Gresham's?'